DUNCTON FOUND

'I'm frightened,' said the youngster, not moving at
all. The wood was suddenly hushed and awed about
them, and the air stilled as the light seemed to
tremble and darken.

'The best way with fear is to turn your snout
towards it and put one paw resolutely in front of
another,' said Tryfan. 'Come now, for the June sun
has summoned us today and beckons us up through
the wood . . . Come, for I have things to say that you
must know.'

Then one after another, with Tryfan in the lead
followed by the youngster and Feverfew protectively at the rear, they set off upslope to find the
clearing in the high wood where Duncton's great
Stone stands alone and mighty, always ready and
waiting for anymole that comes to it in humility and
faith.

DUNCTON
FOUND

The Duncton Chronicles 3

William Horwood

ARROW BOOKS

Arrow Books Limited
20 Vauxhall Bridge Road, London SW1V 2SA

An imprint of Random Century Group
London Melbourne Sydney Auckland
Johannesburg and agencies throughout
the world

First published in Great Britain by Century 1989

Arrow edition 1990

Photoset by Deltatype Ltd, Ellesmere Port
Printed and bound in Great Britain by
Courier International Ltd, Tiptree, Essex

ISBN 0 09 968300 8

Contents

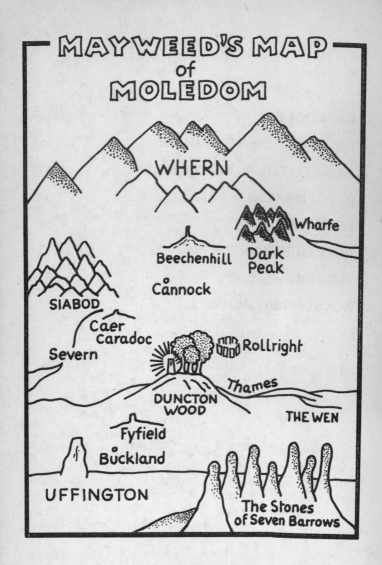

Prologue

So now is he come to moledom, with no name yet but 'Stone Mole'.

He came of a blessed union, but one mysterious and strange, discovered only in the light and Silence of the Stone itself.

His father was Boswell, White Mole, wise mole. Mole we have learnt to trust and love. Mole who in his passing left his only son, not to guide us, but for us to guide.

His mother is gracious Feverfew, born a Wen mole and the last of an ancient line whose final and greatest destiny is to nurture the mole upon whose fateful life our story must now turn.

Whilst to Tryfan, Boswell bequeathed the task of watching over the Stone Mole and helping Feverfew prepare him for the challenges yet to come.

You who remember Duncton as it was when the present histories began and who accompanied Bracken and then Tryfan on their dread tasks, do not weaken now. For the challenges that face the Stone Mole must become your own. His life will be shaped and made, and brought to fruition, sweet or bitter as the case may be, by the actions and thoughts of allmole, of whom you, by your care, your love, and your doubts, are one.

Blessed Boswell knew that moles find it hard to keep faith at the hardest time. So, long ago, he spoke of the first who would follow in the Stone Mole's path, and said that female she shall be, and by her example would light the path for all. Unknown yet to us! To be discovered best by moles with open hearts and courage, and snouts inclined towards the Stone.

So now, you who once prayed for Bracken and petitioned for brave Tryfan, pray for these two who follow them. First for the Stone Mole, whose birth you witnessed and whose life has now begun; next for she who will understand his life and his example first of all living moles, and show us how to honour it.

    Let us choose our companions along the way wisely and well, for we journey but once and need at our flanks moles who have it truly in their hearts to help us to that place we lost even as we first knew it; but where, once more, may be our Duncton found.

PART I

Rites of Midsummer

Chapter One

June; and in the hushed cool depths of Duncton Wood sunlight dappled through the branches and across the great and lovely beech tree trunks. A light that travelled on to every nook and cranny of the wood's floor and shone where dry leaves curled and the lightest of breezes lazed along the grey tree roots and then lost itself amongst the green leaves of dog's mercury.

June, and the light of a summer's day, a light so pure and good that it seems to renew everything it touches, so that the humblest flower, the most nondescript patch of chalk soil, the most gnarled of surface roots, seemed resplendent and shiny new.

This is light that heralds the coming of Midsummer, when all moles know they may petition their dreams to the Stone, and hope that such troubles and despairs as they have will find their solutions soon enough to bear the waiting, and then be gone.

That same light, that June morning, caught the fur of two moles who had come to the surface and were looking upslope towards where the Stone rose hidden among the trees. One was Tryfan, born of Duncton, now returned and never wishing to leave again. Once he had the nervousness and eagerness of youth about him and his fur had been glossy and black. Now he was much older, his face and back scarred by fighting, his fur patchy in parts and greying now.

The suppleness and grace of youth had gone, but in their place was now the quiet strength of a mole who had learnt to put his four paws on the ground and only move them when it is necessary.

His sight was not good, for he had never fully recovered

3

from the savage attack by the dark moles of Whern, and so to know and enjoy all that was about him he had to listen as much as he looked, crouching still with his head a little to one side to hear the rising summer sounds of a wood and a system as venerable as any in the whole of moledom, though one that had fallen now on difficult times.

The second mole was Feverfew and she crouched at his side. She was younger than Tryfan, though not by many moleyears, and like him her body was worn with experience and life, as well as the scars of scalpskin that had at one time ravaged her. But strong she was in spirit and now snouted out the good day all about her with evident delight.

They remained in comfortable silence for some time, as moles will who know each other well and trust each other more, and from the occasional touches they gave each other and the slight nodding of a head or pointing of talons to indicate some new leafy wonder of the morning and the slopes above, anymole who has ever been half in love could tell that these two were a pair, and as close in love and caring tenderness as any pair could be.

'Well, Feverfew, if today's not the day to take the youngster up to the clearing and show him the Stone I can't imagine what day would be!'

'Ytt ys, myn love,' she replied, speaking in the soft and rounded accent of the old language of the Dunbar moles, the colony in the distant Wen where Tryfan had first found her, and from which she had trekked alone so bravely to join him in Duncton Wood and give birth to 'the youngster' and so begin a destiny that all moledom had waited for.

'Where's he got to, tunnelling or exploring?' Tryfan spoke of Feverfew's son with a special love and affection, for though he was not his by birth it was his task, ordained by old Boswell himself, that Tryfan should rear the pup equally with Feverfew and be to him what a father would have been. Out of all males in moledom, Boswell had chosen Tryfan of Duncton to be his main guardian, knowing that the pup would be the Stone Mole, come at last to show moles how to hear the Silence of the Stone.

'He cums nu herre along,' said Feverfew, turning to look at a tunnel exit which lay a little downslope of them. Tryfan followed her gaze, wondering, for though it was true that Feverfew could hear better than him yet sometimes it seemed to him that her knowledge of where her son was and what he was doing was more than physical. Never having reared pups of his own he was not familiar with a mother's sense of what ails her pups and when they need her. But even so Feverfew's instinctive knowledge of the mole seemed exceptional, and made all the more poignant and difficult for her the changes in recent weeks towards his independence which this day seemed about to mark.

Her day-by-day task was nearly done and now it was for Tryfan to take over and begin the training in scribing and lore which both of them knew had become the Stone Mole's own desire and need.

As they waited for him to appear it seemed that at the exit Feverfew had pointed to all the light of the June day began to gather and, special and clear though it already was, yet there it seemed more bright.

Then he emerged, first a snout and then a young paw, the light clear about him and seeming to radiate and shimmer over the trees and leaves above, to mark out the place for anymole that watched.

He came out on to the surface and, as Tryfan and Feverfew had before him, stared up in pleasure and wonder at the day all about. His eyes were wide and innocent, his fur still soft, his form just gaining that touching gawkiness all youngsters have as they pass beyond being youngsters and their body takes on a will of its own and grows now here, now there, and they, bemused, cannot yet find an adult's comfort in it.

He ran quickly over to Feverfew's side, but it was to Tryfan that he spoke.

'Will you take me to the Stone today? You said that

5

when Midsummer approached and the sun was bright, you would. Will you *today*?' His eyes and manner were eager and intense.

'Yes, yes the time's come.' And there was something about the mole and his way that filled Tryfan's eyes with tears, though he was not sure why. Some premonition, perhaps, that one day, upon this young mole's slender and innocent back the weight of moledom's greatest cares and troubles would be placed.

Then, staring upslope once more among the lichen-green and sinewy trunks of the beech trees that rose up towards the highest part of the wood, Tryfan sought out a route towards the Stone.

Yes, yes it was time he was taken to touch the Stone and be told his sacred heritage. Tryfan snouted about slowly, quite unconscious of the fact that he bore himself so very peaceably these days that his solid, easy stance calmed those about him, and made them wait instinctively on him as if to hurry him would be to try to move moledom itself. Tryfan *was*: that was what his training, his years of living in a world about which he had never ceased to care, and his faith, had made him.

As Feverfew and the Stone Mole waited for Tryfan to decide on a route upslope, he himself was thinking of something quite different as he stared at the play of light among the trees. It was this: that surely somewhere there in the light and shadows about them, unseen and perhaps never to be seen again, Boswell was with them, watching over his son as he watched over all of them and always had – with love and with hope that they would find their way to Silence.

'Yes . . .' whispered Tryfan roughly, his eyes filling once more with tears, for now he was growing older and he felt sometimes the loneliness that wisdom brings, and wished that Boswell was there to talk to and ask questions of. Why, there were so many things he wished he had asked when he had the chance . . . when he was *this* mole's age. He grimaced ruefully, the play of emotions plain

6

upon his lined face, and wondered what he could possibly teach the Stone Mole. Something or other about living, he supposed.

'Thiden is the daye, thiden is the houre,' Feverfew told her son gently. Then, putting her paw to his flank, she said to Tryfan. 'Latte us goe now, myn dereste luv, alle thre togider, to showe hym whar he was borne and tel hym wheretofore.'

'I'm frightened,' said the youngster, not moving at all. The wood was suddenly hushed and awed about them, and the air stilled as the light seemed to tremble and darken.

'The best way with fear is to turn your snout towards it and put one paw resolutely in front of another,' said Tryfan. 'Come now, for the June sun has summoned us today and beckons us up through the wood . . . Come, for I have things to say that you must know.'

Then one after another, with Tryfan in the lead followed by the youngster and Feverfew protectively at the rear, they set off upslope to find the clearing in the high wood where Duncton's great Stone stands alone and mighty, always ready and waiting for anymole that comes to it in humility and faith.

Chapter Two

For days after his birth they had not known how to name him, for 'Stone Mole' is no name for a mole to live by. But a name is more than some moles think, for with it is inherited something of everymole that bore that name before, and offers the chance of passing something on to namesakes yet to come.

Few names, if any, are all dark, but some seem so more than others. So is Mandrake dark, and Rune; so is Bracken good and stolid, and Rose a name for moles whose lives give much to others. But how to name the Stone Mole?

Tryfan knew that his own naming came with his father Bracken's first sight of him when, as a newborn pup, he climbed higher than his siblings and snouted upwards, making a form whose shape, Bracken said, reminded him in miniature of the solitary peak near Siabod on whose summit the Stones rise.

Remembering this Tryfan felt he should be the one to name the Stone Mole, and so for several days after his birth he huffed and puffed about it, looking this way and that for an inspiration that did not come.

But one day, as mothers will – as mothers must – Feverfew whispered nothings to her pup as he nestled contented at her belly. And Tryfan, allowed near for once, smiled to see them both content, and barely heard the words she spoke . . . 'Yowe are myn sonne, and may yowe bee the sonne for alle of us. . . .'

Myn sonne. Owre sonne.

She spoke the words not as mole speaking mole speaks it, but accented long as if she said 'sowne', which the flowers are when the wind blows hot on a late summer's day and the seeds scatter and drift to hide in the earth's warm heart until a new spring comes.

But 'sonne', however pronounced, meant something else as well. Tryfan, knowing the traditions of the Dunbar moles of the Wen as he did, and having read many of the texts in their crumbling library, understood Feverfew's natural play on words and that she was saying that the Stone Mole was not just her son, or Boswell's, or both, but that he was the sun that would shine upon them all and bring them new life.

So much Tryfan understood, but he felt more instinctively, not fully understanding the way his thoughts ran, or towards what end. For in the moment he knew that for Feverfew 'sonne' meant several things, his own thoughts moved on from that and he remembered a day – a warm *sunny* day! – when he had first arrived at Beechenhill, and had the sense that in that good place, which seems to lie at the very heart of a natural beauty moledom has forgotten, a part of him had come home.

Beechenhill, whose mists and sun and curving fields, whose height and favoured prospect give it a wider fuller sky than most other systems he had ever seen. Beechenhill! A place where a mole such as the Stone Mole might have done better to be born than in outcast Duncton. Yes, Beechenhill.

The very place to which Mayweed and Sleekit, acting on a similar instinct, had taken Tryfan's two pups by Henbane and so saved them, for as surely as the sun rose each day Tryfan felt that Wharfe and Harebell were safe and hoped that one day they might know him, or know at least that he had cared.

And thinking that, Tryfan trembled and then whispered as he looked on the Stone Mole pup: 'His name could be *Beechen*, my love, after a place which all moles who visit it learn to love. A place of good moles, loving moles, moles trusted with my own. It is a worthy name.'

Feverfew thought, and touched, and whispered, and the pup turned and came closer. She whispered it yet more, annexing the name to him and to herself, and as she did so she did not see the tremble in Tryfan's flanks, nor

9

guess the sweet sorrow in his heart, nor see at once the tears that ran down his face. But when she did. . . .

'Myn luv!' exclaimed Feverfew, concerned.

'Well, a mole may cry if he likes,' mumbled Tryfan, looking at Beechen and then at her. ''Tis something about the name and his vulnerability. I fear for him, Feverfew, and wonder what you and I can do for one marked out as he is.'

'Luv hym trewe,' said Feverfew, touching Tryfan's face gently where his tears were. 'Feare nat, the Stane ys his fader and we fynde favowre to watch over hym. Wan that we yaf doubts and troublis we wyll togider aske of the Stane ytys holpe and yt wyll guyde us tway. Beechen ys nowe hys nam.'

So Beechen got his name and Tryfan knew that one day, whatever other places the Stone Mole might visit, he would go to Beechenhill. Then Tryfan was thankful that the Stone had ordained that his own pups were living there, and might learn of their father from Beechen while they, in their turn, would be witness to Beechen's coming, and give what support he might need.

Beechen's puphood was as other moles', and he was raised in the same burrow and tunnels which in long moleyears past had been Rue's, the mole who bore Bracken's first litter amongst whom was beloved Comfrey himself.

In those modest tunnels Feverfew chose to settle, and though the soil was not as wormful as some in Duncton, that mattered less since her need was only for herself and a single pup.

Despite the public nature of his birth, and the fact that it was witnessed by so many in Duncton, afterwards there was a communal sense that Feverfew and her pup needed privacy, and so, though all longed for the day when Beechen would go among them and be of their life, her tunnels were left in peace. A few did happen by, mainly females who longed for pups of their own and were cursed by the sterility which plague, stress and consequent disease seemed to have cast forever on that system. But none of these few moles got a sighting of the pup, and they were gently deterred by Tryfan from coming yet awhile.

So Beechen grew unseen, as young pups should, learning what Feverfew told him, her dialect words the first he ever heard. Later, when he was adult, her soft accent and sometimes curious turn of speech stayed as his own, and gave his words a touch of timelessness that ran from the past and forward to the future.

His eyes opened but a day or two after he was named, and from the first he seemed quick and curious, falling over himself to get at his mother's milk and then, when full, not sleeping as other pups do but gazing in her eyes and then turning from her to venture from the encirclement of her paws.

Not that, at first, he dared go far, nor risked going anywhere when great Tryfan was about. Yet Tryfan was gentle with him, and Beechen soon found the confidence to crawl all over Tryfan and tussle with him as that mole allowed himself to be buffeted by the pup's young paws. His fur then was fair, and Tryfan wondered at its softness, touching it with his gnarled cracked paws, discovering that when life starts it is so soft and tiny it's a puzzle it survives.

The cold time of April passed with the pup barely seeing the surface above, nor being allowed to feel the blasting of chill winds upon his fur, or the showering rain that fell so easily through the still-leafless wood.

But in the first days of May, by which time Beechen was well grown for one of his age, and already talkative, Feverfew allowed him to quest his nervous way out of the tunnels towards the light and bright air above.

He ventured as far as an exit, poked his snout out, heard a run of wind through budding trees, and rushed back down to safety once again. But curiosity drives a mole up and out, and Feverfew was beginning to want to be on the surface once again, and so as the days went by Beechen was encouraged to venture out with her, and learnt to know the sounds of the wood, and associate them with comfort and not danger. A rustle of leaves was Tryfan coming, a flap of wings was but the harmless blackbird's way, and the youngster could forget for a little his need of his mother as she groomed and rested in the first warming suns of May. But then strange sounds: the tumbling of a branch, a rook's rough call, and he was away and down, back to where he was safe.

Rook? Feverfew told. A rustle of leaves not always stern Tryfan's paws? Feverfew explained. A hooting owl at night? She warned.

Yet Beechen's curiosity overcame his fears and he ventured out again and further still, too far now for Feverfew to leave him be for long before she must follow him, thankful she had not other young to fret over.

So far Tryfan was Beechen's only other company, and Tryfan had to serve as a whole tribe of siblings, playful, irritable, generous, silent, always there but different and unpredictable until learned, just as siblings are.

In those molemonths of May, Feverfew delighted to see Tryfan's smile and the way that so powerful and strong a mole could be so gentle with one who often tried him hard. For Beechen was sometimes more than boisterous, and as that May gathered strength and he grew more, he was not always easy in his response.

But Tryfan spoke with him, calmed him, laughed with him and even at him when he must, and troubles subsided and moments of harshness soon went. The youngster learned to listen quietly as Tryfan and Feverfew talked, each weaving stories of the past for the other, and myth as well, for moles like to talk and remember what they have been told and add something of themselves to it.

Of the Stone they often talked, and to it they spoke and prayed, Tryfan in his Duncton way and Feverfew as Wen moles did, with quiet passion. But neither spoke to Beechen directly of it, letting him absorb what they did and said, and in his own time ask.

Yet in the end it was to neither of them that he first

12

directed such questions, but to one of those moles who, from mid-May, began to come into the small orbit of their lives. These were naturally all adults, since no other pups were born that spring in Duncton, and mainly those who had been closest to Tryfan and Feverfew at the time of Beechen's birth and who, by virtue of the Seven Stancing that was then made, were his natural guardians. So old Skint and well-made Smithills came, interested more in talking to Tryfan than to the so-far untried pup. Bailey too, who played with him much in those days, for Bailey was ever a mole who understood the young, and perhaps in his playing came a little closer to the beloved sisters, Starling and Lorren, he had lost. Marram came by too, though he was mainly silent, a mole to trust and respect for the journey to Siabod he had made, but never one to talk unnecessarily. At that time the only female who came there was Sleekit, mysterious Sleekit, Mayweed's mate, a mole who knew much and in time would impart much. Beechen was a little afraid of her, but curious, and always took stance near her when she came. For he had learned from Feverfew and Tryfan's talk of the pups by Henbane, and how two of them, Wharfe and Harebell, had survived Whern with the help of Sleekit and Mayweed, and been partly raised by them. When he dreamed of having siblings, as he sometimes did, it was of these two unknown moles he thought; but Sleekit was too formidable a mole for him yet to dare ask her to tell him of those dread days.

Nor was it to any of these tried and tested moles that Beechen finally put his first serious questions about the Stone, but another. One we know, one we love, one more devoted to Tryfan than anymole alive.

If ever appearances were deceptive, and a mole looked one thing but in his nature was quite another, this mole was he. Patchy of paw, rotten of tooth, calloused of flank! But intelligent of eye, quick of brain, humourful of nature, great indeed in his lean, slight stature; huge in his humble spirit . . . He came into Beechen's life quite suddenly one day, and, as with other moles whose ways he crossed and whose lives he changed, he came at the right time.

Beechen had wandered further from his home tunnels than Feverfew would have wished, and she, distracted by visitors, had somehow lost sight of him. But the wood had opened out alluringly and he had gone on until it had suddenly seemed to darken with the approach of evening. His natural fear of the unknown caught up with him and he had turned to run quickly back to more familiar surroundings which, to his consternation, he had not found. Instead the wood and its trees seemed to confuse him, the tunnels he ventured down for help scented ominous, and he had tried to keep calm but was failing miserably. It was then, as panic began to overcome him, that from behind and from nowhere, it seemed, an alarming mole appeared.

Beechen reared up in a not unimpressive stance of self-defence, but one in which he could not seem to prevent his back paws shaking, as the mole raised a paw of greeting and said, 'Trembling tot, stupefied by my sudden and unexpected appearance, note my smile: it is astonishingly friendly. Note my stance: it unasserts. Remark upon my pathetic form: not likely to cause harm.'

'Whatmole are you?' asked Beechen doubtfully.

'Inquisitorial Sir, I shall tell you. I am a humble mole, a nearly nothing mole, an almost anonymous mole!'

'You're Mayweed!' said Beechen, relaxing.

Mayweed grinned, his teeth livid in the bad light.

'You're Sleekit's mate. You're Tryfan's friend. You're. . . .'

'I'm many things, still-growing Sir, son of fecund Feverfew.'

'They said you speak strangely.'

'Who, when, why, and how did they say it?' demanded Mayweed.

'Well . . .' began Beechen.

'Ill!' declared Mayweed, his eyes lighting at the devious possibilities of verbal play.

14

'Unwell!' said Beechen.

'Ailing,' said Mayweed, delighted that Beechen was able and willing to join in his game.

'Um . . . hurt?'

'Unhealthy,' said Mayweed immediately.

'Er . . .' But Beechen stopped, unable to think of another word expressing the same idea.

'Diseased, injured, harmed, wounded, and afflicted, much-yet-to-learn-but-trying-very-hard Sir,' said Mayweed, beaming with satisfaction and frowning as he thought of a dozen other words he might have added to the list but deciding against uttering them out loud.

'Well!' said Beechen, smiling.

'Well indeed this mole me, Mayweed by name, agrees,' said Mayweed finally.

So the two moles met and became friends, and not for the first time in his life, nor the last, Mayweed guided a mole back to safety who had got himself lost.

'I didn't know I was lost,' said Beechen in surprise as they came back to familiar paths.

'Serious state to be in that, self-losing Sir, *very* serious.'

'I'd like to talk again,' Beechen said as they parted.

'Loquacious lad, this mole will return. He always does. He knows where losing's to be found, he knows where darkness lurks, he's been where all moles go if they are to go beyond themselves and helps them through. Mayweed understands. What will Sir wish to talk about?'

'The Stone,' said Beechen. 'And Boswell.' With that he was gone, and it was Mayweed's turn to look surprised and even perplexed, and then to grin into the fading light and turn away, wandering on the surface for a while, then underground, following the course of his memory of Boswell, and stopping to think in awe of the many uncharted ways of the Stone.

When they next met Beechen simply asked Mayweed to show him how to route-find, which Mayweed did in his own peculiar way: beginning by getting Beechen completely and utterly lost within his own familiar tunnels.

'Lost lad, feel it, and enjoy. Being lost is nectar to a route-finder's soul; being lost, contrary to popular conception, is *most* enjoyable. Humbleness adores it, loves it, longs for it. Being lost! Too rarely happens to him now, not here in Duncton.'

'But isn't it very big?' said Beechen. 'You can't know all of it!'

'Too-eager youth leaps to his first confusion: "know". For "know" he imagines you mean "remembers". Humbleness remembers more than most and therefore knows more routes than most, but that is not how he route-finds. Most moles never route-find, they go along so desperate to keep their talon-hold on what little they know that they become confused the moment – as you now have, very average Sir – they lose hold. In short, they learn the way, remember it, and inevitably when they put a paw out of line get lost. In fact, humbleness avers that most become so afraid of becoming lost they go nowhere new at all which, he mildly suggests, is far worse than being lost since it is next to being dead.

'A lost mole, like you, is therefore in a learning situation, as the moles of the Word put it so curiously. A learning situation! Mayweed loves it! Ha, ha, ha! A *much* better way of progressing is to assume you are lost from the beginning and must deduce each junction afresh. Exciting, that! This way? Or that way? Thinking keeps a mole young! Now . . . which way? Let us commence!'

The theory was over, for the time being, and poor Beechen, bewildered by the way Mayweed had got him lost in tunnels he should know, looked around in some panic as Mayweed darted this way and that, round and round, now here now gone, his snout disappearing and reappearing all over the place.

'Clueless Beechen, a tip. Crouch down. Groom. Ponder the pleasantness of being alive. Forget you are lost. Let your body remind you what your mind has forgotten: *you*

16

can never be lost, since *you* are *here*. Look at your paw! Here. Look at the mark it makes in the dust. Here. Hear your nervous breathing. Evidently here! So *you* are not lost.'

Beechen pondered this, relaxed, and eventually said doubtfully, 'But I don't know where I am.'

Mayweed beamed with pleasure as if Beechen had fallen into a trap he had intended him to.

'Befuddled Beechen, wrong yet again. Crucially wrong. Think and learn, for this is the only way to become a route-finder. Don't say, "I don't know where I am" but "I don't know where *this place* is". See? Understand? Appreciate?'

'Sort of,' said Beechen, who sort of did. Certainly he felt less panic-stricken than he had and, now he saw that his problem was not himself but the place, it was easier to keep calm; and certainly, he realised suddenly, there was something familiar about those walls.

Mayweed watched delightedly as Beechen snouted this way and that, scratched his head, breathed more deeply and, with the sudden sense that might come to a mole who falls headlong into a void and after whirling about lands safe again on his four paws, he saw where he was.

'But we're *here*!' declared Beechen with a sudden rush of recognition. 'But . . . !' And he felt, and looked, angry at himself and the world for fooling him into thinking he was lost when he was not lost at all.

'Yes, yes, yes, yes, yes, yes, yes!' Mayweed said, almost shouting the words. 'You see, you know, you feel, and marvellous . . . you've *found*, young Sir.'

'But . . .' protested Beechen.

'Ah! Astonished and marginally annoyed youth wonders how humbleness here got him to feel lost in the first place? Humble he is clever at such things. Humble he has made a study of such things. Humble he excels at it. By turning this way and then that way, by taking the young innocent's mind off the route he was going, by making what was familiar become so unfamiliar that the

17

bemused youngling could not even see correctly what was in front of his paws. We are in tunnels he has passed many times, but have come from a direction abnormal and stopped in a place and at an angle abnormal. Result? Confusion, panic and a sense of feeling lost. Dear oh dear, now bloodied Sir, and this is but the beginning!' Mayweed laughed again, scratched himself, thought a bit, and finally told Beechen to take him to the surface and find him some food.

When they had relaxed and eaten, Beechen asked, 'Will I ever become a good route-finder?'

'With persistence and application, and a touch of genius – yes, Sir will,' said Mayweed contentedly.

'Will you teach me?' asked Beechen.

'Will you learn?' replied Mayweed, his eyes bright.

'Yes,' said Beechen seriously. There was a pause, and then Beechen boldly asked, 'What exactly is the Stone?'

'That's persistence!' said Mayweed. 'No sooner recovered from being lost than he rushes headlong into a most existential maze. Modest me had guessed that bold Beechen would soon seek the portal to that arcane world, but had vainly hoped that in the bewilderment of getting lost Sir would forget his interest in such things. Me, Mayweed, is not one to say much of the Stone. Tryfan knows it best. He was taught by Boswell.'

'Who's Boswell?'

'Ah! Quick and speedy brained Sir, the questions will come thick and fast now like sounds in a badly made tunnel, and Mayweed will not be able to cope. Tryfan will give you better answers than Mayweed. . . .'

'I heard Tryfan say to Feverfew that you know more about the nature of the Stone than anymole alive.'

'He did?' said Mayweed softly, his bright eyes suddenly moist. 'No, no, great Tryfan cannot have meant that, and anyway youngsters had best keep silent on what they hear until they know it to be true for themselves.'

'What's scribing?'

'Sir will never stop now!' said Mayweed with a sigh.

Then the sounds of approaching mole across the surface relieved him of the need to answer more and instead he asked, 'Whatmole is that, young Sir?'

'Tryfan, and he's tired.'

'Correct but incomplete. He comes from where?'

'Don't know,' said Beechen.

'That's because loquacious lad was talking so much and asking inadequate me so many questions he forgot the route-finder's cardinal rule, which is to keep half an ear open for sounds and clues, for they help, every one of them. Tryfan comes from upslope, some way towards the Stone.'

Which, when he reached them, Tryfan confessed he had.

'But not from it. Nomole's been there since Beechen was born. They're waiting. Eh, Mayweed?'

Mayweed sighed and nodded.

'This mole asks a lot of questions, peerless Tryfan, and so he should. Indeed, humbleness himself asks lots and will never stop. He'll die asking questions, for that's the way of route-finders. However, while he knows whatmole to ask (usually himself), burgeoning Beechen here is asking the wrong mole and should in Mayweed's judgement direct his questions to you yourself, named Tryfan.'

Tryfan laughed but Mayweed did not even smile. Then as Beechen, bored by their conversation, turned from them and snouted a little across the surface, Mayweed said quietly, 'Mayweed is made afraid by the youngster's questioning. The nature of the Stone? Who was Boswell? The truth of scribing? The way to go . . . ?' Mayweed looked full into Tryfan's eyes, wavering. 'When I am with this mole I am full of fear for moledom,' he said simply. 'I feel I cannot help him or guide him as I can other moles. I feel close to tears.'

Tryfan nodded and touched his old friend on the flank.

'You are not alone in that, Mayweed. The mole is growing fast, he questions everything. But if he now asks you of the Stone and Boswell, it is more than he asks myself or Feverfew.'

Mayweed grinned and said, 'See how he has drifted off
. . . he must ask the questions but is afraid of the answers
we will give. Youth, patriarchal Tryfan, is a touching
thing but *aren't* you glad you've left it far behind?'

Tryfan smiled.

'When I was first told by Boswell that one day the Stone
Mole would come, I thought he would come complete, full
grown, ready to guide us. But. . . .'

They stared across the woodland floor to where
Beechen, seeming so young in the soft May light, touched
a root, gazed up at a branch, scented at some leaves and
then simply settled down to look out through the speckled
shade that spread over the wood's wide floor.

Tryfan continued, 'But he has come newborn, a pup,
and is in all our care. Each one of us in Duncton must give
to him what we can, striving to teach him all we know,
whatever he asks we must answer it truthfully. When
moles fear answering questions asked it is because they
fear something in themselves, and do not trust what the
Stone ordains. Answer his questions, Mayweed, and tell
others in Duncton to do the same. For soon now he will
leave the home burrow and I shall take him to the Marsh
End. There, as Midsummer comes, I shall teach him
scribing as I taught you at Harrowdown one Midsummer
that seems long ago. Be not afraid, Mayweed. Here he is
among good moles, moles the Stone wished to be here. We
are his guardians and until he is ready to guide and teach
us, we must all be his teachers.'

They watched Beechen for a little longer until, aware
perhaps of their silence, he came running back to them,
his eyes alight with the beauty of the wood.

'He's teaching me to route-find,' Beechen told Tryfan,
going close to Mayweed.

'Then you have found the best mole in all of moledom to
teach you,' said Tryfan. 'Now come, your mother would
talk with you.'

As they left, Mayweed watched after them, trouble still

in his eyes. He stared at Beechen's still slender haunches, but finally his look was for Tryfan.

'You I'll watch until you have no more need of me,' he whispered. 'This mole Mayweed loves Tryfan, and what great Spindle began in Uffington this mole will conclude. Who knows what ways lie ahead, but while you trouble yourself with the Stone Mole's rearing, I'll trouble myself with watching over you! Slower now you are, Sir, your fur patchy like mine, and Mayweed sees ways ahead for you which may be hard to find and fathom. But humbleness will be there.'

Then, as the two moles stopped at an entrance to go down, Beechen turned and looked back across the wood to the place from where Mayweed watched them. He saw Mayweed, and for a moment his body was quite still and his left paw a little raised. Mayweed saw the look in his eyes, and knew it. It was the look of love, terrible and strong, and before it a mole might quail. And at his raised paw there seemed a light, and Mayweed knew that he was blessed and that moledom would be guided, if only it knew how to see, and hear. That time was yet to come, but for now, here, in beleaguered Duncton, the moles had a task to teach a young mole all they knew, and it was a great and good one.

As June began they all noticed that Beechen grew withdrawn and difficult, asking questions to which he seemed not to listen to the answers, staying near moles he seemed not to want to address, making silence, making sudden outbursts. If there had been other youngsters about it might have been easier for the adults there, since he could have vented his confused needs.

Now, too, he began to wander far, but he seemed not to want to talk to anymole and none reported talking with him, though sometimes he was seen over on the Eastside or near the Marsh End. He seemed not to attempt to go near the Stone or out on to the dangerous Pastures and he came back to Feverfew for rest or food, but she knew his time with her was very nearly done.

'I am muche afeard for hym wandering far,' Feverfew would say when she and Tryfan had time to be close.

'We all are, my love, but it is of more than shadows in Duncton that we fear for him. It is the darkness of which the grikes are a part that I fear. I know Whern's ways. Rune may be dead, as Mayweed and Sleekit witnessed, but Henbane will have taken charge. Mistress of the Word! She will have cursed her father for not killing Boswell when they could have done. Now his son is come, which surely they must suspect, they will not rest until they have taken him. The day will soon come when they know or guess he is in Duncton Wood and he will have to escape from here. Now he has things to learn, and we must try to teach him, for that is our task. I shall take him to the Marsh End, my dear, and there teach him what I can of scribing, and then too other moles of Duncton – the many who have waited so long and patiently to see him, and who have left him well alone – shall come to tell him what they can. If he is the mole I think he is, he will listen well, and learn, and what he learns from us will give him much that he needs to know when he goes out in moledom and takes word of the Stone.'

'Hee ys myn sonne,' said Feverfew quietly, for talk of learning and journeying, guidance and the Stone, upset her. She who had borne him did not want to let him go. So as the sun of June brightened and grew clear, Feverfew grew apprehensive.

Today, historians of those times seek signs of what Beechen was to become in the few scraps of stories that are told about him then. Some say he had healing powers young, and even by the end of May was curing moles; others say that he made a journey to the Marsh End and spoke words of prophecy.

But it was not so. Tryfan himself, who left records that make the matter plain, tells us that until a certain day in mid-June, Beechen was pup and youngster like any other with nothing much to mark him out except, perhaps, a

22

certain grace of form and the common sense intelligence of a mole who needed to be told things that mattered only once.

In the last few days before he first touched the Stone, as if he was beginning to understand that he must at last turn his back on puphood for all time, he slept badly and suffered nightmares, but recovered soon enough. Whatever darkness passed through their tunnels in those final nights vanished and their youngster slept as deep and sound as every youngster should.

At last a dawn had come which called Tryfan and Feverfew out into the wood. The whole of moledom seemed to wake about them as they groomed and ate, a day of beauty and change when a mole might take up his task. They felt that in travelling through the dark nights past they had grown nearer each other and nearer a joyful day to come.

'A day of sunshine such as this one,' said Tryfan softly, looking about the wood he loved, 'a day when Duncton is found once more. I think I shall be gone by then, and you, my love! Our tasks will be done and other moles will be where we are now, to turn about as we do and rejoice in what they see. Theirs to inherit what we leave behind, as we have, and our parents before us. Theirs to guess at what we knew; theirs to know what we cannot.

'But this sun shall be the same, and it will warm their fur as it warms ours. And the Stone shall be there and be the same. Touching it, they shall be nearest what was good in us. Touching it, we can reach out to what will be best in them. The Silence they strive for will be the same as that which, Stone willing, we will have found.'

Then Tryfan and Feverfew were close and touching, and the light was on them and in the dew about, and all Duncton Wood felt it was at one and, if purposeful, would have no need to doubt.

It was a little later that same June morning that Beechen came to the exit nearby and saw the sun, and all knew this was his day to touch the Stone. Then, with all of moledom waiting as the sun rose high, they had begun the trek up towards the Duncton Stone.

Chapter Three

The same June sun that lit their way that morning shone down its special light in other places in moledom, and upon other moles. Some saw that light well, others darkly.

All moles know – even those whose systems have long been in the control of the grikes and whose faith, if such it can be called, is of the Word – that there are seven Ancient Systems in moledom, where the Stones rise true and moles of faith seek to abide.

Most, like Duncton, Rollright, Avebury and Fyfield, have long been taken over by the grikes, and the Stone followers broken and dispersed. Yet even then a very few followers scraped a living nearby hoping that one day better times would come and they could open their hearts to their special Stone and touch it once again.

But two systems of the ancient Seven had been deserted altogether, unoccupied by grike or follower. One was Uffington, where Boswell served his novitiate and where he had been captured by Henbane of Whern and lost to moledom for so many years.

The other was the least known of the seven: Caer Caradoc in the west, where in recent times only a vagrant family of moles had lived, of which only one had survived, living alone and mateless, wandering the hills of the wild Welsh Marches, keeping faith with the few followers of the Stone in those parts who, leaderless and systemless, clung on to their faith with that stubborn obstinacy and pride of place that marks out the moles of those wormless parts.

He had been named Caradoc by his father, after the Stones whose destiny it was to have him as their guardian, and already he has played a part in our history, for he it was who first guided Tryfan's emissaries, Alder and

Marram, on to Siabod where for good or ill they went to show the besieged Siabod moles how they might best resist the grikes.

Of that we will soon know more, but now, today, this June, we discover the ragged and hungry Caradoc climbing the steep slope towards the Stones that are his birthright and his burden.

For days before had he travelled, driven by some inner need, from the western hills into which he had wandered, back to a system moles, and time, seemed long ago to have forgotten. Through honeysuckle ways he went, among the meadowsweet, and then finally up the remorseless bracken-covered slopes above which Caer Caradoc looms dark, its flat fell top out of sight from below.

Slowly at first and then with quickening step he was drawn back up to where his life began and where, he had no doubt, it must one day end.

In those days none but those in Duncton Wood itself knew who the Stone Mole was, or even whether he had come. That secret so far was Duncton's own to be revealed only when and how the Stone ordained. Yet many across moledom guessed that somewhere he had come at last for a star had shone, and while grikes and unbelievers protested that it was but a phenomenon of the skies, the followers were sure it was more than that, and that the star was the Stone's own sign that its mole had come and soon their faith would be tried and tested hard and they must try to be ready.

Such a believer was the vagrant Caradoc, and such was his fervour that those few friends he had and trusted with his thoughts said privately among themselves that Caradoc saw signs of the Stone in everything, even the passing sheep!

Caradoc cared not, and when that inner call came to return to the Stones he loved most of all, he had heeded it. Now, this June morning, as he returned at last, the light seemed especially clear, and the ground to tremble with purpose and hope.

26

The going was rough, and lesser moles might have cursed the dew that encumbered their paws and made them slip as they struggled upwards. But faithful Caradoc saw only the bright light caught in the glistening drops and was glad that he had health and strength to climb the slopes before him. He lingered sometimes to catch his breath and admire the special green of the leaves of tormentil and wonder at why it was he almost smelt the sense of change in the air that morning. Then his breath recovered, and with the prospect of the Stones themselves and the flatter fell getting ever closer, he went steadily on, speaking out his prayers and offering his faith and life aloud, as moles who spend too much time alone sometimes do.

If the seeming weakness of his harried body belied the evident strength of his spirit and ability to press on it was because of a special belief he had – and which he expounded to all moles who would listen –that one day to this deserted, bereft place, where most moleyears the wind blew cold and the snows lay hard, to this very place the Stone Mole himself would come. Aye, and he'd give his blessing and these long years of Caradoc's lonely faith and courage would find their reward. For surely, inspired by the knowledge that the Stone Mole had come even here, moles would return once more to Caer Caradoc, and though the soil was not so wormful as in the vales below they would make the system live again.

A few more yards, a little more effort, and there he was once more, before the Stones he loved. To those who knew the Duncton Stone, the Caradoc Stones were modest enough, but to Caradoc himself, who knew no other and whose faith was great, no Stones were more grand, nor ever could be. Certainly, though modest in size, their stance was noble and sure, and few prospects in moledom are more striking than the vales and hills they watch over, east and west, north and south. He felt his heart lift in joy and his faith renewed, for this was a good place to be, one where a mole might feel himself well found and know that one day, if moles had strength enough, then moledom could be made aright once more.

Aye! The sun shining among these Stones, and the breeze across the glistening grass and in among the bracken and bursting heather, why that gave a mole good faith! Yet more than that struck Caradoc as he looked about over the hills and finally to the mountains of the north and west where, visible that day, the mass in which distant Siabod and Tryfan rose. He gasped at a sense he had that today – today and nearly now! – there was great power in the earth and a trembling promise of life and death, of light and dark in which, if a mole was to know the Silence which was a follower's best intent, then he must look to himself afresh and not flinch from whatever task he now faced. Aye!

Then Caradoc went forward to touch the greatest of the Stones, but even as he reached up to do so he pulled sharply back, hesitant and fearful, looking about him as if there were shadows near and he should protect himself. But though there was nothing, only light and his imaginings, he crouched down before the Stone, and decided not to touch it yet.

'Not time,' he muttered, not knowing why and taking a humble stance. 'No, it's not time yet. But I think it will be soon. There's something about the light this morning that tells me that I'll know what to do and when.' He fell silent and kept his snout low. His flanks shivered a little though the day was warm.

'I'm scared, that's what I am,' he said to himself, 'and I want others near me. A mole can't go on alone forever.'

Then he spoke a prayer: 'Send moles, Stone, send moles who have been vagrants as I have, send them to Caradoc. Send them one day that they may see the light as I do, and share the beauty of the Stone. Let those nearby come to Caradoc and those near other systems go to their own. Send moles to this place and make it live again. Grant it, Stone, if it be thy will. Grant too that I may find a mate and know the joy of seeing my own pups run and play among these Stones which in all my life have only known one pup's laughter, which was my own. Grant it if it be thy will.'

So Caradoc prayed, so he waited, and the sun was warm in his fur and though he saw it not himself – for his snout was as low as his humility was great – that sun made his fur shine as it never had before, as he waited for his time to touch the Stone again.

While Caradoc waits we must travel on, to visit a system whose name we have heard before, but whose dry grass ways and proud Stones we have so far left unvisited. We must venture there to witness the beginning of a life of dedication to the Stone, by a mole who shall in time be much loved, much loved indeed.

If a mole might choose a day he might first travel where we go now, let it be a June day such as this, when the sun shines bright and blue harebells blow across its chalky grass and the great rising beeches of its knolls cast welcome shade across its venerable Stones.

It is to great Avebury we have come, set most southerly of all, a system with history and holiness enough that it should be no surprise that from it a great mole might one day come.

But long now has been noble Avebury's suffering, long and remorseless. For to it the plagues came hard, and after them the grikes visited in force, killing most of its adult Stone followers and perverting its young towards the Word to make them derelict of spirit, and much demeaned.

In all the chronicles of grike outrage few are as sad as that inflicted upon Avebury, whose young were forcibly mated with moles of the Word, and whose happy rhymes and rituals and dances of seasonal delights were reviled and mocked, their performance made punishable.

But there lived in the grike-run Avebury tunnels one old female who could just remember the time before the plagues and the Word, which meant she could remember the Stones themselves, and was the last surviving Avebury mole to have touched them.

Her name was Violet, a worthy Avebury name, and by that June morning, when the Stone Mole in distant Duncton was being taken to the Stone, she was old indeed, and near her time. She had escaped punishment and Atonement of the Word by feigning vagueness and stupidity, but those few who knew her well knew she was more than she seemed, though none could ever have guessed how much.

The grikes let her live because she pupped well and reared her young clean, and she had in her time given guardmoles sturdy, well-found pups. But latterly, growing older, thinking her mating days were done, the grikes had let her go among the few pathetic local males who remained. With which she mated nomole knows, but into pup she went, fecund to the last, and in the cycle of seasons before the June we come to Avebury, she pupped a final litter.

She reared them hoping that among them would be one with whom she could share her ancient irreplaceable secrets of the Stone. But though she was hopeful for a time of one, named Warren, he insisted on becoming a guardmole and so she could not trust him to be silent. She knew the Word used sons against mothers, for that is in the vile nature of its way.

Somehow she survived the winter years, and come the new spring, the very same the Stone Mole had been born, Warren mated, and had young. Violet, growing blind now, was allowed to visit them, and when she did and she touched them with her withered paws, she felt the Stone's grace come to her, and knew there was one among them the Stone's light had touched. A female, sturdy and good, who soon showed a nature Violet knew well indeed for when, so long before, she herself was young, before the grikes came and moles ran free among the Avebury Stones, it was her own.

30

The mole was called Mistletoe, but from the first she was known as 'Mistle'. When May had come, and Mistle was beginning to speak well and learn the world about her, Violet had asked Warren to let the youngster leave the nest and live in her old burrow, to help her now she was infirm and found it hard to take worms and clear out summer tunnels.

Which Warren agreed to, persuading his dull grike mate that one less pup was one less mouth to feed, and his old mother had earned some help in her last moleyears.

Then, when Mistle had come, Violet found ways to begin to tell her of the Stone; subtly, gently, and, as is the way with youngsters when adults treat them as they would themselves, Mistle understood the special nature of such talk and that it was secret to herself alone.

When June came Mistle unexpectedly asked her grandmother, old now, blind, and unable to travel far, to take her to see the Stones.

'Hush, my dear, that's not for us to speak of.'

'But you're not afraid of them like other moles, are you? I've heard you speak to them.'

'And what think you of that, my love?' said Violet, not denying it. She knew she talked to herself these days, and to the Stones as well, no doubt.

'I . . . I don't know. I don't think I'm afraid of the Stones.'

'Have you told others you've heard me speak to them?'

'No!' said Mistle vehemently. 'They wouldn't understand, though I know you do.'

'Understand what, my dear?' said Violet softly, her voice trembling. She felt the Stone was guiding them.

'That the Stones are *there*. They always have been. They're like the ground itself or the sky. And . . . and. . . .'

'Yes, Mistle?'

'I . . . I . . . I'm frightened,' whispered Mistle, her mouth trembling. 'It's . . . I mean . . . what they teach about the Word being the only way is wrong. I *feel* it's

31

wrong because the Stones *are*. I . . .' And then she wept, and told Violet her fears and how recently they had mounted up in a confusion inside her. 'And that's why I wanted you to take me to the Stones, so I could see for myself and decide whether they're old superstitious things like the eldrene says, or something else. *Do* you know what I mean?' There was anguish on Mistle's strong face, and courage, too, and though Violet could not see it her paws touched Mistle and she felt it in her.

'Shush, mole, and let me tell you what I have not dared tell anymole since I was barely older than yourself. I am of the Stone. Before it was I raised and by it shall I die.'

Mistle looked relieved and came closer to Violet, and touched her as she spoke.

'The night you were born there was a star in the eastern sky and I knew that night hope was rekindled across moledom, and nurtured in many old hearts like my own. A few days later when I was able to touch Warren's first litter, I felt the Stone speak to me as I touched you. You have been touched by the Stone, my dear, though why and what for I cannot say; and why it spoke to me, who is not much of a mole and has not long to live, I do not know.

'But there you were, my dear, and I prayed that the Stone might grant that you could come to me so I might teach you what I can. A light shone the night you were born, and your life will be lived by that light, and true to it you must be.'

The two moles were silent and close for a time, as if they were in the presence of a truth that needed no words more. Then Mistle said, 'When I cried it wasn't just because of what the eldrene teaches, and what I felt about the Stones *being*. It was something more than that, and it makes me so afraid. It's something that's coming, and sometimes I dream about it, sometimes I feel it when I'm awake. But it's like something I have to touch to know but I can't reach it, and when I do I won't have the strength . . .' She wept again then, and Violet held her and knew that what her granddaughter was beginning to sense was a task she would have, as all moles have though few know it.

'You shall have the strength, my love, for the Stone gives to nomole a task that he or she cannot bear. You shall have the strength and courage.'

'Will you tell me about the Stone?' asked Mistle.

'I shall teach you all I know, all that I was taught, and all that living has taught me. But you must listen and learn well, for there is not much time. . . .'

'Are there other places that have Stones? Are there systems where moles are free to touch them? Will you tell me about them?'

'I'll do that right enough, and pray that one day such rights as we once had will be ours again. Now come close, mole, for I'll whisper the first thing you must learn, which are the names of the seven Ancient Systems, each of which has a Stone or Stones.'

'Is Avebury one of the Seven?'

'It is, my dear, and as faith in the Stone lives here still in you and I, so I believe does it live in all the others, and waits for a time which I think may be just beginning. Now, these are the other names . . . There's Uffington to the west of here, and Fyfield beyond that. Then secret Duncton and grand Rollright which with us makes five. The last two are far to the west, and one's Caer Caradoc and the other Siabod. . . .'

So secretly did ailing Violet begin to tell young Mistle what she knew, interweaving her tales with the lore of the Stone, and telling of its rhymes and rituals.

'The only one of those I've heard of is Duncton,' commented Mistle. 'It's where outcasts and miscreants get sent.' She shuddered, because even if she was too young to have known the purge of diseased and outcast moles, most who remembered it did not fail to talk of the horrors when, at the behest of Henbane herself, Avebury and other systems had sent their worst on a trek westward to Duncton Wood. The pathetic or the troublemakers were sent there still, and allmoles felt that Duncton loomed over them as a threat, the sentence to which was a sentence of death.

Violet nodded silently and said, 'I remember all that well enough, but even so I'll warrant there's moles to trust in Duncton still. 'Twas always a place of mystery and magic in my parents' tales, and they said it has a Stone the equal of any of ours, and we've a good few as I hope you'll one day discover! Mayhap Duncton's as bad now as they say, mayhap not. But, mole, I'll say this – the Stone has its ways and gives its protection as it knows best. I've never left these parts, but if ever I had been able to do so, of all the other systems it would have been to Duncton I'd have gone.

'Now, listen you,' added Violet playfully, to mask the seriousness she felt, and the sense of wonder, too, 'I'm going to teach you some words you'd best remember, for nomole else in Avebury knows them. They've been spoken for generations and are as much a touching to the past that made us as these touching paws of ours make us one. I'll tell you a secret, my dear: all my life I've spoken these words every time I should, but since the grikes came, which was when I was young, I've said them just to myself, hoping that one day there would be a mole to pass them on to. Now I'll teach them to you and pray that one day you'll have space to say them before the Stones themselves, or others you've taught will.'

'What words are they?' asked Mistle, her eyes wide.

'Words to wake the day with, words for Longest Night: words to eat a worm by and words to heal the sick; words that make foolish moles forget themselves so the Stone is free to do its work through them, words to settle the young; words to win another's love when love seems strange; and, aye, words of Midsummer when moles thank the Stone for bringing their pups safely into adulthood.'

'When will you start teaching them to me?'

'Today, now. . . .'

So Violet began, day by day that June, to teach all she

knew and could remember. Until one morning, *this* morning, the very same upon which Tryfan and Feverfew led the Stone Mole towards the Duncton Stone, the same as that when Caradoc settled down before the Stone he loved for the right time to reach up and touch it; this morning a strange and abiding calm came to old Violet. She went to fetch Mistle to her side but had no need to for Mistle came running out of the lovely morning sun, as if she already knew.

'I heard you calling!' said Mistle.

'Did you, my love?' whispered Violet, who had not called at all.

'What can I do for you? Food? Clearing? Grooming? Learn more words?' Mistle giggled, for she had learnt so much she sometimes joked of it and anyway, this morning, why, it was strange and special and a mole shouldn't do anything much but *be*.

'I want you to show me the morning,' said Violet softly, 'and describe all you see. My poor eyes tell me only that the light is bright, but my heart tells me more. Take me up into it towards the Stones, and be my sight.'

'But the guardmoles . . .' said Mistle doubtfully.

'They'll let us be. The Stone will see to it. The day I've waited for so long has come sooner than I expected, but I'm ready now and you're to help me.'

'What day? Help you do what?'

But Violet was already off and up towards the surface, huffing and wheezing and a little uncertain of her way. Yet she struggled on and Mistle, much concerned, ran after her and caught her up.

'We're to go to the Stones, my dear. Now, this morning. 'Tis sooner than expected, but I want to touch them before my time's done.'

'What do you mean?' cried out Mistle, suddenly frightened, though as fearful of the frailty that seemed about her grandmother as of the dangers of trespassing where moles were not allowed to go. 'We can't go there. 'Tis not allowed,' she added, trying to restrain Violet. But

35

both moles paused as a male voice, deep and gruff, said, 'What's that, lass? What lies ahead where you two may not go?'

It was Warren blocking their path across a field into which Mistle could not quite see, though she sensed there were great shadows there, and more, much more.

'Stones, mole, that's what,' said Violet. 'Stones that sent you here today to let us through. Stones that'll show you your task as well one day.' Violet spoke firmly, even a little roughly, as a mother can when she's old and her son is grown.

'You'll neither of you go any further, for amongst the Stones I can't protect you. Now. . . .'

'Then there'll be the blood of a mother and a daughter on your talons, Warren, and guardmole though you be I know that could never be your way. If you can't come with us, then bless us and say goodbye for to the Stones we're bound as you too should be. There's light all about today, and it protects us and guides us. I'm old and unafraid and I'll touch the Stones once more, and show them to your lass.'

Poor Warren, strong though he was of limb, felt weak before his mother's words and the day's clear light. Troubled, too, and much afraid, for he loved them both and would not see them harmed.

'Go then, and I'll watch over this way the best I can until you come back. There's not many grikes about, nor guardmoles, and I don't even know why I came myself.'

'The Stone sent you,' said Violet with a smile. Then she touched her son, as he did her, and Mistle touched him too.

'I'll watch over you,' he called after them, 'but be quick about it.'

So Mistle led Violet on the way among the Stones whose lights and shadows fell before them and made a way where time seemed to have no purpose, and where each Stone they passed whispered its strength into Mistle for the days and the years of the life she would live; a way whose light and direction would lead her not only to the very heart of this history of Duncton Wood, but on to the heart of the Stone's purpose itself.

They came at last to the Stone Violet instinctively knew to be the one within whose orbit she was raised. High it rose, and the sun was golden on its flanks, the sky blue beyond and white where drifting cloud went by.

'Will you touch it?' asked Mistle, still awed but unafraid.

'For now we'll crouch before it, and later, perhaps, when the time is right, we'll touch it, you and I, and this old body will have done its work and seen the Stone's Silence into another mole's heart.

'That's it, you see, my dear: we may not be much in ourselves – too troubled by life and one thing and another – but we always carry Silence somewhere in our hearts and, however humble we may be, and unfulfilled, we can pass the feeling of it on. Mayhap one day a mole will come who can know that Silence and still live. That's what my good father told me, and it's what I'm telling you. So crouch now and listen out for Silence, and when the moment comes we'll touch the Stone.'

'Can I touch you while we wait?' asked Mistle.

Violet did not reply, but only nodded and looked tired, the sun seeming almost too bright for her old skin and fur.

'Are you all right?' asked Mistle going closer and seeming in a subtle way almost to grow up as she spoke these words.

'I'm tired, my dear, and I've been from the Stones far too long. But I'm here now and you're with me, and we'll just stay until it's time to touch the Stone.'

Then paw to paw and flank to flank they waited, old and young as one, and Violet's Stone rose silently before them, its shadow shortening towards itself as the sun rose higher still.

Chapter Four

Now we turn our snouts to Rollright, another of the ancient Seven, and a place where a mole lived who was much liked by Tryfan and his friends, though they had not met for many a moleyear.

His name was Holm and he was a muddy, marshy mole who lived in comfortable squalor with Lorren, herself of Duncton born. Both had survived the coming of the grikes under Henbane and the tragic evacuation of Duncton Wood that ensued. Holm was without siblings, but not so Lorren, and since those days she had seen neither Starling her sister nor Bailey, whom she remembered fondly as a stolid and determined younger brother.

But that was past, and now, today, this bright day, we are in Holm and Lorren's burrow, and find Holm silent. He usually was, leaving words to Lorren, who liked to talk. But when Holm spoke he said what he meant and all moles knew it. A mole of few but pertinent words, and one renowned as a route-finder, taught by no less a mole than great Mayweed himself.

Holm was small, and when he was not muddy he was dusty. He had ways and methods of his own – darty ways, quick jerky ways, ways by which a snout followed by a head popped round a corner and stared. One moment he was there, listening to Lorren saying that it was an especially nice day atop and did a mole's heart good to see it and bless me if it wasn't just the kind of day Starling and young Bailey would have liked if they were here, which they were not . . . and the next moment Holm was gone to the surface, only his tail and back paws showing as he snouted out the good sun. Then with a wriggle he was all gone, but still near, up above, and Lorren gazed at the burrow's roof as Holm moved about.

She was as proud of Holm as he of her, and even if she had never in all their days together quite managed to get their burrow in neat and tidy shape, why there was happiness there.

A shambly, untidy, dusty kind of happiness which made for dishevelled but obedient youngsters, each of whom loved their parents and carried good memories of them when they left to make their own way. All were moles who had learnt about the Stone and even if they became persuaded of the Word by Rollright's unusually easy-going eldrene, whose disapproval of followers was accompanied only by stern warnings, they felt sufficient love and loyalty to their parents not to inform on them, but rather to put their faith in the Stone down to eccentricity; and in Rollright, the eldrene made such indulgence easy, for her guardmoles chose a comfortable life and let sleeping weasels lie.

So Lorren had had her broods of pups, and she and Holm had been left unmolested by the grikes, and were content now to have lived through their first adult spring without young, and find the muddy peace which they had long looked forward to. . . .

Holm suddenly reappeared, eyes bright and staring. His mouth was open a little and he looked uncomfortable, even desperate. He was preparing himself to speak. Lorren waited.

'Got to go,' he said. 'Stones. To them. Rampion to guide.'

'Rampion?' said Lorren. 'But we haven't seen her for weeks. Too busy with her young.'

Rampion was their daughter by an early litter, and she loved them both dearly and came often to see them when she had time. She lived to the south of the Rollright Stones, and was one of the followers who at times of ritual covertly visited the Whispering Stoats, the cluster of Stones that lie south of the main circle which itself was banned and too dangerous for mole to visit. The Stoats had become the followers' meeting place.

'To Stoats she'll go today, but then to Stones. Must not, must she?'

'Well, no, though why you should think . . . I mean, how you could know?'

'Not without me to guide her,' said Holm, cutting her short.

Then suddenly he was gone and Lorren was left staring, aghast. A bit of sunshine wasn't an excuse to go gallivanting off to the Stones where a mole could get hurt by guardmoles, if not worse.

But barely had she opened her mouth to call after him than his head popped back down the tunnel and he blinked at her.

'Holm won't be seen. Holm was taught by Mayweed. Holm's safe as burrows. Don't fret. Holm loves you.'

Then he was gone and poor Lorren was crying, for it was not his way to say his love out loud, though she knew it to be true, and he only would have done so if there was something to fear. Then she grumbled a little to herself, for he must have known his words would make her cry.

'Must tidy up,' she said purposefully to herself, sniffing and wiping her face with her dusty paws. 'But he's a good mole, the best, and one day the Stone will grant his greatest wish.'

It was a touching tribute to those two's care for each other that when Lorren prayed it was of Holm she thought, and she usually ended up asking that one day he might be allowed to meet Mayweed once more, in whose company the part of him that was a route-finder felt most at home. That would be a day!

While Holm, in those moments he asked for the Stone's blessings, always found time to request that his Lorren might be reunited with her long-lost and much missed siblings, Starling and Bailey. Now, that *would* be a day!

Holm had been right. Rampion was on the surface in the enclave made by the Stoats, not meditating or praying but nervously snouting up at the bright sun, and at the shadows it seemed to cast all about.

'You!' she exclaimed, with surprise and relief in her eyes.

He nodded, but said nothing. His presence was sufficient words for her, and in the way they had there was need of no words more to explain why she was there, and why he had come.

Then he was off, and she following, leaving the familiar routes back to safety behind them as they moved forward across the field that lay between the Stoats and the prohibited Stones. Sunlight lit their way, the same that reached everywhere across moledom that day.

He took her by a surface route to near the Rollright circle, then underground to what she guessed was the buried base of the Stone that rises at the centre of Rollright's circle. Light filtered down through cracks in the sheep-worn soil above, and Rampion was surprised to see that the chamber's floor showed signs of use. A mole had been this way before, and recently.

'Me,' said Holm, answering the query in her eyes.

'You!' said Rampion in surprise. 'But you never told us. I thought Lorren was the active follower.'

Holm's eyes were wide, staring at the wall of stone and then at the cracked roof above.

'We have different ways, but the same purpose. Best way in a pair. Only way.'

'Can we burrow to the surface and touch the Stone? We could escape back down this way. . . .'

'Nearly. Not yet. Too soon.'

But he took her right up to the wall of Stone, though guarding against either of them touching it, and then, wrinkling his diminutive snout, he gazed at the roof more closely. The light came not just from the cracks there, but shimmered as well in the root tendrils that came down from surface plants, tiny shoots of grass, and the white-green of plantain roots. The roof looked frail and thin, and there was the sense of great light above it, waiting to be let in. Holm touched the trembling soil and it gave a little, letting more light in.

'Won't have to wait long. When we thrust out we'll touch the Stone. Grikes will see. Will chase. But we must do it, Rampion. It will be time to show the Stone Mole that this system knows he lives. All the Seven must try to do it. Holm feels it. Holm was taught by great Mayweed more than just routes.'

'I'm scared,' said Rampion, for suddenly her world seemed vulnerable, waiting for something that would change everything she knew.

'He's scared too,' said Holm quietly. 'Needs us now, needs all of us.'

Then he was silent once more, and in the half darkness of the chamber father and daughter waited for the moment when they must take their courage in their paws and break out into the light and touch the Stone.

We have but one record of the followers dying near or at the site of one of the ancient Seven that morning, and it is a most strange one and portentous.

For at Fyfield an incident occurred which was not scribed by moles of the Stone, but scrivened that same day by an eldrene, and one very different from the easy-going eldrene of Rollright.

Her name was Wort, eldrene of Fyfield, and all we need say of her now is this: had she not lived then many a follower and more would not have died. What Rollright gave way in indulgence and indiscipline Wort made up a hundred times in cruelty and persecution of those of the Stone.

Thus it was, in pursuance of vile followers (as it seemed to her), that on that June day she found herself with a cohort of guardmoles watching over the Fyfield Stone, and there apprehended three moles who, following that same urge or call we have noted already, had bravely made their way towards the Stone.

Wort killed them personally. Her talons in their

choking throats, she watched their eyes dim and glaze in the bright sun as the sounds they made faded, and they died. Afterwards Wort, ordering her guardmoles to stand off for a time, went to the Stone itself to desecrate it with the blood of miscreants that she carried still on her talons.

No mole in moledom hated the Stone more, nor saw more easily the dangers to which its temptations exposed moles of the Word. 'Seek out and destroy all those of the Stone, for they are evil and their vile faith is infectious' might have been her motto.

We know that she stanced before the Fyfield Stone alone, we know she reached out her talons to touch it in mockery and contempt. And we know what happened next, in her own scrivened words: '"Beware!" I warned myself. "For even here, the blood of moles who deserved to die still wet on my talons and fur, the temptations wait. This Stone seems beautiful . . ." This was a test! I resolved to wait until I was sure I was not corrupted or belittled by the Stone, but its Mistress, just as the Master of the Word is Master of all. So I waited that morning, that beautiful morning, and felt joy in the testing of my strength, and sighed and wept before the Fyfield Stone as I waited for the moment I would know the test was won and I could touch the Stone with impunity!'

So scrivened the eldrene Wort, and we shall see how, in its mercy, the Stone dealt with her, and how it was that of all unlikely moles, she was at one of the ancient Seven that special morning.

Now to Siabod. The mole we meet here has a name we know: Glyder, and we know him to be old indeed, but not stricken with the infirmity that indulgence in a wormful soil brings. His life had been active, and he had led the moles of Siabod through many troubled times and, living as he did in a system of steep tunnels and slatey ways, he had always been fit and well. But lately he had begun to slow, and the talk of younger moles had passed him by for he had heard it all before, too many times.

We who have followed Duncton's story to this June morning when Glyder climbs, know that his mother was Rebecca, mole of Duncton, and that through her he was Tryfan's half-brother. He was the wise mole who commended Alder and Marram to his peers, and from Alder had heard of Tryfan's existence and his mission. If there was a single disappointment in his life it was that the Stone had never put him and his brothers, Y Wyddfa, Dafydd and Fach, in the way of meeting Tryfan and his kin.

Well, a mole cannot have everything he desires and in any case the Stone provides more than enough to the mole who has eyes to see it, and a good body to feel it.

This spring past, as Glyder had begun to drift towards what wise Siabod moles call the heights, all of that had begun to seem past history, old history, and he had lost interest in it. First one brother, Y Wyddfa, had died, then Dafydd and Fach. Their passing left him the last of his generation, and feeling lonely, and he had decided to leave Siabod and live his last few moleyears by himself and contemplate that which he had spent his life guarding, the Stones of Siabod.

Glyder had prepared his moles as best he could for the future, entrusting their continuing resistance and strategy against the grikes to Alder, and the preservation of the Siabod ways to the many moles, middle-aged and younger, who had travelled with their elders to safety in the Carneddau.

Then, with gruff farewells to his friends, and final salutations exchanged with Alder, with whom he had achieved so much, Glyder, slower than he once had been, shakier too, and his fur grizzled grey and in places thin, set off down towards the Ogwen Vale, not telling a single mole his true intent. Which was, quite simply, to climb Tryfan and touch the Stones. Of what happened after that he neither thought nor cared, but assumed that one way or another his life would be over.

It was several days before he reached Ogwen, and two

44

more before he had climbed up the untidy slopes that rise to the west of Llyn Ogwen and across the boulder-strewn levels that run there. He decided to stay for a time until the thaw came and the heights above were at least approachable.

March had passed into April and then May, and Glyder's wild retreat had changed from survival to celebration as he breathed the good high air and knew at last a freedom he had always sought. The sun began to rise high enough to shaft down into the darker corners of Ogwen, and on the days it did he would gaze at its play across the black mural heights of Y Gribin, of Glyder Fach, and the sheer walls of Tryfan, wondering how he had ever dared to think he could climb to such heights.

But as the snow and ice on the rock faces above began to melt, Glyder heard and scented twofoots come and go. At first they troubled him, but he soon grew used to them and wondered if he was indeed quite mad, for, lacking mole for company, he began to find a comfort in their presence.

Early one morning a solitary twofoot came his way, up out of the mist and through dawn light past the rocks where he had his home. He heard its breathing, clinking, clattering passage and, in addition to its normal sweet scent, he scented fear. This was enough to alert him, for he had not thought that twofoots suffered fear. The way the twofoot went was strange as well, for it led into the nameless cwm above Glyder's tunnels, beyond which, surely, no creature but raven could safely go. Yet to Glyder's astonishment, the twofoot began to climb, its passage ponderous and slow, its breathing and grunt echoing about the high cwm. Higher it went, and the scent of fear hung unmistakably in that cold air.

Yet before it Glyder himself did not feel afraid, but, rather, curious and in some awe, and he went up to the very spot where the twofoot had begun to climb, and smelt and observed twofoot things whose colours almost blinded him. Purples, oranges, and greens. . . .

Then, as the sun got brighter, the twofoot above was

silent and still, but for occasional stresses of movement and a gasping, moaning, whispered fear. And suddenly a slip, a jerk at the thing that lay snaked and colourful about the rocks, and a darkening, heavy cry and fall, almost on to where Glyder stanced. And blood and the deep unmistakable sound which all creatures know: the sound of pain.

For the first and only time in his long life, Glyder found himself within touching distance of twofoot, and its smell sickened him. Yet he stayed where he was and met its gaze, which fluttered, and dimmed, and gazed again. The twofoot was dying.

It was there and then that Glyder of Siabod had a revelation that perhaps nomole in all of moledom's history had had before; or if it had it was not recorded until, later, Glyder's was. It was as simple a thing as ever could be. For watching over that twofoot Glyder understood that after all it was but a creature like himself, with life and death, with light and shadow in its form. Like weasel, like rabbit, like owl. Glyder lost his sense of fear and knew all life was one, all one.

But the twofoot lay dying, and he prayed for it. Its eyes were on his again, and then they were gone once more. But breath came from it, and life still, and scent.

He prayed again in Siabod and then turned his snout up beyond the creature towards great Tryfan's flanks, and knew he must begin to climb. Crevice by crevice, higher and higher, always beyond his questing paws. Night had come, and he had drunk rainwater in a cleft, and eaten the bodies of beetles where worms could never be.

He had slept, and woken with the dawn, and climbed another day, higher and higher, until suddenly he had found the plant he had often sought, the white and starry idwal lily, so rare that a mole who saw it was much blessed. There Glyder had rested one last day, vowing to start the final climb up to the unreachable Stones above at the very crack of the next dawn if the weather was set fair. By the idwal lily he slept, its scent no more than a wraith of peace on the wind.

Morning came, that same morning that came to all moledom that day, and Glyder woke in the deep shadow that daily besets the west side of Tryfan and watched as the sky paled, and the sun began to lighten the great heights of Y Garn and dread Twll Du, which rise massive across the Idwal Cwm.

Then, taking for his only sustenance the pure water he found in the clefts near where the lily grew, he began his climb again in shade, knowing that he would only see the sun that day if he reached the top where the Stones themselves were. As for living afterwards, he doubted that he would, for there would be no food so high, nor for days to come in his descent.

So, commending himself to the Stone's care, he climbed, and as he climbed the morning's light spread itself wondrously across rock, and water, stream and hidden cwm, far far below. And the only sound that accompanied him was the wind's quiet rush, and from far away the muted sound of roaring owl.

'For them too, and the twofoot below, I'll climb this day,' Glyder said to himself, 'for the Stone is for all creatures, aye, even for the twofoot.'

Though the broken, savage rocks beset him, yet still he struggled on in shade as the rocks on the slopes of the Carneddau to his left and the Glyders to his right were warmed and coloured by the clear sunlight.

Then, his breath all gone, his paws faltering, his mouth dry, the massive rocks seemed to flatten ahead, and he was there where nomole had ever been, unless it be a White Mole or a holy mole, or a giant of legend old.

As he went forward for the final part, he came into the sun's great light, and so bright was it that he could see no more of the two Stones than a rising whiteness, glistening and shining into the great sky.

The wind was quiet, the world spread all about, and the light full in his old paws. He moved a little to one side, to stare up at the Stones without the sun in his eyes and saw their grey sheer rising sides, and then he looked far beyond them to the dark rise of Moel Siabod, the place of his birth.

He wanted to touch the Stones, but something held him back. He looked down at his sturdy paws, and at his talons worn with age and climbing where nomole had been before. Old Glyder stared up at the Stones and drew his talons back. Time yet to touch them. Time now to go closer still and settle, time to meditate and wait.

'Aye!' he whispered proudly, feeling his strength and knowing his weakness too. 'I'll not hurry to touch them but be ready for when it's right. But make it soon, Stone, for a mole could die up here!' The sun rose still, and the air was quiet.

So Siabod. Now to Beechenhill and four moles resting in the early summer grass, two sets of siblings.

The eldest pair, Betony and her brother Bramble, were the offspring of Squeezebelly, leader of the Beechenhill moles. These were the two who, as youngsters, found Tryfan near this same spot and led him to the Beechenhill Stone where, for a time never to be forgotten by anymole who heard, he spoke of the tasks of the Stone and how a mole finds courage to fulfil them.

The second and younger pair were Wharfe and his sister Harebell, two of the three moles born of that fated litter that Tryfan begot by Henbane of Whern. All were autumn moles, born the previous October, and they still had about them a touch of youth. Their third sibling was Lucerne, whom Henbane kept and raised, but his existence and full darkness were not yet known to them.

Wharfe and Harebell had been brought covertly to Beechenhill by Mayweed and Sleekit, and their care entrusted to Squeezebelly himself, that they might grow up privily, their true origins unsuspected. Nothing indeed was to be said to them until, when Squeezebelly alone adjudged the time was right, they must decide for themselves the path they must follow.

Betony and Bramble had become their watchers and

friends, keeping them close when they were young and enjoying their company now they had grown and were nearly ready for what adulthood would bring. There was about Wharfe and Harebell a natural authority and strength, which had already begun to reveal itself. Harebell had a quality of grace and intelligence that seemed like a shining of light across her fur and in her eyes, and though there was natural cheer in her face and way yet somewhere within her, too, was a watchful sadness as if there were things in life, dark things, that she was preparing herself for.

Wharfe was bigger than her, and stronger by far, and though he knew it not he had about his limbs that same strength which Tryfan had had when young. But more than that, he had an extra strength, checked for now, which showed only when he was angry, which was rare, and which had the hint of Mandrake of Siabod about it. Perhaps it was in the rougher edges of his fur, or the purpose of his talons, or the way his great head turned and stared, as Mandrake's once had, at wild clouds as if in search of something lost. If this was the counterpart of Harebell's hint of sadness it matched it well, and expressed what these two moles had suffered when, within moments of their birth, they had been taken from their mother's teat, at her behest, and secreted far from Whern's harmful influence.

The sun had risen slowly that morning, and by its brightening light in leaf and dew they had taken their slow leisure. Then settling down near where the streamlet runs, and watching the sparkles in its flow, they talked again of what the future held. Each said they would travel to see the Stones of the Seven Systems, whatever grikes might say, and each agreed that of them all they wished most to see the Duncton Stone from which great Tryfan himself had come. From that way, too, the Stone Mole would surely come one day as well, to all of moledom – and certainly to Beechenhill!

But then for a moment a chill had come to the air, the

kind that Harebell knew made Wharfe uncomfortable, as, for a few seconds, nomole else but she noticed he stirred and looked northward, his eyes bleak and wild, his spirit lost. There a darker cloud moved in the sky, threatening to mar the beauty of the morning, rolling and rising in the sky. He saw it and so did she, but the others, staring and thinking of the south, had eyes only for the light of the sun.

Wharfe crouched up, grew still, glanced briefly at his sister, and then down towards the south again as if to forget what he could not.

'What is it, Wharfe?' asked Harebell with concern. The others became concerned as well.

Wharfe looked at them all and smiled and said, 'We are each other's greatest friends, brother to brother, sister to sister, and wherever we may go we shall be as one. Soon, sooner than we know, we shall be apart. But a day must come when we shall be one again. Then . . . we shall meet at. . . .'

He paused and was silent.

'The Duncton Stone!' said Bramble with excitement, liking the dream.

'Here, on this very spot,' said Harebell, smiling.

'I don't know,' said Betony, capturing Harebell's deeper concern.

The three turned to Wharfe, for him to decide, but his question asked he seemed to have lost interest and turned back north to gaze at the dark mounting cloud that seemed to be bearing out of nothing towards them, right across the northern sky.

Then he was wild again, staring this way and that, distressed.

'I thought I heard. . . .'

'What did you hear?'

'A note. Deep, like a calling to us all. Didn't any of you hear it?' He seemed surprised and he looked troubled. The dark of his fur and powerful form was mirrored by the terrible approaching sky behind. Still the sun shone bright, but the day had a shadow across it.

Then quite suddenly there *was* a note, deep and haunting, mournful, quite short, yet in its effect as persistent as a hungry pup's cry.

'We're wanted!' cried out Wharfe with certainty. 'It's as it was when one of us called when we were young, and the others knew he was needed and must go quick.'

The others looked at him in alarm, and at the coming clouds, and then reared up in readiness as he himself reared up, turned and said, 'I'm needed by the Stone. Now. We're *all* needed, and I don't know why. All *moledom's* needed. Can't you feel it?'

He turned and began to run back upslope and Bramble, who least understood the terrible urgency of the moment, called after him, 'You never said where we would meet to be together again. You never said. . . .'

'At our own Stone, at Beechenhill: there we must go now, and there one day we'll be needed and we'll meet again. At the Stone of Beechenhill. . . .'

Then Tryfan's son by Henbane was gone upslope among the grass, faster than they could follow up the long, long way towards Beechenhill's Stone.

As he went, quicker and quicker, urgent against the darkening sky, the June sun faltering on his back, the others came after him, and moles they passed watched and wondered what the fuss was about before they too stared up at the forbidding sky, and began to think a storm was on the way for the air was restless, and heavy, and the light now strange indeed.

While on ran Wharfe, leaving his sister and friends further and further behind as he strove to reach the Stone before the darkening sky overcast it with shadow and driving rain. As he went he felt that in some terrible and mysterious way the very future of moledom was in his paws. Yet not just in his own: in *all* their paws, to make or mar as they themselves decreed.

North now, beyond the Dark Peak and into the turbulent shadows that confuse a mole that travels on from there.

Past fair Grassington. Past the crag of Kilnsey and then over the River Wharfe, which marks the edge of Whern and gave Tryfan's son by Henbane his name, and up the limestone terraces that form Whern's westward flank.

No sun there now. Its light has gone and June seems all unknown.

Lucerne is abroad.

Lucerne come with his mother to take pleasure in the livid and corrupted sky.

Lucerne, dark one of the three. Henbane's own, cherished and cosseted by her, reared for fell purpose and darkest of intents, the hope for redemption of generations of moles who chose scrivening and dark sound.

Lucerne, a mirroring of his brother Wharfe, but a reflection seen in the black alluring depths of an evil pool. Eyes and body much the same but biased too well to elegance, his body and limbs making their stance too well to trust. His arrogant beauty abnormal and most sinister.

Just as one forebear, Mandrake, was in Wharfe's rich veins so another's blood had seeped like disease into Lucerne's: Rune's own.

'What is it, my sweet?' asked Henbane, smiling from the shadows of Whern's tunnels where she preferred to stay.

'The light I hated has gone out across the fell and darkness is going south from here, as I decreed it should,' whispered Lucerne. He turned and, though almost an adult now, he bent to suckle her, his smooth mouth to her sleek teat, his paws to her flank in a perverse adult copying of a pup's natural need. While sensuously, Henbane stroked his fur.

'The light is gone,' he whispered once more, lifting his head from her belly and her thin milk streaked on his well-made cheek.

'Good,' said Henbane. 'Good.' But there was distant weariness in her eyes, as of a mole who, finding her task almost complete now, begins to doubt its worth. To reassure herself she came out into what light there was and caressed Lucerne's flank. He did not respond, and his eyes were alert on the billowing sky.

'I want to see the Stone,' he said. 'Soon.'

'There are many, my love, too many for a single mole to see. What would you do with the Stone?'

'I should have it for the Word. I would touch it, and speak out the Word and pervert its power to our use.'

'Perversion' was a word that Lucerne liked to use. He used it well.

Behind him distant thunder rolled. A great white flash lightened the sky. Wind came, and sudden violent rain. For a moment Lucerne seemed afraid.

With a smile, Henbane offered her teat once more and Lucerne seemed almost to go to it. Then lightning came again as he hesitated, and its light flared across her body and at her wet teats and he seemed to see her as if in horror and disgust.

'Come suckle me, my love,' she said.

The lightning was violent about them and the thunder huge, and suddenly, impulsively, with hatred in his face, he turned on her and struck her.

'No more,' he said. And with a cry that combined loss with discovery of something new he turned back to relish the scene as rain poured down and his fur shone bright with wet. Appalled, hurt, stricken more in heart and mind than body, Henbane retreated to shelter from the rain, and Lucerne's wrath.

He did not look at her again, but cried out: 'I shall kill the Stone!' And he arced his talons sharp across the sky. Then from high above him, as if at his command, cracking thunder came once more.

Lucerne laughed with pleasure at the dreadful scene and raised his paw as if to touch a Stone which none but he could see. The sky murked with driven rain and the cloud was untidy and lowering over Whern's greatest height, and the storm passed on across moledom to the south and Henbane was gone, and Lucerne triumphant and alone.

Chapter Five

As Beechen and Tryfan continued their trek towards the Duncton Stone that bright day, the way ahead remained rough and needed clearing, and Beechen said more than once, 'Is it near? Are we nearly there?'

His voice was the more nervous because Feverfew seemed to have dropped behind now, and he knew it was not because she could not keep up with them but because this trek represented his passing from her main care to Tryfan's.

Then Tryfan disappeared as well, in among some heavy undergrowth, branches and twigs cracking as he went to find the way ahead.

Tryfan looked back and could not see Beechen, though he could hear him, so he called out to him to stay where he was while a way was found . . . He was annoyed with himself, for nomole knew Duncton better than he and yet that day he felt disorientated and could not seem to keep in touch with his own paws. Each way he looked was beguiling, and the air now was warm on the wood's floor, its scents deep and rich, the soil wormful. Strange! The soils here should be drier and the tall beech trees that surround the Stone clearing must be near. But the ground seemed different and undulating wrong . . . downslope *here* and the wood filled suddenly with the strangest wraiths of light as if there were unseen moles about. Tryfan crouched down in awe.

While Beechen, seeing Tryfan go ahead and then disappearing beyond some bramble stems, ran quickly after him to find him once again. Except that when he reached where Tryfan had seemed to go he was not there. Only sunshine, and the whispering breeze high above, and then, as he turned, it seemed the brambles turned as well and suddenly frightened he ran back the way he had come, except when he got there it was not. He was alone and lost.

Lost? No, no . . . Mayweed's lesson came back to him. *He* was *here*: his paws, his snout, his breathing, he himself. Here. Mayweed . . . and bringing back to himself an image of the strange mole, Beechen felt comfort and calmness. He was not lost. He was free. And the Stone was near. He need only . . . what? Mayweed told him to feel his way forward, or back, or whatever way felt best. Make where he was familiar and using that go on, never ever panicking. . . .

So Beechen, very nervous it is true, but still himself, still not panicked, went on. All was leaves, dried twigs and poky branches, and the sticky fronds of cleaver caught at his flanks like soft alien things trying to pull him from his path. What path? Confused again suddenly, beginning to feel tearful, the sound of a mole crashing about nearby hunting him, coming to take him. So soon did Beechen forget Mayweed's lesson and suddenly, blindly, ran on. The sun was bright and whirling in his eyes, the branches jolting and shaking past him and he might then have cried out in fear had another voice not cried out first:

'Here. *Here!*'

She was there, a young female and an older, too, at a Stone among great Stones, but distant and seeming unreachable as he went, for they got no nearer. Yet 'Here!' they cried.

'What is your name?' he seemed to say.

'Mistle,' the wind whispered. 'Waiting for you to come at last.'

'No, no, no, but you must come to me,' he said, for as he reached her and her Stone, and the old female with her, she was gone, and the Stone she showed him yet to be, and there was the first hint of cloud in the sky, and dark imminence.

Then the undergrowth was gone, and the trees seemed to fall away and a thin and ragged mole called out to offer help.

55

'Here, mole. Aye! *This* way. I have waited for you so long! Caradoc's my name.'

'But you must come to me . . .' whispered Beechen again, running towards him but finding as he did that the ground steepened and grey rocks rose where Caer Caradoc had been, and the air was cold and the wind strengthening.

Above him now Glyder beckoned, and called out directions, and said it was not far to climb.

'But you . . .' said Beechen, nearly in despair, for though they were so near they still had far to go, and he was but one to help, and weak, and darkness was looming on them all and his paws were weary and his breathing coming hard.

Then that wild place was gone, and trees were near again, and another female calling from a circle of Stones. A male was near her, small, eyes bright. Both sympathetic, summoning him to safety among their Stones if only, as they got nearer still, the circle remained substantial and the Stone where the female bid him come would stay where it was and be touchable.

'Here, Stone Mole, *here*!' cried Rampion.

But her circle was gone, and as it went past him there went another, barely seen: Fyfield, where a grike mole strove to touch the Stone and called out for him to come.

'Here!' said the self-righteous voice of Wort.

Everywhere were moles who needed him, yet offered help.

Or almost everywhere. For now Beechen found himself where tunnels once had been and holy burrows, but ruined now and desolate. The white bones of moles were scattered across the great high hill of Uffington and nomole was there. The Blowing Stone was hereabouts but too far off for a lost mole to find and reach before the darkness came.

Then his paws were running, running where others had run before, but he needed help now for a great grim darkness was coming – too great for him to bear. The moles had scattered from this place, and the sun's warmth was draining from his fur, and his body was shivering and he was afraid.

'Help me!' he cried out across the deserted hill, which changed even as he seemed to see it to a place of beauty called Beechenhill.

'Here!' cried Wharfe. 'Here, now . . .' And Beechen knew the darkest terror of them all.

But even as it took him and he began to feel the pain, 'Beechen!' said a voice so old, a voice he knew, a voice that was the sound he sought. 'Beechen.'

Old, grey-white, limping, his eyes warm, his good limbs bent, rising beech trees all about him across a clear wood floor.

'Beechen, help me now.'

The old mole turned and the youngster followed him, turned into the clearing filled with light, light like his eyes, and Beechen caught the old mole up, who turned and smiled.

'Come, my son,' he said.

There before them rose the Stone whose sides caught all the colours of the sun as it rose straight and true towards the sky.

'You know my name and who I am?'

Beechen nodded.

'Then help them touch the Stone. Help them for me.'

'I am afraid.'

'They are as well. Help them now, it is for me.'

Then the old mole limped towards the Stone, whose light was great and whose sound was Silence more than ever mole had heard. As Beechen tried to follow him, the light was gone, and Beechen found himself before the Duncton Stone.

The June sun was there as the sounds of the great wood fell away below and Beechen strove to reach up a paw and touch the Stone.

But how hard that is, how frightening, and the only consolation he felt was that across moledom were a few striving moles whose names he had known but which he now forgot, and all were there for him.

'Help me!' he cried out again and the few who were waiting heard it well.

Caradoc, guardian of Caer Caradoc.

Mistle, before Violet's Stone in Avebury.

Glyder at the Siabod Stones.

Then, at Fyfield, Wort: alone, afraid, judgemental, reaching up towards the Stone against which she tested herself and felt fear.

'Help me,' she whispered, an unknowing echo of the Stone Mole's plea.

Then Rampion, of Rollright born and bred, true mole: she strove to touch the frightening Stone.

All striving, all reaching out their paws, six at the seven Ancient Systems, one more needed to make the seven up.

'Help us now!' cried Beechen, his body beginning to tremble with the strain. The air was heavy about, the sky trembling with darkness coming.

But that prayer was not heard or felt where once it might have been. Not at Uffington, the first of the seven Ancient Systems but last this special day to find a mole to help. None there. Only a place now of memory, where prayers were lost among the ruined tunnels and ended with the white bones of long-dead moles. Not there. A new Seventh was now needed, and with it the change that moledom had so long sought. As the stars shift in the sky so now occurred reorientation across the Stones of moledom. New strength for old. Tradition dies and is reborn. Only so can such prayers be answered.

'Help us!' cried out the helpless Beechen one more time and, turning its back on sterile Uffington, his prayer fled north to Beechenhill and a darkening sky and the approach of sweeping rain. But still where its Stone rose there was light. Brighter than everywhere else about, but threatened, and a mole desperate to reach it now, and desperate with tiredness.

'Too late! I am too late!' cried Wharfe, striving to run forward still as other moles followed far behind.

So he ran to reach the shining Stone before cloud and rain obscured it from the sun and a moment that would never be regained was lost for ever. From where does a brave mole's strength come? Faith? Stubbornness? An ordination of the stars? No, mole, it comes from the Silence where he was made, the Silence that most lose. From there it comes, and it is allmole's heritage.

As Wharfe felt the first spits of rain across his face he found his final strength. The ground levelled off and the Stone was there and he too tired to feel afraid. Even as the first full drop of rain plunged from the sky he reached up his paw and placed it on the Stone, and the wet fell glistening on his flesh and fur.

'I offer my life and all my striving to the Stone,' he cried, 'and my help to all who need it!'

'And I!' cried out Caradoc, far away in the Welsh Marches where he had waited alone with such faith for so long. 'I offer my help!'

Then too did Mistle touch at Avebury, and Glyder for the Siabod moles. Then Rampion of Rollright born. And in Fyfield the wise Stone accepted Wort's touch too, though she was of the Word and her intentions were most evil. Yet six moles touching, and using their strength to help him touch as well.

For then it was that Beechen reached up, and touched the Duncton Stone, and spoke the words that mark the acceptance of his great ministry to mole: 'Stone, who made me, help me serve their need and know thy truth that through me they shall know it too. Teach me to know things as they are: the light and the dark, the noise and the Silence, those that take and those that give; help me to so love them that they shall hear thy Silence beyond the life I dedicate to them.'

So prayed Beechen, where Tryfan and Feverfew found him, crouched before the Duncton Stone, his left paw touching it, and all about him the sense of others near, and holiness, and Silence. They went to him, and touched him with their love and were silent with him before the Stone.

The sun darkened before the clouds that came and mounted up. Dark clouds of warning and trial. The sky cracked, and from it rain fell and shrouded all moledom in its wet and noise.

Yet Beechen knew only joy and said, 'I am not alone. There are others with me though I remember not their names. But they shall wait for me. They shall know me and help me until, back here where I was born, and where I come today, I shall be born again and they shall know me, and know themselves.'

And his tears and those of his mother and of Tryfan were at one with the rain that fell; and the good soil of Duncton knew it, and the Stone as well.

Yet, as they turned from the clearing, the Stone trembled and over its wet facets the reflections of the clouds still went. A mole had dedicated his life to the Silence, but great was the darkness, and a mole but small. The Stone trembled in Duncton and began to wait.

While in one place only across all of moledom the sun shone again that day, bringing to life the wet faces of its pale scars and high fells. At Whern it shone, and on Lucerne its light fell, and his eyes narrowed against it and liked it not.

He turned back underground, his eyes dark and his mouth cruel, his body bent towards a future grim that would start where he himself began, by the still pool of the Rock of the Word. So to there he went, and found Henbane.

'What shall you do?' she said, for the day of dark and sun, when her only pup had hit her, was a day when life turned and set itself anew.

'I like not the light, nor the Stone,' Lucerne whispered across the dark pool to the Rock of the Word. Then he was silent as he began to plot the final fading of the light, and the destruction of the Stone.

'Its fall shall be your ministry,' she said. 'I shall not oppose your accession when the time comes.'

'No,' said Lucerne evenly, 'you shall not.'

Lucerne turned and stared into her eyes and, powerful though she was and still remained, his gaze was the greater, and she looked away. At the Rock? At tunnels that led to where nomole knew?

'Leave me,' said Lucerne.

Neither Rock nor tunnel was it that she saw as she left. But rather a memory, as faint and uncertain as the light that tried to glimmer at the fissure high in the roof above. A memory before any she had ever caught before. A memory born in this very chamber, when she herself was born. A memory of a momentary shaft of light, lost in the fell years when Charlock her mother and Rune her vile father bore down upon her. Lost until now. And knowing it Henbane, for the first time since that nearly forgotten time when she was still wet from her mother's womb, faltered.

'Leave me!' roared out Lucerne.

Which Henbane did, scattering the sideem that clustered about the higher tunnels, breathless, desperate for the surface and what it had which Whern could never have. Which was light, light of a June day almost done, light that follows the cleansing rains of a storm.

'Light,' said Henbane softly as if she saw it for the first time, and she wept for what she was and what Lucerne had now become. Wept for the life and lives she had lost, and could never find again.

'Help us,' she whispered as she watched the light of that day fade now across Whern, and all moledom too, and saw the darkness come. But whether her prayer was answerable, whether by the Word or something greater than the Word, nomole could know. Moledom faced at last itself, and the answers would lie in what it did, and how.

Chapter Six

As the rain finally eased across Duncton Wood and gave way to a cool evening, Tryfan began to tell Beechen of the events that led to his birth there before the Stone.

Feverfew stayed on as witness to the truth of what Tryfan said, and sometimes when his memory was doubtful or faulty gave her own account, for history is never certain, and its tellers rarely perfect.

Again and again on a particular point of detail Tryfan would say, 'You'll need to look at Spindle's account of this, for he was the one who insisted on scribing things down and leaving good records behind, and though many of the texts were hidden where they were scribed and must one day in more peaceable times be recovered, when he settled in the Marsh End with me he scribed more general accounts of things as they had been, saying that one day it might be useful. Sooner than he thought, I imagine! The pace of moledom has increased since I was your age. But even so, between us Feverfew and I can tell you of the things that matter most and the details can wait until you know scribing. . . .'

Of his journey to Uffington Tryfan spoke, and of Boswell; of the coming of the grikes and the long eclipse of the Stone's light by the darkness of the Word; of the journeys with Spindle and the exploration into the heart of the Wen where he first met Feverfew. Then after that to Whern, and the return to Duncton and the star in the sky that presaged Beechen's birth.

As night fell and the moon rose, Tryfan told Beechen with affection of the many moles, many still unknown and their tasks still unfulfilled, who carried in their hearts the light of hope and faith that one day a leader would come to show them the way out of the darkness which, as many were beginning at last to see, they had helped make for themselves. So he led their talk to the Stone Mole's coming.

'You know who the Stone Mole is, don't you, Beechen?'

Beechen nodded, and stared at the moonstruck Stone.

'It is me, isn't it?' he said simply. Then he added with a touching humbleness, 'But I am just mole. I'm not special. But. . . .'

As he paused Tryfan went closer to him on one flank and Feverfew on the other, and all three stared at the Stone and the dark sky beyond.

Beechen continued softly: 'Sometimes I seem to know I'm more than me and it makes me frightened, but excited as well. I feel there are moles waiting for me but I don't know where or how I am to find them. When I touched the Stone I knew that some of those others were there helping me. But. . . .'

Beechen turned to look at Tryfan, and then at his mother, and there was fear in his eyes, and tears. By that light he looked barely older than a pup.

'I don't have to leave yet, do I?'

'No, not yet,' said Tryfan, barely able to contain the confusion of feelings he felt before Beechen's mixture of fear and simple acceptance of a task whose difficulty and greatness he already sensed. 'You've things to learn, things that we in Duncton can teach you. Your task for now is to listen to other moles you meet and learn from what they say and what they do.

'In the old days youngsters left in the years after Midsummer – those at Duncton went out on to the Pastures and a few, like myself, left the system altogether. I first left Duncton in September and I think your time to leave will be when autumn comes as well, but the Stone will guide you on that. Perhaps some of us will come with you, for you will have much to do and will need help as I did. But there too the Stone will help you as it helped me find Spindle and Mayweed and many others I grew to love. Why mole, leaving's a fear-making thing but 'tis a challenge as well, and there're moles waiting to cross your path and bring you much you never dreamed of.

'But meanwhile you must take leave of your mother for the short time to Midsummer, during which I will take you about the system so that you get to know its tunnels and the moles who live here. We shall live in the Marsh End, and before Midsummer comes you shall learn a little of scribing. Afterwards you shall learn much more, and it may not be easy for I sense there is but little time. The summer years, perhaps, but not much more. I had longer than that with Boswell but never felt I had learnt enough! But for now get some sleep. Dawn comes and we must take our leave soon.'

At one time Tryfan had assumed that the Stone Mole would come ready made but now he understood that his own task with Beechen was to prepare him as best he could, with others' help, for whatever challenges might present themselves. For that it was certainly better he left his home tunnels and lived among other moles.

Tryfan's natural protectiveness towards Beechen had already made him fix on the Marsh End Defence tunnels as the best place for him to be. It was the repository of all Spindle and he had scribed through the long winter moleyears before this summer, and in the atmosphere of texts and learning Beechen must find out all he could of what moles had made of the Stone, and what, too, they had *unmade*.

'Anyway,' Tryfan told Feverfew a little later when Beechen had gone to sleep, 'now that summer's here I feel a scribe's need to go back to the work I left the day Spindle died and this youngster was born. I've a lot to do and he can help me do it and learn a thing or two as well. There's plenty of moles down Barrow Vale and Marsh End way who'll be glad to meet him, and he's a friendly inquisitive youngster and will learn as much from them as anymole else.'

'I shall miss yew tway,' said Feverfew, 'yette does a moule nede silence and tranquylitie after the pasciouns of

64

the sprynge. Watch ovre hym wel, my der, and youseln also.'

'I shall, Feverfew. Nor should you wander far. Midsummer's the time the grikes get active once more and no doubt some will venture into Duncton and poke about. Well, you know the system's ways and how to avoid strangers, and Skint, who knows the ground along the roaring owl way better than any mole, has got watchers organised so we'll not be taken by surprise.'

They dozed together for a while, paw to paw, flank to flank, snout snuggled into the other's fur, and dawn light crept through the trees into the rain-damp wood and bathed the sleeping moles in its softness until the rising sun warmed their fur and dried the moisture at their paws, and they awoke once more.

After grooming and a peaceful meal together, the three said a short prayer to the Stone and set off downslope. The confusions of the day before seemed to have left the trees and undergrowth and they were soon back to the runs and tunnels that had been their shared home since April.

The two males said a brief farewell to Feverfew and then, turning from her, set off downslope once more, the feeling of sadness soon leaving as the rich lower slopes of Duncton Wood opened out before them, and a new and important part of Beechen's life began.

Tryfan's return to Barrow Vale after so long away, and with no less a mole than Beechen the Stone Mole at his flank, was soon observed and caused great excitement. There had been much talk over the time since April of what Beechen might be like, and those few sightings of him that had been made – and what guardians like Bailey, Sleekit and Mayweed had said – had only added to the sense that he was a mole the system might well be proud of, and one worthy to carry the hopes of the many old and beset moles who had felt until his coming that time and circumstance had passed them by, and they had been outcast to oblivion and hopelessness.

So when word went out that Tryfan and the youngster were fast approaching Barrow Vale – no, had *arrived* in Barrow Vale – many a mole put all thoughts of summer tunnel delving, modest exploration and a spot of worm-finding to one side, and under the guise of coming to say hello, came to have a good look at how Beechen had turned out.

Tryfan, less sociable now than he might once have been, was not well pleased by the crush of extended paws and pattings on the back, but he took it with rough grace and was glad to see that Beechen was warm and friendly to all he met, though a little too dazed before so many to say much.

A few familiar faces were among the throng, and these Beechen was especially glad to see: Bailey was there, a mole he much liked and whom he knew had a special place in Feverfew's heart since he had been appointed by Boswell to watch over her coming to Duncton Wood. There, too, he met the quiet but impressive Marram, who wished him well and said that when Tryfan judged the time right he would be glad to tell Beechen about guardmole ways – he had been a guardmole once – and about Siabod where he had journeyed and lived awhile.

'Siabod!' said Beechen. 'I'd be glad to hear about that place!'

They lingered longer than Tryfan might have wished in Barrow Vale and though the intention had originally been to travel on through to the Marsh End that same day, it was decided eventually to stay where they were for the night. Others did the same and as the evening evolved into a night of quiet reunion and story-telling, and later some mirth and revelry mixed (it must be said) with maudlin nostalgia for times past but not forgotten, Tryfan was glad that they had stayed. It did Beechen good to listen to others talking, and to hear the old songs and know what a strange outcast system of moles he had been born into and from which he might yet learn much.

The moles gathered in the great community chamber of

Barrow Vale itself where once, Tryfan explained, the elder meetings of the system were held and where the great and notorious Mandrake held court; and where, too, the sinister Rune, then young, first gained power in a southern system and learnt the weaknesses and the strength of followers of the Stone.

'Before my time,' growled Tryfan in memory of those days, 'but Rune desired my mother and she desired him not. For that, much later, I had punishment enough!' He waved a paw across his scarred face and the moles were silent and serious, for there was not one there but Beechen himself who had not a suffering story to tell about moles of the Word; and the bitterest were those who had been grikes or guardmoles themselves, and whom the Word betrayed.

The chamber of Barrow Vale, so long deserted after the plagues came, was in use again, its floor dust-free and its entrances clear. The sense of age and history that the place had came not so much from the earthen walls as from the roots of the trees on the surface above which gave support and delineation, and in many places – the more comfortable ones – were polished by mole passage or use as resting places, and here and there were pitted and roughened by the sharpening of talons.

Friends of Tryfan, like Bailey and Marram, and Sleekit too who joined the group later in the evening, formed the inner circle of moles near Tryfan and Beechen, along with a few bolder souls who wanted a good look at the youngster. But by far the greater number were those quiet and modest moles, many aged now, who encircled the inner group. Though they spoke little their eyes said much, for they watched Beechen with a touching eagerness and loyalty, and listened to the general talk in some awe.

When Beechen went among them, as he did later with some worms, they were embarrassed and abashed, but mostly pleased that he came so close.

Yet all was not quite peace and tranquillity, for moles do

not mix easily in large numbers, and arguments some-times flare.

One mole in particular seemed to attract a general opprobrium and his name was Dodder. He was an old guardmole, and a senior one at that, who seemed irritable with moledom and inclined to argue with anymole near him, and provoke hostility in others.

'You're not stancing here, you mean old bugger,' said another to him when he first came down from the surface.

'Wouldn't want to, Madder. It's bad enough having to share a chamber with you let alone a patch! You and your kind is what moles like me gave our lives for.'

'Humph!'

And so on. But outbursts like these were short-lived and as moles finally dozed off and judgements of the night were made, most agreed that it had been a successful coming out for Beechen, and the youngster had acquitted himself well. As for the business of the 'Stone Mole' and that, well, a mole got carried away in April by the light of a strange star for he seemed normal enough a mole now he had grown, didn't he? Nothing exactly *holy* about him. In fact, truth to tell, it was a bit disappointing that he was so normal. . . .

But when morning came and everymole had to get on with their day, a good few forgot their shyness of the evening before and came forward and modestly wished Beechen well, and, having heard he was to learn scribing down in the Marsh End, they whispered that they hoped Tryfan did not treat him too hard and that he got out into the fresh air from time to time.

'Thank you,' faltered Beechen, not sure what he was thanking them for and wondering what they knew or guessed about Tryfan that he did not.

Moleyears later, many remembered their first meeting with Beechen at Barrow Vale, and would say, with that nostalgia tinged with sadness that attaches to memory of a world lost beyond recall, 'He were but a youngster then, with eyes as wide as a starling's bill for moledom all about! Whatmole would have thought . . . ?'

But whatever mole *did* think, one at least had special reason to remember those early days, and his story, but briefly told, must be enough to show that even then Beechen, for all his 'normality' and youth, had been touched by the Stone and was already, though he himself probably knew it not, reaching out to touch moledom's heart.

It happened that morning, soon after they set off from Barrow Vale, that they came across a mole, a thin old male, hiding to one side of their route in the gloom of some nettle stems, as if he had been waiting for them to pass so that he might catch a glimpse of them. It was not the first time it had happened – indeed, Tryfan was used to it on his own account for many of the outcasts had had experiences so violent and sad that they were timid and half-broken things; and if disease had touched them as well, they were embarrassed yet pathetically eager for acknowledgement.

Though Tryfan was no longer a mole who bothered much with the niceties of social behaviour – perhaps because he could not see as well as he once could – he always found it in his heart to greet such moles, though if he could he avoided protracted conversations with them. But a greeting, and a touch, and a moment's warmth did not seem too much to give.

On this particular day, and after the lingerings in Barrow Vale, Tryfan was more than eager to get on. Certainly, there was timidity in the mole's gaze, but it was mixed with curiosity and longing too. Tryfan had seen the mole on the night of Beechen's birth but did not know his name, and he had not been among those in Barrow Vale the night before.

'May the Stone be with thee, youngster,' said the mole who, to Tryfan's relief, did not attempt to say more, or come any closer. Indeed, they were almost past him before Beechen stopped and turned and stared back at the mole.

'Come on, Beechen,' said Tryfan, fearing another delay.

But it was too late, and Beechen had gone back to the mole and greeted him.

His face was ravaged by scalpskin, and his paws were swollen, bent and evidently painful. He looked both surprised and alarmed as Beechen approached and half turned to get away. But Beechen was too fast for him and the old mole stopped and his face broke into an uncertain smile.

''Twas just to wish you well, mole. Just to *see* you.'

Beechen stared and said nothing, and the mole said nervously, 'They say you're named Beechen. Not a name I've heard before but sturdy enough all the same.' The mole spoke clearly and well despite his natural diffidence. His accent was local and Tryfan guessed that he had been brought to Duncton from a nearby system.

'What's *your* name?' asked Beechen.

'Me?' said the mole. He seemed to hesitate, which was strange since a mole ought to know his name even if he was diseased and inclined towards forgetfulness. 'My name? 'Tis . . . why, I don't know. I . . .' and his voice slipped into a fading unhappy cackle as if he regarded himself as so worthless he had even forgotten his own name.

Tryfan was ready to bring this exchange to a halt, and urge Beechen back on to the path into the Marsh End when something about Beechen's stance stopped him. The youngster had grown suddenly still, as had the other mole, and to Tryfan's surprise Beechen reached gently forward and touched the mole's face.

'Whatever name others have called you, mole, all these years past, it was not the one your mother used. What was your real name?'

The mole held Beechen's gaze for only a moment or two more before, his eyes softening, his snout fell low and he shook his head a little, as if to shake away a memory too painful to bear here, now, in the light of the present day.

Tryfan felt a tremor of insight and saw that this was a scene, or a version of it, which would be repeated many times in the years to come, as Beechen cut through with a single touch of his paw other moles' doubts and evasions.

'Why, mole,' said the mole, 'how would you know that? Nomole knows my real name.'

Beechen gazed at him and said nothing and the male sniffed and looked frail, as his troubled, half-blind eyes looked here and there for a comfort they did not find. And eventually he wept, and let Beechen touch him once again.

'Nay, you're right. My name . . . my name was . . .' And it was a long time before he was able to say it. But finally . . . 'My name was Sorrel once upon a time, but the grikes took it from me and never gave it back. They took my mate and our young and sent me here. Nomole to call me Sorrel now.'

'Where did you come from?'

'Fyfield, which isn't far off as the rook goes.'

'Sorrel of Fyfield,' said Beechen softly.

'Aye, that was me and proud of it. But not now. Look at me now . . . Look at me.'

Then Beechen spoke, his voice soft but powerful in a way that seemed to still even the leaves in the trees above, and make of the moment something that lived forever.

'You shall be Sorrel again,' said Beechen. 'To a mole that matters much to you, you shall be Sorrel once more. And that mole shall serve me, Sorrel, as you serve the Stone. Now tell me the name of your mate and young.'

'Her name . . . her name . . . They killed her by the Fyfield Stone. Much killing was done there. They killed my own. Her name was Sloe and she was a mole to love. Our young were a female, Whin, and two males, Beam and Ash, taken from us with barely a moment to say goodbye. I told them to remember us and trust the Stone, but the grikes killed Sloe almost before our young were out of sight and . . . and I trust not the Stone. It took as good a mole as ever crossed my path. It. . . .'

Tryfan saw then the light of day across Sorrel's troubled face seem to brighten, and his eyes to clear as he gazed up into Beechen's eyes, though where the light came from nomole could say.

'Trust the Stone, Sorrel, for it shall bring you peace. There are still things you have to look forward to. For I am the Stone Mole and it shall be. But tell nomole of this but

71

that your name was Sorrel once and is again, and you are proud of it. Tell them only that.'

Then Beechen turned back to Tryfan and they were gone, leaving old Sorrel staring after them and wondering in awe about the mole who had touched him, and whose touch he felt as sunlight on his face.

There, later, others found him and said, 'You look like you've seen a ghost, mole. You look. . . .'

'The name's Sorrel,' said Sorrel firmly.

'Sorrel? Is that so? Now have you heard that that Beechen mole's about?'

'Aye, I met him,' whispered Sorrel in awe. 'That was the Stone Mole all right. His fur is so glossy the sky shines in it, and his eyes as bright as spring flowers were when I was young. He knew my name which no other knew, and that name's Sorrel. He knew my name, and touched my face, and told me I was not so old that there weren't things still to look forward to.'

'*What* things?' said his friend.

'Things a mole's promised not to talk about until they happen.'

'Did he really know your name without telling? Are you sure . . . ?'

'He did,' said Sorrel.

Thus many of the stories and myths about the Stone Mole started, with simple moments when the truths of hearts were exchanged, and Beechen reminded moles of who they really were. Such simple stories would, in time, evolve to accounts of healing and of prophecy, of magic and of miracles; and perhaps become unstoppable, even by a whole army of trained grikes. Truly, the Stone Mole was coming, and his name was Beechen.

In June, the Marsh End's secrets show themselves best to moles who are ready to struggle through the thickset undergrowth and debris to where the sun filters among moist greenery and the sweet secrets of pink saffron and the last pale flowering of hellebore.

Yet even in summer this is a part of Duncton Wood that has a dark and clandestine aspect, for the beeches of the higher wood disappear to be replaced by the smaller and closer growing alder, sycamore and stunted oak, all underlain by mucky undergrowth and rotten fallen branches.

A place whose wintertime depression still hung about in the darker pockets of its surface, and where Beechen hurried closer to Tryfan as the older mole went on, and looked about himself a little nervously. Stone Mole or not, he was still an ordinary mole at heart and prone to the natural fears younger moles feel in strange new places.

But the few flowers about cheered him, and a bright cluster of wood-sorrel, their frail green stems and delicate white leaves trembling against the dark of a fallen branch stopped him still with pleasure. But it was the luminescent green of the moss at the boles of the trees that fascinated him most, and the way it seemed to catch and intensify the light.

Then, as if that was not enough and the Marsh End wished to put on its best display for him, they came upon a bank of ramsons along the hollow made by a stream that drains down into the marshes beyond the wood.

Tryfan had to tell him their name, for Beechen had not even heard of them before, and he showed the youngster how the leaves, if crushed, gave off a bitter-sweet smell that healers like.

'My mother Rebecca first met Rose hereabout. She was the last great healer from the Pastures, who taught my mother all she knew of that craft, and she in her turn passed it on to my half-brother Comfrey.'

As Beechen stared in wonder at the ransoms' star-like flowers, Tryfan told him about the Marshenders, the moles who once upon a time were both feared and reviled by other Duncton moles.

'My father Bracken told me that *his* father, who was a Westside elder, used to say, "Where frogs and toads and snails go out, there you'll find Marshenders out!" But they were not really like that at all.'

Which was true, for the very nature of the place – damp and dark and worm-poor – made for a special breed of mole: quick-witted, fiercely loyal to their own kind, thinner and less strong than the big Westsiders but with intelligence, humour and persistence enough to compete with other Duncton moles. In Bracken's day, indeed, Mekkins of the Marsh End had been one of the system's most respected and resourceful elders.

But to moles outside the Marsh End he was an exception: to them, who feared that place, Marshenders seemed a secretive bunch, whose tunnels were poor and whose natures mixed ill temper with a fearful mystery. A place to avoid, moles to avoid in a group, but moles to bully and push around if they could be got at one by one.

'None left now though,' sighed Tryfan, who had inherited a special affection for the Marsh End from his parents, both of whom had reason to be grateful to the place.

'Mind you, enough Marshenders survived the evacuation of the system that if ever the day comes when those Duncton moles who remember the place, or had memories of it passed on to them, can return then I'll warrant Marshenders will reclaim their own before any other part of the system is reclaimed! That's the kind of moles they were.'

'What moles live here now?' asked Beechen, looking about the shady place and glad that Tryfan was there to be his guide as they moved on again towards the special tunnels Tryfan planned to make their home for a time.

'When the outcasts were sent in weaker moles ended up here, it being a place where the stronger would leave them in peace. The Westside was always the most wormful part, while over to the east sturdy no-nonsense moles who keep themselves to themselves always used to live. Little community there! But here, now? Old moles, I think. Many sadly diseased with nothing left but memories of a time of trouble and change like that mole Sorrel whom we met. There'll be more of those before we've done! When Spindle and I first came there were still a good few who preached the Word, and some even who preached the Stone. Well, for some argument was as good a way of surviving as anything else. Lately, I've heard the place has settled down and been depressed for lack of pups.

'By the absence of anymole along our path, I think that most are too shy to challenge or greet us. The more characterful moles tend to be like the ones we met last night in Barrow Vale. But never underestimate moles who live in dank places – they may not seem much but in my experience, for all that they have but mean tunnels and few worms, they're more friendly and hospitable once you get to know them than most moles you'll meet.'

Soon after this they veered eastward and Tryfan began watching out for something above the surface of the wood.

'An old dead oak. Can you see it? That's our destination, for it marks the place we called the Marsh End Defence. Get Skint to tell you all about it. Now, wherever is it . . . ?' And Tryfan went forward slowly, and screwed up his eyes to see a little better.

But it was Beechen who finally spotted the tree, and forward into the thick undergrowth and great fallen branches at its base they went, to be met by the strongest mole Beechen had yet seen and who, judging by his open face and outright pleasure to see them, was a mole known to Tryfan.

Yet he did not immediately address him but, rather, turned sternly to Beechen and said formally, 'Whatmole are you and whither are you bound?'

It was the old traditional greeting and Beechen stammered somewhat over his reply, looking quickly to Tryfan for an affirmation he did not get. That mole was smiling broadly.

'Well mole, what's your answer?'

'My name's Beechen, and I'm bound . . . *here*,' he said.

'And where are you from?'

'The Stone,' said Beechen. 'We were there yesterday morning.'

'You're meant to ask my name now,' said the mole with a grin. And then sternly once more: 'Do it!'

'Well, um, what's your name and . . . and whither are *you* bound?'

Tryfan laughed and waited for the mole's reply.

'Hay is my name, and as for where I'm going, nowhere fast is the best answer I can give.'

Then Hay touched paws with Tryfan and the two, who had not met since Beechen's birth, settled to a talk and an exchange of news. They had not been at this many moments before Tryfan turned to Beechen and said sharply, 'Don't stance about doing nothing. Get some food and don't get lost. Darkness falls quickly in the Marsh End and the owls roost low.'

Beechen did so, interrupting his grubbing-out to listen to ominous rustling of wings in the branches above, and the unfamiliar calls of waterfowl across the unseen Marshes nearby.

He returned to the two old friends and gave them worms.

'Feverfew's glad to have some time to herself again I should think,' Hay was saying.

'Aye. Bringing up even a single pup's hard work, and she's looking forward to a summer's rest. She misses the Wen and Starling, who was a good friend to her after I left for Whern. But . . . moles from their own systems, why, it's the story of most moles here. I'll warrant Feverfew will not be idle for long, but out and about meeting others now she's free of this mole here!' Tryfan buffeted Beechen affectionately. 'But what of the others Spindle and I knew?'

'Well, now, a good few did not survive long after April and the Stone M . . . Beechen's birth. But Borage is still about, and his once troubled mate Heather is more at peace, though pupless still. She's turned to the Stone and been newborn. Far too earnest for my taste, mind you.

Old Teasel's going strong and no doubt you'll see her soon enough. She's up towards the Eastside, and still has her sight . . .' He said no more, feeling it best not to mention the first miracle associated with Beechen, which was the restoration of Teasel's sight on the night of his birth.

'But there'll be time aplenty for us to talk. I've heard it said you've come back to teach Beechen scribing, and good luck to you both! Too much like hard work for me! And no doubt but you'll be doing some scribing of your own?'

If Hay expected an answer to this he got no more than a grunt, for Tryfan was not inclined to talk about the things he scribed, nor had he been even to Spindle himself. He scribed for posterity, against a day, he had said more than once, when most moles would be able to scribe and the art was something allmole took for granted and did not elevate, as in his view the scribemoles of Uffington had wrongly done, into a mystery.

'I heard you two were on your way, but I'd been expecting you sooner,' said Hay, not in the slightest put out by Tryfan's unwillingness to give anything away. He had got to know Tryfan better than most and the two moles had great respect for each other. 'You'll find the tunnels are well aired and dry. Mayweed's been by sometimes and he's made sure the texts and folios you left behind are well protected and that no roof-falls or wall-slides have marred them.

'Other moles stay well clear of the place out of respect for Spindle's memory and your privacy, but there'll be disappointed moles in the Marsh End if you hide yourself away as you did in the winter years.'

Tryfan chuckled.

'I doubt that we'll be doing that. Beechen here's eager now to get out and about and I fear my task will be keeping his snout at his scribing!'

Beechen grinned, and seemed more cheerful than he had been on the way partly because Hay offered hope of new company and friendship, but also because, as he had just learnt, this was a place to which Mayweed came as well, and might come again.

It was therefore with a cheerful heart that he followed Hay and Tryfan into the undergrowth which hides the entrances down into those special tunnels, and then dropped underground.

The tunnels were clean and dust-free and the burrows off them neat and ordered. The soil and subsoil was dark and rich, the soil of a moist place of vegetation compacted through time so that, as Tryfan led them down into deeper levels, the walls hardened and the floor as well.

But a place of strange and confusing windsound, quite unlike anything Beechen had ever experienced before, and he made sure to keep close to the other two moles for fear of becoming disorientated.

'Mayweed's creation, with Skint's help,' explained Tryfan over his shoulder, hurrying on, eager now to get back to the texts he had deserted for so long. 'Even if an alien mole found his way in not only would he become very confused, but others already here would hear him long before he reached them and make their way out by the special escape routes that Mayweed designed. We can hope that such precautions are now unnecessary and that these tunnels will never be invaded, nor need to serve for the purposes of defence and covert attack again. Anyway, since my experience in Whern, and on that long journey home which I could not have made without Spindle's help, I . . . I have not wished to fight again, or encourage others to do so.'

They came to a cunningly concealed entrance down to a new level and Hay went no further.

'Time to go,' he said. 'But you know where I am, Tryfan, and I'll be offended if you don't come and see me soon. As for you, Beechen, don't let him work you too hard. I'm not so sure scribing's good for a mole, especially in the summer months when there's a lot to see and do in the wood. You come and see me as well – *he'll* tell you where to find me. As for food, you'll find worms aplenty near the high tunnels, and I'll be about anyway.'

He was no sooner gone than Tryfan was off down the nearly vertical drop to the next level and then to right and left, down and then along, until quite suddenly the confusion in the windsound died and, after a moment of utter darkness as they dropped to a new tunnel level, they were in a wide and peaceful tunnel, one end of which opened out into the hollow trunk of the great tree Tryfan had pointed out on the surface.

From this a gentle light filtered in, and a yet gentler breeze. The subsoil there was lighter than that above, leached by rains in centuries past and bearing ash and black burnt stems of vegetation, evidence of some ancient fire that must have razed the wood long before the tree, itself now dead, had even been a seed.

So does the present grow from the past, so does the present itself grow old.

It was in a further level below this one that Tryfan and Spindle had decided to spend their last moleyears together working, hidden from sight, secret, protected, to make texts whose future neither could know nor guess.

Down to that hallowed place of scholarship Tryfan now took Beechen. The old scribemole was much moved to see the place again, and stopped in the peaceful light and stared about at where white, dead roots formed walls and buttresses to burrows, and at where the tunnel widened to a chamber in which texts and folios were impressively ranked into the shadows.

'I haven't told you much of Spindle, have I?' said Tryfan gruffly, his mouth trembling and his head bowed. 'I miss him more than I can say. He was as good a friend to a mole as ever friend could be.'

Tryfan went slowly forward among the texts, with Beechen just behind and saying nothing. The great mole reached out a worn talon here and there. He touched a text, he peered in at an untidy burrow.

'Mine,' he said. 'And that's Spindle's,' he added, pointing a little way further on. 'You can make your place there.'

Like Tryfan's burrow, the one Spindle had occupied was delved towards the hollow trunk and an opening into it brought in light and fresh air. The burrow was much tidier than Tryfan's, with a small raised area for sleeping. and a high dais on which, Beechen guessed, Spindle had done his scribing. The only untidy objects in the place, apart from the thin layer of dust that lay over everything, were the three folios of bark that lay askew over the dais which looked as if they had been left by a mole who was due to come back imminently.

'He was working on those before he left for the last time. That was during the day of the night you were born.'

Beechen reached out a paw and touched the folios, feeling strange to see and touch something so palpably of the day just before he was born.

'I think I shall like this burrow,' he said. 'I can feel Spindle's presence in it.'

'Aye,' said Tryfan, 'he would have been glad to see it so used. Spindle's interest was history and his life was spent recording things as they happened in the years he lived. He was a scribemole, Beechen, as I am, but he never called himself such and was always modest about what he did. Nomole has yet seen the works he made, none knows them all, not even myself, for I was busy with my own work, and running here and there. Aye!' Tears were in Tryfan's eyes but he did not cry, but rather looked about with pride that he himself had known such a mole.

'Now, here, in this place in the little time we have before you must take up your great task for moledom, I'll teach you scribing, and here you'll ken the texts Spindle and I made. While Spindle's will tell you the history of our times, mine will tell you something of the teachings Boswell your father made.

'Learn them, ken them, discover how to make your own, but always remember that texts begin with living moles and at their end a mole must put them to one side and go out and live. Unless they help a mole do that they are nothing. A text is but a tunnel made by one mole through difficult territory, so that another may pass through more easily. The difficulty may be in recording it truthfully – as Spindle's was – or in the Stone-given ability to set down such wisdom as seems to be invested in the lives of moles like Boswell.

'Neither book, nor text nor folio will so touch another mole that he needs not the touch at first and last of a living paw to his flank, and the true showing of one heart to another, which is the touch of love. This the scribemoles of Uffington forgot, and yet it was their greatest heritage, the thing that gave their work its purpose and intent. I'm not sure Spindle always remembered it either, for all his sterling qualities. But it is a truth Boswell taught me, and for this reason I have left scribing well alone for long periods, to live my life fully, and learn from other moles.'

'Will you be scribing down here, or just teaching me?' asked Beechen.

'A mole can only help another experience for himself,' Tryfan said. 'Everything else is empty words. So I'll scribe and as I do so, in whatever way seems best, you'll learn, and it will not be easy.'

'What will you scribe?' asked Beechen.

Tryfan hesitated before replying, and looked once more at the texts he and Spindle had made. He went among them again, touched some, and seemed to think carefully before replying.

'Well, mole, it's not that I don't want to tell you, but rather that I fear to do so. Boswell used to tell me that a scribemole had best not talk about what he is about to scribe lest he lose the will to do so in the talking, and I shall heed his advice now. But when I have got some way with it, choose your time to ask me again and I shall explain what it is I'm about. I should like you to know it in any case before . . . before we part as in due time we shall. Perhaps what I scribe you may tell to other moles who otherwise might never know it.'

Tryfan chuckled suddenly.

'But don't look so serious and mystified. When I was

first with Boswell I thought he had great stores of knowledge he was keeping from me. When he said he had not, and that what he did have was simply ways to show me what I had forgotten that I knew, I did not believe him. "You will one day, mole," he used to say impatiently.'

'What was he like?' asked Beechen.

'Sensible,' said Tryfan. 'Sensible enough to know that such a conversation as *this* leads but to reveries and idle chatter and a mole with much to learn had best begin to do so. Now, you take Spindle's burrow there. I have work to do.'

'But what shall I do?' asked Beechen.

'Do?' repeated Tryfan with a mischievous twinkle to his eyes. 'Do nothing. Contemplate. Feel the presence of Spindle who once worked hard here and then make the burrow your own. Contemplate on that.'

'But . . .' began Beechen, feeling this was a strange way to start learning anything.

But Tryfan was gone, and took stance in his own burrow and was silent for a long time.

Beechen took a determined stance in Spindle's burrow and was quite uncertain how to proceed with 'contemplation'. But he might, perhaps, have succeeded in starting to do that had not the silence of the place been broken suddenly by a scratching sound coming from Tryfan's burrow, hesitant at first and then with occasional pausings and dour mutterings, increasing in strength and certainty.

'Scribing!' said Beechen to himself at last, realising the sound was that of talon on bark. 'Scribing!' And he stared at the unfinished folio left behind by Spindle on the day he died, and snouted at it and touched it, and wondered how he could ever make sense of it, let alone find words to scribe there of his own.

Chapter Seven

Dark eyes, cold eyes; eyes that did not blink but glittered as dark crystal in tunnels where light flees.

Eyes that followed Henbane, Mistress of the Word, and eyes she railed at. Since Lucerne had struck her she was like a vagrant mole who wanders distracted across a fell whose edge is a void named torment.

The eyes she saw were the eyes of the sideem who lauded her, who called her supreme, but in whom now she seemed to see only the accusations and contempt she felt for herself.

With Lucerne's foul blow on the surface of the High Sideem at Whern, made as lightning struck and rain fell and he found his adult strength, age took Henbane by the throat. And age would never let her go again.

Doubt, loss, guilt, but most of all uncertainty, ate at her, maddened her, and in the tunnels in which she had reigned from the moment she killed her father Rune with her own talons she now saw only those eyes that stared, and blinked not. And she wandered, muttering and lonely, striking out and killing sometimes, but feeling the cold chill that age can bring.

Yet Henbane still moved with the same terrible grace that had always caused males to lust after her and feel a dreadful longing for something they felt she had and which, unconsciously perhaps, she gave the false promise of giving.

Since the birth of her litter by Tryfan her teats had shown, and they showed now when she crouched down: dark teats set in fuller paler fur that Lucerne had suckled into adulthood. Though her fur was still sleek and her body slim, maternity had given her a certain gravity and stillness which transmuted to something else: weariness with life.

83

Something had broken in her at that moment Lucerne struck her as if the structure of her mind and life had been held together by a brittle tension that, once cracked, destroyed her all.

Or nearly. *She* was not yet destroyed, though her life could never be the same. Yet she whom followers of the Stone reviled, she who caused such agony and sadness across moledom's systems great and small; she whom all good-thinking moles abhorred . . . she did what many better moles could never do. She stared into the dark, still pool that was her life, saw evil, but did not flinch or turn away. She saw its darkness and did not die. She saw herself, and chose to live.

So bear with her now, not in pity or forgiveness – those were never qualities she herself possessed or expected in others – but in respect for the courage she showed when everything about herself seemed dark.

Was Henbane going mad? Many thought it, and some, encouraged by Lucerne, dared say it. But Henbane herself, knowing it was almost true and that her paws took her close to the very edge of the darkness she saw, fearful as the pup that once she was, had the courage to pause, and think, and begin to act.

Hence her muttering, hence her vagrancy; hence as well the fact that even those sideem who said she veered to madness dared not yet deny her sovereignty. While Lucerne watched, and waited, hoped, and began to plot her end, Henbane dared to do the hardest thing anymole can do. Broken, vulnerable, despairing, weak, old, hurting, with nowhere yet to go, she dared start life again.

But how? In a most extraordinary and courageous way. The Mistress of the Word dared cast the Word from off herself, and she did it by living in her mind one final time the vile traditions she had been taught, first by her mother Charlock, then by her father Rune, and forcing herself to see them for what they were.

To make sense of Henbane's tragedy a mole of the

Stone, used to light and love and pleasant ways, must dare to travel back in time as Henbane did and learn how the Word was made in those distant years before the tunnels of Whern had heard the sound of the paws of mole.

Long had they waited for their time, with but the sound of chill water to drip the millennia away.

Blizzard snows come early above Whern, violent and heavy, and at the very dawn and beginning of its dubious celebrity, its fells were blanketed in white with just chill wind enough to stir the stiff, dead matt grass tops, and whisper warnings of the harsh winter centuries to come.

It was soon after such a fall, indeed on Longest Night itself, that Scirpus first led his disciples, who numbered twenty-four, to the very edge of Whern where, under the overhang of Kilnsey Crag, he left them sheltering and went on alone.

There, more dead of starvation than alive, more despairing than hopeful, his disciples first heard the rush and roar of subterranean water, and the graceful whine of the limestone wind as they awaited his return on a day of unnatural light and dark portents. Waterfalls froze, rocks and moles had shadows, yet the sun never shone; an unaccountable fear fell among the disciples.

That day which marks the start of Longest Night, when the season came to that threshold which marks a change towards light once more, Scirpus journeyed on alone up into those tunnels, to find a place to pray and seek guidance. Guidance he must have found of a most sinister kind, for he made his way without getting lost into the heart of the High Sideem, and from there took the dangerous unknown route to the great chamber on the far side of which, beyond the lake in whose dark light it is eternally reflected, rises the Rock of the Word. There he bathed in the chill waters and after due meditation and ascetic subjugation, had the first of his twelve revelations of the Word, from which the Book of the Word itself came.

These twelve revelations were known as the Twelve

Cleave of the Word, and disciples of the Word believe they were scrivened for Scirpus's eyes alone across the face of the Rock after which, he having learned them, they faded away. For twelve days, with only the icy water of the lake for sustenance, Scirpus stayed before the Rock, and on each day witnessed the revelation of a cleave. It is said that for each day Scirpus remained before the Rock one of his disciples died. Even as he talked a disciple might suddenly seem to stare, his mouth still open with the word he was about to speak, his body stiff and cold; his eyes unshut. Dead.

Twenty-four had reached Kilnsey alive with Scirpus, but by the time he returned to them, his knowledge of the Book of the Word completed, only twelve remained. But worse. To survive, the living twelve had eaten their dead comrades.

The survivors he led back to the High Sideem where, one by one, he took them before the Rock itself and there taught them a single cleave. On pain of death and before the Rock itself, each one swore his cleave would not be taught to a single one of the other twelve. Nor could a cleave be scrivened down. It would be a secret and unwritten Book, living in the memories of twelve chosen moles, or Keepers, with only one, the Master – Scirpus at first – knowing all its words and wisdom.

The early history and lore of Whern is much concerned with the story of the need to protect this arcane knowledge, for clearly, potent though an unscrivened Book may be, it loses all power when part or all of its words are lost through death of mole.

It was to protect the Word that the sideem and the grikes were formed. The sideems' role was within Whern itself, the grikes' role was to protect it from without.

Scirpus ordered that moles be brought to Whern and trained in the cleave of their tutors, who were the Keepers of the Cleave. Each of the Twelve were to have novice sideem, who bit by bit would learn part of their Keeper's cleave. In this way was knowledge of each cleave dispersed and made safe, yet nomole save the Master himself knew – or had power to know – all the twelve cleave that lived on through the sideem and Keepers.

But the time must come when novices are made initiate, and so arose the rite of the anointing of the sideem, which among all the traditions of Whern is one of the most vile. Of that dangerous and ancient rite we shall have more to say.

Scirpus knew that the sideem would need protection from their enemies, the followers of the Stone led then by the scribemoles of distant Uffington. In those days they were more powerful and active than they later became, and persecuted the Scirpuscans even to the very portals of Whern itself. It was to protect the sideem that Scirpus made the grikes.

Many are the legends of how the grikes were made, but most agree that they are a race he spawned himself upon a female culled from the nearby system of Grysdale Lathe. The female was his consort, his release, and among the pups she had (all but this one denied by Scirpus) was one touched vilely by the Word. A mutant throwback to some monster strain, deformed and horrible; but his filthy blood was strong. They named him Grike and Scirpus trained him in the killing arts.

His intelligence was cunning more than clever, but his loyalty knew no bounds and to him, to satisfy his infernal lusts, captive females were sent from the systems nearby. Then worse: corrupted by stories of power and perversion up in Whern, drawn by fascinations whose basis is still hidden and unknown outside the scrivenings of Whern, females came of their own accord to mate with the beast called Grike. And in them he spawned a ghastly family of moles, squat and lustful, of talons merciless and with a creed that said, 'Right is the Word and right are we that follow it'.

Grike's sons were the first generation of grikes, and from his seed, all too recognisable to this very day in many who despise the blood they bear, all other grikes did come.

Mutant were they, of the blood of Scirpus, of the fell darkness of Whern; born of a rapine, cruel heritage whose only credits are loyalty and obedience to the Word and the sideem they were first nurtured to serve.

All this Henbane had always known, though by her day the role of sideem and grike had spread and changed. She had been told it as a story that glorified great Scirpus, and brought honour and a fitting menace to the Word. But now, thinking of it once again, she saw it all afresh and understood that as a speck of poison may befoul the deepest pool so had those two groups of moles, one of blinkered disciples and the other of ruthless servants, befouled moledom's once peaceful and pleasant land.

It was on all this horrid past that Henbane now began to dwell, grateful only perhaps that, so far as she could tell, grike blood mingled not within her own. Small consolation, though, in the deepest of her tormented night. For her blood was Rune's and dread Charlock's and her inheritance was Scirpus's own realm.

But if she was corrupted by it, what was her escape? And where to? These questions were, as yet, unanswerable. For now she was preoccupied with the realisation that the tradition she had inherited, the dark arts she had learned, had made her make evil the one pure thing she felt she had ever made: Lucerne.

For corrupt him she had. With her body she did, encircling him in her own incestuous pride, letting him pass through puphood to youth, and then towards adulthood as one who touched her and knew her as only lovers should. Doing to him what her parents had done to her.

But worse she knew about herself. As Lucerne had grown, but even before his first speech had come, she chose as his tutor, in full knowledge of what she did, Terce, most senior of the Keepers, and most odious.

Terce liked young moles. Indeed, the sideem that served him were always especially young, all clever, some beautiful. But it was as if his sideem career had been directed by the Word itself towards the sole object and purpose of preparing him as tutor for one as full of the potential for evil as Lucerne.

'Yet he was not evil before that mole first touched him . . .' whispered Henbane in her new-found guilt for, among her worse memories of things she did that could never be undone, was that night when *knowing what she did* she yielded her only pup to Terce. . . .

The folios that record the coming of Terce to Whern have been destroyed, probably by his own paw. The minutes of the meeting of the Keepers wherein he was made Twelfth elect have been destroyed – by his paw. All scrivenings relating to Terce's role as Keeper, and tutor to Lucerne, have been 'mislaid'; his work, too.

But in outline at least his past is known, though his parents' names are lost. Of humble birth in nearby Cray, north of Whern, he came. Chosen by his predecessor he learnt the hardest cleave, which is the twelfth, in but eight days. To curb his ambition and his pride he was given the task of sorting out the indulgences of the grike guardmoles of Wharfedale, and, fatally, his single request for a mole to help him was granted. The mole he chose was Lathe, the perfect subordinate. Cruel and unscrupulous was he and, with no more desire but to serve the mole who gave him power, most reliable. Oh yes, those two fulfilled their task and brought the grikes back in control. But worse, they gained dominion over them, some say with Rune's agreement, others say without. The fact was, though, that in the long days when Henbane, with Wrekin as her general and Weed as her sideem aide, conquered moledom's southern part, Terce it was who gained power among the Keepers. Clever Terce it was who stayed clear at the time of Henbane's accession and Rune's demise, and consolidated his hold and was the first to offer his services to Henbane.

'Let me tutor thy son Lucerne,' he said, 'and he shall learn more than anymole but you.'

'He shall be Master when I have done,' she said. And he agreed that Lucerne would. For just as Lathe had no desire to take the place of Terce – his glory being in the shadow of his sponsor's flank – so Terce had no desire to wrest the Mastership from its Mistress for himself. Though whether he might wrest it from her for Master Lucerne was a very different thing. He would.

'Wilt show me the pup, Mistress?'

Which Henbane did, ushering the silent and still timid Lucerne before the intimidating senior Keeper.

Terce gazed at him and reached out a paw.

Lucerne did not shudder at his touch, but stared at him, eyes glittering with pride.

'I would have him learn thy cleave,' said Henbane.

Terce gazed more. Lucerne did not drop his gaze. Terce smiled and Lucerne returned the smile. Terce was pleased to see the youngster unafraid.

'He shall learn it well,' said Terce. 'I shall teach him all I know.'

'Do it harshly, as I was taught,' said Henbane. 'But let him still see me.'

'Yield him to me on Longest Night,' said Terce, 'and I shall make him ready to be Master of the Word, first among his peers, before everymole but thee.'

'Let him have companions for his learning, for I had none when I was young . . . and regret it now.'

'I shall choose them well. But two only, as tradition dictates. And Mistress . . .' Terce paused, and seemed hesitant.

'Keeper, speak plain.'

'Then Mistress, let him suckle thee beyond his puppish years. It will bind him to thee in ways deeper than words can say, but finally it will make him hate thee too, which hate I shall divert to punishment of the followers of the Stone. In such teachings has the twelfth cleave made me adept.'

'I am aware of it,' said Henbane, 'and had already hesitated to wean him. Now I shall not, and nor does he seem to wish it. Even now he sleeps at my teat. Till Longest Night then, Terce, and after that to thee.'

As Terce left the Mistress with her pup he heard that vile refrain, 'Come suckle me and be my love,' and with what relief he smiled! Of what lay behind that smile, and how before he died Rune laid plans with Terce to see a final glorification of his name, we still must tell. Henbane knew *that* not. But she was right to sense that in Terce lay evil deep, and blasphemies beyond recall, and plots that entwined back in time even to Scirpus himself. Oh yes, we are not finished with discovery of evil yet. And the force for good might seem poor indeed if, so far as Whern is concerned, its only champion was but the flawed Mistress, Henbane.

Terce smiled because he saw a plot of Rune's continue to unfold. A plot that used Henbane more vilely even than she had yet been used. A plot that would elevate her son Lucerne, and so herself, but most of all Rune, Father of them all, beyond even the Mastership, and forever beyond mole's ability to dethrone. The first place Rune would wish to be; the last that Henbane, touched by a new light it seemed, would surely wish to be.

So tremble now at Terce's unseen smile as Henbane talks of suckling. And hope the Stone may yet find champions stronger than we have seen.

Which brings us back to where we do not wish to go. . . .

We said before Terce cast his shadow across these Chronicles that, of all the rites, the anointing of the novice sideem was *one* of the most corrupt.

The other is that known as the secret rite by which one Keeper succeeds another, and it goes back to the very beginning of the coming of Scirpus when those twelve disciples died in the shadow of Kilnsey Crag. Shudder at what we must tell: even the sideem whisper it among themselves and look here and there in horror. A Keeper eats the body of the mole he follows.

This was not the only cannibalism of Whern. On Longest Night, to commemorate the revelation of the Word to Scirpus, a sideem –originally one anointed, but now one chosen by the Twelve – was sacrificed before the Rock, his corpse divided into twelve, each Keeper whispering a filthy rubric as he took his bloody portion: 'Oh Word, by his body I thee worship; oh Word, by his blood I thee worship; oh Word, by his death our lives renew in thee.'

Secret and dark that bloody rite became, and fatal was the shadow under which the Twelve lived out their arcane and ritualistic lives, the principal purpose of which was to keep the Word alive and pass it on by rote to novitiate sideem. Their lives dominated by a eucharistic rite in which a mole who has entrusted his life and learning to them must die that the Word might live.

Keeping this nightmare rite in our unwilling minds, we now come, just as tormented Henbane did, to how Rune took power. Though many are the dark stories told of Rune's ascent, few are the moles who know that one Longest Night he was the sideem chosen to die. Aye, taken among the Twelve Keepers before the Rock of the Word, and there arraigned before the Master, Slithe.

There seems no doubt that Rune was chosen to die because they feared him, and most of all Slithe himself, who rightly saw in Rune a mole whose intelligence and purpose was too great for it to be long denied. Every task set him he had fulfilled, everything he had to learn he learnt even as it was told him. As for the notorious trial of the Clints, that maze of surface tunnels carved in limestone which moles must traverse before their anointing, he mastered it *despite* false instruction, the only mole until then ever so to do.

A second attempt on his life was with talons, the sound to be drowned by the rushing water they were near, in which, no doubt, his body would be thrown afterwards. The attack was ordered by some of the Keepers themselves. What really happened none but Rune ever knew, and he never told. Eight attacked him, all were drowned. Aye, moles, *all were drowned*.

It was after that that the Master sent him into the unknown south to report on the plagues and there, hopefully, to die forgotten. There he nearly died, at the talons of Tryfan's father Bracken on the high Eastside of Duncton Wood. Nearly but not quite, for moleyears later he reappeared at Whern, his reputation great now among the younger sideem, his knowledge of moledom unique, and his ambition feared.

The last attempt to have him die was on Longest Night itself when he was summoned to the Rock to be sacrificed.

Even as the Master spoke out the ordination of the Twelve Keepers – that Rune was 'honoured' to be chosen so to die and be the symbol of life to come for other moles – Rune's black eyes shone and his fur glossed darkly. Under sentence of death, and that imminent, his mind, like his body, thrived.

The arcane ritual he had guessed, for the generations of young sideem had seen one or other of their colleagues disappear at Longest Night. To be so chosen was an unspoken fear, but for a maddened and idiot few whose belief in the Word was so profound and their need for discipline so strong that a sentence of cruel death in the Word's name seemed like an honour.

Rune was too intelligent for that. And now, even as the Master spoke, the Keepers' eyes narrowed and their tongues flicked across their mouths and their talons fretted at the arid floor of the Chamber of the Rock, he revelled in the challenge of turning terminal disadvantage to lifelong gain, and, narrow though the way, slim though his chance of success, doubtful the outcome, he found his route and took it.

Its way was words, its authority the Word, its power that which he invested in himself, his strength their weakness, his weapon their own hypocrisy, his method, attack.

'Blasphemy,' he said quietly, the accusative word

whispering about the chamber until it was almost, but not quite, gone, 'would be in my death here as sacrifice, great though the honour. Honour for me, moles, yet dishonour for any who took my life.'

He smiled as if to apologise for the trouble his words might cause them, but what menace was in that smile! He flexed his sharp talons too, as if to remind them that, if pressed, then in pursuit of honouring the Word he would kill before being killed. It was enough to intimidate the older members of the Twelve, and a mole as acute as Rune could see which among them was weak and which was not.

'Blasphemy? Dishonour?' hissed Slithe who, had he been a stronger mole and Rune less strong, would have killed him then and there. But no, he weakened as moles usually did before Rune's gaze and voice.

'Yes, dishonour,' said Rune, and before the stir of dismay among the Keepers could turn to attack he firmly reminded them of the origins of the sacrifice, and that it was only in recent decades that the Keepers had devolved the sacrifice to a mole outside their circle not, he said (as was really the case, as well he knew), for fear but rather because none among them would, for modesty, take so great an honour.

'Whatmole would be so vain as to suggest himself to die?' asked Rune. All the time he watched them closely to find the weakest one, a mole least liked by the others, a mole to whom their dire choice could turn. But before his arguments reached that far he made certain with stares subtle and sinister that each one of them thought that *he* was the one this clever, strong sideem would manoeuvre the others to kill. So each knew fear, and each felt the power of Rune's threat.

Argument set in, fuelled by dismay and fear, an argument among twelve Keepers the consequence of which was one must die. Upon each other others picked, and vote after vote was tied, until at last the Keepers turned to Slithe to make a nomination. So one was chosen and clever Rune was invited to kill him and join in the feast.

Nor did Rune stop there. Inevitably the remaining Keepers chose him to make up their number and so Rune gained access to ultimate power.

It did not take him long to depose the Master, Slithe himself, and he began to lay his plans for the expansion into moledom of the Word's great power based on the experience learnt in his travels south. He did not yet take up the Mastership himself for his power was not consolidated nor the moles he needed quite in place. But some time in that period of upheaval and change he brought in Terce as the youngest Twelfth Keeper for many a cycle.

It was in that period that Rune broke the sideem rule of chastity, daring to cite Scirpus himself as the precedent, and took to himself a mate called Charlock. She bore Henbane, and raised her privily to darkness in ignorance of who her father was. Charlock taught Henbane that her first and only loyalty was to the Master and that to his lusts she must yield. Which Henbane, having killed her mother, did, not knowing that to the crime of matricide she now added the violation of incest with her father. There was but one consolation among all this filth, which was that Henbane was never made with pup by Rune. Nor indeed by any of the males she subsequently took, of whom there were many, mercy be upon their shadowed souls.

But for great Tryfan, all who knew the pleasures of her body died, one by one, killed by Henbane after she had suffered them to exhaust their pleasure, then later, when she tired of killing, by the sterile eldrene, Fescue among them, who vented their distorted lusts on those already used by their Mistress. But in that time Henbane learnt the killing arts and it was said that no female ever learned to kill a male more quick than she, and, when she wished, more slow.

All this was Lucerne's loathsome heritage, and brooding over it that June Henbane saw clearly and ever more clearly how it had infected her rearing of Lucerne, and was the necessary prelude to the freedoms over him she so fatally gave cold Terce.

*

On much else did maddened Henbane dwell and Whern was thrown into disarray as she wandered its tunnels and seemed to see accusation in every face. For June is a busy month when the sideem prepare for the rite of the anointing at Midsummer of those novice sideem who have survived the trial of the Clints.

All this needed the Mistress's attention and approval, and in that Henbane held power still, and knew it. For without completion of the Midsummer rite the younger sideem would not be legitimate and any succession Lucerne had plotted for, which depended on such younger moles, would be weakened. Nor had he himself been anointed, though many argued, including Terce, that Lucerne need not submit to the Midsummer test. The risks might be too great.

For all her seeming madness Henbane understood the power she still held, and that the sideem would not accept Lucerne unless he had been anointed. So they put up with her madness as she wandered, scraping her paws against the sacred walls of the High Sideem and shouting out of dark sound, and incest, and two lost pups, and much more that ate age into her.

But as Midsummer drew nigh, and certain preparatory rites had been left undone by her, the Keepers sent Lucerne and Terce to talk to her.

'Mother,' Lucerne began, hypocritical affection dripping from every pore, 'you are still Mistress and you have duties to perform. I. . . .'

'Yes, my son?' she said. . . .

'I know not why I struck you –' And though there was no apology in the words, he put it in his voice.

It was Terce she watched as Lucerne spoke these words. Apology? Hypocrisy? Half of one and half of another, that was what she judged. But more than that she saw in Terce's eyes belief that if not quite mad she was no longer strong. Strong enough, she wondered, for what?

She smiled because she knew. Not strong enough to

exploit what Terce had suggested Lucerne do and did no more, which was to suckle her until he was an adult. 'It will bind him to thee in ways deeper than words can say,' Terce had said. But now, guessed Henbane, Terce adjudged that *that* was what she could no longer exploit: too weak, too dazed, they supposed, no doubt. But Henbane knew she could. Not now, but one day. Aye, one day; Lucerne still longed for the comfort she could give but which his pride and growing status could not allow him to ask for or to take.

The comfort and potential of that thought would keep her sane, and give her strength and, in some way she could not understand but felt in that remote and tiny part of her that still was whole, would guide her towards something that might take her out of torment yet.

'I have been ill,' she said at last and to their relief, 'yet now the Word does give me strength. For now, with thy help, Terce, and thine, dear son, we shall trust the Word to guide us to the Midsummer rite, and make those preparations we must make.'

She was glad to see they did not believe she would survive. She was glad because their mistake would be her saving yet. They would use her to legitimise the novices during the rite to come and then . . . discard her.

'Come, mother,' said Lucerne, his paw to her flank, 'we shall help thee be Mistress once more.'

'You shall?' she said.

'Yes,' he said.

But she knew his hypocrisy better than anymole, for of that art she must now be Mistress indeed, and for the few moleweeks to Midsummer so she must remain.

Chapter Eight

Tryfan proved a tolerant teacher of scribing in those first moleweeks of June in the Marsh End, for though he wanted to get on with his own scribing while Beechen worked hard to learn the tasks he was set, he knew as well as anymole the excited restlessness that overcomes young moles at the approach of Midsummer.

So a few days before the day itself, when the air was warm and the light good and nomole should be stuck in a tunnel with his snout in a text, Tryfan suddenly declared, 'Enough! Too much, in fact! We're going up to the surface to join in the merriment and make a visit or two.'

Beechen was secretly relieved for on his occasional forays to the surface he had fancied he had heard moles chattering nearby and enjoying the June days, and had wanted to join them.

'Where shall we go? What moles shall we see?'

'I have a fancy to show you the burrow where my mother Rebecca raised Comfrey, though whether or not I can find it is another matter. As for which moles to see, well . . . at Midsummer moles have a habit of going a-visiting, so you never know what moles you'll meet where except that they'll be a surprise and in the wrong burrow. Moles gather and talk and have a laugh and then, slowly, their groups growing in number all the time, they make trek to the Stone for the Midsummer rite.'

It seemed to Beechen that a great change had come to the wood in the short time since they had first ventured underground in the Marsh End.

The leaves of the trees were fuller and greener, the undergrowth thicker, the bird song richer, the soil warmer, and evidence of mole – and other creatures, too – greater and more glorious. Emerging into the busy world once more, he felt happier to be alive than he ever had, and ready for whatever the Stone might put their way.

All around there were delights to the eye and the ear, and had not Tryfan been there Beechen might not have turned any way but round, and round again, uncertain of which way to turn to see the best that was there.

''Tis a grand placc, the Marsh End as Midsummer approaches,' said Tryfan, breathing in the clear air. 'No need to go searching for mole at this time of year; they find each other and enjoy themselves, or used to! As I said before, we'll see what comes!'

What came was another mole, and one they both knew.

'Greetings both, I guessed you might be about on a day like this. Where are you going?' Hay asked them.

Tryfan explained they were looking for a burrow his half-brother had been raised in and that it lay somewhere off to the east. Not being a Duncton mole originally, Hay had no idea where such a burrow might be, but he seemed eager to join them, and so all three went on together.

'If we carry on this way,' said Hay eventually, after a pleasant ramble during which Tryfan stopped occasionally in a vain attempt to get a better idea of where Rebecca's old tunnels might be, 'we're going to come to Borage's place. He's all right, but I'm not so sure about Heather . . . well I mean she's a bit intense for a summer's day if you know what I mean. Ever since. . . .'

With a frown and raised paw Tryfan stopped him saying more.

''Tis nearly Midsummer and we must take moles as we find them, just as the Stone docs.' Beechen knew that Tryfan never gossiped about other moles.

They passed the ruined entrances to several tunnels in an area of the Marsh End that had obviously once been heavily populated. Then, turning south-east and a little upslope, the general air of dereliction gave way to a sense of order and life more appropriate to the season. They entered a clearing that was clean, sunny and had an inviting entrance down into a tunnel.

The moles living there must have been aware of their approach, because no sooner had they arrived but a stolid and worthy snout appeared at the entrance and a burly mole emerged.

Beechen already knew something about Borage from what he had heard. He knew him to be a big mole, one who had been tortured and diseased in his time – the evidence for which was still in the scars on his flanks and the patchiness of fur at his rump.

Before Borage had a chance to greet them, another mole came out of the entrance, a fixed and righteous smile upon her face, and eyes that had a disconcerting way of looking past a mole as if some golden land of goodness lay beyond him.

'Greetings! May the Stone be with you all!' said Heather with general good humour, the warmth in her eyes not failing to hide the sense of surprise and worry she seemed to have at being visited by three moles all at once. 'The Stone does us an honour!' she went on, without complete conviction, 'to bring to our humble burrows no less a mole than Tryfan and. . . .'

'Beechen,' said Beechen.

'So you're Beechen, are you? A solid-looking mole I must say, and a great credit to Feverfew, if I may say so. Yes, very good, very good. May the Stone be with you, Beechen.'

'Er, thank you,' replied Beechen, finding himself smiling inanely in response to Heather's continual beatific smile.

'You've grown since the night you were born,' said Heather. 'May the Stone be praised!'

'He'd look pretty odd if he hadn't,' said Hay lightly, but Heather ignored his irony and, seeming eager to put a seal on her comments about Beechen, added, 'Blessed be the Stone indeed, aye! Welcome to the Good News!'

Tryfan, evidently anxious to avoid too much evangelising, said hastily, 'Beechen, Borage here knows more about Buckland, the grikes' southern base, than most. You should talk with him.'

'I will tell you what I know of Buckland,' Borage said, 'but not now. Today is not a day for remembering that dark place.'

'The Stone –' Heather began yet again, but Hay interrupted her.

'We're in search of some tunnels Tryfan wants to see,' he said. 'So we'll be off now, Borage . . . Heather.'

'Then I shall come with you,' beamed Heather and before Hay could say anything to stop her Tryfan said, 'A good idea, mole. Both of you come. The more the merrier. I want Beechen to meet as many moles as he can.'

'It's being pupless that has done this,' Borage whispered to Tryfan as they set off. 'She means well.'

'It isn't bad to love the Stone,' Tryfan said soothingly.

The group now comprised five moles, and Beechen had little doubt that soon along the way they would meet others, for there was a sense of infectious adventure about their journey which, it seemed, gave it a life of its own which any individual among them could not control, and certainly, Tryfan was not trying to do so.

As they went along Heather talked loudly to Beechen of the goodness of life and of the Stone, while Hay nudged and winked at Beechen saying, 'It'll get worse before it gets better, and could get very bad indeed if we meet the wrong moles. It only needs . . . oh no!' Hay looked wildly about with mock alarm as they turned a corner and found, approaching them in a desultory kind of way, an old female. Snouting at the undergrowth she was, and singing tunelessly to herself.

'Moles coming,' she said quite loudly, putting her ear to the ground and then her snout, and then looking up.

'Teasel!' said Heather with distaste. 'One whose entire life was based on deceit. One into whom the viper Word once burrowed. Out of the way, mole. Tryfan and I are on the Stone's business!'

'Teasel is of the Stone, as you are, Heather,' Tryfan said firmly, and went forward to meet the mole whose sight appeared as poor as his own.

101

'Tryfan!' she exclaimed in pleasure and surprise. 'Bless me, if you've not come back to us again! And not a minute too soon seeing as Midsummer's almost on us. Where's that pup you were looking after, eh? Where have you hidden him?'

'Why 'tis Teasel, getting younger by the day,' laughed Tryfan, touching her close and then stepping back to look at her. 'You haven't changed a bit since I last saw you.'

'Would it were so. But you're older, mole, and thinner, and your face . . .' She reached out a paw and touched his facial scars tenderly. 'I've missed you, I have, Tryfan, but since I always spoke my mind to you I'll not lose the chance now. A system needs its leader, so you'd better make sure you're seen about a bit more. Scribing and that, hidden away where none can find you, let alone see you . . . it's not right, Tryfan! It's not your task.'

'I'm not the system's leader, Teasel, not in the old way any more. I'm not sure systems need leaders like that now.'

'Stuff and nonsense!' said Teasel. 'Moles don't go anywhere of their own accord, they need a mole to guide them.'

'And where should we be guided?' asked Tryfan quietly.

'Away from here where there's so much misery and loneliness,' said Teasel.

'You'll find that wherever you go,' said Tryfan, 'and you might find worse beside. What we're looking for is right here, under our snouts waiting to be found. I always knew that before but I didn't believe it.'

'Show me then,' said Teasel. 'Come on, mole, show me!' But Tryfan crouched in silence looking at her, and there came to the group a sudden quiet and a feeling of loss, as if all there sensed something important was missing and none knew what to say.

'Well,' said Teasel, looking suddenly very old and quite ill, her fur sagging on her thin old bones, ''tis sorry things we are to be so miserable before Midsummer's Night and with that pup of yours to think of. Where is he, Tryfan? I'll not let you be until you tell me. . . .'

Her voice faded for she could see by Tryfan's look that the mole next to him was the Stone Mole himself. And now she came to look at him – or she saw his eyes on her, bright and clear, with a look direct and true – why, she felt all a-fumble with herself, not knowing for the moment what to do at all.

'What we're looking for is right here under our snouts,' Tryfan had said a moment before, and as she realised whatmole Beechen was she sensed around him, and through him, and in his presence, something greater than them all, which stilled a mole's mind and put peace in his paws.

Hay later reported that there was something about Teasel's trust and faith that made such a moment possible, and helped them all see what it was that Beechen held of the Stone about him.

'He was an ordinary enough mole for most of the time, or so it seemed,' he recalled, 'but sometimes when one of belief, like Teasel, was with him it was as if together they made something far more than the two of them, and those of us watching were touched by the light that flowed between them. 'Twas then that what some called miracles might happen, and healings take place, and beset moles come right in the mind, as if they only needed to see the light in his true gaze to be at one again.

'Some think it was there all the time, but it wasn't so. Why, I had seen him a good few times before that moment with old Teasel, and, to be truthful, I had been disappointed since he seemed nothing special at all. A wholesome lad, and likely to be a good scribemole and even a fighter if need arose, but nothing more . . . But once I saw him as Teasel saw him I never forgot it, and, having seen it, a mole would have followed him to the end of moledom and back just to see it once again. . . .'

Whatever Teasel saw, or sensed, she at least was not long overawed by it. Her natural good nature made her come forward and touch Beechen with the same warmth she had touched Tryfan and say, 'Welcome, mole, welcome. Let me look at you. Why, I remember you when no more than moments old and now look! Full-grown, near enough. There was such a light about you that night as dazzled all moles who saw, and as for this mole, she regained her sight that very same night, as all moles know but none do talk about. Well, I do! 'Tis true as I'm standing here, but you'll not remember that.'

Beechen shook his head.

'I'm Teasel, as you'll have gathered, and I daresay Tryfan here has never mentioned my name to you. But here I am, for what I'm worth, and if there's anything a mole can do for another I'd do it for you.'

Tryfan saw that Beechen had no idea what to say to this, though his paw was touching Teasel's in an affectionate way, so Tryfan explained that they were in search of some tunnels and since others had joined in the fun he hoped she would as well.

'Whatmole lives in the tunnels you're seeking?' asked Teasel.

'Now? I know not. Once it was Rebecca, but that was before your time. Before allmole's time but my own, and by then she had long since left the tunnels and moved on. But Comfrey showed them to me.'

'Aye,' said Teasel vaguely, more interested, it seemed, in Beechen than lost tunnels, ''twas before I came.'

They wandered on chattering, arguing, laughing, and occasionally pausing to admire the wood.

'Do you know if you're any nearer these tunnels you're looking for?' asked Hay at last.

Tryfan shook his grizzled head and looked about in a puzzled way.

'I'll tell you whose tunnels we are near,' said Teasel, 'Crosswort's!' Hay and Borage groaned, but Tryfan suddenly brightened and his snout rose and scented at the air.

'It's near here!' he said, going forward quickly.

'But this is *Crosswort's* patch,' said Borage.

'Crosswort indeed!' said Teasel testily to Hay, and he too looked reluctant to stop at the place.

'Well this *is* the place,' said Tryfan, snouting about.

'She'll not be pleased to see you!' warned Teasel. 'Sullen mole she is, and when she's not sullen she'll sooner bite your head off than pass the time of day.'

'This is *definitely* . . .' began Tryfan with mounting certainty.

'The Stone is not with her *at all*,' said Heather, 'and the last time I tried to bring her the Good News she used some very unpleasant language. It was a great effort of will on my part to find it in my heart to ask the Stone to forgive her, though I was finally able to do so after I recalled the story of – '

'You're right, Heather,' cut in Borage, 'she's not exactly a friendly mole.'

Even as they talked a mean grey snout appeared at the nearby entrance, followed by mean grey eyes, followed by wizened little paws. Female certainly, unappealing definitely, and yet 'cross' would not be quite the word though 'cross' was scribed across her lined face and into her indignant eyes.

If ever a mole was making an effort to be nice this was she. For her face, despite its natural self, was trying to smile; something that clearly caused her much difficulty and pain.

But not nearly such pain and agony as she suffered as she spoke, or rather spat out with profound displeasure a word her mouth found difficult to encompass.

'Welcome,' she said.

A collective air of such surprise came over the little group that had the miserable trees about that place suddenly broken into song and danced about none of them would have had the energy left to be amazed at all.

'"Welcome"?' intoned Hay, astounded.

'Yes,' Crosswort hissed, 'welcome.' She began to look as if she was feeling ill with the horror of it all, and in the tone of a mole who can hardly credit what she herself is saying, she added, 'I was expecting you. I hope you had no trouble getting here. Please to come down and make yourselves at home.'

'"Please to come down"?' repeated Teasel, perplexed.

'"Make yourselves at home"?' said Hay faintly.

'Something's very odd here,' said Heather, 'unless . . . aye! The light of the Stone has touched her! Blessed is he who bears the Good News when he sees lost moles such as thee, Crosswort, born once again!'

Fortunately Crosswort missed this nonsense as, eager to take them underground, she had turned back into the entrance with a general instruction to follow her.

So down they went into tunnels Tryfan only just remembered from the single visit he had made to them before in the company of Comfrey. Comfrey himself had remembered them better, for he had been raised here by Rebecca, with a diseased female called Curlew for company whose tunnels these had been and who had taken Rebecca in. Now the tunnels seemed small and dark, and though they were clean enough they were dank and restricted.

Crosswort went fussing ahead of them, saying she had not had time to get *every*thing ready, that she had not been told there would be so *many* of them, and would they *kindly* mind the walls and where their talons went since the soil was friable and likely to scatter.

But when they eventually reached the communal chamber of the place the atmosphere changed unexpectedly.

'Er, welcome,' said Crosswort again, looking over her shoulder at somemole within whom she seemed afraid of.

One by one they squeezed through the small entrance and into the cramped chamber that was the system's only communal place. And one by one they saw, stanced comfortably and crunching with pleasure at a chubby worm, a mole they all knew. One who looked up and smiled toothily at them with very great glee.

'Sirs and Madams, humbleness wonders what kept you so long,' said Mayweed, utterly delighted with the surprise and sensation created by his presence in so unexpected a place.

'Stunning Madam,' said Mayweed turning to Crosswort and raising a paw to quieten the exclamations of surprise and pleasure among the others that had greeted the sight of him, 'now is your chance to be generous to a fault. Shall we be wanting food? We shall. Shall you fetch and carry it as a host mole should without complaint? Indubitably you *will*. Alas, appalled Madam, seven hungry moles stanced in your tunnels and waiting to be served – torment would be bliss compared to this, would it not?

'But as you grub about for some worms above and mutter to yourself about the injustice of it all, ponder this: you shall hear good conversation here, and stories, and come to share in such jollities as sensible moles indulge in during the last days and nights before Midsummer's Night, and moles will ever after say "Remember *that* occasion when we had more fun than for many a year? Why that all began in Crosswort's tunnels!" You shall be the envy, until-now-painful-to-know Madam, of generations still to come, and moles shall regret they were not here. So worms, Madam, and plenty of them!'

Mayweed's friends greeted this speech with delight, and more than one of them called after Crosswort to bring *at least* two worms for them personally, and possibly *three*.

These arrangements made, the moles settled down as Mayweed, who seemed for the moment to be in charge, said, 'Perplexed Sirs and Madams, you are wondering, I know, how modesty himself just happens to be ensconced here. Bold Beechen – and a special welcome to you, young Sir, since this Midsummer in Duncton Wood would be a sorry thing without your presence, seeing as you are the only hint of youth that our poor old outcast system has – is especially perplexed. But perplex no more.

'Mayweed had come to get you up and out from the

Marsh End when Hay arrived and asked where you were going. Hearing that your intention was to come to Rebecca's former tunnels, and knowing your pleasure in finding them would be diminished if I led you straight to them (for finding the route is half the fun), and diminished still more if Crosswort had not been prepared for your arrival I decided to come on ahead.

'Knowing that her welcome can sometimes be austere, even to humbleness myself, I came to prepare the ground. In short, I threatened her saying, "Miserable mole, you will for once in your horrible life be pleasant to some visitors and if you are not then I, Mayweed, an humble mole, will make you regret it!" Those are the very words I spoke and she responded to my unwonted aggression by swearing, cursing, and striking. Accordingly (since a mole who makes a threat should carry it through) I kicked her here, buffeted her there, and generally did what moles do not expect Mayweed to do. Her anger knew no bounds for a time, but Mayweed did not weaken and, inevitably, she wept. Weeping is good for moles. Humbleness confesses that on rare occasions he has done it himself. Not much another can do for a weeping mole but shut up, which is what I did, though the waiting would have been more pleasant if I'd had food on paw. Eventually, she was quiet.

'"Lachrymose Madam, now lapsed into muteness," I said, "do I have to go through this entire rigmarole again or can this route-finding modesty who is me, Mayweed by name, settle down and await the worm a guest expects?" This she brought and I then instructed her how to welcome you. Which done, I have stanced peacefully here and enjoyed eating said rotund worm. Madam now seeks worms for each of you and, in the difficult circumstances she has faced, and faces still, Mayweed humbly suggests she has done very well indeed and deserves consideration and cautious respect. Why cautious? Because if others are not as direct with her as I have been she will revert to being the Crosswort she has always been. Crossworts are made, not born. If others treat her honestly, as I have, and stay their ground, then she may reform for ever. But ask her yourselves! Here she comes!'

Indeed it was so. Crosswort had reappeared with several worms, fat ones, and laid them, with a gesture that might almost have been meek, at the entrance of the chamber. For a moment not a mole spoke, but then, spontaneously, several cried their "Thank yous" to her and welcomed her back, insisting that she took stance among them and shared out the food gathered so far.

'The Stone has blessed thee!' declared Heather, but nomole encouraged her to say more, least of all Crosswort who, still unbelieving that she was in company in her own tunnels, was experiencing a new-found feeling called enjoyment and was staring around her in growing amazement. Then, when Hay buffeted her gently and said he would come and help her gather some more worms for they would soon be needed, her pleasure was complete. Was not Hay a good strong mole to look at, and *male*, and helping *her*? Crosswort almost fell over herself in her eagerness to be obliging and if, as she went, residual habits of complaint still surfaced – ''Tis going to get too warm down here', and, 'Maybe one other mole might have come to help' – they were easily lost beneath the rising tide of her new determination to please.

If Beechen's introduction to these outcasts, who had found their way to Duncton Wood in such cruel and trying circumstances moleyears before, had been warm when he first met them at Barrow Vale, what began to happen now was warmer, rowdier, jollier and even more memorable.

Though sometimes moles addressed him, for the most part he stanced quietly in one corner and listened as the conversation and stories began to flow from one side of the chamber to the other and moles listened to each other with pleasure, amusement and criticism, both good-natured and bad.

Tryfan set things going with a moving account of how Rebecca had come to be in this very chamber moleyears before, with her teats dangerously engorged after all her pups had been killed by Mandrake. What a silence fell as Tryfan described in his deep voice how good Mekkins, the greatest Marshender of his time, had found one of Bracken's pups by Rue and brought him to Rebecca!

'I heard the story from Bracken himself, for he crept on after Mekkins to make sure his pup, runt though he was, found love and safety,' said Tryfan. 'He said it was a close thing but the pup did take milk at last and so both moles lived.'

'What was the pup's name?' asked Teasel.

'Why that was Comfrey, and nomole more gentle nor more loving than he was ever leader of a system. He was my half-brother and I loved him true, and the Stone where he died, which overlooks the great valley in which the Wen lies, is called Comfrey's Stone.'

'More worms, and another tale!' cried Hay.

'While Madam supplies the former, you, happy Sir, undertake the latter!' said Mayweed, which Hay very willingly did, saying he could not move them to tears as Tryfan had done, unless it be the tears of laughter, for a funny thing had happened to him on the way to Duncton Wood. . . .

Which *was* a tale to make a mole cry with merriment, for Hay was a mole who could turn even a grike into a joke and get away with it. After which the moles were silent for a time, exhausted with laughing, until Heather offered to sing them a song or two she had learnt when a pup, which all agreed would be a good idea provided there was no mention of the Stone or doing good in it, at which Heather fell silent, saying that there *was* some mention of the Stone, but that wasn't her fault, was it? And anyway. . . .

An argument ensued in which Heather became very passionate until, to everymole's astonishment, Crosswort told her to shut up or get out since she was host mole, and until Heather had started speaking everymole had been having a good time.

Teasel said she didn't mind singing a Stone-free song about butterflies provided *they* didn't mind her cracked

110

old voice and if Borage could oblige by singing bass and Heather the descant, which she was good at.

So troubled moments passed to pleasant ones, and humorous anecdotes replaced historic tales. As the hours went by not a mole there did not contribute their mite, not even Beechen who, remembering a tale Spindle had scribed regarding his journey back to Duncton with Tryfan, repeated it to general applause.

Outside darkness had fallen, and after Mayweed had suggested, and Crosswort had graciously agreed, it was decided that they might as well make a night of it and not go hurrying back to their different tunnels. The hoot of a tawny owl clinched it, and led to a legendary tale of owl-killing, which Mayweed told.

It was as he was nearing its climax, which was as convoluted and strange as some of the routes Mayweed took across systems, that, hearing a sound above, Crosswort slipped out and up to the surface to see whatmole was there. Raised voices soon interrupted Mayweed's narrative.

'But I've got guests and you can't come in!' they heard Crosswort say, reverting dangerously towards her normal mode.

'Guests? And I not invited? I, a mole who has tolerated your miserableness too long to think about? *Guests?* If true, which I very much doubt, it is discourtesy of the lowest sort typical of a mole of the Stone. If a lie then it is a damned one and I shall have to insist you let me in!'

'Keep your voice down, Dodder, or they'll hear you.'

'Hear me? Hear what?' His voice was louder now. 'Hear about you, that's what they'll hear. Hear about your broken promises and infamy. You're not the only female alive, you know. By the Word, they'll hear all right. Hear how you deceived a poor, broken, old mole into thinking that here in this miserable wood was one mole at least who had a spark of care in her. One who had led this old but not entirely decrepit mole to raise his hopes and think that his final years might not, after all, be eked out in complete solitude; his burrow and tunnels not empty for ever of another mole!'

If the moles who had arrived at Crosswort's tunnels had been amazed by the welcome she had earlier given them, they were even more so now to discover that such a mole, notorious for her disagreeableness, had an admirer. The six moles had abandoned all interest in Mayweed's tale and waited now with bated breath for Crosswort's reply.

'I never promised nothing,' she hissed, doing her best to keep her voice low but not quite succeeding, so that her whispers only added more drama to the exchange. 'If there was even a hint of anything, even a tiny tinge or insinuation of anything it was on the understanding it was strictly private and between ourselves and nomole must know. Now all of Duncton will know and I shall be laughed at even more than. . . .'

'Yes, mole of the Stone, floozy follower, think only of yourself and think of no other. Guests, eh? Well, you've another one now, and he'll tell them about a mole he once knew who raised his hopes by offering happiness to an old military mole who had served his cause well, and then dashed them back to the ground because she's concerned about being laughed at. I reject you, Crosswort! I rebuff you! And I now enter your mean little tunnels with the intention of exposing you to the so-called guests you claim to be entertaining.'

Then, suddenly, his voice was raised even louder.

'Guests? I should have realised. Guest, singular; sex, male. That's it, isn't it? I have been deceived! By the Word, he's going to feel my talons before he's done. No! Don't try to hold me back! I am trained in killing! I shall advance now and challenge him and fight to the death. If he wins then may you be miserable with him. If he dies then I shall kill myself in any case and two corpses shall be the reward of your deception! *Guests?* Let me get at him. . . .'

The moles below looked at each other in alarm as geriatric paw-steps pattered towards them from the tunnels above.

'It's the former guardmole Dodder!' whispered Hay.

The paws stumbled about a bit, and then headed towards the chamber's entrance as Crosswort, hysterical with rage and embarrassment, ran along behind shouting at the old mole to stop before he made a fool of himself.

But too late. In burst Dodder through the tiny entrance of the burrow, withered paws raised, brittle talons extended, eyes narrowed as he peered about in the murk for his adversary and rival. Beechen saw he must have been a large and imposing mole once, but now he was aged and short-sighted.

'Filth! Scum! Deceiver!' he cried, circling about ready to fight. As he did so his eyes adjusted to the light and he saw not one mole but seven, and all of them reposed in a lazy and comfortable way with welcoming smiles on their faces and not a trace among them of rivalry or deceit.

There was a very long silence as Dodder retracted his talons and slowly resumed a normal stance.

'I see,' he said, 'that you did not lie and I have made myself look a fool. Worse, it is I, a mole who should know better, who has committed the discourtesy.'

Much humbled, and yet retaining his very considerable dignity, Dodder turned shakily back to Crosswort and said, 'Hit me, Madam, on the head. Hard if you like. Then I shall leave and interrupt your company no more. Strike, Madam! See, I do not flinch!'

To everymole's surprise there went over Crosswort's face a look of genuine concern and sympathy as she said, 'I'll do no such thing, and now you're here you'd better stay, even though you are right to be ashamed of yourself. Really, Dodder . . .' And a perspicacious mole, who knew a little about males and females, would have noticed that in addition to the concern on Crosswort's face was a look that might almost have seemed affectionately respectful, as if Dodder's wild display of anger and jealousy had convinced her of something of which she had not been sure before. . . .

There the touching moment might have been well left,

and the pair been allowed to find another time to explore further whatever it was that lay between them, had not Heather risen from the shadows at the far end of the chamber and, pointing a talon at Dodder while taking frenzied hold of Beechen's shoulder, declared, 'See, Beechen! See the face and fur of the sinner, hear the arrogance of its voice, know the vicious nature of its mind. Its eyes shall be smitten by thy might, oh Stone, its ears deafened by thy Silence; and its Word broken as the slow-worm breaks under the wrathful paws of thy representatives.

'Disappoint us not, Beechen! Grow strong and vengeful! Punish the wrongdoer, for yours is the power and many are those that await your just anger as a sign to follow your cause. Disappoint us not!'

As this outburst ended, Dodder, who had listened to it in growing disbelief, said, 'She's not addressing me, is she?' Then, when he realised that Heather was, he muttered, 'The mole's mad, quite mad.'

'"Mad"?' repeated Heather incredulously, and letting go of Beechen she approached Dodder with a threatening look on her face.

But Tryfan stopped the argument getting any worse by reminding them that it was Midsummer, a time for reconciliation, and, anyway, they were all tired. A few more stories, a few songs, and sleep. Then in the morning they could move on, and, since Crosswort had given them such a welcome, it was for her to choose where they went to.

'Get us all some food, Beechen!' he said and, as Beechen did, all agreed on one thing at least: that Beechen was a fine-looking mole, and well-behaved, and a credit to them all.

But the day had been long and his impressions many, and soon after Beechen had brought them some worms and the talk continued unabated around him, he fell asleep, beginning to understand the strange and varied nature of the community into which he had been born.

When morning came, and the moles, lazy from the night before, had groomed and pottered about the surface for a bit, Crosswort announced that, as hers was the decision, they would all go and visit Madder, Dodder's neighbour and enemy, and she would not hear one word of protest from anymole at all, especially former guardmoles.

'Madder!' fulminated Dodder to himself. 'Pay a visit to Madder! Humph!'

But again the day was warm and good, and the mood of the rest of the company a cheerful one as they set off upslope into the Eastside.

Dodder's temper improved and for the first part of the journey he enjoyed himself, welcoming Smithills and Skint to the group and generally being friendly. But as they came near the area of his tunnels, and of Madder's, he grew belligerent once more and told anymole who would listen what a terrible mole Madder was.

'Be warned, Beechen,' he said quietly, not wanting Crosswort to hear his complaints, 'when you set up your own tunnels, find out what your neighbours are like first, and what their habits are. Madder is what I would call an undisciplined mole. But you'll see, you'll see.'

They did. No sooner had they arrived at Dodder's patch – or what he said was his patch – than they saw two moles crouched on the surface, one confidently eating a worm, the other looking embarrassed.

'That's Flint, whose tunnels lie adjacent to them both,' whispered Hay. 'He's never sure which side to be on.'

He was interrupted by the mole Madder who, the moment he saw Dodder and the moles with him, leapt to his paws and shouted, 'We thought you'd come back, you miserable old bastard, and here you are. Ex-guardmoles and other such filth and scum had better not put so much as a talon on my territory or they'll regret it. These others are welcome, of course, but as for you . . . bugger off down into your tunnels before you feel my talons.'

Dodder did no such thing but, rather, pulled himself up

115

into his most impressive posture and stared imperiously at his enemy. Madder was forced to do the same, whilst making a vain attempt to tidy himself up, pulling and tugging at his fur to do so. But the truth was that, though rather younger than Dodder, he did not have that worthy mole's bold bearing, or if he did it was masked by the sorry mess his fur was in. For though it was thick enough, even glossy, yet it never seemed to have discovered the knack of lying flat and in the same direction. It stuck out here, it stuck out there, it stuck out in the wrong direction everywhere.

His eyes, unfortunately, were no better than his fur. Not only were they placed a little awry on either side of his head but they were astigmatised, so that one pointed too far out and the other too far in and a mole found it hard to decide if Madder was looking at him, and even harder to find the right place to look back.

The posturing of the two seemed to be coming dangerously close to blows when Crosswort moved swiftly between them and said, 'Well really, Madder! What a welcome to give me on my visit to your burrow!'

'By the Stone, 'tis Crosswort. Damn me but . . .' A look of some alarm came over his face as he looked first at her, and then at the crowd of others and realised the implications of such a visit. Worms to find, smiles of welcome to smile, general disruption. . . .

'Yes, Madder! We've come a-visiting, *all* of us, and I shall be very displeased indeed if, so near Midsummer, you cannot find it in your heart to be *pleasant* to Dodder and the rest of us.'

'But . . .' said Madder, a look of considerable misgiving on his face. He began mumbling excuses: 'So much to do . . . tunnels somewhat untidy . . . worm supply poor for the time of year. . . .'

'Madam,' said Dodder, 'in the absence of courtesy and politeness from this dishonourable mole, and his obvious but may I say typical unwillingness to welcome us –'

'Be quiet, Dodder!' said Crosswort. 'Well, Madder?'

116

'Yes, well. Very well. Very happy to be well and able to welcome you *all*,' he said, adding more urgently and quietly and hoping, perhaps, the others might not hear, 'Though I had intended my earlier invitation to be just for yourself, Crosswort, so we could . . . you know . . . get to know one another.'

'He's at it already!' cried out Dodder. 'Whispering, plotting, shirking his social responsibilities. Yes, this is the mole of which I spoke . . .' Then, turning to Beechen in particular, he continued. 'Note him well. This is a mole who is as ill-disciplined mentally as his appearance might lead you to believe. If I say, and I do, that he is a mole of the Stone, I mean no rudeness to Stone-followers in general. But, well' –and here Dodder smiled rather thinly, and with a certain smugness too – 'I flatter myself that my appearance is a better testimony for the Word than this shambles you see here is for the Stone. Stay smart, young mole, stay smart.'

'Fine! Very fine his words, but what a miserable evil character they hide,' responded Madder immediately, not moving a single molemite. 'I mean no disrespect to the rest of you, but I am surprised to see you in his company . . . and I am sorry if I seem rude, but while I'm willing to be visited by everymole else I am not having an ex-senior guardmole, who has the blood of followers on his talons, inside my tunnels.'

Tryfan suddenly reared up, dark, glowering and powerful, as if the very ground itself had broken open and an ancient root burst forth.

'Speaking for myself,' he said with such calm authority that all the moles were hushed and Madder slowly dropped his paws to his side, 'I am tired and in need of food. I am sorry that Madder feels as he does. I am sorry that Dodder seems inclined to provoke him. But most of all I am sorry to see talons raised, for violence is failure.'

'Aye,' said Hay suddenly, 'we're all tired of you two arguing, and it's about time it stopped.'

'But they like it,' piped up the timid Flint, 'they love it.

117

They're not happy unless they're quarrelling. They *need* it.'

There was silence at this and then Hay and Teasel laughed.

'Well said, my love!' said Teasel, as Dodder and Madder glared at each other.

'What's more,' said Flint in a confidential voice, as if he imagined that neither of the protagonists could hear, 'if you were to attack one of them the other would defend him.'

'Here's the mole you should be choosing, Crosswort: Flint. He's got common sense.'

'I have asked her, as a matter of fact,' said Flint, 'but so far she has refused me.'

'Paradoxical Sirs and Madams, and diplomatic Flint, humbleness is like Tryfan – hungry. Can we eat?'

'Madder?' said Crosswort sternly.

With that, and a resigned look at Flint, Madder led them off and down into his own tunnels.

He may have been all aggression and accusation above ground, but below it he was a very different mole, as if his own tunnels oppressed him.

Which, if they did, was not surprising, for they were a mess. Indeed, so messy were they, so disorganised, so utterly unkempt that the group as a whole was struck rather silent, for a mole likes to make a pleasantry or two when he visits another's burrows and in Madder's it was hard to find anything very positive to say at all.

'Er, very snug,' said Hay uneasily, snouting up a wide tunnel which seemed blocked with dead weeds.

'Not big but *interesting*,' said Teasel, who was beginning to regret that she had ever mentioned how moles used to go a-visiting.

'Humph!' said Crosswort shortly, looking about with disapproval all over her face, and pushing a pile of soil out of her way.

Madder was clearly aware of the bad impression his

118

tunnels were making, for he hurried here and there making a futile attempt to tidy ahead of the incoming moles – pushing a pile of herbs into a corner in one burrow, and back-pawing some dead worms out of sight as he ushered them all a different way. All the while he muttered excuses about being unready for moles and having no time to keep order in the way he normally liked to.

Eventually they assembled in a cluttered burrow and looked about uneasily at each other and, almost to a mole, refused Madder's offer of food as, giving up further pretence at tidiness he attempted to be hospitable. He had gathered up a particularly neglected and suppurating worm from somewhere, its tail part all covered with dust, and was now offering it about.

'Ah! No thanks, I eat too much anyway,' said Smithills, patting his ample stomach.

'Me?' said Skint, a look of alarm on his normally stern face. 'No, no, I don't eat at this time of day.'

Smithills, always mischievous and full of fun, turned to poor Hay and said, 'He's always hungry, he'll have some food.'

'No!' said Hay. 'I mean, well. . . .'

'Mole, I'll have it if I may,' said Tryfan suddenly, 'and Beechen will eat it with me.' To his credit, Beechen succeeded in appearing as if he looked forward to the grim prospect while Madder, clearly relieved and pleased that such a one as Tryfan himself should accept his food, attempted to wipe the dust off the worm and spruce it up a bit as he laid it before Tryfan.

It was a strange and touching moment, and while some moles there, like Dodder and Crosswort, might well have considered Tryfan foolish for taking such dubious food, most others appreciated his kindness and felt indirectly admonished by it.

But what had greater impact was the way he now gravely regarded the sorry worm, looked up at Madder, whose eyes gyrated nervously this way and that, and asked, 'Would you have a grace spoken in your burrow?'

'If moles of the Word and others don't mind, I'd like it if you did,' he said. 'Yes I would!'

'Well then . . .' said Tryfan, silently reaching out a paw to Beechen who was looking about with too much curiosity at that serious moment, and stilling him, 'there's a traditional Duncton grace which you might like to hear. Beechen has learnt it and can say it for us.'

The moles stilled, several snouts lowered. Dodder seemed about to speak but said nothing. Crosswort wrinkled her brow as if a grace was rather a threat, while Heather closed her eyes tightly and pointed her snout in the direction of the Stone. Mayweed grinned, and Skint and Smithills settled into the easy stance of moles who knew Tryfan of old, and liked it when he encouraged the traditional ways.

Beechen waited for silence and then, in a clear strong voice, as Tryfan had taught him, spoke the grace:

> The benison of ancient Stone
> Be to us now
> The peace of sharing be here found
> And with us now
> This food our life
> This life ours to give
> This giving our salvation
> The peace of sharing be here found
> And with us now

As he spoke he reached forward and touched the worm, and it seemed that the worm so unwanted, and Madder's attempt to share it which had been so rejected, was transformed into something of which all moles there must have a part, whether of the Stone or not.

When the grace was over, Beechen ceremonially broke the worm and took a part of it to each of the moles.

''Tis ours to share,' he said each time he proffered the food, and the followers among them replied, 'Shared with thee', while Dodder and one or two others simply took the

120

food and whispered 'Aye!' to signify their acceptance of the sharing.

Then when the last piece had gone to the last mole Tryfan said softly, 'The benison of Ancient Stone be to us now,' and the moles ate their pieces in companionable silence.

They rested then, and talked among themselves, and, with Dodder on one side of Beechen and Madder on the other, he heard both their stories and learnt how it might be that in strange and troubled times such as had beset moledom, a mole of the Word and a mole of the Stone had ended up living in adjacent tunnels in a system of outcasts.

'Would you really defend Dodder as Flint said?' Beechen asked Madder quietly.

'Flint shouldn't have said that but I might, yes I might. He may be what he is, and done the things he's done, but he is a Duncton mole now so he's one of us, isn't he?'

When Beechen asked the same question of Dodder, he replied, 'Young mole, I would, but keep it to yourself. In a military situation he would not know where to begin, whereas a trained mole like me would.'

Later Tryfan turned to Madder and said, 'I've been told your surface entrances are worth seeing, mole. Would you honour us by showing them to us all?'

At this Madder looked surprised and pleased.

''Tis true enough, Madder, isn't it? I've just been telling Tryfan you've a way with plants and trees.' Hay spoke encouragingly.

It did not need much persuasion before Madder led them through his untidy tunnels, pushing this and that out of the way and into still more untidiness as he went, and took them into tunnels different from the original ones and delved by himself, which threaded their untidy way up among the living roots of ash and out into a place on the surface such as few of them had ever seen the like before, though many must have passed nearby on their travels through the wood.

It was most strangely overgrown: strange because there

was order to it, strange because in that dry part of the wood it seemed pleasantly moist, strange because wherever a mole looked there seemed something more to see, something more to draw his eye. Strange because there, among that growth and the wondrous light it cast and the soft shadows it made, Madder was a changed mole, and one in his element. Up here in the secret places he had made for himself all the oppression of his tunnels left them, as it left him. He darted here and there, touching and tending to the plants and growth all about, and talking as he went. Even his disordered fur seemed more ordered there, unless it was a trick of light that made him look . . . well, as neat and tidy as neat and tidy can be. Such he seemed, such the place he had made was. The plants that formed the backdrop to this place of peace were yellow nettles, tall, proud and bright. Making them seem even brighter was the thick ivy that grew up the trunk of the ash behind and from which, too, trained it seemed by Madder himself, came a few strands of dark leaves along the ground.

'The yellow nettle's at its best now, but it will fade soon as all flowers must. But as it does, and the sun begins to harden north again in the years of July and August, why my eyes delight in the ferns that I have let grow here. . . .'

He pointed out a clump of fern they might not have noticed, for its leaves were still small and unopened, and it half hid itself beyond a root.

'Ferns like darkness and a little wet, and when the sun catches at their leaves and turns them shining green the darkness of their place sets them off.'

'It's just a fern,' grumbled Crosswort, unconvinced.

'"Just a fern"!' laughed Madder with the genuine delight of a mole who knows others are wrong but that when they see the error of their ways and drop their prejudices what a delight they have in store for themselves!

'Perhaps so,' he added, leaving the others to judge for themselves. Which they did, and found in Madder's favour.

122

There were so many more things to see in this enclave of peace Madder had made by his tunnels' exit that the moles were reluctant to follow him as he hurried on to show them other treasures.

The wood seemed to open past the fern into a path, crooked and secret. It was arched over with the russet stems of wild rose, and its floor was softened with crunchy beech leaves which gave the route a dry, good scent. As they went they lingered, for here and there the path branched up some tempting byway, or opened out into a prospect a mole could not simply pass by. He or she must linger there, and stare, and think that moledom must be great indeed if in so small a space there was so much to see.

'It's not easy to keep up,' Madder said. 'Voles *will* use it as their run – I can't think why – and when the wind comes from the east, which it has a lot this June-time, the under-leaves are disturbed and need attending to. So much to do!'

'Looks wormful,' said Borage.

'Wormful? Oh, I don't eat the worms hereabout,' said Madder with faint disapproval. 'That would only increase my work, wouldn't it?'

'Er, yes,' said Borage, supposing it would.

Madder hurried on until the path opened out into a second enclave very different from the first. It was dominated by a great holly tree, whose shining leaves gave dark light to the place. Other leaves had fallen from it but lay undisturbed on the ground, brown with their points yellow-dry.

Beyond it they climbed to a raised area of ground at the top of which was some exposed chalky soil. Such places occur across the Eastside of Duncton Wood and occasionally in the high wood too. The soil seems to rise above the level of the humus, or perhaps some natural minor anticline of strata creates an exposure over whose top the wind is always sufficient to clear what leaves fall there. A process aided by the liking other creatures have for such exposed spots across the wood's litter layer.

As the moles ascended the little rise they saw the spoor of rabbit, and there was the whiff of weasel there as well.

'We all come here,' said Madder, as if he thought moles were no different from the other creatures and were all one in the wood. 'There's three kinds of trees grow in this part, the ash, the oak and the beech, and I can see the light of them all from here. Swaying and graceful for the ash, its leaves soon gone; green and airy for the beech, its leaves the true whisper of these woods; and the oak, not so great in Duncton as in other places I visited when I was younger, but a solid presence all the same. All have their ways and, as my mother used to say, a mole never learns them deep enough.

'This is the spot I stopped at when I decided that I was going to have to stay in Duncton Wood, like it or not. I felt at peace here for the first time since leaving my home system. I thought, well, there's no river to scent nor coots to call here, there 's no sedge to watch rise and hear the stems rustling, there's no yellow flag opening out all pretty in the wind; nor kingfisher's dart, nor trout's sudden splash, nor any of the sights and sounds of the Avon that I love. But, mole, there's new things to see, new things to hear, and many a new thing to scent. And there's places aplenty to make good with plants as my mother taught me, and none to harass, and none to spoil.

'That's what I said to myself when I came. And so I thought it was as I found things I'd only ever heard of. Beech tuft all slimy on the beech, and slipper orchid down among the ash, and baneberry to scent out downwind of it on a July day, and its black berries to warn a mole of sin and shame. I come here when I want to think.'

Then suddenly, to everymole's alarm, Dodder, who had said nothing at all for a long time past, turned to Madder and said, 'I must say I would not let my tunnels get into the mess yours are in. But then. . . .'

He looked about the lovely ways Madder had led them on and added, 'But I'd say you've got something I never had. Yes, and never will have.'

'Which is what, surprising Sir?' asked Mayweed softly, with a quick glance about and a gleam to his eye that stopped others saying anything to spoil the moment.

'Ability to make a place feel like home,' said Dodder, 'and not like temporary accommodation. Your patch would scare the paws off most guardmoles because it's got the whiff of insubordination, but I'll be quite frank, Madder . . . I envy it.'

For once Madder's paws stopped fretting at his fur and a glimmer of real pleasure came to his skewy eyes as they settled in their eccentric way on Dodder.

'You . . . like it then?' he said with touching and genuine modesty.

'Best place I've seen in Duncton,' said Dodder with certainty. And then, evidently finding it all right after all to say something nice to Madder, he dared to add, 'Apart from the neighbours, of course. No imagination. Complainers. Moles of the Word or . . . !' Pausing, Dodder enjoyed the joke at his own expense and beamed expansively at Madder, then at Crosswort, and finally at Flint . . . 'or moles of no particular belief at all.'

'Well said, formerly grouchy Sir!' said Mayweed, and everymole agreed, and felt relief that peace could be established between the two rivals on such a delightful day.

Others, seeming to have heard that Tryfan was about with Beechen, joined them during the course of the afternoon – among them Bailey and Sleekit – and the moles talked, and slept, and grew excited at the prospect of Midsummer by the Stone.

Skint told the story of how Tryfan, guided by Mayweed, had once rescued him from certain death at the paws of a patrol in the infamous Slopeside of Buckland. Teasel showed how, if a mole tumbled the petals off a briar stem, she could tell of his past and his future and moles queued up for the privilege.

But when Beechen tumbled the petals so a pattern might be formed, a breeze blew and the petals drifted through the wood, and far out of sight.

'What's it mean?' said Beechen, but Teasel only smiled in a troubled way and said she knew not, and the sky was darkening, and they had all best travel on, and bide by Madder's choice.

'We'll go to Feverfew's,' said Madder, a popular choice and one Tryfan greatly welcomed, for he knew that his consort would be awaiting him and Beechen, for the morrow was Midsummer, and all moles must go to the Stone.

As they wandered on upslope, for Feverfew's tunnels lay that way, Mayweed lingered by Teasel and said, 'Woebegone Madam, what was it you saw in the fall of petals young Beechen made?'

Teasel shivered.

'The night he was born his touch restored my sight, but would I had never regained it if it had meant I did not see what those petals showed. He'll need moles near him. He'll need us all. Nomole can go so far as he must and not need help.'

'Madam, he has us all,' said good Mayweed, and Teasel's gaze followed his own as they watched the moles go forward up the hill with Beechen in their midst, laughing and at ease.

'He's so young,' whispered Teasel, 'and I wish Midsummer did not have to come; but it must, and a mole grows old.'

'Metaphysical Miss, a mole does, even those as humble as ourselves! And we slow, yes, yes, yes; and we worry, yes, yes; and we wonder. Yes?'

'Yes,' agreed Teasel.

Mayweed grinned and together they followed on after the others, as fast as they could.

Chapter Nine

In the moleweeks since she had reluctantly agreed to help Lucerne and Terce make preparations for the Midsummer rite, Henbane, beleaguered Mistress of the Word, confronted an enemy greater and more subtle than any she had ever faced: her own desire for the truth about herself, the Word, and the making of Lucerne.

Something was wrong but she did not yet know what. Something must be done, but of its nature or implications she knew nothing. Only a mole who has tried to face such questions can fully know the isolation she began to feel.

For Henbane had lost faith in the Word, but found no comforting substitute to cling on to, as the nightmare reality of what the Word was and had been under Rune and herself, and would more than likely continue to be under Lucerne, became progressively more clear to her. The first insight had come in that appalling moment when Lucerne had struck her; its revelations of horror continued to come upon her in the days and weeks afterwards, like ungovernable waves of flood water down a tunnel in which a mole is lost.

All was terrible doubt and uncertainty, and the pain of a mole who hates herself for what she is and what she has done which can never be undone.

Not that the sideem or even Terce yet knew it. But they mattered not to her now: it was what Lucerne was becoming that beset her, and him she feared, for she guessed that he now suspected her commitment to the Word and would be wary of all she did and said.

They were a blighted mother and ascendant son, circling each other as they waited for the other to make a strike, though each knowing that that moment would most likely come on, or very soon after, the Midsummer rite. Until then each needed the other and each must play the game of honeyed words and hypocrisy.

In that hiatus period in the High Sideem, the main thrust of Henbane's thought was this: what was the nature of the education Lucerne had, and what, if any, was the weakness in him that it left behind? Where, in short, was Lucerne vulnerable?

Mixed with this was a mother's guilt, a mother's shame, a mother's tortured recall of a puphood which she knowingly maimed, of a youngster she helped corrupt . . . and whose outcome, terrible and now unstoppable, would soon have its triumph. She knew with certainty that once Lucerne had gained the legitimacy that the rite would give, all his striving would be for Mastership, and all Henbane's for survival, and her life.

So, as mother and son exchanged their pleasantries and smiles of hate, with Terce hovering between them both, his dissembling art experiencing its greatest test, Henbane strove to make her plans or, more accurately, strove to understand the nature of the son she had made, that she might know how to destroy him.

Her task would have been easier, and its outcome more certain of success – if filicide can ever be called 'success' –if she had understood *why* she thought thus. But so far she did not, nor why, at the end of her life, she should even attempt to redress wrongs too great for mole to contemplate.

Henbane had not had a sudden revelation of the truth, but, rather, something harder for a mole to contemplate, which made her contemplation of it all the more courageous. For as good and evil are the light and shade of the same thing, in the same fleeting moment when Lucerne had hit her and she had seen the evil of the Word she had glimpsed as well something greater and more beautiful than she could ever before conceive.

Once glimpsed, that 'something' – that light, that Silence, that fierce fire burning towards the truth – becomes a portal that can never close, beyond which a mole sees fearsome things of beauty not seen before.

But Henbane had, though all too briefly, seen the light itself before. At her own birth, shafting down in the chamber of the Rock, a light before which Rune and Charlock had trembled. To that distant, unconscious memory something in Henbane had returned, and that light it was that cast itself now across her life and made her see anew what she had barely seen before.

These recollections of her life became her torment now, for she saw that, despite what she was and all she represented, life had given her much whose beauty she had not recognised or which she had affected to despise.

There must have been many such memories for Henbane then, but we who have followed her story know for certain only a few of them. Some seem surprising now . . . like the memory she had of Brevis, scribemole of Uffington and the mole who, along with old Willow, was snouted at Harrowdown on her direct command. At the time she had discounted their bravery, only now did she wish she might have talked to them, two different moles, both wise, whom she had killed with barely a moment's thought. Two of many such. . . .

But if such a memory was representative of many, a few stood out alone and by themselves, and none more so, perhaps, than that evening and night when she and Tryfan of Duncton had known each other in her chambers in the High Sideem. Passion and delight, abandonment, and they had made love. Now, moleyears later, for the first time in her life she knew loss and regret – for she knew their time together could never be again, and she saw too late its full beauty, its goodness. Yet she marvelled that such light should have been known to her, and of all places *here*, in Whern. And she wept that she had not treasured or honoured it, and ached and sighed with remorse.

Which regretful memory led to the last and greatest realisation of all, which had to do with Lucerne. For the result of that union with Tryfan was, significantly enough, the only pregnancy she had ever had, the only life, as it now seemed to her, she had ever made.

She wept now at the memory of how Tryfan's pups grew inside her, so slowly, as if knowing that it would take time for her to even sense that here, at last, was something good to come of her, something unsullied by the Word. Despite her weakness in the days before her time came, despite all fears, and most of all despite the loss she knew would result from what she did, she yet had the courage to command Sleekit to take those pups from her. In the event two were saved – or at least got out alive.

'May they be safe, may they be strong . . . may their parentage be forever unknown that they live in anonymity . . .' she whispered often to herself those days before Midsummer.

But the third pup, Lucerne, had not been got out of Whern, but had been hers to keep and in that keeping she had for a time found new and terrible strength. For him she had killed her father Rune and later, had not the Rock sounded its dark sound in her soul and kept its corrupting hold upon her, she might still have saved him too.

But that power overtook her, along with dynastic desire, and she committed him to the joyless Word, and did to him what had been done to her. Worse, she did it well. Worse still, she even denied her troubled self to do it, denied the memory of Tryfan, denied that same urge that had but a short time before made her make Sleekit take the others.

Then, when the pup was ripe for joy, for life, for the sun and air and love she herself had been denied, she let him have it not.

'I gave him up to Terce . . . I gave . . .' And she remembered, and her talons curled in an agony of hatred at herself to have so abused the single trust her life had left her with. Of all that she had done *this* was the worst to think upon. Yet, however evil Henbane's life, it *was* courageous to look back. . . .

So it is we find her, as Midsummer approaches, acting out the part of Mistress of the Word, listening to sideem confessions, licensing the preparations for the terrible rite to come, while all the time struggling on bravely with thoughts that dwelt on what she might not have done.

To her credit there must have come a day when her thoughts moved on from regret to reality and asked the treacherous question: what might now be done? For reasons that will soon be plain enough she did not think that Lucerne was redeemable. He was what she, and Terce, and ultimately the Scirpuscan Word, had made him. Again and again she returned to those questions: what was Lucerne's weakness? How might she exploit it?

In the internecine troubled world of Whern she knew that Lucerne guessed at where her thoughts were aiming. So his concern, and Terce's too, was to contain Henbane's power to what was essential, to surround her with spies, to so encumber her with work and assistance that she had not time or opportunity to make whatever undermining plans she might wish to make.

'Once Midsummer is over and she has fulfilled her task . . .' purred Lucerne.

'Yes,' said the Twelfth Keeper, and said no more. The very essence of such moles as those is ambiguity and vagueness so that when the moment comes and they move one way, nomole may accuse them of not having kept the option open to move another.

But where *was* Lucerne's weakness, if he had one at all? The weakened Henbane sought to know, surrounded by threat and the knowledge that when her duty was done they would have power to dispose of her. *And would do so.* So it was that over and again she thought of his education since Longest Night in the light of something two moles alone knew – herself and Terce. She as Mistress, he as Keeper of the Twelfth Cleave. For it is part of the Word's creed that nomole should be perfect, and part of the Twelfth Keeper's duty is to ensure that sideem moles each have a weakness which, if need be, a Master or Mistress can exploit. *That* poisoned secret is the greatest of the Twelfth Keeper's art, a canker in the summer rose. She

131

knew Terce must have put such weakness into Lucerne but did not know what its nature was.

'What is his weakness?' Henbane asked herself a hundred times. 'May I be granted that discovery. . . !' It was the desire to know the answer that drove her tormented mind to look back again and again at all she could recall of Lucerne's dire education at Terce's talons. . . .

We said it would be an unpleasant duty to make a record of this education and so it is, but a necessary one. For let all those who make or bring forth pups reflect upon the duties *they* may have, and how the nature of the contribution to Silence they make, or mar, may be dependent on the love, or lack of it, they show their pups.

For know this well: the seasons turn swift, the pup a parent soon becomes, and the measure of a mole is the quality with which he or she learns to live with the past to make something of the present which enhances the future. Nothing is more real in the present, nor more challenging, than the pups that depend on a mole. Nothing. No success is more satisfying than this; no failure more undermining. . . .

Lucerne began as any pup begins, with bleating, with suckling, with messing, and with life. Bonny he was, though dark and intense, but in fertile times many such are born. They do not all become the monster he became.

Seeing him, feeding him, encircling him, Henbane felt great joy; but hearing his bleats and not knowing their meaning, seeing his distress and not knowing distress is normal, suffering his demands and having no joy or patience of herself to set such suffering by and see its triviality, Henbane was confused and angry in herself.

In that dark place where Lucerne was born, surrounded by moles distorted by training, mainly male, mainly with a learnt distaste and fear of females, Henbane found no others to turn to. Few mothers can have been so ill-prepared within themselves, or so ill-placed within moledom's great expanse for such a great yet simple task: the rearing of a pup to maturation, with love.

Had she but known it she had already done more than many such mothers could have done: she had fought for her young, she had helped them all survive, and from some instinct deeper than time itself she had seen that two of them were taken from her to safety.

That much was true, but the reassurance of it was not hers to have, and nor in that hateful place was there a single mole to give such reassurance, or to help her with the simplest things to do with a mother's love. Yet even so, despite everything, she had the courage to have doubts. For when Lucerne the pup was gay, and she saw his simple happiness, and she took him by his neck and carried him to the surface and the sun, she knew, deep down, that all was not right.

'My love, my sweetling, my own delight,' she purred, words which vile Charlock never said to *her* with love. She cried to see him happy and feel in herself an inability to respond, and worse, the tightening of incoherent anger as he demanded love. Strange anger that feeds upon itself and turns impotence into a sense of uselessness, and forces a mother to put upon a harmless pup the anger and frustration she felt for what had once been done to her. Pity her, that she knew not how to stop the hatred of the mewling thing that grew side by side with love, as black ivy entwines the sapling sycamore.

She was a mole perverted by her parents from the course of normal love and was no better prepared for the defence of her pup than a crippled mole on the surface is against the marauding owl. And yet within her there was decency and the propensity to love, and crippled though she truly was she faced not one owl but ten or a hundred with a courage few mothers ever show.

Again and again she recalled Terce's persistence in asking that the pup be delivered to him on Longest Night that his training might then begin.

133

'It is the due time then, Word Mistress, the due time for such a one as he.'

She said yes and yes again, yet still he persisted, as if the very process of making her angry and guilty about parting with her pup to him was part of his Twelfth Keeper's art.

Henbane, no fool, challenged him.

'Oh yes Mistress, I am aware that my diligence annoys you. It must be so if the pup is to be prepared fully for what is to come. I say again, he must hate thee if he is to fulfil his task.'

'What task had you in mind, Twelfth Keeper?'

Did Terce then hesitate? She watched his reaction minutely, as skilled at observation as he at impassivity. She saw no hestitation, and yet knew his answer was not the truth.

'Why Mistress,' said Terce, 'to be Master after thy Mistress-ship. To be thy worthy successor.'

No, no, no, no, no. There was more. Something Rune had planned. Something. . . .

'You were made by Rune, Keeper.'

It was as near to an accusation of falseness as she ever got.

'I can be unmade by thee!' said Terce smoothly. His eyes were as cold and fearless as her own could be.

'Well, he shall come to thee. He shall. But. . . .'

'Word Mistress?'

'Shall he be tutored with other novice sideem, as I ordered?'

'I have chosen but two to serve their novitiates with him, Mistress.'

'Tell me of them.' Henbane had been surprised to find she felt jealous of these youngsters and was also surprised to see Terce falter a shade as if, realising this, he knew that one or other of those he had chosen would give her cause for jealousy. And then she remembered that Terce desired hatred between son and mother, and she smiled. One of the novices would be hers to destroy if she so willed – the payment to her for suffering her son's hatred.

134

'I have chosen the first after much thought, and the second by instinct though in response to a vow before the Word.'

Again, Henbane was surprised, for such vows were rare, and rarely extracted from a Keeper, least of all from a Keeper of the Twelfth Cleave.

'The first is Clowder, of Hawkswick born. I nearly took his father a cycle ago but he was flawed. We have over-watched his young, and Clowder has all the qualities of his father – intelligence, pugnacity, astuteness, plus something more. He is that rare mole, a leader who yet will serve another in whom he has faith. If I may put it this way, Mistress: as you served Rune in your campaign in the south so shall Clowder serve Lucerne. I shall make him worthy of his great task.'

Great task? Terce knew something Henbane did not. Terce *planned* something more than he now said. Again, Henbane detected the vile talon of Rune in this.

'The other novice, what of him?'

Terce faltered. Genuine? An act? Henbane could not tell. She disliked the mole, but acknowledged to herself that he was a master at what he did, and as such was fitting tutor to her son.

Terce replied, 'I know not, but the promise of a sideem before the Word is a sacred thing. I know not. . . .'

'You *know* not, Keeper?' It was an astonishing admission, and Terce came as near as he ever did to looking sheepish. The moment quickly passed as he repeated once more that the choice was instinctive and such choices had not failed him before.

'Tell me,' said Henbane coldly.

It seemed that he had got a female with pup, which is a Keeper's privilege if it is done discreetly and outside the confines of the High Sideem.

Henbane, all powerful, could afford to laugh.

'And you promised what to her?' she said, eyes light as she added a purred afterthought: 'You make me think that

Keepers aren't as dry and dead as they usually seem, Terce. Tell me, whatmole was your mistress?'

' 'Twas a female came a spring before but could not find sponsorship. Her name was Linton, but she was not strong enough to be sideem.' He paused fractionally and Henbane saw it.

'You're doubtful, mole. You still think sweet of her who was strong enough to make the Keeper all novices fear make a promise by the Word.'

Terce did not smile.

'She had the touch about her, certainly. I promised if she was with pup then I would take the best born of her litter to be novice, whether he seemed fit enough or not. By the Word I promised it.'

'And who to choose this "best born" who shall serve his time with *my* best born?' There was sarcasm in her voice, and a measure of dislike. If one was to be sacrificed to Henbane's jealousy this would be he.

'Last month Linton sent word that the youngster was ready and even now I await the return of my colleague, Lathe, with him. On such matters Lathe is discreet. I shall honour her wish and her choice, for in my judgement a mother who has born and reared her young, if she is intelligent and respects the Word, as Linton is and does, is the best judge.'

Henbane smiled sweetly.

'You seem to have much experience in these matters for one who is a sworn celibate. But no matter . . . you shall let me know when this "best" mole comes: what his name, and what his character.'

'Mistress, I shall.'

And days before that fateful Longest Night he had.

The loathsome Lathe had brought the youngster privily up through Whern and into the High Sideem to Terce's chamber. At first, seeing the youngster, Terce was inclined to smile, even laugh, which was very rare, if not unknown, for him. The youngster Linton chose was female.

Terce laughed because he appreciated Linton's humour.

'I refused her,' he whispered to himself, looking at the comely elegance of the female, 'but this one I must train.' But incest was not in his mind, or even crossed it. His perversions lay at first remove in others' lusts.

'Your name?' he asked the youngster, who was, after all, of his own seed.

'Mallice, father,' she said. Her eyes were not afraid. They were his own. Her spirit was Linton's, her body young. Laughter first, now pride he felt. And then fear, terrible. *For she was not strong and even if she survived the Midsummer rite, which surely she could not, Henbane's jealousy would take her.* Perhaps he had underestimated Linton to so devise a punishment of him.

'You are accepted,' he said, 'but if you ever call me father again in that same moment I shall kill you.'

'I understand,' she said, and what he understood was that Linton had reared her to hate him. It was a pretty challenge.

He took her to the Mistress of the Word and the Mistress laughed even more.

'Well,' she said, staring at Mallice, 'you have a motley crew of novices for the Midsummer rite, Terce. An ungainly clever mole called Clowder, a daughter whose mother seems to have named her well, and my son Lucerne.' She turned to Mallice again and fondled her, to Terce's intense displeasure. 'Why, truly this mole was sent by the Word. She pleases me, though I wonder if she shall survive the rite. She seems too weak . . .' Henbane's eyes looked as cruel and malicious as they ever had.

'I warn you, Terce, and make an ordination of the Word. Train your trio of novices well and see that all survive, for if one does not then you shall die as well. I shall see to it myself. May the Word help you the day the rite comes by. Meanwhile I shall give a mother's love to my Lucerne and entrust him to thee in the dark hours of Longest Night.'

'Mistress, forgive me but . . . remember to suckle him. It is meet that you do.'

'I know it,' hissed Henbane.

All this she remembered, all of it. And even more of that Longest Night. . . .

It had been in a small antechamber, adjacent to the Rock, that the life of the then-innocent Lucerne was committed to Terce and seemed to kill forever a sense of joy within herself. Henbane remembered all the details of her last small journey with her growing son, his trust – how hard and falsely won! – his eagerness, his eyes that were wide with interest and intelligence; eyes that were beautiful. Yet behind it all was fear of the unknown, a fear that might have turned to terror had he or Henbane suspected what was soon to come.

But such suspicions were not held, and so it was that an innocent pup, a little afraid of the adult world, but one that might have served his fellows well, trotted obediently at Henbane's side that Longest Night, going inexorably towards a doom about which *despite his fears* Henbane would only say that it was for his betterment.

Even then he felt an inner doubt.

'Why?'

The question he had asked again and again betokening a determination which, if perverted, might become a persistence for evil.

'Because thy time for growing up has come, my love. I can't always look after you. I have things to do. And Terce can teach the Word better to you than I can. He is trained to it. But. . . .'

'*Why?*'

'It is the Word's will. As I was taught so will you be. You can't be a pup for ever. And anyway, I shall love you more if you do it, and be proud of you.'

'*Why?*'

'Lucerne, be not afraid. Terce is kind and will care for you. Lucerne . . .' But even to the end young Lucerne cried.

138

Oh yes, Henbane remembered all of it, and the slow and skilful bullying and threats of withdrawn love she used to mould the pup she made to her dark wilful will, even to the last moments. His mouth trembling, desperate to trust but trusting not. . . .

'Will it be all right? I mean . . . I'll be able to see you? Often?'

'Yes, as often as you need.' *Need!* A weasel word, but what youngster knows to ask, 'Who will judge what I'll need?' What youngster could guess that the one he trusts most in all the world will commit sole judgement of that crucial need to a mole like Terce? Such betrayal of love leaves an infection more malodorous than the worst scalpskin or murrain. It can destroy a mole and often does.

In torment, Henbane remembered how the nights before Longest Night Lucerne awoke screaming. But how much greater her torment that even at the last moment, as they turned a corner into the antechamber where Terce waited, she still had doubts and could have acted on them.

'Why didn't I? Why?' Bitter her torment, more bitter than death when life is much loved. Bitter as a life laid waste.

Then the dark corner was turned, Lucerne looked up at her with a final instinct for survival, and she said, 'It will be all right,' echoing his fear that it would not.

Then as Lucerne gave the last brave smile that marked forever the end of his innocence, the cavernous limestone walls widened, and there, enshadowed, waited Terce, calm, assured, certain of his power. Smiling.

At his side were two moles no older than Lucerne himself.

They stared in awe at Henbane and whispered, one after the other, 'Word Mistress! Word Mistress!' and deferentially inclined their snouts. And then they looked at Lucerne, and he at them.

'This is Lucerne,' said Terce.

'Clowder,' said the male. Awed but malevolent.

'Mallice,' said the female. Awed and calculating.

As Lucerne joined them and Terce turned to take them to the secret chambers to the north of the High Sideem where the long and arduous training would be carried out, Henbane felt utterly bereft.

'Too late,' she whispered as they went.

So Lucerne's education began.

Even now the full horror of sideem training is not wholly known. Nothing like it exists in all the experience of moles of the Stone, not even during the most ascetic and obsessive periods at Uffington. The only detailed account of it is that scribed by Mayweed at Sleekit's dictation moleyears after she had left Whern and turned her back on the Word, and lived in Duncton.

Truthful though she was it seems likely that her account is incomplete, though whether from fear of unknowingly tainting those who might later work on Mayweed's text, or because she blanked out memory of much that happened, is hard to say. Certainly it was part of the sideem training that the sideem *did* forget. But the arcane rituals, the harsh austerities, the self-abuse and punishment, the use – to death – of youngster grikes from outside Whern, the training in interrogation and torture, the inculcation of a creed of indifference to all but those who confessed the Word and Atoned – all these Sleekit gave some account of.

We do not know all, but it is enough to say that during the long moleyears between Longest Night and the Midsummer rite, Clowder, Mallice and Lucerne were in the talons of a Master corruptor, and by the time June came round what innocence, what kindness, what true care for others they might once have had was all gone. A kind of cold glittering dust of age had settled on them, the knowingness of moles who have seen more than moles should see, done more than moles should do, whose dreams and frightening fantasies had been lived out and made satiate; moles whose training had aimed at but one thing: to teach them how best to turn others to the service

of the Word by making them masters of the use
corruption of other moles.

But if that was the norm for the sideem – the norm that
Sleekit later partially described – the training of those
three by Terce had one further aim, unique in the dark
annals of Whern, though originally prophesied by Scirpus
and made real by Rune posthumously through Terce.

Clowder and Mallice and Lucerne were to be a trinity
whose sole purpose was the final ascendancy of the Word.
The New Age which Rune had begun, and Henbane had
continued, was to find its fulfilment through Lucerne with
those two on either flank. This had been Scirpus's belief and
Rune's desire. Now it was Terce's task to see it to fruition.

So his training did not make ordinary sideem out of his
novices that cycle. The three he made were to be arch-
sideem and together do and be what a single mole could
not: one to lead with strength – Clowder; one to corrupt –
Mallice; and one whose name would be used to exalt for
ever the honour and inviolability of the Word – Lucerne.

Let us not mince words.

By mental torture Terce did it. By deprivation in
darkness. By starvation. By abuse at the talons of moles
brought in secret for that task alone, and then killed. By
utter satiation of adolescent lust. By rote learning of the
Cleave words to exhaustion. And the only deference ever
shown to Lucerne, and that an evil one, was that he was
allowed to suckle his mother still.

Dark, dark and never-ending those moleyears must
have seemed. Sadism and masochism touched with the fire
of delight. Memories and frightened youngsters done to
death as sacrifices to the Word. Blood on talons. And all
about the great dark subterranean lake north of Dowber
Ghyll, on whose banks Terce made them live, and in
whose waters he made them submerge themselves almost
to death itself, that they might be the more ready for the
Midsummer rite to come.

Nomole but Terce could have performed his task so
well.

And Henbane saw the progression of Lucerne's training, for daily she fed him, daily she suffered his hatred of her failure to take him out of there, daily she saw the change. She was witness and aide to his corruption. She was party to evil.

'I WAS evil. I am evil. I killed my son's innocence, which is the joy in life; now I must kill him.'

This was Henbane's summation of her role in those moleyears and its inevitable consequence. But how to kill a mole whose very training had left him powerful, and at whose flanks went Clowder, Mallice and Terce, three moles dedicated to his ascendancy, which must give them power and glory too?

So again and again she asked. 'What is his weakness?' and prayed (to what power, provided it was not the Word, she did not care) that the day would come when she would know. And that that day might come before Midsummer, before it was too late.

Chapter Ten

As Midsummer dawned across bleak Whern, the black and awesome darkness in the subterranean Chamber of the Rock of the Word began to weaken towards light, and the sinister shapes of moles to show themselves.

The novices awaiting the terrible rite of acceptance to the sideem had long since gathered, and now formed a mass of moles in the lowest part of the chamber, which ran down to the edge of the lake, on the far side of which the Rock itself rose.

Gradually through the night all twelve Keepers had taken up their stances about the edge of the chamber, except for its furthest, darkest, higher part where nomole but the Mistress of the Word might go.

As the distant rising sun began to play its light at the contorted fissure in the roof high above, all was still and waiting. No sound but the drip and play of water and the high-pitched call of bats above, disturbed by the light, shifting their roosts, uneasy.

Then the Twelve Keepers, as one, began chanting the long gradual which is the preliminary to the rite; a chant whose ancient and subtle timings announce and follow the slow progress of the great shaft of light which comes down into the chamber once the sun is high enough.

At first showing, the shaft of light is but short and stays high among obscure crevices, but then as the gradual continues and the sun above rises, it strengthens deeper into the chamber and brightens all in its path.

The awed novices watch on until suddenly, in a moment they never forget, it reaches the spot where, most mysteriously, the Mistress or Master of the day is revealed in meditative stance: still, fur ablaze with light, eyes impenetrable pools of darkness, ready to give the command that even the most confident novice must dread.

The chant of the gradual deepens and grows louder, the novices feel themselves drowning in its sound as the shaft travels on to the very edge of the lake. As its first dappling reflections shoot out and up and on to the face of the Rock far beyond, the Master or the Mistress speaks.

So, that Midsummer morn, Henbane spoke.

'Begin,' she said.

None but a sideem who has survived the ritual can know the shudder of awe, fear, dread, excitement and terror that overcomes the novices at that moment: '*Begin!*'

Lives hang now in the balance, and as some will surely *end* before the day is out, so, truly, do many indeed *begin* again, changed and wrought darkly by the most testing of the rituals of the Word.

As Henbane spoke the command that Midsummer day a mortal silence fell over the gathering, and the gaze of the novices was concentrated with a fearful intensity on the solitary shaft of light that even now moved on, half on the lake's shore and half into its deepening edge where, pale green, the limestone shore shelved out and then was gone into the shimmering chill of the water.

The shaft's brightness served only to make all the rest of the chamber seem dark, but for the massive dappling of the light's reflections on the water that played back and forth across the Rock and would remain much the same for some hours yet until, its journey across the lake complete, it reached the face of the Rock itself and rose back whence it came, towards the darkness of the night. But by then many of the young eyes now hypnotised by the light would be drowned and dead, and see light no more. It is – or was – one of the great ironies of moledom that moles of the Word celebrate Midsummer during the day, whilst those of the Stone made their ritual when that day ended, and night returned. But for now . . . suffer the Word's vile way. . . .

Henbane remained elevated on that rocky outcrop on the

far side of the chamber behind which a high cavern runs into which no sideem may go. There are the remains of previous Masters, their body shapes preserved in the slow encrustations which form as ceiling water drips and water trickles out of unseen tunnels and runs on to feed the great lake.

It was up one of those tunnels, tiny, dark, almost unexplored, that Mayweed had led Sleekit moleyears before, each carrying one of the pups Henbane had borne after her mating with Tryfan. Nameless then, Wharfe and Harebell later, they had been carried past the surface cemetery of the Masters and up into the darkness, their escape made the easier by the awe in which the sideem held that place, and the reluctance with which they followed Henbane's command to pursue and kill.

Indeed, not a single one of the five sideem who had obeyed her command had returned, lost in the swilling darkness of the tunnels and perhaps taken by drowning into the dread Sinks into which failed sideem are sucked. For in Whern such tunnels are inclined to flood, and moles to drown. There, too, it was presumed, Mayweed, Sleekit, and the pups had been lost and now none but Henbane herself, hoping with a mother's hope that those pups survived, believed them still alive.

More than once Henbane cast her gaze behind her towards that cavern and the distorted shapes of the Masters dead; her gaze settled on the newest corpse there: Rune's, the father she killed. Already the surface of his body was slaked and hardened with shining crystals of lime, his black talons turned a milky white, his back sheening into the grotesque and arching form of a centuries-old Master behind him, his snout extending beyond its normal length and dribbling with the drips of that wet place. At his rear, past his distorted right paw, the biggest of the feeder tunnels stretched away to blackness, half blocked by his body. Water trickled out from it; water that might become a flood. Henbane shuddered and turned back to watch the rite commence.

145

Although at first the mass of moles might have seemed in no special order, in fact to one who knew them it was plain that near each Keeper those novices attached to him had gathered. Apart from Henbane herself, four moles stood out from the rest and these partly by virtue of having taken their places immediately under the spot where she had stanced: Terce, Clowder, Mallice and Lucerne.

Such was his chilling authority that Terce would have been noticeable at any time in any company, but there, that day, for this rite, this quality he had was especially marked.

His large thin body was so still that a mole looked twice to see if he was alive, to which the clues were only his open staring eyes and the just perceptible in and out of his breathing. A little below him, to his right, was Clowder, full grown now and dark, his gaze pitiless, his physical power overt and frightening; to Terce's left flank was the mole many had looked forward to seeing – Mallice, his daughter. The likeness was unmistakable, for her body and head were thin and dark like her father's, the eyes similar. Though smaller than both Terce and Clowder there was a quality to her eyes and set of her jaw that warned a mole not to cross her path, the more so that Midsummer day because like others there she was afraid, and fear made her beauteous face look vicious.

The last of this quartet was Lucerne, who had taken a place of special privilege behind and above Terce, and nearest of all to his mother Henbane. The most frightening thing about Lucerne was the fearlessness with which he seemed to face the coming rite. From his dark eyes there came a look of utter confidence overlain with tension and concentration. He did not look like a mole who could fail.

Taken together, these four presented a formidable front and from their position might almost have been taken for a protective guard about Henbane; or else a custodial guard, which many there knew was more the case.

Few truly believed that the Mistress was cured of the

madness that had overtaken her earlier in June, and Whern was rife with rumours that these four moles, led by either Terce or Lucerne himself, had nurtured her back to sanity for this day's rite, and that alone. After . . . nomole could know. She would have fulfilled her task. Lucerne would be legitimised by the rite and ready to take her place, leaving Terce, his tutor, the second most powerful mole in moledom. If Lucerne wished so to do, none there would gainsay him: the sideem would rather have a strong Master than a failing Mistress.

Other lesser rumours abounded too, of Mallice especially, and of how Lucerne and Clowder had used her – with her acquiescence – and even, darker still, how she and her own father, Terce . . . but few moles there dared stare at her for long. She seemed to sense when others gazed on her and turned her narrow eyes on them, and left a mole feeling marked for future vengeance if he displeased her. She had something of the power and allurement of Henbane, but none of her strange charm. But now . . . all that was as nothing before the reality of the rite to come.

'Begin!' Henbane had said, and as the echo of her solitary command died away in the high darkness of the Rock the First Keeper came forward.

He was an old, thin mole of withered mouth, but dignified, and he advanced into the water and turned to face the way he had come. As he did he signalled a novice forward and a male broke ranks and came to him. The Keeper began the low chant, in little more than a guttural whisper, which is the start of the ancient liturgy of anointing, his voice cold and strangely powerful in its whispering age, and finding awesome echoes in the distant Rock. Light seemed to thunder down about him as he spoke, and the black water of the lake stirred and lapped away with his movements into the darkest corners of the chamber.

'Forasmuch as all moles are conceived and born in shame and weakness, spawned of lust and born out of the flesh; forasmuch as born moles cannot please the Word until they have Atoned; forasmuch as allmole without instruction of the Word and mandate from it will die cursed in everlasting pain, and unfulfilled, the Word ordains that chosen moles go out into moledom's bleak places to convert the lost and blind, to destroy the mindless and the wilful, to set example in word and deed and bring Atonement to those cursed.'

The First Keeper paused and stared about, his front paws dropping half submerged into the water. He stared down at the mole before him who crouched at the very edge of the lake, his snout low.

'By words and deeds!' the First Keeper cried out suddenly.

'Is it not so?' spoke Henbane sharply.

'It is so!' the Keeper whispered back.

'Forasmuch as this mole has been admitted to the knowledge of the Word,' continued the Keeper, the other novices now utterly transfixed and staring, 'may he thank the Word for its complaisance and its pleasure and now be grateful to stand trial in the chill waters of the Word's judgement. To be found worthy is to live; to be found wanting is to die and journey to the Sinks and there repent his failure in just and everlasting torment. Art thou grateful for this chance?'

'I am,' whispered the novice humbly.

'Art ready?'

'I am,' he said yet more softly, his flanks visibly trembling.

'Then prepare now to submit thy will, and the last vestiges of thy shame and vanity, to the Word's power and might, here, today, now, before us thy witnesses.'

'I do!' said the novice.

The First Keeper now laid his paws on his pupil's head, and Henbane spoke out the following words in a commanding voice:

'Of those before us now, some, mighty Word, are unsure and weak, their desires false, their intentions misaligned from thy intent. May thy dark waters punish and damn them and we be witnesses to their shame.'

'May it be so,' said the eleven other Keepers.

'And more than so,' said Henbane.

This was the signal for the First Keeper to raise the mole before him and turn him to face the Mistress.

'The novice Brenden, born of Howke, I present to thee for ordination of the Word,' he said.

'Dost another make avowal for the novice Brenden, born of Howke?' said Henbane.

'I, Fourth Keeper, declare the same,' said that Keeper, coming forward.

'Novice Brenden, art thou ready to make the declaration of assent before the Rock and these witnesses?' said Henbane.

'I am,' replied the novice.

'By this rite thou shalt be sideem or die inglorious. The sideem are the only true representatives of the Word, privy to its secrets, privy to its power, privy to its purpose. They profess the faith in the scriptures uniquely revealed to the Master Scirpus even in this holy place and scrivened by him, whose creeds and articles must be proclaimed afresh by each generation.

'For this great task thou hast applied, for its training thou wast accepted by the First Keeper, and thou now find seconding by the Fourth. Your testing time has come. In the declaration thou art about to make, thou wilt affirm thy loyalty to the great inheritance of faith, of inspiration, and of guidance through the Master or the Mistress of the day.'

Henbane stopped speaking and a dread silence followed before, faltering at first and then gaining in confidence, the novice Brenden replied in the prescribed words.

'I, novice Brenden, borne of Howke, will so affirm and declare by belief and trust in the Word and the power of Atonement.'

Then Henbane spoke again.

'A sideem is called to lead and care for allmole towards the service of the Word, and to show the cursed the way of Atonement. It is his duty to watch over the spiritual health

149

of those in his care, to reward virtue, and to punish without mercy and in the manner taught by the articles of the Word all those infected with error, or who lead others to error in their ways. He acknowledges the absolute power of the Master or the Mistress of the day and teaches others to do the same, that the sideem may be as one, and through their sage ruler follow only the true way.

'In order that we of the High Sideem may know your mind and purpose, and that those amongst your peers chosen to survive the rite may be witness to your declaration, you must now make the declarations I, your Mistress, put to you.

'Do you believe, so far as you know in your own heart, that the Word has called you to the office and work of the sideem?'

'I believe the Word has called me.'

'Do you accept the scrivened Word as revealing all things necessary for salvation of mole?'

'I do so believe.'

'Do you accept the doctrine of Atonement, that the original sin of mole may be eschewed and divorced only through austerity in the Word's name?'

'Truly, I believe it.'

'Will you accept at all times the judgement of the Master or the Mistress of the day, and the discipline of the sideem?'

'Gratefully I so accept.'

'Will you be diligent in your study of the Word, in prayer, in discipline, in the upholding of truth against all error?'

'By the help of the Word, I shall.'

'Will you strive to shape your life even unto death, according to the Word?'

'Humbly, I shall.'

'Will you be witness of the Word and its true prosecutor at all times, always?'

'As I have been taught, so shall I be.'

'And now, before we ask novice Brenden to make the

final declaration, let us speak thus for him: Holy Word, if it is your will he lives, give him the strength to perform all these things that he may complete that task he has begun in your name.'

'Be it so!' cried out the assembled Keepers and novices as one.

'Then let the Rock be witness to thy faith, let the waters of the lake cleanse thy body, and may the Word have mercy on thee if error lurks within thy heart.'

With these words, Henbane ended the Declaration of Assent, which is the first part of the liturgy of anointing, and nodded sternly at the First Keeper to continue.

In a daze, it seemed, terrified certainly, the novice mole backed slowly into the lake until his rear part was submerged and his balance only kept by the firm hold the Keeper had taken of his right shoulder. It seemed quite certain that the quality of the Word's mercy was about to be tested.

The Fourth Keeper, who was the novice's seconder, now came into the water too and, crossing his left paw over the First Keeper's, he grasped hold of the novice's left shoulder.

'By this anointing may he be judged,' said Henbane as the two Keepers placed their talons around the mole's throat and, with an almost violent movement, arced him back into the water with a splash so that he was suddenly totally immersed.

Sleekit's account of what that baptismal act is like says that nothing before prepared her for the jolting shock of the freezing water on her face, snout and eyes, which seemed like sharp stars of pain. To add to the dismay of the moment was the complete disorientation and vulnerability a mole feels in such a posture, made all the worse by being held there until the breath began to burst in the lungs, and panic set in.

Then, said Sleekit, as sudden as the submergence, is the re-emergence into the bright and blinding shaft of light from the fissure high above. Talons, sharp and pressing, turn the novitiate about to face the Rock even as the swirl of dark sound made by the echoed chant of moles against the Rock seems to present a new drowning, and one yet more terrible.

Then the Keeper whispers an urgent, 'Swim! And may the Word be with thee, mole! Swim and remember all you have been taught! Keep to the left, and do not pause or falter for a single moment. Swim!'

Out into the frightening, chilling, numbing cold of the lake and through the blinding light towards the Rock, which seems to recede with each desperate stroke, seems too far, for the cold numbs the mind almost as fast as it numbs the body. A terrible crushing thing about a mole's flanks which causes pain between the paws, which stirs at her and seems to seek to suck her down.

So Sleekit told Mayweed and so must it have been for the novice Brenden of Howke as, with the eyes of all upon him, he set off to swim out and make his scriven mark upon the Rock, and then swim back. Anything less was failure. To turn back too soon, the task incomplete, meant a taloning to death by his tutor Keeper and the seconder. To linger too long, to slow, to lose orientation, to succumb to the cold and begin to wander, that meant death as well: the sucking death among the currents that run strong and deep near the centre of the Rock.

'Keep left! Always left!' was the traditional advice, and generation after generation of novices wondered why the tutor Keepers were so insistent on it, so boringly repetitive.

But now that novice began to know, by the dread Word he knew! The water was a tightening clasp of cold about him as he passed beyond the shaft of light into the dappling darkness there, and heard what he had been warned he would hear then: the sound of his own frightened and desperate gasping echoing back as dark sound from the Rock ahead.

'Turn it to your purpose,' he had been told. 'Feed on its strength to make more strength, or its weakness will weaken you.'

But he *did* feel weak, and panicky too, for from the uncharted darkness beneath him he felt the first entwinings of a current, cold and powerful, diverting his paws as they sought to swim him forward. His breath came fast and desperate, and the dark sound worsened into weakness.

That novice tried, as so many had before him, to call upon the long moleyears of training he had had, to conserve his strength to swim resolutely forward to the left side of the Rock and through the strait of death he now found himself in.

'To the left, to the left,' his chattering mouth sought to whisper as he saw, nearer now, the ghastly dark maw at the centre of the Rock in which water slurped about and towards which the unseen current began to drag him, and into which a failed mole flounders before he is lost to the eternal damnation of the Sinks.

'To the . . . left?' The memory of his training was leaving him, despair was overtaking his desperate paws, the dark sound echoed back his own slow drift towards surrender and whatever he had been taught seemed beyond his grasp now, lost in the confusion that overtakes a mole succumbing to such death.

His paws reached forward towards the Rock. *The left! The left!* faint memory said – but the left was drifting away and the dark centre was coming nearer and the lake's current growing stronger and remorseless.

Fatally he paused to look around for help that was not there, and saw only a shaft of light and the distant shapes of moles, as the current bore him on into the very centre of the dark sound of his own fear. Fear palpable; fear tangible; fear felt as growing pain, and his strokes, such as they were, grew wild and desperate, the Rock huge above him, and on its face the scrivens none had ever seen so close but those about to die.

Then he screamed, the novice Brenden born of Howke, and of his scream the Rock made a dark sound more dread than any yet heard. Like a black talon to pierce and turn in a mole's gut it came, worse than a snouting it was, and only another scream could he make as the dark water sucked him and turned him as, with one last desperate surge of rational strength, he reached up and touched the Rock even as he was swept into its maw and beyond all hope, ever, of recovery.

A final despairing scream, the scrivening scratches of his paws along the lowering ceiling of the cavern which lies beyond the maw, and then rock abrading his head, water sucking him beneath it, pain all through his body, and the last hopelessness of a mole who knows that all his life's trials, all his hopes, all his fears, all of everything, even love, even first memory, were leading him to nothing but this dawning hateful unredemptive terror, and the beginning of the bursting of his lungs.

So the novice Brenden was lost to the world. Gone but for his last scream and scratching which redoubled in the Rock's dark echoes and cast a deep fear and dread over the remaining novices. It was a sound that made the Keepers seem the very agents of judgement and death, and made the Mistress Henbane – dark and still, alluring and merciless – the very embodiment of the Word itself.

'Next!' she said, and the First Keeper's second pupil stumbled forward, and the rite began again.

Three more died before one survived, and that the last of the First Keeper's group. An ominous beginning, and enough to cast a pall over that Keeper's future. By the pupils let the tutor himself be judged, so saith the Word.

But when he who survived clambered ashore the palpable fear that had haunted the chamber was over-ridden by an extraordinary zeal. If one could, others might. The possibility was there. It *could* be done.

The Second Keeper began his round of anointings, and throughout that Midsummer day, deep in the black heart of Whern, the rite went on. The ominous beginning gave way to a run of survivals as the shaft of light travelled on across the lake towards the Rock.

Then, at the thirteenth anointing, and on to the Fourth Keeper's group, another death; and another after that; and then a third. Now a grim and dour mood came upon the witnesses to this rite, for moles others knew were dying and more would die among those who waited with nothing to do but stare in growing awe at Henbane or the Keeper performing the ritual, and envy those who had survived.

Over these survivors a striking metamorphosis had taken place. The light of success and confidence seemed to have settled on them, a hard cruel light of moles who have been tried and tested and now feel exclusive, not recognising as worthy of respect any who have yet to prove themselves. Such demeaning of others in the survivors' eyes is a prime purpose of Whern's Midsummer rite, and prepares such moles for the tasks of subjugation and tyranny soon to come.

Meanwhile, among those waiting, were brooding Clowder; Mallice; and Lucerne.

It is part of the Twelfth Keeper's great art to keep the stolidity and confidence of his own group intact as the rite wears on and his novices face a double undermining – from watching moles die, whilst having to face longer than any other group the new power discovered in those who have survived.

Terce seemed to have done his work well, for none of his three pupils flinched or looked unsettled as the day progressed. Their stances were relaxed and sure, and at different times each of them sunk into a whispering meditation. The only perceptible difference was that Terce moved closer to them, and they to him, so that they seemed to form almost a solid mass of mole, formidable and fearsome. Even Mallice, the weakest of the group, seemed to have gained composure.

Above them Henbane stanced her ground unmoving, and yet a watcher might have perceived a change gradually come over her as the rite's progress led to the Tenth Keeper's charges (one dead) and then the Eleventh's (two out of four lost into the Rock's maw).

155

Few yet knew for sure, though many guessed, of the struggle that had developed between Henbane and Lucerne in which, so far, Terce had played an ambiguous part. Henbane, who had been hemmed in ever since her return to a semblance of normality by Lucerne and those sideem Terce had set to the task of over-watching her, had agreed to participate in the rite only because she had no other choice.

She did not trust or love her son. Thus far her sole intent was to try and undo what she had done, which was to help others and the Word make of Lucerne's life a growing evil. Yet she felt powerless and had watched over the course of the rite with growing despair and self-hatred. Those lives that were lost in the maw of the Rock were wasted lives, pointless lives, and she was herself the very instrument of their doom. Yet what confusion swirled inside her as the dark sound swirled without, for each time she raised her paws, each time she spoke that dread word 'Next!', she found it harder to keep her composure, harder not to scream out her self-misery.

But she knew well enough that Terce, Lucerne and the others, whatever else they might be, were her guards, and from here there was no easy escape. After the rite was done, and Lucerne legitimised, she knew her life would be forfeit. So what to do but hope, even at this last hour as the rite continued, that some way of stopping Lucerne might still be found.

Outwardly calm, Henbane had inwardly debated long and vigorously what she could yet achieve. Kill him, her son! It might be just possible if he had been nearer. Had she not killed Rune in this same place? Yes, the thought occurred and recurred as the day went by. But if she failed . . . if others stopped her . . . then her ignominy would be a glorious beginning to his reign. And, too, killing was not to her talons' liking any more. Life was what they craved; the life and light they should have known before. . . .

Or hope, perhaps, that he might not survive the rite? That had been her wish when the day began, and before. It would be a fitting end. But watching him, seeing his confidence, seeing that lesser moles than he survived, sensing the confidence that Clowder and Terce seemed to have as well, she doubted that he would fail. Only Mallice seemed weak. That mole might fail, but not Lucerne.

Yet suddenly then she relaxed and seemed to know what to do, and Terce seemed to sense it for he tensed and kept looking at her, his mind puzzling over what she might have thought of. Well . . . he was prepared for all things. The plans of the great Rune, of which he was the executor, would go on.

The last of the pupils of the Eleventh Keeper stumbled back to land, and already, with but the last three to go, a mood of excitement had come over the assembly. With Lucerne, son of the Mistress, to go, and Mallice, daughter of the Twelfth Keeper, there was a certain gratuitous interest in the success or otherwise of the remaining novices.

Interest, excitement . . . and tension, too, which came most of all from the Mistress herself. Never had she stanced so still, never with such fearsome authority, and never had her fur seemed so full of light and graceful age, and her eyes so impenetrable.

'Next!' she said, and Terce nodded to Lucerne, and slowly Lucerne rose and followed the Keeper to the water's edge. The rite began as it had so many times already: the tutor Keeper went out into the water, he turned, he raised his paws.

Behind him the great shaft of light began at that moment to shine at last upon the Rock itself, at its dark centre, where the water flowed deep and dangerous and whence the bleakest suckings came. What had been obscure before now became clear, for the watching Keepers, the newly anointed sideem and the three waiting novices could now see all too well the terrible nature of the cavern into which the lake flowed. Above that dark place the light of sun – direct at the base, reflected and dappled above caught at the great scrivenings of the Rock and made them seem like wild scrivens across a great sky, beautiful and awe-inspiring. The dark sound muttered, water lapped and, once, high and unseen, a bat shrilled.

As Terce opened his mouth to summon Lucerne into the water and begin the Declaration of Assent, Henbane hunched suddenly forward, the first movement she had made for hours. It was enough to shock and still the watching moles.

'Not him,' she whispered. 'Not my son. I judge him yet unready.'

A buzz of excitement and alarm went among the watching moles. The implications were all too plain. Unanointed, Lucerne could not assume any power at all. Unanointed he was less than he had been before, for the others who had come through had something he had not.

For a moment Lucerne himself was still, and then he turned, glowering, while higher on the shore Clowder moved in anger, and Mallice too. Indeed everymole but one seemed disarrayed by Henbane's quiet and brief announcement, and that one was Terce.

Lucerne seemed about to speak, to shout perhaps, and Clowder ready to rally at his side; a hushed whisper of apprehension went among the moles. Terce alone was calm, the counterpoint to Henbane's icy stillness.

'Novice Lucerne,' he hissed, 'return to thy place. It is thy Mistress's will.'

But was there reassurance in his voice? Had he foreseen this move of Henbane's? Had he already made his plans? Or was he taken by surprise as well and wished his loyalties to remain ambiguous? None knew then, none truly knows now. At all events, he stayed calm and made but one change that others knew of, which was that when the Mistress said 'Next!' once more, after Lucerne had grudgingly resumed his place, Terce nodded not at Mallice as he had intended but at Clowder.

The reason was plain enough. If the next that went failed then the Twelfth Keeper's position would be weak indeed. Of Clowder and Mallice the former was certainly the more likely to succeed, and his success would surely encourage Mallice when she went, and thereafter . . . not a mole could doubt that Terce was thinking of a way in which Lucerne might gain Henbane's permission, if not peaceably then by force.

Clowder came forward past a grim-faced Lucerne in a chamber now cast down into a silence of suppressed excitement. The shaft of light was strong on the Rock, from the maw of the cavern now came the loudest suckings yet heard and the lake's water lapped hungrily at the shore. Not a mole but Terce and Clowder moved.

'Forasmuch as all moles are conceived and born in shame and weakness . . .' Terce began the rite once more, raising his paws over Clowder's head, his words finding a clear and distant echo all about the chamber.

There was about Clowder's anointing an assurance that even the strongest moles had not yet shown, and a confidence in the way he rose from submergence and turned, unaided by the Keepers, and began to swim steadily towards the Rock. Not once did he falter, not once deviate, not once slow. But on he went steadily, driving the dark waters before him, the grunt of his breathing powerful, and dark sound subservient to his strength. On, on, watched in awe by the other moles, unperturbed by the occasion, certain of success.

Indeed, his reaching the Rock was almost an anti-climax, for he made his scrivening swiftly and then turned and was coming back, water flowing off his face and back as his body rose with each stroke he made, looming nearer and nearer to the shore once more. He emerged and shook himself dry without the support of anymole, stared balefully around at Henbane, then, instead of joining those other moles who had made the swim successfully, he returned to take stance at Lucerne's side.

'Next!' commanded Henbane icily, and Mallice rose and went past Lucerne and Clowder and advanced towards Terce, her father-tutor, and the rite began once more.

The watching moles regarded Mallice's progress through the rite, from Declaration of Assent to the moment of immersion, with less interest than they might before Clowder had swum. His triumph had made the whole rite seem easy and had released among the survivors a mood of cheer and renewed excitement. Lucerne seemed diminished and the once-feared Mallice irrelevant; whatever plottings lay between Terce and Lucerne, whatever failings the Mistress might have, she was in the ascendant once more and the survivors could relax and look forward to the pleasures of being acknowledged to be sideem.

It would be hard, impossible perhaps, to say quite why or when they began to pay attention to what, only gradually, mole after mole realised was becoming a scene of profound tension, climax and change in Whern.

Mallice spoke her responses quietly, and though clearly nervous there was something impressive about the almost pup-like sincerity and fragility she seemed to emanate as Terce loomed over her and Henbane and he progressed through the now familiar Declaration of Assent.

Moles seemed to sense that something powerful, something sacrificial, was taking place and that now, in Mallice, a mole most feared for her dark self-centred beauty and closeness to three such moles as Terce, Clowder and Lucerne, there rested something greater than all of them.

Perhaps it was the tension in Henbane's voice that gave away the fact that if *this* mole failed then the Mistress would in some way regain power. Perhaps it was the subtle frailty in Terce's voice, as if at this last moment of the rite he was revealing the attachment he had to this mole, whom all knew to be of his own blood; an attachment that betrayed him and marked him out for dismissal and death. They felt his fear for her.

But more than that there was something in the way the demeaned Lucerne watched her through her rite, something of an attachment which until then none had guessed. Not love, for that short word was never one for Lucerne's use; nor lust. Nor even liking.

160

Need . . . that was it. *Need*. There was a kindredness between these two, one prevented from taking part in the rite, the other – moles now began to guess – who would almost certainly not have strength for it. Was *this* then Henbane's intent in barring Lucerne from the rite, to rob Mallice of the support his success would have brought? To isolate her? And so destroy them both?

If this were so it found confirmation in the strange protective stance that Clowder had taken, and the way he looked malevolently at the Mistress, and then at Terce, as if waiting for a word of command to raise his paws and talon Henbane to death.

Indeed, so overt did his restless anger seem that several Keepers now began to move nearer to Henbane as if, recognising her right to power still and her success in wielding it, they would not allow Clowder or those of his ilk to attack the Mistress of the Word.

But understand this well: this was all unspoken. This was but in the minds of those who watched. And the mole who kept all in control, who kept the anger and the evil there unspoken and contained, was Terce. Still, calm, in control; and all about them the dire whisper of dark sound as the Rock, seeming to respond to what they did and thought, echoed back their silent struggle all about.

Then Mallice was submerged and, rising, she was turned to face the Rock and with the familiar last whispered advice that goes to such novices, 'Keep left! Keep left!' was gone out into the unforgiving lake.

She swam more slowly than great Clowder, but steadily enough at first, and in good line. The shining maw was to her right, her strokes were steady, the lake lapped darkly, the dark sound did not grow unkind.

But just when she seemed in reach of the Rock and as the moles began to relax she gasped, suddenly and audibly, and the dark sound cruelly gathered in the Rock above her, and she gasped again, and her distress began to deepen.

Now Mallice declined towards the fateful and terrible

161

ending that the watching moles had already witnessed so many times before that long Midsummer day. Her strokes grew weaker and when she finally reached the Rock it was to falter and slide to her right along its lowering edge, such scrivening as she made weak and pathetic as she tried to push herself away and turn to swim the long impossible route back to the shore across water that swirled and raced with the dragging currents of the lake.

Her gasps were almost screams, her strokes became more frantic, her progress back slowed, she half turned, she saw above her the rising Rock and the maw of its sucking cavern and she cried out these memorable words, cried out as no other novice ever had before: 'I shall not die! Your power, Word, is in me! I shall not die!'

On the shore the moles most affected by her fate were dumb and still. Terce loomed in the water, staring; Clowder hunched forward, one paw advanced as if wanting to reach out and bring her back. On Lucerne's face was . . . what? What word exists for a feeling others do not feel? No word at all. Loss, anger, despair, kindredness . . . strange pride.

'I shall not die!' she had said, and Lucerne looked . . . *proud*? Even as the waters sucked her towards eternal pain? He did! Hunched forward like Clowder, eyes narrowed, snout thrusting, his elegant flanks and fur that caught the dark light of the chamber expressive of a mole about to thrust his talons into the very heart of time and turn it to his use. His breathing quickened, he sensed his potent time was almost come.

But now something more came to that hateful chamber as the others there, seeing Mallice so near death, wishing to align themselves to the one who would win the unspoken contest that was taking place before their eyes, instinctively began a dark chant to urge the female of Terce's seed on to her death.

Slowly Lucerne looked around at them. The guttural chant whose principal refrain might have been *Die, die die!* was amply matched by the snarled and torsioned curls of

162

their mouths and teeth, and the swelling of their reddening eyes. Die, and the rite is done and we can begin our celebration. Die, and our lives as sideem begin. Die, for thy lingering keeps us from what we would the sooner have.

It was a chant whose driving rhythm found like echo in the Rock that now soared above Mallice's pathetic struggling form as, drawn down by that sucking current beneath the lake's surface, she desperately tried to reach up the Rock's slippery face and the cavern's roof to hold herself from the grasp of death.

Her talons scraped and scrivened at the Rock and she began to add her own scrivenings to the ancient and evil ones already there.

But . . . *'Die!'* the chant cried out to her.

'Die!' the Rock above echoed back, sending out a sound so vile that horror came to all who heard it, and their eyes widened and their senses seemed to attune ever more to where there was weakness in that great chamber – which was where Mallice struggled and where, the only one there absolutely still, her father Terce, Twelfth Keeper, his reputation dying in some strange evil way out on the water before him, stared too.

Weakness there seemed now in that mole of towering strength, Clowder, for he too was still and staring and helpless as the companion of his training moleyears continued to die before his eyes.

Little wonder that such mite of pity as there was that day in that place was all unseen. Yet may the Stone be praised for what it gives, pity was there. Coursing as a single tear down one mole's face: Henbane's. She who had most to gain from the death of Mallice was the only mole there with heart enough to pity her. So far along the hard way towards the light had Henbane travelled, so far but no further.

For no others tears flowed, but rather her eyes hardened as she remembered that in the death of this mole Mallice some measure of hope that Lucerne's growing power might be stalled remained alive. So Henbane pitied, but did nothing more.

Then a strange forbidding silence began to fall, as if the dark sound had reached its peak of frightfulness and found no more moles on which to dwell and swell its evil. So, an echo turning back on itself, it began to die and the moles there began to know a fear worse than any they had so far felt, now or ever before: a fear of a silence they had never even suspected existed before in which a mole, truly, as the Word taught, was nothing.

In that silence the moles witnessed an astonishing thing: Mallice still alive. Mallice clinging to the Rock, cursing, blaspheming, fighting for life and not sucked in, her talons tight to some cornice or cleft at the maw of the cavern and the dark, angry flow of the lake water at her body. Her screams had gone, her gasps had gone, and now in the silence the moles heard the answer to their guttural chant for death: the short, sharp breathing of a mole who has a will to live.

'I shall not!' whispered Mallice, and each mole heard those words as a charge against themselves. Each mole trembled, each felt anger, each felt frustration. She who should be dead was not. The Rock seemed defied. The Rock was demeaned. And yet there was glory in that moment, and revelation, and, surviving but yet unsaved, Mallice dared to laugh.

Then Lucerne moved. Forward. Slowly. As if dark shadows had taken life and moved out into the light. As if the chamber's very shape was being realigned.

'Tutor Keeper,' he said, ignoring his mother Henbane utterly, 'I shall make the Declaration of Assent. Now!'

'He shall not!' cried Henbane.

Clowder turned towards her, and seemed half inclined to attack her then and there, but Terce whispered, 'Novice Clowder, thou art not a sideem yet. The rite is not concluded. But it is the Mistress herself who blasphemes. This mole seeks to make the Declaration and he cannot be denied.'

Henbane stared powerless as Clowder turned back towards Lucerne, hunched over him protectively, and nomole there to stop him or defy him as Lucerne entered the water, turned and began in a rapid powerful voice to speak out the Assent.

'I believe . . . I so believe . . . I believe it . . . so I shall be!' he cried, uttering the responses boldly as Terce spoke his own part of the litany and that of the Mistress as well. Shock at such seeming blasphemy was palpable about them and some of the other Keepers stirred uncertainly, wishing to protest, but the light and the power of the moment seemed gathered about Lucerne and so confident, so overpowering was the speed and utterance of his litany, so at one with the darkness and the light in the chamber about him, so matching it was the defiance that came from the struggling Mallice out at the very portal into suffering, that nomole there dared gainsay it, or him. And nor, for good measure, would any have tried but with the certain knowledge that even as they spoke their protest Clowder would have raised his talons and dashed the life from them.

Then Terce signalled to Clowder to come to his side, and the two moles – one most senior Keeper of all and the other the most recently anointed sideem – sought to reach forward and immerse Lucerne in the holy sanctifying waters of the lake.

But even this he would not have.

He waved them back imperiously and then, alone and untouched, he turned to face across the lake towards the Rock. He dipped his paws in the water, he raised them and tumbled the water's shining darkness in cascades upon himself.

'Word, to thy service I commend myself,' he said. 'Anointed by thee alone. To thy care I commit my body, to thy will I commit my soul, to thy purpose I commit my life.'

With this he thrust off into the water and swam out towards the Rock, but not to the left, nor to the right, but straight to its darkest heart and very centre where Mallice awaited him.

Nomole who witnessed that fabled moment in Whern's dread history, save Henbane alone, ever gainsaid the dark glory and evil wonder of that moment. But for her it seemed a moment of turning evil.

Out swam Lucerne, swift and sure, and if Clowder's swim had seemed powerful his appeared as if preordained to triumph by the lake and Rock itself.

The waters drew him on, the shaft of light cast down upon the Rock and dappled now in reflections as he went lighting his way.

This was the Master in the making. This was Scirpuscan power reborn. This was of such power that anymole who saw it would follow him for evermore. Anymole but Henbane.

To the right flank of Mallice he went, defying the current that ought to have swept him on, turning without seeming to need to touch the Rock for support at all.

'Return to thy life renewed! I, thy Master now, so order it!' he cried out to Mallice. Dark sound whispered, strength came to her, and she who had so nearly died now swam out against the current and defied it. Back towards the awestruck moles she came, across the dappled water, as Lucerne watched, his power beyond questioning.

Then he turned, stared up at the Rock and then, as the waters seemed to surge and raise him up, he reached forward his talons and scrivened bold and mightily across the Rock's great face.

Such dark sound sounded then that moles covered their ears in fear, moles closed their eyes in terror, and moles sought vainly to bury their snouts in the unyielding ground.

Then, when that sound began to die, they looked back across the lake, and saw Mallice coming and Lucerne protectively behind. While on the shore Clowder waited for the mole who, the moment he touched the shore once more, must surely be acknowledged Master; and for she who, saved by him, would be his consort and mistress.

So they stared, and might have stared on had not a sudden movement to their right reminded and alerted them that the Mistress was witness to her own supersession. They turned as one and saw Henbane turn before them, back and gone into the cavern wherein the Master-dead lay encrusted by the flow of time.

'Take her!' cried out Terce. 'By my power as Twelfth Keeper I order thee to follow her to where the Masters of the past lie still, and take her!'

So it was that Lucerne's triumphant return to shore with Mallice was overtaken by a rush of moles up to that raised place where Henbane had been, and then on to where she had retreated among the encrustations of the past.

The first there saw her at that tunnel's mouth from which one of the feeder streams came down, with the contorted body of Rune, limed over, at her side.

'Take her!' roared her son Lucerne, Master designate, as he reached the shore and sought to scramble up to where she had been. 'All favour to him who gets his talons on her first!'

Ominous and strange what happened next. Unreported until now. Distasteful. A precursor of worse to come.

Henbane seemed unsure, as if to flee was to turn towards an unknown that even now she feared more than the evil from which she fled. But moles advanced upon her, greedy to touch their talons to her hallowed flanks. Greedy for the favour her capture might bring.

Quickly she turned, suddenly she stumbled, and her left paw fell upon the flank of her dead father Rune. So vile, so unexpected what happened then.

Rune's flank cracked. Rune's dead body burst. The encrustation broke beneath her paw and revealed a body rotted into slime and dark tuberous remnants, sliming odorous protrusions that burst and spattered, slid and flowed down towards the moles that advanced on Henbane. The smell was viler than moles had ever smelt before, as if all evil was concentrated in the squirting cracking thing that Rune's body had become.

For a long moment Henbane floundered in her father's body's rotten flesh, then she screamed; and as the odour of what she had disturbed rose up she screamed once more and found the strength to push on past it, leaving its sliming flow in her wake, a wave of vileness that stopped the pursuing moles in their tracks.

Some pulled back; others, too late, found their snouts and mouths caught by the filthy stuff and retched and vomited where they were. While others, behind these ones, were overtaken by the horror of the smell and turned away, deaf to the cries and orders of Lucerne, their paws to their retching mouths, their eyes watering into blindness.

Most strange of all was Lucerne. Such was the confusion of the moles ahead of him that he could not break through; and yet he retched not and seemed unaffected. The rottenness of death had no hold on him.

'Catch her!' he cried, but nomole could obey.

'Then to the surface!' was all he could command. 'Find her and the Word will judge her through me!'

So, out through known tunnels Lucerne led them; the rite was done and power transferred in confusion, and a new Master made and eager to mete punishment on the Mistress whose power he had stolen.

While deep in the heart of Whern, unseen, alone, Henbane fled her father's broken cadaver. Retching, near to being sick, she ran on gasping and desperate, not knowing that those who had sought to follow her were not behind. To flee the rottenness, she headed for light and air. She ran from power to powerlessness, from being the pre-eminent mole of her time to being nothing.

The more she went on and that stench was lost behind her, the more she sensed the freshness of life that lay ahead. On and on, towards the glimmering of new light.

And she laughed, and she cried, and she whispered as she went, 'Lead me, help me on, take me to where those I lost so long ago still live. Lead me. . . .'

She went where good Mayweed had once gone, she ran in the steps of brave Sleekit, she seemed to know that this was how her pups whose names she did not yet know had escaped.

'Help me!' she whispered as she went. And the tunnel helped her on until the air was clear, the light was good and she surfaced high on Whern, into the last of the Midsummer sun and saw its glory across the sky, and its new hope.

'Give me strength!' she said, and as the sun shone upon her aged fur she turned and went across the fells of Whern to seek out what light her life would still give her time to find.

'I shall find you,' she whispered to the pups she had lost so long ago, 'and you shall teach me what I was denied.'

Peace began to come to her and sometime then, among the humble peat hags there, she saw a pool of water. But it was not black or stained as such pools are, but rather seemed as clear as a summer's day, shining with the blue and white of a great sky, and into it she went and cleansed herself.

'By the light that makes this water bright I am reborn,' she said. Then she came out and took a stance on the open surface of the moor, and let the wind dry her fur, and felt the evil that had been her inheritance leave her.

'My name is Henbane no more,' she said. 'Whatever task I still can do, grant that I do it well.'

The Midsummer sun began to fade and gave the mole that had been Henbane, and now seemed nomole at all, the security of darkness to make her escape; the special darkness of Midsummer Night.

The special Night when others, far away from that place called Whern – moles whose hearts are turned not to the Word's dark sound but towards the Stone's great Silence – touch each other's paws, raise up their eyes and pray for those less fortunate than themselves, who wander lost but seek to find the hardest thing of all: the better way.

So, that night, did an old female go out alone at last, free to find the self that once, by a lake dark and forbidding, before a Rock, her parents took away from her.

'Which way?' she whispered to herself. Then with a sigh, and trusting to herself at last, she journeyed on.

Which way?

Moles, let it be towards our prayers she comes.

Chapter Eleven

That same night, in distant Duncton, Beechen was initiated another way, as ancient as that we have witnessed in Whern, but more loving, and before the Stone.

In the great clearing there, with all those moles whose friendship he had made and company he had kept in the previous days of June as witnesses, Beechen took part in that great Duncton rite which marks a mole's passage into adulthood.

Where Tryfan's father Bracken stanced so long before, where Tryfan himself had been, now Beechen was. Many of those who grouped about him, to witness with pride the rite that Tryfan spoke, we know already. . . .

Feverfew, Beechen's mother, was there. Mayweed, with Sleekit at his side. Good Bailey, brave mole, was witness too.

Then Skint and Smithills, and Marram: strong moles all, whom age had worn towards slowness and frailty, but not yet conquered. They were there.

Others, newer to us than these, though most more aged still, the survivors of those outcast to Duncton Wood: Dodder and Madder, between them scolding Crosswort and, watching over all three, good Flint, anxious for peace and finding it this night.

Teasel was there and old Sorrel of Fyfield, their bodies withered but their spirits bright as the stars that began to show soon after dusk crept up the slopes and settled on the wood. Hay was near and Borage, too, and Heather.

All these and many more: moles whose lives this history does not tell but, if time allowed, would surely be spoken of as well. In some way all outcast, all survivors, and now all with humility enough to be awed by the presence of the

171

Stone, and the light of the stars and moon it brought unto itself.

The wood grew darker, great trees became but shadows of themselves, while by the Stone the sense of Midsummer peace deepened, and Tryfan, great beloved mole, leader who preferred no more to lead, mole whose talons had fought their last fight and now touched the ground worn and broken, never to be raised in anger again . . . Tryfan was humble before the Stone and spoke a prayer.

'O Stone,' he said, 'many here have never been before thee at this time. Some from lack of opportunity, others because they are not of the Stone at all but now, being of our outcast community, wish to share in what we are this special night and join their paws to ours. Guide my prayer towards their hearts, guide their hearts to mine, and hear all our prayers tonight, whatever our beliefs may be.

'We pray first for those who are not here, but would be if that chance was theirs. Moles we know, moles we love, moles we have lost but trust are still alive. . . .'

Poor Bailey, ever a mole to shed a tear, shed one then and lowered his snout to his paws and thought of the sisters he had lost: Lorren and Starling. And Feverfew, knowing why he wept, came close to him and put her paw to his and whispered her own prayer to him that by the Stone's good grace one day his sisters might be with him once again.

While Madder remembered his home system by the Avon, Dodder, graceful in age and the Stone's light, reached out a paw and touched the mole who had so long seemed his enemy.

'Next, to those of other faiths than ours,' continued Tryfan slowly, 'we ask that they may trust their hearts and minds before they listen to our persuasions; they may be right, Stone, and we wrong! In thy great heart all moles shall find the place of truth and there learn that many are the ways moles come, many the names they give to thee.

'Last, guide me back into the hearts of those who profess the Stone, including I myself. Imperfect, our spirit but partially formed and far from thy Silence, striving onwards, let us yet be proud of what we are and seek always to dwell on the rising sun of the morrow rather than the fading sun of the day gone by. Let us drive ever forward to thy reality, not falter backwards to the dreams and fantasies that never were. Guide us forward to truth, Stone, not backward to the lie.'

Tryfan was silent for a time, and let the many gathered thereabout think of the prayers he made, or what they wished, and gave them time to say those special prayers a mole can often best say in company of others whose faith strengthens his own, and whose wishes go to absent friends all the better for the company he is in.

At last Tryfan spoke once more.

'Midsummer is a time when Duncton moles like to celebrate, just as they do when Longest Night comes at the end of the December years. But that dark time is a celebration of deliverance and the revels mark the beginning of the coming spring, when life begins once more.

'Our celebration this night marks the moment when young moles reach maturity. It is the time for parents to touch their pups one last time and wish them well of the rich life to come. A time for which the moleyears before have been a preparation.

'At such a time no parent feels his work is done and many do not wish to say goodbye, for it is hard to think a youngster's grown and the need for us is done. Harder to turn back on ourselves and start again, facing our partners or perhaps ourselves alone, and find once more a meaning in what we do reliant on our loving of ourselves and no more upon the loving of our young. For such as these the Midsummer rite is useful, too.

'But here, in Duncton, this clear June, are many who might have had pups but, because of disease and stress and age and the strangeness of where they are, go pupless and are bereft. For them the moleyears past, especially of spring, were hard and bitter times and you, Stone, seemed arid and pitiless. Help such moles now. Let them, with

173

this rite we shall perform, cast off the sadness they put on and see themselves afresh –and what they have, and the beauty of where they are and the great freedoms they possess afresh.

'Yet you have blessed us all. One was born to us, one that we knew as a pup, and saw to a youngster grown. One who will now an adult here become. His presence brings joy to us, and makes this Midsummer rite have meaning for us all tonight.'

Then Tryfan turned and signalled Beechen to come to him, and the youngster – *youngster?* Why he was as full grown now as Tryfan himself, and that mole was already beginning to look stooped by his side! –came, and together the two broke from the great oval of moles and went nearer to the Stone. A cheerful hush came over the watching moles, and friendly jostling took place as older and smaller moles pawed their way to the front and large moles, like Smithills and Marram, pulled back and encouraged the more timid to come forward to get a better view until all could see and watch the rite performed.

'The sacred words of the rite I shall speak this night were taught me by my father Bracken,' continued Tryfan, 'who in his turn learned them from a much-loved elder of Duncton called Hulver. To this very spot they came in the dark days when Mandrake and Rune ruled Duncton and sought to stop such ancient rites as these.

'Yet bravely Hulver came to speak the words, and another mole, Bindle was his name, gave him support. They spoke the rite and Mandrake and the others tried to stop them and struck them down. But my father, a youngster then no older than Beechen now, stanced his ground and finished speaking the rite, and then the Stone alone aided his escape and saved his life.

'Let us now remember brave Hulver and loyal Bindle, and with that prayer send out what strength and faith we have to those moles who, this very night, may face such dangers Hulver and Bindle once faced together here. We know not their names, nor where they are, but we of the

Stone believe that if we speak with love and truthful hearts before a Stone then others near Stones far from here will gain something from our prayer.'

Tryfan suddenly fell silent and seemed beset, and several there, including Feverfew, came a little nearer him. But it was Beechen who reached out a paw to him as if sensing that his guardian was touching some need beyond them all that demanded support.

'Sometimes . . .' began Tryfan, faltering, 'sometimes there may be moles who are not near the Stone, do not know its name, or, if they do know it, only to curse it. Yet sometimes such moles seek something far beyond themselves, whose name they know not. Such moles are brave indeed, for they go into the shadowed unknown places of their minds and hearts, guideless and terribly alone. If such there be tonight . . .' Poor Tryfan faltered again, and his great paw tightened on Beechen's as if he sensed, as if he almost knew, that that night, far away in Whern, a mole wandered, nameless now. . . .

'If such there be tonight we add this prayer to any other sent to him, or her. Or her . . .' His repetition of 'her' seemed to strike a chord in Sleekit's heart, and she turned suddenly to Mayweed and looked at him, and he looked back and wonder was in his eyes, and he nodded to Sleekit to add her prayer to Tryfan's. . . .

'Send thy help to such moles, Stone, wherever and whatever they may be,' she said.

'Aye!' whispered others, all drawing closer together, and 'Aye!' again, and in that moment Duncton became a true community once more, strong enough to send its love beyond itself to moles that needed help, wherever they might be.

This joint affirmation seemed to encourage and strengthen Tryfan once again as, looking up at the Stone and raising his paws to it, he said, 'After my father Bracken and Rebecca went to the Stone my half-brother, Comfrey, whom some of you knew, continued our traditions for many moleyears until, indeed, that dreadful time when the Duncton moles were forced to escape their home system and disperse. It was Comfrey's hope and wish that one day some of those forced to leave would return, and if not them then at least their pups or kin. To them he dedicated this system, and said that surely one day the Stone would bring its peace back here and leave its entrances and exits unguarded by grike, and free once more. I fear that I shall not live to see such a day. . . .'

There was a murmur of dismay at this, but Tryfan raised his voice and continued over it so that it died away.

'While I am sorry it may be so, at least I know tonight that I have lived to see the beginning of that return. In my heart I knew it to be so the night Feverfew made her way into Duncton and bore us Beechen.

'To some of us Stone followers he is called the Stone Mole and others have wondered what that might be. Why, he has wondered himself!' Tryfan smiled at Beechen, and others did as well.

'I shall tell you what I think it might be,' said Tryfan. 'A mighty thing, a thing of which we, all witnesses to his birth, all part of the secret of this first part of his life, may feel proud. Until now I have been reluctant to speak of it, for such a thing is too much for a youngster to bear. But this night, when we watch over the youngster's journey into adulthood, I shall speak, and on this night alone.

'Beechen was made of the union of blessed Boswell and Feverfew, born of the Wen. How this was, or why, I do not know. But I believe it was so, and that my master, Boswell, who taught me the greatest thing one mole can teach another – to love and trust myself – sent his son to us.

'He sent him here to Duncton because he knew that between us we would honour him and teach him all we knew. But more than that: he sent him here where he himself had found happiness and acceptance in the company and friendship of two moles who loved him even more than I did myself: my parents. Here he felt Beechen would be safe to grow and learn all that he would need for the great task he faces.

'Our Beechen, whom we love, cannot now abide here long. He must leave us, he must travel . . .' The moles sighed with dismay at this, and Beechen's snout fell low. 'It will be so,' said Tryfan simply, and sadly, 'it must be so. Moledom has need of him now, and this is what the Stone Mole is. One whom all others need, one in whom all others find their way; one who teaches others what beloved Boswell first taught me – to love and trust themselves. It is a hard lesson to learn, and one a mole often forgets. But without it he is of little use to others; without it, or something of it at least, he may soon be lost.

'Therefore, be proud this night, for in our different ways we have performed the task Boswell entrusted to us. We have brought a single pup through to adulthood, and given him that which he needs to know himself.

'Be not mistaken in this. However humble you may feel, however little you may think you have given him, however unworthy you sometimes feel yourself to be, *you*, by being here, by being willing witness to this rite, by being of our community, have helped nurture him. You are in him now. Your good and ill, your light and shade, your peace, your restlessness. You are his heritage.

'When first Boswell told me that the Stone Mole would come I thought he would come out of nothing, ready formed, to save us all. I was unwise. For good or ill, all moles are born, are raised, are nurtured; the best they do comes of the best they are first given. So had it to be with the Stone Mole. Of all systems for his birth and rearing Boswell chose this one. He trusted us, and knew that though many here are not of the Stone they would somehow honour what was brought to them.

'Moles, you *have* honoured him and his trust, and this special night we celebrate what we have jointly done. Lest any here still doubt my words, and feel they have not yet done enough, think well on this and act upon it in the summer years to come. Beechen shall not leave us yet. Of scribing he has not yet learnt enough, and he must help me finish that last text I shall scribe, which is a communal

Rule. More than that, he must be free to go amongst you all so that he may take what you have yet to give out into moledom's wide expanse when, at last, he leaves us.

'Aye, so he shall; leave us. As others here may. Darkness does not yield to light in peace. It turns and changes and finds devious ways of transmuting good to ill. A far worse war than that one we all have seen is yet to come – one all moles must fight with the spirit of truth and peace, not with talons, or tooth, or anger. To lead us in that war is the Stone Mole come, and to its very centre he must go, which shall not be here though for a time it may seem so. Surely it shall be nearer Whern than this, for there the heart of the evil of our time does beat.'

A shudder went among the moles before Tryfan continued.

'But this is yet to come, and I know no more of it than the shadows I describe and which haunt my mind as age besets me and I know how much there remains still to do. This knowing is the sadness we all must feel as age comes on us and we watch the faltering steps of young moles beginning to take our place.

'For us, here in Duncton, that generation is but a single mole. "Stone Mole" to others beyond this place, and to history; but to us he is but "Beechen", ordinary mole.

'Give to him, in the peaceful time that still remains, what knowledge and what love you can. Show him your hearts, tell him your memories, teach him to know that in all moles there is so much to love. Give him all you can, and he shall make it seem the very light itself to others whom fate and circumstance guide towards his life.'

Tryfan fell silent again as many there, of Stone and Word, whispered their prayers for Beechen and offered him their help, however humble it might seem.

Deep night had come. The brightest stars were out and the moon had risen through the trees and shone down upon the Stone. All was clear light and darkness, and the only movement was seen in the shine of friendly snouts and loving eyes, and talons that touched others with care.

178

It was then that Tryfan began the rite:

> '*By the shadow of the Stone,*
> *In the shade of the night,*
> *As he leaves your burrows*
> *On your Midsummer Night,*
> *We the moles of Duncton Stone*
> *See our young with blessing sown . . .*

> '*We bathe his paws in showers of dew,*
> *We free his fur with wind from the west,*
> *We bring him choice soil,*
> *Sunlight in life.*
> *We ask he be blessed*
> *With a sevenfold blessing . . .*

> '*The grace of form*
> *The grace of goodness*
> *The grace of suffering*
> *The grace of wisdom*
> *The grace of true words*
> *The grace of trust*
> *The grace of whole-souled loveliness.*

> '*We bathe his paws in showers of light,*
> *We free his soul with talons of love,*
> *We ask that he hears the silent Stone.*'

Thus spoke Tryfan, and spoke it more than once that the moles there, including Beechen himself, might learn the rite and pass it on as it had passed to Tryfan.

'I do not forget,' said Tryfan, 'that among us is another than myself who was born in this wood, and that is Bailey. Come forth, mole. We who know his story know of his suffering, his loss, and his courage; and we know of the redemption he found in bringing Feverfew safely to us before Beechen was born. One future Midsummer, when I am gone, I pray that he especially is here to speak this as I taught him. Now I ask that he repeats these words for us one last time, for himself and Beechen too, and for those he has lost and with the Stone's help may find again who surely, this night of nights, stare at the stars and think of those they love.'

So, stumblingly, somewhat, for Bailey was a modest mole who rarely took on a public role, he spoke the rite to show he knew it too, and many, some of whom were not of the Stone, whispered with him, and added to that lovely prayer thoughts of their own that wished Beechen well in the tasks he had ahead.

Then, when that was done, Tryfan went forward and signed for Beechen to touch the Stone as, on that night, the youngest there is always first to do. Then Bailey touched, and others followed, the moles breaking into talk and laughter, good humour among them, and comradeship. Yet in that moment when each touched they felt their touch return in the Stone's great Silence, and knew that even without one another they were not alone.

Last of all to touch were four moles: Mayweed and Sleekit, Tryfan and Feverfew. Silent they were, and close, and they turned back from the Stone's shadow and into the moonlight to see poor Beechen besieged by many a mole who wanted to offer him his help, to invite him to his burrow in the coming summer years and wish him luck and courage in his life to come.

'Madams and Sirs, Sirs and Madams, follow Hay and he shall guide you to a chamber humbleness knows well! Jollity is there, and revelry, and worms aplenty! Stories too, Sirs, and amazements, Madams!' Thus Mayweed directed the moles of Duncton underground into the Ancient System, there to enjoy the revels that traditionally follow the Midsummer rite.

So that finally Beechen and his mother alone remained, with those seven guardians who had encircled them after Beechen's birth: Mayweed, Sleekit, Marram, Skint, Smithills, Bailey and Tryfan.

The light of the moon was in Beechen's eyes, and on the

great Stone that rose above him; beyond, the night sky glistened and shone.

'I feel . . . much loved,' said Beechen, close to tears.

'Then the Stone has helped us fulfil that task that Boswell sent us with your coming,' said Tryfan. 'You'll have to come back to the Marsh End with me for a while, for there's much of scribing you must yet learn.'

Beechen looked both disappointed and concerned, for he had enjoyed meeting so many new moles and there was a sternness about the way Tryfan had said 'come back' that implied it might be harder than before.

But the others seemed not to notice this as, one by one, they touched him, and told him those things they alone could teach.

The last to embrace him was his mother Feverfew.

'Myn owne sonne,' she whispered, 'yow are and wyl ever be alweyes in myn herte with luv and tendrenesse. Lat mee lok on yow nowe.'

So she looked at him for the last time as her youngster, as her pup, and when she was done she let him go with the others to the revels below, excepting only Tryfan.

When they were gone Tryfan came to her right flank and together they stared up at the Stone.

'I yaf latte hym goe myn dere, and I am muche afeard. Soone yow wyl leve me too. . . .'

Old Tryfan did not deny it but moved closer to her.

'Myn luv, what was that moule for wych you made an especyall prayer?'

'Henbane,' whispered Tryfan, 'but I know not why.'

'Yew luved her once,' said Feverfew simply, 'and yow luv her styll.'

'She bore the only pups I had that lived,' he said. 'I thought of them tonight and so of Henbane. She . . . she . . .' And Tryfan wept from some sense he had of Henbane's tragedy.

'She needs thy prayer, myn dere, more than I, for I yaf sene myn sonne growe stronge tonight, and at my syde yow are as wel. Whan shal he leve this place, myn luv? And wherefore?'

'In September when the beech leaves fall he must go. He will have learnt enough by then, and perhaps it will be as well for him to be away from here. I fear for what may come. I have one more thing to scribe before I've done, and I trust I may do it before anything befalls us here, as I fear it might.'

'Doe ytt sone this "one more thing", then wee yaf a somertyme of luv to share,' said Feverfew with a smile.

'A long long time!' chuckled Tryfan.

The sound of laughter and good cheer came up to them from the communal chamber in the Ancient System and, touching each other, they went to join their friends and welcome the best of summer in.

PART II

To the Summer's End

Chapter Twelve

After the pleasures of the Midsummer rite, and the sociable days leading up to it, Beechen had not been looking forward to returning with Tryfan to the Marsh End, and the hard task of learning the real nature of scribing.

His fears were soon justified, but not in the way he had expected. It was not the difficulty of the task that beset him, but a rapid and unpleasant change in Tryfan's behaviour the moment they were back in the deep tunnels of the old Marsh End Defence.

The previously kindly and benign scribemole moved swiftly from pleasant to preoccupied, thence to indifference and finally (as Beechen saw it) to an almost constant irritability that bordered on malevolence.

Curt commands to get more food, complaints about its quality when it arrived (preceded by moans about it being late), maddening grumbles about untidiness in others (from a mole untidier than most Beechen had seen) were not all Beechen had to contend with. Extreme impatience regarding anything to do with teaching scribing, a task which, judging from Tryfan's attitude towards it, the youngster had to assume that he greatly regretted embarking on, probably because Beechen had no talent for it. Whenever Beechen asked for guidance on some scribing task, all Tryfan would say were words such as, 'Mole, you can see I am busy and yet you persist in interrupting me. Copying and more copying is the way. You have plenty of texts about you, and even if your comprehension of them is minimal you ought to be able to get *something* from them.'

'But Tryfan. . . .'

'What is it now?'

'Well, I can't *understand* everything that I'm copying and you don't say if what I do is any good.'

'Can't you? Don't I? Eh? Let's look then, come on, come on . . . Can't understand this? Why mole, it's perfectly obvious, isn't it? Even to a mole of low intellect. Couldn't be more obvious if it spoke for itself, but you don't seriously expect that, do you? Eh? Say something if you're thinking it! I don't like sulking. Now, you were whingeing about me not saying if your copying is any good. Frankly it's not. It's a disgrace. You must try harder . . . Now, I really must get some work done . . . Oh, and as for understanding everything you copy – well! I understand less the older I get. You should be grateful, not aggrieved. . . .'

Added to all this was Tryfan's habit of impulsively disappearing to the surface without saying where he was going or when he was coming back. All he did offer were strict orders that Beechen himself should stay where he was, but if he *must* go to the surface, he should confine himself to the immediate orbit of the nearer entrances.

As if this wasn't bad enough, Tryfan was charm itself when the only three moles who paid them visits – Hay, Teasel and Mayweed – came to call. Laughter, good cheer, the sounds of eating, even occasional song drifted to him from Tryfan's burrow, all of which Beechen was excluded from since Tryfan would set him especially onerous tasks when these visitors came, saying that he could join them once the tasks were finished. But too often the visits were over by then, leaving Beechen frustrated and with the uncharitable feeling that Tryfan was glad he had missed the opportunity for the pleasure of the visit.

Many a time in this period Beechen was inclined to leave and seek his way across the surface above, where he imagined the sun shining and entrances down into tunnels where he might find a warm welcome among moles such as those he had met at Barrow Vale. How he missed the freedom he had enjoyed in the days when he had lived in his home burrow; how he missed Feverfew's warmth and good humour! What would he not have given to listen to Dodder and Madder arguing once more, or even stolid Heather earnestly preaching of the Stone.

What stopped him from leaving was his own obstinacy and determination not to fail, combined (he reluctantly confessed to himself) with a peculiar and growing fascination with scribing and the texts stored so methodically by Spindle outside his burrow.

In fact, as the moleweeks went by, he discovered that Tryfan had taught him sufficient to understand at least the simpler parts of those texts, and the more he copied the scribing the more they made sense to him. Out of sheer contrariness he refused to copy any of Tryfan's texts with the result that his own paw, on the rare occasions he scribed something of his own making, was based on the neat, clerical script of Spindle and, consequently, a pleasure to touch.

As he became more fluent in both copying and understanding the texts his interest in those things that Spindle scribed about, which were many and varied, increased. Places like Whern and Uffington, Rollright and the Wen he knew of from the many conversations about them he had listened to between Feverfew and Tryfan through his puphood. Now he learnt more about them, and about the moles whom Tryfan and Spindle had met on their travels, for they were all brought to life in Spindle's histories. But more than that: Beechen now began to learn about the deeper ideas of the Stone and Silence, of the Word, and of the things that moles did in opposition to each other. Sometimes, when Beechen forgot for a time the unpleasant restraints he worked under with Tryfan, it seemed almost as if Spindle was there and talking to him, and he all ears to hear.

In a real sense Spindle became a much-loved mole for Beechen, and he gained comfort and some wry amusement from Spindle's descriptions of and loving complaints about Tryfan, whose behaviour when he was scribing had been at times no different in Spindle's day than it was now.

Beechen could not help but reflect upon the bold things that Tryfan had done in his younger days, the places to which he had led other moles, for good and ill, and the change in him which became apparent in Spindle's accounts, from a mole who was ready to fight with talon and tooth, and encourage others to do so, to a mole willing to be led by the anarchic leaders of the Westside to within a whisker of death by lynching at the Stone and never once raising a paw to defend himself and so break the pacific creed he had adopted.

Some accounts of this long and difficult period for Beechen with Tryfan in the Marsh End attribute his determination to stay with the scribemole to exceptional fortitude and an almost holy tolerance, which is hard to believe in one so young even if he did have the great destiny that Beechen faced.

But is it any wonder that he stayed, despite all he had to put up with, when, day by day as he laboured to learn scribing, he found himself copying passages like this one from the retrospective diary that Spindle made of the two moles' journey from Whern back to Duncton? It reads thus:

As we came to within a day's journey of Duncton Wood I unfortunately fell ill through eating poisoned worm. Despite the danger we were in, for the place was busy with grike, Tryfan insisted that I stay still, and tended to me. The exertion and difficulty of finding food was great for him, for his wounds were still painful, and I think may always be so, and he had little sleep. I had no doubt that had we been discovered in those several days when I was very weak and barely conscious, he would have fought for my life and been willing to sacrifice his own.

It was during those days that I realised again, and fully appreciated for the first time, that in all the long years of our difficult trek from Whern he had never, not once, complained of the pain he felt or the sufferings he had. A mole whose sight had once been good, and whose body strong, had been reduced by the terrible attack Rune and his sideem made on him to a mole nearly dead. He often thanked me for his recovery, but never accepted the credit which he owed himself. He is not the easiest mole I have known but he is my greatest friend.

And again, elsewhere, here is a passage Beechen transcribed, giving an account of how Tryfan of Duncton helped two moles they had met who were terminally diseased:

He insisted on staying with them for several days but would not allow me near, saying that their condition was infectious and I must stay clear. When I remonstrated with him he said that such moles needed some care and comfort, and since he had little else to give it would be a poor thing if he did not give it. He stayed with them until their deaths, and only when he felt certain that he had not contracted their murrain did he join me again. I prayed to the Stone that in my absence, or if it should take me first, then there is a mole near Tryfan when *his* end comes who gives to him that comfort he gave those moles then, and lets him know to the very end that he is loved and not alone.

It seems likely that in those hard moleweeks Beechen came to understand, partly through what he learnt in this way, and partly through observing Tryfan, that the old scribemole was struggling to put something into his scribing he found very hard to do. Beechen came to see that what he suffered through Tryfan's irritability was nothing compared with the darkness and difficulty that beset Tryfan, but about which he would not talk.

It is certain, too, that Beechen received encouragement from Tryfan's visitors, when he was permitted to see them, though the only mole who has left records concerning the matter is Mayweed, the discovery of whose final scribings has now made a record of Tryfan's last moleyears possible.

Teasel was a comfort, for she never failed to talk with Beechen after her visits to Tryfan – meetings which the older mole was probably aware of though he preferred not to let Beechen know it.

But it was Mayweed who seems to have been most active in bringing some cheer into Beechen's otherwise cheerless life with his brief but challenging visits, several of which he made at that time, and all of which must have given the youngster pause for thought.

'Studious Sir,' said Mayweed, after listening one day to Beechen's many complaints, 'humbleness hears what you say and declares, "Leave now if" and falls silent.'

'What do you mean "Leave now if"? If what?'

'Miserable mole, this less miserable mole Mayweed has absolutely no idea. "Leave now *if* you really think you must", perhaps. Or, "Leave now *if* you are so pathetic and dim-witted that you can't see that troubled Tryfan is doing his best". Or even, laughable lad, "Leave now *if* you have already learnt scribing so perfectly that the greatest scribemole of our time has nothing more to teach you".'

'Of course I haven't,' protested Beechen.

'Then you must stay, sorrowful and frustrated Sir! Must you not? Silence, even grumpy silence, signifies assent. Mayweed agrees with you! Wise decision. Brilliant!'

'But he's not teaching me *much*.'

'Over-expectatious Sir, this mole's glad he's not teaching you "much". A little learning usually goes further than too much, and those moles who feel they're learning nothing at all are often the ones who have learnt the most.'

Mayweed fell silent with his head cocked on one side. There was a twinkle in his eye and so appealing was the strange mole's natural good humour that, despite himself, Beechen grinned ruefully.

'I think I know a little scribing now,' he said. 'Since

Tryfan wouldn't teach me I took to copying what I found in the texts in Spindle's old burrow. Shall I show you?'

'Why not, eager Sir? Impress me!'

Beechen scribed across the floor of the chamber where they were talking. He did it slowly and with some grace and Mayweed was clearly delighted, for he moved to be shoulder to shoulder with the youngster and snouted and touched Beechen's scribing even as he made it.

'All this from memory!' exclaimed Mayweed. 'And in as neat a paw as daisies on a summer meadow! And this young Sir makes so bold as to suggest Tryfan does not teach him! Mayweed's brain must be of limited capacity, humbleness must be dim-witted, humble he, namely Mayweed, must be thick as a rabbit.'

'Well, of course I've learnt something. . . .'

'Ah!' said Mayweed, interrupting him. 'Say no more muddled and confused novice, pubescent pupil, difficult dolt. Humbleness's talon positively itches to scribe, and will now do so!' Then, with a flourish and a wild look to his eye, Mayweed scribed rapidly on the ground in front of him, his script as thin and ill-kempt as his body, and his scribing extremely fast so that dust and soil seemed to fly in all directions as his talons moved.

When he had finished he crouched back and frankly admired his own work. Then, with one of his widest and most ghastly grins, he said smugly, 'Nothing much, but 'tis mine own! Now, as the enthusiastic and good-natured Hay would put it. "Press on, lad! Keep at it! Do not give up!" All of which me, Mayweed, heartily endorses. So farewell!'

When Mayweed had gone, Beechen was left staring after him, a little irritated and frustrated it is true, for a mole never quite seemed to catch his breath and say what he had meant to when Mayweed called by, but also feeling a great deal more cheerful than he had.

He reached out a paw to the route-finder's scribing, and then snouted along it as well. It said, 'The mole Beechen confessed today that he learnt something yesterday. What may he learn tomorrow? To concentrate on the task in paw, perhaps, and talk to mole of things that matter. Thus will he find his way ahead. Signed: AN HUMBLE MOLE OF NOWHERE IN PARTICULAR.'

Beechen laughed and, feeling better and even more determined than he had before, he returned to his burrow and resolved to work even harder at his scribing, to be obedient and do his best to ignore the difficulties of living with Tryfan.

But even so, his patience was sometimes sorely tested, as when, one day, Tryfan summoned him to his burrow and told him to stop whatever he was doing and contemplate worms.

'Worms?' said Beechen in disbelief.

'I do not like having to repeat myself.'

'But why worms?' said Beechen, 'I want to scribe, not look at worms.'

'I did not ask you to look at worms, mole. I asked you to contemplate them. But of course if that is not to your liking . . .' Tryfan shrugged and began to turn back to his own work.

Remembering his determination to be obedient to Tryfan's will, however difficult it seemed, Beechen hastily said that he *would* contemplate worms but would Tryfan mind explaining why, and how, if only briefly. . . ?

'How? With effortless effort, mole. Trying without trying. Thinking without thinking. Being without. . . .'

To Beechen's surprise Tryfan was suddenly expansive and in good humour as he described, somewhat cryptically, how a mole should best contemplate worms.

'. . . being. Your father Boswell told me that novice scribemoles at Uffington were advised to get a worm, stare at it, close their eyes and then imagine it, open their eyes and . . . well, it's obvious enough, I suppose. To contemplate the worm, by all means place one in front of you and look at it. But in the end you must wean yourself from the need to have real ones before you, as a pup weans himself from the need for his mother's teat. He still loves his

192

mother though he is teat-less and can gain comfort without it; so you must still love the worm, and find ways of knowing the worm without the worm being before you. But, you wonder, why bother? Worms are life, that's why. Can't think of anything better to contemplate, can you? Without worms we would not be. *Life*, you see!'

To Beechen's astonishment Tryfan laughed aloud, a rich deep laugh.

'I remember once Spindle and I were contemplating a worm after having found one with great difficulty. He had asked me to explain the very point of Boswell's teaching as I am trying to explain it now. He was making one of his records, you see – no doubt you'll find it somewhere or other. We got the worm and I stared at it for a short time and suddenly, impulsively, I ate it. Spindle was outraged. "Why did you do that?" he asked. Ha!' Tryfan laughed again and turned back to his work.

'Why did you?' asked Beechen, puzzled.

'To contemplate it all the better. The stomach is a better thing to contemplate with than the mind. I'm sure you'll agree with me in time.' As Tryfan continued to chortle to himself until the sound of his renewed scribing overcame his laugh, Beechen was forcibly struck with the sense of what his relationship with Spindle must have been like. Two very different moles, sharing so much. Two *friends*.

Later that day Beechen noticed that Tryfan had fallen silent in his burrow, and his scribing had stopped. Sensing that he needed comfort and cheer, Beechen went up to the surface and gathered some food.

He quietly took it down to the threshold of Tryfan's burrow and laid out a worm there for him.

Tryfan looked at Beechen silently, and Beechen said, 'You miss Spindle sometimes, don't you?'

'I do, mole,' said Tryfan thickly and then, crunching at the food, he continued: 'When you grow old the early times sometimes seem more real than the present. I find myself looking round the corner of a tunnel and expecting to see Bracken there, or Comfrey, whom I loved very much. On the surface I . . . I look to my right flank, where Spindle so often was, and am surprised he is not there. And often, lately, I have missed Boswell. I think Spindle suffered much in my early years with him because I missed Boswell. I am not an easy mole, Beechen. I . . . I fear you may have suffered too these last weeks, but you see I miss your mother and those others I have known.'

'It's all right, I can cope,' said Beechen, disturbed to see how distressed Tryfan had become.

'I wish it was all right, mole! But life is hard and moles try too much to make themselves secure in a world of change. Did you know that your mother and I had young once? No . . . they died and some things are hard to talk about. It is no secret, I think, that the only young I ever had that survived were by Henbane of Whern, and I never saw them. My good friend Mayweed and his consort Sleekit reared the two they were able to get free of Whern. Likable pups they have said, named Harebell and Wharfe. There was a third . . . but he was left behind in Henbane's care. I would like to think that one day you will at least meet the two who got out, and tell them of me. . . .'

'I will,' said Beechen.

'. . . and if you do, tell them that whatever stories they hear, whatever moles may have said, their mother was . . . was . . .' But poor Tryfan could not continue and for the first time in his life Beechen saw him weep.

Beechen stayed close to him, and though he said nothing he knew his presence was a comfort.

'I knew happiness with Henbane of a kind I have not had with any other mole. Deep and passionate. Your mother knows it, so I am not being disloyal. If you ever meet Wharfe and Harebell tell them that in the short time I was with Henbane, their mother, I felt that a part of her was more truly of the Stone than anything I have ever known. Moles have often asked why I went to Whern. I believe it was for those few hours with Henbane, from which I hope one day moledom will see some good come.'

194

Tryfan made a clumsy attempt to wipe his face fur dry of tears, and then smiled ruefully.

'You see, Beechen, when a mole grows old it is of such strange things he thinks . . . As for you, why mole, there are times when you quite remind me of Boswell. Not in size (you're bigger), nor in fur (you're darker), nor in nature (you're more patient) . . . but in understanding. You have listened to an old mole ramble on, you have known how to comfort him, you have known that bits of what he has said have made good sense. You have known what to do and when, all without thinking much about it. That's what being a scribemole *is*, you see. But more than that; it's what being a *mole* should be. You have learnt much. Well done!'

Beechen did not know whether to laugh or cry at this, but much later, when Tryfan was asleep and Beechen had woken in the night, he smiled, for he saw that by saying what he had in the way he had, it was Tryfan who had known what to do, and when; and that Tryfan's teachings were wise and rich. In seeing that, Beechen understood much better what a scribemole was and must be, and how it might be that he would scribe all the better for living through the difficulties of this time with Tryfan.

We do not know, and it is vain to guess, the many ins and outs of the deep meditation that Beechen entered into at this period of his life. As the days advanced a kind of slowness came on him, and peacefulness, and his desire to leave the tunnels and do other things was nearly forgotten.

His consciousness of what he saw in the scribing he made as well as in the worms he brought down into the tunnels deepened, until he saw quite suddenly what might have been obvious all along to anymole that knew it: that the basis of scribing was the sinewy form of the worm, and the more a mole was at one with himself and what gave him life, the easier and more natural did that scribing become.

'But why didn't you say?' he sometimes wanted to ask Tryfan, but he knew in his heart what the answer was: a mole learnt little by being told it, most by experiencing it, whether of scribing, of worms or of life. It was a lesson Beechen never forgot.

Now at least Tryfan was willing to answer questions, though his impatience and preoccupation with his own work, and his ruthlessness in cutting Beechen short if he felt he was wasting his time, soon deterred him from asking anything but what he considered was important and essential.

As Tryfan said in various ways more than once: 'A mole who asks another a question without thinking first, or offers another his opinion without thinking first, or seeks to describe a feeling before he knows truly what it is, is a mole who does another a disservice and discourtesy. Why should your confusion become another's, whose own may already be bad enough? Why should you ask another to think for you when, by doing so, you demonstrate that you are not ready for the thoughts he may provide? Laziness is as much a destroyer of communication between moles as the fear of truth, and since they usually go paw in paw with one another, conversations die many deaths. Remember this, mole, and you will learn the truth of it as you come to meet other moles in the years ahead, especially those beyond Duncton Wood who do not know you so well.'

So it was that one day, and only after much thought, that Beechen went the few moleyards to Tryfan's burrow and there waited in respectful silence until the scribemole seemed ready for him, which he indicated with a sigh at his own work, a relaxation, and then a friendly glance.

'Yes, Beechen?' said Tryfan.

'Would you show me the correct scribing for "soil"?' asked Beechen doubtfully. It was a scribing that seemed to have no logic, and to come in many different forms.

Tryfan thought for a moment, and seemed pleased by the question.

'You won't find any absolutes with soil,' he said, 'for not only does it change its nature constantly, but the way a

196

mole perceives it changes as well. Moles adapt their feelings to where they are and so naturally their scribing changes too, as your voice does if you're nervous or your snout if you're unhealthy.'

'So there's no right way to scribe it?'

'No, no, mole. There's always a right way, but it's always changing. The problem is to know the right way at the time you're scribing it, and that may change from the beginning of a sentence to its end. You will find that in Spindle's scribing "soil" does not much change its appearance from one place to another. He was not interested in such ideas. But in Mayweed's scribing the word changes halfway through itself. A mole of the soil, you see, a mole whose whole life is soil. He's always been a better judge of what's right at a particular time than I am. Perhaps you should ask him the same question. The trick with such things is to know which mole to ask. It's a rare mole that is not better than anymole else at *something*, and a scribemole does well to remember it. Nomole has nothing to offer.'

'There's a lot of variation as well in the word "tunnel",' observed Beechen.

'Well, there would be, wouldn't there? Be a strange world if tunnels were all the same. Mind you, Spindle once told me that the Holy Burrows had a book in its library devoted entirely to local variations of the word "tunnel" compiled by a librarian after eighteen years of research through the Rolls of the Systems. This was one of the books lost when the grikes came but not, I think, one of the greatest losses. . . .'

So it was that the earlier sense of frustration and anger that had overtaken Beechen's mind now began to lift, and he felt as if a storm of rain had passed that leaves the air and land cleaner. There was a shared sense of excited endeavour in the tunnels as they continued their separate work and Beechen now began to discover more and more about the texts around him, and about the nature of scribing.

197

Sometimes Tryfan would volunteer a thought or make a suggestion about how Beechen should approach it. Stance, he said, was important, for a mole cannot scribe well if his back paws are not firm, and his breathing is not good.

By 'scribe well' Beechen understood him to mean scribing words worth scribing, rather than script that simply felt good to the touch.

'I fear my own scribing is not of great elegance, but I never had the training, you see. Spindle's talon is a neater one than mine, but then he was a neater mole. Neither of us, I fear, have that grace and beauty which it was our privilege to discover in many of the texts in the library of the Dunbar moles. The mole who combines grace of form in his scribing with grace of thought will always make scribing that brings a blessing to moledom.'

Beechen did not notice the way Tryfan gazed at him as he said this, the gaze of a scribemole who knows well the strength of the mole he teaches, but is pleased to see his modesty. If Beechen ever gave thought these days to being the 'Stone Mole' he did not show it.

All he said was, 'I'd like to see some of those ancient texts which Spindle refers to in some of his scribings, and which you've mentioned.'

'Perhaps one day you will, if you don't waste too much time dreaming! The texts Spindle saved at Seven Barrows, some of which are earlier than the Wen texts, are certainly memorable and include all six of the Books of the Stillstones. I think that perhaps they are moledom's greatest scribed heritage. Even so, always remember that it is the thought behind the scribing that matters, not the text itself.'

'But are there not *seven* Stillstones?'

'There are, but the Book of Silence, which must accompany the last Stillstone, has never been scribed. Most of us believed that Boswell would be the mole to do it but it was not something he talked of on the journey I made with him back to Uffington, nor when he might have done later with Spindle and myself at Seven Barrows, where we cast the Stillstones for safekeeping.'

'Whatmole will scribe the Book of Silence?'

Tryfan shrugged.

'Not I, that's for certain. I'm having enough trouble scribing the paltry thing I'm about at the moment. No, Boswell was the mole to do it, and I sometimes think he may have done already and it is but waiting to be found as the Stillstones are! One day they shall be recovered and placed together, and when that day comes then Silence shall be known and perhaps its Book as well. I shall be long gone by then, and maybe you as well, Beechen. Now, mole, I hope you have no more questions for I'm tired and still have work to do. . . .'

'Just one more!'

Tryfan laughed, and settled down. The difficult days were indeed over, and a pleasant companionship and respect existed between the two moles now.

'Spindle mentions "dark sound" occasionally, and your texts do as well.'

Tryfan's brow furrowed, and his face became grim.

'Aye, there's a form of scribing called dark sound. Its masters have always been the grikes, though Dunbar himself was adept at it as well, but he used it for good and for prophecy. We've a Chamber of Dark Sound in Duncton, though few know it now for 'tis lost high in the Ancient System near the Stone. My father knew it well, and had the strength to go there.'

'What is dark sound exactly?'

'A scribing that gathers sound to itself which a mole makes and sends it out again perverse, so a mole hears the worst side of himself but alluringly well. Hearing dark sound he seems to see himself do evil things and survive, which makes him all the more eager to do them for real.'

In that way Beechen gradually learnt of the light and shadow of moledom, and of the Stone. Yet Tryfan could still sometimes be perverse. . . .

As relations between the two had improved Beechen

had taken to lingering rather longer on the surface than Tryfan liked him to, but he enjoyed the fresh air and bird-song, and missed the visits of Mayweed and the others which, lately, had tailed off.

One bright morning, at the end of July, he was very late returning, and when he did Tryfan was waiting for him, eyes narrow.

'Feeling like a change of air, mole? Finding my company tedious, eh?' the old mole said.

'Er, no. I . . . well . . . no! I want to learn scribing.'

'Good,' said Tryfan approvingly, 'real dedication. A pity, though, for I'm off to the surface myself. Some moles to meet, some matters to attend to.'

'But I . . .' began Beechen, wondering how he could take back the hollow and over-earnest protestation he had made just before.

'Another time, then!' said Tryfan, stretching his paws out with a contented sigh and then setting off. 'On a summer day like this one a mole feels he has done enough work to last a lifetime. I shall enjoy the break!'

With that he was gone, leaving Beechen feeling as frustrated as he ever had and wondering what interesting moles Tryfan was to meet, and what exciting business he was seeing to.

But the mood passed, and Beechen found himself wondering, not for the first time, about what it might be that Tryfan had been scribing with such difficulty and for so long. All Tryfan had ever mentioned was a 'Rule' but what that was he did not know.

By the time Tryfan came back, darkness had come and Beechen was half asleep in his own burrow. He did not stir when Tryfan peered in at him and softly spoke his name, but he was touched that Tryfan should whisper a blessing on him before retiring to his own burrow.

When Beechen woke at dawn Tryfan was also stirring, but as if in uneasy sleep. Beechen listened to him for a little time and then, concluding that he was likely to remain asleep for a while longer, rose and went up to the surface to groom and find food for them both. Any irritation he might have felt about not being allowed out with Tryfan the previous day was quite gone, and nor did he feel such a craving this day.

Dawn was no more than a dim, grey light in the eastern sky, and the air of the wood was still heavy and cold, the shadows dark. But over on the eastern edge of the wood a blackbird sang, and somewhere else a wood pigeon stirred and flapped. Beechen felt joy to be part of the beginning day, and purposeful, and then eager to get back to Tryfan. Leaves scurried as he searched for food, and he drank from one of the pools of water that formed in among the boles of the trees nearby. Dead lichen floated there, and the upturned downy feather of a young bird, pale against the dark water.

His task complete, Beechen went back underground and, not caring for the noise he made, nor even hearing the normally confusing echoes of the tunnels, he brought himself quickly to the library chamber.

Tryfan was awake and waiting for him. The light from the hollow trunk behind was already brighter.

'Good morning, Beechen!' said Tryfan. 'Another good day for the surface?'

Beechen hesitated so long before replying, knowing that whatever he said might go against him, that eventually both moles laughed.

'If I say one thing you'll make me do another!'

'No, mole, I shall not. You decide!'

'I shall do whatever you would like,' said Beechen, and he meant what he said.

'Why, mole,' exclaimed Tryfan, clearly much pleased, 'I think you need fresh air and company, and to begin once more to learn what you can from the moles in this wood. They each have so much to teach you, and so few of them know it. I have told Hay and Mayweed that you shall be going out into the system, and I've no doubt Teasel will hear of it and track you down. Don't forget to go over to Madder's patch, for he and Dodder will tell you all kinds

201

of things about plants, and the Word, and much else I dare say.'

'But you . . . will you be all right alone here?'

Tryfan laughed.

'To tell the truth I need to be alone for a time. I have put off letting you go for a long time now, but only because I'm reluctant to get on with my task. It's not an easy one! But scribing never is.'

'What *are* you scribing?' asked Beechen curiously.

'It is to be a Rule by which a community might live,' said Tryfan, 'such as the moles of the Wen lived by for many centuries. But though Spindle made a record of the Wen Rule, such a thing is not easy to adapt to a different system and different times as we have here.

'In the months ahead I want you to come back to our tunnels here from time to time and discuss with me what you have learnt. I would come with you but you will learn more without my help now. Sometimes you will need to come back and think and meditate alone, and perhaps I shall need your help as well for certain tasks – I'm not as quick as I used to be, and you know I cannot see very well. My sight is getting worse . . . but no matter, it serves me well enough for this last task of mine.

'So off you go and meet some moles. Take my love and wishes with you, mole, and if they ask of me, tell them good things and that I am proud of the community of which I am part!'

Beechen embraced rough old Tryfan, and said he would come soon to tell him what wisdoms and truths he had learnt.

'Do so, mole,' said Tryfan. 'I shall miss you each day you are gone.'

'As you miss Spindle?' said Beechen, looking at the neat burrow he had taken over from the cleric mole.

'Aye, as I miss that great mole, and Boswell, and so many more. But they are here with me, Beechen, *here*.' And Tryfan waved a paw over his great lined and scarred body, as if to say each sign of age and wisdom marked a mole's passage through his life.

Beechen smiled, and gazed on Tryfan, and was gone. And the scribemole watched after him, tears in his eyes, though they were not unhappy ones, and he whispered, 'As those moles were to me, Stone Mole, you shall be to moledom evermore.'

Then he turned back to his burrow, and the deserted tunnels and empty burrows had no sound but that of summer far above, and the scratch of his talons slowly scribing once again.

Chapter Thirteen

As Beechen begins to explore summer in Duncton Wood and prepares himself for the world beyond it, other moles, their names, like his, unknown as yet to the resurging forces of the Word, were making preparations and journeys too.

To each in turn we must soon go, for these are the moles who had made their way that auspicious June day to each of the Stones of the Seven systems, and had been moved to pledge their future to the Stone Mole's cause.

Caradoc at Caer Caradoc; old Glyder in the shadow of Tryfan's heights at Ogwen; Wharfe, Tryfan's son, in Beechenhill; Wort, vile eldrene and torturer of followers in Fyfield – strange one to count among those honoured to pledge themselves to the Stone . . .; Rampion, daughter of Holm, courageous and faithful upholders of the Stone at Rollright. They shall find their tasks and we shall come to honour them.

Which leaves but one of those six: young Mistle, the only one of them born by the light of the same star that marked the night of Beechen's birth. . . .

We left her apprehensive and trembling on that June day when she and Violet had stanced before the Stone in Avebury, so close together that their flanks touched. The same day, the same few moments indeed, when Beechen in far-off Duncton had sought help from allmole to touch the Stone and so take up his task.

The light about Mistle and Violet grew ever brighter, but not so that it blinded a mole, but rather infused all that on which she looked with a glistening or shining quality which brought out its colour and shape. For this reason the Stone, the grass from which it rose, and even their own front paws, seemed more real than anything Mistle had ever known, and for a long time she was conscious of nothing else, except that there was a look of joy and faith on Violet's face, and from her blind eyes there came tears of growing joy. Long had she waited for such a day, and now the day had come.

Then they felt a gradual sense of tension and stress about them, and a growing unease, which made them take stance closer to each other, and to the Stone. Yet they were not afraid for themselves, still feeling the protection of the Stone, but rather it seemed they felt afraid for somemole else.

Violet began making a prayer, and though it was not one Mistle had ever heard her speak before, yet she ever afterwards remembered its words:

> *'Great Stone*
> *Comfort of our lives*
> *Our good protector,*
> *Assuage the fear of the troubled one.*
>
> *'His name we know not,*
> *His being we have not seen,*
> *His love is not ours to share*
> *But he is of the Stone,*
> *And our own.*
>
> *'Great Stone*
> *Comfort of our lives*
> *Be comfort now to him.*
> *Our good protector,*
> *Protect him.*
> *Assuage his fear.*
>
> *'He knows not our names,*
> *Our being he may never see,*
> *Our love may not be his to share*
> *But we are one in thee, Stone,*
> *Tell him that we care.'*

Why did troubled Mistle falter and cry out when she heard Violet speak these final words? And why did she repeat them once again?

'Tell him that we care.'

But so she did, and as she spoke Violet touched her paw and said, 'Now, mole, now the Stone awaits your touch, and this mole we pray for awaits it too. Reach and touch, my dear, and help me do the same, for I cannot see and it feels so far.'

Then each helping the other, with the light of the Stone shining in their eyes, and feeling humble and weak, they moved forward, reached up, and touched the Stone.

We know now that in doing so their paws joined those of Caradoc, of Glyder, of Wharfe, of Wort, and of Rampion as they, in their own systems, touched their Stones as well. Thereby Beechen, Stone Mole, was given the strength to take up his great task.

Of that Mistle did not know, nor could she have guessed. Yet as she touched that Avebury Stone it did seem to her that there were others beyond the Stone, in that inner circle of Stones where Violet had said that nomole but a holy mole might go and in the old days none ever had. Yet there moles seemed to be, half visible and calling out to Mistle, and where they were was Silence too.

She found it strangely hard to touch the Stone, or keep touching it, and both needed to make an effort so great that Mistle began to shake and Violet herself finally fell back, unable to touch for long, and dropped away then from the younger mole's view.

There was a crying or a calling sound from out of the light where the stranger-moles danced, like the cry of pups out of a tunnel, and even as Mistle felt her touch weakening yet she knew she had only been able to touch the Stone so long because others were helping her, and she now wanted to know their names. But they too were weakening.

As they slipped from her ken she felt as if she was losing friends she had sought all her life and yet had never known until then that she sought them or that they might exist; friends who wanted her as well. Yet now was not the time, now they could not reach her.

So she cried out for their names, and the Stone's light was bright as they called back to her, but for *her* name, seeming not to hear her call. They needed her as she did them, and like her could not quite reach out far enough.

'Mistle, I am Mistle . . .' she cried after them, but they seemed to despair and slip away at last until she alone was left and touching, but for the one they had all sought to help.

'I am Mistle,' she whispered again as her touch weakened, 'hear my name.' Yet even for him, for whom Violet had said her prayer, and whom they had been helping, she could not seem to call quite loud enough so that he would hear.

'Mistle,' she whispered, and lost touch with him and with them all, and with the Stone.

'Violet, help me,' she said, unwilling to turn from the great Stone that rose above her. 'I can't reach them! We must help him but we cannot without each other and we cannot reach ourselves. Violet, help us!'

But it was not her grandmother's voice that responded, but a deeper one, her father's. Warren had come after them and now stanced close, and put his paws to Mistle's flanks.

As she turned to him he said, 'Shush, mole, the guardmoles will hear you and know where we are. . . .'

Violet, grandmother and mother, old mole, frail mole, lay weakly now, staring at Mistle and the Stone.

'Did you hear them. . . ?' began Mistle, unable to find words to express all she had heard and seen.

'Yes, my love, oh yes I did,' whispered Violet. 'Now you must go, my dear. . . .'

Mistle looked around her wildly, and no sooner had she heard the approach of searching guardmoles than she saw them, running and angry among the other Stones of the outer circle.

'Make a run for it, lass,' said Warren, 'I'm not sure they've seen you yet.'

'But I can't leave Violet, I can't . . .' The thunder of grike paws was in the ground approaching, but behind her beyond the Stone, the sound of Silence lingered, and though only a faint echo of what it had been it was louder to her by far than the grikes' paws and she was not afraid.

'You must go now, Mistle,' said Violet. 'Warren will watch over me here until I. . . .'

'Until what?' shouted Mistle, though she knew what well enough. She saw that Violet was nearly of the Stone and very soon would be safe at last.

'Where must I go?' said Mistle, panicked suddenly not by fear of the grikes but the growing realisation that she was about to leave the mole she loved most in all of moledom, the one who had cared for her and taught her; a panic the greater because moledom seemed to beckon her, and it was large and she so small and uncertain of herself.

'Go and seek the moles who sought to know your name, my dear, go to them. . . .'

'Did you hear them, Violet, did you see them?' whispered Mistle in wonder. 'They were trying to help the mole you prayed for, as I was, and they wanted to know my name, but they couldn't hear.'

Old Violet nodded her head, and she smiled and touched her paw to Mistle with great love, even as grike shouts came near and guardmole voices said, 'They're there, they're over there!'

'Run past the Stone, my love, run to the sanctuary of the inner circle of Stones. The grikes won't find you there.'

'Go lass, go!' said Warren urgently, moving from her to stand guard all the better over his mother.

'But that place is not for ordinary moles, Violet, you *said* it wasn't. You said . . .' But the grikes were almost on them and Mistle knew she must run for her life, and that the Stone had ordained this, all of this, and that Violet was safe now, so near her Stone, and could never be hurt or harmed again.

'Go now, my love, let me hear thee go,' said Violet, her blind eyes full of tears, 'and remember through all your fears that you are much loved, so much loved.'

Then Mistle turned from her, went blindly past the Stone and fearfully began to make her way towards the awesome inner circle of Stones within whose enclave she had heard the sound of Silence, and seen moles waiting.

'This place is not for me,' she whispered as she ran.

'It is for thee, it is for holy moles,' called Violet's gentle voice after her, though now it seemed to come from all the Stones about. 'For thee I lived, in thee I have put my love and my knowledge and my faith. Go now and seek the moles who seek you, go now, my dear. One day you shall find them and in their light and love know mine again.'

These strange words were the last she ever heard Violet speak, but they helped her on her way as from behind her shouts came louder and the angry guardmoles came and Mistle passed beyond their reach into Avebury's holiest place.

She must have slept protected by the Stones, for when she woke she was unharmed. But more than that, it was to a night as dark as the day that preceded it had been bright. Through it, as trembling and fearful a mole as there ever was, young Mistle escaped eastward from Avebury.

Away she went, a shadow in what hidden and secret ways she could find, afraid and yet feeling that she was guided by a power far greater than herself which, though it could not save her from danger and hardship, would at least show her the way she must try to go. If she faltered or slowed it was the hope that she would one day find those moles who had touched the Stone with her that drove her on.

When a new dawn came she hid herself and slept straightaway, without eating first. Afterwards she remembered only waking as dusk fell once more, and continuing to take what obscure ways she could, and always hurrying on, stopping only to hide from moles she happened near, daring to go near no sound of living things at all lest they were guardmoles or some other danger.

So, in darkness, for nights without number, Mistle made her desperate escape from Avebury. Friendless, lost, uncertain, weak, guided only by the belief that somewhere ahead, some day, she would reach those other chosen moles.

The way she instinctively went was eastward, which eventually leads to Uffington and beyond to Duncton Wood, both of which Violet had spoken of as being places of sanctuary.

The route from Avebury is slow and tortuous for mole, for the ground is often cut across by dykes and streams, and where it is not there are dangerous fallow fields and open pastures for a mole to navigate. But perhaps it was these very difficulties, and the grikes' reluctance to pursue for long a mole over such ground, that helped Mistle survive.

So, alone and wandering she went through the dark, lost and lost again, forever hearing danger all about, so tired, often barely able to go on. . . .

'. . . *Must* go on, must push one paw before the other, moles behind now, moles coming to take me, great moles . . . but can't stop now, stopping so tired, too tired to . . . and those moles I want to find *not* yet found. So tired and I am failing them. Must go on, must. . . .'

'Ah . . . hem! Er . . . hello? Aahm . . . Miss? Are you dead? Praise be she *is* dead! But no, wait . . . alas she breathes. She gasps! She mutters. She lives, poor mole. Lives only to die again! Ssh! Stop struggling to live. Lie still. *Miss*, for the moment *die*!'

Mistle woke from whatever nightmare she had been in and black night was gone and a bright sun was on her face. She felt a hesitant paw at her shoulder and through her painful peering eyes she saw a mole, male, staring at her worriedly.

She started in fear, then stilled in utter fatigue and resignation to have been taken, but he said urgently, 'Die,

Miss, or play dead!' And before she could summon up energy to say anything his paw was removed from her and she sensed – or rather smelt – other moles near. Large moles, not-nice-at-all-moles: *grikes*.

'Sirs,' the voice went on from somewhere behind her, now addressing the arrivals, 'it is but I and my poor mother, sadly dead, dead and never saw her only son again.'

Mistle lay as still as she could, her mouth open, ants and fleas scurrying through her fur and at her snout. Why, she must have collapsed here, utterly. The fleas and ants evidently thought her dead! She did not have to act, she felt very dead indeed.

'Plague?' said a grike voice.

'Never, Sir, she was a clean mole.'

'Looks pretty poxy to me.'

'Looks *dead* poxy!' laughed another grike.

'You insult my family and me by even thinking such a thing.'

There was laughter, of two or three moles, and Mistle was relieved that they did not seem to want to come near her, but, rather, seemed to have moved away.

'Only Cuddesdon would claim a plague corpse as his own flesh and blood!' she heard one of the moles say. 'Anyway, your mother died in Buckland years ago. You're a fool, you are.'

'Where's some worms, idiot?' said another.

'Ah, yes, they at least survive. Back five paces, right fifty paces and left two paces and you'll find a nice damp wormy place. But Sirs, you said I could have the next I found.'

'The worms are ours now, mole. If you want food, eat *her*.'

They guffawed in a loud, crude way and Cuddesdon said, as if he was offended, 'The dead should be as honoured as the living.'

'Honour buggery,' said one of the grikes, laughing, and then, to Mistle's utter relief, she heard them trek off and out of earshot.

211

'Their language is quite shocking and disgusting,' said Cuddesdon to himself.

Then he put a paw on Mistle's flank again.

'*Are* you dead?' he asked.

She tried to speak, and knew that the word she wanted to say was 'No!' but it would not come out of her mouth, which only moved a little, and she had not even the strength to brush the ants away. She tried to look at him.

'I'm as good at finding water as finding worms,' said Cuddesdon from out of the bright light of the sky that made such pain in her eyes every time she tried to open them, 'but I don't have the strength to drag you there. If you can't move you'll die. And if you don't die soon they'll find you when they come back. So all in all it would be better if you concentrated on living, and moved.'

With that he prodded her sharply several times, first in the flanks and then near the snout, so that she started involuntarily and, finding some resource of strength she could not have guessed she had, she rolled over, crouched up with difficulty, and looked at him.

He was definitely male, no older than she was, thin, with inquisitive restless eyes and dirty talons. He had an expressive face, and at that moment it showed watchful curiosity.

'My name's Cuddesdon,' he said.

'Mistle,' she managed to say.

'As in "toe"?' he said immediately.

'Yes,' said Mistle, for whom words just then were painful things to search for in her brain and were retrieved with difficulty.

'You look as good as dead, which in the circumstances was just as well. Must be a story in how you got into that condition, and being me I intend to hear it. First, water. Nothing like it for resuscitation. Follow me!'

'The grikes . . .' she began nervously.

'There's only those three about, and they're eating, so that will keep them occupied, what with their hypocritical graces to say before and their belches to make afterwards.'

He laughed, and spoke of them as if they were mischievous rather than fearful superiors, and his confidence helped her rouse herself to movement.

He led her by easy paths through growths of soft green wheat among which a dry June sun played. Insects buzzed about, and above their heads the swaying shoots revealed a blue sky in which, unseen, a skylark sang.

Despite the recent proximity of the grikes, and Cuddesdon's warning of what might have happened to her, she felt ever more safe as they went, and all about her seemed soft and enchanted.

Ahead of her Cuddesdon slowed, turned and stopped.

'Can't you go a bit faster?' he said.

'No I can't, and anyway I don't want to,' she replied, rather surprised at her own contrariness. But she had never felt so weak and yet so content at the same time and everything, even the mole staring at her, seemed so *beautiful*, and she felt as if she had never seen anything like it before, except for Violet at the Stone that day. . . .

'It seems long ago,' she whispered.

'What does?'

'Since I escaped. Has Midsummer been?' She remembered Violet had said that it was not so far off now . . . but perhaps it had passed.

'And gone,' said Cuddesdon. 'Nearly July now.'

'Where are we now? . . . I mean. . . .'

'Water first, then a nice safe hide, and *then* questions and answers,' said Cuddesdon firmly. But though he was masterful with her it was not done roughly as the guardmoles in Avebury would, and she felt comfortable in his presence and glad, for the time being, to be looked after.

They went through another field of loose sown wheat, and though the ground was dry there was the scent of moisture in the air which suggested water ahead. Cuddesdon paused frequently to let her catch up, but even so she was feeling progressively more tired.

'Is it far now?' she asked.

'Don't know the place any better than you,' he said, 'but water scents near, doesn't it?'

She snouted about a bit. So it *was* that that made the air seem good. Water! Well if this was water that was coming it was of a different and much better sort than she had ever known at Avebury. Purer, deeper, clearer and not brackish-scenting at all.

They went on, broke clear of the wheat and passed through a hawthorn hedge to find themselves at the top end of a pasture, more verdant and sweet-smelling than any she had seen before. Where she came from the grass was thick and rough, and the soil all chalky. Here the ground seemed to stretch forward into a sun-filled gentleness, all greens and fresh colours, which invited a mole downslope to explore its secrets.

'Further than I thought,' said Cuddesdon, looking back behind them as if to check how far they had come, 'but not *too* far. Come on!'

But Mistle was already on her way ahead of him, and trying not to stumble and fall in her weak haste.

'I'm not sure we should go straight across such an open field. If the grikes come . . .' said Cuddesdon doubtfully from behind.

But with each step that Mistle took she felt more certain that she was safe, and anyway the slope that now rose high behind them felt like a barrier protecting them from the three grikes, and this place she was entering was a new world. Whatever had guided her so far was guiding her on now; and she was thirsty, and wanted to drink!

But she paused to let him catch up with her and, indicating the slope above them, said, 'Well I'm too tired to go all the way back up there. I *never* want to go back again!'

'So this is a break for freedom, is it?' he said, more to himself than to her. 'Here, now, Cuddesdon takes a step into the unknown. A step to freedom. Oh, all right – I suppose I always knew it would happen in an unexpected way like this. Let's go then.'

On they went, the field levelling out before them towards a rise of bushes and trees among which they could scent that water flowed. The sun was in the grass at their paws, and the air sweet, and soon there was nothing at all cautious about their progress. Freedom! That was the word Cuddesdon had used and whether it was the idea of it, or something about the day and the place, or both, they seemed intoxicated with it. The dappling light ahead, where water ran, drew them on and on, until they did not bother to watch for other moles, or predators, or even for cows' feet on the ground.

'Look!' said Cuddesdon.

'Yes . . .' sighed Mistle.

For they had reached the bank of a stream flowing gently just below them, cool, clear and inviting. Swirls of water passed slowly before them, in quieter spots they saw water weeds swaying back and forth beneath the surface, their flat green ends breaking through into the blue light of reflected sky.

On the far side of the stream plants bloomed of a richness and colour and form that Mistle had never seen before, and she stared at them in wonder. One in particular had serrated and shining leaves and stood boldly out in a great clump; among the leaves were the brightest yellow flowers she had ever seen, each one a little sun unto itself and together a dazzling display. Beyond the far bank another field of wheat rose up, with poppies at its edge shivering in the light wind, and in the distance over it, black wings shining with the day, a rook flew slowly. Her gaze fell back to the flowers.

'But they are like suns,' she said in awe, suddenly feeling very grubby indeed, and all her tiredness and thirst coming back.

'Marsh marigold,' said Cuddesdon. 'Splendid I know, but is it worth becoming an outcast for? Yes! Certainly! Why not? Let's die for the sake of flowers! Now, Mistle, since you're thirsty, drink; and since you're filthy, cleanse yourself! And I shall watch out for my former masters,

215

though they're so lazy that I doubt they'll follow us this far just after eating. Later perhaps. . . .'

So she drank the cold water, and felt its current rise up against the right side of her snout, and then splash against her paws. She went forward a little into the water and felt its chill come into her as the light of a clear winter morning comes in at a tunnel entrance.

She drank again and felt ever more reborn, and seemed to see again the light of the Stone, and hear an echo of Silence, and felt sure the Stone had sent her here.

She had never in all her life immersed herself in water but she did it now, timidly at first but then totally, out into the slow stream, feeling its cold freshness take her breath away as it penetrated her fur. Then light scattered in flashes about her as her own splashes fell across her eyes and she sighed and gasped with pleasure, rolling and turning as if to let the water wash away not just the grime, but also the recent moleyears of living under the stress of a forbidden faith.

'Mole! Mistle mole! Be careful.'

Mistle pulled herself upright in the water, orientated herself to the bank and saw she had drifted downstream and that Cuddesdon, wary of the water it seemed, was doing his best to run along the rough bank and keep up with her. She tried to touch the bottom of the stream, could not find it, panicked, and then floundered forward towards him until she felt the gravelly bottom and was able to pull herself out, tired and cold, but laughing.

'It was wonderful,' she said simply, turning her face towards the warming sun and closing her eyes.

'Wonderfully silly!' said Cuddesdon. 'You might have drowned. At least you could have said you could swim!'

'I didn't know I could,' she said, shifting her right flank to get the sun full on it. 'Where I come from there are no streams to speak of.'

Cuddesdon said, 'Ah!' in an abstracted way, looked around to see how much cover from searching eyes they had, and then, seeing that Mistle looked very tired and seemed about to fall into a deep sleep, prodded her gently into moving further along the bank until he got her to a place among deep grass where they would be safe enough for a time, and might burrow if they chose.

'Won't the grikes come looking for you? Won't they notice I've gone and realise I wasn't dead?' She asked these questions wearily, as if remembering that she might be in danger.

'Probably. But it's a sunny day and those lot don't worry about what they can't see, and they've got other things to think about. I've wandered off before and they'll expect me to be too cowardly not to come back. But this time I think I really will stay away.'

'Ohhh . . .' sighed Mistle, relieved and too tired to ask more questions. So long as she was safe . . . she stretched out, letting the warm sun dry her fur, and closing her eyes again so she could enjoy the blissful feelings of peace that were overcoming her. She yawned once, sighed again, and drifted off into a long and dreamless sleep.

When she came to, the sun was still shining, the grass was still warm, and though every limb in her body ached she felt good. She opened her eyes and saw that though Cuddesdon was dozing now he had been busy, for a pile of food was ready and waiting and he had delved a temporary burrow whose earth rose loamy brown behind him.

She stared at him and saw he looked older than he seemed to be when he talked. His face was worry-lined, his brow permanently furrowed, his snout not quite straight. His general appearance was grubby rather than dirty, as if he had better things to think about than his appearance. She noticed unpleasant scars on his flanks and knew what they were, because a lot of moles in Avebury had them: they were where guardmoles had taloned him.

The moment she moved he opened his eyes and said, 'Eat, then drink. *Don't* talk or you might not stop.'

'All right,' she said. And she did, slowly, feeling quite at ease with him.

'Do you know where we are?' she asked eventually.

'I was just pondering that very question and I do believe that we are looking at a stream which becomes a river which leads to the great Thames itself. If so, then this is what moles south of here call the Kennet. I deduced all that from what the grikes have been saying these past few days.'

'Which way's Avebury from here?' she asked.

He pointed to the north-west.

'And Uffington?'

'Off up that slope to the north-east, over the chalk and then a long, long way.'

'I'm off course then,' she said.

'Why? Avebury's not where you're from, is it?'

She nodded and he laughed.

'In that case, mole, you certainly would not have been killed by the grike platoon, assuming they had the intelligence to question you before they killed you. We were on our way to Avebury and only diverted south because the going got rough and somewhat less wormful than it had been. Mind you, they would have taken you back there, which might not have been pleasant. Avebury's like Duncton: once in, moles don't easily come out.'

'Why were they going there? And . . . and who are you?' she asked.

'They had been sent by Wyre himself to assess Avebury.'

Since it was plain that she did not understand who Wyre was, and was therefore uncertain who he himself was, Cuddesdon, in his own idiosyncratic way, quickly re-assured her.

'Wyre is the sideem in charge of Buckland and supreme commander of southern moledom. Can't say I'm a close friend of his, of course, but you can take it from me that he's a mole others obey. Most unfortunately for him, though it causes some followers I know a bit of mirth, he is unable to go out and about much at the moment since he has, so they say, galloping scalpskin. He must have been a bit too thorough about poking his snout up into the notorious tunnels of the Slopeside and caught it there. Perhaps the Word was displeased with him!'

Mistle, who knew nothing of such things at all, though she knew of Buckland, looked alarmed at this reference to the Word.

'Don't worry, I'm not a grike if that's what you're thinking. Nor am I of the Word.'

Mistle gasped at this, since she had never in her life heard a mole openly admit such a thing, except for Violet.

'Why, you may ask, was I in their company?' he continued. 'Answer: I'm a craven coward and when a guardmole says jump I jump. I was sent along to serve them, which mainly means food-finding and tunnel-making, both of which I happen to be rather good at.

'I am also prudent and cautious by nature, which is why I am alive today. Though come to think of it *this* . . .' he waved his paw about in a general way to indicate the whole adventure of their escape from the grikes . . .' is hardly prudent. So perhaps I'd better revert to my true self and ask who you are, where you're from and, as old moles of the Stone ask, "Whither are you bound?" '

'Well, you know I'm from Avebury. . . .'

'You *say* you're from Avebury!'

'I never lie,' said Mistle immediately. 'Never ever!'

'Right! Fine! I take it back. You're from Avebury.'

'I certainly am. And . . . as for where I'm going I'm not quite sure. *Can* I trust you?'

'You can.'

She giggled and said mischievously, 'How do you know I'm not a grike?'

'As I know where worms are, mysteriously. You look like a fleeing mole to me, got into trouble and then out of it by the skin of your teeth.' They were silent for a little, looking in a friendly way at each other.

Then Cuddesdon exclaimed. 'Avebury! Impressive that. I did not think moles got out of there very easily. One of the ancient Seven and all that, and very heavily guarded on Wyre's orders. Like Duncton Wood, Fyfield and Rollright, it's *watched*.'

'Well I got out,' said Mistle vaguely.

'Tell me,' said Cuddesdon.

'Well,' said Mistle calmly, 'perhaps it would be better if you told me about you first.'

'Fair enough. My parents were brought to Buckland before I was born – in fact they met there and what they had in common was they came from the same system. In fact, they were the only survivors from their system. Fate played a paw in bringing them together, you see. My father died before I was born, my mother died soon after and all I know about either of them is the name they left me: Cuddesdon. It's where they came from.'

Cuddesdon paused for dramatic effect until eventually Mistle said, 'Well . . . do you know anything about it, like where it is?'

Cuddesdon shrugged and pointed a paw in a north-east direction.

'All I know about it is that it is over there and it has good views.'

'Of what?'

'Moledom I should think. But something in my bones says it's a good place to start.'

'Start what?' asked Mistle.

'Something or other,' said Cuddesdon, frowning. 'Something worthwhile. Yes, that'll be it: something worthwhile. It's not very nice having no parents, no siblings, nomole at all. Nor is it nice to have to say, "I was born at Buckland." It's not my idea of a home system. I long ago decided to leave and find a way of getting to Cuddesdon and there start . . . something. I met a follower of the Stone and he made me think his way was better than the Word's, and that gave me the idea that what I start will be a system of the Stone. But the older I get the more I realise that I don't know anything about the Stone – at least not much. When it came down to it that mole I met didn't know much either but what he did know sounded pretty good, and combined with what Cuddesdon's like, with views and that, starting something there can't be bad!'

'How do you know it's got views?'

'My mother told me. Do you know why I didn't mind having to go to Avebury?'

Mistle shook her head.

'Because it's got a Stone. It's renowned for its Stones. I mean real Stone Stones. That's why the grikes don't like it, and guard it so well. Well, I've hardly ever seen a Stone at all since the grikes aren't keen on them and there aren't any at Buckland. I have seen some since we left but I didn't know what to do when I found them, and they just sort of stood there.'

Mistle laughed and crunched a worm.

'I don't think it's especially funny,' he said.

'I'm enjoying myself,' replied Mistle. Then suddenly and quite unexpectedly she remembered Violet, and Avebury, and felt weepy and homesick and said, 'But. . . .'

Immediately Cuddesdon raised a paw, 'No "buts". Problematic things, "buts", with a negative life all their own. "But" is a grike word, like "mustn't", "can't", "shan't", "sin", "punish", "Atone" and, by degrees, "snouting" and "dead". So if you want my company no more buts. Now . . . I told you about me, you tell me about you. Where were you heading for before you collapsed in a heap? Was it Uffington you said?'

'Beyond it to Duncton Wood I should think,' she replied.

'Oh! Well ask a silly question and it seems with Avebury moles you immediately get a silly answer. Duncton Wood: nice place to go if you want to catch an infectious disease and live miserably until you die.'

'Violet, my grandmother, said it was a safe place for a mole to go.'

'Violet, your grandmother, must be a mole used to

living dangerously if she described Duncton Wood as safe. It's about as safe as an owl's nest. Your grandmother must be mad.' But seeing his remark had brought Mistle close to tears again, Cuddesdon said with surprising gentleness, 'I wish you'd tell me about the Avebury Stones . . . and Violet.'

'She didn't mean safe from talons. She meant safe for . . . well. . . .'

'Yes?' said Cuddesdon.

'For moles of faith.'

'What faith?'

'Just faith,' said Mistle, so used to keeping quiet about the Stone that she could not bring herself to mention it now, even though every instinct in her told her that Cuddesdon was a mole she could trust.

'Wait a minute!' said Cuddesdon as much to himself as her. 'Don't tell me you're a genuine unadulterated follower? I mean a follower of the Stone? No "ifs" and "buts"? The real thing?'

'Well . . .' began Mistle, her doubts about Cuddesdon fading before his evident surprise and delight. 'I'm not sure what you mean by "follower" exactly, but. . . .'

'A follower is a mole who knows which way to take but isn't sure how to do it, or where it's going. You learn how to do it as you go and, and. . . .'

'. . . And eventually it doesn't matter where you're going because your faith will take you there!'

'Why yes!' exclaimed Cuddesdon. 'That's how I feel about setting off to find the system where my family came from and starting something. I know it will be all right if I can only keep going even when I've no idea what's coming next. That's what faith helps you do! It's when I've tried too hard to do something that I've failed.'

'Yes,' agreed Mistle, 'and it wouldn't have been any good me trying to predict that I'd be here with you today. I couldn't even have imagined it, or thought that with three grikes on our tails and likely to hurt us if they found us, I'd have taken stance here in the sun by such a beautiful river

222

feeling, well, *happy*. Violet always said there was no point thinking about tomorrow because unless you sorted out today it wouldn't be any good anyway. Maybe being a follower helps you sort out today in readiness for tomorrow, and it's being ready that makes it all right.'

'Violet sounds as if she is quite a mole.'

'Was,' said Mistle softly. 'I think she's gone to the Stone now; I think she must have.' She looked at Cuddesdon with a growing realisation that she would never see or talk to Violet again and tears came to her eyes once more. But though she did not cry she let herself feel sad for a time before continuing. Cuddesdon looked at her sympathetically for a few moments and then, enjoying the warmth, extended his snout along his paws and closed his eyes as the sun beat down.

'She would have liked today,' said Mistle eventually. 'She would have liked *here*. She would have liked you.'

Cuddesdon half opened his eyes but said nothing, thinking his own thoughts.

'Fancy me finding a genuine Stone follower!' he said at last. 'Well, that's a bit of luck. Tell me how you came to leave Avebury, tell me. . . .'

But he did not need to ask her more, for suddenly she wanted to talk and tell it all, and cry, and sometimes even sob; but most of all she wanted to talk about Violet, and say how much she had loved her, and that she knew she would not see her again, but all she had said, all she had taught, was here in her heart and she would never forget it, not ever. . . .

Cuddesdon listened in utter silence, and sometimes as she spoke his eyes filled with tears as well; and when she was silent he waited patiently until she started talking again. And then, when she was finished and had been quiet for a time, she said, 'I feel better now, much better.'

'I said I'd never really seen a Stone,' said Cuddesdon. 'Well, listening to you I realise how little I know. I was moved, of course, but most of all – and to be quite frank – I was *enthralled* by what you said. It is incredible! I want to know all about the Stone, all about the rituals, all about the prayers, all about everything. Then I'd know how to be a proper follower.'

'But it isn't like that . . .' began Mistle. 'It's just . . . well . . . it just is. It's easy and you're sort of making it seem hard. Anyway, you're a follower already.'

'Am I?' said Cuddesdon earnestly.

Mistle laughed and crunched another worm.

For the first time in all the long time they had talked the sun went in, and Cuddesdon stanced up, wandered about a bit, came back and said, 'We had better make a move.'

For a moment he hesitated and then he said, 'Are we going to travel on together? I mean. . . .'

'Of course we are,' said Mistle, 'aren't we?'

There was a shy silence between them, the shyness of two moles who each want to stay together but are not yet certain of the other's reaction to the idea. They looked here and there – in fact everywhere but at each other – but the day seemed to be conspiring for them to journey on together and, as if to put a seal on it, the sun came out briefly once more.

A silver dace rose in the stream and took a fly, the circle of its surfacing travelling downstream, widening and distorting until it was lost in the watery light ahead. Then with a dash and scurried rush of wings from among dry grass a damselfly crashed and dangled for a moment from a spider's web in the grass above them, its long blue body and black sheening wings catching the sun. Its legs battled furiously, its body righted itself, and its free wing banged at the air until suddenly it was free and hovering, and then gone over the stream, and off to the east.

'You know when you asked where I was going and I said Duncton Wood? Well, it wasn't the whole truth,' said Mistle impulsively. 'If we are going to travel together I wouldn't want to begin on a lie. Violet said that lying is like taloning both yourself and others around you at the same time.'

'What do you want to tell me then?'

224

'I think I *am* trying to get to Duncton but the reason is that I'm looking for some moles I saw, or thought I saw, and I thought I'd most likely find them there. I didn't tell you the whole story about leaving Avebury. You see, really I didn't know I was going to leave until after I touched the Stone. . . .'

So he listened and she told him the rest of the story, concluding by saying that she believed she had been guided from Avebury, and the moles she saw would one day be real, and they had all been trying to help a mole, and it was so hard to explain but. . . .

'. . . But no buts!' She smiled. 'Does it all sound strange to you? – because it does when I talk about it like this.'

'No. It all sounds no more strange than what I didn't tell you . . . You see, it's not just Cuddesdon I'm looking for, but a mole as well. He's called the Stone Mole. It's about all I know of the traditions of the Stone that one day he would come. Well . . . I've heard that a lot of followers seem to think he has come, and is alive. And . . . *I* think so too. He's sort of in the air at the moment, and I think if I can find him I'll know what I've got to start at Cuddesdon when I get there.'

'The Stone Mole?' whispered Mistle, awe in her eyes.

'Apparently there was a star in spring, just after I was born. Followers say he came then, they say he's come to moledom now. Surely you've at least heard of him. . . ?'

She nodded, for Violet had told her that moles believed the Stone Mole would come, but she had thought it would be far in the future in another age.

'He's really come?' she said quietly, staring at Cuddesdon in wonder and remembering the sense she had had at the Stone of them all helping another mole, *one* mole; a *particular* mole. She felt suddenly afraid.

'Will you. . . ?'

But she did not need to ask. Cuddesdon was at her flank and holding her protectively.

'You're trembling,' was all he said.

'Yes . . .' she whispered, her teeth chattering, but not with cold. 'It was when you said "Stone Mole". I *know* he's come. When I touched the Stone I felt him here and that he needs us, everymole of us. And . . . and. . . .'

She lowered her snout and wept, and Cuddesdon held her closer until she was ready to say more.

'I was born on the night that star showed,' she whispered at last. 'Violet told me about the star and she thought that one of the litter my parents had would be special. After I was weaned she picked me out, persuaded them to let her have me and reared me herself . . . It was him we were trying to help, it was *him*.' And she wept again, and Cuddesdon held her and knew that he had been right: it had been meant that they should meet, for the Stone wanted them to make their way towards the Stone Mole together.

'We had better cross the stream before it gets dark and start our journey,' he said gently.

'Yes,' said Mistle. Then without asking if he could swim she went down to the stream and, checking only once to see that he was close by, she swum out into it, head high, and her eyes on the darkening eastern sky beyond the far bank.

When they reached the far bank they clambered out and she said, 'You see, you can swim. It's not difficult.'

'You're right,' agreed Cuddesdon, shaking the water off his fur.

Then they climbed the bank together and were gone, leaving only the poppies swaying against the evening sky to say where they had been.

Chapter Fourteen

A glorious high summer, so long heralded by the clear days of June, duly came, and the lovely vales and glades of Duncton Wood settled into days of warmth and hallowed contentment.

It was as if the wood sensed that it too had its final role to play in Beechen's rearing, and must show him its finest part so that when his time came to leave he took such memory of it that he had only to speak of the wood where he was born and all who heard it would feel its textures and see its light.

Each dawn seemed ushered in by the soft call of wood pigeon, echoing and re-echoing among the leafy branches high above the wood's floor; until, the air grown warm with sunshine, the pigeons shifted high above, and a moment's flap of wings here, or a shudder of flight there, marked the real beginning of the day.

Then, far below, moles awoke and peered about, and listened to the sound of scurrying birds astir once more, as night foxes slipped out of sight, and badgers returned to sleep in their setts on the Eastside slopes.

The tunnels sounded merrily with the movement of moles, and the dry summer surface stirred with busy paw and hungry snout as they groomed and ate and began another day in a succession of summer days that seemed to have no end.

At noon, when other creatures quietened, the moles looked about for company and, choosing a spot where the sun came down – and was likely to do so for a good while more – settled to talk and gossip, or just rest together in companionable silence. What pleasant thoughts those old outcast moles then shared, regretful at times, no doubt, but finally thinking that if a mole had to end his days somewhere far from home then such a summer in such a system as this was as near to dream come true as he might have.

That good summer, when Beechen roamed freely and in safety through his home system and was generally made welcome where he went, memory and nostalgia were in the air. Those moles who had survived such hard lives at the paws of the grikes and now found themselves cast together in old age in Duncton discovered a new harmony after the Midsummer rite, and in the long years of summer felt it safe to talk pleasurably again of a past many had sometimes found painful to recall.

Most sensed that, like it or not, they were near their end. They had survived plague, the invasion of their systems, outcasting into anarchy, dreadful murrain and disease, but now the Stone (and for some, like Dodder, the Word) had granted them peace and security in a system time seemed almost to have forgotten, and into which the grikes no longer came.

Tryfan had rightly sensed that they would be willing to impart to young Beechen what knowledge and wisdom they had or he could discover, and so it proved. It was as if he was their only future, their only immortality.

If a mole seemed weak and likely to die then others would seek Beechen out and say, 'Mole, visit this one now . . . she be close to her time and would talk with you before she goes . . .' Others, too shy and timid to seek Beechen out, would find their friends had brought him to them, and that he seemed almost timid himself, and not at all the fearsome mole the name 'Stone Mole' might have made them expect.

'Why, you're but a mole like us . . .' they began in wonder, as he took stance by them and reached out and made them feel more themselves than they had ever felt.

What was it that such moles said to him? What wisdom did they, often unknowingly, impart? Why were so many anxious to tell him of themselves?

These questions, asked even then, before Beechen's

task made his name known to allmole, will find many different answers as this history tells its tale. But we may guess now that it was of modest things they spoke, of memories that meant much to them, some happy, some troublesome, which had been restless in their minds and needed telling.

'What would you tell me?' he would ask, and they might reply, ' 'Tis barely anything, mole, hardly worth the mentioning, but when I was young there was a tunnel, see, beyond which I had never dared to venture. Then one day . . .' And so they would start, and tell him how they learnt to learn. Others spoke of love known, some of regret.

But some spoke only of trouble, of something they had done which they wished might be undone . . . and more than one, and those not just of the Word, told of murders made or hurts they had inflicted which, had they their time again, they would not do.

'Never forgiven myself, never, never,' a mole might weep. 'Can't get it out of my mind, that I did *that*. You think twice, Beechen, before you let anger or fear overtake you, think a hundred times. Love's the only way, though I should be ashamed to say it for I've never given much love to anymole . . . Aye, hurting hurts most the mole that does it. . . .'

Beechen listened and nodded, and sometimes he wept too, and not a mole talked to him but felt better for doing so, and better able to face the days still to come his way.

No accurate record exists, or could exist, of Beechen's wide wanderings those summer years. We know only that he adopted two centres to which he returned frequently, and from which he would set out re-fortified. One was the tunnel system of the mole Madder, whom he had met when he had first gone a-visiting, and whose quiet surfaces seemed to provide him more than anywhere else with places to be at peace. When he was there his only company, apart from Madder, was provided by Dodder and Flint in whose new unity moles saw proof of

Beechen's gift for bringing harmony where there had been disorder. There was a general understanding that when Beechen was at Madder's place he was to be left alone.

The second centre to which he retreated was the old Marsh End Defence, to which, after Midsummer, Tryfan had retired once more to complete his scribing of a Rule for community. There Beechen resumed his studies of scribing by snouting through the texts Spindle and Tryfan had left, as well as those texts which Mayweed, in his eccentric way, had contributed. Beechen himself scribed of the moles he spoke with during those summer years as if by so doing he transmuted what they had told him into something of himself.

But to make such scribings was not the only reason Beechen returned to the Marsh End, for it seemed to have become clear to all that the old mole needed help now to find food on difficult days, and Beechen would watch over him when he chose to take a quiet stance on the surface and, for hours on end it seemed, reflect on the passage of another day's light and the ever-changing cycle of decline and revival in the wood's life.

When Beechen was in residence with Tryfan these were tasks the young mole took upon himself. But when he travelled forth as Tryfan had bid him, and learnt the many wisdoms others in the wood chose to impart, strong Hay stanced close by Tryfan, with Skint and Smithills to back him up when sleep or other duties called him away. And then, in August, Feverfew moved into the Marsh End Defences.

We have said that Beechen travelled about the system 'in safety', and so he did, but only by virtue of the labours of other experienced moles who watched over him. In a sense *all* the moles had become his guardians, but so far as external dangers from the grikes were concerned it was primarily the now frail Skint who directed things.

Nomole knew the system's defensive needs better than Skint, who, when Henbane invaded Duncton, had given Tryfan and Mayweed the time they had needed to lead the moles who lived there then to their fateful escape.

Now Skint was older, and the moles available to him who had strength and skill for watcher duties were but few, so their task could not be one of active defence but, rather, simply of watching out for signs of grike activity near the cross-under, and preparing a warning system against the day when the grikes entered the system once more.

It was Skint who mainly kept such fears, and precautions, alive, for he was always distrustful of the grikes, however certain it seemed they would now leave Duncton alone.

'The day the Word is forgotten is the day we can stop being on our guard, and that day is a long way off,' he would say. 'As long as I'm alive I'll keep half an eye open for its dangers.'

Skint used various moles for watching duties, with Marram and Hay in the fore, and Mayweed and Sleekit as formidable roving sources of intelligence. Teasel, who had survived the original anarchy that followed the system's outcasting by spying and passing information from one rival outcast group to another, was a useful ally, and her loyalty to Tryfan and natural good sense made her a mole Skint trusted.

Smithills' role was one of companion and support to Skint, but those who knew him did not doubt that should the need ever arise Smithills would give all that remained of his aging strength to the mole who had journeyed at his flank for so long.

Skint had long since confided to Tryfan that he believed it would be after Midsummer that danger from the grikes would loom once more. They would be free of whatever young they had reared by then and eager for action in the summer years. More than that, summer was the time when, traditionally, the sideem postings were changed, guardmole patrols were rearranged, and what had been static and unchanging since the previous winter was liable to be upset as sideem and guardmoles, eager to impress their superiors and show they could do better than their predecessors, poked their snouts about and caused trouble.

'I'll warrant that the day will come when somemole or other of ours down at the cross-under will blab about Beechen's presence in the system, and some over-eager sideem or other'll hear about it,' said Skint. 'Well, if there's need for a warning I'd like to be the mole to give it!'

Tryfan was content to leave such arrangements in Skint's capable paws, and knew that such was the good feeling among the moles in Duncton now that nomole would betray them but by accident caused by infirmity or senility. A mole could not prevent such things. In any case, the Stone would ordain when word of Beechen's presence went forth, and when it did he knew that Skint's watchers would do as good a job now as they had in times past, and all must hope that Beechen stayed well hidden until able to make good his escape. But if, on the other paw, they were spared grike interference until the autumn years then Tryfan had no doubt that Beechen would be ready to slip safely away from the system, and that some among them would be able to help guide him on his way.

Meanwhile, both Tryfan and Skint knew that one reason for the system's being left alone was the dread reputation it had gained for violence and infection – indeed, it was part of Skint's strategy to encourage the more diseased-looking moles, if they were able and willing, to wander down to the cross-under and let it be plain that disease was indeed still rife in Duncton Wood.

Such ventures were not, however, without danger for two or three such moles had failed to return, and the body of one of them had been found murdered next to the cross-under, presumably by bored grikes doing guard duty who were, perhaps, less afraid than they once had been of infectious disease.

So Skint's precautions seemed sensible and he found just enough willing watchers to maintain an adequate cover of the cross-under and neighbouring areas.

Of all this Beechen was either not aware or not interested, but even then, as later in his life, he showed scant regard for his own personal safety as far as moles of the Word were concerned. He had grown to be a strong mole, not over-big nor especially aggressive, but physically more than competent, and with a grace and beauty that even in a system of normal moles, and not one in which age, infirmity and the ravages of disease were the norm, he would have been striking.

His fur was now more grey than pure black and it lay naturally well, and had such a good sheen that it seemed to glow with light. His snout was sure, his paws and talons well set, his voice male but gentle.

Yet, though others found strange peace in his presence, he was not himself untroubled, and at times seemed distressed as he had been in the last months of his puphood. Those who knew him well knew that in some way he felt that the demands the Stone would one day make of him would be too great, while the strangeness of his conception at Comfrey's Stone, and the mystery of Boswell's death there, seemed as something he could not resolve.

Tryfan scribed of his attitude to the Stone then in this revealing way:

I know that when he spoke to others he spoke not of the Stone. I know it because they told me, and told Feverfew, and were enough surprised by it to mention it especially. Several times I heard that moles asked him about the Stone and to this he would invariably reply, 'Tell me what you know of it yourself', and would say no more than that.

The truth is that in the very period when so many moles thought Beechen was showing little interest in the Stone his thoughts were almost constantly upon it, and profoundly so. In his periods of retreat with Tryfan their conversations were much concerned with matters of the

Stone, and the indefinable problem the memory of Boswell seemed to present to him. Again and again Beechen quizzed Tryfan on all that he could remember of what Boswell had done and said, and he worked at those texts in which Tryfan and Spindle had recorded Boswell's words.

We know of this as well from a record scrivened by the former sideem Sleekit, Mayweed's consort, of conversations she had at this time with Feverfew, which include this brief memory:

> She told me once that when Beechen visited her he often wanted to know about his father and his making at Comfrey's Stone, but that she could not remember much. She said it was as if he half remembered his father but that the memory eluded him and he wanted to capture it again. 'Boswell-moule was as yff an dreme to hym thatte hadde ben trewe and wych he gretely soughte yet gretely was afeard to knaw another time. Yette strang was hys nede to knaw, poore moule, ytt peyned hym muche.'

Moles tend to forget how remarkable Sleekit was. Not only was she one of the few female sideem who had survived the rite of Midsummer, but she was probably the only one in all the long centuries since the time of Scirpus to escape the cold teachings of the Word and turn her heart truly towards the Stone. From her, surely, Beechen had much to learn, not just of faith in the Stone, but something of the true nature of the Word as well; and more than that, of dark sound.

Beechen, then, was seen and known throughout the system that summer, and at some time almost everymole must have met him, and shared time with him. His worries and concerns were as well known as his delights, and his sense of burden and self-doubt where the Stone was concerned must have been general knowledge. The

234

few healings that he did – some called them miracles – before he left Duncton had not yet occurred when, at the end of August, the first incontrovertible evidence of Beechen's powers of control over matters beyond himself was witnessed by two moles. The incident began almost casually, when to her great surprise Sleekit discovered Beechen stanced quietly up by the Stone.

'Why Beechen, you look as if you're not so much praying before the Stone, as waiting for somemole to come.'

'Perhaps I was,' replied Beechen, turning to her with a smile.

'But I thought. . . .'

'. . . I didn't like this place? You've heard the Stone worries me?'

'Something like that, yes,' said Sleekit, reflecting that while it was true that a mole always felt better for Beechen's direct and open gaze, there was some personal discomfort in the fact that he did not make idle conversation, and was willing to gaze on in silence such that other moles were inclined to babble on to fill the silence until, stopping at the sound of their own nonsense, they found themselves speaking to this young mole whatever was deepest in their hearts.

But Sleekit stayed silent, and at peace. She was a mole who had found her way, and knew it, and throughout Duncton had gained great respect, as much for this quiet restraint and sense of having arrived at spiritual peace as for the fact that she lived with Mayweed, the most eccentric and strangely beloved mole in the system.

Beechen looked ruefully behind him at the Stone, and, going to her in acknowledgment of her seniority said, 'Curiosity brought me here, not reverence! I was just wondering if all the rumours about the Ancient System of Duncton are true and there really are old tunnels down there, and dark and dangerous places. Tryfan's the only mole I know for sure who has been down there, but he would never talk about it when I was a pup, and certainly won't now. I was sort of hoping to find a mole who might, well, guide me down there . . .' He grinned ingenuously.

Sleekit laughed and said, 'The Stone has granted your request sooner than it is reasonable to expect. Mayweed has sometimes taken me into the periphery of the Ancient System, and I see no reason why I should not guide you there myself – not that there's much to see these days. Though why you need me I don't know, since from what Mayweed's told me you're already as good a route-finder for your age as any he's known. Mind you, I would not recommend going into the deeper central tunnels of the old system.'

'Is it dangerous then?' asked Beechen.

'To a mole that lets it be, and one who allows dark sound to kill his spirit, very. But . . . it's wise to be cautious. Even Mayweed is reluctant to venture down into those tunnels.'

'Dark sound? Tryfan has told me of it but I have never heard it.'

For the first time Sleekit looked discomposed. Her intelligent eyes went blank as she remembered her own most striking experience of dark sound, which was at Midsummer when she was a novice sideem, and she barely survived the swim over Whern's deep lake to scriven at the Rock of the Word.

Beechen's eyes were deep on her, and she sensed that now, today, she was being tested by the Stone, and that in the hours ahead she might – no she *would* – need all the self-discipline and courage at her command.

It was not Beechen the young adult before her, but Beechen the Stone Mole. It was his eyes that gazed on her, and continued to gaze on her, challenging her to lead him into the Ancient System, even to its deepest parts, and there to hear dark sound. Sleekit trembled and was afraid. But. . . .

'Come,' she whispered finally, and she led him down into the Ancient System, to a place that seemed far away from the light and safety of the rustling summer surface above.

*

It was in the course of that same day that sturdy Marram, doing a turn of duty with another mole as watchers down on the south-eastern slopes near the cross-under, first gained proof that Skint's fears of a grike resurgence of interest in Duncton, and general aggression towards followers, might be justified.

It began harmlessly enough when Sorrel, the second mole, the same Sorrel whom Beechen had come by in Tryfan's company when he had first entered the Marsh End, wandered past the hidden Marram and into the cross-under itself. By this device, and the grike reaction, they had often gained information about what was happening beyond the cross-under, for the grikes were not necessarily unfriendly, or unforthcoming.

Generally, it was the guardmoles' habit on these occasions to warn the Duncton wanderers back and, since they were invariably infirm (though less so than they seemed), to give them time to get clear. Often the guardmoles would laugh and ridicule the vagrant, and venture towards him and point him back in the right direction with friendly oaths if it was a male, and scurrilous ones if female. Brave Teasel, who had become well known to the guardmoles over the moleyears, invariably gave back as good as she got, and as a result gained time to see if there were new guardmoles about, or any change in number or attitude.

That day, as Marram covertly watched, it was plain that things were very different indeed.

As Sorrel approached the cross-under, two new guardmoles, not known before, came marching out towards him as another mole, young, slight and mean of appearance, watched coldly from the shadows of the concrete uprights of the roaring owl way.

'Name and origin?' demanded the larger of the two guardmoles.

It was unfortunate that it was Sorrel and not Teasel playing decoy that day for she might have known better

237

than he how to deal with the challenge. A laugh, feigned stupidity, even silence might have been enough to get him away from the danger; but he did none of these things. Perhaps he was feeling tired and ill that day – certainly his scalpskin looked livid and his limping painful indeed – for to Marram's horror he replied aggressively, 'And what's *your* origin, mole? Malicious and murky. And your name? Filth.'

Even then another guardmole, one perhaps used to the occasional intransigence and madness of these outcast moles, might have ignored Sorrel's outburst blaming it on the irascibility of old age. But the new guardmole who had confronted him took the old mole's words as, in truth, they were intended and grew angry. Yet despite everything he might still have preferred to do nothing and avoid further contact with a diseased mole but that the vicious-looking one in the shadows nodded a quick order to apprehend Sorrel – an order the hidden Marram saw, and one which the guardmole obeyed.

He advanced on Sorrel, and looming over him thrust the points of his talons under his snout.

'Did I hear what you said right or was it a trick of the wind?' he said menacingly, eyes narrowed.

'You heard right, filth,' said Sorrel, speaking with some difficulty because of the guardmole talons in his chin. 'It was bastards like you killed my kin in Fyfield.'

At this the other guardmole came forward and, without warning, taloned and buffeted Sorrel several times in the side until he collapsed, bloody and winded. Then together they dragged him, breathless and only half conscious, to the watching mole.

Brave Marram crept forward to hear and see better, and perhaps find an opportunity to intervene.

As the third mole approached the gasping Sorrel and moved into the light, Marram recognised from his youthful authority and the humourless intelligence of his cold eyes that he was sideem, and not one he had heard of at the cross-under before.

With mounting concern Marram watched from the gully that runs parallel with the roaring owl way as the sideem circled Sorrel with distaste, waiting for him to recover from the beating he had had.

'Your name?' whispered the sideem as Sorrel came to. Then, when Sorrel did not immediately answer, he thrust a single vile talon in Sorrel's ear, and twisted it until that mole screamed.

'To make you hear the better . . . your name?'

'Sorrel,' whimpered the old mole, eyes wide in fear as the sideem's talon poised barely a hair's breadth from his vulnerable snout. He was not acting any more.

Then the sideem made a statement and asked a question which sent a chill of apprehension through Marram's body.

'Sorrel,' he said, with false and loathsome friendliness, 'followers of the Stone persist in coming here to try to enter your system. Do you know the mole they're searching for? Eh? *Eh?*' Now his talons were on Sorrel's snout and the other moles had come closer and were resting their own talons on him to prevent him breaking free, or attacking the sideem, though either course seemed an unlikely option for so infirm a mole, which made their precautions seem grotesque as well as cruel. The sideem suddenly, and expertly, applied sharp and pointed pressure to Sorrel's snout, and the old mole screamed again.

Though Marram was very near to intervening, he held himself back a moment more to see if the sideem revealed anything further.

'Yes, Sorrel,' continued the mole, 'they think there's a mole in your Duncton system called the Stone Mole. Well? True?'

Marram, who knew the torturing ways of the sideem too well to doubt that it would not take long for them to find something out from poor Sorrel that might give away Beechen's presence, now showed all his courage and resource.

Instead of rushing blindly forward to the rescue, he

239

went quickly down the gully away from the cross-under to where he could climb up on to the Pasture and turn back towards where the moles were as if he had happened by. He limped and went slowly, to make himself less dangerous-seeming, and indeed it was not until he had almost reached the three moles of the Word, intent as they were on getting information from Sorrel, that they heard him.

The bigger of the guardmoles swung round, but even as he came forward Marram limped past him very fast and gained the far side of the cross-under as if he was trying to escape the system altogether. In fact his purpose was simply to see what other guardmoles might be near to give these three support, and the happy answer was that none was near enough to undermine Marram's purpose.

Even as the guardmole called after him, and the others paused in their assault on Sorrel, Marram swung back suddenly towards them, still maintaining his pretence of limping, and came directly at the guardmole as if he could not hear what he was saying.

It had been a long time since Marram had last fought, and not since his departure from Siabod had he wished to fight again, for his way was peaceful now, just as Tryfan's was. He knew that physically he was no match for three younger moles, and could not hope to rescue Sorrel, and prevent the news of Beechen's presence leaking out, by force. But he had not forgotten the value of boldness and surprise.

Judging his moment well he suddenly surged forward and, in what could easily have seemed an accidental and lucky thrust, taloned the larger of the guardmoles painfully on the snout. As he did that he stumbled, or appeared to, and let his left paw buffet the sideem away hard against the concrete wall behind him, where he slumped winded and furious.

In the moment of confusion he had caused he was able to put a powerful paw under Sorrel's shoulder, raise him up and thrust him bodily back towards Duncton's slopes, then he turned and faced the astonished remaining guardmole, and with a smile said apologetically, 'No harm meant, not by him nor me. No harm . . .' and he backed hastily away.

The first guardmole was thrashing about in pain and surprise, his eyes watering and his shouts of anger echoing about the damp cross-under. The sideem seemed dazed and slow to comprehend what had suddenly happened to them.

So only the second guardmole pursued Marram who, urging Sorrel to make good his escape back into the system, stopped limping and loomed his full height intimidatingly back towards the grike who, perhaps sensibly, drew to a halt.

'He's just an old fool that one,' said Marram, 'let him die in peace.'

The guardmole stared up at the now formidable Marram and, thinking better of attacking, took the easiest way out.

'You better bugger off, mate, before my mate and the sideem come to. Get yourself lost, and stay lost.'

'Why?' said Marram, at his most authoritative.

'Because he's not the only new sideem they've sent, and Duncton'll be in for a visit if you don't keep your bloody snouts out of sight. Now . . . *this* won't have done any of us any good and the last thing we want is to come searching your Word-forsaken system and catch disease. Wouldn't be too pleased if we had to do that, wouldn't be too friendly.'

'You're new here. Changes in the patrols?' Marram dared ask.

'Changes all over bloody moledom, chum. Now scarper!'

Which, thankfully, Marram did, following on after the redoubtable Sorrel, and ensuring that their escape up into the wood beyond the slopes above was swift, and complete.

★

News of this incident and its obvious implications for the system spread rapidly through Duncton Wood and it was not long before Tryfan was dragged from the Marsh End by Skint to hear the report at first paw by Marram and the unrepentant Sorrel. They met, along with a growing number of excited moles, that same afternoon at Barrow Vale and there told their tale in full. Marram's modest and brief account being graphically filled out by the still-outraged Sorrel, who showed off his injuries and, far from exhibiting signs of weakness as a result of what he had suffered, seemed rather to gain strength as the afternoon progressed.

As soon as he had heard the news Skint had quietly and efficiently deployed other watchers down towards the cross-under, in case the grikes sent out a revenge party; at the same time moles like Madder and Dodder on the Eastside were evacuated to Barrow Vale and that side of the system cleared.

But the cross-under stayed quiet, guardmoles were seen there doing no more than their usual duties, and the threat seemed, for the time being at least, to subside.

Meanwhile, at Barrow Vale, Madder made a rousing speech against all sideem and grike guardmoles, and was ably seconded by Dodder, though the latter avoided casting aspersions against the Word itself. Then there was a renewed demand for yet another recounting of Marram's splendid rescue, followed by an increasingly serious discussion about the dangers implicit in a new regime of sideem at the cross-under, and, worse, the grim news that the grikes might be on the rampage across moledom once more.

All there knew how vulnerable to attack they were, all realised that the days of their contented and happy summer were getting fewer, as old Skint had long since warned. All feared that. . . .

'Aye, but where's Beechen?' said one of them suddenly, provoking general alarm. Moles ran here and there looking for him but found he was not among them. None had seen him that day! He might very well be in danger! Quick! Find him! Save him!

Tryfan calmed them.

'He's no fool,' he growled, 'and is not one to go on the south-east slopes unaccompanied. Panicking will help nomole. Where's Mayweed? He's the one who'll find him.'

'Humbleness is here, and he is, trenchant Tryfan, the one to find him. Or, looking at it another way, *he's* the one to find *us*! Get it? Yes? No? Not got it? No? Are we dim tonight? We are! Mayweed humbly takes your leave and will seek him here and seek him there and, in the end, find him, as one day moledom will, everywhere.'

With many a mole shaking their heads at this cryptic statement, and some still wanting to rush off and search for Beechen themselves, Mayweed turned around several times, snouting north, east and west, before turning resolutely southward and upslope, towards the Stone and Ancient System, and saying, 'Yes, Sirs, Yes, Madams, yes, yes, yes!'

Then, humming cheerfully to himself, and winking at Tryfan while leering confidently at Feverfew, he said, 'One half of me is better than the other half, and the better half knows where bold Beechen is. To her me, Mayweed, humbleness, will go. Southward! Farewell and good night!'

He paused for dramatic effect, a sudden stir of wind up on the surface obligingly marking the moment, and with that and as dusk settled over the quiet wood, he was gone. . . .

From the moment Sleekit had led Beechen down into the peripheral tunnels of the Ancient System she felt uneasy and disorientated, as if she was doing something difficult, something she had never done before, and doubted her own ability. However much she reminded herself that her consort Mayweed had brought her here without mishap, her heart still pounded uncomfortably, and nor was her well-being helped by the distant murmurs of dark sound that the tunnels seemed to carry.

Had it not been for the fact that Beechen seemed quite unaffected by the sound and followed quickly behind her without any apparent doubts about her ability at all, she might easily have surfaced and made good her escape from what felt like the tightening talons of danger while she still could. But, in truth, as well as the sense that she must not let Beechen down there was also that sense of mission a mole gains when personally challenged to do something from which to back down is an admission of defeat. So she went on.

Not that initially there was much direction to their exploration other than that provided by curiosity, whim and the necessity of turning one way or another because the tunnel ahead was blocked. The part of the system they first entered, which was made up of tunnels of an ancient arched style which the Duncton moles did not employ in their later colonisation of the lower slopes and Marsh End of the wood, had clearly been damaged in every way they could have been. Apart from the roots of trees and undergrowth, which in Bracken's day had been benign but since seemed to have grown malignant, dry summers had cracked the soil. Creatures like voles and weasels had broken into burrows, and squirrels and foxes and, in one place, badgers had vandalised stretches of the Ancient System so that only moles with eyes to see could make out the remnant tunnels and chambers that had once known such glory. Now they were open to the summer sun, desecrated by bird muck, lost among the tumbling of fallen trees and branches, all but destroyed.

It said a great deal for the quality of such tunnels as remained that there was windsound at all in these broken subterranean ways, and suggested that despite appearances even these ruins had links with a deeper part of the system which was whole and undamaged. It was towards this that their seemingly random route appeared to go, and as they went Sleekit had the frightening sense that they were being inexorably led towards a place to which she did not wish to go. She knew that place's name, for Mayweed had told her, but as yet she had no wish to tell Beechen.

How long they wandered thus that summer day, now below ground, now forced above it by some invasive root or broken ceiling, she did not know, but there came a time when the tunnels began to become more whole, the windsound to grow more sonorous, the hint of dark sound more treacherous, and their route to turn back westwards, towards the centre of the High Wood, beyond which was the Stone itself.

It did not surprise them that here the tunnels were less damaged, and, eventually not damaged at all, for the beech trees were larger and more ancient, and their thick canopy of leaves above, and the many-layered covering of dry beech leaves below, smothered and prevented undergrowth and kept other creatures out. At first they chose to make slow progress, snouting about the tunnels a bit, listening to the subtle windsound, and then darting up to the surface to ascertain where they were.

But finally the ruins were all behind them, the tunnels deepened, and they committed themselves to pursuing their exploration underground.

The nature of the soil had changed, being drier and harder, with a sub-soil underpaw that was nearly chalk. Here they found tunnels of extraordinary high elegance, deserted and dusty, and in which the ancient moles who had made them had used flints to great effect as buttresses at corners, and exploiting their shiny surfaces to cast light from vents into the dry surface leaves above, and to carry the subtlest of sounds forward.

There was now a quite unmistakable whisper of dark sound about the tunnels, and again and again Sleekit paused and asked Beechen if he was sure he wanted to go on.

Eventually he stopped, stanced still and gazed at her in the direct way he had. 'I think it is *you* who does not want to go on,' he said. 'It is your fear you question, not my own.'

'I . . . I hear dark sound,' whispered Sleekit, ashamed that her fear was so obvious to the younger mole.

'And I hear confusion,' he replied. Then, coming close and touching her, he said gently, 'You know, I must go on towards such confusion until I find it. That is my task, Sleekit. I will go on alone if you . . . if you feel fear. But I think Boswell's teaching to Tryfan was that nomole helps another by shielding him from his own fear, or merely by showing such fear can be conquered. My going on alone would not help you, and nor, since my task seems to lie with allmole, would it much help me!'

Beechen even smiled as he said this, and Sleekit felt much moved at his concern for her, and his courage.

She said, 'My dear, I am afraid. I have known dark sound before, but I was younger then and perhaps I had more strength than I have now.'

'Was it when you were a sideem in Whern?' he asked. 'You've never told me about any of that, and nor anymole else as far as I know, because I've asked.'

'This is hardly the place,' said Sleekit, looking around the shadowed arches of the tunnels and listening to the distant and ominous sounds that came to them.

'Don't see why not,' said Beechen lightly. 'If a mole waits for the right time and place he might wait for ever. Tryfan always said Boswell said that *now* was the best time of all.'

'Tryfan has a lot to answer for!' said Sleekit. But then she smiled and said, 'But you're quite right, I haven't spoken of it. I'm no different than most of the moles in Duncton who want to forget. I sometimes feel lucky just to be here and alive, and have no wish to remember my past.'

Beechen stared at her silently, and she at him.

'Well, are you going to tell me?' he asked at last.

Sleekit sighed and said, 'I suppose I must!'

It was then, and in the now ominously whispering tunnels of the Ancient System, that Beechen first heard a full account of those events that had led to the invasion of Duncton by Henbane moleyears before. Then Sleekit found it necessary to tell Beechen of Whern, of the sideem and of the Word. Of the Midsummer rite at Whern she told, of the Rock of the Word and of the Master Rune.

Then too he heard the real truth of Henbane, of her violation and corruption by Rune, of the strange mating with Tryfan and of their even stranger love which was light discovered in darkness, and how Tryfan had been all but killed by Rune's sideem.

Then of how Mayweed discovered her Sleekit told, and that Henbane had borne Tryfan's young, and two of them had been rescued by herself and Mayweed and taken out of Whern to Beechenhill.

'Wharfe and Harebell,' Beechen said. 'Tryfan told me of them.'

'Yes,' said Sleekit. 'And through their rearing I learnt to love Mayweed, and he to love me. We have not young of our own, and nor can we have for disease makes a mole sterile. But we saw those two grow towards maturity and left them in the care of the leader of Beechenhill, Squeezebelly. There is no better nor more stoutly faithful mole than he.'

'What of the third pup?'

Sleekit shook her head.

'I know not. We left him in that dreadful place with Rune and Henbane to fight over him. I know not. . . .'

'But you have an idea?'

'I know only that if he survived he would be raised a sideem, and because of his birth he would be favoured. If he was favoured and well trained, then Tryfan's son would be thy enemy, and the Stone's.'

Around them, suddenly, the windsound strengthened, and there was the rumble and roar of dark sound as if other moles were in that place, threatening moles.

'Sleekit,' whispered Beechen, 'I think that mole is alive. I feel he is alive. And I think . . . I think I know where I must go after Duncton.'

'Not Whern, Beechen!' said Sleekit urgently. 'Never

247

there. For they shall kill you and moledom shall die with you.'

'Not Whern . . .' repeated Beechen faintly, but whether he was simply echoing what she said, or whether he had another place in mind, she could not tell.

The light in the tunnels had faded, and there was the sense of dusk about the place.

'We must go back to the surface,' said Sleekit with a shiver. 'We must continue here another time.'

'No, no,' said Beechen, 'we must continue *now*. And you shall come with me despite your fears. I shall show you the way beyond them now. I know the way. I have been learning it from the first hour of my birth. Come now. . . .'

Yet even then he lingered, as if reluctant to take up the challenge that he felt lay before him.

'Tryfan told me that he loved Henbane.'

'It is true. I know my Mistress much loved *him*. In their union I saw the first good, the first light, I ever saw in Whern. Tryfan opened a portal in Henbane's heart which I believed could not, would not, be closed again. She . . . she . . .' Sleekit lowered her snout.

'Yes?' said Beechen.

'She was not as evil as she seemed. She did evil, but she was not all evil. And always, always, there was in her what other moles – moles that might be good, followers as well – often did not quite have. She had *life*, Beechen, and seeing that and witnessing what I did when Tryfan loved her, and how she bore their young with courage I have never seen before nor known myself, I knew that moles who *live*, which is to say moles who have courage to experience what comes their way, may finally, whatever else they may have done, find their snout turning towards the Stone's light.'

'Others think her evil.'

Sleekit made a strange reply to this. She said, 'Others once thought my Mayweed to be a mole of no account. I have loved him as I loved her, despite what all others say.'

'Perhaps you have an eye for the light of truth,' whispered Beechen.

Sleekit said nothing to this but instead declared with uncharacteristic passion, 'I am fearful for them both. What will become of my Mayweed? What has become of Henbane?'

There was no reply but in the windsound, dark and light, of the tunnels about them.

'I often think you know more than you let others know,' said Sleekit.

It did not seem to be Beechen, a young adult, who replied.

'I may know more fear than they, it is my heritage and my task,' said the Stone Mole, his eyes bright in the darkness about them, his form almost lost in the chalky shadows where he stanced.

'Now, you have told me of the dark sound of Whern. What of this place, and the sounds we have heard all day? Tell me!'

But all Sleekit could do was to repeat the little she had been told by Mayweed and Tryfan, about a place Bracken had called the Chamber of Dark Sound, wherein moles had once died in their pursuit of Mandrake. Stories of times past before the plagues, fearful stories.

'Then let us face these fears and find that chamber!' said Beechen boldly.

So, with dark shadows all about, they turned into those side tunnels from which the dark sound came loudest. By slow degrees the tunnels deepened and the surface noise of the rousing wind seemed further off. Yet in places light from a rising moon began to reach down to them through the cracks and crevices of the surface above, and the windsound and dark sound in the tunnels increased and grew more troubled until at last Sleekit was forced to pause and let Beechen take the lead, for her courage was deserting her again.

Whatever lay in the tunnels or chamber ahead was echoing their pawsteps back to them, but all turned and distorted and painful to the ear.

'It is like the sound I heard the Rock of the Word send out,' said Sleekit.

'Then follow close and let us face it,' said Beechen.

A short time after, the tunnel widened and Beechen led Sleekit into that fabled chamber into which nomole had gone since those distant days when Mandrake had wandered madly there.

Great beyond sensing. High beyond seeing. Long beyond telling. But far ahead of them across its width was the rising, shining, flinty and scrivened face of the chamber's west wall. At its base, centrally, but dwarfed by its size, was the portal that led on to the whispering sinewy sounds of the Chamber of Roots.

But this was no ordinary portal. It had been delved such that rising from it, all around, across the whole face of the wall, was the image of the cruel open beak of the owl whose image was formed by the carvings or scrivenings which made the dark sound.

The flinty wall shone and reflected dark light, and the slightest pawstep or breath seemed instantly to be echoed back from its scrivenings, all distorted and fearful.

Beechen stared across the chamber in awe and wonder but then, seeing the portal, he said without a moment's hesitation, 'That is our way. That is where we must go.'

'But the dark sound . . .' whispered Sleekit. 'It will grow worse as we go nearer to it. It is like the Rock of the Word, made to disorientate a mole, and then destroy him.'

There was no doubt that she was right. For as their eyes grew used to the strange light of the place they saw that scattered across the floor were the gaunt remains of moles who had been in the place before them, which they guessed must be the bodies of henchmoles who, in times past, had pursued Bracken and Mandrake. They saw then, too, that the portal was partially blocked with fallen flints and more bodies of moles, but all broken and crushed.

'Do not be afraid,' said Beechen, reaching out a reassuring paw to Sleekit. 'This is the way we must go.'

Even as they started to move, and their paws scuffed the hard uneven floor, dark sound reverberated back at them from the wall and to Sleekit it seemed that the air of the chamber was full of the violence of things hurled by a wind whose sole purpose was to destroy her spirit and break her body.

Only the form of Beechen ahead of her kept her from losing herself in the confusion of sound, only the touch of his paw kept her on course. And then he stopped suddenly, as if he heard something beyond the dark sound, and something even more fearful. Then, horror in her heart, she heard it too.

Desperate pawsteps, and a desperate crying voice. A mole in terrible desolate fear. A mole lost who called a name.

'What is the name he calls?' said Beechen, turning to her.

Louder it came, nearer, from the very portal towards which they struggled, pawsteps and a cry, lost and nearly hopeless now.

Then she knew the name it called. It was her own.

'Sleekit! Sleekit, help me now! Help me for I am lost, lost . . . Sleekit . . . help. . . .'

Then slowly through the portal he came, pushing a way through the death and destruction there, now with the strength of desperation, now feebly with the weakness of hopelessness. Mayweed. Route-finder. Lost. Speaking in a voice that was not his normal one, yet more nearly his own than any he had ever had. Poor Mayweed.

Sleekit looked, and looked away in fear. She did not have the strength to go further across the Chamber of Dark Sound and help him.

'Go to him!' Beechen cried to her, as she knew he would.

Again she looked, again stared helplessly, again she looked away.

'I cannot help him,' she whispered. 'The sound is too dark for me.'

She could not move. It was like a freezing day in winter, when the cold is so penetrating it stops a mole's mind and he sees all move slowly and in silence beyond his power of control. Thus she watched as Mayweed stumbled into the Chamber of Dark Sound and saw as he staggered here and there along the edge of the scrivened wall, crying out in agony, seeking with his paws to stop the sounds that were destroying him, yet still calling for her. He seemed blinded by the noise, for he did not see them where they stanced immobile watching him.

Until before her eyes poor Mayweed slowed and collapsed and began to cry, terrible cries that were like those of a pup lost from everymole. A pup lost in darkness. Sleekit looked away again.

'Help him,' commanded Beechen then. 'One chance more you have.'

Help him? So Beechen must have spoken – though so strange that chamber's sounds, and so confusing, she felt it was the scrivens of the wall that spoke.

But help him she could not. Her only saving in that place was Beechen's proximity, as if about him was a sense of Silence that gave her space just to survive. To leave him and go to Mayweed was too much for her to do.

'Help him,' Beechen said again.

Mayweed was a lost mole now, lost in some memory of puphood, lost again in that place in the Slopeside of Buckland from which once he had only just been rescued, and from whose darkness his life had ever since been one long striving to escape.

'Sleekit, he was lost, and found, and now is lost again. *I* cannot save him, I can save nomole except that knowing the Stone through me they may save themselves. For this have I come, to show how we may help each other. You and Mayweed are as one, so find the courage to leave me here and go to him. Use all your training, all your love, and go to him where so long ago his mother left him. Help him. Teach him as he has taught so many others it can be done. Here he is weak. Here he is dying. Through you he can

252

survive and be stronger still that one day he shall have the strength for his final task, which is to guide Tryfan into a darkness beyond imagining.'

'His final task?' whispered Sleekit, knowing that if she took her eyes off Mayweed now she would not have the courage to look at him again.

'As a mole is loved so shall he love, so show him the way now, Sleekit. I think he had come in search of us. He came to find us and nomole knew better than he the dangers of this place or the torments it might bring. Despite that he has dared come and it has nearly killed him. For you and me he did it. His love has given you the strength to help him now. Use it, return it to him.'

Then in that dreadful place Beechen stood aside, and for a time Sleekit felt the full force of dark sound upon her and thought that she would die. Yet somehow discipline and faith came to her, one learnt of the Word, the other discovered of the Stone, until with Mayweed's cry weakening before her she found the strength to advance through the blizzard of darkness that beset her, and go to him.

'My dear, my dear . . .' she said, and she reached him, and put her paws to him, and comforted him, and like a pup he wept and cried that he was lost.

'Yes, help him so,' said Beechen, and with love she did, and held him where he had fallen, and encircled him, and whispered safety to him, and the security of love.

Then all about them the dark sound began to die, and peace fell on that place, and from the eyes of Beechen came a light of love that seemed caught in the scrivens of the walls of the chamber, a light that was the light of Silence.

Then the Stone Mole went to those two striving moles and touched each of them, and they felt a healing in their hearts and knew that they were safe, and the chamber held fear for them no more.

'Follow me,' said Beechen then, and weakly they did, and it seemed that each pawstep they made, each piece of debris they cleared to make a path back through the portal, brought forth a gentle sound from the scrivened wall above.

They passed through into the Chamber of Roots, and paused there within sight of the roots that formed a vertical and ever-shifting screen through which only moles of faith might go.

Mayweed, half supported by Sleekit, said nothing, but stared at the roots which were lit, it seemed, by the luminescent tendrils of the smallest of their number high in the chamber's roof, carrying some light of their own, or taking from the surface above something of the moonlight there.

Beechen seemed barely interested in the roots, but Sleekit noticed that when, briefly, his gaze fell on them they stilled, absolutely, and all sound went, and an enchantment of Silence fell over them and the chamber they commanded.

Beechen sighed and said, 'Come, we have heard and seen enough. This chamber can wait its time once more when Duncton shall be found again. Our tasks are different. Come, we must go to the surface and make our way to Barrow Vale, where our friends are concerned for us.'

They reached the surface, and, before they set off downslope, they turned back to touch the moonstruck Stone and all stanced together in the night with the Stone's light upon them.

'I shall never forget you, nor this place, nor the moles who have taught me so much,' said Beechen suddenly.

Neither said a word, but both came close and knew that already Beechen was beginning to say goodbye to the system that had made him, and they sensed that the time for his leaving was drawing near.

Mayweed separated from Sleekit and stared up at the Stone. Still he said nothing.

'What are you thinking, my love?' asked Sleekit. Tears were on brave Mayweed's face.

He spoke no long words in reply. Nor strange words.

Nor smiled, or leered, or grinned, or anything of that. Yet he was more Mayweed himself than humble he had ever been.

'What do you feel?' whispered Beechen. It might have been the Stone itself that spoke.

'Feel?' repeated Mayweed in wonder. 'I feel no fear.'

'And you, Sleekit?'

'The same.'

With his left paw Beechen reached out to Mayweed, with his right to Sleekit.

'Tell nomole of this, or of what I shall say now. Soon I shall leave and travel where I must. Both of you shall come with me, one all the way and the other but to see us safely begin a journey of which all moledom must know. Mayweed, you shall be the one who must turn back. With Tryfan lies your task for he shall need your guidance one last time.'

'Shall I see Mayweed after that?' asked Sleekit fearfully.

Beechen shook his head.

'The time remaining in Duncton is all the time you have. You have heard Silence today, you have seen light, and you shall not want other company than your own. This shall be your time and shall prepare you for the parting soon to come.'

'But whatmole shall need me so much that I must leave Mayweed?' said Sleekit, staring at the Stone.

'Tryfan's own shall need you. And I shall need you. Many shall need you.'

'But . . .' began Sleekit.

But Beechen gazed on her and she was silent.

'Tell nomole of the dark sound you have conquered or what I have said to you. Nomole, not even Tryfan yet, will understand. Now . . . we must go to Barrow Vale. Take me there for I feel weak now and need your help. Guide me there, and then be to yourselves alone until the time comes that your final tasks begin.'

'When will that be?' asked Sleekit.

'When the beech leaves of this High Wood begin to fall,

255

and autumn heralds the coming of moledom's darkest winter.'

Above them in the night, wind stirred at the high branches of the beech trees and down into the clearing a few leaves fell, their green turned prematurely to brown.

They turned to Beechen and saw in the white moon's light that his fur was drenched with sweat, and his eyes fearful, and that he was fatigued beyond sleep. Then together they helped him turn from the Stone, and led him downslope towards Barrow Vale.

Chapter Fifteen

Marram's alarming discovery that the grikes' observation and patrolling of the cross-under had become more strict, and that they might be poised to re-enter Duncton Wood, was but part of an extraordinary resurgence of the grikes about which much of moledom, to its cost, already knew.

The magic calm of Duncton's summer years, which had made possible that slow education of Becchen in the true ways of mole, community and Stone, would have seemed but a lost dream to many beyond the system's boundaries.

Long before those first early autumn leaves fell at Beechen's paws in the Stone clearing that August night and warned of harder times to come, the harder times were already spreading fast from the north; with that a new name for horror spread forth as well.

Lucerne's.

'Yes, that's the one. Great Henbane's son. Master of the Word soon, if not already. Oh yes, accepted by the Keepers. He'll change things a bit . . .' the gossip went.

For those quiet followers, ignored or beset according to the effectiveness of the eldrenes who ruled their systems for the Word, it was becoming a name to whisper in terror and dread. 'Change' in Lucerne's paws meant persecution once again, but worse than before; far, far worse.

While for those moles of the Word who wanted a quiet life, and wished to maintain the lip service to the Word and ordinary indulgence many such invaders had assumed since Henbane's days, it was a name that struck fear in their lazy hearts; and pushed them into arbitrary acts of violence and suppression against known followers of the Stone to prove that they were still capable of doing their jobs.

But for zealots of the Word, always few, not always in

power in the systems where they lived, it was a name that gave new hope of judgements to be made, of just Atonements to be enforced, and the chance to gain power once more and renew the faltering glory and power of the Word.

'Master Lucerne, to thy cause I shall dedicate my life, to thee only, Master, blessed Master, the Word's gift to us. . . .'

So did reverent zealots whisper his name, and so was it encouraged to spread before and ahead of the vanguard of Lucerne's young sideem who came down upon moledom from the north rapidly that summer, moving from one system to the next as they began their new and ruthless work. . . .

But before we turn our disconsolate and dispirited paws in pursuit of Lucerne's sideem, and wonder in horror at what they did and how they did it, it is best that we do not lose sight of what lay behind the young Master's remorseless drive to bring the Word to eternal ascendancy and cause faith in the Stone to be forever broken.

Let there be no doubt about the monstrous powers for leadership and organisation that Lucerne's bloodline and training had given him. This was no ordinary mole. This was no ordinary evil. This was no shadow that the light of the next rising sun would cause to flee and be quickly forgotten.

This was a corrupting, infecting darkness that might – nay, that surely *would* – enshadow moledom forever, and leave it a stinking, fetid place where the light of love and faith had quite gone out. This was the darkness beyond the Stone's light finally come to earth in molish form. This was dark sound corporeal.

Of such evil was Lucerne.

So far as we are fortunate in anything to do with such a mole, we are fortunate to have the record Terce made of those times, routinely scrivening, day by fell day, the decisions and actions which the new leader of Whern took

– though often called 'Master' his inauguration was still to come. Yet he was Master in all but name.

We have seen already that for Terce the rise to power of Lucerne was part of a scheme decreed by Rune in the days when Henbane was with pup, and when Rune guessed his own days might be few.

Rune did not imagine or even guess that he would die at Henbane's own talons. Rather, his intention was to choose the best of her pups for nurturing towards his final and obsessive ambition, and hope he had at least a little time to set his nominee on the way to power before he died. But though he could not guess his end, he made plans against it being premature. Terce was that contingency.

In finding Terce, and giving him penultimate power, Rune showed his genius for discovering and making loyal those who could best serve his purpose. This is not easy for any leader of moles, whether he leads for ill or good. Great subordinates must subsume themselves to their leader's purpose, and while showing intelligence and initiative must yet be loyal and subservient to the higher aim.

But already Rune had shown that when he needed to he could find the mole who served his purpose best. His consort Charlock had known how to rear Henbane to make her all-powerful to all but Rune himself. Weed had known how to spy on Henbane and yet keep her trust. Wrekin, the great mind behind her invading army, had known how to stay impervious to Henbane's charm and yet retain her support for the control of the guardmoles that he needed.

As Rune judged moles' strengths, so he judged the moment of their weakening, when they lost their value to him, and then he took power back from them. So he arranged for Wrekin to be dismissed. So he judged well when Henbane should be summoned back to Whern, where, we must assume, he deliberately allowed the mating with Tryfan to take place. Did he foresee the need for new blood in the line? Did he instinctively understand what damage it might do to the Stone's power if the very

259

mole that must one day lead the Word's final assault on the Stone was spawn of great Tryfan of Duncton, noblest of the ancient Seven?

We know, from Terce's scrivenings, that Rune did. We know for sure that his intent was to choose one of Henbane's pups and make him Master.

Though he died before he could see them reared, so well had he chosen his Twelfth Keeper in Terce that his design stayed alive in powerful and remorseless paws. All unknowing, even after she seemed to have broken free of her father by killing him, Henbane allowed Rune, through Terce, to sway her life. The Word did well the day it left Lucerne alone to suck her teat. Terce, adept at the persuasive arts, smiled at how easy it would be to take control of Lucerne and corrupt him to the Word.

But how much more he must have rejoiced in that mole's formidable intelligence and driving purpose, and found in it proof of the Word's wisdom and divinity; and confirmation therefore of Rune's as well.

Divinity? *Rune?* Aye, that, in a word, was Rune's purpose: divinity. To corrupt even the corrupting Word to serve him and all his kin forever more. To establish himself as Father of the Masters yet to come who would be makers of the eternal golden age of the Word. Thereby would his seed be most glorious and alive and hallowed for all time. Nomole can live forever, but through others' bodies Rune sought to live and make of himself what even Scirpus had never become – accepted as divine of the Word.

Such had been Rune's aim, and such now was the sole intent of Terce's life through Lucerne. In Lucerne, therefore, Terce found the perfect agent for Rune's posthumous purpose; while in Terce, Lucerne found the perfect agent for his own. It was a marriage made in darkness which, if it was ever to be put asunder and moledom to be saved, would need more than ordinary mole, and more than ordinary circumstance.

Knowing this (and guessing too that there might be

more to Terce's plan than we yet know) we will not be surprised at the speed and ruthlessness with which Lucerne and Terce affirmed their hold on Whern.

Three Keepers opposed Lucerne (and if they had not he would have claimed they had, to give him opportunity early on to demonstrate his ruthless purpose for the Word, and to intimidate those who might yet harbour discord!).

Lucerne did not stain his own talons with these early opponents' blood but, rather, let it be known through Terce that it was not the will of the Word that such moles live.

Nor was Terce ever seen to murder, though his own profane delight in blood, the murky sadistic doings that he did, would in time be known, and feared, and were a part of his campaign on Rune's behalf.

No matter. Two moles had the ear and trust of Lucerne and Terce: Clowder and Mallice, and both even from those early days took up special roles which, as time went on, would expand as Lucerne's power did. Clowder became to Lucerne what Wrekin had been to Henbane: campaigner, general of his forces, conductor of his strategies, second in command of war and fighting.

But Mallice . . . there is no equivalent of her in all Whern's history. Consorts to the Master there had been; female Keepers there had been; 'eldrene' to the sideem Henbane had herself been. But not all three in one, responsible for what a mole might call the execution of the dark interior of Lucerne's policies.

Mallice it was who, from the first, in her chilling and calculated way, took to herself the execution of Lucerne's orders for killing, elimination and disposal. She would become his spy. Her narrow eyes would watch for him, her dark interfering snout would scent out anymole or anything that endangered her lord. And see it dead.

With her own talons she killed those first three Keepers, but it would not be long before she discovered the supposed delights of corrupting others to do the same, and her evil genius found out other spies and killers for the

Word and so gathered to herself a web of murderous power such as nomole in moledom's history ever had before. Like infectious murrain spreading across the body of a mole from one tiny spot, the killings began within hours of that Midsummer rite when Henbane fled the Rock. They would spread far and wide and finally engulf moledom in an orgy of tortured death, and all in the Word's great name.

Up on the surface Mallice killed those first three, by the light of day. A blinding thrust into those old Keepers' snouts and a fascination with their slow throes in death. And let us not avoid what happened after. Lust for her Master; desire for him alone. He who had saved her from the lake, by whose commandment she killed those three and in time would murder her way across moledom. She killed and felt at once a desire rampant and wild, her mouth moist for him: *that* was the vile effect killing had on Mallice. As if in taking life she found an unbearable desire to re-make it through intercourse with evil. Unstoppable, palpable lust. A mole who could only make love by making death first. Such was the consort of the mole Terce sought to make divine.

And Lucerne at such moments? Cold as ice before her need, but ice he knew served only to inflame her more. . . .

And wherefore? For young, of course, for pups. For heirs to the evil that he was. So that divinity would thrive and live on, which, if it proved so, would make Mallice a mother of divinity. All of them corrupt! All vile! Infection! Stain! Have mercy on us, Stone, who face such a gathering storm of evil from the north. . . .

Be sure that others died as well before Lucerne felt that Whern was his. A good few older sideem who had served Henbane rather too loyally for their own good; Terce suggested that they die. Lucerne agreed. Mallice did it, and was no doubt eager once again for Lucerne's lust.

Yet there were more . . . four newly anointed novices

were killed as well, as having been hostile to Lucerne in the past and not to be trusted with the onerous work that now lay ahead of the sideem and was essential to the grand scheme of things. In the mounting excitement of that summer they would not be missed. So far, such eliminations were discreet, yet the hint of them added to the menace that lay behind the charming face of Lucerne. Discreet and successful, as all else he did seemed to be.

Indeed, in only one regard can Lucerne and Terce be said to have failed, and that concerned Henbane.

So swift had been the Mistress's exit from the system through the secret way Mayweed had first used that those moles Lucerne sent after her failed utterly to find her.

But later they knew which way she went from the dead and dying that she left behind. The first of it they knew was a scream they heard on the slopes above Dowber Gill, where they found a new sideem taloned out of the way, one who had not been weak at all but more than a match (a mole might have thought) for aging Henbane. Not so.

Later that day, further to the south but higher up the fells, two more were found, one dead, one dying, yet neither showing any sign of struggle. Their eyes were open and fixed on some puzzle they had seemed to see, and across their breasts were what appeared no more than the rough caress of talons.

What had they seen? Did Henbane stop them with her charm, and did she confront them with the real truth of the Word, which was its essential lie, and therein lay their fatal perplexity? We think that in some way she did.

A fourth sideem they found crying at the Providence Fall, surrounded by its towering walls and falls of rock, his cries muted by the roar of the stream nearby. He spoke no sense but the word 'Mistress', nor could they find a clue how he came to be there. But there he was, and nearly mad.

'Where is the bitch?' roared Clowder, for he knew well enough what Lucerne's final victory needed: Henbane herself, and her punishment; and her dead body seen and witnessed.

Henbane merely disappeared meant doubt, and suspicion that she might return, and even the thought of such a possibility belittled the perceived power of the Master yet to be. Which, if one day he was to be divine, had best seem absolute.

They searched Providence Fall, as they had searched the southern slopes, but found no sign of her at all.

Lucerne and Clowder pondered, but it was Mallice who seemed to know best what to do: 'Send messengers to the watchers on the heights, and on the southern and western scars; send messengers northwards. Order them to describe Henbane in all those systems she is likely to come to, do it swiftly and reward her captor well. And let her live.' The eyes of Mallice glittered, and Lucerne nodded, thinking.

Still he stanced, dark as night, eyes narrowed, fur shining, claws curled sharp, snout strong, the very image of a Master, and with that power his mother had: to attract all others' eyes, and hold them, breathless and afraid as if some force was about to break forth that might consume them all. Even his most ordinary words seemed heavy with portent at that time.

At last he said, 'Her flight makes our task easier, for a Mistress should not flee and by this alone, whatever support she might have had will all be lost.' Then he thought some more, and added to the suggestion Mallice made: 'The messengers shall say that she is accursed of the Word for craven cowardice. If she is found then at my command alone she must die, at the talons of the mole I shall appoint.'

Here Mallice almost shivered with delight, for Lucerne's gaze fell on her and she knew who would win that task. What ecstasy that would be, to take the life of her consort's mother! And why pity the bitch? Had not *she* in her time killed her own mother Charlock? So does evil thrive upon itself.

'If she is not found,' continued Lucerne, 'then let all moles know she is accursed to suffer slow disease and painful death. It is the Word's will; I speak it.'

'The Master speaks a curse on Henbane,' went the whisper throughout Whern and far beyond. 'If anymole or system gives her sanctuary, knowingly or unknowingly, then they'll be cursed as well. Let allmole be on guard and, taking her, bring her back to Whern. The former Mistress Henbane, blasphemer against the Word, is outcast by the Master Lucerne! So ordains the Word!'

To such threats and imprecations we must leave Henbane for now, and to the ordination of the Stone, and wonder if such a mole as she has been would find forgiveness, and guidance, and be given one last chance to redeem a mite of goodness in herself. However hard our hearts may be, however unforgiving, yet we must remember that the Stone is merciful, and trust it more than we can trust ourselves in matters affecting other lives.

Even as the first decree of the Master went out to surrounding grike systems, Lucerne himself, no longer wasting time concerning himself with what for now he could not further influence, turned his attention towards how to harness the new-found energy and excitement that had come to Whern following his success on so auspicious a day as Midsummer itself.

He gained acclamation by resisting all suggestions that his ritual accession could take place that same Midsummer day, sensing instead that it would better serve his purpose if he delayed his accession to a time when other triumphs could be celebrated, and more moles than sideem might see his Mastership conferred. Meanwhile, he continued with the false modesty of preferring others not to call him Master, though his eyes glittered when they did.

He quickly arranged with Terce that the three dead Keepers should be replaced by Mallice and Clowder and himself, and made it known that when he became Master then in deciding which sideem took the Keeper's place he left vacant he would give favour to that mole that most impressed him with his vigour in pursuit of the Word's way in the summer years to come.

In such ways did Lucerne often sow the seeds of

265

ambition and doubt, plotting and deception, among those who served him, causing them to watch each other, and be suspicious of each other all the time. He held sway by doubt, and fear, and favour.

And often with promises of a better dawn.

That same night, indeed, keeping the initiative he had gained, Lucerne gathered the sideem in one of the larger chambers of Whern and spoke rousingly to them of the future. He told them that there were many important tasks for those who wished truly to serve the Word. The time had come for sideem to accept the challenge implicit in the original flight of Scirpus from the south, which was that when the day came that the Word was triumphant then its position must be forever consolidated and confirmed *and that its centre must move south once more*.

Few then realised how radical this suggestion was. To move the very centre of the Word from north to south! It might, in the end, demote Whern to a secondary place in the Word's ordinance.

The sideem were aghast, though few but Terce, perhaps, understood that by divorcing the sideem from Whern and leaving his own guardmoles there – which was his intent, and what he did – Lucerne secured all power to himself of the Word's spiritual home. Powerful indeed would be the mole who controlled which moles might make a pilgrimage back to Whern.

A few sideem dared criticise. Lucerne was too clever to risk killing these, though Mallice noted who they were and marked them down for posts obscure and dangerous where they might easily be eliminated if Lucerne so decreed. Instead, he dazzled them with words which of themselves were but rhetoric, but imbued with the majesty and menace he gave them, they worked for him well enough.

'Must we of Whern be fugitives?' he cried out to them. 'Must we always be victims of the Stone's malevolence? Scirpus led us here from the south that we might survive and know the Word. Here he found the Word, and the

Word lived in us and thrived in us. But Scirpus did not ordain that we stay in this high harsh place forever but rather bide our time, as we made ready to turn on the foes of the Word and take back what is rightfully ours; bide our time until the time is right. So our fathers bided, towards a great day to come when the Word is proclaimed for ever more. The time is now. That day is come!

'Now, with thy support, I, Lucerne, grandson of Rune, will lead you back to the wormful place from which our ancestors of the faith were unjustly driven. There we shall go to cleanse the tunnels and burrows so long defiled by followers of the Stone; to make such moles Atone, to bring succour and support to those who, these moleyears past, have shown allegiance to the Word.

'They cry to us from the wilderness of the south and we shall hear them! They cry for our help, and we shall give it. They cry, and we shall succour. This is the will of the Word. This *is* the Word.'

Profane adoration was in the eyes of those who heard, and no face was still, none quiet. Anger, tears, supine love, all the passions of blind faith were there upon the faces of those who heard.

'Great shall our tasks be. To wreak punishment to the undeserving, to bring strength to those who suffer of the Stone, to bring peace at last to moledom. And you who have been anointed this days of days, you who have heard the dark sound of the Word and been blessed by it; you whose fur is still damp of the baptismal waters of the Lake of the Rock – you shall be my example, you shall be the new apostles of the Word, you are its great crusade.'

Hushed were the young sideem, in awe of the image of themselves he presumptuously made, ready even then to rise up and do his bidding.

'My friends, when moles look back upon this great time, and wonder where it was best to be alive, and for what, your deeds in the months and years to come will tell them this: in Whern it was best to be, and for the Word. They shall revere you, they shall remember you, they shall speak your name in awe and say, "He was of Whern, his life was committed to the Word, he saw the challenge before him and did not flinch or falter before it." '

Then he was silent, sweat shining in his fur, breathing heavily with the effort of his speech, his proud look demanding of loyalty, and commanding of support.

Then among the new sideem there went a rippling chant of excitement and acclaim, ever louder and more rhythmic as they took up what he had said and cried out, 'A great crusade! We shall make the crusade of the Word!' And the tunnels of Whern roared and shook with their clamour.

With such words as these did Lucerne win the sideem to his heart and persuaded them that their bright future lay in leaving Whern and crusading south.

Yet having won them to that course he then deliberately made them wait, saying they must show patience and so test their purpose and commitment for the trials to come. Perhaps he sensed that it was yet too soon to commit the moles of Whern to any radical move from the place that they knew as the very centre of their faith. Nor did he himself, who had never yet moved out of the system, know much directly of moledom beyond and, listening perhaps to Terce, he decided to . . . bide his time.

It had become the expectation in the summer years at Whern that sideem who had been serving in the field – often in far-off systems in the south to which journeys took many a molemonth or even years – returned to Whern and made their reports of what was apaw. Rune himself had been sent on such a venture south, and found trouble too when he returned and strove to persuade Whern to take advantage of the weakness of moledom after the plagues.

As he listened to the reports Lucerne saw a way to give the younger sideem tasks that would test them out and keep them occupied until he was more ready to begin the great crusade. The new sideem took journeys here and there in the company of older sideem, to find out what they could of the strengths and dispositions of followers of

the Stone and of the Word. At the same time he sent a
sideem in whom he had most confidence on a fast course to
south and west, to supplement that information which
other sideem brought back.

Old were put to work with young, sideem were forced to
try out their skills and authority, ability found favour over
rank, and all over Whern things began to change. Not that
the routines of meditation and chant were any less;
indeed, it was Terce's strong belief, and Lucerne's
consequent command, they should be more. The Word
was a living faith, moles must meditate each day, the
obeisances must be made, and nomole to avoid confessions of their transgressions from the spiritual austerities
of the Word. As old worked with young, so must old
confess to young, and young lead in the sonorous liturgies
of faith.

An atmosphere of ardent restlessness came over Whern.
Tunnels once still and darkly peaceful now echoed to the
sound of pawsteps as moles came and went, or stanced
about in ever-changing huddles to talk of where they were
going, what they were doing, and, as the moleweeks went
by, where they had just come back from. And over all was
the menacing glitter of new-found zeal in which moles are
judged and found wanting in the harsh light of reborn
faith.

Hearing them, seeing them, listening to the reports they
brought back to the Keepers who, though still nominally
led by Terce were plainly dominated by Lucerne, nomole
could doubt the future Master's qualities of leadership.

At one sweep of his taloned paw, it seemed, the reverent
hush and slow rituals of elderly sideem had been replaced
by a young cadre of moles who brought health, speed,
intelligence and enthusiastic loyalty to Whern.

Although the Twelve Keepers had traditionally
gathered in a place not far from the Rock of the Word,
Lucerne moved their meeting place to a smaller, lighter
and more informal chamber which had been part of the
suite Henbane herself had occupied, and which had a

portal overlooking the roaring Dowber Gill. From a similar portal nearby Henbane had hurled the odious Weed, and perhaps it was partly this threatening and well-known memory that made him like the place.

But more likely was the fact that the chamber had fluted galleries among its walls, mostly secret, which ran high through the chamber and other antechambers nearby. These had been used by Rune to spy on moles, and had been known to few other moles but Terce.

The echoing acoustics of the place were such that sound travelled from the chambers and tunnels below and a spying, secret mole could hear what others, thinking they were private, said.

Terce introduced this place to Lucerne, and he permitted only Mallice there. It was her secret haven, her listening place, and there, unseen, she heard much that the sideem whispered to one another. More than that, she arranged for certain moles to talk or confess to one another in the antechambers, and heard as clearly as if she had been their confessor all that they said.

So were many trapped; so, many judged treasonable; and, it must be said, some apparently loyal discovered.

'Trust that one not, Master,' she would say. Or, 'Ask him what he would do if he was beloved of a follower, and watch his face for lying, for I know he is.' Or, 'She has disease and would not let you know lest you pass her over for a more healthy mole. Yet she is loyal, my Master dear, so treat her not too hard . . .' Yes, there was charity of a kind in Mallice's heart. Charity to those most blind and loyal in their faith to the Master and the Word, and in that order. As for 'Master dear' and 'love Master mine' and similar cloying endearments, anymole who must unfortunately record the life of Mallice, consort to Lucerne, cannot avoid her use of them. It was her way; and she spoke them with a sickening adoration all the worse for the contempt and utter cruelty she showed other moles.

All this, and the promotions, demotions and dire punishments that resulted from it formed part of

Lucerne's gradual tightening of control over Whern and the sideem through July and August.

By then, naturally, most had heard the rumours of Henbane's ousting and came cautiously into Whern, unsure of themselves and what they should say to preserve themselves. Lucerne and his cabal were already gaining a reputation for ruthlessness, and it did not help that quite senior sideem, with moleyears of experience behind them, would suddenly and inexplicably disappear.

These, invariably, were moles known to have been shocked by what had happened so summarily at Whern and, unable to keep their feelings secret – or overheard by Mallice – made it plain that Lucerne could not rely on them. In any case it was part of his strategy to make clear that it was the young who were to be favoured, and who might gain the quickest advancement in return for absolute loyalty to him.

Yet Lucerne was no fool, and nor was Mallice, and they were well able to judge that some moles, though their loyalties might initially be in doubt, were too valuable to eliminate for reason of the knowledge they brought back of place and mole.

Lucerne also quickly realised that if he was to move the main caucus of the sideem south it must be done during autumn and before the winter came. Which being so, the young untried sideem would not have time to travel too far south and report back to him. He must, then, formulate his strategy for the great crusade on information provided by older sideem; and if there were those among them who were deserving of punishment then their names would be scrivened down against the day when they could be dispensed with and replaced with younger and more zealous blood. Yet whatever the shortcomings of the older sideem, the reports they brought presented to Lucerne and his Keepers a picture of decay and danger too consistent to be doubted. And, as events subsequently showed, one accurate enough to make the formidable strategy for the renewed imposition of the Word that

Lucerne and Terce developed soundly based and almost certain of success.

A record exists of these reports since it was the habit of Terce and his clerical minions to scriven all they heard verbatim, as Lucerne himself would have heard it.

With the initial reports Lucerne rarely interrupted to ask questions, and only slowly did his questioning begin. Until then he left such questions to older and more knowledgeable Keepers than himself, and saw what mattered most to them. It was as if he chose to listen first and learned to comprehend what he heard, though there is some evidence that he was simultaneously, and no doubt with Terce's guidance, going through old reports from the previous cycles of seasons which had also been routinely kept.

When, at last, in the final quarter of July he began interrogating for himself, his questions have startling point, and are invariably well informed. This was significant enough, for all who faced his questioning afterwards said that they had never met a mole who had a better grasp of the strengths and weaknesses of the Word over moledom, or of details of individual systems which even moles who had visited and lived in them sometimes did not have.

But even more significant is the difference between what Lucerne rapidly became most interested in compared to what the sideem, especially the older ones used to easier ways, were prepared and able to report.

Again and again in the scrivened reports we find Lucerne interrupting some hapless sideem with, 'I don't want guesses or answers that you think we would like to hear. I want facts, facts, and more facts.' And then again, exasperated, 'Mole, you are wasting our time, we cannot base a crusade upon surmise. How many days' travel is it between those systems, if fair weather? And how many in foul?'

What Lucerne, with Terce and strong Clowder at his flank, showed interest in were matters such as the incidence of followers in one system as against another; or the spread of disease among moles of the Word, or the dispositions and strengths of guardmoles between different systems; or with things that seemed trivial to the irritated sideem, like effective and ineffective route-ways, the numbers of moles in one place or another, and even the dialects spoken and patterns of soil and worm supply.

Often the reporting sideem were much discomforted by such questions, for they had not thought to ask them, and certainly did not know the answers. So it was not long before Lucerne had gained the reputation for turning these debriefings of sideem into rigorous trials of a mole's abilities, and not a few were left in little doubt at the end of them that they would not have much future in the coming crusade. Others emerged strongly as moles of resource and intelligence who, it seemed, had only needed a change to such leadership as this to show their potential for the Word.

While the new sideem, as Lucerne no doubt intended, were given clearly to understand that when they returned to give their reports they must expect a thorough interrogation, and be ready with answers which went beyond comfortable affirmations that the way of the Word was being observed.

By the beginning of August certain persistent themes in all these reports had emerged to which Lucerne and his advisers gave great importance, and which helped shape the crusade's initial strategy.

First, despite the ruthlessness of Henbane's original invasion of the south, and the efficiency with which eldrene and attendant guardmoles had been installed in all large systems, belief in the Stone was not dead, but, rather, hidden and sometimes tolerated. It was plain that in those areas near three of the ancient Seven – Rollright, Duncton and Fyfield – the Stone was alive in moles' hearts, and seemingly gaining strength once more. Only in Avebury did it appear wholly eradicated.

The impulse behind this movement by followers of the

Stone was the belief, prevalent since spring though with no evident source or basis in fact, that the 'Stone Mole' had come. Whether or not such a mole existed was disputed – the reports Lucerne had got were so far ambiguous and conflicting – but it was plain enough once the reports had been pieced together that a belief prevailed that he was alive, and that he lived in or had come from the troublesome system of Duncton Wood.

But if these areas gave cause of zealous concern, what was happening further west was a source of outrage. Lucerne seems to have been already aware of the name of Alder, the former guardmole who had taken over the military leadership of Siabod, and sometime that July he and Clowder became aware of another great mole of those parts, Troedfach of Tyn-y-Bedw. There were no reports of anymole of the Word ever seeing him, but enough of rumour and occasional hearsay from captured Stone followers to make clear that he was the mole who held sway among the rebels along the Marches.

Even in a few places north of Whern systems lived in open rejection of the Word and seemed impervious to attempts to correct them.

'They persist in their inclinations to the Stone for their system was founded long before the coming of the Word,' Lucerne heard one of his new sideem report.

'Do you know of these systems?' Lucerne asked Terce.

'They have been discussed by the Keepers in times past,' replied the Twelfth Keeper carefully, 'but have been felt to be of little consequence. We cannot monitor every system. When Ribblesdale was taken to the Word these few systems, which I believe lie on its western side, were judged to be beyond the limit of our need.'

'Well?' said Lucerne turning to a young sideem. 'And are they of consequence now?'

The mole looked uncertainly between the Master-to-be and Terce, not liking to be caught between the two.

'Tell the truth, mole,' said Lucerne gently and with a smile. 'I shall know if you do not.'

'Perhaps they were not once,' replied the sideem, 'but it seems that the infection of their belief is spreading into the systems of Ribblesdale itself.'

'Have not the eldrene sent guardmoles out to warn and correct?'

'They have, but to no effect. Accordingly I visited them myself.'

'Good, very good,' said Lucerne. 'No harm came to you?'

'I was not threatened, but. . . .'

'They would not hear the Word?'

'They listened politely and told me I was "misguided". I asked what their belief was and all they said was, "Words will not touch your heart. Live with us and you shall know." I warned them of the Word's vengeance if they sent missions into Ribblesdale. They said they had not. They said it was for nomole to spread any faith, including that of the Word. I said the Word *is*. They said maybe. They never once threatened though I heard it from guardmoles who went there that it is not advisable to attempt force or do violence of any kind against them. I asked them of this and. . . .'

Terce shot a glance of approval at Lucerne. This surely was the kind of report he liked.

'. . . and they said they would never knowingly kill a mole nor let another kill. For this reason they would resist attacks upon themselves. Guardmoles had used force against them so one of them had to stop them.'

'*One* of them?' said Lucerne.

'Yes,' said the sideem coolly. 'One alone stopped eight guardmoles.'

'Killed them?'

The sideem shook his head. 'Disabled them.'

There was silence at this extraordinary report.

'It is not the first time, nor the second,' said the sideem. 'I understand the first thing new eldrene do in Ribblesdale is to try to make these moles Atone, but they have never yet proved amenable.'

275

'What is the name of this recalcitrant system?' asked Lucerne.

'Mallerstang,' said the mole.

'I will hear more of this from you,' said Lucerne. 'But not now . . . You have done well. We shall talk again about this Mallerstang.'

But probably the most notorious example of systems in successful opposition, for it was one which had long been known yet never successfully suppressed, was Beechenhill where the already legendary rebel Squeezebelly was said to still lead effective opposition to any grike or guardmole or sideem who dared show his snout in those parts. This was most certainly a system of the Stone. Unlike the moles of Mallerstang, Beechenhill moles were prepared to kill to protect the continuing error of their ways.

Such is an outline of the catalogue of opposition to the Word of which Lucerne had been made aware by the time summer reached its height in August. At the same time he had gathered much intelligence about individual sideem and eldrene, and was beginning to make dispositions among those who might take over lax systems, or go to the support of undermoled ones.

' "Lax" is the proper word, Terce. *Lax*,' said Lucerne one day. 'Most systems are of the Word, most are under no physical threat of the Stone, and where the Stone predominates are but marginal areas such as the west and Beechenhill where they are well contained by us. But . . . infections easily spread. My mother's campaign was not consolidated as a young sideem's early training is consolidated by the austerities and disciplines imposed by his Tutor Keeper. We shall be the very Tutor Keeper of moledom, and cleanse it of the rebellion of spirit! I like not permissiveness and negligence . . . We shall appoint new moles to the guardianship of the main systems, and give the eldrenes power once more to force Atonement. Moles must suffer to be cleansed.'

But perhaps the appointment that concerned him most was that of Wyre in Buckland, which was still the stronghold of the south. Wyre had gained power under Henbane, but reports of him now were ambivalent and contradictory. In his time he had certainly been a strong and decisive mole but it seemed that since the spring he had been ill with scalpskin and had lost the confidence of some of those at Buckland. Certainly there was news of increasing restiveness in the systems south of Duncton Wood. But the reports were patchy and too vague to make it possible for Lucerne to decide on what detailed action to take there.

'What is clear,' he told Terce at this time, 'is that we know enough to know we have just cause to mount a crusade against the Stone, but we know too little in any detail to be able to do more than plan a general strategy . . . I *must* know more. I must have facts. I must have a sense of where to attack first, where to attack hardest, and in what ways the followers' faith in the Stone is vulnerable.'

Terce agreed.

'Our sideem shall become better trained in gathering information,' he said.

'And more regular in providing it!' interrupted Lucerne. 'But for that we need to move our centre south.'

'Which is what the Master Rune always said must be done,' continued Terce. 'And to a system easily reached from north and south.'

'And one that is placed to mount a campaign against the west side of moledom,' said Clowder. 'I like not the reports from the Marches, nor that we have lost credence in Siabod once more. Yet . . . it is a long time since we campaigned and we shall have things to learn. What happened to the mole Wrekin, Henbane's general?'

'Retired,' said Terce. 'Dead, I think. He came from north of here.'

'And Ginnell?' asked Clowder.

'Wrekin's second-in-command? He is in the west still. I have never met him, but I hear good of him. He has sent reports regularly, but never uses sideem. Like Wrekin before him, sideem worry him.' Terce permitted himself the briefest of cold smiles.

'I think we should talk with him,' said Clowder, turning to Lucerne.

'I agree,' said Lucerne.

'Shall I recall him?' said Clowder.

'He is not a mole to treat casually,' said Terce, 'and might treat a simple recall as an insult.'

'I know that, Tutor Keeper, I know it well,' growled Clowder. 'But with respect, he will as like talk more sense to me than a thousand namby sideem who wouldn't know a military report from their arse if they heard it with their own ears.'

Lucerne smiled. He remembered his mother saying that the military mind and the sideem mind were different things. Clowder was at least anointed, and nomole could doubt his loyalty to the Word, but if he was to be to Lucerne what Wrekin had been to Henbane, then just such blunt directness and impatience was what he would need. No harm would come of conflict between Terce and Clowder, provided neither felt the other had the upper paw.

'We shall move south to a system I shall name,' said Lucerne, stopping their argument before it got further. 'To it we shall summon Ginnell and he shall tell us of the campaign along the Marches, and of Siabod. If he is the mole I have heard he is he will know a great deal more than that. You shall serve with him for a time, Clowder.'

'*With* him?' repeated Clowder slowly.

Lucerne stared at him unflinching.

'As his subordinate, then. Yes, why not? A little humility will not hurt. You will have things to learn and he shall teach them to you.'

Clowder was speechless. Terce relaxed and looked a little smug to see Clowder discomfited.

'And you, Twelfth Keeper, surprise me,' said Lucerne turning on him suddenly. 'You have not even thought to establish whether Wrekin is alive or dead. Supposing alive and living north? What if moles of the Stone find him? Had I been told he *might* be alive sooner then our chance of apprehending Henbane might have been better.'

Terce looked puzzled. It was Clowder's turn to be amused.

Lucerne leaned menacingly close to Terce and the two moles eyed each other coldly.

'Wrekin is the only mole apart from Tryfan of Duncton I *ever* heard my mother speak of with respect. Might she not have fled to him? If there is even the smallest chance that she has then we should investigate it, should we not? I cannot stress enough how important it is that she is found, or her fate discovered. Moles must know that she is dead or else she robs the Mastership of strength. I am displeased, Terce.'

Terce's face betrayed no sign of emotion.

'I shall see to it.'

'Aye, you shall. And if Wrekin is alive then Clowder will wish to speak with him.' He paused and for a moment allowed himself to look both weary and disappointed.

'We shall win no crusades if we are vain . . .' (and here he looked at Clowder) . . . 'or lax . . .' (and now his gaze shifted to Terce). Then he turned and left them, and where he had stanced was left the sense of cold silence and threat.

Terce smiled bleakly.

'He shall be the greatest Master ever known.'

'He shall indeed, Tutor Keeper,' said Clowder, 'and the Word's will shall be done.'

They watched where Lucerne had gone, and Clowder added wryly, 'But the way he takes us shall be harder even than the training you gave us.'

'I know it, and it pleases me,' said Terce.

When next they saw him Lucerne was charming once more, and decisive. He came in the company of Mallice.

'The rest of the Keepers have been summoned and will assemble shortly. Meanwhile I shall tell you what they shall agree to do.

'The Keepers and main body of the sideem shall leave for the south in three days. The Word shall guide as to which system will form our new centre.

'But those new sideem who have already proved themselves worthy to gather information in southern systems to aid our strategy shall go forth as I dictate. They shall return as winter sets in to the new centre we have found and there preparations for our crusade shall be made. Many shall be given their chance of the Word, and non-sideem shall be listened to.

'Meanwhile we are surprised and displeased that there are moles as near as Ribblesdale who persistently flout the Word. We shall need to make an early example that allmole knows the Word is not to be taken in vain, or ignored, or mocked, and that its representatives are to be obeyed. Accordingly, Clowder, you shall go to Ribblesdale immediately and destroy utterly this rebel system of Mallerstang. Such an exercise will give cause for Ginnell to respect you when you rejoin us further south and meet him. I know you will not fail, but I wish that destruction to be on such a scale, and in such a manner, that when news of it is known nomole who hears it shall doubt the power of the Word, or that it shall take vengeance on those who turn their snout from it. It shall be an example for other zealots to follow. Do you understand?'

'They shall be destroyed in a way that all that hear of it will not forget it, nor doubt the Word's power for just retribution,' said Clowder. Nomole who saw his eyes glinting and his fur bristling, and the way his huge talons tore restlessly at the soil in front of him could doubt it would be so.

'Mallice, I have a different task for you: Beechenhill. Send out spies to discover its weaknesses. When the time comes to destroy it I would have it done well, very well. But that time is not yet. It shall be after we have gone south and when this Squeezebelly will have decided that we prefer to leave well alone. Discover what you can of the place and the moles within it.'

'I shall,' she said, her mouth curled to a cruel smile, her eyes warm upon her Master.

'The Word shall be with you,' he said.

'And I?' said Terce.

'It shall be with thee as well!' joked Lucerne. But his smile was brief as that which Terce tried out. 'You shall stay with me, Tutor Keeper, and watch over this migration south. Do it with ritual, do it with pomp. Make moles know it is ordained of the Word, and the Word shall guide us.'

In such a way, thoroughly and with decision, were the first orders of the great crusade of the Word given and final preparations put in paw.

By the end of August all those leaving on tasks had gone, including most of the Keepers and sideem who would help establish the new centre in the south.

Those that remained were a body of picked sideem and guardmoles who would garrison Whern and seal it against incursion from anymole but those come with permission of Lucerne and Terce only.

It was a clear, sunny day, with the colour of autumn spreading over the bracken of the fells, and the heath in mauve bloom in the distant parts.

Lucerne had made his final obeisances at the Rock, and gone to the surface and slowly made his way, in the company of his faithful guardmoles, down to the limestone scars on the western slopes through which the ways lead on to Kilnsey, Grassington and the south.

The river Wharfe wound its way southward in the valley below them, and parts of the trees along its banks were already turning brown.

'The Word be with thee, Master!' said one of the faithful who was staying at Whern to Lucerne as he finally left.

Lucerne deigned to smile.

'I am not Master yet, mole. But with the Word's guidance and the support of moles such as thee then may the day come swift when the Stone is shattered into a

281

thousand pieces across moledom. Then I shall return to this hallowed place and hear once more the wind across its fells and in its tunnels.'

'Then shall you be made Master and all of us able to rejoice in your triumph?'

'May it be so, mole. The Word be with thee.'

With that Lucerne left Whern at last, accompanied by Terce and a pawful of sideem, and the great crusade began.

Chapter Sixteen

September came to Duncton as it did across all moledom, with rain, grey weather, and day after day of blustering winds. Moles poked their snouts out of their burrows, scented at the wet in the air, scurried up to surface exits, peered at the swaying branches above and scatters of wet leaves below, and sighed.

The peace of a long summer was over and the restlessness of autumn had come back again. Tunnels to delve, entrances to repair, burrows to clear and clean, realities to face once more.

If, as the September winds blew on, most moles in Duncton became resigned to this, they sensed as well that, from the moment of the coming of Marram and old Sorrel back to Barrow Vale to tell of their near escape at the cross-under, all of them were on the verge of change. Their time with Beechen was nearly over and, as all youngsters must (for that was how so many of them still thought of him), he would soon be gone.

As if to confirm the truth of this, and to prepare them for his parting, Beechen retreated from them. To Madder's place he went first of all, but then down to the Marsh End to be with Tryfan. When, as on some days he did, he went to the surface, it was plain that he needed to be alone, and moles left him so, to think and meditate as he wished. Yet often when his thoughts were done and he rose from the meditating stance he had taken and turned to go back underground, he would find an offering of food left for him; or some old mole, a friend, watching over him, and saying he had stayed, 'Just to make sure you weren't disturbed . . . just to be sure.'

Then he would go to them, and gaze on them, and touch them with a smile of strange sadness, and go on his way.

Some dared asked him to bless them, and this he quietly did. Others, probably more than we now know, asked for a healing; but they had no need to ask, for those that needed healing or comfort found it came in the touch of his paw, in the warmth of his eyes. But always, always, he whispered, 'Speak not of this, it is between thy heart and the Stone; others need not know.'

Perhaps too, a tender few, when he had gone from them, cried and whispered after him that the Stone might give him strength, and show its mercy. Then the September wind would rattle the branches and a gust of rain come down and they would turn to find shelter and think of that summer, and the young mole who had touched their hearts.

Many such in Duncton, old now, infirm, their joints aching with the damp air, knew that they would not see a summer ever again. A few blessed days yet, perhaps, when the rains cleared, but not such a long time of warmth and time for friendship. But then . . . there would be moles like Beechen to live after them, and with the Stone's help their shoulders would be broad enough to carry the care that youngsters never dream of, and in their turn teach their pups what they had learned.

With such thoughts as these Duncton prepared itself for the harder moleyears to come. But so far as we know only one, and that was good and sensible Teasel, upon whom old age had settled with a smile, took it upon herself to trek all the way to the Stone one brighter day to pray for him.

She had seen him up on the surface of the Marsh End one recent day past, and thought at first it was just the imminence of leaving that oppressed him. But then she had passed the time of day first with one group of old moles, and then with another, and finally with a third, and she'd thought suddenly, Why, Beechen's *lonely* here. We've given him what we could, and he's given back more than many might; now he needs to find others younger than us who will give him, why, yes, who'll . . . well I *hope* they will. Or *one* will at least!

It was then, with humour and care in her eyes, she had trekked to the Stone and petitioned it in her homely way.

'Stone, he's pining for something of which he doesn't know the name! It's a mate *he* needs to finish off his education, for the words of others can never give the secret wisdom a mate's touch brings. Stone, if you're listening to me, you send him a love for himself alone, for he'll be a better mole to serve your purpose if he's known a female's touch. And make her sensible and strong, like me! No airy-fairy nonsense now! Why if I was younger I'd offer him myself, but these young moles don't know a good thing when they see one. Remember, Stone, it's a mate he wants!'

It was a prayer as good as any other, and lest mole think that the Stone does not respect such prayers, nor listens with pleasure to such good laughter and chuckles as old Teasel then allowed herself, let him know that the Stone was brighter for her prayer, and passed into her paws the sense of being young again, and sent her scampering through the wood, not noticing the greying sky at all but knowing only the warm pleasures of her own good-natured thoughts and, though the summer days were all but done, that a mole could still enjoy herself!

But there were few moles able to be as cheerful as Teasel. The sense that a time of trial was coming was too strong for them and they were oppressed by it, and frightened. Which being so they said among themselves that they hoped old Tryfan would show his snout again, and maybe the Rule he had been scribing for so long could now be shared with them, and it would bring some comfort.

'Is Tryfan ill?' they asked one another, and those closest to him in the Marsh End.

'Is he ill?' a few asked Beechen. 'You would know.'

'No, no, he's well. He's nearly ready now, nearly done. He's slower than he was, but my mother's with him all the time these days, and helping him. He wants to speak of the Rule he's scribed. Have patience, he'll do it soon enough. . . .'

285

'Just asking, mind, just wondering.'

Then Beechen smiled and whispered, 'It's all right, I'll tell him that you cared,' as he went on his solitary way through the wood he loved and which had been his only home.

It was the autumn equinox, when the moon is slight and September's end is near, and the sense of darkness drawing in is on all moles, that Tryfan came out of the Marsh End to tell of his Rule.

Nomole could quite say why they knew to go to Barrow Vale, for no announcement was made, and the only change of note was that the weather cleared towards a final few warm days even as, almost as a mole looked, the last of the beech leaves turned and the high wood was cast in golden brown.

However it was, moles seemed to know and one mole said to another, 'Tryfan wants us at Barrow Vale, he's to talk to us and speak his Rule.' Even as moles said this others whispered, 'Beechen will be leaving us now. The leaves are only hanging up there because the weather's calm again. Come a new wind and they'll all be down and he'll be gone.'

Such was the strength of feeling that they must be there to hear Tryfan speak that even moles so old now that they had not been out on the surface for molemonths past bestirred themselves, and groomed their fur, and polished their frail talons and called out, 'If there's anymole can hear me, come and help an old mole up! I'll be no trouble. . . oh, you heard! It's only me! Bit past climbing up to the surface, just need a push and shove. . . .'

While others, hearing from friends who knew they could not make it alone, asked that somemole come by and give them a paw, and early, mind, for they wouldn't miss hearing Tryfan talk, not for the world, and would be fretted if they were late.

So that mild autumnal day the wood was astir early with moles wending their way to Barrow Vale from north and south, from east and west. Few went alone, for if they did not meet friends along the way they stopped by to help others, and slowly came by tunnel and by surface routes, supporting the lame, or guiding the blind.

'Is my fur straight? Eh? What did you say? Oh, it is . . . is it? Are you sure? Eh?' So on they went, some blind, some unsteady on their paws, most very slow, but all with hope and purpose in their gait, and determination to reach Barrow Vale and hear what they would hear.

When they reached the great root-riven chamber of Barrow Vale, they paused, looked timidly or boldly about according to their natures, found a place and crouched down to wait, excited and restless.

Occasionally one would say to another, 'Where are. . . ?' And search about and, failing to find them, would send a fitter or more able mole off to fetch them. Teasel collected several in this way, and Hay as well, while, to everymole's astonishment, even strange, pupless Heather appeared helping some old mole along.

Though there was no sign of Tryfan by noon, Beechen came by and went among them, saying he was sure that the old scribemole would not be long and that Feverfew was bringing him. He had not been so well and was working at his Rule until the very last.

'A scribemole's work is never done,' he said, 'and even if it is he thinks it's not and might be better!'

The old moles hearing him smiled and looked shy, not knowing what a scribemole did exactly, but glad that Beechen at least understood. He was a clever mole, a *credit* to them all to have made him, and a mole could hope that Tryfan, when he came, would say as much. And a great deal more, perhaps! Anyway, he'd be here soon enough and they'd find out.

Bailey came, and Marram, who brought old Sorrel with him and made him comfortable near some friends of his. Then, when noon was over and the sun's shafts angling back another way at the entrances, Beechen looked concerned, and went to one mole after another and softly spoke to them. Some shook their heads, others looked about and pointed out other moles as if they might know. . . but they, too, when Beechen went to them, shook their heads.

Then voices, and several arrived at once – first Madder, then Dodder after him, with Flint close behind, all talking at once.

'Ssh!' commanded Dodder when they came into the chamber. 'Don't talk so loud.'

'It's not me who's talking,' replied Madder.

'It *was*, and knowing you that's no surprise,' said Dodder.

Beechen saw them, came to them, and asked if they had seen Crosswort.

'Unwell,' said Madder.

'Unfit,' said Dodder.

'Unwilling,' explained Flint.

Beechen gazed silently at them, and they looked guiltily at each other.

'I'll get her,' said Flint.

'By the Word you won't!' declared Dodder.

'While you're arguing I'll. . . .'

'You'll do nothing of the sort,' said Crosswort, coming up behind them. 'As for you,' she continued, addressing Beechen, 'you've got other moles to worry about than me! But where's Tryfan? Late? Or just slow?'

'He's coming,' said Beechen with a smile, 'and he won't be long.'

He looked about the chamber, and could not remember so many of the moles being all together, and he tried to see if any weren't there, if any were missing. There were some, a few, but even as he thought of them they seemed to arrive by surface or tunnel, or one of their friends, reading his mind, said, 'I know she's on her way, wanted to take it slow and by herself, wanted to enjoy the wood. Don't fret, she'll soon be here.'

Skint was among the last to come, explaining that Smithills and two other moles would not be along since they had agreed to stay over on the south-eastern slopes as watchers for the day.

'Got to have watchers all the time now,' said Skint, the only thing said all day that cast a doubt into the chamber.

'Aye . . .' sighed Sorrel, ' 'tis wise to be prudent now, as I know to my cost. . . .'

'He's going to tell us about his nearly getting killed at the cross-under again,' said a mole.

'Let him, it gets more exciting every time!' replied another.

The morning had passed by with surprising speed, but then new moles were always arriving, and there was plenty to observe and moles to greet. But when, during early afternoon, the sun came out, moles stretched and some went back out on to the surface, and a mutter of impatience went about the place.

But suddenly everything changed once more as Mayweed and Sleekit arrived, and a buzz of welcome greeted them. Mayweed was a mole who knew where to be at the right time, and they guessed that Tryfan would be along soon now.

'Sirs and Madams,' said Mayweed with a cheery leer, 'greetings to you all and everymole from each of us; me Mayweed and my loved one. Seen us lately, no? Not at all! Been unseen, haven't we?'

'You certainly have, Mayweed!' shouted out a mole. 'Where have you been?'

'Canoodling,' said Mayweed. 'Giving Sleekit all of humbleness's time!' He grinned and Sleekit smiled with pleasure at his side. There might have been a ribald joke or two in younger company, but perhaps not even then, for there was such great peace about them both, and a certain sense of unspoken intimacy that it did a mole good to see it. Not much of *that* about in Duncton Wood these days, love and . . . canoodling.

Several moles, and not all females, could not help whispering among themselves thoughts which summed up to one pithy sentence might have been, 'Mayweed's looking older than he did, and Sleekit younger: that's what love can do to moles.'

'We're all older than we were,' the more judicious replied. 'Everymole of us but Beechen there.'

They might have added Bailey too, who, at that moment hurried out of the tunnel that was the most direct route to Barrow Vale from the Marsh End, and from where everymole expected Tryfan himself to come.

Only Beechen was younger than Bailey, and ever since he had lost contact with his sisters, Starling and Lorren, so many years before he had worn a permanent look of frowning puzzlement and loss on his face, but he still looked like the pup he had been then. Unlike most he erred to plumpness, and this, perhaps, gave him a more cheerful look than some of the cadaverous aged moles could manage.

Bailey looked around at the assembled company, grinned briefly, and said, 'They're coming now. Won't be long. I'll stance by you, Skint, if I may.'

Excitement mounted and suddenly a hush of expectation fell as from that same tunnel the sound of aged pawsteps came, slowly, and low voices, one gruff, the other soft.

Then a shadow fell across the tunnel's entrance arch as a mole reached it, and seemed to fill it up as he paused and gazed out on the assembled moles. Behind him another shadow moved and all light was blocked out in the tunnel behind them both.

There was silence as they felt Tryfan's eyes upon them. Then he came out slowly and light fell across his face and a hushed whisper went among them before they settled once more into expectant quiet.

The scars over his eyes seemed deeper than they had ever been, and his eyes were shadowed and unfathomable as he stared at them. His head shook a little as he looked about, and his paws were great before him, their talons thick, lustreless and worn. His breathing was heavy and rasping and he seemed uncomfortable, as if in pain.

He carried a slim bark text pressed against his body under his right paw but it was beginning to slip and Feverfew, who was at his right side and half supporting him, pushed it back to where it was more secure.

Tryfan said nothing but peered about among them as if looking for somemole but was not able to see him. Feverfew came forward and whispered to him, and pointed a talon to where Beechen had stanced halfway round the great chamber. Tryfan looked that way, muttered to himself, nodded his head, and then slowly went round the edge of the chamber.

Moles shuffled as he passed, some smiling, some reaching forward to touch him, some lowering their snout in shyness or in awe. He seemed to see none of them, but rather to be concentrating on getting himself to Beechen's side.

When Tryfan reached him the two moles touched each other with such affection, and Beechen helped Tryfan turn and face towards the centre of the chamber with such obvious love and care, that there was an audible sigh among the watching moles. Some, like Teasel and Madder, did not mind that others saw them shed a tear or two.

The place where Tryfan had taken stance was near a surface entrance, and light flooded on to him. They saw then that his fur hung loose now at his flanks, for he had lost weight and his sides were thin. Where the light caught his ragged fur it showed that it had turned grey in places, and even white in others. Here and there his rough old skin had no hair at all. He looked like a mole near his time.

Yet stanced as he was at that moment, there was not a single mole who could not tell what once he must have been. His shoulders still had a powerful set to them, and though his head shook all four of his paws were firmly on the ground. But the natural authority he had was not just physical: his spirit seemed to loom within him, and strengthen him. He stared out at them, a mole needing his partner's help, but more fearless now than he had ever been.

'Where's Skint?' he said, peering about again, concern on his face.

Skint was almost opposite him, and plain for all to see. 'I'm here, Tryfan, here . . .' said Skint moving a little. Tryfan turned in his direction and said, 'Come closer, mole, come where I can see you. Yes, that's better.'

Slowly, and with care, he went forward a little, Feverfew on one side and Beechen on the other, and in a bright spot of light on the chamber floor where all could see it, he placed the text he had brought.

Then he went back to where he had been, his breathing heavy, and he said, 'Is Mayweed here?' Nothing could have made plainer than the way he stared at the ground and simply turned his head a little to one side as if to hear better that his sight was failing him.

'Concerned comrade,' said Mayweed, 'humbleness is never far away from you. Mayweed loves you and will not willingly leave you ever again.'

Even then Tryfan did not look towards where Mayweed was, off to his right paw, but lowered his snout still more as a small smile came to his face and crinkled the corners of his eyes. He looked up, then, and there was much gentleness and wisdom in his face, and those closest to him saw that his eyes glittered with tears.

'Yes, I know, Mayweed, I know,' he said slowly. 'It means much to me. Are all of you here?'

'All that could get here,' said Skint, 'all but Smithills who is watching at the cross-under, and two others with him.'

Tryfan nodded his understanding, but said nothing, staring instead at the text which lay in the light before him. Another silence fell, filled only with the occasional scrape of a paw, or sniff of a snout, or sound of bird-call or rustle of breeze from the wood above.

Then, at last, he spoke again.

'You know that I am Tryfan, born here in Duncton, and sent from here by the Stone to guard over Boswell on his journey to Uffington with the Stillstone of Silence. You know that Boswell ordained me scribemole and gave me a task which was to help prepare moledom for the coming of the one we call the Stone Mole.

'As time passed, moles I loved gathered about me, the first among them being Spindle, my dearest and my oldest friend. He went to the Stone the night Beechen was born, but his son Bailey is here among us. Other moles who travelled with me are here and some I met before my return to Duncton Wood.'

Tryfan paused and spoke their names slowly and with love, as if he thought of each mole as he came to him:

'You, Skint . . . and you, good Mayweed . . . Smithills who is not here . . . Marram . . . Feverfew, my dear partner now. . . .

'Others too I have grown to know and love since I returned to Duncton Wood . . . Hay, who was the first mole Spindle and I met when we came back; Teasel, who trusted me; Borage, Heather, so many moles . . . Some I have come to know only recently: Dodder, Madder . . . aye and many more I would name and touch as well if time allowed. But you know of this yourselves, you know it well.

'It is not given to moles to know many they can truly call their friends, for moles – or *this* fallible old mole at least – does not have so much love or energy that all moles may share it. I wish he did! A mole should count himself lucky if he can choose his friends, and blessed if he chooses well.'

Tryfan smiled and the moles about him relaxed.

The pleasant sound of an afternoon breeze through the high branches of the mixed trees about Barrow Vale came down to them, and though the sun shone for most of the time at the entrances there was enough cumulus cloud about to shade it from time to time and bring a moment's darkening to the chamber.

'I have scribed a Rule for the future use of our community, and there it is, that simple-looking thing.' He waved a paw towards the text before him. 'Because only a few among you can scribe or understand scribing, most of

293

you will not make sense of a word it says. Do not worry about that for, as you shall discover from what I say, most of you know what it says already. This Rule is what we are and have become. . . .

'But even so, I want this afternoon to say something about rules in general and this Rule in particular. I hope you will want to listen, and not mind if I ramble a little at times. My thoughts, like my paws, move more slowly than they did.'

He paused again and a slow smile lit his face up, and he looked around first at Feverfew on one flank, and then at Beechen on the other.

'I was fortunate to be born here in Duncton, into a community with great and ancient traditions as many systems blessed by the presence of a Stone have had. Like them, like many of your systems, the moles who lived in my youth have long since been scattered, and most are now dead. Perhaps all of us here are the last survivors of the communities from which we came, and perhaps the Stone intended that to be. Yet in my heart, in my very spirit, I feel that something of the community I was reared in is still alive. And I know, or think I know, that there is not a mole here, not one, who has not brought with him to this place something of the community that was *his* heritage. Not all of it is good, but most of it is, because moles are basically good and as they forget pain and turn their back on its memory, so they turn their back on darkness if they have a chance.

'*If* they have a chance. I wonder if there were any moles who, seeing each of us outcast here, for different reasons and in different ways, would have thought he would have such a chance. Yet here we are, and slowly we have made community among us, *good* community, better indeed than that I remember from my youth. I have come only recently to see that that is so, and to believe that in its wisdom the Stone wished me to return to the system of my birth and be a part of something being made: *us*; what we are today; community. That is what this Rule is all about.

294

'I have met many moles in my travels, I have talked to them of the communities they knew and made, I have observed communities of which I was not a recognised part. I have wondered often what it was about some that made a mole feel whole, and others that made him feel so separate that something in him fails to thrive. He is but part mole.

'Some of you know how much the community I briefly saw at Beechenhill near the Dark Peak meant to me, especially those like Mayweed, Sleekit, Skint and Smithills, who also visited it.

'They can speak for themselves, but for myself I learnt much about community there. It was Squeezebelly, the mole who led it without seeming to do so, who told me that it was change that kept his community alive, and faith that gave it heart. And when I asked how long the system had been of the Stone, he told me he had no idea, but by faith he did not mean the Stone so much as faith and trust in themselves together to do the right thing.

'Many of you know that when Henbane of Whern had young by me, Mayweed and Sleekit were able to take two of them out of Whern, and it was in Beechenhill they were placed. From that system, too, Feverfew and I found the Stone Mole's name. I do not know why the system meant so much to me except that it has to do with its power for community, and in that I am sure the Stone Mole's task will lie.

'Beechenhill revealed something, Whern something more, but in my final years it is what has happened here in Duncton that has guided me most of all. *You* all guided me. Outcast, frightened, suffering, angry, you and those who came but have not survived, made a community strong enough that Boswell felt able to entrust his son to us. Here, without thinking about it, doing our fallible best, I think we have shown what a true community might be. What then is a "true community"?'

Tryfan looked at the moles – the community – gathered about him and in his strong way smiled and said, 'Why, a mole need hardly ask the question when surrounded by such moles as you! But Autumn's on its way now and the tunnels must be prepared for the winter soon to come. A good time this, for pondering.

'Well then, a community should admit all that come to it, *all*. Every last one. Moles of the Stone should welcome those of the Word; moles of the Word should do the same to those of the Stone. A community excludes none, even those whose behaviour makes them seem to reject it.

'A community is made of moles committed to its life, not before their own but equally to their own. And when, as always happens, a mole finds himself and his community in conflict he had best expect himself to be the one who's wrong! Let a mole suspect himself before he suspects his community. And when a mole is most certain he is right, let him feel most certain that he is wrong!'

Tryfan smiled again, a little ruefully, and there were moles aplenty who smiled as well, for they knew well how often they had put themselves first before others.

'A community is a thing where truth is told, not lies, for a mole who lives by lies, or is forced to do so by the lie of others, is a mole not living in reality at all. As for what truth is, a hard thing that! Wiser moles than I may put it better than I can, but the mole who truly knows himself knows it best of all! Boswell spoke the truest things I heard, but even he was sometimes wrong! Which, being so, the more certain you feel when you speak the more wary of yourself you should be, and the more moles whom you love and trust say you are wrong the more you should doubt you are right. Where communities speak without fear then common sense is common!

'But this being so, a community founded on truth is hard for moles to live in, especially at first, because it challenges everymole within with the truth. It does get easier, as many of us know, until it becomes the only way.

'But we cannot expect all moles at all times to be at one with each other. Everything but! A community argues. But if it argues with love and speaks with trust and everymole learns to listen hard, then however difficult things are it has the consolation of knowing that it cannot stray from the path towards true community. Even so, a community may try often to flee from itself but always a majority of its members know it has nowhere else to go and so its moles share a willingness to come home and start again. Often it may do this, and it is right that it should. Such conflicts and their peaceful resolution are the best signs that it is succeeding.

'I have observed that at some time or another a community seeks to place one or a few in command of itself, and thus to avoid having to make decisions for itself. Most systems of the Stone had elders in the old days; all systems of the Word have eldrene and guardmoles.

'The arguments in favour of leaders of one kind or another seem so overwhelming, and the desire of moles to abrogate responsibility for them is so great, that few communities escape them. Moles are so used to their systems having leaders that they cannot imagine being without them, because they have never experienced it. They rightly think that only confusion would result. I said *rightly*. What they do not know, and do not want to risk discovering, is that true community can only lie beyond such confusion, wherein each mole is valued for what he is and discovers his own pride. We here have suffered such confusion. Had it not been for Henbane's edict to outcast moles here I doubt that any of us would have discovered the community we had, or found the courage to make it. So, unknowingly, does darkness lead to light. There were those who complained that I was not leading you in spring. But the Rule you helped me make forbids that anymole should ever lead. A community that goes that way is a community afraid of itself and one that destroys its core, which is that each individual has something special to give and must be heard. Moles do not like to be leaderless, but so they must be if they are to be a true community.

'But if some moles seem to have greater gifts than others then the community must not let them forget that whatever pride or power they feel thereby is nothing against the honour and responsibility they gain from serving those they love. But in truth nomole may judge if one is more gifted than another, or gives more to all. In true community all help the others to give equally by learning to value what others give before valuing themselves.

'And for this trouble what does a mole get? Safety to be himself and to trust others to let him be. Comfort, when his way seems lost. Joy. Love. A certain hard-won freedom. A sense of pride.

'When a mole grows old in body, and feels weary, and he asks himself what it was he lived that was good, why 'tis of other moles he thinks, of things he shared, of moments when he was accepted as himself and others loved him. Think on your own lives, remember what moments you most value, and you will find that so it was and is for you. It is most strange but in true community a mole is most himself.

'But it is not easy, and a community must forever be on its guard against excluding others. I was born of the Stone, and I am a scribemole in its service, but I no longer believe it is the only way . . .' There was a murmuring of surprise at this, and even doubt, and Tryfan had to raise his voice to quell it as he continued: 'If it was the only way then how can it be that I have met so many moles reared of the Word, some of whom are here now, I think, who have taught me so much? Marram, Sleekit, Dodder, Skint, Smithills, and many more.

'Most may now espouse the Stone yet all were taught the Word when young. No, no, the Stone is but one way, and a community, whatever faith it has, will accept all others to its heart even if *they* believe *their* way is the only one. Aye, even then. A heart is changed by example not by words. How can an example be known if it is not experienced and shared? By opening itself to others always and for all time a community exemplifies itself to others. Thereby as well it grows and changes all the time, as a set of tunnels changes with each new occupant. How great the noise he makes! How little the change he truly makes! But give him no freedom and send him away, then how dead those tunnels will soon be!

'Some say that the great tunnels of Uffington were destroyed by the grikes. But I, who was there, and who was taught by Boswell himself, say this: Uffington had died long before that. So had Duncton. So, I believe, has Whern.'

Tryfan was silent for a time and the moles stared at him, and at each other, and muttered among themselves or were silent, according to their understanding and interest in what he was saying. He moved forward a little, perhaps to bring their attention once more to the text he had scribed.

'But, of course, a community is only as good as the individuals of which it is made, and they are fallible. They *are* fallible.

'I was reared in this system by Rebecca, and by my father Bracken. They were near the end of their lives when I was born and I now think I gained by that, though before this summer I had not thought much of it at all. Indeed, I did not think of such things until Feverfew came among us by the light of the Stone Mole's star and gave birth to Beechen, who was sent to us by Boswell.

'So Beechen, too, had a mother, as I had, who was older, and though I am not his father it was that responsibility I took. This summer you have shared that responsibility as well, and in your different ways given much to Beechen.

'What you gave to him he has shared with me and so helped me understand much that I did not before and so enabled me to scribe a Rule. This text you see here is that Rule, and each of you has helped make it, each one of you.'

Tryfan said these last few words slowly, staring around at the moles, and then back at the text.

'I said a community is only as good as its members, and this is so for ours as well. We are, most of us, old now, and all near our time. Many who saw Beechen's birth are no longer with us. Many here will not survive to Longest Night. I think a time of change is coming to us once again and that our community is imperilled as it often has been in the past. In its present form it may soon die. Oh yes, it may. Whatmole here has not sensed the darkness coming? Whatmole did not shudder when he heard of what happened to Marram and Sorrel at the cross-under?

'So now, our Rule. Well, such a thing is nothing new, Uffington lived by one for many centuries, which helped the scribemoles conduct their lives of learning and worship, but it was large and complex. I believe that Whern has a Rule as well, though it is secret and unspoken, and in the paws of the Master or Mistress of that place, and a group of elders which they call the Keepers.

'The Dunbar moles, living in the Wen, had a Rule as well, scribed by the great Dunbar himself, and it is one I know. I kenned it in the Wen, and when we came back here Spindle copied it down from memory. I have referred to it often in making this Rule and have been much struck by the many wisdoms you have shared with Beechen this summer which Dunbar also knew.

'But in one important way is our Rule different from his. His was written for the Stone, whose rituals and liturgies help make up its form. A mole might think that the Dunbar moles appointed the Stone as leader instead of a mole, but a leader just the same. That community died. Moles forgot to think for themselves. Our Rule assumes the Stone wishes each one of us to be himself before it, not a pretence of what he ought to be.

'Nor does our Rule desire moles to be any more humble or reverent before the Stone than they would be towards themselves and each other. The Stone is what they are when they are part of a community striving to be its very best.

'As for such Rules as those of Uffington or Whern, the Rule we have made is very different because its purpose is different. It is to help individuals join community and keep their commitment to it, and bring themselves nearer to it. It is not a set of rules to be used in judgement if they are transgressed.

'From this you may guess that our Rule is positive. It is as my mother Rebecca was: positive. She was what Dunbar would have called "a mole of the rising sun". She preferred to lead a mole towards what he could do, rather than admonish him for what he could or had not done. Moles of the rising sun believe that moles so reared learn humbly to love themselves and so find their lives filled with daily wonder at what they are; such moles are at the very heart of true community.

'Then, too, our Rule is concerned with the reality that is now and here about us and not with a world of perfection yet to come. This is why lies and deceit do not help a mole but hinder him and the community in which he lives for they mask the reality all need to know.

'But to know reality, and see it plain, requires discipline, and that *is* hard. Again and again you have in different ways told Beechen that a mole's life will be hard. Lying simply seeks to ease the pain.

'Our Rule helps a mole with that by showing that hard though the truth may be, hard though right vision may be, lies and obscurity are finally harder. They are a confusion a mole makes about himself and become ever harder to escape.

'Yet what of change? How do we escape from confusion? How do we learn to give all we are to the communities in which we live? The Word teaches that a mole must Atone for both what he has done wrong and what he has not done right before he is judged worthy. In short, the Word punishes mole for being mole and says that only through punishment and suffering can he be saved.

'Our Rule does not point a mole that way, and nor do I believe it is the Stone's will that it should. Rather we say that as nomole is perfect so all moles will, to some degree,

301

carry their confusion with them. That is their reality. But the way to help them escape it is not through punishing them, which merely confirms that a mole is wrong, but by teaching them that at any moment, any time, they can turn back towards the rising sun, which is the light of the Stone, and see that by reaching out towards it they can cast off their confusion in a moment. In a moment.

'This turning to reality – which may take years to come, or but a moment – is what the scribemoles of old called grace. But we have almost lost the word, for its meaning lies in wonder and belief and those we have almost lost. Grace is not a state that stays. As it comes it may go and a mole will not find it again unless with patience and with discipline he turns his snout towards the rising sun once more.

'Yet I know that many of you have been so graced here in Duncton, and often without trying, and without Atonement or austerity or punishment. You have turned a corner, seen the sun with truth, with your eyes open wide, and left your confusion behind you. How can this be, that the diseased and outcast have found grace, and in throwing off confusion have begun to find community? And more than that, though none of us is perfect and all of us slide back into confusion, how have we been able to give Beechen so much to take from here?

'This answer lies, too, in the Rule you have helped me scribe. Many of us came here angry, and full of dark purpose, and full of hatred. We loved not our neighbours, we trusted not our friends. We hurt others because we were hurt ourselves. So did this outcast community begin, and in its painful birth did many die. Yet, slowly, left alone with but the Silence of the Stone to heed and the wise cycle of the seasons to attend and listen to, which shows us daily what we creatures are and were and will become, which is not much unless it is seen for what it is, which is everything . . . we have each stopped striving for what we could not have. Some have stopped complaining, some have found the peace that lies in the simple burrow, some have found that by listening more they need say less; and many have learned to raise their snouts from their own miserable concerns and see the eastern sun rise each day and know the joy of it, and feel their own true worth.

'So, gradually, within ourselves and learning from one another, we have ceased to strive so hard for what we did not really need, and found how greatly wormful is the soil which the Stone has given us. Then, getting older, growing slower, striving even less, we have turned the corner and seen the sun.

'The Rule you helped me make tells much of this. Its way is finally not hard but only seems so when moles are lost in their own confusion. Yet how slowly do we learn not to be afraid of what we are, or ashamed, or sad. We *are*, as the rising sun *is*, and because the Stone knows us, and knows what we truly are, we can accept ourselves without deceit. There is great peace in that and it is the Stone's great gift to us, and somewhere in the whole acceptance of it we shall discover Silence.

'All these things, and the way towards them, are in our Rule. We know them, we have learned them, and we have given them as best we can to Beechen. They are the simple things we know which the striving of our lives has made us too often forget.

'Moledom has forgotten them. And now its longest winter's night is coming and it is ill-prepared. All our lives it has been coming, all our lives.

'Yet there is hope. As if it knew that such a time would come, our forebears, of which we are but the living part, made a myth of the Stone Mole, and said he would be a saviour. We thought he would be more than us, stronger, wiser, better, more powerful.

'But he has come and he is but ordinary mole. He is like us. Outcast here like us. Flesh and blood like us. Fallible like us. Afraid like us. Boswell, White Mole, bearer of the Seventh Stillstone which is of Silence, sent his son as Stone Mole and honoured Duncton with his rearing. For better and for worse we have done the best we can and now, on the eve of the long winter to come, we must do that which is the last thing of our Rule. We must trust ourselves to let him go.

'To make him free to leave us, to make him know we trust him to go forth, is the last and greatest gift we have. As in the nature of our welcome does our community grow stronger when new moles come, so in the nature of its farewell is that strength preserved. Our rite of Midsummer has helped prepare us for his parting, and him as well. Now must the parting be. It is a moment all moles who have pups must learn to face with the same trust with which they must learn to face the rising sun.

'Beechen is our youth, his is the light of the rising sun we saw, he is the love we gave without asking for any in return, he is the gift we give to others. As our communities gave to us so we gave on to him; and if, as I believe, he is the Stone Mole Boswell sent, then he will pass on the spirit of the Rule we made to allmole in its time of greatest need.

'His teachings, which are our wisdom, shall light moles through the great darkness. He is not more than us, but us ourselves. But as we are weak, so shall he be, and if our strength was not enough in him so then shall darkness prevail.

'I pray that we have done enough and that Boswell's trust in us shall be fulfilled.

'As for this Rule, which is but a dull echo perhaps of what we have put in Beechen's heart, it might with advantage be placed where the great scribe and cleric Spindle hid the texts we made when he was alive.

'If the Stone wills it, and moledom survives the deep winter of doubt and dark sound, others will one day find them. It was my brother Comfrey's greatest wish that pups, or the pups of the pups, of those survivors who escaped Duncton Wood would one day return. I pray they will, and find this Rule, and ken it well, and having kenned it put it to one side and through living by its tenets discover things we knew.

'Where that place is I do not know, but Mayweed does.

304

He shall choose a mole to take the Rule with him, that another knows as well.'

'Practical patriarch, I have chosen already!' said Mayweed with a grin. 'Bailey is the mole.'

'But . . .' Bailey began to protest.

'Oh but "but" Bailey *is*! Do we not all agree?' A rumble of good-humoured 'Ayes' and 'Yeses' and general affirmation greeted this. 'The community decides, the Sirs and Madams acting all as one! Incredible. Tryfan's optimism already proven justified. Relief!'

Tryfan smiled and held up his paw.

'But one more thing I shall say, and if I sound too much like a self-appointed leader then gainsay me at once. Let Beechen leave us tomorrow. Let good Mayweed guide him, and Sleekit go with them. With the Stone's help they shall be enough to get him safely out of Duncton.

'We who remain shall have a new task now: to face with all the will at our command as a community the trials that lie ahead. Once before when the grikes came here I fled, and now I wish I had not. The whole burden of our Rule is that nomole gains by fleeing darkness.

'When I returned here with Spindle I told him that I would not leave again. Nor shall I now, though everything suggests that the grikes may soon be upon us once again. This shall be our task, our greatest task, perhaps, old though we are. We shall face the moles of the Word as if they were our returning kin. We shall not strike them. We shall not hurt them. We shall show them what we are, which is a community that strives for nothing other than what it can best make within itself of love and of the Stone.

'We shall feel fear. We may be hurt. We may well be killed. But if anymole here can tell us now a better way than just to be what we are when they come then I would know it.'

Nomole spoke, or said that Tryfan spoke anything other than what they felt, fearful though it was.

'Tomorrow then, at dawn, with the rising sun, we shall accompany Beechen to the south-east slopes and from there, going the dangerous way by the top of the roaring owl way, which Mayweed knows, he and Sleekit shall lead Beechen from us. After that the Stone will guide them all.'

Tryfan said no more in general, but stanced down, took food, and talked with the many who came to him in the long evening and night that followed. Throughout that time Beechen was with him, and Feverfew, and many came and touched them.

Until, when it was still dark with night, the moles made their slow way through the wood, some by tunnel and some by surface until they reached the high edge of the wood that faces to the east and south.

The roaring owl way was quiet, with just an occasional gaze coming along its length. Wind flurried at the undergrowth, beech leaves scattered down, and just before dawn, when the sky was beginning to lighten, Mayweed and Bailey returned from the Ancient System where they had hidden the text.

They went to where Beechen was stanced, with Tryfan and Feverfew at either flank, and joined them. Then, too, Skint and Smithills, Sleekit and Marram as well, and moles saw that all the seven guardians of Beechen, who had gathered at his birth by the Duncton Stone, were gathered round him once again.

In the east the sun began to rise and all moledom lightened towards dawn.

'In the days of Uffington,' said Tryfan then, 'it was the tradition in the Holy Burrows for a blessing to be said when a scribemole set off on a journey into moledom. So shall I say that ancient blessing of the Stone now for Beechen, and say it with the love we all here feel.'

He turned to Beechen and placed his great paw on the younger mole's right paw and in the whispering silence of the dawn spoke these words of the Stone:

> *May the peace of your power*
> *Encompass him, going and returning;*

May the peace of the White Mole be his in the travel.
And may he return home safeguarded.'

As the moles said their last farewells to Beechen the slopes
below them began to glisten with the sun in the morning
dew.

Each of the guardians, but for Mayweed and Sleekit
who were going with him, said goodbye. Then Beechen
turned to Tryfan and Feverfew and spoke privately to
them. Old Tryfan embraced him fiercely, his great body
and rough paws clasped tight over Beechen's shoulders,
then Feverfew spoke softly to him last of all and told him
never to forget he was 'muche-luved, sow muche-luved'.

Then Mayweed and Sleekit led him away, with Bailey to
accompany them a little downslope. The sun's rays grew
ever brighter as they went and the watching moles screwed
their eyes up to see them go. But when the sun had risen
high enough for them to look again, Sleekit and Mayweed
and Beechen had gone.

All they could see was the roaring owl way, and the
dewy tracks of moles in the Pasture grass. And there,
stanced still, was Bailey, his right paw raised towards the
slopes below.

Behind them the wind flurried at the great trees, a few
leaves scattered across the slopes, and one by one
Duncton's community turned back into the wood, to seek
out its tunnels and prepare itself for its time of great trial.

Chapter Seventeen

Yet summer still lingered on in Siabod, the first place from which moles might have expected it to be gone. But there it was, with fair winds and bright skies over the mountains, as if to bring a few extra days of ease to a place that might most need their memory in the times of trial to come.

The Siabod moles, scarcely believing their good luck, were in expansive mood and garrulous as they stanced about in groups at the entrances to the tunnels of high Siabod itself and enjoyed every last moment of the summer's end.

Their leader, great Alder from the south, had good reason to be pleased. He had chosen this time as one for a gathering of all the rebel leaders of the Welsh Marches, knowing he took the risk that if the weather was hard fewer moles might come and an opportunity for uniting the rebel Welsh forces before the winter years would be lost. But the Stone granted fair weather, and over twenty leaders had come to represent systems large and small all along the Marches, each with a story to tell, each with hopes to share, each looking for support.

The high Siabod range of mountains and the neighbouring Carneddau to the north shone with autumnal colour as the persistent sun caught the green lichens on long-exposed rocks, and highlighted the mauve rafts of heather across the moor. Its rays turned black peat hags into rich dark brown, and even the sheer rock faces beyond moles' reach, wet from earlier rains, reflected the bright sky.

The idea for the conclave had been wily Caradoc's, who had trekked the rough way over from his lonely stronghold of Caer Caradoc in the centre of the Marches in August to persuade Alder that such a meeting was needed.

'Ever since June I've been on my paws, trekking first to the south and then back up to the north and now here I am,' he had explained. 'I've talked to all the rebel leaders you know and some younger ones you don't, and had word passed on from some I've never met at all. They need to come together soon, Alder, or they'll go back to their retreats in despair and be lost to our cause.

'They're isolated, they're losing hope, and many have but few moles left who'll follow them. They know that the grikes along the eastern front under Ginnell have not weakened, and still occupy the valleys below Siabod itself.

'Only two things keep them going now. One is knowledge of what you've done in Siabod, and how you've taken back the higher tunnels from the grikes so that there are still moles who watch over the holy Stones of Siabod. Pride in your achievement here makes them battle on to defend their own systems.

'The other is the whisper – no more than a rumoured hope for most – that started when the eastern star shone in spring and moles said that the Stone Mole had come.'

Alder, a great strong mole, his body creased with effort and worry, but his muscles good and spare and his fur still healthy, eased his paws along the ground. Caradoc was the mole who had greeted him so many years before when he and Marram, sent from Duncton by Tryfan, had first arrived at the Marches, and he was a mole he had come to love and respect.

Alder knew that sometimes in the dark, long moleyears of struggle in the harsh Siabod wastes the moles he led had lost touch with the very thing they fought for, which was their belief in the Stone. But there was always one mole he could rely on who would remind everymole he met of why it was they fought, and that was Caradoc.

'Mad Caradoc' some called him, 'obsessive' was the word that others used. But that was behind his back or when he was off on one of his lonely treks to seek out some isolated system of moles and bring to them inspiration of the Stone, and tell them that one day peace would come and the Stone's Silence be known. Given half a chance he would tell them too of Caer Caradoc, and how one day, within his lifetime if the Stone spared him long enough, the Stone Mole would come even there, and the once-great-system, which like Siabod was one of the ancient Seven, would be reborn.

Alder was a fighting mole, reared to the Word, trained as a guardmole, but converted to the Stone by Tryfan who rightly saw in him the makings of a great commander. That had been a long time ago, and since then his greatest friend Marram had turned his back on fighting and on Siabod, and had gone south-east once more because he believed the Stone Mole was coming.

Nothing happened in the winter years that followed but then, just when everymole was giving up hope of any sign at all, that strange star shone again in the spring.

'I tell you, mole, he is in moledom now,' Caradoc had told him then. 'He *is* here. If we can hold on to our faith he will send guidance to us and we shall have something great to fight for. You'll see!'

Caradoc had not been the only one affected by the eastern star. Old Glyder, for long the leader of Siabod, had finally turned his snout towards great Tryfan itself and gone to 'touch the Stones' which Alder knew was a Siabod mole's proud way of saying 'to die'. He had been the last of the four sons born to Rebecca of Duncton in the far-off days when she had come to Siabod, and apart from Gowre, the son of one of his dead brothers, no other issue remained, all killed in the long years of fighting the grikes.

But Gowre, born the previous spring, had matured well and proved a good fighter, and before he left Glyder entrusted this last descendant of Rebecca's offspring to Alder's care and the lad had done well and in time might gain the respect of the Siabod moles. Alder hoped it might be so, for he had grown tired this summer past and was ready to pass on the responsibilities of leadership in Siabod to a younger mole.

Then Caradoc had returned in August and repeated his hopes of the Stone Mole, and Alder had stared at him and heard out his passionate words, half doubtful yet half in wonder, and grateful that the Stone made such moles as Caradoc to remind others of what truly mattered.

'Send out messengers, Alder, summon a conclave of leaders such as they had in the old days,' urged Caradoc. 'It'll give your younger moles useful journeys to make and I'll guide and watch over them. Ordain that the meeting should be at the end of September before the weather worsens. And make it here, where those who come can see the Stones that rise on Tryfan. You'll not regret it. . . .'

Alder had finally raised his paw with a laugh to stop him saying more and said, 'You're right, Caradoc, I had something like it in mind myself, though on a smaller scale. But yes . . . there's sense in such a meeting, for we have no knowledge of what strengths and weaknesses we have, and how many moles we can muster to our cause all at once should we ever need to do so. I believe that one day we shall have to do more than harry the grikes in the valleys and defend our strongholds. Just doing that means we're the ones who gradually weaken and lose faith, while the grikes led by Ginnell sit and watch us die. He's a clever fighter that one.'

'He was well trained by Wrekin who was a great general,' said Caradoc. 'It was a pity he was on the wrong side. And now Ginnell. . . .'

'Aye, but there'll be a way. Two can play at waiting.'

'What is it you wait for, mole?' said Caradoc. 'For the Stone itself to come trekking to your burrow and tell you to get moles off their rumps and invade the east? Eh?'

Alder laughed again and nudged a thin Siabod worm towards Caradoc.

'If we had advanced at any time this past cycle of seasons, and if we did so now, we would be defeated. Why, as you've implied yourself, we're out of touch with each other and unable to do more than defend the ground each of us knows best. East of the Marches is all grike-held, or was according to the last prisoners we took. I know the grikes, I was a guardmole myself and I know our rebel moles are no match for their order and discipline. At the moment we're good only for raiding and harrying.

'No, Caradoc, I'll not lead moles I love to their deaths. We need something to turn us into a force the grikes will respect, but Stone knows what it will need to be, for I don't. A different and younger leader now than myself, that's for sure! A better cause, too, than mere hatred of the grikes and Welsh pride in defence of holy Stones. I hoped that when the Stone Mole rumour started in spring that something more would come of it, and it might guide me. But it's faltered, hasn't it? Our moles' hopes were raised but to no purpose. Moles can't live on hope, and nor can their fighting spirit. So we're waiting, Caradoc. Can *you* tell me for what?'

'Aye, I can. 'Tis the Stone Mole'll come, as I've always said he would. He'll be the one. . . .'

'But he's not come, Caradoc,' said Alder mercilessly. 'The reality is he's just a dream moles speak of – and nomole better at that than yourself! I believe you, but others . . . no, you'll have to produce more than words if ever we have a conclave here that's to do more than argue with itself.'

To Alder's astonishment Caradoc had stared at him blankly for a moment or two, tried to say something, been unable to find the words, and then lowered his snout and seemed about to cry.

'Why, mole . . .' began Alder, glad they were alone, for the Siabod moles did not easily understand tears unless they were of rage. 'What is it? I didn't mean. . . .'

'Yes, you did and I'm not blaming you!' said Caradoc weakly. 'It's been hard, see, keeping my faith: hard and lonely. But something happened in June which I've not told you about which has made it harder still. Have you noticed a difference in me since you last saw me? Eh? Look at me and tell me.'

312

Few moles were better at judging others than Alder. Leaders must know how to choose the moles that follow their orders, great leaders must know best of all: as for leaders of Welsh moles, where everymole fancies himself at least equal to every other and is proud of his independence, why, to lead *them* a mole must be a fine judge of character indeed.

Alder was such a mole and looked at the mole he knew so well and the question forced him to put into words what he had until then only suspected might be true. But, but. . . .

'Go on, Alder, I've known you longer than any here. There's never been a lie or untruth between us, nor ever will be so far as I'm concerned. What do you see has changed?'

'But Caradoc. . . .'

'Speak your heart to me, Alder. It's all I ever want to hear.'

So Alder looked at him and knew what it was he saw.

'When I first met you by the Stones of Caer Caradoc I thought that never in all my life had I seen a mole so alone. In that high place, the Stones all about you, and two great southern guardmoles, intent on murder for all you knew, came along. But there you bravely stanced and faced us. Your strength of purpose has never failed in all the time since then, and your inspiration has kept our snouts pointing towards the Stone. But since June you seem. . . .'

'Yes. . . ?' whispered Caradoc.

'There has been a change. You've seemed even more desolate, even more alone. That's it, isn't it? You've been more alone.'

Caradoc's eyes filled with tears as he nodded his head mutely, and when Alder reached out a great paw to him, his shoulders hunched and he began to sob.

'Something happened, something I have dared tell nomole, see? I know that many laugh at me and think my head's soft with living up at Caer Caradoc with neither mate nor mole; they've heard me say too many times that the Stone Mole will come even to that place and that one day . . . one day. . . .'

Then, just as Mistle of Avebury had unveiled her heart to Cuddesdon that summer, and told of moles who had touched the Stone in June with her and called out for her name, so Caradoc told the same story to Alder.

'I felt the Stone Mole near,' he concluded, 'and he needed us, Alder, all of us. He needed us so much. But one by one we did not have the strength to keep touching the Stone, like when you're a pup and another stronger than yourself is winning the fight and you have to give in . . . Well, mole, I gave in, I let go the Stone and I felt I was losing those others I fancied were doing the same. Since then, all summer, I've trekked the Marches seeking them and I shall feel lost until I find them.' He paused, stared intently at his friend, and said, 'Well, Alder, you tell me what moles would say if I told them of it as I've told you today.'

'They'd say Caradoc had finally gone mad,' said Alder evenly.

'They would. And what do you say?'

Alder hesitated, for he sensed that Caradoc's self-respect, if not something more serious, depended not just on what he said but how he said it. He looked away and over the mountains. What could he say? The mole was sincere, he believed what he had said. He . . . and then, quite impulsively, Alder turned back to him.

'Old friend, I believe what you say is true. I believe that the Stone Mole will come. We shall have the conclave that you suggest, and we shall hope that this elusive Stone Mole shall send a sign that will give me the strength and authority to inspire the moles of the Welsh Marches to remain steadfast through the coming winter years.'

Caradoc stared at him in gratitude.

'You really believe?' he said in wonder. 'You know, Alder, what happened left me with a sense of loss greater even than that I felt when father died and left me as the only mole at deserted Caer Caradoc. It is a kind of ache in the heart and I know I shall not rest until I find those moles or the Stone Mole comes. I shall not rest. . . .'

For a long time after he had finished Alder gazed on the strange mole as he fretted restlessly at the ground. Caradoc was tired, more tired than a mole should be, and the odd story he had told seemed to have sapped his last reserves of energy.

'You shall sleep,' said Alder gently. 'And when you have recovered I shall summon as many young moles here as you think we need and you shall send them north and south, the full length of the Marches, and tell them what leaders to summon here. It shall all be as you wish.

'But more than that, we shall ask for moles to volunteer to cross the grikes' lines to the east and see what we can find out about this Stone Mole to guide our conclave. It is a task we can entrust to the late Fach's last-born son, Gowre. Now sleep, Caradoc, and rest.' And as Alder's quick and orderly mind worked on the organisation of the conclave Caradoc nodded his head silently, turned back into the Siabod tunnels, found a place to lay his weary body and, with thanks to the Stone for Alder's faith in him, he fell asleep.

The conclave had finally gathered at Siabod in the last days of September as they had planned. The moles met in one of the high slate-walled chambers for which Siabod is famed. Those great warriors were dwarfed by the bleak, black verticals of the walls, and the drip-drip of water echoing down tunnels which slope off into freezing darkness.

Even on a sunny day there are many places where the light is grey and cold. Strangely, it is when there is snow and ice on the surface that the light in those chambers is brightest, and it glistens and shines on the water that seems forever to run on the slate at the entrances.

The windsound of the high Siabod is famous, too, for it echoes and re-echoes down the grim tunnels, and if for a moment it seems lost beyond recall it is because in the unexplored darkness of that place it has come to a void, or a corner which nomole knows or will ever see, pausing there before striking a wall once more, somewhere beyond, and it comes back hollower, more distant, more distorted than before.

An awesome place Siabod, yet quite without the sense of evil and dark sound that we who have travelled with the Duncton moles know unpleasantly well from the tunnels of Whern, and the sterile deeps of the inhospitable Wen. Nor was the place as gloomy as it might have been, since after such a warm summer and with the weather remaining fine, the tunnel air was warm and sunlight filtered in. But still, and forever, the water dripped, and there were darkening falls beyond clefts in the slate from which chill draughts sometimes blew and where nomole among those gathered, brave though they were, would ever venture near.

Alder, with an astute sense of history and occasion, insisted that many of the younger Siabod moles came to the conclave chamber as spectators, leaving a few trusty guards across the lower slopes and beyond.

As Alder took his place and looked about him he saw that the faces had changed a good deal since he had first met the moles of the Marches and Siabod. At the conclave of Capel Garmon years before, moles like Cwmifor, Manod and Wentnor of Mynd had been at the fore, but they were now dead or in retreat beyond recall. So too was the great Clogwyn of Y Wyddfa, whose acknowledgment of Alder's skills had marked his general acceptance in Siabod. Sadly, many of the younger moles who would have been leaders now if they had survived the fighting against the grikes were gone as well: Lymore, Blaen-cwm, and, most tragic of all, the great strategist Stitt of Ratlinghope.

Yet, as the present leaders had arrived, Alder took comfort in the survival of some great moles, and the emergence of new ones. From that original meeting at

316

Garmon, two at least were still strong enough to hold their own in any company: Clun, a mole of stocky physique and with a ribald sense of humour, and Gaelri, one of the Pentre siblings and an able tactician who time and again in recent years had made such good use of limited numbers against greater odds.

While a third now towered above them all, in physique, intelligence and the sheer power to lead: Troedfach of Tyn-y-Bedw. As much as moles like those deferred to anymole along the Marches they deferred to him. He had come out of the obscurity of his small system in the south-western interior, taken over the gap left by the death of Blaen-cwm, and now commanded the extensive and vital network of systems that lay south of Caer Caradoc.

Only Alder himself was regarded more highly, for, alone of anymole in Wales, he had led his moles to reoccupy a position taken by the grikes and kept them at bay; and more than that he had done it in fabled Siabod – and he not a Siabod mole at all!

There were, along with these familiar leaders, a number who had come up from the south and who led smaller systems in an area where the grikes were, perhaps fortunately, weak. Of these moles Alder was struck most by Gareg of Merthyr, a clever-looking mole with the same natural authority that Siabod's Gowre had and, like him, still young enough to learn.

Alder heard that he had travelled the Marches in search of Troedfach while still barely more than a pup, and that great mole had trained him well and sent him south once more to gain experience.

Meanwhile, Alder and Caradoc had hoped that the small party sent out under Gowre's leadership would have been back by the time the conclave began, and able to give information about the disposition of the grikes, but it had not yet returned. The conclave had to begin without Gowre and the talk to be wild and only locally informed. Inevitably it had been Troedfach who drew a mole's attention, with his rough black fur that matched his

317

growling voice, and his huge paws and shoulders that were scarred from a thousand fights. Grike prisoners had reported that his name, along with those of Alder and Caradoc, were the only three that the grikes knew, and they spoke them with respect and fear.

Troedfach's brooding presence had dominated the conclave from the start, and at first he had argued for attack before winter, believing that a hard push east could make the grikes turn tail and run.

It was a popular stance, and one many favoured, and Alder wished he had had an ally such as Stitt had once been, knowledgeable of strategy and appreciative of the fact that once such moles as these were off their own ground and in the lower vales to the east against an organised foe they might fare badly indeed.

But Troedfach, for all his belligerence, listened to argument as well, and was generally inclined to accept Alder's advice before his own instincts. In his heart Alder knew that if Troedfach ever wanted to he could lead a great strike against the moles of the Word, whatever Alder said.

Alder was therefore relieved when on the second day of the conclave Gareg of Merthyr was prepared boldly to disagree with Troedfach and argue for caution.

'It's not for lack of courage or will,' he had said, 'but knowledge of what we can do and can't. If I'm to rouse the moles around Merthyr then I'll need to do more than tell them how boldly we talked in Siabod!'

Troedfach had nodded his head in rueful acknowledgment of the younger mole's concern and agreed that too much was still unknown for any proper strategy, though he hoped there wasn't a mole in the conclave who doubted for one minute what he was *inclined* to do!

So the debate went to and fro on the second day, and as the afternoon wore on Alder and Caradoc began to despair that anything would come of it for the future, unless it be simply that these moles who so rarely met together had got to know one another better and seen Siabod.

318

But then suddenly a change came over the meeting as a whisper went about, an exciting rumour, and moles paused and looked at each other. One of the Siabod moles who was acting as a watcher came apologetically into the meeting, went to Alder, spoke softly to him and the great mole went outside.

As he did so the rumour gained voice. ' 'Tis Gowre! He's back! And all the others who went with him but one. No, no, he would not say a thing until he spoke to Alder. . . .'

The conclave was not kept in suspense for long. Alder returned with young Gowre at his flank, and others of his small party. All looked travel-worn and weary and several, including Gowre himself, bore signs of fighting and stress, but there they were, safe enough and ready to report.

Silence fell as Alder said, 'You know well of the mission on which Gowre was sent and you see him here now as I do, returned home safeguarded.'

'By the Stone's grace!' said Troedfach.

'Aye, and his own exertions!' said another. There was rough and respectful laughter among the moles, for not one of them had not some scar or other to show for grike attentions, and all of them knew the danger Gowre must have run.

As they looked at him now they saw that his expression, and those of his companions, was grim. There was defiance in their eyes that put foreboding in a wise mole's heart for it meant that where they had been they had seen trouble, and it was coming this way.

'What he has told me briefly is of great importance to our debate, and tired though he is it is right he tells you himself . . .' A ripple of excitement went among the moles, and then a hush fell as Gowre moved forward to address them. He was a powerful mole of typical Siabod physique, with a proud snout and intelligent eyes. Those who, like Caradoc, knew him before that day saw the mission Alder had wisely sent him on had put a certain age into his face, and a certain necessary strength into his talons.

Gowre, evidently tired, did not waste words, or spend time reporting how he discovered what he had. The details could wait, and would make a good tale everymole would hear in time, but meanwhile the facts were clear enough.

'Ginnell is still in charge of the grikes, and his base is where it was before – opposite Troedfach's position south of Caradoc,' said Gowre. 'But for the time being there won't be any advance or change of position – Ginnell has gone some way north.'

'Do you know why, mole?' asked Troedfach.

'Yes, we know why well enough,' said Gowre immediately, looking round at his companions who nodded their agreement, 'or shall I say we know what the grikes know. There have been great changes and all the grikes are talking of them, for in June Whern got itself a new Master of the Word. . . .'

There was a flurry of surprise and talk at this news, for Gowre's brief had been merely to find the strength of the enemy, not to investigate power at the very heart of the Word's base. He had done well.

'Henbane is deposed. Her son Lucerne has taken her place. We understand he is heading south as his mother did before him, and that a new imposition of the Word is to come. Ginnell has been summoned north to meet this mole Lucerne, and we may presume that when he has his commands they will not include a withdrawal from these parts. We know little of the new Master except that he is greatly feared. That, in essence, is what we discovered, and. . . .'

'And your source is a good one, mole?' interrupted Clun.

Gowre looked at the mid-Wales leader wearily but with confidence. There was a flicker of distaste over his face as he said, 'The best. The Stone was with us. We intercepted a sideem of the Word, and one who has met this Lucerne.'

'You took him prisoner?' asked Troedfach.

'We *had* him prisoner,' said Gowre. 'He killed one of our number, and unfortunately was killed in his escape.

But we got enough out of him before he died to make us think that we who fight for the Stone against the Word still have much to fear, but even more reason to fight on. . . .'

But one other thing Gowre's mission had made plain: Siabod was not central enough to be the base for any counter-offensive against the grikes. If the grikes could be pushed back from the valleys to its east, and the line along the Marches fully established then not only would Siabod be more secure but the centre of their campaign could more safely move east.

'Aye, it's what some of us have . . .' began Gareg impetuously, before Troedfach raised a paw.

There was silence.

'What Gareg was about to say is something older heads than his have said before,' growled the great mole, 'and they were right as I believe he is.' He chuckled and said, 'Go on, mole, I'll not take your moment from you.'

'Caer Caradoc is the natural centre,' said Gareg eagerly, 'and we in the southern Marches never forget that it was once one of the ancient Seven which in their wisdom the scribemoles of Uffington established along these parts. We all know it's deserted and poor of worm, and nomole, not even the grikes, seem to think much of it. But that's because they have their eyes on Siabod and we have our eyes only on defence. If we are ever to move eastward then no better base could be found.'

'I agree,' said Gowre, warming immediately to Gareg, 'for we ourselves ventured up there while we were away. It *should* be occupied again.'

'And soon, too, while the weather's dry. The place'll be hard as great Wyddfa itself to conquer if bad weather comes and we are on top!' said Troedfach. A new excitement and purpose had come to the conclave and they seemed all to want to talk at once.

If there had been doubt before about whether or not to advance east it was laid to rest now. All agreed that by the time they got their forces moving, so much might have changed in moledom that they would be moving too much into the unknown.

Better to stay in their known positions, to establish even better defences, and concentrate their energies immediately on ousting the grikes from the valleys east of Siabod. While some said that Caer Caradoc could be quietly occupied by contingents of moles from Troedfach's powerful territory to the south, and Gaelri's to the north.

'And what . . .' began Alder, when everymole had had his say and all had agreed that the second day had been a useful one and that on the morrow the details were all that needed to be worked out . . . 'what has our friend Caradoc to say about all of this?' There was a general and affectionate laugh, for Alder was not the only one who had noticed Caradoc listening with his eyes half closed to the mounting tide of the debate suggesting that the system he had patrolled so long alone should suddenly be re-occupied.

'What do I think? I think the Stone will guide us well but I fear the way will yet be hard. You all know I have always believed that one day moles will come back to my Caer Caradoc. But in my dreams their return was peaceful, and the Stones were honoured, and it was a place once more for young moles to be raised in. I still have that dream, and while you younger moles raise your talons for what you think is right there'll be me and others like me to remind you why we fight at all. For one day the Stone Mole shall come even to Caer Caradoc and I would have him find peace there, and moles who love the Silence of his Stone.'

' 'Tis well spoken, Caradoc,' said Alder looking at young Gowre, 'and. . . .'

'Aye! 'Tis so!' growled Troedfach with a meaningful glance at Gareg.

'. . . and let nomole forget that only as long as the Stone is truly in our hearts shall our talons truly strive for peace.'

It was with this timely reminder that the second day of the conclave ended. The moles groomed, and ate, and talked in groups, the younger Siabod moles serving them, listening wide-eyed to their tales of courage and fortitude.

Later, as the evening drew in and the air began to chill, Alder found himself with Caradoc and Troedfach out on the high northern slopes of Moel Siabod alone, looking across the valleys. The sun was setting behind great Tryfan, and its highest part, where the sacred Stones rose proud, was clear.

They watched the evening darkness coming in for a while until Troedfach said, 'You spoke well, Alder, when you spoke of the Stone. Some of these young moles. . . .'

Alder laughed.

'We were the same when we were young, or at least I was. But their spirit is what we're going to need. I'm not sure that I'll come with you to Caer Caradoc – Gowre's got things to learn and he can go in my place.'

'No, mole, you're the one to come, not him.'

'But they'll follow you, Troedfach, and you know the ground better than I. The centre of the struggle's shifting, and others must lead it now.'

'Let Gowre prove himself here awhile,' said Troedfach. 'Let him help you oust the grikes from the lower slopes and then leave him in charge. He can make his mistakes in safety here – leading a small party's one thing, fighting a long campaign's another.'

'Well I'd like to see Caradoc once again at least,' admitted Alder, 'and it's the nearest I'll ever get to English moledom again. The Stone banished me here to redeem the wrongs I committed as a guardmole.'

Troedfach chuckled and buffeted Alder cheerfully.

'For a southerner you're not a bad Siabod mole.'

'Well, the truth is I love the place,' said Alder looking across the mountains, 'as much even as Caradoc loves Caer Caradoc.'

'More perhaps,' said Caradoc strangely, 'for it's the Stone Mole I love most now.' Troedfach and Alder exchanged glances, but Alder gave nothing away of what was really on Caradoc's mind.

Dusk came on and as dew formed on the rough grass about them, a light mist gathered in the valley below. Skeins of it drifted across the heather and peat fells that dropped away before them, and lingered where slatey outcrops of rock stood out.

Below them, in the dark valley, a lost curlew called and from somewhere another answered mournfully.

By some instinct that made the moles and place seem one, several youngsters and females came out and stanced near Alder and the others. All stared mutely at the distant peak where the Stones they guarded rose, too far to see, but their presence powerful. One of the females quietly sang, 'Help us Stone, for we are troubled and we do not know how best to serve. Help us now.'

Alder heard the words and knew that it was for such moments as these, when there was a holy mystery in the hills to which these proud and secretive moles had never forgotten how to respond, that he loved the place and had made it home.

He watched the running mist below and remembered years before, coming up these very slopes when he had first come to this place, Marram had been at his flank. And waiting for them, where he stanced now, had been . . . had been. . . .

Movement. More than mist. Sudden movement across the slopes below.

Several of them saw it all at once and hunched forward, staring and tense.

A skein of mist slipped by a rock, and where it went pale movement was again. Then the clatter of loose scree down into the gathering darkness below, and then one of the sharp-eyed youngsters said excitedly, ' 'Tis mole!'

The mist shifted again and they all saw that the youngster was right: it was mole indeed! An old mole, his fur pale grey and unkempt, plodding up the slope towards them.

He was large, or had been once, and still had the sense about him that he was. He paused and stared up at them, and then, snout down, came steadily on.

It was Caradoc who spoke: 'By the mighty Stone 'tis great Glyder himself come back from the dead!'

There was such awe in his voice that two of the youngsters ran back in dismay while the females closed ranks, as if to protect the young from danger.

'It *is* Glyder!' said Alder clearly and with astonishment.

'But that mole's long dead, isn't he?' whispered one of the youngsters.

'He looks alive enough to me, bach,' said Troedfach with admiration on his great dark face. Then Alder and Caradoc hurried down the slope to greet the noble and ancient figure who climbed steadily on to meet them.

Slowly to Siabod he had come, climbing the slopes he had once roamed free moleyears before, pausing to ponder perhaps the flow of the years' changes that had snatched him from the near-death of Rebecca's birthing on the high slopes into years of combat against the grikes.

Uncertain whether there were grikes about he had taken the western slopes. As he had got near to the main northern entrance to the higher tunnels he had been astonished to see, as he puffed and peered his way up the final stretches, what had looked like a whole army of moles waiting for him, and looking scared out of their wits. Times had changed indeed!

'Old friend,' said Alder, coming downslope with Caradoc and embracing the once-powerful Glyder, 'I thought I'd seen the last of you. You said you'd die in Ogwen alone, your body out on the surface for owl fodder.'

'Aye, well I'll die soon enough, Alder,' said Glyder tetchily, 'but the owls don't seem to want me yet though I've given them chances enough coming here. Taken me weeks. You must have known I was coming and thought I was invading all by myself, for I've never seen such a tough-looking reception for a solitary old mole.'

'You didn't know we had summoned a conclave then?'

'Know? Whatmole to tell me? I live alone. Nomole visits Ogwen. None. No, no, I came looking for some moles.'

'What moles?' whispered Caradoc in surprise and then in growing recognition of something that Alder could not immediately see.

Glyder turned his gaze on Caradoc, and for the first time the two looked at each other. Perhaps Alder saw better than either of them what happened next. Wonder, awe, even fear, came into their faces, and then a look of joy and relief he had rarely seen in all his life.

'I have waited long and journeyed far to meet thee, mole,' said Glyder at last.

'And I thee,' said Caradoc.

'Are there others of us here in Siabod?'

Caradoc shook his head. They talked only briefly, but it was enough to confirm that each had experienced the same phenomena of touching and loss at their respective Stones in June.

Glyder looked at Alder as if uncertain.

'I explained what happened to him,' said Caradoc quickly, 'and he believes me.'

'And you reached the sacred Stones of Tryfan, Glyder?' asked Alder.

'I did, but I thought nomole would believe me.'

He looked at Caradoc again and neither mole spoke.

'There is much to say, much to discuss,' said Alder as the others came down the slope wondering what the delay was.

'It is for this I've come back to Siabod,' said Glyder simply.

'For what?' asked Troedfach in puzzlement as he reached them.

Glyder stretched out an ancient paw and gripped Troedfach's own paw with it and fixed a piercing gaze on him.

'Not for bloody talons, mole, nor for wasteful struggles,

326

but to tell you of a vision that I saw and cannot forget.'
Then he added in a lighter voice, 'But first I'll hear of what
changes there have been, and how the grikes were driven
off; and I'll eat; and if I've the strength I'll sing an old
Siabod song or two when night comes and then. . . .'

'What then?' asked one of the awed youngsters eagerly.

'Why, mole, if there's time I'll do what Siabod moles do
when there's nothing left to do and nomole else to fight
with talon or word – I'll go to sleep!'

There was a great cheer at this, and when they had all
paid their respects to the old mole they led him upslope
into the tunnels of Siabod to sing of the past, and talk of
the future.

Gowre's arrival had created excitement, but Glyder's
appearance the next morning at the final session of the
conclave caused a sensation. There was something
dramatic and Siabodian about his reappearance, and long
before the session started the great chamber was packed
with moles.

He came in slowly, supported by Gowre, his one
remaining relative, muttering and complaining to himself
and undaunted by the sight of so many moles.

Silence fell as he looked irritably about him and, leaning
on Gowre even more, he ascended to the higher part of the
chamber. The whisper went round, ' 'Tis indeed Glyder!
Still alive!' and before Alder could say much by way of
introduction or explanation Glyder himself growled, 'Yes,
'tis Glyder of the sons of Rebecca, Glyder who turned his
back on fighting and struggle, Glyder who has been eating
the scrawny worms of the Ogwen in a silence that would
do some of you no harm. I've come back, see? And shall I
tell you why?

'One reason was to see a mole and that I've done, that
I've done.' He smiled, his eyes gentle suddenly, and the
few who were close enough saw him exchange a glance
with Caradoc.

'Also because I wanted to tell whatever moles I found

here something. Didn't expect to find a conclave, but that's the Stone's will. I'll say what I must once and that's that. If just one of you remembers it, if one of you passes it on, it'll be enough.'

He fell silent, thinking, but when eventually he did speak it was quite suddenly and passionately.

'Ogwen's not a place a mole goes to improve his physical health. It's cold and mostly wormless and a mole has to work hard to stay alive. The sun rises late up there and stays on the sides of the mountains where a mole can't easily reach it. When it comes down into the cwms at midday it's not there for long, and in any one place barely at all.

'Yet I was glad enough to get there after my brothers died, glad to be alone. Lead a system like Siabod for long enough through times like these and you get tired of talking and struggling and fighting. So tired that most moles die of it – that and the cold.

'I expected to die in the winter years. Would have suited me. Old mole, seen a lot, done a lot, last of his generation. Glad to go. Sometimes in the dark times I cried out to the Stone, "Let me die now, Stone, let me hear the Silence! You've had my brothers, my pups, almost all my kin, and now have me." And I took stance beneath Tryfan and stared at the Stones, and let the rain and ice and snow hurt me. But I didn't die. I felt like an old fool. Eventually I gave up offering myself and went off wandering Ogwen looking for worms. Not many about! Lost weight along with fur! Scraggy as a chick that's fallen out of its nest.'

Glyder stretched out a scrawny paw and looked ruefully at it, and then round at his flank. His skin hung loose on him now as it does on a mole grown old who was large and muscular in his prime. Behind him in the gloom there was the hollow sound of water dripping among the slate faces.

'Lost track of time, I did, and sometimes I tried to work it out. I knew when summer started, though. The ice and snow thawed and the ground was wetter than a mole likes and water running underpaw. Brought the worms out that did, and drowned them along the ways. Flowers grew then among the wet, and where water dropped down the cwm sides all scattered by the wind, moss grew greener than any I've ever seen. Took to eating beetles then. In Ogwen moles can't be choosy.

'Even the beetles didn't stir my appetite when the warmer weather came. I stared at them and they stared at me and I looked up at the two sacred Stones on Tryfan and said, "There's a beetle down here in Ogwen and he's not worth much. What's his name?" The Stones and the beetle knew!'

Glyder laughed to himself much as he must have done back in May. Then he pursed his mouth and shook his head.

'Slugs aren't much to eat either, but as I said moles in Ogwen can't be choosy. Ate a few and they didn't seem to mind. Said to the Stones, "Who's the lucky one, the slug or me? Who'll get to the Silence first? The slug, that's who. Why didn't you tell me years ago the Silence was in my stomach?"

'Up in Ogwen the Stones' voice is the wind and speaks better where the rocks rise sheer, and best where the Stones of Tryfan stand. I said to the Stones, "A mole could climb Tryfan if he tried. Especially a mole who was less than a beetle and a slug." The Stones did not reply immediately but I knew they would soon enough. Always do in the end. The Stones let you know when you're ready.

'Mid-June it was when the twofoot came clanking up the cwm. Scared the daylights out of me so I hid under the scree and felt it pass. Clank, clank up to where the green moss grew under the cliff that rises at the back of the nameless cwm. Silence. Even the ravens shut up. Stones spoke to me in the wind and I heard the twofoot fall, heard its cry. Like winter rock-fall in Castle y Gwynt its moans were. Went to see. Climbed up the green moss where the waterfalls dripped. Twofoot lay still. Paw bigger than my body and white and scented like over-ripe honeysuckle. Not nice. Paw bloody, and while I watched the blood turned from red to brown. Twofoot moaned and his gazes were on me, head big and furred.'

Glyder's voice had dropped and he had half turned to stare at Caradoc, to whom his remarks seemed addressed. Sometimes he so far forgot where he was that he referred to himself as 'Glyder' as if it was another mole he spoke of and not himself.

'Said to the Stones, "What shall I do?" and the Stones replied, "Watch over it." So Glyder did, and he scented it dying. So twofoots die like us!

'When the first sun came on the cliffs above the twofoot stirred but his gaze was dimming. Said to the Stones, "Shall I pray for it like for a mole?" And the Stones said, "Like for a beetle, like for a slug." Old Glyder felt joy then because he was not afraid any more. What's there to be afraid of when you're part of everything? That makes fear being afraid of yourself. So I prayed for the twofoot with dimming eyes. I went close, see, and when the sun came down on him his scent changed to nothing much and his eyes dimmed.

'That day Glyder started to climb Tryfan and touched the Stones. Saw moledom from the top, moledom where the twofoots live! Twofoots where us moles live. . . .'

Glyder seemed unaware of the buzz of surprise and disbelief that went round the moles at his matter-of-fact statement that he had climbed Tryfan. Most seemed very doubtful that he could have meant what he said.

'Right to the top?' called out one of the younger Welsh Marches moles disrespectfully, looking around him with a knowing smile.

' 'Tis what he said,' growled Troedfach and the titters died away, though a good few moles still looked dubious.

'Yes, yes,' said Glyder irritably, 'but that wasn't it, see? It was the twofoot.'

Most looked at him uncomprehendingly.

'*Needs* the Stone, like us. And beetles and slugs and all of us. But the twofoots . . . it's where the future is, where the Silence will be found. I knew it when that twofoot's

330

gaze dimmed; I knew it on top of Tryfan where the wind was still. I know it now. It's what I've come to tell you. It's why the Stones kept me alive. Listen. There are many paths to Ogwen, all easy to find. But it's taken me all the moleyears since June to find the way out again and that twofoot never did; so it's got more to learn than we have. Stop the fighting, moles! Tell yourselves and your enemies the Silence will be found where the twofoots are. Aye, where the roaring owls go. Silence there for mole!'

'Death more like,' said a mole.

'Shush!' said others, for strange though Glyder's words seemed there was a peaceful certainty about them.

'Listen,' he continued quietly and more slowly as if he had grown impatient with his audience and had little energy or desire to say much more. 'A mole's fortunate if he gets a quarter of what he wants in life, see? *Very* fortunate. When he reaches the end of his life as I have he'd best not regret a thing. No point in that! So he looks about and sees others making mistakes or making good and he thinks to himself he once went that way as well. He hopes others'll do better than he did and if he's a fool he'll offer advice thinking others will take it. Or maybe he'll just hope that some of these younger moles will get to do those things he never quite had time for, and good luck to them.'

Some of the moles were getting restless now, for Glyder's speech had slowed and his mind seemed to be wandering. The old mole had said enough, whatever point he had tried to make he had made for long enough, and surely it was time he shut up and let them get on with more important things . . . But not all felt that way. Among those listening were those who felt that Glyder's words were guided by the Stone and these were enough that they kept the others' restlessness at bay.

'Moles,' he said urgently, 'when I saw the twofoot's gaze dim I heard the beginning of Silence. Turn your gaze towards where you most fear to look and there may be what you most wish to find.'

With this final comment Glyder fell silent as suddenly as he had begun and stared round at the moles about him. As his voice died his body seemed to shrink and grow smaller and Gowre had to stance firm again to hold him up.

'I've said enough, Caradoc, I've spoken all I know. It was what the Stones wanted me to say I saw in Ogwen: the rest you and I know and I'll stay silent from now on. Now I'm tired and have need of sleep. And when I've slept I'll have need of help, for now I've finished Ogwen calls me back that my spirit may be near the Stones and free again.'

So did Glyder's speech end, and though he was led away by Gowre and much more was said when he was gone, it marked the true end of the conclave. Some said he was mad, others just old, and a few felt inspired; but none ever forgot his speech, for when a mole opens his heart as he had done then his words stay alive until those who heard them are ready to let them into their own life. There were many such who heard him that day, many more than ever knew.

Later Alder tried to dissuade him from going, but only half heartedly.

' 'Tis for the best I leave,' said Glyder. 'Let Gowre see me home. I shall tell him what I know of his kin on the way. A mole knows but little if he doesn't know that.'

Alder nodded his assent, and Gowre was glad enough to go with Glyder. He, too, sensed the conclave was over and felt strangely moved to be taking his uncle from Siabod, as if on the first stage of a new journey.

The following morning, as the other moles who had come to the conclave began to leave to east, north and south, those two moles slipped quietly on to the cold surface of west Siabod and thence, by slow degrees, down towards Capel Curig and the way towards the cwms of Ogwen. Caradoc accompanied them a little of the way, and Gowre let them take their leave of each other privately, stancing a little way off and staring at the hills' slow rise towards Ogwen.

When he looked again it was Caradoc who had departed first, trekking back through the dewy grass towards Moel Siabod. He did not look back.

'A mole doesn't need to,' said Glyder, reading Gowre's mind, 'not when he's so alive in your heart you know the Stone's a shared blessing, and you'll see him again one day.'

Glyder chuckled at Gowre's obvious bewilderment and said, 'Now help me back to the peace of Ogwen and I'll tell you of your father, and your Siabod uncles, and what Alder has told me of Tryfan. We've had too little time for kin these moleyears past, too little time for the Stone. Now listen – and support me as we go – and I'll tell you all I know of how a female from Duncton came to be where she shouldn't be, which is in the high slopes of Siabod at the wrong time of the year just as she began to pup.

'It was all a long time ago, see, and starts with a mole you'll not have heard of who was bigger even than your father was. . . .'

'What was his name?' asked Gowre, looking at the long way ahead and thinking ruefully that since Glyder could only move very slowly maybe a tale would pass the time.

'Mandrake,' said Glyder, and even as he spoke the name a shadow seemed to pass across the slopes above them, and Gowre half turned and stanced to protect them. But there was nothing there but exposed rock and a fold in the ground.

'Aye, it might have been him. They say he came back in spirit after he died before the Duncton Stone, and now he watches over his kin across these slopes and sees they come to no harm. Now, where was I?'

'Mandrake . . .' whispered Gowre softly, looking nervously about and beginning to wonder who was protecting whom.

'Aye,' began Glyder once more. 'My kin and your kin, mole, and as true a Siabod mole as ever there was. I'll tell the tale as a mole should, from my heart to your heart, and one day you pass it on as I do now to your own kin. And tell them to stance proud, and know the Stone is for them. You'll tell them that?'

'I shall,' said Gowre with sudden feeling. 'I shall!'

'Then listen, and I'll begin.' And Glyder did, as he made his last trek towards the sacred Stones it had been his life's task to protect.

PART III

Darkness Falls

Chapter Eighteen

Lucerne of Whern, not yet ordained but already undisputed Master of the Word, the lost Henbane's dread son, perverse and distorted mole whose love of others – whose love of anything – began and ended with himself, was not content.

Which, being so, meant those around him trembled for their lives and feared the tortured deaths his ire could mean. Where Lucerne and his cabal sideem went, there moles were hung to death; where Lucerne smiled nomole laughed; where Lucerne laughed other moles would die. Where Lucerne was, the air seemed dark with threat and doom to those committed to love and truth.

We find him now in a large and elegant burrow delved in the sandy soil in Cannock, a system south-west of the Dark Peak; and before him, trembling yet defiant, their eyes filled with a look of blind faith and adoration of the Stone that sickened him, were three followers found in hiding up on Cannock Chase.

Great though their pathetic faith was, he noticed with contempt that it was not so great that they did not very frequently dart fearful glances at the two moles who stanced on either side of them. The Stone, it seemed, could not protect them from reality.

One of the two was the guardmole Drule, huge of paw and pigged of eye, whom Lucerne had found at Kinder Scout on the crusade's passage through the Dark Peak, committing wanton murder on young female moles of the Word who had been found enjoying their pleasures with followers of the Stone. Today Drule is notorious, then he was unknown, but Lucerne had already seen in him exceptional and obedient zeal to the Word's will, combined with total loyalty and a useful cunning that might serve him well, and forthwith appointed him his bodyguard. Drule soon became a mole – the kind a leader such as Lucerne will sometimes need – to whom the very darkest deed could be entrusted and word of it would not leak out. Even from Mallice would some of Drule's secret acts for Lucerne stay concealed, and though she herself was never quite afraid of him yet most moles always were. It was one of Lucerne's perversities to enjoy the way that cleverer moles than Drule felt obliged to be nice to him, and smile in sympathy with his doltish grins, and laugh uproariously at his cruel and ignorant jokes.

The other mole was sideem Slighe, who looked inoffensive, being small and bland and with a face that bore a vacuous smile, and in all but one thing *was* inoffensive to a fault. He was a sideem whom Terce had found to help with the organisation of the crusade, rightly judging him to be efficiency incarnate and just what Lucerne might need in the molemonths and years ahead. An active Master of the Word needs a master of detail at his flank. Slighe was he; his constant presence and willingness to carry through the Master's policies left Lucerne and Terce free to discuss strategy. And more than that, his perverse and analytic intelligence could find possible problems and potential dangers to the Word where others, not even Terce himself, saw no harm at all.

It gives us only pain to expose the true nature of Slighe's revolting tastes, which were insatiable where young and uncorrupted male pups were concerned. He was among the most perverse and wicked moles attracted to the Word.

Meanwhile, know that these two had responded to Lucerne's request to bring some such followers of the Stone as these we find him now with, for he had wished to talk with them, saying, 'Before we decide our best course it is the Word's will that we come to understand such moles, what gives them their faith, and what their weaknesses are.'

Terce had disagreed, seeing only danger in such intercourse with Stone followers, and being content that the reports the sideem were daily sending now from all parts of moledom gave all the information they could need.

'But Terce, you cannot defeat moles' minds without knowing how they work. You taught me that yourself. I have no doubt that we will eradicate all followers we can find, but it will be costly, and by knowing how they think we may find quicker and more thorough ways.'

So Lucerne had overruled Terce's wish yet Terce did not much mind, for had he not trained Rune's grandson to think for himself? So he had shrugged, repeated his warnings, and said no more. Lucerne might, after all, be right, he often was . . . and Terce knew he owed his continuing position to his ability to be flexible.

For several tedious hours Lucerne had discussed the Stone with the three moles during which Terce, at his side, had not spoken a single word. But at last in the past hour, to his relief, he had seen as the others had that Lucerne had become bored and dispirited.

The moles of the Stone did not yield up to Lucerne's arguments or implied threats, but that might not have mattered had they offered good argument of their own for him to enjoy. Instead, it seemed, they revealed nothing but faith, based merely on their rearing and without any proof of the power of their Stone at all.

'These moles seem not to *think*,' he said with exasperation, 'nor to have been trained in any way. They are ignorant of their faith.' This was said in front of the three followers, who merely smiled at this outburst.

'Master,' Terce said, 'I doubt that many of our moles could give a better account of their faith than these followers could of theirs. You have been trained too long, and lived with only sideem too much and so expect too much.'

What seemed most to anger Lucerne was that not only did they not yield to him, but they were unwilling to name any other mole who was a follower, and responded to the suggestion that such names might be tortured out of them by saying – and this is when the sickening faith came to their eyes – that if that were so it would be the Stone's will and there was nothing they could do about it.

'But you tremble, mole, when Drule comes close to you. You know that but one word from me would have his talons finding out your pain. What is your faith worth that you trust it so little to protect you here?'

Drule clashed his talons together and widened his eyes and chuckled, quite delighted with himself. The three moles smiled thinly, looked at each other, and one of them replied, 'We trusted you, Sir. More we cannot do. As for fear, well, we are but mole. If you were us, threatened and powerless, would you not feel fear?'

'I should not,' said Lucerne, disliking the inquisitorial manner of the mole, 'for all is of the Word and I should submit to its will.'

Silence fell, and it was then that Lucerne's discontent began to show. He wanted better argument than faith. He wanted more information than such untrained believers as these could give.

'Shall I kill them, Master?' said Drule, reading Lucerne's thoughts.

'You said . . .' began one of the followers, fear in his eyes.

'He jests,' said Lucerne immediately. 'I said you would go free, and so you shall, in time.'

He smiled the smile that few moles could resist and the moles relaxed, even the guardmoles in the shadows at the rear of the chamber. Drule looked sulky, Slighe calculating, while only Terce showed no expression at all.

'Take them, feed them, keep them until I give orders they can be free,' Lucerne commanded the guardmoles.

'Thank you!' said one of the followers. 'Yes, thank you! The only way forward is what we have said these few hours past – mutual love and understanding – shared responsibility, a willingness to listen to the other side. . . .'

340

Lucerne raised a paw.

'You have made your point more than once,' he said. 'Speak of it again and Drule will pull your tongue out with his teeth. A speciality of his.' Drule bared his teeth and the moles looked shocked and then smiled, and even managed a shaky laugh as several of the guardmoles chuckled. Drule beamed.

'It is but the Master's joke,' he said, with ghastly irony.

Yet was Lucerne serious? His eyes did not smile, and nor was Drule's good cheer entirely convincing. There was terrible menace in what Lucerne had said. The mole shut up.

'So . . . you shall be cared for. Take them.'

The moment they had gone Lucerne said, 'Well, and shall we kill them?'

Drule shrugged indifferently. Such decisions were not his to make.

Slighe said, 'They have served their purpose, Master. They have no further information to give us, and gave us little anyway.'

'Terce?' said Lucerne. He liked to hear what others said before making judgement on such things.

'I was wrong, Lucerne, and you, as often enough to depress an old mole like me, were right.'

Lucerne smiled faintly but with pleasure at this flattery.

'And so? You have not spoken a word since they came.'

Terce thought for a little and then said, 'To me the most important thing was not what they said or did not say, but what they were.'

'What they were?' said Slighe, frowning. He liked facts and clarity, not subtle ambiguity.

'They were grateful,' said Terce, 'and gratitude is weakness in a mole and something easy to exploit.'

'Grateful?' mused Lucerne. 'Tell us more.'

'They were grateful in two different ways. First, of course, because you spared them. But that is unimportant. Then secondly, by talking to them you gave them legitimacy and for that they were pleased as well as grateful.

341

'No doubt that could be dangerous, but dealt with right then we could bring many followers out into the open. We could engage them in debate and discourse and so discover for ourselves their numbers and dispositions. Knowing which we could strike where and when it hurt them most. In the name of the Word we could strike, having first proved them to have been dishonourable. We reached out a paw in peace, they talon it, they are in the wrong, and we are seen to be right to punish them.'

Terce shrugged: such was the way of the Word, was it not?

Lucerne understood his meaning and the nature and promise of such strategy.

'This has attractions,' he said, 'and I shall think on it. Meanwhile keep those followers close by, treat them well, and when I am ready I shall try to see them one more time. Whether we release them or ask Drule to show them to the dark burrow I do not yet know.'

He smiled at his euphemism for murder, and the others smiled too. Cruel smiles, bleak smiles, smiles of indifference, as fitted their different positions, and all pitiless.

The great crusade had started as Lucerne wished: simply and well. He had had no wish to raise hopes too high too early, for raised hopes create expectations, and unfulfilled expectations in moles make them dissatisfied and harder to command.

The Keepers had led the new sideem south through Grassington and then over the Dark Peak. There had been nothing but welcome for them, though in some systems – especially as they passed through the southern Peak which lies near to Beechenhill – Lucerne could have wished the welcomes had been warmer. But then the systems that failed to enthuse for the Word had been noted down by Slighe. Apathy was punishable.

Inevitably, the new sideem were eager to see punishment for crimes against the Word begin but Lucerne was cautious, especially about creating sympathy for followers

342

of the Stone. What reports he had had by then made clear that the policy of restraint and indoctrination rather than the savage suppression that followed Henbane's invasion had been slow but sound.

If there was to be punishment it had best be against lax moles of the Word, for that would intimidate other moles of the Word and put new zeal into them while lulling the followers of the Stone into false security.

Nevertheless, Lucerne decided to yield to the demands of the new sideem when they reached Ashbourne, which lay conveniently close to Beechenhill and was to be the place where Mallice left him for her investigation into that system. Winster, the elderly eldrene of Ashbourne, had been proven lax along with some of her guardmoles and they were snouted after a formal hearing by the Keepers.

It had been the first snouting in public Drule had done, and it gave him pleasure. All the new sideem attended, their faces bearing that look of unbearable smugness that righteous moles who suffer from an excess of zeal have when they see others justly punished. Slighe made a fool of himself – not when the guardmoles screamed but when the eldrene was snouted. Females, in pleasure or in pain, he could not bear. Their blood sickened him.

Soon after they left Ashbourne Lucerne sensed that another swift trial and punishment would consolidate his reputation for just ruthlessness that the recent events in Whern followed by the snoutings in Ashbourne had begun to make. The over-fed Fennybor, sideem of Belper, was a suitable victim none would miss and he was force-marched by Drule for three days with the new sideem until he was hung up to die on the wire of a fence that others might see that the Word was harsh on those that abused its trust. Terce spoke the address at Fennybor's death and suggested it was allmole's duty to report those that were slack in their prayers and observations, or spoke ill of the Word.

A pall of suspicion and prayer fell on the new sideem after this, and everymole was careful to observe the Word to every last scrivening of its rituals. Not a worm was eaten but that a grace was said over it first; not a new sideem went to sleep but that he spoke the grace of the protection of the Word, and made sure that others knew it; and made even surer that if another lapsed then it was reported.

In such ways did Lucerne begin to assert the Word's might upon all about him, choosing moles to punish none would miss and avoiding, as yet, too much aggression against the Stone.

The weather was wet and unpleasant for much of September, and the progress, though steady, was slow. But the crusade crossed the southern Peak and into the bland lowland beyond, and there Lucerne followed his instinct and veered south-westerly. It was sometime then that one of several sideem sent out earlier than the main party from Whern located him and was able to report the existence of the largely deserted system of Cannock.

The Cannock system lies to the south of that wild and wormless place that gave it its name, Cannock Chase. The only moles that live there are youngsters from adjacent systems finding their strength, or outcasts no system wants. Or, as in Lucerne's day, followers of the Stone.

It was here, while making a patrol of the Chase, that guardmoles were later to pick up those three followers Lucerne was to spend time interviewing. But that was yet to come, for when he first arrived he had no time for indulgences, and wanted only to ensure that he had made the right choice and finally he felt he had.

Cannock is a place quite wormful enough for a winter stay, and perfectly suited to Lucerne's purpose. It lies as near to the centre of moledom as a mole could wish, if his desire is to set in motion an extended campaign against the Stone which could most easily reach its insinuating and destructive talons to even the most secret lost places of moledom where faith in the Stone might still lurk.

Apart from its location, Cannock had little to commend it. The tunnels were intrinsically dull and of no interest compared to the cold and subtle splendours of Whern, but Lucerne was pragmatic enough, too, to see the advantage in living in a place where sideem would not wish to be for long: such places test moles, and bring out the best and expose the weakest; such places do not invite others to take them over or to oust those who control them. What was more it had no Stone, nor evidence of any nearby, and that was to the good. Sideem did not like Stones and Lucerne was glad to pander to their fear, though he himself wished he had time to venture further south and see the great Stones of the Ancient Systems there of which he had heard so much. That perverse pleasure was still to come.

What also attracted him to Cannock was its relative proximity to Beechenhill. He sensed, for reasons he could not articulate, that this was a system of importance in the struggle for the Word, and its destruction would do much to hasten the decline of the Stone. He was already impatient for the report of it that Mallice would bring, and in any case disliked it when she was far from him. But he knew well that her power must not rest on his favour alone and she must win respect with an important task of which she made a success.

Nor was Cannock so far south that Clowder need be long delayed once he had finished matters satisfactorily in Ribblesdale. Indeed, the moment Cannock had been chosen as a base, Lucerne had commanded Slighe to send out messengers to key route points so that returning moles knew where to come and the swiftest ways were discovered and made known.

Soon reports started to come in from the moles Lucerne had sent out from Whern, and they tended to confirm the view that rumours of the Stone Mole's coming had aroused followers to meetings at Stones up and down moledom, and to other blatant affirmations of their faith. Yet not one single sideem had yet been able to report a specific sighting of this supposed mole, which supported Terce's belief that the rumour was mere projection of a need followers had for a leader.

345

In the meantime the news of the Siabod and Welsh moles was more disturbing. Soon after his establishment at Cannock Lucerne had, at last, an eye-witness account of the routing of the guardmoles from the tunnels of high Siabod from a senior guardmole sent by Ginnell himself.

Lucerne heard how the guardmoles had yielded to an extended campaign of Siabod attack in March and, encouraged by that success the revolt had spread through the interior of Wales and even spilled over its borderland with orthodox moledom. Since August and September things had gone quiet, and Ginnell had been planning to come once he was satisfied that the western front was in capable paws.

It was from this same source that Lucerne first heard the name Caradoc, the 'mad' mole whose base was the high and desolate stronghold of Caer Caradoc, from which he got his name.

'Nomole that I know has ever even seen him, though other of the rebel leaders are known to us – Troedfach of Tyn-y-Bedw Ginnell has seen, and Alder was, in times gone by, a guardmole himself.'

'I had not been informed of that,' said Lucerne with a frown. 'Siabod led by a former guardmole? This is a mole I would like to submit to the Word's punishment and I have no doubt that in time he shall be.'

'But Siabod is a terrible place, Master, barely worth the trouble of holding it, which is why Ginnell was willing to retreat east. . . .'

Had Ginnell's aide known Lucerne better he would not have been so tactless as to talk of 'retreat', for Lucerne impatiently cut him short and said, 'The Word does not care if the paws freeze off mole in Siabod – it is not the place that matters but what it represents. *Must* I be surrounded by moles who do not understand this?'

He fell into a terrifying silence which the aide had the good sense not to break. Eventually it was Terce who diplomatically moved the subject on: 'Alder, Troedfach . . . give us other names, mole, more names. Slighe, scriven them down, scriven them!'

The aide saw a chance of recovering his position and was grateful to Terce for providing it.

'There's a clever young mole called Gareg in the south, and another, Gaelri, we know about. There's Caradoc, of course . . . prisoners we've taken swear by *his* name and tell us he spreads the belief the Stone Mole will visit him personally one day.'

'Always the Stone Mole!' said Lucerne coldly. 'Always! These prisoners of yours, do they give much away?'

'Any prisoner will say anything, Master, if he's asked the right way. But . . . no. Torture's not the way to get them to do anything but lie, or curse you by the Stone. And Ginnell's not one for such means.'

'Like Wrekin before him,' said Terce.

'I wonder if Drule might know how to make such moles talk,' said Lucerne with a sparse smile. 'When will Ginnell be here?'

'A week or two, Master. He is most anxious to come.'

'Dismissed,' said Lucerne.

'Always the Stone Mole!' exclaimed Lucerne again, when the aide left them. 'I tell you this, Terce, the first mole who brings me positive evidence that this mole exists, and is alive, will find gratitude and favour from me.'

Slighe said, 'Is that a decree, Master?'

'A decree? What. . . ? Oh, the Stone Mole? Yes. Yes, make it so. Tell all those sideem that leave Cannock for task work now to say that the Master Lucerne will show the Word's gratitude to he or she who brings credible report of this Stone Mole.'

'I shall.'

A matter that also recurred to exasperate Lucerne at this difficult time of news-gathering and inactivity was the question of the status of Wyre at Buckland. That he was still alive was not in doubt – indeed, initial reports from that system and systems nearby were good and suggested that the Word and its representatives were generally feared. Lucerne had been relieved to learn that Wyre, acting on his own authority, had ordered a strengthening of guardmole vigilance, and quelled further revolt with brutal and decisive measures against well-chosen systems.

But while that was all well and good, Wyre himself – who had originally been chosen by Rune to replace Henbane when she returned victorious from her southern campaign – seemed to have become a reclusive mole. No report gave an account of meeting him; all was at second paw by moles who had heard this or seen that but knew nothing definite of Wyre himself.

The problem seemed to be that he had been ill with scalpskin, and perhaps he still was.

'We need something more than hearsay, Terce . . . if he needs to be replaced then the sooner the better. If he is avoiding contact because his ailments are too serious then that itself is disloyalty and disobedience, and must be punished.'

'At least two sideem have sent reports from Buckland but because they were unsatisfactory another has been despatched by Slighe.'

'It may be we shall need an example in the south,' said Lucerne ominously. 'A *striking* example and one nomole shall forget. Wyre must be old now.'

'Four longest nights,' said Terce. 'Almost my age.'

'Old indeed, Senior Keeper. Old enough to dispense with, don't you think?'

'It may be so,' said Terce, his face a study in inscrutability.

'Well, we must know soon. See to it. Nomole is indispensable; none irreplaceable.'

'No, Master,' agreed Terce.

'Nor can just enquiries of the Word simply be ignored by moles because it suits their circumstances. Such attitudes weaken us and by this fact alone are blasphemy against the Word . . .' Lucerne's voice rose, his body hunched and he looked dangerous and angry as he did when all was not just so and he was therefore not absolutely in control.

'It is not what moles do but what they think and feel we must be wary of and seek to change. This we must make our sideem understand, Terce, or else all we do in the field shall be undone in moles' minds. That aide of Ginnell's, for example, did not understand that it is not Siabod that is dangerous but the *fact* of it. It is not Beechenhill I shall destroy but the spirit of rebellion and insubordination which its continuing existence represents. The crusade we shall fight shall seem to be about talons and strength but in reality it shall be about concepts, and the winning of moles' minds. Do you understand me, Terce? Will *they*?'

'I understand you better, Master, every day. If I may say this with no disrespect to your grandfather, the Word speaks more clearly through you today than it once did through the Master Rune.'

Lucerne smiled with pleasure to hear this but then he protested as if for modesty's sake and said, 'But without his work, and the work he did through my mother Henbane, our task would be hard today. Your task is to help me be sure that the new sideem understand our intentions. Clowder, Mallice, Slighe and the others will win us physical power under my leadership, but spiritual ascendancy is where, finally, the true task will lie. When allmole *knows* the power of the Word, and believes it, and feels love for it, only then shall the Stone finally die. This is no easy thing, but am I not right to think that it is the final object of the Twelfth Cleave in which you trained us, and will be its greatest triumph?'

'You are right, Master,' whispered Terce soothingly.

At times like this Lucerne's manner became so intense and his eyes so fierce that he trucked no argument or obstruction, and it would have been a brave mole who confronted him. Terce knew well his Master, and his frustrations. He noted, too, the positive reference to Henbane and observed now, as he had in the moleyears since Henbane's flight from Lucerne's life, that when Lucerne was at his most serious and intense he invariably mentioned his mother in this way, as if forgetting the

349

contempt and hatred for her which he claimed to feel, and often expressed, and instead revealing the ambiguity of his attitude towards her.

'The Word always has a solution,' said Lucerne finally, 'and through me it shall be found. That is my task. Now tell me, Terce, what do you know of the Rolls of the Systems at Uffington?' He asked this last question without pause, but Terce knew from his calmer expression that Lucerne had passed the peak of his anger and frustration and was himself once more. In all his experience with Rune, with Henbane, with other Keepers, Terce had never met a mole more capable of clearing his mind and heart of things that a moment before had seemed to overwhelm him, and move on positively to focus on something else.

'The Rolls?' repeated Terce, collecting his thoughts and smiling with sudden pleasure to be servant of such a Master.

'Slighe mentioned them to me,' said Lucerne impatiently.

'Our understanding is that in Uffington's heyday it was every scribemole's task to go forth into moledom and bring back a report on the systems he visited. These reports came to constitute the great Rolls of the Systems, kept in the libraries of the Holy Burrows. Perhaps unwisely, the library was destroyed by the Mistress Henbane's henchmoles.'

'Very unwisely I would say. What were the Rolls used for?'

Terce looked surprised.

'Control, of course, though the scribemoles would not have called it such. Their existence made it possible for successive generations of scribemoles to know the history and disposition of each system – what mattered to it, what moles had been important to it and so forth – and so be able to judge how best to act when problems arose.'

'Information *we* might have used,' said Lucerne acidly. 'Should we not now do the same?'

'In a manner we do. The reports of the sideem are filed and stretch back over the centuries, though until Rune's day they were but modest things and irregularly kept.'

'If you mean some of the scrivenings I've seen in Whern they were useless, Terce. We can do better, and if we are to consolidate the power that we have and maintain it well we *must* do better. We cannot rule without knowledge. We shall make a Scrivening of the Systems to match any Rolls ever made. It will inspire travelling sideem to know that their reports are part of something that will last forever.'

'Where shall it be kept?'

'Whern. Only in Whern. The mole – the Master – who controls such a scrivening shall hold great power for the Word. It shall give idle sideem something to do, and never-ending tasks on which to employ sideem with whom we are displeased. It shall be most useful to us.'

Terce nodded. 'Slighe and myself will arrange it,' he said.

In such ways, through the autumn years of September and early October, was Lucerne's strategy for the crusade developed and its continuing success ensured. Doing everything with patience and order, and so far with only sufficient violence to consolidate his power among the sideem, Lucerne succeeded in gaining in strength even as he learned about moledom.

By mid-October most of those new sideem who had set forth with specific reporting tasks had come back, and the gist of their reports been made known to Lucerne and the Keepers. Although some key questions had still not been answered, and he had yet to meet with Ginnell, or learn the truth of Wyre, Lucerne seemed to have instinctively felt that the time to give a more specific and uniting task had come. He knew that winter would soon be on them all and that if sideem were to reach the further destinations he would want them to go to, he must lose no time. What was more, the gathering sideem were growing restless for all knew they would be given new tasks and most were impatient for more important ones than they had before.

351

Lucerne was inclined to act quickly, and it was Terce who urged caution.

'Wait until we have word from Clowder, wait for Mallice's return. They were moles anointed with you, they will wish to be involved. And Ginnell . . . he may feel disregarded if he finds the sideem went forth without due consultation, especially if guardmoles are involved.'

'You are right,' said Lucerne suddenly, 'and I am overtired. I shall give them a little more time. Why is Mallice not yet returned?'

'You miss her, Master?' said Terce.

'I do, Terce. But she is your daughter – do you not fear for her? Her task is a dangerous one.'

'I trust the Word, Master. I know it will protect her.'

'I trust it will. But I *am* tired, and Cannock begins to bore me. Reports, interrogations, planning . . . I shall leave it for a time. You shall take my place.'

'But Master . . .' began Terce, much alarmed, for Lucerne had never been far from him, and never beyond his control. Nor did Terce enjoy the idea of absolute power.

'I have need to find the Word again,' said Lucerne quietly. 'Now where is Slighe? Guardmole, summon him!'

Slighe, who was never far away, came hurrying in.

'Master?' he asked.

'I am leaving Cannock for a short time . . .' Slighe's face showed the same alarm that Terce's had and Lucerne laughed aloud. 'I shall be safe enough! The Word shall care for me! Now listen . . . our planning is almost done. When I return it will be to set the next stages of the crusade in motion, and once it begins I fear it will have a life of its own and we who lead it shall not get much rest. So, briefly, while I have time, I shall seek my way with the Word.'

'Surely Master . . .' said Slighe unhappily.

'But . . .' tried Terce again.

'Meanwhile I have a task for you and Slighe which will keep you occupied enough not to worry about me, Tutor

Keeper.' He smiled as he used this old way of addressing Terce. 'In consultation with the new sideem, but in secrecy of our true intent, you shall together begin to group the sideem and guardmoles into threes. Each group shall be able to act independently and alone, and each must contain the skills of scrivening and of fighting. For this reason one at least shall be sideem, one at least guardmole. The third may be either, or simple helper, according to your judgement. Place all the new sideem in this way. Slighe has already made scrivenings of the different systems according to their loyalty to the Word and the strength of Stone belief within them. The systems must each have a group of three moles nominated to it; begin to match them to each other, though I shall make the final choice on my return. So, that is all. If the Word wills that Clowder, Ginnell and Mallice return while I am gone, then brief them thoroughly. I shall wish not to waste time when I return.'

'It shall be done,' said Terce.

Lucerne raised a taloned paw.

'Do not have me followed, Terce. I would be alone. Not even Drule.' Terce flicked a glance at Slighe and looked apologetic. Sending a trusted guardmole to follow the Master had been exactly his intent.

'I mean it, Terce. Whatever mole you send after me I shall kill and that would be a waste,' said Lucerne at his most charmingly chilling. 'Like anymole, the Master has need to be alone at times. Now I shall leave.'

'Master?'

'Yes, Slighe?'

'Just for the scrivens . . . have these groups a name?'

Lucerne paused and thought.

'Call them trinities. It is a fitting name and the sideem shall like it.'

'Trinities,' whispered Slighe, playing with the word.

'Trinities,' repeated Lucerne, and with that he left.

So began the trinities, the most hated and feared of all Lucerne's creations.

So began as well that extraordinary and mysterious interlude in which, briefly, Lucerne was lost to the sight of all the moles of the Word in Cannock, not excepting even Terce himself.

'Keeper Terce? A question.'

'Scrivener Slighe?'

'Where has the Master gone?'

'The Master seeks a mole I fear he shall not find: his mother Henbane. It is a need he does not know he has. When Mallice is with him he forgets that need, for she ministers to it. Now she is gone that ache has returned. He will not find Henbane, I think, but no doubt he'll find a female soon enough. Some little slip of nothing who'll not know the mole who's come to her.'

'I do not like not knowing where my Master is,' said Slighe.

'Nor I, Slighe, much more nor I. It was a mistake that I let Mallice go so far from him and for so long. I shall not permit it ever again.'

'But he is Master, he can do as he wills,' said Slighe.

'No, Slighe, he is the Word's servant, and he cannot. Do not forget that. *Never* forget it. Upon your understanding of that will lie the final fulfilment of your task for which, I may remind you, I preferred you myself.'

Slighe stared at Terce and blinked. His eyes were empty of emotion.

'We have a task, Senior Keeper,' he said at last.

'Scrivener Slighe, we have.'

It was in the few days that Lucerne was gone that first Clowder and then Ginnell came at last to Cannock. Terce briefed them on all that had been happening and made his own record of their news.

'Tell nomole of this, Clowder,' he said, when that mole had finished his description of the terrible events for which he had been responsible in Ribblesdale, beside which few massacres in mole history compare except, perhaps, that in Weed and Fescue's day on the Slopeside of Buckland when the clearers were all killed and Tryfan and other followers barely escaped.

Ginnell, a grizzle-furred mole of spare body and few words, and an impressive grasp of the strengths and weaknesses of moles of the Word and Stone alike, gave detailed reports to Terce as well.

Neither mole could credit that Terce did not know where Lucerne was.

Terce merely sighed and shrugged, saying, 'He wished to be alone. He is *mole* as well as Master, Clowder.'

'Humph!' said Clowder.

'Nomole knows where the overall commander *is*?' said Ginnell incredulously.

'He knows where we are,' said Terce.

'Well!' said Ginnell, who expected moles, even Masters, to be where they said they would be.

'He will soon be back,' said Terce.

'Aye!' chuckled Clowder. 'He will! The Master, or rather the Keeper Lucerne as he still is, is probably with Mallice, and if not with her then with a wench, and a young one. He likes them so! Eh, Terce?'

'It is possible,' said Terce carefully.

'Well, when he comes back let me know,' said Ginnell.

'We will,' said Clowder. 'Mole, we will.'

Clowder knew his friend and Master well, but Terce, who had made him what he was, knew him better.

Even so, until now, the truth of Lucerne's brief disappearance from Cannock that October has not been known. We can only make a surmise from a certain record made much later by a certain mole whose name . . . whose name is best for now left unspoken.

However it was, however it will be, that mole much later, when the events of this history became but shifting shadows and passing light across forgotten fields, had good reason of his own to venture forth into the moors that lie north-east of Cannock Chase. Good reason to talk to moles along the way, good reason to point his snout upmoor and press on and answer when a mole asked, 'Greetings, mole, whither are you bound?'

'To see the Five Clouds. Can you direct me to them?'

'Aye, mole, you're not far off. A day to the north-west of here and you'll find them. Keep to the streams, there's food along their way.'

It was not mole country, yet that mole pressed on and saw at last five overhangs of millstone grit darkening the skyline above and beyond. In their lee, far under them, he met a mole he had sought for many a molemile past. She might have been as old as the dark grit that overshadowed the isolated but homely tunnels she and her kin had made. Dark though her fur, overhung the place, yet her eyes were bright as speedwell.

He saw her and he saw her kin in the system thereabouts, generations of her making, and his troubled face looked pleased. She saw him, and her peaceful eyes looked troubled.

'Do you know who I am?' he asked her.

'I can guess who you might be.'

'Can you guess why I might have come?'

'I can. How did you know?'

'He never forgot,' said the traveller. As the old female's eyes lightened with pleasure, he asked softly, 'Will you tell me?'

She stared at him, and when the youngsters who came near stopped to stare as well, she sent them away.

'Shall you ever speak of it?'

'It is part of moledom's history and my own. I may speak of it, I may scribe of it: there is no promise I shall ever make I cannot keep.'

She was silent a long time, and for some of it she turned and gazed at the Five Clouds above.

At last she said, 'I have never spoken of it. Why must I do so to you?'

'Look at me, mole, look well.'

She did, and she nodded and she sighed. Then she did

356

speak, and that stranger mole made a record of what she said.

I did not know his name. He was young, he was like nomole I had ever seen or ever saw again. The sky was in his fur so bright it was as if it had never been there before. I was afraid of him and asked him whither he was bound. When he made no reply I said, 'Are you going to Beechenhill?' In those days that was a system outcasts and followers of the Stone sought out for refuge, and the Five Clouds and the Roaches beyond was a safer route than most. We often saw such vagrant moles pass through.

'Are you in trouble with the grikes?'

It was then he gave me the only dark look I ever saw upon his face. It made me cry. He asked me if I was of the Stone and I said I did not know what I was. I had gone there to escape such things. But if the Stone was like the Five Clouds then yes, I was of the Stone. And if the Word was of the Five Clouds, then the Word was for me. I was surprised that he asked me what they were and so I took him there. It was October, yet warm and he was male, and I was untouched by mole. Before he came I had felt so young and gay, but the moment he looked at me I felt I had waited for him all my life, and as if my life had been long. I took him upslope a little way to see the Five Clouds better than we could from here and when he saw them he said we must go to them. I said nomole should, and he said he was not 'nomole'. He took me there, and beyond to the Roaches themselves where the scent of pine makes the rounded rocks and wormless soils seem light and heady. There above the Five Clouds where I thought I could never go, nor have ever been again, we mated. For a time he was everything to me. I never knew there could be such joy with anymole, nor have I ever known it since. His talons were both rough and soft, wild and free, his body strong. Yet sometimes he was like a pup in my paws and

357

even said himself that if I'd been able I should have suckled him. It was but lovers' talk. Sometimes he seemed but a pup. . . .

I do not know how many days we wandered there. On the last day I pointed east and said, 'Beechenhill's there. Was that where you were going?' He said, 'I know 'tis there. I know.' If he had not been so strong, so fierce at times, so assured unto himself, I would have said he was afraid. 'Promise me you'll never go there, never.' I did. I would have promised anything.

We wandered slowly back downslope to here where he left me and where you find me now. I knew he would not come back.

'What was his name?'

'I never asked his name,' she said, 'not once. Nor did he ask mine. When we needed a name we took it from the earth or the air or the sky as we made love. He was most beautiful. He made my life.'

'Did he ever say where he had come from, or whither he was bound?'

She shook her head.

'Do you know who he was?'

'He chose not to tell and I not to ask. Why should I change that now?' She looked around and saw the youngsters born of her own youngsters' young. They were curious and creeping near once more. She looked very old and yet her eyes were so filled with that short memory they seemed as young as those of the pups that ran to her.

'What's he want?' asked one of them.

'To talk of the Five Clouds,' she said.

'Oh, them! When's he leaving?'

'Don't be so forward, don't be so rude,' she said, laughing.

'He's going now!' they said. 'What did he want?'

She said nothing but watched the mole leave, dark, his fur shining with the sky, and long before he paused to look

back and raise a paw and call farewells she had turned
from the sight of him and followed the youngsters to play.

Such is the record that mole made, and it remains the only
clue to where, that October long ago, when darkness was
poised to fall across moledom's pleasant land, Lucerne,
Henbane's son, might have been.

Lucerne came back to Cannock as secretly as he had left.
Now he had been there, then he had been gone, now he
was returned as Terce had said he would: full of the fire of
crusade, impatient to begin.

'The sideem are all here, all waiting, all eager, Master,'
said Terce, with Slighe in attendance. 'The trinities are
named; Clowder has returned and Ginnell arrived. All is
ready.'

'All? Is Mallice here?'

'She is not, Master.'

'I am displeased.'

'But your . . . journey. You . . . were . . . satisfied?'

'Satisfied?'

'With where you have been.'

Lucerne looked at Terce in such a way that Terce never
asked that question again. Nor, when she later heard of it,
was Mallice ever fool enough to ask. Nor anymole. What
was had been. What would be was what mattered now.

'Have Clowder and Ginnell reported?'

'Fully.'

'Good news?'

'Excellent.'

'It is well. You will brief me now before I see them. It
will save time. Meanwhile, Slighe, let it be known that
tomorrow, early, the whole chapter of sideem shall meet
and then I shall make known the nature of the task the
trinities will have. After I have spoken with Terce, and
talked with Clowder and Ginnell, we three shall meet
again and arrange which trinities will go where. It will be a
long night, Terce.'

'But the beginning of a longer night for the followers of the Stone,' replied the Twelfth Keeper.

'You are nearer to the truth than you yet know!' said Lucerne, his eyes bright. 'Now brief me.'

Of the full horrors and pitiless slaughter that Clowder was responsible for at Mallerstang in Ribblesdale we shall soon know more. It was the first of the new massacres in the name of the Word. Everymole, male or female, old and young, that Clowder and his guardmoles found in that quiet and peaceful place was killed in a rapine orgy of violence. The moles of Horton, judged pure of the Word, were nevertheless forced to see Clowder's work for themselves, trekking up the bloody slopes of Mallerstang. Lest there be any doubt at all of what a mole's duty was, the eldrene and the senior guardmoles of Horton were forced as well to snout some moles Clowder ordered to be kept alive for that purpose.

To this day the slopes of Mallerstang seem to hang heavy with that massacre, and in October, when autumn comes, then if the sun shines those desolate slopes seem red. 'Aye, red with the blood of innocents,' as the locals say.

'It is well done,' said Lucerne. 'We shall have Clowder tell the full story to the chapter of the sideem tomorrow. It will encourage them and make their duty clear. Mallerstang shall be an example for us all of how the Word made angry wreaks vengeance on the wicked and the sly.'

Early the next day Lucerne spoke to the full chapter of the sideem. There was a change among those who expectantly and eagerly waited for him to speak compared to those who had heard him in Whern at Midsummer after the ousting of Henbane. Now there was a harder and more certain air about them all: some had scars from travels they had made, some seemed older by far. But the most part of the difference was in the confidence and spirit they had. The weak ones had gone and those that were left, or the older sideem who had survived the testing times of interrogation, were resolute and self-disciplined.

Before Lucerne spoke, Terce told the moles about the trinities and Slighe assigned them to one and to a system, so that each knew with whom he would serve his task and where he must go, though none knew yet what the task might be.

There was mounting excitement and curiosity about this when Clowder rose and gave a cold, impartial account of the destruction of Mallerstang. He told how those moles had mocked the Word, and why its judgement had been merciless. Awed silence met the end of his account, and then such cries as a rabble makes when it feels victorious and its evils seem justified. Cries which ask for more and call for death on all those not on their side.

In this atmosphere of brimming violence and hatred, Lucerne at last rose up. Instant silence came. The speech he made was a long and passionate address, though in Terce's record of it the full power of it is lost, and the passion diluted. But the record shows that all who heard it rejoiced to be so led, and to be given tasks of the Word that would lead inevitably to the destruction of the Stone.

As he spoke on, there came an adoration to the sideems' faces, and when he smiled they laughed, and when he laughed some were moved to tears.

'Help him, Word!' they cried out.

'Blessed be our Master!'

'Your Master? Nor yet even Master of the Word. For I am not yet ordained. Nor shall I ever be . . . no, not ever be.' He paused and the silence was so great that if a mole had dared breathe it would have been heard.

'No, my fellow sideem, I am not ordained. And this pledge I give thee as I give it to the Word we serve and which makes us and gives us our life. When the task we begin this day is complete, on that night will I be ordained. By the whispered Word, by the bloodied Stone, by the drift of cloud, by the rasp of just talon; by the shout of triumph in thy hearts shall I be ordained. When that night comes, that dread night for those that fear the judgement of the Word, when that night is here – that night when

361

rejoicing fills the heart of those who have no fear of what they do – *then* shall the Word judge me Master. But what night shall that be? What shall it be to us?'

'Tell us when, Master!' shouted a sideem.

'Master, tell us what we must do that you shall be ordained.'

'You must fulfil your tasks,' he said simply, his voice suddenly calm, his eyes watching for their response as he paused and wiped white spittle from the corner of his mouth.

'What is our task?' another said, his voice pleading with Lucerne to say.

'To go forth obediently in those trinities in which you have been placed. To go to those systems to which you are nominated.' He stared at them, playing with their terrible desire.

'But what shall we do?' one asked at last.

'Do that which is most hard. You shall . . . listen. Listen to the followers of the Stone. Listen for the deceit and fraud they call Silence. Listen and scriven the names, the places, the strengths, the weaknesses, the *everything* of the followers.'

They looked at each other in bewilderment.

'Is that *all*?' a sideem whispered to another.

'*All*?' cried out Lucerne with feigned rage. 'This "all" shall be the very essence of the Stone's destruction. The Word would know the strength of its enemy. The Word would know the places where its enemy dwells. The Word will know it *all*. You shall gain their trust; your trinities will be made welcome; the eldrenes and the guardmoles shall defer to you; you shall use every means at your command to find out the where and the what of the followers, except for this.'

Lucerne raised a paw and extended a single, shining, sharp, curved talon.

'There shall be no violence. Yet. There shall be no punishment. Yet. If you are mocked, or reviled, or

362

threatened, you shall smile and not respond in kind. Yet. You shall only listen.

'But as the Word is mighty, as the Word is great, together we shall make such a scrivening of the systems that we shall know where the Stone is, and what it is, and how it shall be destroyed.

'This is your task. And it shall be done swiftly, for the Word is impatient to give its judgement on those moles that mock it by their belief. Remember this. For every blasphemous word you hear ten Stone followers shall die; for every sideem mocked or threatened shall one hundred followers die; for everymole that dares to turn his back on the Word to face the Stone, his mate, his pups, his kin, all his vile kind shall be judged eliminate, and punished to death.'

'When shall this be?' they cried.

'When?' whispered Lucerne, his eyes narrowing and black. 'I wish to tell you when but I dare not for even here, among us now, the Stone lurks. Aye, moles! Here, it stays. You shall know when it is too late for the traitor Stone to turn and warn its spawn. But know this at least.' The darkness seemed to gather into Lucerne's face. His talons rasped the ground and a whisper of dark sound encircled them all. He hunched forward and they all moved a little closer, as if what he had to say was the darkest secret yet.

'By virtue of the tasks your trinities shall now fulfil, the Word will have the darkness of justice and vengeance fall upon the Stone. That shall be the night I am ordained. Then shall we all be celebrants of the Word, then shall we all be ordained in the power of its judgement.'

This was what Lucerne said and it was enough, with the more detailed briefings Terce and Slighe then gave, for Cannock to buzz with excitement and for the sideem to set off across moledom in their sinister trinities, with purpose and intent.

All the day following, moles left Cannock, hastening away to fulfil their tasks. Many came to say their farewells to Lucerne. Others, who knew him less well, lingered for the chance to smile and simper at him in the hope of winning his notice and favour. Ginnell was briefed to hold the western front until Clowder sent new orders, and those would come before too long. Nor were small matters left forgotten. The three followers Drule had been keeping were released. 'They shall instil trust and confidence,' said Lucerne, but these were words that Drule did not understand and so he frowned.

'Worry not, Drule, you shall have more work than you could dream of soon enough.'

Within a day Cannock was emptied of sideem and the infection of the Word began its remorseless progress across moledom once more.

It was in the days following, when Lucerne began to be restless and uneasy once more, that Mallice at last returned from Beechenhill.

'You have been long gone,' he said.

Mallice smiled and caressed his flanks.

'Where I have been are pleasant and surprising things,' she said.

'Beechenhill?'

She nodded.

'Pleasant?'

'Mmm, my dear. Very, very pleasant. You will be pleased.'

'Tell me, mole,' he growled.

'At length, or briefly and most sweet?'

'Briefly.'

'Your kin live there.'

'My kin? You mean Henbane?' There was terrible hope and terrible anger in his voice.

Mallice laughed.

'No, no, my dear, much better than *her*. Your *kin*, your lost siblings.'

'My siblings?' repeated Lucerne faintly, as if he did not understand the meaning of the word. She nodded slowly, taking her time. As Lucerne could twist a mob about his paw, so could Mallice play with him.

'Yes, yes, my love. Sweet Harebell and strong Wharfe. Your *sister*. Your *brother*.'

'In Beechenhill?' he said, aghast.

'Oh yes, yes it is indeed so. And something more, though since you said I must tell you only *briefly* . . .' Mallice giggled.

'Tell me,' he ordered impatiently.

'You will not be proud of them. They are both, it seems, such *worthy* followers of the Stone.'

'If this is true. . . .'

'It is, Master mine, it is most true. And since it is, what will you do?' she asked, mouth moist but eyes wide and innocent.

'Something moledom shall never forget,' said Lucerne most grimly.

'Good, oh good,' purred Mallice. 'I *know* it will be good.'

Chapter Nineteen

Those moles who have never been to Beechenhill may wonder how it was that this system held out so long against the Word. But moles who have been that way, and lingered to stare at the running streams, or been beguiled by the light mists that make the same elusive valleys seem different each time they are travelled, will understand. Beechenhill is not an easy place to find, let alone invade.

Even if a force of moles made their way towards its higher parts, and negotiated its labyrinthine and confusing limestone tunnels to reach the point where the system's modest Stone rises and looks on the hills and vales all about, their coming would have been long observed, and the moles they sought long gone.

It is indeed a blessed place, and upon its surface and its tunnels the Stone must have cast some very special light in that early time when the Stone created moledom and Balagan, the first White Mole, came.

Not that Beechenhill had in times past avoided its share of plague and trouble, or more recently not felt a warning of the darkness coming. Indeed, ever since that strange day in June when Wharfe had so suddenly left his sister and companions and been driven by a kind of madness to rush and touch the Stone, it might be said that Beechenhill had been on its guard.

Beechenhill moles, always close to the Stone and its auguries, took such things seriously, and they did so then all the more because Wharfe's touching of the Stone had been followed by rearing storm clouds in the northern sky, and a dreadful downpour of rain so violent that it drove dangerous torrents of water into the tunnels and killed seven moles – four drowned in their chambers before they made a move, two dashed by torrents against protruding rocks and one more, though nomole knew how she died, Squeezebelly himself found her staring at the raging sodden sky, dead as if she had seen something that made her want to live no more.

The rain stopped, the ground soon dried, but that storm left a pall in all moles' hearts that seemed to blight the summer and left a warning all about. Great Squeezebelly became a thinking, planning mole, sensing trouble ahead, bad trouble, trouble worse than anything he had known before.

But for that, at least, his system's long and noble history of dissent had prepared him well. In his younger days his father had taught the lower routes of tunnels and surface to Squeezebelly intimately, and shown him all the likely routes an invader might take, and the options of retreat and hiding which Beechenhill moles could exercise to confuse and demoralise even a persistent invader.

Despite his girth he made sure he knew his system still and it was knowledge that Squeezebelly had used well and wisely in the difficult years it was his fate to live through as leader of the only system of significance in the north which successfully held out against the grikes.

Rune was already dominant in Squeezebelly's youth and the evil potency of the Word and its moles' ways well known to the Beechenhill moles who made forays down to the lower slopes of the Dales and saw the terror, destruction and cruelty that followed in the wake of Henbane's long drive south.

It was through this dangerous and fraught period Squeezebelly matured, and few moles were as indomitable as he in defending the Stone, the system, and the moles in his care, against the evil Word. By making it easy for invaders to lose their way in the alluring slopes and vales that lie below Beechenhill, and difficult for them to gain access to the higher ground, the Beechenhill moles preserved their sacred autonomy.

But more than that, through some happy mixture of topography and climate, of aspect and geology, of history and living tradition, the Stone had blessed that happy place and, despite all, its moles remained open-hearted yet not easily fooled; cunning, yet not secretive or sly; physically strong, yet not aggressive and bullying in their ways; realistic and yet never forgetful of the love they felt for the place in which they lived and the sense of faith to which they had been reared.

All these great attributes Squeezebelly personified, and added to them a humour and rough good nature which sometimes hid other qualities he had: intelligence and common sense, and an ability to see that nomole must ever for a moment stance back into laziness nor forget that if the Stone is to be properly served then it demands never-ending attention and self-honesty.

These were the qualities which made him the mole he was, and built for Beechenhill a reputation that went wherever moles went, whether friends or foes, for all spoke alike of it in awe.

As the years of Henbane's rule had gone by, and Beechenhill had become more and more solitary in its resistance to the grikes – who rationalised their failure to subdue it by talk of its unimportance – those few moles remaining who held fast to the Stone in their hearts, and loved liberty of spirit even before their own life, were drawn to Beechenhill as an afflicted mole will always go where warmth and welcome is, and shelter too.

It was through such fugitives that the moles of Beechenhill and the one who led it so ably, despite their isolation, were able to keep in touch with moledom's strifes and troubles, and to know much of what went on.

It was always a surprise to visitors that while grikes had so far found it hard to penetrate the higher tunnels of Beechenhill, wandering strangers and followers of the Stone usually succeeded in doing so in safety, despite the grike patrols about it.

One reason was that Beechenhill maintained good relations and contacts with moles in neighbouring systems that, outwardly at least, were of the Word. Such moles were used to spotting vagrants of the Stone and guiding them into safety in Beechenhill. At the same time, the system had developed an effective network of watchers, mainly young moles, male and female, who knew the tunnels and were deputed to hide themselves around the periphery of the system, keep in touch with friendly neighbours and guide newcomers upslope if they were adjudged to be safe and not spies.

But watching was a dangerous task and so, knowing that at any time one might be taken by the grikes and tortured for his knowledge of the system, Squeezebelly ordained that each watcher knew only a limited section of the tunnels into Beechenhill. Sadly, watchers were taken from time to time, but this policy had contained the knowledge they revealed and the Beechenhill moles were able to counter any information the grikes gained by rapid adjustments to tunnel alignments and seals.

As for friendly moles, they were vetted on their way upslope, and none would have got through without experienced moles knowing about it. Since watching was a service that all Beechenhill moles must perform for a period, Wharfe and Harebell had both done their turn, though Squeezebelly had been much concerned for them when they did; but he judged they would be better for it and through May they had both performed their duties well.

In all the time of Squeezebelly's rule only one group of moles had ever succeeded in evading all the grikes and watchers around Beechenhill to make their way unnoticed to the very heart of the system, indeed to the Stone itself. They were Tryfan and Spindle, guided most of the way by the mole Mayweed.

When Squeezebelly heard that a mole had reached the Stone and was talking to Bramble and Betony, his own youngsters, he had laughed in his deep and cheerful way and said, 'Then by the Stone this is a visit that shall bring great blessing on us. It was meant to be, and ordains the coming of some change to moledom I cannot foretell.'

In this open spirit Squeezebelly had listened on that never to be forgotten day when Tryfan had preached of the way of non-violence before their humble Stone, and he had sensed that somehow here the future for Beechenhill surely lay. He began then to believe it might be possible that in Beechenhill, a system never aggressive but one which raised its collective talons only in its own defence, and that more by retreat and cunning than confrontation, here was the embodiment of how all moles of the Stone should be. For if Tryfan's words had been right, and non-violence *was* the way, the way forward must be for moles to learn to defend themselves when needs must without hurting others. But how can a mole defend himself from moles who seek to kill him and destroy his faith without hurting another?

It was this great and difficult paradox with which Squeezebelly had wrestled since Tryfan's visit. And if others said there was no answer to it, and where would they be if their fathers before them had not sometimes had to kill the grikes to survive, Squeezebelly found comfort and indirect confirmation that there was a solution to the paradox in the fact that the Stone delivered to him and his system, of all the moles and places in moledom, Tryfan's two young by Henbane.

When strange Mayweed and dark Sleekit brought those young moles to him and told him the truth of their parentage, Squeezebelly felt he saw at once the significance of it. Few moles would in future be better placed to resolve the conflicts of moledom and find a middle way between the Stone and the Word – between life's paradoxes indeed – than a mole or moles who had been born of the union of the Mistress of the Word, Henbane of Whern, and great Tryfan of Duncton Wood, the first mole who dared take the light of the Stone into Whern itself.

So he watched over Wharfe and Harebell well, put them under the care of his own two young, and was not in the least surprised that it was Wharfe who, of that happy

370

quartet of friends, emerged as natural leader, a mole who might one day take over the leadership of Beechenhill too.

Of his own pups he was proud, but had no illusions: Bramble was a dreamy mole, whose love and skill was the history of Beechenhill, and who learned and recounted all the tales Squeezebelly told, and knew by heart the names of all the many moles who had over the molecyars visited the system from outside. Betony, on the other paw, was as sweet and loving a female as ever lived, and his only grief for her was that though he watched her love for Wharfe grow and mature over the years, he was wise enough to see it was not returned. Wharfe was made of sterner stuff than Betony, and would only ever see her as a friend.

As for the last of the four, Harebell, she was more graceful, more alive, more alert than any female Squeezebelly could remember, and he hoped that when her time came she would find a mate worthy of her, and her young would be a credit to the system that had adopted her.

In the moleyears of these four youngsters' maturing, Squeezebelly was often moved to take stance at places he loved in high Beechenhill, and harbour the innocent hope that perhaps Beechenhill was the place which, secret and protected, sacred and much loved, the Stone had set aside to be a last bastion in its hour of greatest need, the place perhaps of its redemption. Here, believed Squeezebelly, great things would be, and he prayed that its moles would be worthy, and those four young ones would be especially so.

It was Squeezebelly who best understood the significance of Wharfe's extraordinary rush to touch the Stone that June, and guessed that with the torrential drowning of the moles afterwards in tunnels never yet bloodied by the Word's dark talons, Beechenhill's trial was beginning; and perhaps moledom's too.

In the moleyears of summer that followed June Squeezebelly noticed that Wharfe became preoccupied, even sullen, and was inclined to wander off by himself. At first he put it down to that normal change that comes to a mole when, matured, he or she begins to feel the restraints of the home system and, at the same time, to look more seriously for a mate. In Squeezebelly's younger days such thoughts arose in the dark snug winter years of January, not at the height of summer. But he was a wise and philosophical mole and had observed that the stresses of the plague years and the grikes had made moles, even sensible ones, behave in most curious and untraditional ways.

But neither Bramble nor Harebell seemed to think that was it at all, and the older mole eventually got a better and more significant explanation from his daughter Betony.

'Something happened when he touched the Stone, but he won't say exactly what. It's upset him more than he admits. Do you know what he does when he goes off by himself?'

Squeezebelly shook his head and scratched his ample flank. No he didn't and his bulk was now so great that he was disinclined to follow younger moles about and try to hide behind thistles to see what they were doing by themselves!

'Well, I'll tell you. He's looking for a mole or moles unknown. He stares into everymole's face that comes along hoping he's going to see what he's looking for.'

'Which is what, Betony?' said Squeezebelly, much puzzled.

'He won't say. All I know is he's not looking for a mate because I asked him outright and he said he wasn't and Wharfe never lies, which is a relief. I think it's got to do with the Stone.'

'Ah!' said Squeezebelly, and decided to wait for Wharfe to tell him in his own good time which, since the mole was looking uncharacteristically miserable, in sharp contrast to the glorious summer, would be sooner than later.

Meanwhile Squeezebelly kept him and the others busy with training and watching tasks designed to strengthen the system's defences and retreats, and made them develop, as a final safety measure, one or two special routes out to the north and west, in case a full-scale evacuation should ever become necessary. It was not an option Squeezebelly himself would ever take, but perhaps there could be a case for some of the younger moles to be got out one day.

Naturally moles asked him what was apaw, and he told them something of his fears and hopes as well.

'When or how the grikes might come I know not, but we must be vigilant. Equally, the Stone will give us guidance and we must be ready to hear that too, for the Stone works in mysterious ways and what it wants us to do is not always easy to discover.'

'But haven't you any idea at all what we're looking for?' asked Harebell.

'He'd tell us if he knew,' said Wharfe.

Harebell grinned.

'He didn't always tell us we were going the wrong way in the tunnels before we got lost when we were pups! That is before he got too rotund to go the more secret ways!'

All of them but Wharfe managed to laugh, Squeezebelly especially, and he patted his large stomach and said, 'Pure muscle, my dears, not a mite of wasted flesh at all! But listen. Over the years I've learnt most and been challenged best by the followers the Stone has sent here to visit us, Tryfan himself included. They always come in summer, so be observant when they come and see if there isn't one who can give us a clue to what we're looking for.'

Summer is ever a time for visitors, moles in other systems growing restive then, and that summer was no exception and a good few moles passed through in late July, and more in August. In return for the warm welcome such moles got they were as usual asked to pass on their knowledge of moledom beyond Beechenhill, and so Squeezebelly saw that his moles were kept informed and outward-looking. It was in August that they had confirmation for the first time of rumours of changes at Whern, and that Lucerne, son of Henbane, had taken over as Master of the Word.

This was news indeed, and inevitably resurrected once more the old stories told of Henbane and her southern invasion, and the graphic accounts given of her by Mayweed and Sleekit when they had brought Wharfe and Harebell into the system with the help of Skint and Smithills, both old friends of Squeezebelly.

Always at such times Squeezebelly had to ask himself how much longer he must keep the secret of Wharfe and Harebell's parentage from them, and whether he was right to keep them in ignorance at all. He had noticed that Wharfe in particular seemed to have doubts about the truth of the idea that Mayweed and Sleekit were their parents, and in fact had never directly asked if it were true – as if he was afraid of what the answer might be. Sometimes both moles said that they would like to see Mayweed and Sleekit again, but moles were used to wandering and separation, and in those times to permanent loss as well.

So when the news came that Henbane had been deposed and had gone missing, the time did indeed seem to have come to tell them the truth and one day in September the opportunity arose.

It was shortly after Wharfe had returned from a dangerous reconnaissance down the Dove Valley towards Ashbourne, confirming an escalation in grike guardmole activity, and he was in Squeezebelly's burrow with Harebell and their friends Bramble and Betony.

It was one of those friendly family occasions, when the chatter may be idle but the feelings are close and deep; such a time indeed when moles who love each other may say things that matter much to them. It seemed an ideal time for Squeezebelly to say what he had so long wanted to, and the presence of his own two seemed to make it more appropriate.

But it was Wharfe who spoke first, and quite unexpectedly.

'I'm sorry,' he said suddenly, 'about being so morose all summer but ever since June. . . .'

There was silence in the burrow. He had said at last what all of them had thought at different times, and only Betony had dared raise with him.

'I should have spoken before.'

Harebell nodded silently.

'But it's not been easy.'

'Never is,' said Bramble.

'Let him get on with it,' said Betony.

'Well . . . I don't know where to begin. Well I do. It was the day I touched the Stone, in fact the moment I touched the Stone. The day it rained.'

Nomole spoke, all remembered.

'I had this feeling as I touched the Stone that there were others touching with me.'

'But you were alone,' said Betony. 'We didn't reach you till ages later.'

'I know, but I don't mean moles you could see, or even moles that were there. It was like . . .' And then he tried to tell them what it was like – as Mistle had tried to tell Cuddesdon, as Caradoc had tried to tell Alder, as Glyder had told nomole but Caradoc, who had known already.

Perhaps they found it hard to understand exactly what Wharfe was trying to describe, but when a mole they all knew so well, and who was of them all the strongest and on whom one day soon the responsibility of leadership would fall, when such a mole expressed grief and loss they believed and understood the strength of his feeling well enough.

'Why didn't you *say* before,' said Harebell. 'Perhaps we could have helped.'

'The moles who I felt touch the Stone with me seemed so real. As for the one we were all trying to help, I *know* he's real, as real as any of you. I *know* that somehow one day I'll meet him.'

'It's a him, is it?' said Betony with relief, as if she half imagined that had it been a female she would have stolen Wharfe's heart away. They all laughed, as families do at such moments.

'Has the thought crossed your mind that it was the Stone Mole you were "trying to help"?' said Squeezebelly.

Wharfe nodded and shifted his stance, his strength and dark fur in contrast to Harebell who was lighter in both colour and weight.

'I'm sure it was,' he said. 'Maybe we're all of us – us in Beechenhill, followers in other systems, moles like Henbane and that Lucerne in Whern – all part of something that has started with the coming of the Stone Mole.'

'If he *has* come,' said Bramble. 'It's such an old myth the Stone Mole one, going right back – seems strange to think it's happening for real in *our* generation. But perhaps when a mole like Rune of Whern takes power, or moles like Boswell of Uffington and Tryfan of Duncton Wood start trekking about, then everything follows inevitably from it.'

Silence fell again until, in that indefinable way moles who know each other well sense that one is thinking of something he is staying quiet about, they knew that Squeezebelly was holding something back. He shifted about restlessly and then sighed and said, 'Well, I knew there would never be a good time, a best time. A mole can't get everything right!'

'What is it?' said Betony immediately, a frown on her face. She had rarely seen her father discomfited.

It was then, quietly, privately, he told them the story of how Wharfe and Harebell had come to the system. From the very beginning he told it, how Tryfan had trekked north preaching non-violence until he eventually reached Whern; how he had met Henbane there; and how he mated with her and then been all but killed by Rune's sideem. The rest they knew, or had heard from others over the moleyears – of how Mayweed and Sleekit had rescued two of the three pups born, and brought them to Beechenhill, of how . . . but neither Wharfe nor Harebell heard more, so dumbstruck were they to learn who their parents really were.

'He was our father?' said Wharfe in astonishment.

'Henbane was our *mother*?' said Harebell.

'She . . .' began Squeezebelly.

'You should have told us before!' shouted Wharfe.

'Yes, you should, and *you* must have known as well!' cried Harebell, turning on Bramble and Betony, both as shocked as their siblings by adoption.

There was anger; there were tears; there was sulking. Then each in their own way grew angry again – now with Squeezebelly, now with each other, and finally with Tryfan. Through it all Squeezebelly stayed sadly calm, pointing out again and again that nomole – not him, not Tryfan – does everything right all the time.

'But Henbane!' shouted Harebell in disgust. 'Tryfan with Henbane!'

'He was not an easy mole was Tryfan, but none I ever met or ever hope to meet was truer to the Stone than he,' said Squeezebelly, feeling the anger needed a response. 'What he had learnt of the Stone he had learnt in courage, and Bramble and Betony here remember better than any of us the preaching he made, and what a great mole he was.'

Betony nodded, her paw to Wharfe's, tears in her eyes while both Harebell and Wharfe, still appalled, glowered at the rest of them.

'You would have been so proud of him,' whispered Betony to Wharfe, and meaning well she added tactlessly, 'and now I know the truth I can see that there's something of him in you. He was so dark and big and forbidding.'

Wharfe looked utterly outraged.

'And me?' said Harebell miserably, waving a paw over her grey fur and flanks. 'What is there of him in me? It's *Henbane* that's in me!'

Squeezebelly went to her and held her close in his great paws while she wept, and if there were tears in his own eyes he did not care. When she had quietened he said, 'I have never seen Henbane, but I met moles who knew her, none better than Sleekit who loved and cared for you as if you were her own. She told me that when this day came and I told you the truth that I must say this. That until the day Henbane met Tryfan, Sleekit would have pitied any pup of Henbane's. But after that day something of great love and light was born in her Mistress (as she always called her). Something she had never seen before, though it must always have been there.'

Squeezebelly spoke slowly and with such a sense of concern and tenderness for them all that the atmosphere in the burrow quietened.

'Sleekit said that as Henbane grew with pup her feelings for her pups – for you – changed from indifference to love; when she felt your movements inside her it was as if she understood something about the nature of a light she had glimpsed long before, and known again only when she and Tryfan had made love. The more these feelings grew, the more afraid she was of the threats to you – not only from the dark intent of Rune and the sideem around him, but from herself, for she knew she had been corrupted.

'She asked – she begged – Sleekit to take you from her once you were born, even though she knew she would not want it and might resist. She felt she would not have sufficient love for you to fight the corruption she had suffered; she felt she would be unworthy of you. This was a most courageous thing for her to ask, and one that Sleekit said caused her much suffering as the time for your birth came. Yet she said it again and again. Through her contact with your father, Tryfan, she had for the first time seen something of the light, and she wanted her pups to know it too, even though she felt she could not have it in her own life.

'Be angry with her if you will, but she did more to show her love for you than many parents ever do. And at the end, when you were born and helpless, she fought with her whole strength for you, and made it possible for Sleekit and Mayweed to rescue two of you at least, and bring you out of Whern. Be proud of her as well. As for your grey fur, Harebell, which you think may be as

Henbane's was, well, mole, that tells me only that your mother must have been most beautiful. And if such as Tryfan loved her, and made you in union with her, why then I am sure the Stone in some way blessed their union, and that one day moledom will also see that it was blessed.'

Squeezebelly fell silent then, and not a mole in that deep burrow doubted that each was much loved by the other, and in some strange way much loved by the Stone.

'But . . . this Lucerne,' whispered Harebell at last, 'he is our brother. The Master of the Word is our *brother*.'

Squeezebelly stared at them, and at his Bramble and Betony, and he said, 'We live in times I do not always understand. Since Tryfan came here I have felt that the Stone has chosen Beechenhill for something no other system will know. All these years, all these decades, since long before I was born, since the coming of the first mole himself, perhaps, the Stone has blessed this system and kept its moles in health and faith, as if it knew that one day it would need a place most fitting to the light it casts, and the Silence that is all its own. More and more I believe this great event is near. I believe it has been nearer ever since the Stone Mole's star first showed. I believe your strange birth of parents supremely of the Stone and of the Word is part of this event.

'And if I had to look into the future and say what might be, I would say to both of you that if the day should ever come when you meet your brother Lucerne then more than your own lives will depend on how you conduct yourselves with him. I believe all of moledom will tremble in that hour, and in time all moledom will know of it, for better or for worse.

'Your father preached before our Stone, and spoke of the non-violent way. I do not know what that way may be, yet always I strive to find it. Where he is now or what happened to him I cannot tell. Your mother was the very head of the violence that the Word wreaked across moledom, yet she gave you the chance of life before the Stone, and now she has power no more, but more than that I do not know.

379

'What I do know is that I, and through me Beechenhill, was entrusted with your lives. We have reared you here as best we could, in a community which knows the Stone's light. Why, if either of your parents could see you now, as I can, then I think they would be as proud of you as you should feel of them.'

So Squeezebelly spoke, and nomole could doubt that he had fulfilled his task in those two moles. They looked at him with love, as Bramble and Betony did, and though they did not think it then, they one day would: that they may have lost first their parents, and then the two moles who saved and reared them, but in Squeezebelly they had found a mole who had ever showed them as much of love and faith and honour as the truest parents ever could.

'And now,' he said, 'I think you must decide if you are to keep this secret or tell other moles. We shall all do as you wish.'

'Secret,' said Wharfe, 'though I hate to take that way.'

'Secret for now,' said Harebell, 'though I hate it too. But moles might not understand. . . .'

'For now only,' said Wharfe. 'But one day we must tell.'

'So be it,' said Squeezebelly. 'Bramble? Betony?'

'We shall not tell,' said Bramble.

'I shall never say,' said Betony with a smile towards Wharfe.

The number of visitors to Beechenhill had been declining since news of the changes at Whern had come into the system and by mid-September no visitors at all were seen, and few even heard of.

The weather had worsened, and as autumn came across the southern Peak, grike patrols increased in the peripheral areas, not only in the east and south, but more ominously in the less populated west and north as well.

Then, like shadows gathering, the news filtering into Beechenhill became more grim. A watcher went missing on the eastern side; two vagrants who, it seemed, had been trying to reach Beechenhill from the normally safe west were found slain by grikes.

Then in the last third of September news came from followers in Ashbourne that a great massing of moles was taking place, and soon after that an account of the snouting of the eldrene of Ashbourne, and three of her guardmoles, one of whom Squeezebelly knew to be a brave and secret supporter of the Stone. It was a great blow, for Ashbourne was a system that was traditionally friendly towards moles of Beechenhill and it seemed that the new regime of the Word was being thorough in its job if it was killing its own when they were deemed to go astray.

It was against this darkening background that Squeezebelly ordered a retreat into the more central and safer part of the system of moles who lived around its edges, while moles like Wharfe were sent out on missions to watch for grike movement and change. There was a sense of fear about the tunnels now, and all knew that the dangers Squeezebelly had warned about for so long might be soon upon them.

But for several days, and then a week, and then two weeks nothing happened. Several of those out on missions returned and reported no grike moves against Stone followers. The tension eased and there came that dangerous sense that the danger was past, and soon surely the Stone would send them better news. And so at first it seemed.

Wharfe had been sent to the north-west with three other moles including Bramble, and they had ventured a good many miles beyond Beechenhill itself and seen some evidence of grikes and even patrols up the Manifold Valley, which is the complex western boundary of Beechenhill. But beyond it, on Grindon Moor and north to Revidge Heath, there were no grikes.

It was as they turned back to make the long trek home, and were seeking a safe passage across the Manifold at Ecton, always a grike outpost, when Wharfe had turned a corner among the rough grasses above Ecton that he found himself face to face with a greying tough-looking mole. He seemed alone and regarded them gravely and kept utterly still, appraising them without fear or aggression. Wharfe had rarely seen a mole in such circumstances so self-assured, and asked with typical Beechenhill calm, 'What is your name, mole, and whither are you bound?'

The manner of the mole's reply, as much as its content, took them by surprise, for though he was one to their four he spoke quite without fear and indeed with considerable authority. He had a strong northern accent, and had he not spoken slowly they might have had trouble understanding him.

'Neither my name nor my destination need concern you yet. Where are *you* from?'

'Ours is the power to ask,' said Wharfe with a smile.

''Tis of no consequence,' he said coolly, settling down and smiling back in a way that they found disconcerting. Wharfe had a most uncomfortable feeling that he was out of his depth, and certainly he did not know quite how to proceed. The mole, who though a good deal older than him was evidently fit and powerful, eventually said after the silence had grown uncomfortable, 'We could stance here facing each other all day and learn nothing.'

'Or you could respond to our greeting and give us your name and destination,' said Wharfe.

The mole said nothing.

'Or at least where you are from,' added Bramble.

The mole seemed to think about this and finally made a positive decision to reply. But it was clear he felt neither threatened nor under duress.

'I'm from Mallerstang,' he said, watching Wharfe for a reaction.

Mallerstang . . . a name a mole would not easily forget, and one that stirred a memory in Wharfe of something told him once. Mallerstang! Aye, a memory of something Squeezebelly once said.

'You know the name, or have been told it,' said the mole

matter-of-factly, as if he could read Wharfe's mind. 'Then let me speak another name: Medlar. Mallerstang and Medlar. What stirs in your memory now?'

Bramble, whose love of legend and history was well known, whispered something to Wharfe who listened, nodded, asked a question, and looked at the Mallerstang mole with surprise.

'I see the names mean something to *you*,' said the mole to Bramble.

'They do,' said Bramble. 'Medlar was a mole from your system who came this way long ago. He came with another whose name we cannot remember.'

'Roke,' said the mole.

'That's it!' said Bramble. 'Roke!'

At the mention of this name the mole's look softened and he smiled with pleasure. He turned from them and called out, 'Come, it is safe, these moles shall not harm us.'

To the surprise of Wharfe and the others, all used to trekking and the arts of hiding, two moles who had seemed but shadows in the grass rose up and came forward and stanced one on each side of the mole's firm flanks.

'My name is Skelder,' said the mole. 'This is Ghyll,' he said of the mole on his right, a younger male of two Longest Nights. 'And this is Quince.'

Though little smaller than the other two, she was more slight, and like them had about her a peaceful air and open, honest look combined with purpose and intelligence. She was about Wharfe's age.

'Roke was my kinsmole,' said Skelder, 'and as your friend may know he travelled south with Medlar as far as a system called Beechenhill. There they stayed for a time before Medlar travelled on and Roke returned to Mallerstang. He had good memories of Beechenhill and said it was a blessed place and worshipped the Stone most truly.'

'What is it you want?' asked Wharfe.

It was Quince who spoke, her eyes on Wharfe's.

'Sanctuary,' she said. 'Do you know where Beechenhill is?'

383

'We are of Beechenhill,' said Wharfe not moving. 'Why do you seek sanctuary?'

'The grikes have destroyed our system,' said Ghyll, 'and we are the last survivors.' Wharfe stared at them horrified, a horror made all the worse by the resignation in their eyes.

'We have travelled far to get to you,' said Skelder. 'We knew of no other system to go to. We thought your system might be safe. We thought . . .' He spoke with such sincerity and lack of self-pity that Wharfe knew he spoke the truth and was deeply of the Stone. Indeed, all of them were moles for whom faith had put into their faces, and into their stances, all that was noble in moles, all that anymole might trust. He had been doubtful and kept them talking while he assessed them, but neither he nor his companions would question them more.

'Come, we shall guide you to Beechenhill,' he said. 'It is two days from here by the route we shall take to avoid grikes.'

But luck was not with them, for though they passed Ecton and the river safely, on the slopes of Ecton Hill they ran into a patrol of grikes. It was an ambush and well planned and Wharfe thought ruefully that perhaps they had talked too long in the open when they first met these moles and had been seen.

The grikes, five in all, followed their normal strategy and charged suddenly and violently. Strike first, ask questions after was their usual tactic and one before which Beechenhill moles were inclined to retreat if they could, and if they could not then to act stupid and escape later. Each was a tactic that had worked for generations, but on this occasion it could not work. The grikes were large and fearsome to a mole, and perhaps because they were outnumbered seemed intent on causing injury. When the questions came, if they ever did, it might be too late. On the other paw the only route for fleeing was downslope back towards Ecton, and Wharfe knew that there were plenty of moles there he would not like to meet.

But as all these thoughts flashed through his mind and he prepared to meet the onslaught of the approaching grikes, the three Mallerstang moles, as if impelled by a common mind, began to move as one. The effect was, Wharfe afterwards remembered, most odd, as if he and all the other moles but those three were not moving at all, while the Mallerstang moles seemed to drift forward in a movement so fluid that between its beginning and its end there seemed barely nothing at all, but for a paw striking a grike here, a talon caressing a grike snout there, and a shoulder buffeting a grike over there. All in silence. Then normality returned, and everything was still but for the sound of the breeze in the moorland grass, and the heavy, pained breathing of grikes.

Two of the grikes were unconscious on the ground, a third was lying still and staring as if made mute and quiet by what he had seen, a fourth was picking himself up and beginning to flee, and the fifth was fleeing already, long past them down the slope.

'They are not hurt, and will come to very soon,' said Skelder calmly. Ghyll and Quince moved to his flank. 'Come, lead us from here quickly before they do so.'

Soon they reached tunnels Wharfe knew and then moved on swiftly to Beechenhill. In the rare moments they paused, Wharfe tried to get Skelder and his comrades to explain how they had stopped the grikes, but they only shrugged and said they did not like to hurt moles, it was not their way.

Their arrival at Beechenhill caused considerable excitement, and as soon as they had eaten and rested they were brought before Squeezebelly in the main communal chamber of the system near the Stone. When Squeezebelly heard who the moles were he greeted them warmly.

'Mallerstang?' he boomed. 'Of course I know of it! Medlar and Roke? They came here before I was born but my father spoke of them. But. . . .'

Wharfe told him briefly of how it was the three had come to Beechenhill and he looked at them sombrely.

'I could have wished your visit here to be in very different circumstances,' he said. 'Tell us what happened.'

Skelder told them, slowly and terribly. Of how the peaceful Mallerstang moles, whose system lies on the slopes above Horton-cum-Ribblesdale, had heard of the coming of a group of grike guardmoles and sideem, led by a mole of Whern called Clowder. Of how their elders had been tricked into meeting these moles and trapped in a place where they could not defend themselves at all, and all killed.

Of how the other Mallerstang moles, who though adept at individual and small-group combat, were not experienced in group warfare and were successively massacred.

'Face any one of us with two or three of those moles and we will disable them without hurting them,' said Skelder with feeling, 'but face us with such a disciplined and ruthless force as that and we will always be defeated.' His account wore inexorably on. . . .

Chamber by chamber the grike guardmoles massacred the Mallerstang moles, who made the mistake of massing where they could be caught. Unused to group confrontation, not willing to flee into alien country, they stayed where they were and, in tunnels now struck down by an eerie silence, were killed as if paralysis had overtaken the whole system.

'But didn't more of you flee?' asked Wharfe appalled.

'It is not our way,' said Quince simply. 'We talk, we retreat, we tire those who oppose us. Then we let them live among us, and they see our way is right. There are – were – many moles in our community who came from grike stock, and many other kinds of moles besides. We do not fight, we do not flee; we *show*. In the face of such absolute violence we did not know what to do.'

'Then how come you three survived?' said Bramble.

'Chance. The turn of shadows. As the random fall of rain across a field may leave a patch dry, so we three were missed. We heard the killing, we stayed still when we realised the numbers involved, and we were missed. We were not even together, but separate, in places over-looked. When the grikes went we found each other, and when they came briefly back with moles of Horton, we hid. That was the worst moment. We heard them killing prisoners. That was the worst.'

Skelder shook his head, resigned.

'Moles cannot stop the rain, or the sun, or the cycle of the seasons, or death. Death has come to our system and so it was long ago forecast. We three are the survivors, and that too was ordained. It was meant to be.'

To Wharfe it seemed astonishing. Why, if such a catastrophe happened to Beechenhill, he would . . . he would. . . .

'What would you do?' asked Quince, her paw on his, her gaze penetrating.

'Weep,' he said.

'We have,' she said. 'And when the tears were done, and we saw there was nothing we could do in Mallerstang, we resolved to come to Beechenhill because of what Roke said of this system long ago when he returned to us.'

Nomole said a thing, none dared look at another. What could a mole say in the face of such events?

It was Quince who broke the silence, wanting, it seemed, to move on from memories which hurt so much. She turned to Squeezebelly and asked, 'Did your father tell you what happened to the mole Medlar?'

'Oh yes, I know what happened to him, though it was not my father who told me, but a mole of Duncton Wood called Tryfan. *His* father met Medlar, and indeed was trained in fighting by him.'

'Defence,' corrected Quince. 'Medlar would have called it "defence", not "fighting".'

'Defence then,' said Squeezebelly with a wry smile. 'Medlar was a great mole, and he went on to Uffington and there became Holy Mole.'

A look of great joy came to the faces of the three Mallerstang moles.

'Did you not know this?' said Squeezebelly.

'We could not,' replied Skelder, 'but Motte, one of the greatest elders of Mallerstang, who prophesied much that has happened, including the survival of three moles from such a massacre as we witnessed, also said this: "A mole shall come out of Mallerstang, and into moledom go, and shall rise to wisdom in the greatest of the systems of Stone and Word." '

'Then his prophecy came true,' said Squeezebelly. 'You shall all be welcome to stay here for as long as you wish,' he continued. 'Beechenhill has benefited greatly over the years from such fugitives as yourselves.'

But if the news these moles brought was grim, the next that came brought the threat of grikes much nearer home.

One evening in October Squeezebelly was enjoying a chat with Skelder, Wharfe and Harebell when they were interrupted suddenly by the urgent arrival of a watcher, one of those who had gone with Betony and two other moles to patrol the south end. He was obviously tired from his journey, and had been injured in a skirmish. In his eyes was a look of great concern.

'What is it, mole?' said Squeezebelly, his normal good cheer fading from his face.

''Tis your daughter Betony,' said the mole. 'She's taken by grikes.'

Betony! A mole they all knew and all loved. Sweet Betony.

The watcher's story was soon told. The four of them had come upon a solitary vagrant female on the slopes above Ashbourne. She said she was of Tissington and was seeking passage into Beechenhill with two other moles who were in hiding nearby . . . It sounded like a simple ambush and they kept her talking while vetting her, much as Wharfe had done when he had met Skelder. She was most convincing and gave a name the watcher later had good reason to think false.

Then, quite suddenly, the group had been attacked by

several grikes at once, the female herself being the first to strike a blow. No amount of courage, faith, or attempting to see the shadows of those attacks had saved them. The watchers had been caught, one killed outright, and then they were all interrogated. In this the female, far from being harmless, proved the cruellest of them all and soon seemed to sense that Betony might be especially knowledgeable of the system.

They used the vilest tortures on the other watcher and soon Betony could not bear to see his agonies any longer.

'She tried to lie, telling untruths to save him, but that female seemed able to detect the subtlest lie, the subtlest truth. My friend was hurt more when she lied, and it was not long before they discovered that Squeezebelly was her father.'

The listening moles looked at each other, horrified.

'Then the female ordered that my friend be released and Betony was taken away. Even as they turned from us I saw the remaining grikes were preparing to kill us. I shouted to my friend and turned and ran for the tunnels. They chased us but we were in ground we knew. We were able to pick one off, and then they turned back. I . . . I turned to follow them, but there were too many . . . I could not save her, Squeezebelly. I could not. I would have given my life for Betony.' He lowered his snout and wept.

Squeezebelly, Wharfe and Harebell stared at each other blankly. Then Squeezebelly barked out orders to some moles to go to the south end and see what they might find . . . but all knew it would be no use.

'What were their names, these grikes?'

'There were so many . . . but the female's name I heard, a different name from that she gave us first.'

'Yes, mole?' growled Wharfe.

'She was called sideem Mallice.'

'May the Stone protect her if she harms Betony,' said Wharfe angrily. 'I shall lead the search for her myself.'

'She knows so much,' Squeezebelly said softly. He stared dumbly at Wharfe and Harebell, the possibilities too terrible to speak aloud.

Chapter Twenty

Like an old mole who knows how to pace himself on a long journey, the River Thames gathers its strength but slowly as it travels across southern England from its source in the high Cotswolds to the distant eastern sea marshes and flats which lie beyond the dark Wen.

Before twofoots came and made their crossing points, the great river was a barrier which few moles crossed, and those that did remain as giants in the legends of the past. Of these, none is better known than Balagan, first White Mole, bringer of the knowledge of the Stone out of the dereliction that lies north even of Whern itself, who crossed the river in one single mighty leap; and where his seventh leap thereafter took him he founded Uffington.

But although the Thames flows generally eastward all moles know that in the centre of its course it makes a great meander north, whose loop forms the north and eastern boundaries of the great vale of Uffington. Duncton, bounded by the Thames and using an outcrop of chalk to rise clear of its more marshy ground, marks almost the northern limit of this great meander; while the Holy Burrows of Uffington watch over the vale from its southern side, perched on the chalky Wessex uplands wherein, yet further south, lies Avebury.

Between these two is that magical and secret country, verdant and fluvial, whose quiet and gentle systems were the homes of the first scribes of Uffington. Charney and Stanford in the vale, Shellingford and Grove, Marcham and Lushingmarsh . . . Fyfield, another of the Ancient Systems, is there and from these places, and many more about them, came the great scribes of the past.

It was not by chance that Rune ordained that in this hallowed vale Buckland should become the very centre of the southern grike campaign. Where better to base the campaign of terror and repression that, by Tryfan's young adulthood, had all but destroyed the gentle and ancient culture of the Stone?

Yet though the spirit of the Stone may have been driven from many of these ancient sites, topography does not change. When October comes, and the seasonal fruits are rich and the hedges and the trees are all russets and yellow brown, thought of the Word's darkness easily slips away from a mole positive enough to see the light about him. For then the Thames is at its most gracious and fulsome, and all across the vale there flows and drifts that easy sense of the misty autumn beauty that living water always brings.

While jays and squirrels build their stores, and soft fungi emerge stiffly from the dew-wet grass and leaf litter, then after tunnel-clearing is done moles venture out and snout at the fresh moist air. They peer at the huddles of earwig and ladybird in fallen bark, and leave them be, content that the worms will be food enough when they flee the coming frosts to deeper ground and be on paw when they're most needed.

It was as such an October started that Beechen, together with Mayweed and Sleekit, found his way into this great vale.

Even with Mayweed to guide them they had not found escape from Duncton Wood as easy as they had hoped. Mayweed had done as Tryfan thought he should, and climbed the embankment of the roaring owl way planning to take a northern course until a safe crossing point could be found. Safe, that is, from roaring owls and grikes waiting on the far side. Once this had been accomplished Mayweed had intended to take route to the north, using one of the smaller cross-overs to reach the far side of the great Thames, and thence by quiet paths to Rollright, which is not too far beyond.

Rollright was Beechen's choice because it was his great

desire to visit first another of the Ancient Systems and, though not the nearest, Tryfan knew it to be not too difficult of access – or so he and Spindle had found when they had come down from the north. It seemed a sensible choice, and all the more so from Mayweed's point of view for his old route-finding friend Holm lived there and would make them welcome.

But it had not worked out like that.

Once up the embankment of the roaring owl way, Mayweed had twitched and quivered his snout north and not liked what he sensed at all.

'Grikes Sir, grikes lurking, grikes nasty very much. Waiting for such a break-out as this. And since humbleness has two responsibilities today, bold Beechen and sensuous Sleekit, he prefers to proceed with especially extreme caution.'

For the most part Mayweed had to shout this over the screech of roaring owl which raced past them in a never-ending stream of noise and fumy wind. Beechen and Sleekit had been forced to find cover as best they could among the grass and debris by the way, with strict instructions not to look at the roaring owls.

'Their smells are bad enough, Sir, but when their gazes start at dusk, beware! Intoxicated and then hypnotised, a mole is likely to wander where he shouldn't until he gets used to them, and such wandering leads to death, even for Stone Moles. Humble me has got away with a lot in his worthless time but even he would find it difficult to find a form of words which he could use to Tryfan and your mother which would pass over the grim truth that moledom's greatest hope had been squashed flat within sight of Duncton Wood. Not a good beginning, Sir! Not one to inspire others to follow in your paws. No, no, not good at all.' Mayweed laughed wryly, and Beechen grinned, but took the warning seriously.

This counsel given and repeated several times, Mayweed eventually turned tail and led Beechen south. Perhaps they would be able to cross the way in safety and find a route right round the cow cross-under which is the only direct exit from Duncton Wood.

They travelled all day and at night took unpleasant refuge along the way and waited for the dawn. Still unsatisfied Mayweed pressed on south and for another day they braved the continual race of roaring owl and occasional harassment of kestrel.

Throughout all this the inimitable Mayweed made observations and gave constant advice which he thought Beechen might find useful.

'Keen sighted Sir,' he said after one especially frightening kestrel-stoop on them, 'it isn't that our feathered friend the kestrel likes our flesh, because he doesn't. It's bitter to him. It is rather that (astonishingly enough) they mistake us for voles, in whom they have a consuming interest. Ha, ha, ha! Moles should therefore look carefully at the stooping kestrel and decide if he has brains. If his eyes are close-set and his tail and wings have a doltish look, flap your paws and look madly molish and he'll take the hint and fly off.'

'And roaring owls?' laughed Beechen. 'Do they like us?'

Mayweed grinned and said, '*Like* us! Stop one and ask it and let humbleness know the answer!'

They spent another uncomfortable night along the embankment.

'Begrimed Beechen,' Mayweed said the next morning. 'We apologise, do Sleekit my consort and I myself for this unexpected inconvenience and filth but there we are! What is a mole to do? It *is* a mole to do! Ha! See? He smiles, my sweet and dusty love, our ward sees the joke! But seriously . . .' And Mayweed wrinkled his snout and glanced here and there . . . 'me, Mayweed, has felt better going south. There's something wrong with going north. Something not quite right.'

'Perhaps we *should* be going south. Perhaps what's wrong is thinking we should go north,' said Beechen reasonably. 'And anyway, Fyfield's down this way and that's an Ancient System every bit as good as Rollright is according to Spindle's texts.'

'Not only well informed but brilliant Sir, that is true. Let me point my snout south with that in mind and see what we get. Humph! We get, we get. . . .'

'We get something very appealing,' said Sleekit. 'We get off this roaring owl way towards the area where scribing first started.'

At this a remarkable change overtook Mayweed.

'We also, we also . . . oh, humble me, we. . . .'

In the space of a few moments poor Mayweed had turned from his normal self to a mole who seemed frozen to the spot with fear.

Sleekit went immediately to his flank, put her paws tenderly to him, signalled with her eyes to Beechen to do nothing and stay where he was, and said, 'What is it, my love?'

'Buckland, the Slopeside tunnels black as night. Humbleness never wants to go back there. That's south as well, and not far from Fyfield.'

'But you don't have to go there, Mayweed,' said Sleekit.

'Don't I, Madam? Can you be sure? You cannot. Mayweed trembles because what Beechen said was right – we *should* be going south, that was what was wrong. Rollright, which is where we're meant to be going by common consent, certainly does not seem to be south since it is in the opposite direction. But then if humbleness can state a truism of travelling: the longer way is often better or, as nomole has been brainy enough to say until this moment, the hasty mole dies first. Yes, yes, the way *round* may be the only way. It *is* the way. But me myself do not want to go that way because Buckland lies there waiting.'

'Well . . .' began Sleekit.

'But it is the way we must go, isn't it?' said Beechen with authority. 'It *does* feel right to me.'

Mayweed nodded his head sadly, shook it wearily, then nodded it again.

'I shall go alone,' said Beechen. 'We're clear of Duncton and I can find my way from here.'

But Mayweed went quickly past him, took several paces on along the way, turned round and leered in a rueful manner, and said, 'Promise me one thing, boldness: if our "right" route goes anywhere near Buckland, let alone the Slopeside, you, Beechen, can go first.'

With that, having agreed to give themselves up to the free and vagrant spirit that often leads moles with the courage to follow it to where the Stone intended they should go, Mayweed led them down the embankment of the roaring owl way and south into the Vale of Uffington.

The details of the route they initially took, in what has become known as Beechen's First Ministry, have been the subject of much research and argument, and few facts about the early weeks of their journey can be established. We know only that Beechen, used as he was to all moles being friends, had a natural wish to talk with anymole they found. Therefore it was with great difficulty that Mayweed and Sleekit persuaded him to be cautious, at least at first, and to proceed slowly. Their advice prevailed in those early days and Mayweed or Sleekit – the one thin and scarred with scalpskin, the other elegant and with all the authority her sideem training had given her – went on ahead to sound out moles they met.

In fact, however, there seems no evidence that Beechen was much noticed, nor any that they suffered interference from guardmoles or grikes. They could not know that the part of the vale they had entered, though theoretically under the thrall of the Word like the rest of the south, was but thinly populated by grike. The policy long since adopted by Wyre in Buckland had been to put his resources into the bigger systems, draw moles into them, and let the smaller systems in between die. This had made sense in the wake of the plagues and the first invasion, for there had been few moles about. Wyre knew that some outcasts lived in the less populated areas, but the occasional foray of guardmoles, a few prisoners taken and cruel examples made was enough to keep moles in the centres where they were and those outside lying very low indeed.

The moles who had survived were the more cunning and wily ones. Most were of the Stone, and if they were not they had their own reasons to live and let live and kept whatever little faith years of devastation had left them to themselves. What was more, by that October the young these free-thinking moles had borne in the spring were long grown up and, though wary of grikes, still had all the nerve and naivety of youth, and so had dared take tunnels in the more wormful places.

It was this kind of laxity (as Lucerne's new sideem termed it) which was soon to be the target of the great crusade, and had Beechen delayed going forth into the vale until November he would have found a very different and much darker scene.

Indeed, had he and Mayweed not decided that their right route from Duncton was south, and gone north instead, they would have travelled straight into that advancing tide of darkness that Lucerne had sent out from Cannock.

As it was, by journeying to the Vale of Uffington that October it might truly be said that the Stone had guided them to the place in all of moledom most ready to hear the truth of the Stone, and to recognise the mole of all moles best suited to preach it. In those crucial first molemonths of October it was still possible in that part of the vale for Beechen to move freely among moles who worshipped the Stone in relative safety. More, even, than that: they found a place where there were young adult moles with the rearing and nerve to dare listen to one who would preach of the Silence of the Stone, and to follow him.

We may guess that in the first weeks of their journey Mayweed and Sleekit warned Beechen many times against being too open about the Stone. But in any case, it is certain that he first wished to do what Tryfan had advised moles should do: listen and listen more. Then listen yet again, and only when the heart is loving and the mind is calm, speak.

This Beechen must have done, but since secrecy and deceit were never his way, and he believed that a mole must stance on all four paws, it was not long before he felt he must state his name, his system and his faith as clearly as he could.

Yet astonishingly, the earliest record of Beechen outside those in Duncton Wood – but for the brief record of those times that Mayweed himself later came to scribe – is one made in a short scrivening by an anonymous sideem in Blagrove, a minor grike system that lies between Duncton and Fyfield.

Blagrove. Two outcasts, one diseased, the other a Stone-fool. Warned them yet they gave their names readily: Mayweed and Becknon. From the east, no system noted. Becknon spoke of the Stone and I warned him again, but he continued his foolishness. There are more such Stone-fools about since the summer years and something must be done.

The scrivening does not mention Sleekit, who was perhaps hiding lest she should be recognised as a fellow sideem, but 'Becknon' must be a mis-hearing of 'Beechen', and clearly the moles were free to move about.

The reference to a 'Stone-fool' suggests that in the vale at least there were enough moles who had been maddened by disease and past troubles and the stresses of a vagrant's life that they dared to speak of the Stone openly. It is clear that until then the grikes had no need to punish such moles, seeing them as harmless and better left alone, but the comment 'something must be done' is an ominous precursor of the new repression soon to come.

But if Beechen and his friends succeeded at first in remaining little noticed it was not long before Beechen's name became more widely known among followers in the vale.

No single incident seems to have made more certain that this would be so than his healing, at Dry Sandford, of the mole Buckram. It seems that word had reached a small colony of moles at Sandford, a heath which lies a little to the west of Blagrove, that a mole most truly of the Stone was about, and perhaps already there was the hint that he was a healer. However that might be, a mole appeared one day where Beechen and the others were eating and asked if one of them was of the Stone.

'We are all of the Stone,' Beechen said softly, gazing on the mole. 'Whatmole is it that troubles you?'

The mole, whose name was Poplar, seemed astonished at this reply, and faltered, 'Nomole, none at all. It was just that we heard you might . . . we thought you could . . . is your name Beechen?'

He saw that it was.

'A mole told us that you spoke of the Stone. Well, we would like to hear what you've got to say.'

'Whatmole troubles you?' asked Beechen again. 'It's for that you want me not my words.'

'Will you come?' said Poplar hastily. 'Please.'

So they had gone, climbing the dusty way up to Sandford and finding there, on a nondescript slope of pasture above a brook, a few meagre burrows and five moles.

It was not long before Beechen had them telling of whatmole it was that put the fear he had straightaway seen in the mole's heart. The little colony had started a cycle before, with Poplar and his mate, and they had three autumn young of whom one died. The surviving two, both females, made tunnels nearby and a male outcast had come by in the spring and taken one of the females to mate, though as yet there were no young.

'We live a peaceful life, we avoid the grikes, we meet others like ourselves in the higher heath where the guard-moles do not bother to go and there, in our way, we give thanks to the Stone. But in August our peace was shattered and our lives are now in jeopardy. We dare not move from here and yet we hardly dare stay . . .' It was plain from the faces of the others that they lived in great fear.

'You did not ask us here to learn of the Stone, did you?' said Beechen impatiently. Poplar was silent.

'It is our talons you value, not our hearts,' said Beechen. 'A mole finds it harder to help another who dares not speak the truth directly.'

Poplar's snout was low.

'Well, mole?'

Poplar nodded his head and then, looking up, he blurted out, 'I don't know how you know but you're right. We heard there was a Stone-fool passing near. They said you were a strong-looking mole in the company of two others, though I didn't realise they were old. But even so I thought if you came the one who threatens us might be afraid and go away.'

Mayweed looked at Sleekit and said, 'Ancient Crone, fellow "old" mole, we will not be of much use up here. Food? Certainly, withered Mayweed thinks. Sleep? Why not? he would say. Let us listen and feel old and eat and sleep when we will.' With that he fixed poor Poplar with one of his most ghastly grins, showing what yellow teeth remained in his mouth, and fell silent again.

'I didn't mean, I mean . . . well.'

'Tell us about this mole. Why does he make you so afraid?'

'He's diseased!' said one of the females.

'He threatens us!' said her sister.

'He says he'll kill us if we try to go away,' said Poplar's mate.

'Or tell the grikes we're followers of the Stone.'

The mole's name, it seemed, was Buckram. He was a guardmole with murrain and well known in those parts as having been cast out of Fyfield. He was said to have killed fellow guardmoles who threatened him, and had terrorised a succession of the small outposts of moles he had settled near. One day at the end of August he had appeared at one of the little meetings of followers up on the heath and shouted at them, and then taloned and wounded one of the males who had remonstrated with him.

'He said terrible things,' Poplar explained, 'and disrupted our meeting. Then when it was over he followed me rather than any of the others, not saying anything. We thought he would leave us but he didn't. He took over a burrow on the slopes above us and now he often threatens us as we've told you. He takes our worms and drinks in the stream where we like to, although there are plenty of other places. Nomole among those around here will help us drive him off because he's got murrain and it's getting worse. Recently he has been more violent and taloned and buffeted me out of his way by the stream. He's a *trained* guardmole. He's very strong and. . . .'

'What do you want me to do?'

A look of hope came to Poplar's face.

'Drive him away. You look strong enough to me, and since you must be outcasts you could stay on near here. You could all find room here. The grikes won't trouble you.'

'But my heart would trouble me,' said Beechen, gazing on them all and a look of terrible despair came over his face. 'You say his name is Buckram? Take me to him. Now.'

'We can point to where he lives,' said Poplar eagerly.

'Is there a Stone on the heath where you worship?'

'Why no, the nearest is at Fyfield. But nomole can go there and come out alive.'

'Would you like a Stone to rise above your burrows?'

'Why . . . yes. We're followers, aren't we? But there's no Stone here and never has been.'

'There is a Stone here, Poplar, but you cannot see it. It rises where Buckram waits.' Beechen leaned forward and touched the timid Poplar on the paw and gazed on him so that Poplar could not take his eyes away. 'Your Stone is where he is, and as he waits so it waits as well. See him truly, mole, and you shall see thy Stone.'

Poplar stared in awe at Beechen, and then as Beechen drew his paw away, the mole raised the paw he had touched and looked at it as if he expected to see more than a paw.

'I don't know what to do,' he said, and then turning to his family he said again, 'I have never known what to do.'

'So you ask another whom you barely know to do something for you, not even knowing what it should be? No, mole, *you* go to him. Go now, and ask him here and you might learn what it is you must do. He shall not harm you any more than you can bear.'

'I am afraid.'

'Then take these moles with you, for they are what you most love, which he will know. Go together, ask him to come with you, and we shall wait for you.'

'But . . . but . . .' began Poplar, but somehow, almost in a dream, he signalled the others out of the burrow and then followed them. At its exit he turned back and said, 'Whatmole are you?'

'You know my name.'

'Yes, yes I do,' said Poplar. 'What shall I say to Buckram? What happens if . . . ?'

'The Stone you shall see rise before you will tell you what to say. Now think no more but with thy heart. Go to him.'

And so they did, and Beechen and the others followed them to the surface and watched as they timidly went up the slope together, staying close for fear of what Buckram might do to them.

They saw the group stop and Poplar go forward. They guessed that he called out Buckram's name, for they heard a roar of rage and saw a great mole emerge and tower over Poplar.

Then all seemed quiet, all still, all caught in silence. Then Poplar turned from Buckram, and the great guardmole, his face livid with raw murrain, his paws bleeding with ulcers, his flanks open and fetid, followed behind him as meekly as if he were a pup.

They saw that in Poplar's gait and eyes were wonder and strange pride as he guided the diseased guardmole back to where Beechen had taken stance.

When they reached him it was Buckram who started to

401

speak first, his voice rough and broken, yet his hurt body restless and stanced as if ready to fight.

'He said . . . the mole said . . . he told me. . . .'

'What did he tell you?' asked Beechen, going to the stricken mole and putting his paws where the sores were worst. 'What did he say?'

But Buckram could not speak, for his hurt snout was low and his great ruined body seemed unable to support itself more.

'I said you were the Stone Mole,' said Poplar, staring at Beechen in awe.

Then he turned slowly back to Buckram and, reaching out his paw, touched him on the flank. Already the sores were healing, healthy skin growing in their place. 'I said you had come especially for him. I said, I said. . . .'

There, on that dry slope, where no Stone was, there rose a mighty Stone made of the rock of faith and shining with the light of faith. For there moles turned their fear to love, and with their love they touched one who they thought could give them nothing in return.

'Can you see your Stone now, Poplar?' asked Beechen.

Then Poplar looked at the moles about him, and saw them in a light brighter than he had ever known before, and he smiled and said that the Stone was there and he could see it, and knew he would always see it now.

From this time on news of Beechen's coming began to spread, though confined at first to those few moles who had found safe places to hide and made their lives in the obscurity of the more inaccessible parts of the vale. How the news spread none can be quite sure, for Beechen always asked moles not to speak of what he did for them, saying that it was a matter between them and the Stone alone.

But moles will share the excitements that come into their lives, and even if they try to keep them secret others will see the light in their eyes and soon find out. Indeed, is not community a sharing of such light?

They stayed a few days more with Poplar and his family to see Buckram through the dark lone time that followed his healing, and even in that short space moles came over the slopes and up the brook side to meet the mole they were beginning to hear whispers of. Beechen turned none away, but when the bolder among them asked if he really *was* the Stone Mole he would say, 'I am of the Stone and if you see the Stone in me you see only the truth in your own heart.'

Beechen spent time with Buckram, who before murrain had infected him had been a senior guardmole in Fyfield, and one much given to punishing others, and those of the Stone. But the eldrene, Wort, believing his spreading disease to be a judgement of the Word, ordered him to be outcast into the vale that his murrain might infect followers of the Stone.

That was the beginning of long moleyears of isolation for him, in which he learnt that nomole wanted him, and the only way he could make any respond to him was by making them afraid. Their fear was his only comfort, for through it he knew he was still ordinary mole.

'Why did you follow Poplar?' asked Beechen.

'I wanted to frighten him. He had what I didn't have, his health and family and a place. I thought . . . I don't know what I thought. He was there.'

'The Stone is there, always there, and you can hit it without hurting anymole but yourself.'

'But *I* couldn't strike you,' said Buckram in alarm, thinking that Beechen meant himself.

'But some moles could,' said Beechen, 'and one day I fear they will.'

Suddenly Buckram reared up, and in spite of his weakness and the newly healed sores they could see what a fierce and terrible mole he was. 'Take me with you and let me protect you,' he said. 'I shall let nomole harm you!'

But Beechen made no answer, though the light of utter faith was in Buckram's eyes.

When Beechen judged it was time for them to leave, Buckram asked again that he might go with them.

'What can you do for me?' asked Beechen.

'When my strength returns it will frighten those that threaten you,' he said.

But once more Beechen made no reply.

Then, when they had said their farewells and started downslope from Poplar's place, Buckram pulled himself from his burrow and came after them. Poplar and his family followed and listened as, for a third time, he begged to be allowed to travel with Beechen.

'What will you tell moles that threaten me?' asked Beechen, gazing on him.

'He'll tell them where to go!' said Poplar.

'One shake of his talons and they'll dare not harm you, Stone Mole!' said Poplar's mate.

But as Beechen smiled and shook his head, Buckram lowered his great brutish snout and muttered, 'No, no I'll not do that. Not ever again. No, I'll tell them not to be afraid, for I was afraid once and now I'm not. I'll tell them that.'

Then Beechen looked at him with pleasure and joy and said, 'Then I shall have great need of you, and you shall be with me, and be near me, for the day shall come when I shall be afraid and need your help.'

Then Buckram looked at the Stone Mole with love, and knew the Stone had given him a task that he would follow all his life.

'For now, Buckram, you shall stay here and grow strong. You shall help these others with your strength and faith to worship the Stone which will guide you in what to do. And mole shall remember the name of this place, and say that here at Sandford Heath was faith in the Stone reborn.'

'When shall I come to you?' asked Buckram eagerly.

'When the last tree is bare and the frosts begin, your work here will be done. Seek me out then where you first denied the Stone. I shall need such a one as you at my flank. Seek me there.'

The wondering moles watched as Beechen went on downslope, accompanied only by Mayweed and Sleekit.

404

'What did he mean, "where you first denied the Stone"?' asked Poplar.

'Fyfield,' said Buckram simply.

'But you were outcast from there. They'd kill you if you went back.'

'The Stone will guide me in safety,' said Buckram, 'just as it guided me here.'

During the autumn and early winter of that time Beechen, Mayweed and Sleekit wandered within the limits of the northern part of the Vale of Uffington, and wherever they went moles gathered to listen to Beechen and to seek healing. Sometimes the numbers were small, no more than families of moles such as Poplar's of Sandford Heath; at other times news of his coming went ahead and all the moles of a system were waiting to greet him.

It was a time of great happiness for him, when he had time to talk to the moles he met and learn much from them of their lives and experiences, listening as he had learned to do from the moles of Duncton Wood.

Now, too, for the first time, he met moles younger than himself, and recent mothers, and heard the different hopes they had, and felt their fears, sharing the ordinary things that make a mole's life.

'Is the Duncton Stone *very* big? And . . . and what's it look like?' one youngster asked him, for he had never seen a Stone at all and could not imagine what it might be like.

'It's not big to me, nor to anymole who trusts it,' replied Beechen. 'As for what it looks like, nomole could quite agree for it's hard to see it all at once, and each time you see a new part of it what you saw before seems changed.'

'Oh!' said the youngster, pondering this. 'But it *would* be big to me, wouldn't it?'

The mole's mother smiled and others laughed sympathetically, for they sensed, as Beechen did, that the youngster was afraid of this Stone the adults talked of. They, too, had been afraid when their parents had first talked of the Stone.

But Beechen did not smile or laugh, for he saw the youngster was truly afraid, and was not able to imagine that such a thing could be anything but big. And, being big, he felt it was not for him.

Beechen, ignoring the adults, snouted about the ground and found a small stone which he took in his paw.

'How big is this?' he asked the youngster.

'It's not big, it's small.'

Beechen asked the youngster to stance very still and placed the stone in the hollow between his shoulder blades.

'If you were the Stone and this little stone was the top of it, would it be big?'

'Only just, and then not *very* big!'

'But when you're adult and you've grown, won't it be bigger then?'

'Only just,' said the youngster, shifting about and trying in vain to see the stone on his shoulders, 'because I'll be bigger then myself.'

'And what will it look like?'

'Me mostly, if I'm still the rest of it!'

'That's how the Duncton Stone is to moles who see it right, it's how the Stone always is. It is there as that stone on you is. It grows as moles do and is never far beyond their reach; and they need only know themselves as they can be to know what it looks like.'

Beechen took the stone from the youngster's shoulders and placed it among the others on the ground.

'Which one was it?' asked the youngster.

'What is thy name, mole?'

'Milton,' said the mole abstractedly, staring at the stones. 'Which one was it really? This one?' He picked up one of the stones and held it up.

Beechen shook his head.

'The stone I touched is not yet ready for you to find, Milton. The search for it shall take you and many like you where you may fear to go and there you shall find it.'

*

406

By the beginning of November, Beechen had been warned by several moles of the growing danger of what he was doing. The more he travelled, the bigger the crowds of followers that began to collect about him when he agreed to speak to them, the greater was the fear that the grikes would come to know that here was a mole who was beginning to be seen as more than a 'Stone-fool'. Indeed, everywhere he went there were now those who openly called him 'Stone Mole', and there was an alluring but dangerous sense of excitement, of escalation, of *massing* towards the Stone.

'It will only need one more big gathering like this,' Sleekit observed at Frilford, 'and the whole of the vale will know the Stone Mole is come. One more healing, one more preaching, one more *something* that shows you are truly of the Stone. Is this how you want it, Beechen? Starting something here that we have not the power to finish? . . . I know the grike guardmoles – they will take you and you will be lost to us, as your father Boswell was lost so long ago in Whern. Lost, or worse.'

'What do you think, Mayweed?' Beechen said.

Lately Mayweed had been subdued and quiet and Sleekit had confided that it was because their route had lately taken them towards Buckland.

'Think, Sir? Me, Sir? Humbleness? Confusion's what I think. All going round and me here, Mayweed, without much to do. Boldness has become a leader of moles before my very eyes and I am amazed and task-less. Give me something to find and I shall find it. Leave me nothing to do and darkness and confusion beset me, and the thought of Buckland does not help as, no doubt, my comfortable consort has already whispered in your ear. "Poor old Mayweed," sensuality herself has said, "now nerve-racked." She is dead right as usual.'

'Well,' said Beechen, suddenly dispirited, 'for myself I'm tired. In Duncton there was always somewhere a mole could be himself, but being here, there and everywhere is being nowhere. I think I need some peace, and comfort. I miss Duncton!'

'You're surrounded all day long by moles who need you,' said Sleekit. '*You* need a period of retreat, and if you had one then this excitement around you would die down and we could choose our moments better.'

'Our moments for what?' said Beechen sharply. 'Now is the only moment for mole, *now*. The mole who thinks only of tomorrow forgets today.'

'You know the warnings about Fyfield we've had, and Cumnor to the north. That leaves Buckland to the south, where Mayweed *would* die if he had to go again, and west round Fyfield to the Thames.'

'Yes, the Thames,' said Beechen softly. 'I only saw it from a distance in Duncton. Everymole I meet who's been there talks of it. That and Fyfield I would see. Yes. . . .'

'If Mayweed finds a place that's quiet and safe would you go there for a time?' asked Sleekit.

'If there's peace there, and something that I seek, then yes I would.' He looked at Sleekit deeply and said, 'Perhaps it's for yourself and Mayweed you need it, not for me.'

'For us all,' said Sleekit with a smile.

Mayweed stared at them both, first one, then the other, and then he leered in a general way all about and said, 'Ha! Humble he has a task again! His snout tingles! He shall away and come back another day! He feels himself again. Too many moles, too much of following, too much noise. Madam mine, I love you but I really think I ought to go. Farewell, embrace me, let your touch linger, show this innocent what passion is so that he has reason to come back!'

Sleekit laughed and went close to Mayweed, her healthy fur mingling with his thin, patchy coat, their paws touching, their snouts snoodling, their eyes smiling. Anymole seeing them – and Beechen was the only one who did – saw true partners there, perhaps the strangest and sweetest, and thus far the most secret, in all moledom.

'Don't go near Buckland, my love,' she said, worry in her voice.

'Anywhere but, the exact opposite, contrariwise I shall go, let's see . . . now, yes . . . there!'

As he had said this, he had disengaged from Sleekit and performed an extraordinary turn or two before, as he cried out the word 'There!' he pointed his talons to the far north-west.

'Where's "there"?' said Sleekit.

'Peace and quiet, the river, and what Beechen most needs,' said Mayweed.

'We need peace too,' said Sleekit.

'Madam! Farewell!' and with a laugh and affectionate grin he was gone.

Sleekit stared after him for a few moments and then, turning back to Beechen, she said, 'I hope the Stone will one day find you such love as I have found.'

'The scribemoles of old Uffington were celibate,' said Beechen with a rueful grin, 'and I suppose I'm a scribemole of sorts. Though after snouting through Spindle's accounts of the goings on at Uffington there's reasonable grounds for thinking that not all scribemoles were celibates at all.'

Sleekit sighed and settled down.

'I know all about celibacy,' she said. 'As a sideem I was meant to be celibate and was so too, for years. Even now when Mayweed calls me sensuous I feel I've sinned. I think I withered without knowing it in those years. But I must admit that after I left Whern. . . .'

'With Mayweed,' said Beechen.

'. . . after Mayweed and I left Whern things were rather different. I can remember what celibacy is like, and strangely I can imagine going back to it, though I wouldn't from choice. I've learnt so much with Mayweed – though I suppose we must seem an odd pair.'

'No odder than any other pair when you get to know them. I mean my mother and Tryfan aren't exactly matched, are they?'

Sleekit laughed and said, 'If followers could hear you – it's not how they would expect the Stone Mole to talk!'

'"Stone Mole"! I've no wish to be anything other than what I am – that's what Tryfan taught me, and Feverfew too. *They* certainly weren't celibate! And my father, Boswell, if he *was* my father. . . .'

'Was?' said Sleekit.

'Well,' said Beechen a little defensively, and looking embarrassed too, 'it's not something Feverfew ever talked about. But if he was he can hardly have been celibate!'

'Feverfew wouldn't talk about it, but Bailey was there.'

'All he remembers was the Stone's light and my father . . . Boswell calling out for Feverfew.'

'You don't really want to be celibate, do you?' said Sleekit.

'Well, I mean, well . . . no!' declared Beechen, looking rather young again.

She laughed again and patted him amiably on the shoulder.

'If they ever scribe of you, my dear, and they will, then I'm sure they'll not scribe of this. They'll want to think you pure. I'll say one thing for the Masters and Mistresses of the Word: celibacy was one pretence they did not bother to maintain, though that was the only one!'

'You see,' continued Beechen earnestly, still lost in his thoughts, 'the moles I meet are most of them paired or mated or have had pups, or if they haven't they want them, and I feel they have something I don't understand.' He looked almost comically baffled, but Sleekit was sensitive to how serious he was being. She remembered Tryfan saying that the Stone Mole was *first* 'but mole', and had to be, if he was to touch other moles' hearts. Only after that was he the Stone Mole.

'You know much that they do not understand and which they need to be led towards, just as you led Mayweed and myself through the Chamber of Dark Sound in Duncton,' she said.

Seeing that this did not satisfy the ache in Beechen's heart she added, 'Mole, the last thing on my mind at the moment I met Mayweed in Whern was love and mating. I could not have even dreamed of it happening. Others I know dream and search for it all their lives and never find it. You have told many in the time you have been in the vale of how a mole should not search for what he has not got, but rather be patient with the Stone, and trust that it will give him what he needs when he needs it. If love is to come your way it will come.'

'I know that,' said Beechen softly. 'I believe 'tis so. Yet the longing I sometimes feel . . . remember the mole Poplar, and the family he had and sought to protect? How *much* he had, how much. Yet not all moles know it. Surely mating and pups are the greatest gift the Stone can give a mole, for it is not for everymole to choose celibacy, or to be a scribemole or a sideem. But when moles touch a pup that is their own, then if they have eyes to see, and a heart to feel, they may know the vulnerability and strength of life itself. How can anymole who has truly touched his own pup hurt another? How can he not feel love for all others? Somewhere there the Silence lies.'

'I never had a pup of my own,' said Sleekit, her snout low.

'But you chose another way towards the Silence, and through moles you've known found moles to help you there. And anyway, you raised two of Tryfan's young, which is the next best thing.'

Sleekit's eyes softened in love and memory.

'Wharfe and Harebell. I named them myself.'

'I sometimes feel they are the nearest I shall ever have to brother and sister and I've never met them.'

'There was a third, Beechen,' said Sleekit darkly. 'I saw him with my own eyes.'

'I know it,' he said. 'I know it well. May the Stone help them all.'

'Aye,' sighed Sleekit, 'and my Mistress Henbane, too. As for Poplar, the mole you mentioned, remember how much *you* gave him, Beechen.'

They fell into silence, thinking their thoughts, until Beechen said, 'The darkness that so many feel *is* coming,

Sleekit. I am often afraid, fearing that I shall not have the strength for whatever it is that I must do. I see the love you and Mayweed share and feel that when that unknown future moment comes I fear so much, experience of such a love as you have had would strengthen me.'

'Well, Beechen,' Sleekit said warmly, 'one thing I know. If love comes to you then such dark thoughts as these will fly away in the face of it! At least, they will if what you have is the same as what Mayweed and I have.' She looked away towards the direction in which Mayweed had pointed and then gone, and said, 'Do you think he'll be safe? . . . I mean. . . .'

It was Beechen's turn to laugh.

'The mole that guided Tryfan into Whern and you out of it can be trusted to wander about in these parts by himself safely enough. It's the kind of thing he's been doing all his life.'

If it was a place in which the three moles might find a peaceful retreat that Mayweed had gone to find, then it was increasingly needed. Moles now continually sought Beechen out, and he seemed never to have time to himself at all.

But already there was a growing urgency about each meeting, and a sense of impending confrontation which Beechen did not want and yet could not avoid. Indeed, shortly after Mayweed had gone, before Beechen finally escaped the demands of Frilford, there had been a brief and unpleasant altercation with a group of three moles others had believed to be followers. They were tough and solid-looking, and they had stayed in the shadows at the rear of the chamber where the moles had met. Who they were none knew, but nomole worried too much. Such moles had appeared more than once at previous meetings, though never in force, and since Beechen always said that all moles were welcome to hear him they had been left alone. Lately one such mole, who had a touch of grike about him, had appeared at several meetings, almost as if he was following Beechen about. Nomole knew who he was or where he came from. He rarely spoke and since he looked as if he could take care of himself, few dared try to make him speak. He had asked a question about healing once, and about what moles might be excluded from the Stone, and Beechen had answered clearly and well, saying again that all were welcome, all might find healing.

That same mole had been in the crowd on the occasion of Beechen's last Frilford meeting when the unpleasant incident took place which reminded many of the harsh reality of the Word. Towards the end of the meeting the group of three had shouted and heckled Beechen and tried to distract him. They had mocked him, and warned him that the Word would strike down blasphemers.

One or two larger followers had remonstrated with them, but received only blows as a result, and Beechen had had to calm them. At the end of the meeting he went to talk with the three, with Sleekit and a few others at his flanks, and the three had started to berate him, saying he spoke blasphemy against the Word, was tainted and was scum. Buffets were exchanged between these moles and some of the followers and Beechen himself was mildly taloned and bloodied on the flank, though he struck no blow himself. When he had fallen back, one of the followers was more badly hurt and without Beechen for the moment to control them other followers seemed bent on avenging him and it seemed certain that the argument would develop into the serious fight the moles seemed to want.

It was at this difficult and explosive moment that the unknown mole who had followed Beechen from meeting to meeting came powerfully forward and with buffets to right and left had separated the scuffling moles and then, with a laugh, had reminded them that the day had been long and hot heads needed cool November air. The three troublemakers left and peace was restored.

Beechen found himself face to face with the mole and gazed on him.

'What is it *you* want, mole? Why do you follow me but barely say a word?'

'Is the Stone for allmole?'

'It is.'

'Even of another faith?'

'The Stone will listen to all moles that try to speak true,' said Beechen. 'Send your friend to me.'

'How do you know it is not for myself I have come?'

'It is in your stance, mole, and I see all of thee as plain as I see my own paw. Send your friend to me. Tell him not to be afraid.'

'I shall strive to bring him,' said the mole respectfully.

When he was gone Beechen watched after him and whispered, 'It is fear, Sleekit, fear which governs moledom; not love. I feel fear in everymole about me and it is from that I crave for rest.'

'Come, Beechen,' said Sleekit.

'Come, Stone Mole . . .' other followers insisted. For after the near fight fear *was* there, and for the first time in all Beechen's ministry in the vale the sense of danger that had been about so long found tangible form in the blood that ran from where the talons had cut him.

'We must retreat a little,' Sleekit advised, 'and let things settle down. It is safer for the followers.'

Beechen agreed and decided to make a diversion to Garford, a small system to the south-west of Frilford, but even as he left a follower came to warn him that the Fyfield guardmoles had heard of his coming and had sent out patrols.

'There's much change in the air at Fyfield, and three important moles have come down from the dread Cumnor way and strange rumours are flying about. Some say that a new repression is beginning, others that Stone followers are to be free to follow their faith.'

'Well then, if repression is beginning we cannot do much but *trust* our faith, and if we are to be free then let us be free and bear witness to what we believe. I shall go to Garford, for moles have asked me there. But tell me of this

Cumnor: you say 'tis "dread", and I've yet to hear a good word for the place from anymole.'

''Tis not as big or as important a place as Fyfield, but it has a far worse reputation among followers because of Wort, the eldrene who controls it. She was eldrene of Fyfield but Wyre demoted her by putting her in charge of obscure Cumnor.'

'I've heard of Wort from Buckram at Sandford. For what offence was she demoted?'

'Overzealousness in her punishment of moles of the Word who do not follow the liturgies and practices of their faith. And being too hard on followers unfortunate enough to fall into her paws. Since Wyre's time things have been easier, more tolerant. Moles like Wort became an embarrassment and so they have been put in places they can do less harm.'

'Who is Wort?' asked Beechen.

'Why, Stone Mole, I have said, she is. . . .'

'No, mole, she is more than that . . . Wort. Was it really Buckram who first spoke that name to me? Wort. Sleekit, when I speak that name I wish Buckram was here. Fear, it seems, is catching.'

'Beechen. . . .'

'Come, we must go to Garford, we have much work to do.'

It was two days after they had got to that river-bound system, and found it a pleasant place rising above meadows with (as usual) an over-abundance of followers to hear Beechen preach, that four guardmoles were reported approaching. There was sudden panic but Beechen calmed them, and said he would continue their meeting for the grikes would not harm him or anymole here.

The moles came even as Beechen was speaking and, despite Beechen's protestations, Sleekit caused the followers to encircle Beechen, though many were afraid.

'Is the mole Beechen among you?' said the one who was

415

obviously their leader, 'The Stone-fool who's been preaching about the place?'

Beechen asked his followers to let the guardmole through, and when he was near he said his name was Beechen though whether or not he was a Stone-fool was for the Stone itself to judge.

'That's as maybe,' said the guardmole, looking around boldly at the motley collection of followers with evident contempt. 'My name's Hale and I'm a senior guardmole of Fyfield. You're to come to Fyfield, and you'll have safe passage, in and out.'

'That's a joke!' shouted one follower.

'You've a nerve!' said another.

The guardmole's face was impassive.

'It's not funny and it doesn't take any nerve for a mole of the Word to come among you lot, with your Stones and your fools. For some reason our new sideem want to meet a Stone follower. The name of Beechen has been mentioned, and it didn't take us long to find him, did it? Eh? He's been known about for quite a time.'

'Well, he's not such a fool that he'll come with you, Word guardmole!' said a follower.

The guardmole smiled grimly.

'I don't give a bugger if he does or not. I'm not to force him anyway. There's others gone to find other such moles and one of them will come.'

'No, mole,' said Beechen suddenly, 'only one has to come. Only one *will* come. And I am he.' He spoke quietly and a hush fell among them all.

'Well there's nothing like being sure of yourself, is there?' said Hale.

'What do your sideem want?' asked Beechen.

The guardmole shrugged.

'Their heads examined I should think,' muttered one of his subordinates.

'Shut up,' growled Hale. 'The new Master of the Word has issued a dictate that moles of the Stone are to be heard and their needs listened to wherever they are found. That's all I've been told. . . .'

His voice was drowned by great cheers and shouts.

'That bloody Henbane must be dead!' cried a mole. 'And may she rot in Whern where she came from.'

A look from Beechen silenced the crowd.

'What is the new Master's name?' asked Beechen.

'He's not the Master, Sir,' whispered one of the guardmoles to Hale. 'He's not been ordained, they said.'

'My well-informed friend here says he's not quite Master yet,' said Hale. 'However, whatever his title I can tell you his name is Lucerne.'

'Henbane dead . . .' whispered Sleekit, her eyes lost. 'Then is her pup Lucerne . . . ?'

Beechen reached a paw to her and touched her.

'I am the mole you have been looking for, and to Fyfield I shall go,' he said. 'This mole, Sleekit, shall come with me, but none other: none . . . other.' He emphasised this twice and the clamouring and excited moles fell back subdued. Hale seemed surprised at this, as if he had not expected to see such command in a Stone-fool.

'We shall come now,' said Beechen.

Hale stared at Sleekit once and then twice, as moles often did. Despite her age, she still carried herself with authority.

'Well, I don't care who comes provided they can make a reasonable pace. You'll have safe passage in and out.'

'There'll be trouble if he doesn't, mole,' said one of the bigger followers.

'Mole . . .' said Hale, but it was a threat to one of his own guardmoles who was eyeing the speaker aggressively. 'Come, Stone-fool, let's go,' he said, clearly anxious to avoid further trouble.

'Have no fear,' said Beechen as he left the Garford moles, 'it is as the Stone ordains it. Stay here, pray, be thankful to the Stone if this news is true. Be watchful for yourselves.'

Then Hale led Beechen and Sleekit away and they began to trek to the Ancient System of Fyfield.

The following day, as they drew near to Fyfield, the senior guardmole said suddenly, 'Mole, you *shall* be safe.'

'I know it,' said Beechen peaceably. 'For myself I do not worry, but moles with me. . . .'

'She shall be safe, too.'

'And others?'

'You have no other.'

'One waits for me,' said Beechen.

'He's an odd one, he is,' whispered one guardmole to another. 'Gives up without a fight, comes with us meek as a slug, got no nerves I've noticed, and now he starts talking of a mole waiting for him we cannot see.'

But when they reached Fyfield and were challenged at the first entrance and then let through, Beechen said, 'There's a follower here close by.'

One of the entrance guardmoles said, 'There's no Stone followers here, chum, just. . . .'

'He is here,' said Beechen.

Hale said, 'Right. Anymole been through?'

'Just one. He's in the cells. It's that idiot. . . .'

'Just one?'

'Yes, Sir.'

'Fetch him through here, then, and perhaps we can get on. Quick now!' barked Hale.

'You won't be pleased, Sir.'

'Do it,' said Hale.

The guardmoles, obviously frightened of Hale, scurried away and were soon leading their captive up out of the shadowed tunnel. Great he was, and fierce-looking, but when Sleekit saw him she sighed with relief.

'Guardmole Buckram, what the Word are you doing here?' said Hale, amazed. He turned to Beechen and asked, 'Is *this* the mole you meant?'

'He can speak for himself,' said Beechen.

Buckram stanced before them proud. His fur was patchy but healthy and new fur was growing over his healed sores.

418

'Until now I was not sure,' he said, his eyes full on Beechen. 'But now I know and 'tis not the Word that brought me but the Stone itself!'

'You are welcome, Buckram,' said Beechen. 'Now we are three and we have a task – to bring faith in the Stone back into this ancient place. We shall not be harmed.'

'I thought we'd seen the last of you, Buckram,' said Hale, staring at his healed body in surprise.

'You did. I am not that mole you knew,' said Buckram.

'Humph!' said Hale. 'Still I must say, religion seems to suit you. Last time I saw you, you were trying to kill three guardmoles all at once and Wort as well, and nearly succeeding. No funny business this time, eh?'

He turned to the entrance guardmoles. 'Any others come?'

'Not so far as we know.'

'Well, this seems enough to me! Where are we to go?'

'The Stone, Sir. That's what the sideem said.'

'The Stone!' exclaimed Hale. Then, shaking his head and grumbling as he went, he led the three moles on, with his guardmoles bringing up the rear, upslope towards the Fyfield Stone.

Chapter Twenty-One

Fyfield is the most modest, or least striking, of the seven Ancient Systems. Its origins lie far back in the time of the first rise of Uffington to the spiritual leadership of moledom, and it was the home system of several of the early Holy Moles, with strong traditions of worship to the Stone, and of a rich and poetic tradition of Stone lore and language.

Some say the first library of Stone texts was here, for the system was certainly where the scribemole Audley was born, who was the originator of the Rolls of the Systems. He travelled widely and until his election as Holy Mole lived some of the time at Fyfield. With his final departure to Uffington, however, the library of great texts he had built up in Fyfield was removed to the Holy Burrows and survived intact as a collection there until the destruction of the Holy Burrows by the grikes in Henbane's day.

Fyfield itself lies on a limestone ridge which stretches north and south and which is just high and strong enough to cause the Thames to swing north around it until, at Duncton, it breaks through and turns south once more. By the standards of Whern or Siabod the ridge is no more than a hill, but in those riverine parts it keeps such systems as Fyfield clear of the floodplain of the Thames and its soil, though a little dry, is rich enough to be called wormful.

Its tunnels remain its greatest point of interest, for they are ancient and honestly made, seeming to carry in their rounded and well-carved walls the scent and drift of ages past, when moles feared the Stone more than each other and treated the elders of the system with deep and abiding respect.

Although there was a brief period of expansion of the tunnels westward in medieval times, Fyfield was never a large and extensive system. 'Old Fyfield', which is its original central core, was 'old' before most systems were even a twinkle in the eyes of the pioneer moles who established them.

The plagues whose coming marks the beginning of these Chronicles devastated Fyfield, and the system might have been forgotten but for the fact that its origin as one of the Ancient Seven made it a natural target for the grikes. What was more, however modest the place might be, the fact was that a Stone of undoubted potency and power rose sheer from the central communal chamber of Fyfield, one of whose subterranean walls was formed by the Stone's plunging base.

The grikes naturally avoided this most ancient area of the system, as they avoided the Stones in the other Ancient Systems they occupied, like Avebury and Rollright. Instead they had occupied the newer westward extension of the system, and not only sealed up those tunnels that led into Old Fyfield, but crudely delved new tunnels through the older peripheral ones in an attempt to unify the system around the new centre, and give the disorientated tunnels a new integrity.

There was another more sinister reason for this extensive and only partially successful restructuring of the system, and that was to seek to isolate the central core of Old Fyfield and ensure that nomole ever again entered its tunnels. The proper explanation for this desire of the grikes to expunge from history knowledge and even memories of those tunnels, and the Stone that rose above it, is even now unknown, but rumours of an atrocity so vile, so sickening, and so unjustified have been prevalent around Fyfield since the coming of the grikes though ever since hushed up by them.*

* The extraordinary truth behind these long-stancing rumours was only revealed after the delving expedition of Fewl of Tulwick whose scribing on the matter is now well known and beyond reasonable dispute, though a dissenting view is to be found in the scrivenings of Wordmole Nodblail of Cannock.

It seems likely that Beechen was aware of these rumours even before reaching Fyfield, but if he was not then perhaps as Hale hurried him and the others along to their meeting with the trinity, Buckram whispered a grim explanation of what the strange seal-ups and unexpected turns in the tunnels signified as they passed them by.

If this was so then it helps explain the tough and non-conciliatory attitude in which Beechen appears to have approached his first meeting with one of the new trinities of moles of the Word, created for the purposes of crusade.

The meeting took place initially in the dull communal chamber the grikes had made in that portion of the system called West Fyfield, and it was to there, after a tedious trek, that Hale finally led them.

There were a large number of moles in the chamber, and the atmosphere immediately before Beechen and the others came into it was excited and uneasy. Already three other followers were there, moles brought in from the south of Fyfield towards Buckland way.

These had been brought in unwillingly, and they presented a sorry sight, for they had not believed a word of what they had been told —namely that they would be given safe passage back out of Fyfield and that the new sideem, just arrived, were merely anxious to 'talk' to them. They had not been hurt, but had watched with growing apprehension as more and more moles of the Word — guardmoles, eldrenes and their assistants and finally sideem gathered in the chamber.

Nomole had been quite certain what the other was doing, and the uneasiness was caused by the curious fact that the trinity of moles who had come from the north, though they had taken bold and impressive stance at one end of the chamber, had given no lead at all.

'We understand a Stone-fool is coming to, er, join with us in this friendly exchange of views,' said one of the sideem smoothly, 'and until he comes I suggest those of you who do not know each other make yourselves known. Yes, that would be a good idea I think . . .' After which conversation had been somewhat strained, since the moles in the chamber, already very aware that the visiting trinity was making a report direct to the new Master himself, found themselves under their silent and impassive scrutiny.

What *did* go on was a sometimes desperate attempt by the moles of the Word who had gathered for this strange meeting to behave in a way that they thought might best impress the investigators with their intelligence, devoutness and zeal. Since each mole seemed to have a different idea of how best to achieve this there had at first been general pandemonium. Some prayed loudly to the Word, some adopted meditative stances, some talked loudly of their love of the Word, a few felt the best thing to do was to go and roundly berate the outnumbered Stone followers. Fortunately, three stolid guardmoles had been briefed to stance guard by the followers, say nothing and prevent violence, which at times it seemed their presence alone succeeded in doing.

The wait for the Stone-fool had been longer than expected, the noise had died down, and eventually the gathering was overtaken by subdued expectant chatter, mainly about whatmoles the trinity were, and what their purpose.

Important moles, important purpose, it seemed. The Fyfield eldrene, Smock, was even now stanced near them looking ill-tempered but respectful. They had come only a few days before having trekked from Cumnor where, so it was said, Wort had impressed them by her devotion to the Word.

Smock, more easy-going, had simply obeyed their summons to a private talk, put her system and guardmoles at their disposal, and sent out for followers.

'There's one called Beechen who's got a following, and I've a mind to hear him myself. He's in Garford now which isn't far off . . . and there's a few others we can always find.'

So the followers had been summoned. Meanwhile the

trinity, led by an austere and ascetic young male, Heanor of Nidd, had begun to interrogate senior moles, asking all about the Stone, and ending each interview with the admonition that until further edict from the Master-elect himself, Lucerne (the news of Henbane's deposing had come earlier, in September), no harm was to come to the followers at all *of any kind*. The guardmoles found this hard to take for they enjoyed a periodic expedition to rough up a few followers, but there was something forbidding about the way Heanor gave the warning, and little doubt that penalties would be severe and carried through.

What the sideem's intent was the Fyfield garrison had no idea, but when it was announced that followers would be debated with and senior moles might attend, a great many had crowded in. The sight of the abject followers had caused outrage in some, but the beady eyes of Heanor and the three guardmoles were enough to prevent anymole do more than shout his contempt.

Occasionally Heanor leaned over towards eldrene Smock and, nodding towards somemole in the crowd, asked a question, probably the mole's name. Whisper whisper, glance glance; blink and scriven. No wonder the atmosphere in the chamber seemed to darken as the wait wore on, no wonder the followers looked fearful, and their fur grew haggard and moist with fear.

Then a hush fell and expectation mounted, for a messenger, a humble obeisant mole and one of the few remaining original moles of Fyfield, had come in and whispered to Smock, who in turn whispered to Heanor, who in turn whispered to his colleagues. This Stone-fool, it seemed, was on his way and would be in the chamber soon.

It was into this expectant and strained atmosphere that Hale led Beechen, Sleekit and Buckram a few minutes later. They must have seemed a strange yet imposing sight to the waiting moles of the Word: the aging but upright and bright Sleekit, a mole of authority; Buckram, cured of

424

murrain, whom many there must have known from before; but, most striking of all, the last to enter – the young male Stone-fool, handsome, healthy, open, and certainly not abject.

'Welcome,' said Heanor, the moment they had come in and settled near the other three followers. 'My name is Heanor of Nidd, and I am sideem anointed before the Rock of the Word. We are sent here by the Master of the Word-elect, Lucerne, peacefully and in just spirit. We shall in the molemonths ahead continue to do what we have done already, which is to debate with true followers of the Stone the nature of their complaints and of their fears and to strive to come to an understanding of their doubts of the Word.'

Heanor spoke clearly, pleasantly and well. There was a lulling reasonableness about what he said. He turned to his colleagues and introduced them – a sideem and a tough guardmole whose names are now forgotten. 'And this is eldrene Smock,' concluded Heanor with a suave smile, 'to whom I am grateful for the courtesy she has shown these past days and in whom I am sure the Word is well pleased.'

Smock affected not to be pleased at this and leaned over to Heanor and whispered to him, pointing to Buckram.

'Really? Yes . . . I understand that you are one Buckram, former guardmole apostate to the Word.'

There was an angry whisper among the moles at this. Buckram smiled, shrugged and said, 'Well, I don't know what a postle is but if you mean I was of the Word and now I'm of the Stone you're right. Best thing that ever happened to me.'

Again murmurs ran among the moles. Such openness going unpunished was unheard of, and if *this* was the way the new order at Whern was going to go Word help them all. Yet there was a menace about Heanor that comforted them, and a smug assurance about Smock that made the more astute think this wasn't what it seemed.

'We know not your name, mole,' said Heanor to Sleekit.

It was a moment Beechen, Sleekit and Mayweed had often discussed – whether or not to use their real names. They had long since decided they would do so, for a mole's name is his outward identity to others, and to lie about it, however good the reason, is to demean the self that name has come to represent. Yet in all their discussions they had not imagined they would be asked it by a sideem.

'Sleekit,' said Sleekit boldly, 'of Duncton Wood.' This too caused a murmur, and this too Sleekit had often thought about, and had decided that since she had first discovered her true feelings for the Stone in Duncton in Henbane's time there, she might legitimately claim to have been born – new-born! – there.

The sideem did not react in any special way, and it seemed that even if he knew that the Mistress Henbane had had a sideem Sleekit in attendance he did not connect this mole with her.

'So you are Beechen, or as I understand they say in these parts, a "Stone-fool".'

'Mole,' said Beechen coolly, without any concession to Heanor's seeming politeness, 'what would you have followers do in a system blighted with the blood of moles? Where would you have us turn in tunnels haunted by moles' screams?'

But for a hardening in the set of sideem Heanor's mouth there was no sign that he was upset by this, indeed his eyes retained their suave, if false, smile.

'Mole,' he responded strongly, 'we shall not progress. . . .'

'We shall not!' said Beechen powerfully, half turning from Heanor so that the gathering could see him. But what did they see? Not an abject follower such as the lies and distortions of eldrenes and sideem over the years might have led them to expect, nor a maddened Stone-fool of the kind they had grown used to finding and mocking, but instead a mole of strength who stared at them in a way that impelled them to look and wait on him.

'No we shall not progress *this* way.'

426

Heanor tried again to gain control of the meeting, and said, 'But mole, I. . . .'

'Nor *this* way!' cried out Beechen turning from both Heanor and the gathered moles and pointing his right paw at the three followers who were quite speechless at what was taking place. Indeed, all moles were, for never in any of their memories had they seen a mole, a follower of the Stone furthermore, outface a sideem, grikes, guardmoles and themselves.

'What moles are these?' thundered Beechen. Then advancing towards them, his eyes glinting in his face as the sun shines in pools of water caught in a tree's surface roots, the guardmoles fell back utterly disconcerted by him. Then he turned to the three followers and said in a much softer voice that was full of love. 'What moles are these?' Then he reached out his paws to them and, wondering, they reached out to his and whispered, 'Whatmole are you? Whatmole?'

Beechen smiled and said, 'Go from here and be not afraid. None here shall harm you while I am here. Go now, and speak of this, and say you came to stricken Fyfield in fear, but you left with the fear driven out of you by pride in what you are.'

The chamber was still, nomole dared speak or if they did they knew not what to say, and the three followers looked first at the guardmoles who had been assigned to them, then at the trinity of moles led by Heanor, then at Beechen once more, their eyes wide in awe.

'Are they not free to go?' cried out Beechen, again turning round suddenly and facing Heanor. 'Safeguarded to come, safeguarded to go – so we were told and they. By the Word itself it was said! Well Heanor of Nidd, anointed at the very Rock itself, let us see the truth of thy Word. Let them go from here, they have no place in this!'

Heanor, now looking furious, nodded and the three turned and began to run from the chamber.

'Nay, moles, not like miscreants and outcasts, but like moles born free to go whither the Stone guides thee, and gently. Go gently, and with pride.'

427

'What shall we say to the followers we meet?' one of them asked Beechen as they reached the exit of the chamber unmolested by anymole.

'Tell them that thy Stone Mole has to moledom come, tell them to make ready, tell them to be peaceful, tell them to reach out and love all moles, whether of Word or Stone, as I reach out to this mole now!'

With that Beechen went forward quickly to where Heanor stanced and did what even a mole of the Word would not dare do: he touched Heanor on the shoulder.

'Go!' said Beechen, and they went, slowly, with dignity, staring back down the tunnel to catch a final glimpse of Beechen; slowly, as if they were reluctant to leave him.

Beechen stanced back from Heanor and his two companions who, utterly perplexed by the way their gathering had been taken over, had crouched up. Several of the guardmoles seemed to have come to their senses, too, and were hunching forward so that Beechen and the others seemed surrounded now by moles who meant them harm, though not a word more had been said.

It had all taken but moments, yet Beechen was breathing heavily. The gathering began to mutter and whisper grimly, a dangerous and ominous noise such as the sound a wall of hail makes as it drives towards a mole through a leafless wood.

'We asked you here to tell us of the Stone!' said Heanor, striving to regain his position at the gathering, 'not to see you point a talon here, shout over there, and seek to make a mockery of moles who wish . . . who wish to listen, and to talk.'

Heanor's voice dropped steadily as he said this, and slowed, and a smile returned to his face, if only a strained one. 'We wished to *listen* to those moles you sent away, we. . . .'

Beechen's snout had fallen low, he seemed not to be listening to Heanor at all, his flanks were glistened with sweat and trembling, and he seemed suddenly even more abject than the most beset follower could be.

428

'There is a mole here who doubts me,' he said, turning away once more from Heanor who reacted with a gesture of exasperation, as if this mole was indeed mad. Which might have successfully made others think so to, but they could see Beechen's compelling gaze, which Heanor could not.

'She hurts me,' said Beechen, and the word 'hurt' was spoken as if in pain, and his look was of suffering. But where he looked was hard to say for his head shook this way and that. 'She doubts me and hurts me and she is here, here now, among you. She hates what she most loves. Stone give her thy healing now, show her thy love! She hurts. . . .'

Silent tears came from Beechen's eyes as behind him Smock whispered urgently to Heanor, 'This must stop! Sideem Heanor, this cannot proceed.'

Then as suddenly as Beechen had been beset he was freed of whatever suffering he had felt. Sleekit came to him, and Buckram went to his flank, a little in front, and put a great paw to his shoulder and for a moment, exhausted it seemed, Beechen leaned against him.

'I shall have need of thee, Buckram, great need of thee. Leave me not.'

'I shall not, I shall not,' whispered Buckram. 'Show me the mole that hurts you.'

'She is no more, she has gone, yet when you are ready you shall see her.'

Beechen faced Heanor and said, 'Sideem, I came here in good faith to tell thee of the Stone. I saw a mole with cold eyes, I heard a mole speak words that had no love or truth, and the Stone guided me and told me what to say. I spoke to three moles who feared thee, and gave them courage. I spoke to a mole who hurt me, and directed her to follow the way that leads to the Stone. I was comforted by Sleekit, who saw me born; I was supported by Buckram, a mole who loves me. In all of this you have seen the Stone and its ways.'

'Mole, you have told us nothing of the Stone, nothing at all,' said the one who stanced next to Heanor.

' 'Tis just tricks and impressions and the superstitions of the past,' said the other.

'What is the code or the doctrine in this?' asked Smock. 'Tell us that.'

'You call me and moles like me Stone-fools. Many times have you mocked moles like the followers who come to me for comfort from a moledom you have put in thrall. Foolish I may be, but would I speak to them if they were deaf? Would I smile at them if they were blind? Most of all, could I listen to them if they were dumb? I would not, I could not. I came here in faith to meet you and am silent before your deafness, still before your blindness, and cannot hear the void that is your speech.

'Only by this can I reach you. Yet we shall meet again. The day shall come when you shall see and hear as if you were pups once more, fresh to moledom's light.

'Now, as those three followers have left, so shall we three leave. To the Stone of Fyfield we shall go, and speak a blessing on those whose blood is still wet and whose cries still sound in this system that was beset by moles of the Word.

'Heanor of Nidd, come to the Stone with us, be not afraid of it; and others come as well. Hear the blessing I make, remember those moles that died in faith, and then come with those others that shall follow me to Cumnor and you shall learn more of the Stone on that hard way than by talking here with smiling eyes until last Longest Night itself.'

With that Beechen turned from Heanor, and signalled to Buckram to lead him to the Stone. As the gathering broke up in confusion he left the chamber.

'That mole's mad!' said some.

'It's what the Stone does to them!' said others.

'Blessed Word, punish the sinner, punish the blasphemer, punish the faint-hearted' said a few, snouts low, eyes closed, stanced as if stricken by what they had witnessed.

'If he's going to Cumnor then good riddance,' said one

430

to another. 'If I had my way I'd snout him and moles like him right now. But don't worry, Wort of Cumnor shall do it for us.'

As Heanor and the other sideem and senior moles, outflanked at every turn of the meeting by Beechen, whispered and frowned and reluctantly hurried after him, the other moles there drifted away, chattering wildly. But out of the shadows a mole came, and at her side were dark moles, thickset and strong: henchmoles.

'To the Stone?' one said.

'We'll be seen,' growled the other.

'At a distance we shall follow,' said their mistress, 'and most carefully. I would see this mole at the Fyfield Stone.'

'Heanor should have killed the bugger,' said the first henchmole.

'Heanor should indeed.'

Beechen's stay at the Fyfield Stone was brief and according to Sleekit's account seemed to give him no pleasure, for he was still carried along by that passion that had overtaken him before Heanor. Buckram led him there and Beechen stared but briefly at it, an ancient gnarled Stone, taking firm stance against the moist mild southerly wind that was blowing hard from an unsettled sky, which seemed bent on blowing all things, starting with the ground around them, northwards. Barbed wire whined and rattled at a nearby fence.

Heanor and the others came along behind them, the November wind parting their fur this way and that, and were barely in earshot before Beechen spoke his grace.

Before he did so he said these words: 'Here, and near here, moles have died in anguish that they were forsaken. Here, and near here, the earth was reddened by their blood. Here and near here, the Stone and tunnels trembled to their cries. Let us remember them and speak these words that through the Stone or the power of the Word they may hear them and know they are not alone nor forsaken.

'Omit not these whose cries I have heard
From thy great Silence;
Let them rest now, let them know thy peace.
Omit them not that when the wind blows
And the sun shines, and the cycle turns
Again, their cries are heard no more.
Welcome them to thy great Silence.'

'You spoke of the Word,' said Sleekit when Beechen was silent.

'Aye, mole, you did,' said Heanor.

'Because moles of the Word died here as well, Heanor. Now go, mole. Protect thyself. Pray, for darkness is on you!'

Then Beechen turned to Buckram and Sleekit and, shaking himself as a mole might shake off dirty water in which he has been forced to swim, he said, 'We shall to Cumnor, which followers call "dread", and let all come with us who will. These moles of the Word want to learn something of the Stone. By deed and not by word shall they know of it, for let all followers that are able come there. Let them rise from the burrows in which they have been forced to hide, let them test this new freedom which the Word offers, let them show their faith!'

The fierce wind blew his call before him and he turned northward towards Cumnor to follow it, and said not one word more until their paws were free of Fyfield's soil.

While behind them, as Heanor and those with him turned back down into the Fyfield tunnels, a mole emerged unseen by anymole, and that mole and her two henchmoles watched after Beechen.

'Shall we follow?' said a henchmole. His mistress shook her head.

'Blasphemy we have seen,' she said. Then she looked back the way Heanor of Nidd had gone and added, 'Blasphemy did *he* permit. A task we have with *him* in the holy name of the Word. And then!'

'What then, eldrene Wort?' whispered the second henchmole.

432

'Why mole, the Word's business shall send us back to Cumnor before that fool we've seen, quicker than ravens fly.' They turned in their own shadows, the wind-bent grass shook, and were gone.

The November wind was indeed strong, for even the smooth surface of the river that runs south of Garford was roughened by it, while the leafless willows along its bank whipped violently back and forth over the water.

'Yet,' murmured Mistle looking at the bleak scene, 'yet I feel excited and light, as I did sometimes in the summer years. Oh Cuddesdon, I'm *sure* he's near.'

'Well he better be for then I can rest at last, leave you with him, and go on my separate and more peaceful way.'

'But you wouldn't leave me! I mean if we found him. It would be . . . it would be. . . .'

'Wonderful for some of us, Mistle, desperate for others. But I know what you mean. Since we got to these parts, and met so many who talk of the Stone Mole and say. . . .'

'They say his name is Beechen!'

'. . . And say this Beechen is nearby, or has been their way already, or is coming back . . . and always add that we've only just missed him . . . I admit I have felt renewed excitement about my own mission. But I don't suppose you remember what it was!'

'To go to Cuddesdon and start "something",' said Mistle promptly.

'Oh! Well, yes. I've felt nearer to knowing what it was.'

'Cuddesdon, the Stone Mole *is* real,' said Mistle passionately, 'I know he has come for us, to help us. I know he has.'

'When we catch up with him you'll be disappointed, I'm warning you. So I'd better stay around so you've a shoulder to cry on.'

She laughed and buffeted him in a friendly way, as he did her, and turning upslope they headed into Garford, yet another system of many they had visited where they hoped they might at last find the Stone Mole, of whom they had heard so much.

Since their meeting east of Avebury in June, and their resolution to trek northwards towards Duncton Wood together and give each other what help they could, Mistle and Cuddesdon had learned much of each other, and of travelling safely through a moledom occupied by grikes.

Mistle had quickly recovered herself after their first meeting, and her initial timidity and self-doubt – natural enough in a mole who had been under the thrall of the Word at the Avebury system – was very quickly replaced by confidence and a sense of mission. Before many weeks had passed she had assumed the role of leader of the two, her common sense and ability to make decisions and act on them being virtues which Cuddesdon lacked, but which he was happy to acknowledge and defer to. What was more he recognised that beyond Mistle's intelligence and simple faith was a driving compulsion leading her towards the Silence of the Stone, and he soon found it was something other followers they met recognised and were infected by.

Her love for the Stone's rituals and lore put a natural joy and grace about everything she did, whether it was making a temporary burrow, finding food, eating, or simply contemplating the view. She talked to the Stone as if it was a companion at her side, a companion she could scold as well as praise, or simply enjoy. When she was pondering a problem – such as where to go or where to tarry – she would pray to the Stone aloud. Or, if it was to Cuddesdon she was confiding, then she would speak as if the Stone was just another mole at their flank, and able to hear them, and share their thoughts.

She spoke often, and with great love, of Violet, and it was plain to Cuddesdon, a gentle mole and in later years a wise and much loved one, that a great deal of what Mistle *was* Violet had *made*. It was from Violet, he guessed, that she got her most striking quality of all, and one that quite unnerved him at first, for he was used to moles who rushed and hustled and had no time.

434

For unlike most moles he had ever met, time was not Mistle's enemy, but her friend, and it seemed to stretch itself out for her and make space about those things she did, not the least of which was listening to other moles.

Which Cuddesdon found hard at first because he was not used to a mole who stayed silent when he spoke, fixing him with a firm gaze, and giving him the sense that each word he spoke mattered; which sense made him all the more conscious of what he said, and he thought about it first.

This was one of the things other moles noticed too, and while some found it difficult, and were restive and embarrassed to meet a mole whose silence and attention sometimes made them hear the foolishness in their own words, most responded to Mistle by speaking true, and so feeling more at ease with her and themselves. Indeed, Cuddesdon was astonished at how much others told her about themselves and their faith, almost as if they had been waiting for her especially to come along.

Although they had found out early on where Uffington lay, and how far Duncton Wood was beyond it, Mistle decided they should go slowly at first and enjoy the summer. They had moved east along the valley of the Kennet, learning much of moledom and discovering that there were many like themselves who had faith in the Stone, and professed it still in quiet ways; and many more who had been won only by force to the Word's creed, and still yearned for something they felt only the Stone could give them.

So, gently, but cautiously too, for many grikes were about, they had met many a follower until, one day in late August, learning that new sideem were snooping again and change was in the air, Mistle had said they must go north now and follow their snouts towards the Stone.

'There will be dangers, no doubt,' said Mistle, 'but we must seek our destiny, Cuddesdon, and trust that the Stone will guide our paws and bring us to safety at last.'

They began by climbing out of the river vales on to the

long dipslope of the chalk that rises slowly northwards and which they had been told would take a mole with the persistence to get there across the desolate Lambourn heights to Uffington itself. From there they hoped to find safe passage to Duncton Wood and Cuddesdon Hill.

Though they set off with expectations of travelling swiftly, they soon found the distances were greater than they thought, and that there was something about the route that slowed them once again, and made them bide their time. They were soon struck by how few grike strongholds there were in those parts.

'It's the Stones they don't like,' a cheerful vagrant told them one day. 'And I can't say I altogether blame them. The further and higher a mole goes from here on, the more Stones there are, and the more a mole feels he's being watched, if you know what I mean. You'll not find many moles north of here now, and those you do will be the kind who prefer to be left alone and not asked questions about the Stone or the Word! Either of them are as bad or as good as you care to make them, and both as bad as each other if you ask me. . . .'

It was talk they had heard before, for even those who still dared to espouse the Stone openly would tell of how they had lost touch with their own communities in the hard years past, and complained that the Stone had not helped them.

As they travelled on the soil became less wormful, and the fields larger and barren of trees. When darkness fell there were fewer twofoot lights, and when a roaring owl came along one of the narrow ways its gaze could be seen looking all yellow across the country, and its roar heard long in advance.

What moles there were kept to brook-sides and copses, and seemed furtive and afraid, glancing quickly upslope and away again when Mistle said they were heading for Uffington.

'Derelict that place is, the scribemoles all gone long ago,' they would mutter. 'They said the Stone Mole would come but he never did, he never will. Better you than me going up to those parts. Moles go there and never come back.'

It dawned on Cuddesdon only slowly that when moles said the grikes were afraid of going north towards the Stones near Uffington, they described their own fear as well. Then he had to admit he, too, had a certain fear about going on himself, but perhaps both of them felt that if the other had not been there they might have turned back south again. . . .

'*You* might have, Cuddesdon, but I wouldn't!' Mistle said boldly, and watching her day by day as she pushed on ahead of him, Cuddesdon knew what she said was true, and he berated himself for his lack of faith and purpose.

It was not until mid-September that they found themselves coming on to much chalkier and drier ground where here and there Stones rose before them proudly, and they began to have the sense of being lone explorers in an almost deserted land.

The only moles they came across were solitary outcasts, mainly scarred by disease or desperate escape from grikes, who chose to live out their last years in some unvisited place where grikes would not bother to hunt them. It was one of these who warned them of the territory they were getting near, and told them its name.

'This old place was called Lambourn once, but there's not a mole left here now to give it a name, so nameless it will become once I'm gone,' he said. 'Wasn't raised here myself, but it's a place that will do for a mole who's suffered enough. When I came in February I stopped here because there was another nearby wanted the company and told me its name and little else. Anyway, it gets icy cold upslope of here and full of risen Stones that seem to watch a mole as he goes by.'

'How do you know that if you've not been there?' asked Mistle.

'Went up there in June when that star shone,' said the mole. 'Then all my courage left me and I got back here as quick as I could. You won't catch me going up there again. If you take my advice, which you won't, you'll circle west for a few days.'

'Why?' asked Cuddesdon.

' 'Cos if you don't you'll go slap bang into Seven Barrows, and *that's* a haunted place if ever I heard of one.'

'Humph!' said Mistle shortly.

' "Humph" all you like, young mole, thinking you know better, but you'll find out, you see if you don't.'

'What about the mole who was living here when you came. Where is he now?'

'She. Lost,' said the mole darkly. 'Among them haunted Stones I shouldn't wonder. Mind you, if you should come back, then stop by and tell me what you saw.'

There was longing in his voice and Mistle said, 'Why do you fear the Stones? They do mole no harm.'

'A mole gets lost among them, that's why! I fear them more than I do the guardmoles or the grikes. No, if I must have to do with such things I say a blessing of the Word and think harm to nomole.'

'We'll say a prayer for thee before the Stones,' said Mistle softly, looking into his eyes.

His eyes fell, his snout lowered and his talons fretted at the ground. Behind him the Lambourn Downs stretched up far away and he looked very alone, and lonely.

'That's a promise, is it?' said the mole, trying to make a joke of it.

But Mistle was serious.

'It is,' she said.

'The name's Furze, that's the name to tell the Stones,' he said gruffly, and as they looked at him they knew it mattered to him. In such ways, so many times, did Cuddesdon see how Mistle drew moles out, and helped them dare to show a little of themselves.

They were surprised how soon after this brief encounter they came to Seven Barrows, for Furze had spoken of the place as if it was too terrible to be nearby. But there it was, a cluster of mounds, mysterious perhaps but at first hardly a place for a mole to fear. The Stones, it seemed, must lie beyond the barrows, for the way they came there was nothing else but grass.

They decided to find a place to stay the night where they were, for they had no wish to arrive at the Stones by night. But then, as dusk approached, there was a certain haunting sense about the place which made Cuddesdon fretful and jumpy, and Mistle curious, restless and alert.

'I want to go on,' she said, half to herself, 'even though we're tired. I'd like to be nearer the Stones *now*.'

'Mistle! Night will be on us, there's a heavy dew forming and if it gets any colder there will be mist about and you'll not see a thing,' said Cuddesdon. 'Anyway, this place makes me nervous enough as it is, and what the Stones will be like I hate to think. Let's wait till morning when, with any luck, there might be some nice bright sunshine to light our way ahead.'

But Mistle was not listening. Instead she was staring past the dark mounds of the barrows into the gathering gloom beyond.

'He's coming nearer now . . . or we are. Maybe he's on his way to where we're going.'

'Who is?' said Cuddesdon irritably, starting back when some grass stirred at their side.

'Don't know, but I know he *is*,' whispered Mistle. Then suddenly she was up and off, and Cuddesdon, very reluctant to stay alone, hastened after her.

So it was at dusk and with a mist stirring about them that they reached the great stonefields that lie west of the Seven Barrows, and where in the winter years following the destruction of the Holy Burrows brave Spindle had brought six of the seven Stillstones. Then later, to this same place, Spindle had guided Boswell and Tryfan, and that great mole, young then, had just managed to carry the last Stillstone, the Stillstone of Silence, and hurl it out among the Stones that rise so mysteriously across those fields.

All that was unknown to either Mistle or Cuddesdon then, but both sensed the power of the place and they watched in silence as night fell and the stars grew bright, and the Stones seemed to rise ever higher from the ground. They ventured a little across the stonefields, staring at the scattered remnants and fragments of Stones that lay all about, many smaller than their paws. The risen Stones seemed near, yet as they went they seemed to recede, and move. It seemed that as one appeared another faded away again.

'Don't be afraid,' said Mistle, touching Cuddesdon with her paw as she sensed his awe. 'A mole is safe among such Stones. I grew up near the Avebury Stones and it was with their help I escaped . . . Please don't be afraid. This is a most holy place, Cuddesdon. Can't you feel it all about? I think, I think . . . something began here, Cuddesdon, long, long ago, and that over the centuries many moles must have stanced here as we are now, and felt as humble as we do. Violet said a mole who feels fear among the Stones is really only afraid of something in herself.'

'I'd be afraid if you weren't here,' said Cuddesdon, a little tremble to his voice. 'Where the Stones are not it seems so dark, but where they are it's hard to look, as if there's something light that can't quite be seen, or if it can it won't stay still.'

'Cuddesdon,' whispered Mistle, reaching out for him.

He turned to her quickly and saw in the starlight that her eyes were full of tears, and he went to her and held her close.

'I feel so much has happened here, and *will* happen. There's moles here who have needed help, and others yet to come, and I want to reach out to them all and hold them as you're holding me.'

'You can't help everymole, Mistle, though I sometimes think you want to try. You can't love all of us.'

'No,' she said, and wept and held him in return, 'but you are right: I want to try.'

440

'Is the mole you said you wanted to meet one of the moles here?' asked Cuddesdon.

She stared among the confusing silhouettes of Stones and each one might have been a rearing mole; everywhere she looked seemed shapes of moles that had once been or might yet be.

'I don't know,' she whispered to the stars twinkling above, 'but I don't think so . . . he's like us, just like us; he's now, always now.'

'He?' said Cuddesdon, surprised to find himself feeling suddenly protective and even jealous.

Her paw tightened on his and she smiled in the darkness.

'Yes, he,' she said. 'No, don't let go of me, Cuddesdon. Hold me. I love you, Cuddesdon. I hope we'll always be this close.'

They slept together on the surface, with only a scrape in the stonefield to protect them, and when they woke the early sun was slanting and glinting across the Stones and gravel and made some of the smaller Stones glisten and shine. Yet as they reached out to touch them, they found the Stones' light faded as they got to them and others lit up further away, as a rainbow recedes before a mole who tries to reach it.

As the sun rose up they wandered forward among the Stones, the game of trying to touch a glinting stone absorbing them. Over the plain they went, close as the closest friends can be, pointing new things out to each other, laughing, secure, lost in their pleasures, their journey for the moment quite forgotten.

All sense of time and distance seemed to leave them until they found themselves on higher ground, north of the stonefields. It was early afternoon.

'I think moles will come back here to live one day,' said Mistle, 'and I think Seven Barrows will be occupied again.'

Stretching away below them now the Stones rose up, one here, one there, a pattern to their randomness, and they looked like guardians to a secret place

Cuddesdon shivered.

'Well! I wouldn't want to go back down there among them. You say those six Stones are friendly to mole but they still make me feel nervous. If there's one at Cuddesdon, and a small one too, that'll be enough for me.'

'There's seven Stones for Seven Barrows,' said Mistle following him, 'not six.'

'Six,' he said, sure of himself.

They turned back once more to see who was right, and counted the Stones.

'Six,' said Mistle faintly, 'yes, six.' Then she started forward towards them and said, 'I promised that mole Furze to say a prayer for him before the Stones and I quite forgot. I must go back . . .' Then a cloud's shadow drifted across the stonefields and the Stones seemed suddenly dark and formidable.

'Must we?' said Cuddesdon.

'I'll go alone,' said Mistle, and though Cuddesdon protested, and tried to persuade her that there was probably a Stone ahead where they could say a prayer, she insisted on going back.

'Stay here. I shan't be long.'

So back she went, alone, and feeling all the more alone as she got down among the Stones once more and found that, as before, the smaller Stones glinted ahead of her with a light that went out when she reached each one.

'Where shall I say a prayer?' she asked herself. 'Before which Stone?'

One after another she visited them, hesitating as she stared up at their rising facets, feeling each time that the next would be better. One, two . . . to each Stone she went, three, four . . . and she was growing tired: five . . . six, but there *was* one more. She could see it, just over there, not far. She had been right: seven Stones.

'That's where I'll say a prayer for Furze,' she decided, and went towards it.

As she approached a calmness came to her, and she felt as a mole feels when she reaches out to something in the dark she cannot see, yet knows with certainty she shall find it there. The Stone rose higher than all the others, and as she turned out of the shadow at its base and into the sun she came upon a little stone which caught the afternoon's sun within its depths and did not fade when she got nearer to it.

It held the whitest light she had ever seen and around her other sounds faded, blocked out, it seemed, by the sound of Silence this stone made, a sound she had heard before. It was the same as that at Avebury, but this time no moles called out of it to her, and she was alone.

She stared at the standing Stone not daring or not able to touch it. All was light and white and calm and she felt life upon her body like an ache she could not shed, nor yet wished to.

She whispered her prayer for Furze, and then for Violet, and then for Cuddesdon, too. For so many moles, and others yet to come. She felt no fear and knew that every day would bring her nearer to the mole she sought, every day: for that the ache of life was worth the carrying, for that the Stone would help her help herself survive.

'Help *him*,' she whispered. 'Help them all.'

Then as suddenly as she had found herself by the seventh Stone she found herself leaving it, hurrying away, not daring to look back. But then, as she reached rising ground, she turned and counted the mysterious Stones. There were seven, no doubt of it, and yet they did not look quite the same as they had before. . . .

She turned upslope and ran on and was relieved to find Cuddesdon once more, as relieved as he was to see her return.

'Count the Stones,' she said as she reached him.

He did so.

'Six,' he said at last. 'The same as before. Why?'

'Did you see anything strange about them while I was down there?' she asked.

He looked apologetic.

'I was so afraid you wouldn't return that I don't think I noticed much at all. Why?'

She tried to explain what had happened, though it sounded strange repeating it, but Cuddesdon listened gravely right to the end.

'Don't expect me to say anything useful because I can't,' he said when she had finished. 'But I was thinking. This mole, the one you said you had to meet . . . let's go and find him, shall we?'

'Yes, let's,' Mistle said, suddenly glad to be away from the Stones and back with Cuddesdon. They laughed, and ran on, and did not look back again.

After the stonefields of Seven Barrows, the Holy Burrows of Uffington seemed to Mistle inconsequential. Perhaps it was that she had come to Uffington from experiences of the Stone so deep and intense that whatever she had been told by Violet of this once most holy of systems, she saw it as it was – deserted, wasted, the spirit flown.

True, the Blowing Stone was there, but it did not sound for her and Cuddesdon as they went by. Their past lay behind them, their future spread before them: the ruined tunnels of Uffington were but a place they passed whose time was over.

They paused atop Uffington Hill and gazed down across the vale. Mistle looked, listened to the day and was so still, with her head a little to one side, that Cuddesdon asked, 'What can you hear?'

'The sound of roaring owls,' she said strangely. 'They seem suddenly so loud.'

They had arrived in the vale as the news of the new crusade from Whern was beginning to get about. Grikes were thick on the ground and had they not had by then such long experience of travel it seems unlikely they could have avoided being taken by them. But they did, and Mistle guided them carefully north, pausing a few days here, and a week or so there. Eager to get where she was going but taking it slowly, with that grace over time that Cuddesdon had grown to love her for. And by good fortune, and the Stone's grace, they avoided Buckland.

So it was, sometime just after mid-October, that they first heard the rumour of a Stone-fool, different than others they had heard about, one who preached and made healings; one who had been to a place called Dry Sandford.

'It's him. I *feel* it's him,' said Mistle. 'We shall find him soon.'

But though the rumours increased, when they finally got to Sandford at last the Stone-fool was long gone, and they had also missed another mole, called Buckram, who had set off to find him. But another called Poplar said, 'He was the one called Stone Mole all right, because I saw him heal moles. But he looked like just an ordinary mole, except for when he spoke of the Stone, and when he looked at you.'

'Yes?' said Mistle, gazing on him.

'Well, I can tell you his name was Beechen, and he had two others with him. Old Moles. Mayweed and Sleekit.'

' "Beechen",' repeated Mistle with a half smile.

'That's what I said.'

'Where was this Buckram going?'

'Fyfield . . . but I wouldn't! Grikes!'

'The Stone shall guide us,' said Mistle with a laugh.

When they left, Poplar stared after her as he had Beechen, and he said, 'She looked something like Beechen did, that Mistle.'

Place after place they followed in the tracks of Beechen, until at last, too late, they had reached Garford.

But not too late to learn something strange indeed, told by a mole who heard it from another mole, who heard it. . . .

Cumnor.

'They've all gone to Cumnor, my duck, the whole bleedin' lot of them, 'cept for me and a few who've got more sense. They say the Stone Mole's come, say he was *here*, but you better hurry now if you're to find him.'

'Did you *see* him when he was here?'

The old female's eyes lightened. ' 'Course I saw him,

and when the guardmoles come for him, and when he faced them fierce and proud. "Want to talk of the Stone, do you?" says he. "We do," says they. "Then I'll come," says he, and he went. Next thing we know a follower comes bespattered with grime and says. "To Cumnor, lads, the Stone Mole says to Cumnor." " 'Stone Mole'? who says he's come?" asked one of ours in return. "He was *here*, you daft mushroom," says the follower. "The mole Beechen, *you* know. Bugger me, put a worm in front of a Garford mole and it wouldn't know what to do until somemole else came by and said 'Eat'. Dim isn't in it! That was the Stone Mole who was here, and we're to go to Cumnor for he's to outface Wort and preach of the Stone!"

'That's how it was and I'm looking forward to hearing what a fiddle-faddle of a time they have had when those that survive the grikes and the bleedin' roaring owls get home. Meanwhile, beggin' your pardon and nothing personal, I'm off to get some peace and quiet.'

'I sometimes think,' said Cuddesdon, 'that we shall never quite reach your Stone Mole.'

'No, Cuddesdon, it is not we who shall reach to him, but we who must let him reach out to us.'

'That's very subtle, Mistle. Yes . . . so . . . Cumnor then?' said Cuddesdon with mock weariness. 'Or would that be us striving too hard?'

'Cumnor,' said Mistle. 'I'm not perfect, Cuddesdon, but after that I'll try to stop trying to find him.'

'To Cumnor and beyond then, fellow follower!'

For once Mistle let Cuddesdon lead the way, and she followed after him with love in her eyes, and saw something about him that she had seen more of only recently: that he went slowly now, and with grace, and had discovered that time is not against a mole, but on his side.

Chapter Twenty-Two

Of the madness that the trek to Cumnor became, Sleekit after remembered only one thing: the forgiving of a mole of the Word amidst the wind, driving rain, and a sense of rushing moles, their paws on the ground all about, trekking, trekking.

'Stone-fool!' a voice hissed out of the darkness.

In the wood at Appleton it was.

'Stone-fool, he is here!'

In Appleton, at night, Beechen was stopped by a mole the others knew not. Immediately Buckram loomed up and Sleekit was there, both watching for tricks and traps since Beechen never watched for such things himself. For so wise a mole his innocence seemed strange to those who knew him, yet it was something for which those who knew him best learned to love him.

But Beechen said, 'Mole, you helped us in Frilford. How can I help you now?'

'I have brought a mole who seeks forgiveness,' said the stranger.

Beechen nodded and the mole led him, Sleekit and the still-wary Buckram into the dark shelter of a rotted tree stump where the wind was quieter. A smell of fungi and dampness hung about, and then they noticed something more; the rank odour of murrain.

In the shadows there, his flanks shivering, a mole crouched low, his body afflicted by the final stages of the plague. His eyes wept pus and from his throat there came the sound of rasping, painful breathing.

'What is thy name?' asked Beechen gently. 'And what would you with me?'

The mole who had led them moved near the mole, as protective of him as Buckram was of Beechen.

'He is my father. He desires forgiveness before he dies.'

'For what?' asked Beechen.

But before the mole replied Buckram came near once more and peered hard at the stricken mole.

'Master,' he whispered urgently, 'I know this mole, I *know* him, he. . . .'

'Let him speak for himself, Buckram.'

Beechen stared at the mole and said, 'Whatmole are you?'

'I am one who has been punished but not forgiven,' whispered the mole, every word he spoke a terrible effort.

'What can I do for you?'

'My son said you were the Stone Mole.' The mole stared terribly at Beechen, his flanks heaving in and out with the effort he was making to control his pain, his eyes full of suffering.

Then he said, 'My name is Wyre. I am punished for what I have done but I desire forgiveness.'

'Aye . . . Wyre of Buckland,' said Buckram, confirming what he had first thought.

'What hast thou done, mole?' asked Beechen.

'Much,' said Wyre, 'much that I should not have done.' His son went to him, and tended to him, and whispered comfort to him.

'Then, mole, if you would be forgiven, and more than forgiven, do that which you should do,' said Beechen with sternness rather than compassion. 'Turn your back on the Word, and turn your snout this night towards the Stone. Then all that you need shall be given to you, even in the hour of your death.'

'Where shall I find the Stone?'

'It is here, Wyre, here before you. Waste not my time or other moles', or your son's, searching for what in your heart you know you found long ago but did not have courage to take up. It is here now, mole, and you know it.' Beechen's voice was dispassionate and matter-of-fact. 'Moles of the Word talk much of sin, and their creed is one of Atonement, or punishment, of retribution for sins committed. You are afflicted for the moles you and those at your command have punished and tortured in the name of the Word; your murrain is the infection of their suffering. I judge you not for this – that is for you yourself to do, and I see from your body you have done so. If you would be forgiven you must begin again and be new-born and give up all you have.'

'I have nothing but pain to give up,' said Wyre bitterly.

Beechen looked from Wyre to his son and then back again.

'Mole, you have your son. Tell him to come with *me* tonight.'

'I am near to death and would have my son with me.'

A look of fear came to Wyre's eyes, stronger even than the suffering.

Beechen replied sternly, 'Give what you have up to the Stone, turn to the Silence you have heard so long in your own heart, and you shall find the forgiveness you seek. Through me the Stone has spoken, hear it, mole, and be free.'

Then the dying Wyre turned to his son and whispered, 'Go with him to Cumnor and hear him speak.'

'Come,' said Beechen softly, 'for your father shall not need you more. Come with the other followers and learn of the Stone.'

Then back on to the wooded way to Cumnor they went, north across the heaths where the winds blew from behind and the grass and withered thistles bent the way ahead.*

Many travelled through those nights, and saw that the sky was red in the troubled mornings, red with warning and with blood.

Among those followers, hurrying henchmoles went over the heath, running from the deeds they did. Aye, done in darkness, fled by morn, and a trinity murdered where they were.

* The subsequent history of Walden, son of Wyre, is told in *Tales of Longest Night*.

Heanor, and the other two, turning into the death the henchmoles' talons wrought. And Smock, raised her paws in surprise, but did not find them strong enough to ward off Wort's treacherous blows.

They were dragged privily to the Fyfield Stone and when others came (summoned by the very henchmole who did the deed) Wort pointed to the corpses and said, 'Murdered by the Stone-fool's aides! Treachery! Deceit! Summoned here in peace, allowed to leave in peace, and this is what they leave behind. The Word shall be avenged. The grass where the Stone-fool blessed the dead now bloodied yet again, and in his own name. Whatmole could welcome such a morning? Whatmole could sleep through nights such as these? This Stone-fool shall be punished.'

The Fyfield moles were troubled, but more by the death of Smock (though she had enough enemies to make their dismay equivocal) than Heanor and the others of his trinity. Though he was of the Word had he not let the Stone-fool make fools of *them*? Yet they had seen the Stone-fool leave – he must have been a clever mole to have come back again. So, puzzled still, they cleared the corpses and left Wort by the Stone.

'Cumnor, now?' asked one of her henchmoles.

'Cumnor, moles. And fast. Faster than this filthy wind itself, for I will catch this Stone-fool for myself.'

'Some call him Stone *Mole*. Some say he's the one all waited for.'

'Call him what they like, mole, Wort will see him tortured, and then dead.'

They laughed, and their laughs were ripped from out their mouths by the rushing wind and torn along towards where the Stone Mole travelled on, the laughter of scorn and hate. All, all, rushing now, to Cumnor's high bleak hill.

On a clear day a mole who cares to pause at Cumnor, where obsessive Wort then ruled, and looks across the roaring owl way that offends the landscape far below, may see the hallowed rise of wooded Duncton Hill. It makes a better prospect than the heathy history-scarred surface beneath his paws, for which few have ever had much good to say.

Certainly that windy grey day when followers gathered there, shaking from cold and apprehension, scarcely believing that the Stone Mole would come here, as others said he would – which others? nomole knew! – the place cannot have seemed very much. Desolate, forgotten, a place of banishment for mad Wort, roaring owls incessant below, hopeless grey skies above.

The moles had come in dribs and drabs, very hesitant indeed, and gathered at first at Wootton High, which lies a little to the south. Braver spirits there, who remembered Cumnor before Wort came and knew the routes, led the followers on, singing to cheer themselves, keeping close lest guardmoles attack. Not so fearless that they did not stop again for a time at Hen Wood, and wait for others to join them and give them strength of numbers.

Even then the followers' courage was relative rather than absolute, and on the morning when they made the final push they decided not to go to that part of Cumnor where Wort had made her base – drab Chawley End to the west of the hill itself.

Instead they went straight on north up the hill to its highest point, an open, mainly treeless place, such tunnels as it had unremarkable and stinking of fox and diseased rabbits. No Stone either. All grim.

But it was safer than anywhere else around there, and hard for guardmoles to ambush. But as it was, everything seemed to show that the guardmoles of Cumnor were taken utterly by surprise by the arrival of the followers, and that, even better, Wort was not there.

The two guardmoles stationed at the eastside of the system, which is where the followers came, could scarcely believe their eyes when so many moles appeared in force. They challenged the first they met in a half-hearted way, and then retreated out of sight back to Chawley End, the cheering followers pressing on upslope – cheering, it must be said, to see the grikes retreat for once – but not quite sure where to go, or where to stop. But there is a summit of sorts there, and there they stopped, watching as others came.

It was not long before a brood of grikes approached from the Chawley End, glowering and ferocious, and words were exchanged. But the grikes were outnumbered, and the senior ones seemed to have been told that such a meeting was not, at the moment, against the Word.

What the guardmoles did do, however, was to circle about the followers, staring hard at them as if to remember their faces and talons, and generally to intimidate them.

At first this aggression succeeded in cowering many of the moles, but before long their numbers gave them confidence and they began to support each other and to outface the grikes. When a guardmole asked a mole where he was from he answered with a laugh, 'Duncton Wood, mate, that's where I hail from,' naming the one system everymole knew he could not be from.

'That's right, I seen him there. I'm from Duncton too!' said another.

'Like the others, Duncton Wood, my darling. The *better* part,' said a female to raucous laughter when asked the same question.

The grikes scowled, and retreated to a distance and watched helplessly as the numbers grew. And grew.

Until by the time dusk came the grikes were so outnumbered that any idea they might have had of attack, or marshalling, or simply bullying, had quite gone, and a few were detailed to keep watch while the rest went off to more comfortable quarters.

As for the followers, a few, disheartened by the non-appearance of Beechen, left before night came, but most stanced down in temporary burrows, or took up quarters in such tunnels as still survived at the top of the hill.

Nor did Beechen come the next day, or that night; a few

more left but yet more came, saying that moles they had met had heard for sure that the Stone Mole was on his way, and would soon be there. Expectation rose once more, though there was a false alarm when a small group of moles came up from Hinksey in the east, brought there by that mysterious sense that takes over moles when a gathering of significance is apaw, as if the very tunnels buzz with something going on beyond and makes them restless to find out what it might be.

It was in mid-afternoon of the third day, when the light was glooming and a good few moles were beginning to want to call it off and leave while the going was good, that a sudden rush of excitement passed through the temporary burrows and tunnels and the news spread that he was nearly there at last.

Which he was, for there below on the southern slope, he trekked steadily up from Hen Wood with two other moles close by, many more before him and others coming along behind.

How, from that distance, did they know it was the Stone Mole? It was most strange, but everywhere he went the ways across the soil, the clouds above, the line of woods to left and right, even the disposition of the moles about him, made him seem the very centre of things. If that was not enough there was a quality of light about the place where he happened to be. Wherever the Stone Mole was, moles looked first at him.

He came slowly and gracefully, but a sense of urgency ran like a wave up the slope before him. Among those who had come to hear him were a few who were not well, though ambulant. He stopped by several of these, and touched them, and murmured gently to them and, so talking and stopping as he went, the Stone Mole came among them.

A good few knew of Buckram, or had heard of him, and that he had been healed and was now of the Stone and stood guardian to the Stone Mole – or Beechen, as moles now understood him to be named. Though Beechen was by no means small, Buckram was much larger and stayed always near him, and together the two looked like a large mole that has a larger shadow. Sleekit did not always stay with him, but went among the moles, talking to them, and seeming to find out from them which ones particularly Beechen might himself like to reach out to.

Though nomole said as much, it seemed plain that for a time Beechen wished only to move among them, and come to know something of them before he spoke to them as a whole. Thus, although there was some clustering at first, the moles soon settled down and waited patiently as he went here and there, or sometimes huddled over some-mole who wanted his moment of quiet and prayer. Nomole told any what to do, yet all seemed to know what was best.

Gradually, as the evening drew on, Beechen brought one mole to another, or a couple to a third, and bade them talk to each other, and help each other; some to hold, some to touch, some to repeat prayers he had made. In this way he gradually turned what had been but a gathering of different moles into a group that knew something of itself, and was, however briefly, a community.

Only then was he willing to address them. The moon was already some way above the horizon, the sky for the most part was clear, the lights of the roaring owl way spread into the distance below them, and those of the twofoot place to the east glowed in the sky. Beechen went to the highest place on Cumnor Hill and turned to face towards that one place about them that had no twofoot lights at all.

Its hill rose darkly against the sky, the roaring owl way ran round its south-eastern edge. For a time Beechen stanced staring at it in meditative silence, and one by one, or sometimes in groups of three or four, the followers crept closer to him, for they sensed that he was going to talk to them soon and tell them of things that were in his heart, and which he desired to be in theirs.

When all the moles were settled, Sleekit went to him

454

and put her paw to his shoulder, and whispered to him as if to say, 'Stone Mole, Beechen, these moles are ready now.' The crescent moon was higher in the glowing sky, and a cold, light, westerly breeze came up the hill. But few moles noticed the cold, for somehow the Stone Mole had made the hill on which they gathered, and which had seemed so dangerous when they first came, seem peaceful and in some mysterious way feel like the very centre of moledom.

Round the furthest edges of the circle of moles a few others came, malevolent, eyes narrowed, dubious of what they saw. Of the followers only Buckram saw them, and feeling, perhaps, that Beechen was safe he had thought to take stance at the circle's edge. The guardmoles saw him, his eyes watchful, the moonlight on his fur, and most knew him, and that few had talons as fierce as his could be. His presence alone was enough to stay them and to give the followers a sense of security.

Once Beechen had stanced where all could see him, he turned first this way and then that, as if to acknowledge the presence of all the moles there, and then began to speak. His voice was deep and pleasant, soft at first but then growing more powerful as his stance grew somehow more powerful, so that if this was the centre of moledom all eyes were on him, for he was the centre of the centre. Like a Stone he was, grey, shadowed, moving, talking, his form ever-changing, his words lulling yet penetrating at the same time.

'From my heart to your heart shall I speak and tell of the place where I was born. From here you all can see it –' And he turned again towards the dark, secret hill that rose across the vales – 'for it is Duncton Wood. Aye, it was so!'

There was a murmur of surprise at this, for though the rumours had always persisted that the Stone Mole was indeed in Duncton Wood, few could ever really believe it, for the grikes guarded the system tightly, letting nomole in, and those inside were known only to be diseased outcasts.

455

'To Duncton my mother came in the April years, guided by a mole whose story one day you shall know, and she gave birth to me before the Duncton Stone. Sleekit here did witness it – I was born by the light of a star many of you saw, and my father was Boswell of Uffington, of whom many of you have heard.'

'The White Mole!' muttered a follower in awe, and others whispered in surprise at what they heard. It was now that Beechen's voice grew more powerful.

'Know that I am the mole called Stone Mole, come for each of you, for all of you. The time in which I was born, and in which you live, is a chosen time such as comes but once to each group of creatures across moledom and beyond. A time of testing, a time when darkness is most dark and light must find its greatest powers.

'To show moles the way through this hard time I have come, but as I was made by mole, as I am mole, so shall the worth of my life be made by mole. What I am you have made, what I shall be your courage, your faith, aye and your fear and failure shall decide. May the Stone be with us all, may we have the strength to outface the darkness that besets us.

'Of birth and death of body and of spirit I shall speak to you tonight by telling of Duncton Wood. For there a community did die, and yet was born again, as moles are born and die, and may be born again.

'Know then that there was a mole called Bracken, and he had faith in the Stone and the courage to pursue it. And another called Rebecca, who had faith as well, and knowledge of love and of life. There was a September day, a rainy day, when these two . . .' So Beechen began to talk to them, telling them the story of the system whose outline they could see rising in the darkness behind him, and of the moles who lived and died there. Telling much of Tryfan, telling of how a community must ever watchfully strive to be true to itself and thereby to the Stone.

For some he spoke of what could only be a dream, for their lives had never known community, but only being

456

outcast and under the thrall of grikes. For older moles, and the few who had stayed free of the heavily guarded systems and been told by their parents of the past, what he said reminded them of something they had known, or heard about.

But for all of them it touched on something that they felt they missed, a need to be more than they were – more than they could be – by themselves, the same need that had given them courage to come to Cumnor and know him.

Sometimes moles asked him questions – at first, ones of simple fact about Duncton's Stone, of the incidence of disease there, or where his mother came from. Then, later, others asked him of Stone and faith, and what it was they must do to serve the Stone truly.

He answered all they asked, and sometimes broke off from what he said to be still for a time with a mole who suffered, or to wait while others comforted one who had discovered tears in the night and dared to weep with others near. The night deepened and sometimes from Hen Wood below them came the shrill of owl.

A few moles spoke of doubts they had, or hopes, or fears. Aye, fears came last, and so many when they did. Fear was everywhere.

Great silence was on them then, and even the guard-moles at the edges were rapt and listening, unable to keep their eyes off Beechen. So intent were they, they did not see the dark glint of teeth in the night, and henchmole talons creeping. And eyes that stared from out of the tunnel by which she had come: Wort. But Buckram saw. He did not move, but watched as Wort signalled to the henchmoles to stay where they were, and only she came forward and settled quietly among the followers, eyes as rapt as theirs but full of the hate of fear.

'The Stone is peaceful, Stone Mole, and asks that we hurt nomole and turn our backs on violence. How then do we protect ourselves when the grike guardmoles come? How do we protect our young from the violence of the grike talon, and the eldrene's teaching?'

There was a murmur of sympathy among the moles and Beechen nodded his understanding of the question. After thinking for a little, he told them a story, beginning in the traditional way, 'From my heart to your heart I tell it, as it was told to me by my mother Feverfew, as it was told to her . . . There were once three pups, all male, and one was weak. When he sought his mother's teat he was pushed away. He learnt patience. When he reached for the brought worm it was taken from his grasp. He learnt independence. When he strove to get to the surface one of his brothers blocked his way and got there first. He learnt there is always another way. That mole grew up in a system full of fighting and he knew he wasn't good at that. So he went to an elder and asked what he should do. "Learn to fight," the elder said. He went to another and asked the same question. "Leave the system and live alone," he was told. He went to a third, "Find a mole to protect you."

'So he went to the Stone to pray for guidance, but when he got there the system's healer was there before him. "Stone," he was saying, "there's so much fighting in this system that I need help, but I can't find the mole I need. Stone, send me a mole who has patience, who can think for himself, who can find another way of doing something if the first won't work." Then the healer turned from the Stone and saw the young mole stanced quietly there and said, "Who sent you to me?"

' "The Stone," the young mole said.'

Beechen paused at the end of his tale and looked at the moles on that benighted hilltop, the starlight and glowing sky upon their faces and talons. He saw that some understood his story while others searched for a meaning in it, and a help to themselves.

'I have been asked by some how a mole defends himself against the talons of his enemy, and by others how it may be that the Stone should allow the forces of the enemy to prevail over him, even to death itself.

'Moles, be as that youngster was – healers to your

458

enemy. Know that the Stone does not and cannot save the lives of the just. The Stone is not a wall that keeps your enemy and his talons out, it is a tunnel, a way without portals or the obstructions of any seal, and is ever open to you and your enemy too. It is a way which you choose to be, and to raise your talons to those who threaten you is to close the way not only to them, but to yourself as well.

'Moles see raised talons before them and they think they see the greatest danger. What they see is fear. A follower's response should be the healer's response – fearlessness with common sense, fearlessness with intelligence, fearlessness with joy: with such powers as these at your command the most mighty talons wither and break, the most prideful and evil mole lowers his snout and submits. But raise your talons with fear, seek to strike first, seek to hurt, seek even to kill, and it is yourself and the Stone within you you destroy. Therefore seek the healing way.

'Yet do not be weak, for weakness is a sucking pool which attracts dark things to it; and weakness is often false. The healing mole who trusts the Stone is strong and sometimes fierce, sometimes irritable, sometimes wrong. But he is not weak and does not hide the strong talons of his spirit, or compromise his truth to placate another's darkness.

'Most of all the healing mole listens, and listens again, and lets those who threaten him always know he listens to the words behind the words, and he seeks to fight the talons behind the talons. Even in the face of death his eyes are bright and his ears hear. But if, at last, he is afraid, it is because he is but mole: then shall the Stone come into him and tell him he is loved.'

The night had grown cold, and the moon begun to sink. Beechen turned this way and that suddenly and said in a quieter voice, 'There is one here who hurts me, one who loves me more than many can, and yet hurts me . . .' There was a whisper of surprise among the moles, and Buckram, who remembered him saying the same thing at Fyfield, quickly came close to him and whispered, 'Tell me which he is, Master. Show him to me.'

459

'You shall know her, Buckram. Forgive her and tell her that I shall love her.'

'But if she hurts you. . . .'

'Even more must you forgive her.'

'Master. . . .'

But Beechen said no more but went out among the moles again to talk and touch and share those thoughts they brought to him. Below them the roaring owls quietened and were still, and the twofoot lights went out, but for some across the vales and those along the ways. Then many slept, but where Beechen was Buckram did not sleep, but stayed close, watching through the night until dawn came.

As the sun rose the moles saw that there was frost across the hill, the grass stiff with it, and the moles' breath steamy in the air. They sensed their time with the Stone Mole was almost done; they saw the guardmoles had all gone and felt the time for listening might be over and the grikes be gathering forces. It was best to go.

'Go peacefully,' said Beechen at the end, 'go to your communities, bear yourselves proudly wherever you are, speak of the Stone to those that will listen, and say the Stone Mole has come among you. Live not in fear for what is to come, but in joy for what you have; but if you are oppressed, and the talons of darkness are raised against you, know that the Stone sent me to tell you it is near, through me it is close, through my words it is known.'

'When shall we see you again?' asked a mole.

'You shall hear of me again. On Longest Night I shall pray for those I have met as I have met you. But I have far to go, many to see, and I shall not come this way again.' There was a sigh of disappointment among the moles.

'Others shall come for me as you shall go for me now, and tell moles what I have said. Darkness shall fall over moledom but my star shall be seen again. On that night you see it you shall know that I have fulfilled my task.'

There was puzzlement among the moles, and apprehension, and they looked at one another and asked what he meant.

But he said no more, but began leading them down Cumnor Hill towards Hen Wood even as the sun grew warm and the frost on the open grass melted where they passed, leaving behind them a great swathe of tracks where they had been.

More talked to him as they went, or to Sleekit, and there was scarcely a mole among the many who had come who could not go back to their communities, or families, and say they had not talked to the Stone Mole himself, or the warm and loving female at his side; hardly a one who could not tell a story or a wisdom he had told.

At first as the moles went on their way they stayed close, but gradually as they descended the hill those in front seemed to go faster, those behind slower, and those in the middle to spread out and become even more spread as fences and ditches split them up, and some took longer than others to negotiate obstructions along the way.

Beechen had told them to go peacefully, and there seemed no reason why they should not, for the sun was rising across the frosted fields and glinting on the ice that had formed in ditchwater and puddles, and the day was beautiful. Yet somewhere along the way, perhaps at that moment when most of the moles had lost contact with the group of which Beechen, Buckram, and Sleekit were the centre, hurry and even panic seemed to set in.

It was enough for one mole, fancying that in those northern-facing hollows where the cold and frost was deepest he saw dark movement, to say, 'Grikes!'

'Grikes coming?'

'Attacking!'

So mole thought, or heard, and began then to hurry and rush towards what seemed the safety of the trees of Hen Wood. While others far behind, hearing shouts and thinking the dangers were ahead of them, went cautiously, and more slowly still.

While where Beechen was Buckram loomed ever

461

nearer, ever more watchful, until, when the wood was but a short distance ahead, he disobeyed Beechen's wish and, with a great paw at his side, hurried him towards the wood and, hopefully, away from any danger.

Buckram was well advised to be so watchful. For ahead of them on the south end of the wood, waiting with mounting impatience for the first moles off the hill, grike guard-moles lay hidden, forming a long line across the wood, with others beyond to east and west at less popular alternative routes. Centrally placed along this formidable line, at the common way by which many of the moles had first come up from Pickett's Heath to the south, stanced Wort, her henchmoles at her flanks, watching the wood ahead, listening for sound of mole.

All along the line the guardmoles glowered and looked irritable for they did not like the instructions Wort and her henchmoles had given them in the middle of the night.

'No aggression, no retribution, let moles pass unharmed. Stop only the three I have described to you, and when you stop them do it discreetly and let nomole see you. Get them underground, keep them there, send a messenger to one of us. On pain of death do not harm the three moles if you take them. They probably won't be among the first to come, but be alert to allmole.'

So now they waited, and moved back and forth to keep warm, for they had been in position since before dawn and the night had been chilly, leaf litter was freezing around them, worms going deep.

'Wish the buggers would hurry up, been up half the night already.'

'Aye, dragged from off the hill before that Stone-fool finished all his words. Eerie as a Stone up there, I was glad to get away.'

'Sssh! Sssh. . . .'

'What is it?'

'Mole approaching. Now remember what Wort said. No violence.'

The guardmoles eyed their thick black talons and one looked at another and said, 'What, *me*? You must be joking. I wouldn't hurt a fly.' The other chuckled unpleasantly, and they turned to watch the way moles might soon come.

And come they did, all along that line, some going so fast because they thought they were pursued that they did not see the grikes in front until they were upon them.

'It's all right, you silly buggers, we're just making sure there's no trouble, no punishments here.'

So, relieved, the first moles went through the line, and the others followed thankfully along behind, pausing only to look back and see the grikes were speaking true and letting allmole through.

So the exodus from Hen Wood began. Sometimes a follower would stop and think and go back, realising that perhaps the grikes were waiting for the Stone Mole who, unless he was warned, would come straight into the trap.

But these the guardmoles gave short shrift to, turning them back south, telling them to keep moving until they got to Pickett's Heath where they could go unmolested.

So on they went, their uneasiness clearing, for the day was bright, Hen Wood was behind them, and in their hearts were the Stone Mole's words: to be fearless and trust the Stone; hurt nomole and take what they had learnt back to their communities.

As these first ones broke out of the wood and headed down the slopes to Pickett's Heath, Mistle and Cuddesdon, after an early start from a night in a sandy burrow on Boar's Hill, headed on up towards Hen Wood half expecting that moles might come down towards them that same day.

They knew where the Stone Mole must be, for the day before they had run into a couple of those moles who, losing patience, had left Cumnor Hill before Beechen had got there. They had, of course, been negative, saying he had not come and did not seem likely to, but Mistle was not to be dissuaded and insisted they press on.

In truth Cuddesdon had not wanted to, for at last he had had positive directions to Cuddesdon Hill and knew now, from a mole who had been near it not a molemonth before, that it lay but a week or two's journey away.

'You go on, Cuddesdon, and I'll find you there,' Mistle had said. 'If the Stone Mole is not at Cumnor then I'll give up my search for him and follow after you to Cuddesdon Hill.'

But Cuddesdon dismissed this idea. Had they come so far towards Duncton Wood that he would now turn away from it without her? No, they had not. He would accompany her into Duncton itself, and would stance with her by the Stone and give thanks for the day they had first met, and the protection that the Stone had so long given them. If, after that, she chose to come to Cuddesdon Hill then he would not stop her, but in his heart he knew it would be only as a friend, though a much loved one. He was ever an honest mole and knew he was not the mating kind and, even if he was, Mistle was not for him. It was a different mole than him she needed, one who could give to her as much as she would bring to him – if such a mole existed, which he doubted.

So they had set off that morning over the frosty ground and begun the climb towards Hen Wood, beyond which they knew Cumnor Hill rose, where Beechen might still be found.

But, at Pickett's Heath, they had been disappointed to meet the first moles to have come out of the wood and to hear that the Stone Mole's meeting was over, all moles had begun to leave, and nomole should go up into Hen Wood because the grikes were there.

'But they're not attacking moles?' said Mistle.

'Not yet they're not. But I've heard Wort herself is there, and she's not a mole to stance with idle talons while followers drift by. I wouldn't go up there, mole. There's bad trouble apaw.'

'Did the Stone Mole say where he was going next?' asked Mistle.

'Strange, that. He said he would not be this way again, he had his task to fulfil, but we would know. Said we were to go back to our communities and burrows and hurt nomole, but live out our faith in the Stone. But we're not dawdling here. We got off quick and we'll go on quick. . . .'

'How shall we know him?' Mistle called after the mole.

'By the older female with him, and by Buckram, former guardmole and as big as a tree. As for the Stone Mole, why, it's his eyes. They make a mole want to be close to him.'

Even as the mole spoke to them others hurried by, and poor Mistle, disappointed, stared upslope, uncertain what to do.

'It would be safest to stay here and wait for him. He's sure to come this way,' said Cuddesdon.

'But the further upslope we go, the more likely we are not to miss him,' said Mistle. 'Cuddesdon, you go off to the east, both of us shouldn't risk ourselves, but for me . . . for me. . . .'

'What's for you?' said Cuddesdon.

'I want to see him. I feel so close now, I must find him.'

'Come on, mole,' said Cuddesdon, taking the lead. 'Come on!'

So on they went, Mistle hurrying for once, and others hurrying down past them to left and right, none of them looking like how Mistle imagined the Stone Mole to be.

The higher they went, the nearer the trees of Hen Wood became, the stranger the looks they got, and Mistle's need to go on became more urgent.

They had taken the most central route, which moles at Pickett's Heath had said was the quickest into the wood, and they followed it now, having sometimes to move aside when more than one mole came towards them.

'We're near,' said Mistle, 'I can feel we're near. It's like it was at Avebury, that same calling, oh Cuddesdon, come on. . . .'

Old oak tree branches closed over them as they entered

the wintry wood at last and they seemed to leave the bright sun on the frosty ground behind.

'He may be somewhere here,' said Cuddesdon running behind, 'but there's grikes as well. Mistle, we must be careful!'

But Mistle was not listening, for the track was clear and easy, the slope not quite so steep and she was rushing forward now, eager, hope in her eyes, for she felt him close, he was. . . .

The way turned, Mistle was not looking, the floor of the wood seemed to rush up at her, and she tumbled forward, straight into the paws of a henchmole.

'Well,' he growled in surprise. 'Well!'

He stared coldly at her, and then loomed over her as Cuddesdon came up.

'Look what we've got here, eldrene Wort!' he said, holding on to her and calling over his shoulder.

The undergrowth at the side of the way parted suddenly, and out of it came Wort. Not small but spare, a round, innocent face spoilt by cold, narrow eyes, middle-aged, inclined to stance too close to a mole for comfort.

'What *have* we got? A female!'

Snout to snout, Wort and Mistle stared at each other.

'Why mole,' said Mistle softly, 'I thought you . . .' It was not the way anymole spoke to eldrenes and the henchmole looked surprised, but strangely Wort did not; and nor did she react angrily but rather, for once, she seemed not quite to know what to do.

'This is not one of the moles I am seeking,' she said dismissively, though her gaze lingered on Mistle's face, as did Mistle's on hers. 'Nor is this male. Let them be.'

'But they're going the wrong way,' said the henchmole, letting Mistle go.

'Come on, Mistle,' Cuddesdon whispered urgently, 'let's get away from them.'

'But she's one of them,' said Mistle. 'At Avebury, *she* was one of them.'

'Mole . . .' began Wort, turning back to her, beginning

466

to look at Mistle again, curious, hesitant, yet threatening. 'Why are you going that way?'

Even as she spoke, two other followers came down the way, out of the centre of the wood, as if to affirm the oddity of what Mistle did. Yet it was enough to divert Wort's and the henchmole's attention from them, and to allow Cuddesdon to say, 'We've lost one who was with us, we're just going back to find him.' And, with a paw to Mistle's rump, he quickly pushed her on and got her away from more questions and further up into the wood.

'You looked as if you had seen that mole before,' said the henchmole.

Wort frowned and her eyes glittered.

'The Stone is evil, many its subtle ways,' she muttered. 'I think I *have* seen her before, yes I think I can place her.' Then she said with sudden urgency, 'Henchmole, go after her. Bring her back but do not harm her. Quickly!'

But Mistle and Cuddesdon were not the only moles who had gone through the line the wrong way. Ahead of them a brave follower, who had already passed through the line out of the wood and seen the grikes, had felt so uneasy about going on without trying to give a warning to the Stone Mole that he had crept back and, in the confusion of so many moles, successfully gone up into the wood to warn Beechen.

He had found him and Buckram halfway down the wood, poised at a point where the floor fell away steeply, while waiting for Sleekit to recover her breath from a rush that had been too much for her.

The follower struggled up the slope, and described what he had seen.

'Is Wort there?' asked Buckram immediately, for he knew that mole all too well, and she ruled these parts most powerfully in the name of the Word.

'I don't know what she looks like, but I know there's guardmoles right across the wood – it took me a time to find a way back through.'

'To right and left across this route we're taking?' asked Buckram.

The follower nodded.

As they had talked, other moles had come on from behind until Buckram suddenly found himself in a melee of moles, none quite sure what was happening as some were convinced they were pursued from behind, while others, hearing something of what the follower said, thought that now the dangers lay ahead.

'Right,' said Buckram loudly, his guardmole training coming to the fore as he imposed his will on the group, 'except for the Stone Mole, Sleekit and me, the rest of you continue the way you were going. It's for the best for you to go on and the safest. If guardmoles come this way, jostle them but don't attack. That will give me time to get the Stone Mole out another way.' There was ominous-seeming crashing from below and Buckram responded to it by ordering, 'Now go, the Stone Mole's life may depend on it!'

Which they bravely did, turning from him and skeltering off downslope even as two moles began climbing upslope before them, a female and a male: Mistle and Cuddesdon. . . .

Poor Mistle. Just at that moment when she had seen at last a mole so big among some moles upslope that he *must* be Buckram, and therefore the Stone Mole must be near, most of the moles with him detached themselves and ran confusingly towards where she and Cuddesdon laboured up the slope. Both were tired, for they had pressed on fast, rightly concerned that the henchmoles were following.

They watched helplessly as the crowd of moles pushed into them and they found themselves stopped in their tracks and even for a moment knocked backwards.

It was in those few vital moments of disarray on the slopes that Mistle saw the mole she had been seeking for so long. He was in profile, talking to a female – Mistle guessed it might be the one called Sleekit – and then she saw him turning to Buckram who at that same moment was pointing westward across the wood away from all of them.

Mistle called out, and for the briefest of moments the three moles looked their way, thinking, perhaps, that she was one of those moles who had been sent running down the slope. The mole she thought she *knew* – was the Stone Mole looked directly at her then for the first time, but at that same moment Buckram looked past her and Cuddesdon, and seemed to see something further down the slope below them, something that alarmed him: a pursuing henchmole.

He turned back to the Stone Mole, pointed again westward, and, putting a paw against his flanks, almost bodily turned him that way, shouting to Sleekit to follow them. Mistle saw all this as if the moles were moving very very slowly, and she as well, so slowly that the glance she exchanged with the Stone Mole seemed to go on a long time.

Then she saw him struggle against Buckram's paw, and that he wanted to turn towards her, to come downslope to talk to her. But again Buckram turned and urged him on. She saw his gaze on her faltering and she tried desperately to push herself on, to call to him to say, to say. . . .

'Mistle!'

From beyond the silence of the long moment she seemed locked into – a desperate moment in which she seemed unable to do anything but watch passively all about her – Cuddesdon's voice urgently came.

'Mistle, one of the henchmoles is coming! Run now!'

She turned to look behind her, and saw the rush of moles that had now passed them reach one of the big henchmoles they had met before. Fortunately he too was stopped in his tracks, for the moles were jostling him, but he was buffeting them out of the way and pushing himself on up the friable slope and leaf litter of the wood, gaining ground on them.

'Come on, Mistle!'

Cuddesdon had run ahead and now, as she turned back to flee upslope, she caught one final glimpse of the Stone Mole, hurried westward by Buckram, looking at her as desperately as she did at him, and then he was gone from her sight.

'Mole! Stop, mole!' the henchmole roared from among the trees below.

'Mistle! Up here, *this* way,' called out Cuddesdon from above.

Then other followers crashed down from the slopes above, heading straight for her, and she turned first to right and then to left to avoid them.

'Mistle!' Cuddesdon's voice was further off now and she was not sure where he had gone, for there were fallen trunks and branches to get round, undergrowth, a hollow in the ground, and behind her the inexorable crash of the henchmole closing on her and shouting for her to stop.

Panic overcame Mistle then, and she ran blindly on, going left round a fallen branch knowing that if Cuddesdon had gone the other way it would be hard to find him again for she could not cut back on her tracks without going towards the henchmole.

'Mistle . . .' His voice seemed far, far away, but wherever he was the henchmole was nearer, and she must flee and escape from him. On she went, on . . . until her breath gave out and she desperately scurried in among the leaf litter by a branch and hid, and heard the rushing, chasing, terrible shouts of the henchmole all about and tried not to let her desperate panting be heard.

He came running up nearby and stopped. She dared not move but could see his flank through foliage, going in and out with the effort of chasing her. She stared transfixed, and utterly afraid.

'Shit!' he said.

Then he cocked his head on one side, listened and muttered, 'The bitch is probably hiding . . .' and began to snout about the surface, checking among fallen branches and undergrowth, coming so near that she could hear his heavy breathing and almost count each individual hair of fur as he moved past her hiding place.

'Shit!' he said again, and then turned away and stanced down quietly in the shadows, waiting for her to move. An earwig crawled over her paw, the thin red sheen of a worm's end thinned and disappeared into the ground she had disturbed to her right. The ground smelt damp and musty, and she thought, Think of something to stop yourself moving, Mistle, think of something! But she could think of nothing but the numbing fear she felt. Nothing else.

Only after a long wait did the henchmole, still swearing, finally leave and she felt she could breathe again. But it was not until long after, and the movement of followers through the wood seemed to have ceased, that she dared shift her stiff limbs.

Then dusk came. She felt cold. She peered out into the wood, she saw nomole, she heard nomole. The wintry wood seemed dark and malevolent and she felt terribly alone and wanted to escape it as soon as she could.

But not downslope south where the grikes might still be, nor upslope north where Cumnor was. East, then, or west. She did not know. Cuddesdon . . . at least he must have got away from the henchmole as well. Should she stay where she was in the hope that he might come back? Which way might he have gone? It must be east or west, she had no idea.

'Guide me, Stone,' she prayed, 'guide me now where I can best fulfil my task.' She thought of the Stone Mole, she thought of Buckram leading him away from danger across the wood – west. That way, too, the wood was lighter with the last of the sun, and she knew from experience that if a mole is in danger in a wood it is best she moves towards the light – for coming out of darkness as she does, she can see before she is seen. Yes, it's what Cuddesdon would have done. With a sigh she turned west and hoped she might reach the edge of the dark wood before night or tiredness overtook her.

471

That night was bitterly cold and again dawn showed a frost across the woods and fields, and only the flap of rooks in the high trees. As the wood grew lighter a solitary mole watched three moles approach him. He was a rotund mole, a cheerful mole, a mole who for some time past had been wrinkling his brow and blowing warm, steamy breath on his paws to warm them and muttering, ' 'Tis cold!' But he was a mole who knew how to look after himself, for he was stanced most comfortably in the warmth of a hastily made surface nest of moss and leaves.

He watched the three and said to himself, 'About time too!' Then he squeezed out of the nest he had made, shook his body free of loose material, and emerged from the shadows in which he had hidden and waited to be seen.

The biggest of the three, who was male and very big indeed and had the look of guardmole about him, did not make him feel confident, but he put a brave face on it and called out, 'Good morning and greetings! Would you be Buckram?'

Buckram loomed nearer, looking to right and left in case of traps, and said, 'I am.'

'Your friends must therefore be Sleekit and Beechen of Duncton Wood.'

These two ranged up alongside Buckram and stared in some bemusement at the mole.

'Amazing,' said the mole. 'Absolutely amazing. I have met some extraordinary moles in my time but . . . well, words fail me.'

He beamed at them.

'Who are you?' asked Buckram.

'A friend of a friend. My name's Tubney, *his* name's Mayweed . . . and he is another amazing mole.'

At this they all relaxed. Beechen grinned, Sleekit fought back sudden tears and Buckram, still very much in charge, asked, 'Where is he?'

'Not far, or too far. There *are* guardmoles about and that's why I've come into this wretched wood, along with several others. He spaced us out and told us to keep an eye open. Very amusing, your friend Mayweed, "Keep an eye open and relax, yes, yes, yes!" Relax? I normally do. Bablock moles such as me are not renowned for stressful living. Since Mayweed turned up, took a look about, said our system was exactly what he had been looking for all his life and did we mind if one or two moles dropped in for a shortish stay all very hush-hush and please don't fret, *this* mole has been worried sick, which doesn't suit me at all. He said that whichever one of us should have the indubitable honour (as he put it) of finding you we were to lead you to him, and he would accompany you to Bablock himself.'

'Well if Mayweed said it you had better do it!' said Beechen with a laugh. 'And anyway, I think he'll be anxious to be with his mate again.'

Tubney looked at Sleekit and respectful surprise crossed his plump face. Then sudden embarrassment as if such an impressive and elegant old female should not be kept waiting a moment longer than need be.

'Oh! I see! I hadn't realised, Madam, that you're Mayweed's, er, partner! Well then, of course, please, yes, yes . . . he'll want to see you as soon as possible, so please follow me.'

Tubney turned and waddled off as Sleekit and Beechen, glancing at each other with amusement and shared love for Mayweed, turned and followed him, with Buckram guarding the rear.

The route was circuitous, and they picked up three more moles who had also been deputed to watching duty before they passed under a small cross under and stopped.

'Where is he?' asked Sleekit.

'Supple Sleekit, beloved, look up and see your heart-throb, me!'

They looked up and saw Mayweed leering down at them from the top of the cross-under where, he explained as he scrambled and rolled his way down the embankment, he had been watching lest they did the really sensible thing

473

and came via the minor roaring owl way they had just gone beneath.

'Dreams come true!' he said when he was on all four paws before them, had dusted himself off, and had greeted Sleekit with an affectionate embrace.

'I have found a place where we may rest! Do I see gloomy languor in your stance, bold Beechen? It shall go in Bablock. Do I see frowns on your brow, 'stonishing Sleekit? In Bablock they shall flee. How far? Less than a day to reach a place a mole might seek all his (or her) life!'

'Come on, Mayweed,' said Beechen with some impatience.

'Yes, yes. I see you are as tired as you look, bothered Sir. I shall not witter more!' He turned to one of the Bablock moles and said, 'My new-found friend, go and tell the other watchers that the moles we were looking for are come. We shall go on ahead. Away one and all! Stout Tubney, lead!'

The ground was mainly sloping fallow fields and heath, the earth frosty cold, the route westward and down into the great valley of the River Thames which stretched out below them.

It was plain from the outset that Beechen was in no mood to talk, or even to travel willingly with them. He kept pausing and staring across the great misty vale below and then up and down it.

His mood was in sharp contrast to that of the others who, with the prospect of a place of rest before them, seemed to have found new energy and cheer. Mayweed and Sleekit chattered about this and that as if they were young moles again. Buckram seemed to find much to talk about with Tubney, and so it was only slowly that they all began to realise that Beechen was not himself at all.

He stopped. Sleekit went back to him, and saw to her surprise that he looked tearful, he looked vulnerable, his face looked both young and fatigued at once. All the party stopped then as Sleekit spoke to him. Of what he told her we can only guess — of a sense that he was outcast from

474

them perhaps, of a strange restlessness, of a desire to be alone, and . . . of the mole he had seen so briefly in Hen Wood, one he should have gone back to, one whose gaze he could not get from his mind. One he was going to find – yes, that was it: now!

He stanced up purposefully to set off back upslope then and there.

'Beechen . . .' began Sleekit, at her most understanding and diplomatic. But whatever she said had no effect. He had seen a female, henchmoles were coming, she was in danger, he was going to find her. And he was going alone.

'She wasn't "just" a mole, was she?' said Sleekit.

'I don't know what she was,' said Beechen unhappily. 'She seemed like moledom itself to me. I wish . . . this is ridiculous. I'm sorry. . . .'

The Stone Mole behaving like . . . like the young mole he still truly was! 'He is mole first,' Tryfan had said, and now they saw it. It was as if, after a long trial in which he had had to be Stone Mole to everymole, he wished now to be 'but mole'.

Naturally all of them, and especially Buckram, were against any notion of Beechen going off by himself.

'I saw a mole,' said Beechen again, wishing he had more strength, wishing he could inspire himself as he could others, wishing they would all go away.

'Female?' Mayweed half whispered to Sleekit, who nodded.

'Then good luck to boldness. His friend me, Mayweed, fell in love with sweet Sleekit here at the blink of an eye, at the flash of a talon! Go and find her! Bring her to us! We shall warn her against it but give her our blessing! As for danger, of course there's danger, dire danger. But for the folly of youth the world might not change at all. Let danger be welcomed! Remember that humbleness himself trained Beechen here in route-finding from a pup, and he'll be safe. A mole needs to be alone sometimes. Adventure! Danger! Risk! 'Tis the making of life's blood.

And if true love is the end result what a tale we shall have to tell! We shall decline into our staid ancientness in Bablock and from the safety of our pleasant place thank the Stone that we no longer feel the confusing rushes and faints that drive a mole, otherwise sensible, perhaps even divine, to rush about the place looking for that most elusive and changeable thing that graces moledom's sunny ways – a female to love; or, worse, being pursued by that most ferocious monster a male can encounter, a female *in* love. But humbleness jests and leers knowingly and says to one and says to all, let the poor lad be, he'll be unlivable with until he has been, and then when he comes to his senses he'll be unlivable with again. But there we go, puzzling life. To Bablock then, and he can follow, downhill all the way! Ha, ha!'

Once Mayweed's flight of romantic fantasy was over, he gave Beechen some instructions about the easiest way down to Bablock.

'Now, I'll watch *you* go,' said Beechen, who felt much better for talking to his friends. He stanced on the bare ground as the others, with general muttering and reluctance, despite Mayweed's words, went on down the slope.

'But I don't like to leave him,' poor Buckram could not help saying. 'He saved my life.'

'Warm-hearted but misguided mole,' said Mayweed, 'he may well have done, but if you kept him here now he would make your life insufferable.'

They looked back to wave farewell, but where Beechen had been was nomole now. He had gone.

The second night after the departure of the followers through Hen Wood was even clearer than the first, and the air grew colder and colder as all warmth seemed to flee southern moles and lose itself among the winking stars.

As dawn came the leaves crackled with frost, and every blade of grass at the edge of Hen Wood was bowed under the weight of white crystals.

Mistle stared out at the pale chill scene, her back paws still warm from the earth in which she had rested through the night, but her pink snout tingling with the cold. Despite everything Mistle did not feel as lonely and depressed as she might have, and indeed a wave of entirely new feelings came over her.

What she felt most of all was an unfamiliar mix of relief and guilt. Relief to *be* alone, and free; guilt that she did not miss Cuddesdon more, or seem to worry for him.

But ever since she had so briefly caught the Stone Mole's gaze, and once she had got over her panic at losing Cuddesdon, the sense of freedom had steadily increased. After the henchmole had left and she dared move off once more she had decided to press on west, for that had been the way the Stone Mole was going and perhaps Cuddesdon had gone that way too, though the more she thought about it *his* inclination would have been to go east towards where he had been told Cuddesdon was.

Well, that was as maybe. The Stone would decide . . . and with that consoling thought and tired out, she had made a safe burrow, concealed it, and slept the first night through. The next day she had woken to movement, sensed mole about, heard scurrying, seen two large moles in the distance who looked like guardmoles, and lain low for half the day.

At midday it grew suddenly colder, and the branches of the trees seemed stuck quite still against the pale blue winter sky. Silence had fallen all about and she felt, or sensed – indeed she felt she *knew* – that the guardmoles had gone and it was safe to move on.

The enforced idleness seemed to have cleared her mind and made her calm, and she moved out across the surface to the west slowly, enjoying the darkening violets of the late afternoon shadows, and the sharp crackle of leaves underpaw.

Rooks roosted high, stirring and flapping their wings but not taking off, and she came to the edge of the wood. She heard solitary roaring owl ahead and decided to stop once more and sleep the night through at the very edge of the wood, and take her chances out on the heathy ground beyond the following morning.

She prayed to the Stone, for Cuddesdon, for herself, and then for the mole she had seen, Stone Mole or no. Increasingly, as she grew used to the image of him in her mind, she thought of him as mere mole, male, with eyes that had transfixed her. The thought of meeting him, let alone talking to him, made her feel nervous and she said her prayers to calm herself, but the prayers slid into reveries, pleasant dreams, silly languid thoughts, *summer*-seeming thoughts, as winter night settled down around her. She watched the stars, listened to the wood behind her, and then sunk down into the warmer soil, and snuggled into her temporary burrow and slept.

So it was there that when she awoke the following morning, she felt fresh, alive and good. She watched the light strengthen across the heath ahead of her as the sun rose behind and filtered through the bare trees of the wood, she saw a ragged lapwing alight on the heath ahead and then take off again, she heard the rooks call and argue, she groomed, she ate, she took her time.

Then, when the air felt good and the time felt right she set off, leaving the wood behind her as if she was shedding old fur, and an old life.

'It's November, and cold, and yet I feel as if it's spring!' she told herself in surprise. She thought of Violet, and smiled. How Violet would have liked all this, *all* of it.

Where to go?

Ahead, my dear!

So west she went, until, quite suddenly, the rise eased, the ground fell away, and she saw below her the winding misty vale of what she knew was the River Thames. She could not see its water, for it was lost in lines of leafless trees, misty and mysterious. But north-west of where she was it stretched away and in places the trees along its banks gave way to pasture and meadow and she saw its dark line.

Somewhere on along it, she knew that Duncton Wood must be, the place that Violet had told her to go.

She turned north, and took a pleasant route along the contour line as the heath became fallow fields and hedges crossed over her way. She sensed that to veer upslope north-easterly and go too high might bring her round to Cumnor, but though the sensible thing was to go lower, down towards the river, yet she felt right the way she was.

But she did not feel sensible. She felt *free*, for moledom seemed to stretch out invitingly to her left flank and to her right the ground rose and blocked out the realities of Cumnor and of grikes. Strength came to her paws and she travelled faster, encouraged by the light rather than the warmth of the thin sun that rose behind her, and whose rays were too weak even to warm the ground enough to clear the frost.

A day for today, a time for now, on such a good day she had always wanted to have her first sight of Duncton Wood and now she was beginning to think she might.

Then, suddenly, she knew – *she knew* – she would, so on she went, seeming to be at one with the ground she touched, and the air she breathed, and moledom all about her.

Twice when dark shadows touched the sky she paused and hid: rooks perhaps, heron maybe; but they were soon gone and she pressed on.

Sometime later she paused again to rest and feed, the air cold but her body warm and pleasant with the effort of travelling. The Thames below was more visible, for the sun reached down among its trees now, and the ground ahead had dropped a little and showed the northern view. On she went, over fields, under hedges, sliding across the frozen water of a ditch, keeping high to avoid the streams that must flow from the slope towards the Thames lower down.

On, on, even faster now, for she wanted to reach wherever it was the Stone was safely guiding her with the sun still high and clear, and the day so bright.

The ground eased ahead, the slope fell off to her right, and there, past a hedge, over a small dip of pasture field, there, oh there was the hill on which was Duncton Wood. There!

The light of the sun was on it, and it seemed to rise so near that a mole might reach across the great vale that opened out below and touch it. Duncton!

'Duncton Wood.' She whispered the words and her heart felt full of joy. 'Oh Violet, I got here, I got to Duncton Wood! Violet, it's so beautiful!' she said.

She gazed at its great slopes, and up over pastures to where the wood was thick. Then on to its highest part where the leafless beeches were shining grey, with an occasional holly tree among them to give a touch of green. So peaceful.

The hill was steepest to its left or western side, where pastures dropped down towards the river. Beyond there, moledom stretched away.

Certainty, security, a strong sense of something fitting came upon her, and a sense of purpose too.

'I feel as if I have come home,' she said. 'Home from home. Violet, where you dreamed of I shall go. One day Cuddesdon will find me up there in Duncton Wood. One day. . . .'

Mole near. Mole. She knew it but was not afraid, for the sun and the cold clarity of the day seemed to have driven fear off the face of the earth. She looked to right and to left and then behind her, puzzling because she could not see mole, yet she felt a presence.

She turned from the place she had taken stance, looked back again, and contoured on a little, her route swinging north-east. She was alert but relaxed, the sun at its warmest of the day, her fur glossy, her paws and talons sure. Mole *was* about. She paused to look at Duncton Wood once more, turned to continue and then suddenly saw him there, stanced ahead as she had been, staring at the distant hill.

He turned even as she stopped on seeing him, and he

480

saw her then. They were too far off to speak, too near to shout, so for a moment they just stared, as transfixed it seemed as they had been in Hen Wood.

Then moving at the same time they started towards each other. She dropped her gaze on him then, from sudden shyness or embarrassment. She looked at the ground, she looked up again, she moved, she looked away, she dared to look once more and there he was, and there she was, smiling, each smiling, and the sun upon them both.

'You're the . . .' she began.

'I'm Beechen of Duncton born,' he said. He did not want to be called 'Stone Mole', it seemed. He looked larger than he had in the wood two days before, he looked tired. He was smiling. He. . . .

As so many thoughts rushed through her head she heard herself say, 'My name is Mistle, born of Avebury. . . .'

He came closer, his eyes were clear as purest sky, there was nothing but *him* before her, nothing but him at all.

'I thought . . .' he began.

'. . . that we might not find each other,' she continued for him. Her voice trailed away. 'He's mole, he's *mole*,' she said to herself and relief was flooding into her. She felt her paws shaking on the ground before her, and she saw he was nervous too. More than nervous, he seemed quite terrified. So he is but mole, he's just as I am. . . .

'Is that Duncton?' she asked, seeming unable to turn her head away from him to point the way she meant.

'Yes,' he said looking at her as she did at him, 'where you were looking before.'

'Yes,' she said still staring at him.

Somehow, clumsily, paw almost to paw, they turned together and stared at Duncton Wood, though it might have been in a cloud of mist so little did they see of it, so much did they feel overpowered by the other's presence so near.

'It's beautiful,' she said.

'I have never felt fear like this before,' he said. 'Do you feel it?'

Yes, yes, yes, yes, yes, yes.

'Yes,' she said abstractedly.

Neither said a word, both stanced utterly still staring at what their eyes could not for the moment see.

Slowly, fearfully, shaking, his breathing sharp and irregular, he reached out his left paw and placed it on her right one.

'Mistle,' he whispered. It was a statement, not a question.

She looked at his paw and then dared look at him, dared because he still stared ahead. She felt his fear and it was the sweetest thing. Moledom was in their touch. She looked on him and even as she felt surges of joy and pleasure and relief she said, 'Beechen?'

And this was a question. Many questions. A whole life of questions, a whole life beginning.

He turned to her and came closer still, and their paws reached for each other, and as the release of touch came to their bodies she wanted to cry and laugh, and run and dance. She felt at that moment that she could reach to the sun itself and yet still be on the earth; and when at last he spoke, and when she replied, it was to say as much, and much, much more.

Chapter Twenty-Three

Wort, eldrene of obscure Cumnor, waited two days before she was satisfied that her guardmoles had failed to apprehend Beechen of Duncton, whom she now felt certain *was* the long-heralded Stone Mole.

Being satisfied, she gave strict instructions that her guardmoles were to stay in Cumnor and on no account leave it until she returned to them.

'Where are you going?'

'The Word shall guide me,' she said enigmatically. But then obscurity was of the essence. Obscurity would, as she had frequently said, be their strength and it was the Word's will that obscurity should remain the lot of the Cumnor moles for a little while longer.

But surely, her devotees in Cumnor's Chawley End responded, the Word was displeased with them: they had been presented with a rare, probably unique, opportunity to take this mole Beechen who might be the Stone Mole – 'who *is* the Stone Mole,' she interjected – and the Word had not let them do so.

'Now is the Word testing our fortitude, and exposing our weak vanities,' eldrene Wort lectured them. 'Can you not see that it was *meant* that the Stone Mole was not caught? Let us gratefully accept that it is so and open ourselves to learning and moving on positively from this "failure".'

So obsessive and intense was the faith in the Word of this notorious eldrene that anything that happened to her, or the zealot moles attracted by her ruthless devotion to the Word, was interpreted as 'meant', 'inspired' and an object lesson in 'providence'. The worse it was, the more to Wort's twisted and prejudiced mind it seemed to speak of grace. Plague might hit them – well then, smile, for this is the Word's judgement and retribution on moles who were spiritually weak; she and several of her cronies had been banished from Fyfield to Cumnor by Wyre for overzealousness, then smile again, for *this* was 'the Word putting us into obscurity to prepare us still pure in the faith for the rigours of our finest hour soon to come when we shall be the talons of the Word's final judgement'. And so forth. Dangerous insanity.

Whatever setback came Wort's way, she survived it, turned it, and gained strength from it. Although thus far her obsessive faith seemed to have served her ill such moles do not give up, least of all Wort. Indeed, she sensed the turning point had come that justified everything that had so far happened to her and she believed that now, if she did the right thing, she would be set fair on the way that would lead her to the great destiny the Word had prepared for her. No wonder then that she was turning the failure to catch the Stone Mole into success.

As always at such moments she resorted to passionate prayer: 'Holy Word, mother of my mind, father of my body, cleanse me of doubt, cleanse me of despair, cleanse me of sadness, wash from my outer form the dust and filth of the infections and temptations of the Stone; Holy Word, my mother and my father, guide me.'

She spoke the words rapidly and with terrible intensity and they brought tears to the eyes of some of her listeners.

'Afflict mine enemies with suffering and death, for they are your enemies, Word; teach my mind to know thy justice and help my talons to wield thy punishment on those whose ignorance is an affront to thy great beauty, and whose wilfulness in following the Stone threatens thy great peace.'

She finished and stared at the henchmoles and guard-moles about her. They were a mixture of zealots like herself, male and female, some cruel and loyal hench-moles, and some guardmoles thrown out of more moderate systems locally and now clustered to eldrene Wort and Cumnor as galls to bitter fruit.

484

The eldrene Wort, whatever else she did, knew how to lead such moles. She gave them discipline and the hope that soon they could openly go forth and prosecute the Word's will upon allmole, as its most loyal servants. She pandered to their obscene belief that they were right and all others wrong. In this way, since her dismissal as eldrene of Fyfield by Wyre, Wort had quietly given legitimacy in Cumnor to this group of misfits, sadists, outcasts and obsessives of whom she was the archetype. Her faith was obedience to the Word. Disobedience was blasphemy. A blasphemous mole was no longer mole, and whatever was done to him, however it was done, was justified. She, or the Master himself, perhaps, was judge of what was blasphemous. Since she was obedient to the Word and its sworn agent, to doubt her was blasphemy. Such was the closed circle and harmonic evil of Wort's mind.

In truth, she had a certain dark genius as well. She *was* the first to recognise Beechen for what he was: the Stone Mole. She had been the first to appreciate that if the persistent rumours were true that he was in Duncton Wood, then the moles who controlled the cross-under outside it had an important part to play – something she had long urged, though with the more pragmatic and less prejudiced Wyre, it fell on deaf ears. Which made him a suspect mole in her twisted gaze. So strongly had she believed in the significance of Duncton's role as harbinger of the Stone Mole that in September, without seeking permission of Wyre, she had sent some of her own guardmoles to 'support' the patrols at Duncton's cross-under.

But the cross-under was also on the key routeway between north and south, and so it was that through her well-placed guardmoles she was informed when Lucerne's sideem first came. Better still, the contrast between 'her' guardmoles, and the more easy-going ones already there proved favourable, and the sideem gave them promotion. When new guardmoles were sought Cumnor supplied them. By late September, unknown to the sideem, the cross-under was Wort's.

Therefore, when the trinity led by Heanor first came that way it had been Wort's moles who had thoughtfully directed them to Cumnor first, and so turned Wyre's decision to demote her back against him, for she entertained them well, spoke a language of zeal and faith they liked to hear, and was the first mole in those parts to hear that Lucerne would reward that mole well who first brought him news of the 'Stone Mole'. She had been bemused by their desire to talk to moles of the Stone and relieved that they were to fulfil this part of their task in Fyfield and would not undermine her authority in Cumnor.

She was astute enough to understand the value of the information she had now, and cunning enough not to reveal it. She had thought it likely that the trained and clever Heanor would quickly find out the Stone-fool's true identity and so had risked a return to Fyfield, and soon afterwards assassinated Heanor – making it seem the work of followers of the Stone. Smock, the eldrene, was killed as well.

Wort justified the evil deed to herself by judging that the Word was offended by Heanor's failure to deal with the insults towards it Beechen's appearance in Fyfield had produced. But, with Heanor dead, she was more likely to be the one honoured for discovering the Stone Mole.

Her prayers said, Wort told her devotees what she would do.

'The Word guides me, the Word tells me that our patience shall be rewarded and our hour is coming. I shall entrust my life to the Word and travel to distant Cannock and there seek the direct intervention of Lucerne, our father in moledom, our beloved Master-to-be. From him I shall gain authority to act against the Stone Mole as I must. Did not corrupted Duncton spawn him? It did! Should not Duncton then be laid waste as the Holy Burrows of Uffington was by the Word? It should, and it shall! This

486

shall be Cumnor's great task, for this shall it ever be remembered. The Master-elect shall hear us on this. Your eldrene shall return and lead you and others we shall find against Duncton Wood.'

'But eldrene, the place is outcast and diseased.'

'Mole, you are right – it must be to have produced the evil that is called Beechen. But do not worry, the Word shall be our guardian and protector against disease!'

She then gave instructions that moles in her system must stay unseen and obscure until her return and, her preparations complete, the still-unknown, unmeasured, eldrene Wort, together with two henchmoles, set off north to Cannock, to seek out her dark and driven destiny.

In the space of the short time Lucerne and his sideem had occupied Cannock, the place had been transformed, and what had once merely been a system of dull tunnels now had the gloss of evil; and by that infection the Word brings wherever it comes, the same dark menace that inhabited the tunnels of Whern now occupied the tunnels, burrows and chambers of Cannock.

Mallice, ever attendant on her Master's needs, as on her own, controlled the running of the place, and had established the quarters of Lucerne at the central southern end of Cannock, near enough to the community chamber where moles met to see and hear what went on.

She had grown used in Whern to secret ways and tunnels, and to using spying points, and had some delved in Cannock too. There was little that went on she did not know about, and all was passed on to Lucerne, and much to Terce.

And Cannock had its fearsome place as Whern did: somewhere about which moles did not care to speak.

It lay downslope to the east of Cannock where underground water flowed and had made a place of fluted chambers, deep, moist, echoing, uncomfortable. Under the direction of Mallice it had been delved and sealed in such a way that cells existed there in which moles were easily kept. The one thing they did not die of there was thirst, for water dripped and oozed and formed sucking pools and sumps. These last gave it its name – the Sumps, which was a reminder to anymole that heard it that like the Sinks of Whern it was not a place from which a captive mole easily emerged alive.

The Sumps ran to various levels. The lower tunnels were always chill and damp because into these the water flooded sometimes when heavy rains fell outside: an event accompanied by a roaring and racing of water sound. The air was fetid in the deeper cells, and the light all gone. A mole incarcerated in those cells suffered a life of perpetual darkness, in which the only sounds were the menacing roaring of the water, and the occasional drag of paws when a prisoner from a higher level brought down some stinking food.

Some of the higher cells were comfortable enough, and there were those who, confined but briefly in the Sumps, never guessed the horrors and agonies of moles who survived in the murk and blackness deeper down.

The Sumps' power and organisation was vested in three moles: Mallice, most powerful of all; Drule, who was in charge of the guardmoles who ran it, and was their scourge as well; and Slighe, who kept the records of the prisoners there meticulously, but never visited it for very long himself.

The Sumps served three different uses. One was as a punishment to moles of the Word who had been lax, indolent or blasphemous. A second was as a place of torture of those moles who might have information Lucerne and those who served him needed. A third was as a place of secure confinement for moles, mainly of the Stone, who though not judged and punished might have a use at some time in the future, or be better 'lost'.

And lost was the word, for only Slighe knew the names and locations of all the moles confined, and if he made a slip – and he did – or lost interest in a mole, that mole was truly lost, and left to die in darkness and unloved.

By November the Sumps was in full use, and its wretched tunnels groaned and echoed to the sound of suffering moles who screamed, or coughed or bled their life away. It was a place that drove moles mad and Drule, the expert on its punishments, had quickly discovered – initially to his cost – that confinement in the Lower Sumps drove a mole insane if kept up too long. Twelve days was enough for most, though some had been permanently affected after only eight. Its most efficacious use was as a threat, meted out on those who had been sent down to it before and knew its horrors.

Perpetual darkness, rotten food, the real threat of drowning are enough to make a mole hallucinate and imagine horrors worse by far than any a torturer can inflict.

The Middle Sumps was where most prisoners were kept, eking out their days in crippling dampness, suffering the sadism of the guardmoles, malevolently forced to share cells with moles who hurt or raped them.

The Upper Sumps merely took a mole's liberty, and was slow to harm him physically. Yet even here was a place, a chamber more than a cell, in which certain moles were taken for bloody questioning – for access to it was comfortable and easy for moles such as Lucerne and Terce who had no desire to sully themselves with the realities below.

In the Upper Sumps as well those most pathetic prisoners of the Word in Cannock, youngsters of adult inmates, were kept since they were not strong enough to survive the rigours of the damper cells. Usually alone, always afraid, and if unwanted then fearfully abused. To these poor creatures Slighe came and, if they were male, he would use them and abuse them unto death itself through his perverted lusts. As for Drule, he had the pick of females there and having had his way would pass them on for guardmoles to use. Few of them survived.

How much of this did Lucerne know? Mallice knew all, or if she did not then she was blind and deaf, for she frequently visited the Upper Sumps, and on occasion the Middle Sumps as well. The reason? One word will be enough: torture. Aye, that was what she liked.

All done, all of it, in the name of the Word. But then it might be said that when a mole was sentenced to the Sumps he or she is no longer mole. Only this explains why guardmoles, who in their quarters elsewhere in Cannock could play happily with their young and be affectionate with their mates would, when their leave or break was done, return and be monsters to mole once more. Yet guilt was alive – for how else does a mole explain the fact that nomole spoke of the Sumps?

We too would like to turn our backs from all awareness of the place, but we cannot. A mole we know, and one we were beginning to learn to love, was confined there.

Betony.

Squeezebelly's daughter. Sister to Bramble, adoptive sister to Harebell and Wharfe.

Poor Betony. Suffering Betony. By November she was near death.

Aye, it was Mallice and her guardmoles who had snatched Betony from Beechenhill. From the moment she had realised exactly whatmole she had, which was some hours after her encounter with the party of watchers in which Betony had been, Mallice did not linger, but turned her snout towards Ashbourne, and thence to Cannock feeling her task in Beechenhill was now well done.

Betony was already half broken when she reached the Sumps, for on the journey there Mallice had tortured much information out of her.

Being the sideem she was, Mallice revealed the source of her startling revelations about Wharfe and Harebell being Lucerne's siblings, and living in Beechenhill, only after Lucerne's appetite had been whetted. . . .

'Oh, and Master, one more thing. We have a rather special prisoner, my dear. One you will much wish to see.'

'Then bring him here.'

'It is best we visit *her*,' said Mallice, 'she is not fit to travel far. She has hurt her paws.'

Then quickly she led Lucerne to a cell in the Upper Sumps, in which Drule and a repulsive female henchmole squatted staring at a mole. Lucerne saw that though the mole had been tortured and was limp, she was still alive. Four talons of one paw had been ripped out, two talons of another.

'It was necessary,' said Mallice, nodding at the wardress to leave them be. Drule stayed, smiling.

'Who is she?' said Lucerne, staring at the mole, utterly unmoved by the fear in her eyes, and the continual shudder of pain in her paws.

'She shall tell her name. Won't she?' said Mallice, sliding one of her talons gently along Betony's cut face. 'She shall tell you everything, won't you, my poor hurt love? She shall say again all and more than she has said to me. Then I suggest that Drule has his way with her to find out whatever still remains. There is something about Drule that *repulses* information from female moles.'

'Whatmole are you?' asked Lucerne.

'I am the friend of Wharfe and Harebell, I am their friend,' intoned Betony, a look of utter despair and hopelessness in her eyes.

'Who are they?'

The mole darted a frightened look at Mallice. A solitary tear coursed down her face, made ugly by the scars of her first torturing, which had long since congealed.

'They were Henbane's pups.'

A look of surprise followed by exaltation crossed Lucerne's face, but there was barely a pause before he asked the next question.

'How do you know this?'

'My father told me.'

'Who is your father, mole?'

'Squeezebelly of Beechenhill.'

'And what is thy name?'

'Betony, I think,' she said. Her eyes, though open,

seemed for a moment to drift, as if the mention of her own name brought back a place and time and memory forever lost to her. 'Please don't hurt me any more, I don't know anything more to tell.'

'Oh but you know so much more that you don't know,' said Mallice.

'How came you to know this Wharfe and this Harebell?' He came closer to her, glaring, and she began to shake with pathetic fear.

'Please don't . . . not again. I told *her* they were brought to Beechenhill by the moles Mayweed and Sleekit. They were left for my father to rear.'

Lucerne turned to Drule and ordered him away.

'Sleekit! I know that name,' he said, for once showing his anger. He turned back to Betony. 'This mole is cursed of the Stone, but she has value. Great value. Drule shall *not* have her yet, for once he has done with a mole she is good for nothing more. We must learn all we can of Beechenhill, and she shall be kept alive. Alive, Squeeze-belly will still give much up for her; but dead she will add resolution and righteousness to his spirit.'

Mallice nodded.

'She should have been physically unharmed,' said Lucerne, still annoyed.

'She would have been silent if not harmed,' said Mallice matter of factly. 'Her will was strong.'

Lucerne stared at Betony.

'What are they like?' he asked eventually. Mallice came close to him and tried to draw him away. 'What are they like?' he said again, more forcefully.

Betony looked at him, and into his eyes, and at his flanks and paws and snout.

'They are . . . they are. . . .'

'Yes, mole?'

'But for their eyes they are like you.'

'Their eyes?' whispered Lucerne, who seemed for the first time in this terrible interview to be discomfited rather than merely angry.

'Their eyes are not like yours but like their . . . like your father's. Their eyes are Tryfan's eyes and full of love. Not like yours.'

'My love,' purred Mallice with delight, 'you can make her tell you things she would not tell me.'

Betony's eyes began to close.

'She is not so hurt. . . ?' began Lucerne.

Mallice smiled and said, 'Your consort knows her art. This mole shall not die quite yet. But she is tired and the pain dulls, and she must be allowed to sleep.'

'Be it so. You have done well, better than well. This mole shall be the destruction of Beechenhill. My own siblings there, and of the Stone! Of the mighty Stone! From Henbane they came, of Tryfan were they the spawn. And the Word shall punish them through me, born with Rune's blood in my veins, true Master of the Word. This delights me, Mallice.'

'I thought it might,' she said softly.

He laughed and turned from that burrow, excited and pleased, exclaiming, 'Thou art mighty, Word, and thy servant glories in thy justice. Thy talons shall make of Beechenhill a desolation that such punishments as that of Mallerstang, and others yet to come, shall seem but pleasant interludes on the way to the Stone's agony. Blessed be the Word!'

'Blest be!' responded Mallice as they swept out of that drear burrow in the Sumps where Betony now lived a living death.

So Betony's agony in Cannock had begun, and many the time she had wished to die, and would have done so had she had her way. But Drule's fat mate kept her alive, and when she worsened she was allowed out briefly into fresher air, and as the molemonths dragged by her brain began to dull, her mind to numb, as if something inside of her was protecting her from the terrible reality of her lot. One thing she could not know was that her presence disturbed Lucerne because it stirred that place within his heart which he might have hoped to leave alone, which was curiosity about the siblings he had had at birth. Until Betony came he assumed they must be dead, as Henbane had reassured him they were; but once he knew they lived he was consumed with desire to know about them.

Then too there was the knowledge that Tryfan, his father, had been *seen* and talked to by this vile female who was now his prisoner. Was he dead? He must be. Even if he survived the journey back to Duncton Wood, the plagues and diseases of that place surely would have killed him by now. So often he found his sleep was disturbed with such unanswered thoughts.

'Master mine?'

'Mallice?'

'Come closer to me. It will help you rest and sleep.'

'That mole. . . .'

'Dear Betony?'

'The same.'

'What of her?'

'I would talk with her. I would hear more now of Beechenhill.'

'Again? She cannot tell you more. And anyway, my love, have we not pups to make?' She smiled, she shifted her haunches near and invitingly. Pups were her desire now, pups by the Master, to find an heir, to confirm her supreme position as mother of a Master yet to be.

Since Betony's coming the same thought had consumed Lucerne as well, as if by making young he could in some strange way blot out the void in his life that the loss of Henbane, and then the discovery of siblings he had never known, had created.

He turned back to her, and took her. Oh yes, they mated savagely, and in the way his taloned paws raked Mallice's back, and his teeth bit at her shoulders, a mole might have learned how near love is to hatred, and hatred is to murder.

'Am I your mother that you hate me so?' screamed Mallice with delight.

She was uncomfortably near the truth.

But when they had done, and their energies were spent, then she let him leave her for his long sessions with Betony, during which, it seemed, he did little but stare and ask the same question, again and again.

'What are they like?'

'I cannot say more . . .' whispered Betony.

'You must, or I shall send you to the Lower Sumps again in punishment as I did last time. Tell me one new thing and you shall be spared that place.'

'They . . .' And Betony wept, broken, for every secret moment of her life with Wharfe and Harebell this mole who looked like them had ripped from out her heart. But worse, she had begun to hate them for what her knowledge of them made this mole do to her.

'Blessed art thou by the Word, Betony,' he said to her, 'acknowledge me as thy Master, let this be thy Atonement to the Word, let the Word's power take the shadow of the Stone from off your body.'

'But . . . b – ' She gazed through eyes brimming with tears at the ragged scars where her talons had been, stared at the flattened damp floor, and at the shadowed walls and high fissures where dead light lurked. Somewhere a mole screamed, and Betony dared to say, 'B-but the Stone is all I've got.'

'There is no Stone.'

Where does a mole find such courage as Betony so long found, where such hope?

'There is,' she said, 'and it shall find you out.'

By mid-November the report-back by the trinities was underway, and every day seemed to bring members of the sideem back to Cannock with news of the followers and the Stone.

Lucerne and the Keepers seemed permanently convened, considering and weighing up the evidence as it came in, and there was an atmosphere of confidence and excitement about the tunnels, and suspense as well.

Although Lucerne and Terce had kept their thinking secret, the sideem talk in the tunnels was accurate enough about its general direction. The Keepers were debating where and when a punitive strike might be made for the crusade, such as Lucerne had all but promised them back in October before they had set off. Where, and when . . . and how complete?

The answers sideem gave depended on where their own reports had taken them. Those returning from the east had seen widespread abuse of the Word and argued for swift and thorough retribution.

Trinities from the Midlands and west lowlands up to the western front itself, where the Word was strong and followers few and isolated, agreed that a strike was needed, but argued it should be limited to making an example of one area or system.

Between these two extremes were the views of those trinities who had returned from the south-east, the old heartland of Stone belief where the once-powerful Holy Burrows of Uffington were. Strange and sombre news had come from that important quarter, for the trinities deputed to Buckland returned with the news that Wyre had died of murrain and Buckland was leaderless; and, worse, that the trinity led by Heanor of Nidd had been murdered by followers in Fyfield, a system of symbolic significance since it was one of the Ancient Seven of the Stone.

This was especially annoying to Lucerne who had instructed that trinity to enquire of Duncton Wood and whether Tryfan, his father, had ever returned there from Whern as some said he had. If he was alive . . . But this appealing line of thought was broken by the pressing news that several Buckland trinities had received positive reports of a Stone-fool who followers in those parts were daring to call the Stone Mole, which put the Master-elect in some difficulty. . . .

'Difficulty, Mallice?'

'Yes, it's what the gossips say: that the Word will be

debased if you let the murder of Heanor pass without retribution, yet if our guardmoles impose it they may create a martyr if this supposed Stone Mole should be taken and put to death. . . .'

'We need a single devastating strike of the kind I led on Mallerstang,' said Clowder. 'Having kicked my talons on the Western Front for so long I no longer believe that that is the place for it. Ginnell argues that we should take Caer Caradoc, also one of the Ancient Seven systems of the Stone, and I agree with him. As I was leaving the Marches it was being reoccupied by followers, and but for your order that there should be no violence yet, we should have taken Caradoc by now. But when the time comes it will not be hard.' Clowder shrugged and smiled briefly before he continued.

'I think Beechenhill's the place now. Our sources have given us all the information we are ever likely to need to successfully invade it. It remains a symbol of resistance to many moles, particularly in parts north of here, and is a living insult to the Word. Let us destroy its blasphemy forever that all moles know such resistance is not the way. It is the kind of gesture we are looking for, and I do not think followers in the south feel sufficiently strongly about it to use it as a rallying cry.'

Lucerne raised a paw to end the discussion.

'There are still more reports to come. The Word does not desire us to act quite yet. Longest Night is probably right, and we have time to muster our strengths to south or north or west, whichever we finally choose.

'The strength of the Stone followers does not seem to me as great as we had feared, and if anything our position has become more secure since the trinities went out than before. We shall ponder the matter a little more yet. It hurts nomole and can only benefit the Word if our sideem argue and gossip and grow angry in the tunnels outside this chamber for a little longer.'

'Well,' growled Clowder with a grimace, 'I only ask that it is not too long – at every turn I take a sideem seeks to ask me what the Word shall decide, and to lobby me to tell it what it should do!'

'I like being lobbied,' said Mallice, 'it teaches me so much about the greed of mole. . . .'

It was into this busy, contentious, sanguine scene that the eldrene Wort arrived a day or two after the Keepers' adjourned debate.

Although the guardmoles who patrolled the approach routes to Cannock were under strict instructions not to allow through moles who were not sideem or members of trinities, Wort made short shrift of any attempt to stop her. She had not journeyed so far so fast to be stopped by a mere guardmole and nor was she impressed one bit by the fact that the successively senior guardmoles who came to get rid of her were *un*impressed by her title of eldrene of Cumnor.

The henchmoles who had come with her were utterly exhausted by their journey, but Wort, like all moles who have a mission and know they are right, radiated purpose and energy.

'Take me to the Master-elect!' was virtually all she was prepared to say, except for repeating that she was. . . .

'Yes, "eldrene of Cumnor", you have said so before,' said yet another mole summoned to deal with the trouble-some arrival.

'And I shall say so again until you begin to show some sign of *action*. We are here to serve the Word, and in my view your lethargy comes close to blasphemy. I have important information for the Master-elect, and he shall hear it from me direct.'

The eldrene Wort was aware that it would do her no good to reveal her information to a mole too unimportant to know how to deal with it, apart from the very real risk that another mole might annex it to his advantage.

So she made a nuisance of herself until, eventually, a sideem was summoned, and to him she revealed but one thing: she had seen the Stone Mole.

'I would talk to the Master-elect about this matter.'

'Eldrene, do you know how rarely even a sideem gets to talk to the Master?'

'Master-elect is his correct title, mole. I assume the reason sideem rarely "get to talk to him" is because he knows they have little to say. I have a great deal. Now get off your rump and do something about it.'

'Mole . . . !'

'I'd do it if I were you, mate,' said one of Wort's henchmoles wearily, 'it'll be easier in the long run.'

So, mole by mole, never daunted, Wort clawed her way up Cannock's hierarchy until at last she found herself ushered into the presence of an inoffensive and quiet-seeming mole about whom she knew nothing but that his name was Slighe.

After whispering with the sideem who had finally brought her to his chamber, he turned a mild gaze on her and said, 'Well, and will you talk to me?'

'In the name of the Word, I shall talk to anymole who serves the Word's purpose. What is your task?'

'I organise the place,' said Slighe blandly.

'Then, mole, forgive my bluntness, but organise the place so that its Master is informed that there is a mole can tell him of the Stone Mole.'

Slighe smiled faintly and his eyes hardened. The Sumps seemed an inviting place to send this difficult female, and yet there was something about her that impressed. He measured his words carefully, for he knew that sideem Mallice was listening in.

'Eldrene Wort, I ask you to believe everything I am about to say, everything.'

Wort blinked and stared at the mole. He might look mild but she sensed that at last she had met a mole of power.

'If you do not tell me enough to decide which mole of several, *including* myself, might be the best recipient of your information then you shall not leave Cannock for a very long time, during which you shall see neither the sky nor feel the wind at all. If you *do* tell me but you do not trust me to decide to whom you should speak, then the outcome will be the same. Therefore, mole, speak.'

Wort gave a bleak smile. In Slighe she had met her match.

'The Stone Mole is one Beechen of Duncton. He is not a Stone-fool or an imposter, or mad. He is the Stone Mole. He has such power over followers as nomole of the Word yet knows. He is evil come to moledom. I have seen him, I have seen his power, and I tell you this, sideem Slighe: if you do not believe me, if you abuse the trust I place in you by failing to tell the right mole the importance of what I have said, then it will not matter if you imprison me forever, for forever shall not come. The Stone Mole shall come and the Word shall be destroyed.'

It was Slighe's turn to blink. Then a shadow crossed the portal of his chamber and he looked past Wort and her henchmoles and saw Mallice.

Mallice smiled and nodded, and as Wort turned to see who it was had entered Mallice said, 'I think, Slighe, that our Master-elect will wish to listen to *this* mole. Please inform him.'

A few moments later Wort was shown into the presence of Lucerne himself. Mallice was with him.

'My love,' she said. 'I think it wise that Keeper Terce is present.'

Lucerne nodded to Slighe to get him while he continued to stare at this strange female.

'Sideem Slighe has told me briefly what you have said to him,' said Lucerne pleasantly. 'Now tell me, is not Cumnor adjacent to Duncton Wood?'

'It is, Master-elect,' said Wort, impressed. He was the first mole in Cannock who had heard of it.

'And *I* am impressed as well,' said Lucerne.

Wort was startled. It seemed the Master could read her thoughts.

'You are not nervous of me. Most moles who meet me are afraid, and not just the first time.'

'I am in awe of nothing but the great Word which my life serves,' replied Wort. 'Before it we are all servants, including you yourself. Insofar as you are its greatest servant, so shall your greatness as Master be judged.'

As she spoke Terce entered, and hearing the last of what she said looked as surprised as Mallice. Lucerne merely smiled, but a dangerous smile, for Wort trod dangerous ground.

'And the Mistress Henbane, would the eldrene Wort say *she* was a great Mistress of the Word?'

Whether or not Wort was aware of the danger she was in in giving her opinion of Lucerne's mother it was hard to tell. Her earnest face betrayed nothing but faith and certainty.

'The Mistress Henbane was made Mistress by the Word and in the Word's name, as one day you shall be made Master. She dishonoured the Word by failing to address her task in the south-east for she did not destroy the infection of the Stone and it thrives even where the moles she appointed place their paws. I cannot judge if any could have done better. I know that many would have done worse. Perhaps we all dishonour the Word by failing to be as we should be. I know I do. Yet I try and I trust the mighty Word knows it. Did Mistress Henbane truly try? I understand that you are in a better position to judge than I.'

'A good reply, Master-elect!' said Terce with a smile.

'A clever reply,' said Mallice.

'What is it you wish to say to me?' said Lucerne.

'Moledom, the very Word itself, faces a greater danger than anymole yet seems to realise. The Stone Mole has come and is among us. He. . . .'

'Have you *seen* him, mole?' said Lucerne.

'I have seen into his eyes, I have felt his talons on my heart, and if the holy Word, which is my mother and my father, will forgive me, if he had taken me with his body I should not have been closer to him than I have already been. Master-elect, evil is upon us, and it is to warn you of that evil that I have come to you.'

501

Not a mole said a thing, nor even looked at each other. The mole was either mad or inspired, and whichever she was she put fear even into *their* hearts. Lucerne nodded his understanding of the seriousness of what she said and with a polite, 'One moment, eldrene Wort,' turned to his aide.

'Slighe, postpone the audience I have this afternoon. I would talk with this mole.'

'Master-elect,' said the indefatigable Wort, 'I have not eaten today, or yesterday.'

'You look remarkably fit.'

'The Word has been my sustenance, but what I have to tell you may benefit from food.' They all smiled broadly, even Terce.

'So be it. Eat, drink, groom, and then tell me what you must.'

In this way did the eldrene Wort first come before Lucerne at Cannock: purposeful and assured in her service to the Word.

While she was absent Lucerne said, 'A remarkable mole, Terce.'

'Frightening,' said the Twelfth Keeper.

'Mallice, what do you make of her?'

'I think,' she said in a measured way unusual for her, 'and I hope I may not be wrong, that we have been waiting for a mole like her, and she has been sent to us by the Word.'

By the time Wort came back Clowder had been summoned and Drule as well, for Lucerne sensed that whatever it was the eldrene had to say they all should hear. When she returned Lucerne stanced her comfortably down.

'Tell us something of thyself, mole, for the words a mole speaks are more easily judged by knowing who she is and where she comes from,' he said, at his most charming. 'Take your time, miss nothing out. Slighe shall scriven it, but pay no heed to that.'

This said, the most powerful group of moles in moledom fell silent to hear how it might be that not only they, but even the Word itself, faced the greatest danger it had ever known.

'I am born of Nuneham, which lies close by Duncton to its south,' began Wort, adding quickly and with pride, 'but my father was the guardmole Sedge, born in the north.

'We were well taught of the Word and I saw its wisdom young and was able to make modest service to it while barely more than a pup, which brought me to the notice of the eldrene's assistants.*

'From Nuneham I was sent to Buckland shortly before eldrene Fescue went to serve in Duncton Wood, and after the changes that followed the then worthy Wyre's coming I was honoured with the appointment as assistant to the eldrene of Fyfield, a system to the south of Duncton.

'It was not long before the Word called the eldrene to its final service and I assumed command at Fyfield and there rigorously imposed the Word.† It was my sole purpose to see that the Word was observed at Fyfield, and since those days I have ruthlessly put down anymole who has preached the Stone, or encouraged others to do so. More than that I have felt it my duty before the Word itself to treat as blasphemers anymole, be he grike, guardmole or even sideem who without just cause has been lax of the Word.

'When the winter years were over we in Fyfield and several of my more reliable colleagues in nearby systems became aware of an upsurgence of interest in the so-called "Stone Mole", whose coming had been predicted by

* Wort's long and despicable career as persecutor of Stone followers did indeed start young. Among the 'modest services' she performed while still a pup at Nuneham, was to spy on followers, whose numbers she pretended to join. Her reports resulted in the routine torture and killing of several leading followers, including her mother, one brother, and an uncle.

† There is evidence, not conclusive, that Wort murdered the eldrene of her time; and further evidence, reliable, that she ordered that the sideem Gerne be put to death when he threatened to report his suspicions of this murder to Wyre.

followers after the showing of a star in the east. I had seen it myself: impressive, but an aberrance in the sky. Deviant moles might be forgiven for thinking it presaged something strange, though we in Fyfield, failing instruction on the matter from Wyre who I believe had become infected by murrain at that time, concluded that the star was a warning from the Word to be vigilant at all times. I trust I was not mistaken in issuing such a command.

'Interest in this "Stone Mole" now increased and it came to my notice that a number of Fyfield moles who, despite our precautions and efforts had fallen victim to the evil wiles and persuasions of the Stone, had made their way north-eastward towards Duncton saying that he was "coming there". The guardmoles were warned that such journeys must be stopped, and it became necessary to put two of these moles to death as an example to others. They were snouted by me personally at the Fyfield Stone.

'I pride myself that no moles from Fyfield thereafter joined that foolhardy march of moles that sought the Stone Mole, which was nothing less than a march to blasphemy, but I heard reports that elsewhere followers persisted in doing so. I strove to warn Wyre of this but he was unavailable even to eldrenes, and I was told he did not believe that suppression was wise or even of the Word, which shocked me.

'Even though there was for a time an assemblage of followers near and about the sole entry into Duncton Wood so great that it was almost beyond the power of the sideem and guardmoles there to control them, Wyre did nothing. I resolved that if in future the Word should put into my paws the power to control that cross-under of Duncton I would quickly disperse those followers in the name of the Word. It is one of my great prides that I was able to do this.

'I confess I expected the interest to decline as spring came and brought with it the normal birth of pups and need to concentrate on rearing. So far as Fyfield was concerned, I believe that with a few minor exceptions this was the case. I cannot say that I was then aware of the extent to which interest in the Stone Mole persisted, and that many still believed that he was near and continued to visit Duncton Wood. It is said always to be a goodly place, and stances proud of the river and roaring owl ways that together circumscribe it,' said Wort. 'I have not visited it myself but I am told by moles who have that it has a mighty Stone at its highest point and moles go there in trembling and awe. For myself, Master-elect, who have seen several of these Stones, including the one at Fyfield, I do not understand such fears and think them unnecessary and degenerate. The Word protects allmole that has true faith in it. As for the rest of Duncton, it sounds ordinary enough with wormful and worm-poor parts as any system has. It has an area called the Marsh End which is dank and harbours disease. The place has been little visited by mole since the Mistress Henbane made it outcast.'

'Yet you have said this Beechen is "of Duncton",' said Terce. 'How do you know?'

'He himself claims it,' said Wort. Spittle had formed a minute froth at the corners of her mouth, and her talons were tensed angrily as if she expected the arch enemy Beechen himself to appear in the chamber at any moment. There was a look of obsession about her, or perhaps it was merely that related curse of mole, sincerity without softening of humour.

'In view of the disarray in some other nearby systems, and the seeming laxity of the guardmoles at Duncton Wood itself, I felt it incumbent on me to depute moles I trusted to watch out for developments regarding this so-called Stone Mole. Various stories were heard and rumours went about, and they were sufficiently appealing to followers that three emerged from the slime of their own secret deceit in my own system and attempted to perform some heathen ritual at the Fyfield Stone which was, naturally, out of bounds to all moles in the system but for the patrols.

'They were caught and I decided to punish them myself

505

before the Stone. It was as they died that I felt for the first time the corrupting temptations of the Stone, and knew I was being tried and tested in my faith to the Word.

'I ordered the guardmoles away and decided to prove my faith in the Word. Master-elect, no words can adequately express the trial I then went through. For it seemed to me that the Word sent its temptation in the form of a mole of surpassing beauty who I saw as a light. This mole called out to me, and others with him called as well, and they asked me to touch the Stone in that mole's name as if by doing so we should help him.

'The light was beautiful, the day like no other I remember. I wept and felt pity for that mole, but always there was a corner in my heart that said, "Thou art of the Word and for the Word and the Word is here to strengthen you!" Only when I felt strong again did I reach forward and touch the Stone, believing that to do so was not to yield to the Stone but to show it and that mole that I could touch it with impunity.'

'Eldrene Wort, why do you believe that this mole who, in your own words, was no more than light was the Stone Mole?' asked Mallice.

'Because I later saw the mole in corporeal form and saw the same light about him, and felt the same presence. I am not in doubt of that and nor shall you be.

'But before that, and after what I call my vision in June before the Fyfield Stone, I gave certain of the guardmoles strict instructions that if a young charismatic male mole was apprehended or seen I should be informed *directly*.'

'I do not fully understand, eldrene Wort. You gave out a description of a mole you had only seen as "light"?'

'I had the sense of what he might be. I made a guess that he was young and male. The reason I did it was because I believed this mole was sent to test me before the Word, and that in his presence I knew evil disguised as goodness. It seemed imperative that as few other moles as possible knew of his whereabouts before I apprehended him. Forgive me, Master, I. . . .'

Lucerne nodded his head and said, 'Wort, your testimony is as impressive as any I have heard, the more so for your attempt to try to make clear something that is not clear. Say what you have to fearlessly. The Word shall judge you well for this! You are a credit to the office of eldrene.'

'Well then,' she continued, almost falling over her words in her eagerness now to get to the heart of her report and to tell of the experience that had so obviously made such impact on her, and her face darkening.

'The order I had given came to the ears of Wyre of Buckland as well as the punishment I meted out on those three blasphemous followers. He sent moles to depose me from my office at Fyfield, demoting me to Cumnor, an unknown and empty place north of the system I had grown to love and in the very shadow of infamous Duncton Wood.

'But since Wyre acted in the name of the Word I was obedient and went without argument. But the Word was merciful and prevailed on Wyre's representatives to let those few moles who wished to travel with me to Cumnor to do so. This was a further test of my faith in the Word, for I saw that by taking honour and power from me, and giving me but a few moles to direct, I was forced to examine my faith and the way that as an eldrene I gave leadership to a system. I believe that in Cumnor the Word was not disappointed in me, and it was not long before it sent other moles of the Word, disenchanted by the laxities the rule of Wyre at Buckland had encouraged, to serve with me. So it was that there were enough moles in Cumnor for me to send some to the Duncton cross-under and there gain acceptance and finally dominance. In that way the Word was at least well served at that place where, the followers of the Stone believed, the Stone Mole might be known.

'But in fact it was from other moles who joined me in October that I at last heard of a Stone-fool preaching and healing in the vicinity of Frilford who sounded like the mole I myself had already "seen" at Fyfield. Then one of my informants who pretended to be a follower offered to get me into one of this Stone-fool's gatherings.

'Despite the great risks involved – not only of my being recognised by followers, but of my being tempted by the Stone – I knew it was my duty to go. To lessen the chances of being recognised I went unaccompanied by my guardmoles.'

'And what did you see?' asked Mallice impatiently.

'Evil masquerading as something beautiful!' exclaimed Wort. 'Much that was alluring and corrupting!

'The meeting was held in a high place east of Frilford, windy and wormless. There are few tunnels thereabouts, and those mainly used to avoid the patrols. An eldrene prepared to get her paws dirty learns much. My informant led me well, and although here and there we came upon other moles going the same way, all followers no doubt, we kept to the shadows as they did and did not linger to talk. There is something privy and filthy about Stone followers. They have not the pride of true moles of the Word.

'However, I reached the chamber where the meeting was held without being challenged or even having the necessity of identifying myself at all. Only later did I realise that this seeming openness is a lure to attract moles of the Word who might otherwise fear to go. So cleverly does the heathen Stone make its converts!

'I kept out of the way well at the back, but found a good vantage point so that I could view others there and all that took place. I was able to identify two moles I knew to be guardmoles – moles I have yet to bring before the vengeance of the Word, and one or two others who had minor positions in the Fyfield system.

'I will not dwell at length on the happenings in that burrow prior to the mole Beechen's appearance, except to say that there was some chanting and songs using old and now forbidden tunes with words full of reverence for the Stone. I noted a number of moles there were evidently crippled, and others I saw were badly diseased. They were

508

a sorry bunch! Nevertheless I stayed and since excitement in the chamber was rising in expectation of the coming of the Stone Mole, whose title was chanted and called out a good deal, nomole was much interested in me.

'The chamber was rank with the sweat and smell of so many, and the air was getting ever hotter when a sudden silence fell and at the far end of the chamber, by an entrance guarded by two or three larger moles unknown to me, two moles came in. Both were elderly – a scalpskinned male of no consequence and a female of the same age, but healthy.

'A pity you did not know their names,' murmured Terce.

'But I did!' said Wort, affronted. 'For emboldened by not being challenged I asked a follower nearby, since my own informant –- who confirmed the names later – had stayed clear of me lest I was found out. The moles were Mayweed and Sleekit.'

Terce and Lucerne looked so astonished that Wort paused in her narrative and said, 'You know those moles?'

'We have heard of Mayweed,' said Terce quietly. 'And Sleekit is a former sideem, assistant to the Mistress Henbane. Well! This is indeed remarkable, Master-elect.'

'It is, Tutor-Keeper Terce. Continue, Wort.'

'After those two the one called Stone Mole arrived. There was pause before he came in, in which the excitement mounted even more and I confess I felt faint with heat and the blasphemy of being in such a place, and whispered prayers to the Word to protect me. . . .

'But then he came. He came alone. Alone into that heaving, noisome, ghastly chamber . . .' She paused and her eyes stared behind Lucerne and Terce as if she saw again the sight she had seen then. What was most extraordinary about that pause, which was marked only by the matching pause in the scrivening talon of Slighe, was that Wort's attitude towards Beechen was plainly ambivalent as if, recalling the moment, she could not even now decide whether to talk of what she saw with alarm, or awe.

The moment lasted long enough for the doubts arising from that ambivalence to be sown in any listening mole's mind – and then her manner veered towards condemnation and hatred as she said with quiet intensity: 'The Stone Mole is a young mole, male, handsome, healthy, and has eyes that a mole cannot easily look away from. He looked briefly about him, and as he did I knew him to be the mole I had seen as light before. Then he smiled, and his smile was that of innocence, and he spoke and his voice was soft to the ear. Oh, beware this mole, moles of the Word! Beware the words he speaks, the temptation he brings. Though I have said this to nomole, I fear the power that he holds! Aye, I fear! Evil is in his form, which is good and strong; evil is in his words, which are pleasant and reassuring. Evil is in his ideas, which dwell upon the unthinking mindlessness of a Silence to come. But most of all, evil is in his eyes, which draw a mole as do the gazes of a roaring owl, and blind him, and paralyse him, and lead him to his doom.

'This was the nature of the evil I saw then, this the allurement of a mole who enthralled all who heard him that night but me, guarded as I was by the Word's wisdom and truth.

'But yet I witnessed power. Others will deny it, others will not tell you the truth, for they will fear it, or be seduced by it. But I saw it, and witnessed it and tell of it now. I said that chamber was hot and fetid before the mole Beechen came: yet the moment he entered it was cool and sweet-scented like the grass in June, and moles who had been restless and excited grew calm and easy. Evil! I said there were cripples there, and the diseased. I saw it, and witnessed it: they called him "Master", and their Master spoke of the Stone. The beset went to him and were touched by him *and they were healed*. I saw a mole who could only move by dragging himself along aided by others healed by the touch of his Master's paws. I saw that mole return to his place unaided. I saw a mole blind, his eyes rheumy with murrain, with his sight restored, the filth plucked from his eyes by the talons of that mole. And I saw an idiot mole whose words were an incessant jumble of filth made whole again, and able to speak plain. Evil. All of it evil and vile.

'But a greater trial for this servant of the Word was yet to come. I will not – I cannot – properly describe the course of that night, except to say that the healings were interspersed with prayers and incantations to the Stone of an ancient pagan kind. Sometimes the mole Beechen spoke them, sometimes moles present uttered them, crying them out, most frightening to see.

'But it was when the mole Beechen asked that moles touch each other in love that my trial came. I did not feel the Word desired that I join in such a rite and, accordingly, pretended to touch the mole at my side on the flank, though I touched him not.

'Even at the moment of my pretence the Stone Mole cried out as if in pain and said, "Which mole among you touches me not?" And then again, "Which mole among you loves me not? He who touches another with his heart touches me!" Then for the third time when I did not touch a mole he cried, "I tell you there is one among you who despises me, and who touches me not. The Stone will know her, the Stone will come before her and the Stone shall forgive her, for at the moment of my passing she shall cry out to me as I cry to her now, and she shall touch me when all others fear to. Her name will be reviled but she shall be forgiven. I have known her already and shall know her again. So may it be for all moles who fight against the Stone, that in the end they shall be forgiven!"'

Her voice had changed as she spoke Beechen's words, or supposed words, becoming soft and chanting as her face adopted a curiously beatific and gentle expression which only succeeded in highlighting its essential inflexible poverty of spirit.

Then her manner changed violently as she denounced, in a rage the more shocking for the calm that had preceded it, all she reported Beechen as having said.

511

'Evil, Vile evil! The abyss was before me and I felt the urge to leap forward into its dark depths. I, devout mole of the Word, servant of thee, Master. Strike me! Talon me! Hurt me! For I felt then the temptation to cry aloud, to touch, to know this false Silence of which the Stone followers speak. Even I felt it!' Her voice, which had started the denunciation in loud anger declined now to a whisper of abject horror as if she felt herself corrupt, and almost corrupting.

But then Wort's innate self-righteousness emerged once more, and an officious smug look came over her face, quickly masked, though not entirely successfully, by a sickening modesty.

'But I did not yield. The talons of the Word were about me, and they did comfort and guard me. The moment of temptation passed and I was left stronger and fiercer in my support of the Word and recognition of the subtle and surreptitious nature of the Stone and the mole who is its representative in moledom. I saw he was a mole whose beauty masked a seductive horror greater than moles of the Word yet know. I witnessed it twice more, once in Fyfield where this Beechen took the meeting away from your sideem Heanor, and again outside my own system at Cumnor.

'Master, as I stance here before you, I would have killed him there and then with my own talons . . . and I thought of doing so. But the Word chided me and said "Are you to take the law of the Word in your own paws? Are you to judge the punishment? This must be the work of the Master alone. He shall decide. Tell him what you have seen, and he shall judge and he punish." So seemed the Word to speak to me and this is what I have come to say to you.'

For a long time after she had finished Lucerne continued to stare at her, utterly still. No testimony ever brought before him had ever been so stark or clear, nor its warning more plain.

Then Terce came to Lucerne and whispered to him, and Lucerne nodded, looked at Wort, and nodded again.

'Master-elect,' said Wort, seeing this, 'if I have done wrong then punish me. I did all that I did in the name of the Word.'

'I know it, mole. Now tell me, what is thy Master to thee?'

'The source of all truth about the Word.'

'Would you lie to your Master?'

'May the Word strike me into eternal suffering if it should be so.'

'Then answer me this question, eldrene Wort, and answer it truthfully, for if you do not eternal suffering may be yours sooner than you think.'

'Master-elect?'

'What do you know of the deaths of Heanor and those in his trinity?'

Wort seemed surprised at the question, less for its implications as for its unimportance.

'I killed them myself, in the name of the Word. They had abused the Word.'

'And Wyre?'

'Not him, he died naturally. But the eldrene Smock I killed.'

Lucerne smiled cruelly.

'Then, mole, you have robbed us of both a trinity and the eldrene of Fyfield.'

'It was just, Master-elect, you would have done it yourself had you been there.'

'Drule, Slighe . . .' said Lucerne coldly, 'take the eldrene Wort outside, watch over her, and await my summons to come back here.'

Wort's eyes widened in dismay as she saw the dreadful Drule and Slighe bear down on her, but she said nothing when they led her away.

'Well?' said Lucerne.

'A dangerous mole,' said Terce.

'Not one I would want to share a burrow with,' said Clowder.

'Well!' declared Mallice, admiration in her voice.

513

'I was impressed by her,' said Lucerne. 'We have either to punish her for a succession of blasphemies and abuses of power which few moles can have ever exceeded, or we give her a task to suit her many abilities. I favour the latter.'

'You have a task in mind?' asked Clowder.

'Several. She has that quality even a lot of sideem lack: an ability to think for herself and do something about it.'

'It is a pity she takes herself so seriously,' said Clowder.

'Is it? I think not – it may be the very quality we need if such a mole is to fulfil the function which I think the Word intended for her. She is a mole of formidable resource and courage, and she is as loyal to the Word as anymole we are likely to find. We need moles we know can keep a secret, moles strong enough to report only to us.'

'But she has no experience wider than the one she recounted, and nor is she sideem.'

'A mole does not have to be sideem to be useful to the Word, and to ourselves. There is something absolute in the faith this mole has and in the rightness of what she sees and does that I like, and which I think will strike fear and respect into the hearts of all those under her.

'But most of all I like the darkness of her mind, the secrecy in which she prefers to live and work. I have no doubt she does not reveal to her right paw what her left is doing without pondering it first. But she needs others to watch over her, just to be sure she does not decide *you* have blasphemed, Terce, or *you*, Clowder! Let alone myself, of course! Let's get her and the others back in here.'

When they came in, Wort looking somewhat subdued for she thought she was to be punished, Lucerne said to Drule and Slighe, 'Range yourselves by this mole Wort! Aye, so!'

The three moles stared about uncomfortably. Drule glowered, Slighe blinked, Wort looked uncertain of herself.

Lucerne smiled benignly.

'You have been too long confined in Cannock, Drule.'

'Master?'

514

'And you as well, Slighe.'

'But I am here to serve *you* Master-elect.'

'Quite so. As for you, eldrene Wort, words fail to express the admiration I feel for you. You shall continue to be known as the eldrene Wort of Cumnor though Fyfield shall now be yours to command as well, and the moles within it. But in truth you shall be something more than that, for you shall work for the good of the Word with Drule and Slighe as your comrades in crusade. Aye . . . no need to protest, Drule, you will do it very well and it will not be for too long. Nor you, Slighe, more action and less scrivening will do your talons good. Yes, you shall all have a very special task, which must be done by moles I trust always to tell me the truth, whatever they may tell other moles.'

'What shall be our task, Master-elect?' asked Wort, immediately taking charge of this gruesome trio.

'To investigate ways and means of seeing that Beechen of Duncton is punished of the Word, and finally made dead with such dishonour that it will cast a pall of shame forever over the faith of which he is supposed to be the greatest son. How you will do it I cannot tell, and you shall report back on that. Meanwhile together, and with those moles you shall now have at your command, eldrene Wort, you shall make a strike that we need and have long debated.'

'What strike?' asked Wort.

'Explain to her, Slighe, now, so we are all agreed what it is we are talking about.'

Wort listened intently to Slighe's succinct account of the debate that had overtaken the tunnels and conclaves of Cannock in the moleweeks past.

'I see,' she said at the end. 'I see. Yes.'

'Yes?' said Lucerne.

'Oh yes, Master-elect, I understand. Moledom needs to see the *power* of the Word and be impressed by its great might. What may be obvious to moles like us may not be so to those less thinking or devout. We must begin to curl

515

the talons of the Word about the Stone Mole in readiness for the Word's just vengeance.'

'Yes?' encouraged Lucerne. He liked this mole's mind.

'Then we must destroy where the Stone Mole first thrived. As the Holy Burrows were laid waste so must we lay waste Duncton Wood. The place is already feared and outcast, and followers and moles of the Word alike regard it as diseased. We shall purge moledom of it, and the moles who still struggle to live there.'

'But Tryfan shall not be touched. If he be alive I shall deal with him myself. 'And I stress we shall not punish the Stone Mole with death, yet,' said Lucerne. 'Cut off from his home system, driven from the peripheral tunnels and burrows that give him succour, we shall let him wander pathetically across moledom, growing ever more isolated and weak. It would be most fitting – would it not? – if Duncton Wood were destroyed on Longest Night, for that is the night I shall be ordained Master of the Word.'

'But that leaves us little time,' began Slighe.

''Tis a long way to travel by then *and* organise,' said Drule.

'The Word shall guide your talons as it guides mine!' said Wort fervently. 'Blessed be the Word!'

'Blest be,' whispered Lucerne.

'Master-elect, I would have liked to witness your ordination on Longest Night,' said Slighe, reluctant to set off quite as soon as the irrepressible Wort.

'My dear Slighe, you shall. I shall be ordained on Longest Night in the blood of the moles you choose to destroy by Duncton's Stone. Let our time of rejoicing be as a blasphemy to them, let the Word be so well pleased with us that we can outface the hallowed Stone in its name, in the very place that spawned the Stone Mole. And if the Word *has* spared my father, why, what pleasure for me, what an honour for him, to see his son ordained.' Lucerne laughed at his irony and said acidly, 'It shall be the last thing he sees.'

'Aye, let it be so!' they all cried, satisfied with the fitting

516

justice of their intent, all but for Terce. Though he too cried 'Aye!' he looked uneasy, and shadowed.

'To Duncton then!' said Wort, triumphant.

'To Duncton it shall be!'

But when all but Terce had gone Lucerne said, 'Twelfth Keeper, what troubles you?'

But what really troubled Terce he would not say, for beyond his Master now was the sacred destiny of Rune.

'Be ever wary of the Stone, Terce. Its cunning is more clever than moles know. The way to ascendancy of the Word lies closed indeed to the Stone's suffocating light.'

'What troubles me, Master, is the Stone,' said Terce, who found that the best lies were those nearest to the truth. 'The Duncton Stone is said to be one of very great power. Even Master Rune respected it. It may belittle thee and thy ordination.'

'I suppose it may, Terce, but we shall be nothing if we do not try to be everything. I find the eldrene Wort's reminder of the Stone's power timely, most timely. Yet it is that very fact that puts me in mind to be ordained in Duncton. Is their water that for anointing?'

'I think not, Master-elect. The scrivenings describe it as being on a hill.'

'Then the tears of followers shall be our cleansing and their blood our anointing.'

'Yes, Master-elect, they shall have to be.'

Chapter Twenty-Four

Moles have ever the need of a place to dream of, a place to where they may travel in their mind and be happy once again, when they are beset, when the aging body aches, when the heart pines for loves and friends once known and times remembered.

A place simple and right, with its parts so harmonious that though each may be but modest and unremarkable, together they seem to make perfection in real life.

Some – perhaps many – will say there is no such place but in memory, which so easily removes trial and tribulation to leave a remembrance in a sunlit glow without a threat in sight.

Others will smile and say it was really so, just as they remember it, and that it was no dream. So do adults remember their days as pups, and they are right, for puppish days may well seem sunlit when the menaces and threats of life are borne by parents.

Yet there is one happy group of moles who knew a reality that really was as good as memory of it later claims. These are moles who know, or knew, an adult love. Not the first love, which is often blind (and all the better for it!), nor the second, whose passion may not last, but that later love of moles who look each other in the eyes and know each other as they really are, and love them still, and grow with knowledge to love them even more.

Such moles in old age, when describing what they once had, will say that she, or he, was most beautiful, *the* most beautiful, and where they lived, why, it *must* have been a goodly place for sure: did not their love thrive there?

Yet, when all is said, some places – a very, very few – have about them a harmony of parts that makes others remember them with special fondness. Happy the mole who falls in love in such a place, or having found their love renews it there.

Such a magic place was, and is, Bablock, along the River Thames. Quiet, modest, secret as a sunlit vale deep in a wood is secret, and with that extra quality which nomole can arrange or pre-ordain: surprise.

One moment a mole is trekking on a way along a riverbank, the next he is in Bablock Hythe. One moment a mole is coming off the heathy slopes above the river valley, the next he turns a corner, snouts round a bend, peers under a fence and blomp! he is in Bablock Hythe.

Yet where it begins, and where it ends, nomole can accurately say, and many a mole, in all other respects intelligent and sensitive, may pass right through from one end of Bablock to the other, and not remark a thing.

In short, the Bablocks of moledom do not simply find their moles: moles find them as well. Indeed, moles can lose them too, if they lose touch with themselves, and swear that their Bablock is the dullest place. While others, quite lost it seems, can be stanced in a Bablock all their lives and not know it until one day – one very happy day – they look about themselves and say, 'Why, I never knew it until now, but this *is* Bablock Hythe!' While all about them dance with relief and say, 'He's seen the light at last!'

When Mayweed set off from Frilford that early November in search of a place where Beechen might rest in anonymity for a time, he only half knew he was looking for a Bablock. That half was made of a nagging doubt about his life with Sleekit, whom he had loved devotedly since the moment he so dramatically discovered her in the Providence Fall at Whern.

Devoted he may have been, but Mayweed was always a mole travelling a route to somewhere he never quite arrived. So being peaceful and content, stancing still, watching the day's butterflies go by, was not his nature. It left him uncomfortable, as if something dark might come along from the route behind and overtake him once again.

So on he went, taking those moles he loved along with him on his sometimes frantic way.

His consort Sleekit, on the other paw, was a still mole. Trained in Whern in the ways of meditation and discipline, naturally reticent, intensely loyal, she found contentment in thoughts, and stancing quiet. Her love for Mayweed was a mystery to many, but perhaps in him and his aching restlessness she found an outlet for that nurturing love she had only ever been able to show to Wharfe and Harebell in the all too brief period when she and Mayweed reared them, first in the Clints of Whern, then in Beechenhill.

Yet, in that strange interlude with Beechen in the ancient tunnels of Duncton, when Mayweed had been beset by dark sound and she had gone to him, something changed within them both. Beechen had warned them then that before long they would part, and advised them to make the best of their time together, for it was now limited. Which they had done since then in Duncton Wood, and would have done more had not the darkness begun to fall across the wood, and the imperatives of Beechen's escape from it become paramount. So, once more, had Sleekit found herself travelling on with her love with little time to themselves.

Did she complain? Not once. She travelled with Mayweed during Beechen's First Ministry, and did what she had to do to help them both. But that day when Sleekit said that Beechen was tired, Mayweed had seen that Sleekit was tired as well. Seen their whole life together for what it had been for her, which was journeying and travail, in concert it is true, but not in peace.

So when he left them, and Sleekit, loving and knowing him as she did trusted him to be safe, and said not one word of how much she would miss him while he was gone, Mayweed knew in his heart that he was looking for a Bablock for them both. A place where finally, in that little time they had left for one another, he hoped Sleekit might feel secure, and loved, and content to know that he was content as well. A place that would see the culmination of their love, a place to take them to its heart and let them love it as true as they sought always to love one another.

As for Beechen, why, he could take his chance with them! Yes, yes, yes, he could! He was young, he had strength, he had no need of a Bablock! No, no, no!

So in a cheerful spirit, and more partisan to Sleekit's needs than Beechen's, Mayweed had set off to find a route that led to a place where a mole might most wish to take his much beloved.

Where, when, how, or why he came to Bablock we do not know nor care. But, one day his route at last took him along the River Thames, and he turned a corner, and watched a cloud, and pondered a coot, and debated a worm, and came upon a mole stanced quiet, and watching the river flow by.

'Plump Sir, you look content!'

'I am.'

'Contented mole, may humbleness ask what you are doing?'

'Nothing much.'

'Ah!'

'There's nothing much to do in Bablock Hythe but what I'm doing. It's always been like that and always will I hope.'

'Rotundity, this place sounds good to me,' observed Mayweed, stancing down, 'the sort of place I'm looking for.'

'It's a lot better than the place where you seem to be hurrying to.'

'Where's that?' asked Mayweed, curious, and grinning.

'What an astonishing grin. It's almost a leer. I haven't been leered at for a very long time. No matter. You look as if you're going somewhere *busy*.'

'No, no, no, no, mistaken mole, that's exactly where I'm not going.'

'Well have a worm and stance still because you're not going the right way about it.'

Mayweed, who delighted in moles who used words as he did, settled down and crunched the proffered worm.

'Mayweed is my name,' said Mayweed eventually.

'Tubney,' said Tubney. Who added after a very long pause during which he stared at the river that flowed past them in a deep dark way, 'What sort of place *are* you looking for?'

'Humble me does not ask for much. He is in love and wishes to find a place which is quiet, peaceful, doesn't mind a visitor or three, and is not likely to be invaded by grikes, or anymole else come to that.'

'You've arrived,' said Tubney, 'so have another worm.'

'Forgive humbleness for raising a doubt, but how can Sir be sure? How can Sir not have a fretful talon or a restless tail or twitching fur for thinking that just beyond where he now is is not something better? Is Sir not curious?'

'Um. Curious?' said Tubney slowly, frowning and staring at the slow water, and then at the sky. 'Am . . . I . . . curious? Well, I suppose I am, sort of.'

'"Sort of"!' exclaimed Mayweed. 'Sort of Sir, a mole cannot be sort of curious. Curiosity is an absolute where he personally is concerned. If you are curious you fall off your paws satisfying it. If you're not . . . you're dead.'

'Clever but untrue my friend,' said Tubney. 'The reason I am contented with where I live is because everymole who ever comes here looks about and tells me that I should be. Now, taken together, they have travelled more than I ever shall so it makes sense and is much easier to believe them. Of course they could be wrong, which is why I'm *sort of* curious to see if they are right. But not *so* curious that I can be bothered to find out. Take yourself, Mayweed. Have you travelled much?'

'More than much. Show me a route and I may well have been along it.'

'Just what I thought. Now, go and look around Bablock, say hello to a few moles, pass the time of day with them, and then come back here and give me one good reason why I should leave the place.'

'I shall!' said Mayweed. And he did.

He explored the wormful tunnels, he said hello to the pleasant moles, he wandered the bank of that wide and curved part of the River Thames along which the system lies. He looked at the swirls of slow water, he followed the progress of a feeding coot, he stanced still and listened to the water's flow, and he scented the meadows and the leafless winter hedgerows beneath which the berries of cuckoo pint shone red and bright.

Nearly a day passed in such wandering before his route took him back to Tubney's place.

'Well?' said Tubney.

'What did Sir say the system's name was?'

'Bablock Hythe.'

'Perfection.'

'Almost but not quite, otherwise it would be too dull.'

'Explain, explain, please, please!' said Mayweed, increasingly delighted with Tubney.

'Well, you see, visitors *do* come. Some have said they are a nuisance and that without them things would be perfect – to use your word. But it is in the very nature of visiting that visitors leave. If they did not they would be residents. And what do I find when visitors leave? Peace, Mayweed. Blissful, delightful, unutterable peace. So my welcome is warm to visitors because being restless they will go and when they go I am reminded of what I had forgotten I have.'

'Philosophical Sir, I shall scribe that down, since it seems to contain a deep truth about happiness.'

'Ah, well, if you can scribe that makes you an interesting visitor, which is, of course, a mixed blessing. Interesting visitors tend to impose themselves a bit, make moles question things, can be disruptive. It can be hard while it lasts, but then when they leave. . . .'

A blissful smile spread across Tubney's cheerful face.

'Yes, when interesting visitors, especially ones who have been *very* interesting, finally leave, dear me, it makes

523

me almost glow to think of it! The sheer joy of seeing their rears disappear down that path, the unadulterated pleasure of knowing they are going to be interesting somewhere else for ever more and *not* here. Mayweed, have you any idea how pleasant that is and what joy it gives me to think of it?'

'Sir is sufficiently eloquent to have given me a very good idea indeed. But one last question: what about moles in love? Are they good moles to have in Bablock?'

'On occasion we have had those. Charming, delightful, brings tears to my eyes. They tend to like the riverbank at night, and that sort of thing. They look at the moon and occasionally race about. More mysteriously they stance for hours on end staring at each other, which seems strange when you consider that everything else around here is so much more interesting than mole. But I am thinking of young love, I suppose. Mature love, the kind of love that a mole such as you might indulge in is altogether different. Oh yes. That's me, you know. A mature love.'

'She is . . . ?' began Mayweed hesitantly.

'. . . dead? No. Absent with leave, as mature loves should often be. Visiting upslope. Doing what she enjoys doing while I do what I enjoy doing which, as you now know, is nothing much.'

'May humbleness ask the name of your love?'

'Crocus. I'll tell you the story one day.'

'Pups?'

'Dozens. Hundreds. All gone now, all gone . . .' A tear slowly coursed down Tubney's face.

'Why mole, Mayweed, me, he's sorry, he. . . .'

'Sorry, mole? What for? My tears are tears of joy. I shall never forget the day the last of our pups declared in an earnest voice and not for the first time that he was off and then, to my unabated joy, he left! Now that was a day worth waiting for.' The smile returned.

'Marvellous mole, Mayweed has the feeling that Bablock has all that he is looking for.'

For the first time a look of genuine concern came to Tubney's face.

'You're not planning to come and stay as a resident are you?'

'No, no, a mere visitor. With Sleekit my consort, and Beechen my, er, well, just a mole I know.'

'But just visiting?'

'Yes, we shall eventually have to leave.'

Tubney relaxed.

'Then, dear Sir, you and your friends shall be very, very welcome here in Bablock Hythe.'

Mayweed could not at that point have known about Beechen's visit to Cumnor – since the Stone Mole himself had not yet decided to go there – but he might well have guessed the intention and direction of Beechen's final gathering for his First Ministry.

So Mayweed scurried about and plotted an escape route out of those parts which would avoid all the complications of Cumnor. Rollright, north of Duncton, had been their original objective and soon, Mayweed sensed, it would be wise to go there.

Meanwhile, and despite Tubney's affectation of not doing much, Mayweed wasted no time in enlisting the aid of the Bablock moles to the Stone Mole's cause.

'Imagine, new-found chubby chum, how much greater your feelings of relief and delight will be if you leave your system for a time, help others, show your sense of responsibility towards endangered moles of the Stone, and feel you and the moles of Bablock have done something useful.'

'"Useful"! "Responsibility"! "Leave"! "Help others"!' moaned Tubney. 'Why *should* we? Isn't it enough that we provide a welcome refuge for those who find us?'

Mayweed stared at him and said nothing.

'I mean to say,' continued Tubney uneasily, 'these moles you want us to help you rescue – "rescue", a word redolent of danger and disturbance which makes me shudder – can't they rescue themselves?'

'Supposing the grike guardmoles descended on you here, selfish Sir, would you not want to be rescued?'

'Ah, yes well . . . I should have explained. I *am* a guardmole, second generation, third order, reserve, retired. You see my father was sent here and, well, he took one look at the place and decided to stay and sort of let it be known that he had died in the course of his duties. Drowned, in fact. Toppled over into the river and drifted off. Enquiries were made, questions asked, guardmoles snouted about a bit, and then they gave up and he emerged from hiding.'

'Does nothing bother Bablock, then?' said Mayweed.

'The eldrene Wort at Cumnor tries. We had been left well alone for *years* and then she sent a couple of very odd moles down here, ranting and raving about the Word, saying blasphemers should be snouted et cetera and so forth. We gave them plenty of worms and a very enjoyable time and said we completely agreed with them and it *was* shocking. They went back satisfied but feeling guilty, as sincere moles who overindulge themselves are inclined to. Bablock was put out of bounds to them after that but we get one sneaking down here occasionally and we have a thoroughly enjoyable time pretending to be austere for a few days and agreeing how shockingly lax moledom is becoming.'

'Incorrigible Sir, you impress me. But now I under-stand that my friends are about to go to Cumnor and may need help. . . .'

'Oh yes, no doubt of it, they will. They are coming tomorrow, or perhaps the next day . . . in fact some followers have already arrived and the Chawley End moles are most flummoxed about it.'

'You *know*?' exclaimed Mayweed.

'Of course. One cannot be indolent all the time, just most of it. As for your friends, is it true that one of them is the S—— M——?'

Tubney mouthed 'Stone Mole' but did not speak it aloud.

Mayweed laughed.

'Yes, staggering Sir, yes!'

'That's what Crocus said. She's thrilled, of course. Delighted. If only for her I shall bestir myself, just as soon as we have found out what Wort and her henchmoles are doing.'

'But won't they immediately come down here?'

'No, they won't, not in force. A mole does not, as Crocus's cousin rather crudely puts it, poop in his own back burrow. Anyway, you have, I believe, worked out an escape route?'

'You constantly dumbfound me, Tubney,' said Mayweed.

'By Pinkhill?'

'No, Swinford. It's quicker and less likely.'

'Dear me. Swinford. That's most daring, most energetic, very vigorous.'

'It may be, Tubney, but just think how you will feel when we finally leave.'

'I do, all the time. Now relax, for your fretting talons and busy leer quite put me in a sweat. All is in paw, when we've been told what's happening we'll set off towards Hen Wood and be ready to collect your friends. Have a worm or something, tell me a tale, *relax*, you're in Bablock now. Things will work out as they should.'

Which, apart from Beechen's unexpected desire to be alone and leave them on the very threshold of Bablock after their rescue from Hen Wood, they did.

'Relax!' Mayweed said more than once to troubled Buckram as, having looked upslope and seen Beechen gone, the great mole lumbered miserably along feeling that he had failed in his duty.

'No good *telling* him to relax, Mayweed,' observed Tubney as they continued on. 'Nomole relaxes if they're told to. No, you leave it to Bablock to sort him out. It'll take a day or two – perhaps three in his particular case –

but believe me there's something about the air in Bablock, and the way the river flows, and, and. . . .'

But he had no need to say more for the moles had turned the corner and crossed the mysterious boundary that took them into the world that was Bablock.

The frosty ground stretched ahead of them, and the pale sunlight slanted down across the tree-lined riverbanks, and all over the great meander of flowing water whose sound and scents dominate the gravelly terrace on which the Bablock system sits. The last of the autumn colours were dotted here and there, and as Sleekit came to Mayweed's flank the two paused to stare as Tubney, kind and thoughtful that he was, led Buckram on, talking to him non-stop to take his mind off Beechen.

'Sensuous love, this is the place I found for us,' said Mayweed.

'Mayweed, you always surprise me, from the first time I saw you until this moment.'

'Humbleness thought hard and decided his beloved needed a place to rest and enjoy his company to the full. Bablock and the moles in it will provide it. Indolence and pleasure ooze out of every tunnel, and lie like sweet-scented nesting material on every surface stance. Madam will have noticed that the air here makes her Mayweed wax poetic.'

Sleekit sighed with pleasure, touched him close, stared about, pulled him nearer to the river and closer to herself, peered down into its waters, sighed again, stanced down, stanced up, snouted here and there, sighed a third time, and said, 'Will Beechen really be safe?'

'Mayweed does not know, though he fears for him very much. But he thinks the Stone is with Beechen as it is with us. Let the mole be, he needs time alone and thinks he is in love. Let him wander a bit. It does a mole no harm. The Bablock moles are not as idle as they like others to think, and no doubt Tubney will see that moles are watching out for him. When he's ready he'll come here and we can show him the pleasures we have found in the place.'

'How long can we stay?'

Mayweed settled down, extended his snout along his paws, stared at the water and then northwards upstream.

'I would like to get you both to Rollright by Longest Night. I. . . .'

'It's enough, my dear, it's all I wish to know. When you say we must leave, we shall leave. Until then I'll pretend we have forever here.'

Which, with much pleasure, she did, as the clear skies that brought frost across moledom continued, and moles enjoyed days of pale sunlight, and shining nights when the bright stars seemed to conspire with every dream that lovers, young and old, might have.

While in the secret places along the heaths above Bablock, and down to the icy meadows where Whitley lies, two moles began to know their providential love.

Beechen and Mistle, the nervousness of their first meeting soon gone, discovered the joy that complete acceptance by another, both in body and in spirit, brings. Blind such love may sometimes be, irrational as well, yet to those lost in its continuing discoveries time, place and circumstance seem all moulded to suit the lovers' ends.

Some have said that Beechen, being what he was, should not have fallen so in love. Others that surely Mistle, faced by such a mole as him, could not but feel her love thwarted by the awe she felt, so that it was not love but adoration. And there are those who would pretend that those two young moles had a love so pure, so ideal, that driven snow would have seemed mucky by comparison.

Not so. All untrue. Forget their antecedents and their destiny; think only of two moles driven by that ordinary need young adults always have for a union that gives strength through sharing to the struggle to make sense of the great conflicts and dilemmas that moles and moledom always present. Stone Mole he may have been but, as Tryfan never tired of reminding those in Duncton Wood, he was *first* but ordinary mole, with an ordinary need to love; and in that sense Mistle was but ordinary as well.

Yet for all that, one thing was extraordinary about their love, which was that from the very first its nature, its context, its very life, was of the Stone. If ever the love of two moles shone with the light of the Stone it was that of Beechen of Duncton Wood and Mistle of Avebury. The meaning and context pairs so often search for in vain, wondering why once passion is spent or why when conversation is done there is a void, those two had discovered from the very first.

Their love was not just of the Stone but was its celebration too, and so once their nervousness was done, wherever they went in those special November days, the Stone was with them, and shone about them.

Like Mayweed and Sleekit, they watched the bright night skies, and they wandered the still and frosty mornings when mists made the Thames mysterious; they heard nature's sounds and knew its austere winter scents and felt at one with themselves and with their world. Reverence was in their every movement; but quietness, too, and fun.

Historians have picked away at that short time of private love they had, scribing of some detail they've grubbed up or guessed, but that is not our way. They had their time, they discovered love, and if in the tunnels that they found or made, or by the whitened riverside they made love, then let us say that we believe it was true love, and leave it be at that.

If a mole would know how they were then, let he or she remember their first true love, and imagine them to be well blessed by the Stone's light as well. The Stone made those two as one and let each of us celebrate it as we will without the tittle-tattle of gratuitous surmise.

At the end of November the skies grew cloudy as the wind veered east, and the rains swept in, driving across the Cumnor Hill and bringing downpours on its western slopes and on to Bablock, where the river ran.

The frost was gone, the trees dripped, the river changed colour and rose a little, and Beechen said to Mistle, 'I think it's time we went to Bablock now.'

So, by tunnel and wet surface, the wind driving their fur this way and that, laughing and sharing with pleasure even the rough day, they tumbled like two pups into Bablock Hythe, where Tubney, alerted by the most discreet of watchers, found them.

'Welcome, Beechen, here at last!' he beamed. 'And . . . a friend?'

'Mistle,' said Beechen with a smile. 'Of Avebury.'

'Well! Welcome, Mistle of Avebury. What rain! What a turmoil up above!'

'It's not so bad,' said Mistle, 'once you're out.'

'Ah, the young! It's a lot better once you're in,' said Tubney. 'The others will, I think, be pleased. I say "I think" because you see they have been in Bablock long enough to have forgotten that moles exist outside it.'

Mistle looked about the tunnels with pleasure, shaking her fur dry and not at all surprised to find that a place she and Beechen had looked down upon from the heath above for the exciting days past should be as pleasant and homely on the inside as it looked from out.

'Let's explore!' she said. Which they did, despite the mild protestations of Tubney who thought that perhaps he ought to tell somemole or other that Beechen was in fact *here*, and had brought with him a most elegant, a most pretty, a most. . . .

'Tubney?'

It was the voice of Crocus, and it was to be obeyed.

'Yes dear, coming.'

So it was Crocus who was the first to know of their coming, Tubney being discounted in the matter altogether once it was discovered that the Stone Mole Beechen had a female friend with him.

'Are they together?' Crocus might have been heard asking.

'Yes, I think so. I mean they seemed to be, they came through the same entrance wetted by the same rain.'

'Well then –' (a listening mole would have also heard), 'we'll have to find a very different burrow than the one I had in mind. A private burrow, with its own entrance and exit, and with views of the river. Yes. Leave it to me!'

'My dear, I was intending to. . . .'

'I shall tell the others myself, immediately I have arranged a burrow for the two young moles, but you can tell Mayweed since you're the only one who ever knows where he is.'

'He's with Sleekit usually, not doing very much.'

'Well, I don't know, you might have *said*.'

Said what! Tubney did not know, and when Crocus had gone off to be busy he went his leisurely way saying, 'Dear me, rush, rush, rush.'

But Tubney was wrong to think the others had even half-forgotten about Beechen. The moment Sleekit set eyes on him once more, she saw and understood the changes that had overcome him. He stanced more solidly, more proudly, and there was a touching shyness about the way he introduced Mistle to them both.

'My dear,' said Sleekit warmly, 'you are most welcome, *most* welcome, and I am only sorry that Beechen's mother Feverfew is not here now to say so as well, for she would be pleased, I know she would, and many times!'

'Mistle Miss, my name is Mayweed, and humble as I am, a mole of merely slender stature, yet my rejoicing for you both is greater than the greatest mole's.'

Indeed, so great was their joy to see Beechen, so genuine their delight in her, that tears came to Mistle's eyes and she turned to Beechen to hold her for a moment and said that she for her part wished Violet was still alive to see how happy she was, and how generous and welcoming moles could be.

As for Buckram, when he saw Mistle he was protective-ness itself, and took Beechen to task for not bringing her to Bablock sooner lest they had been caught out by grikes.

'Didn't see a guardmole once, Buckram, nor anymole.'

'Well, Stone Mole, 'tis the last time I let you out of my sight!'

What nights of conversation they all had, what days of shared leisure, and what excitement it was for the Bablock moles to hear the tales Mayweed told and which Sleekit confirmed. How hushed they were at Mistle's account of her escape from Avebury, and what tears were shed by Crocus when she spoke of Violet. How appalled to hear of Whern, yet wanting to know more. . . .

Then Buckram would tell them darkly of Fyfield and of Wort, yet make clear as well that not all guardmoles were bad, but rather simply caught by a faith that demanded loyalty before conscience, and by moles who ruled by fear.

Many a tale was told, and by Tubney, too, who could turn the conversation this way and that, and lighten it when it grew too dark, and make it more serious when they had enough of jokes.

While all delighted to see the joyful spirits that radiated wherever Beechen and Mistle went, and the way those two moles' very being spoke of the Stone without mentioning its name.

December came, the winds changed once more and in place of rains came murk and mists and heavy skies which loomed so low that mist drifted across the top of Duncton Wood off to the north, and obscured its highest trees.

There came a day when Tubney found Mayweed by himself staring at the dark water of the Thames. It was midday, but the light was poor and all colour had left the grass and trees along the bank.

'You look downhearted, my good friend,' said Tubney.

'Mayweed is, but trying not to be. He, his love and his friends have had a time they will never forget here in Bablock Hythe. But the time has come to leave and humbleness does not want to go. Longest Night is coming soon, and he knows that Beechen and his Mistle will wish to celebrate it near a Stone, and Mayweed senses that Rollright is the place.'

For a long time Tubney said nothing, but stared dolefully at the river flowing past. A moorhen peered out of some reeds, seemed to dislike the world it saw, and disappeared. A cold mallard, its feathers ragged and its colours all faded, drifted sideways down the river past them, looking as if it had lost the will to paddle any more.

'My dear friend,' said Tubney, 'I shall be miserable when you have gone, not happy at all. I have enjoyed every moment of your company because you make me laugh.'

'Well,' said poor Mayweed, much moved by Tubney's testimony, 'well . . .' And tears coursed down his face. Then he said, 'Mayweed has been lucky to have many friends in his life, but he says this now, having thought about it often during this time in Bablock: of all the friends he's had, of all the moles he's loved, there is nomole in all of moledom he would more prefer to sit with by a river and do nothing much with than Tubney of Bablock. Tubney has taught humbleness something many moles find very hard, and wherever he goes he hopes he will have the self-discipline to stance down at least once a day and do nothing much, and when he does he will say a prayer to the Stone for a mole he once knew in Bablock Hythe.'

The great river flowed then, as it flows still, and the new-found friends stared at it and wept in the December gloom that they should be so soon parted. Then, when they felt they had wept enough, one sniffed and said, 'Rotundity, special stoutness, we must go!' And the other sniffed and replied, 'Amazing mole, if you must you must, but Bablock will not see your like again.'

That same evening Mayweed announced that they must leave, and a final night of revelry and cheer brought their stay in Bablock to a fitting close.

The following morning, early, the moles gathered to set off, and their Bablock friends gathered with them, except for Crocus, too moved it seemed to be able to face saying goodbye in the open.

Tubney made a speech, and said that never had Bablock

534

known such exciting, interesting and joyful guests, and he hoped they would travel in safety.

Before he finished he turned to Beechen and said, 'As for you, Beechen, and your love Mistle, we here in Bablock have treated you *ordinarily*, just as we would wish to have been had we been able to come to your system. But we would not wish you to think that because of that there were not many times we would have wished to call you Stone Mole. We too saw your star, we too awaited your coming, and we are honoured by the Stone that you should come here.

'Longest Night will be on us soon. We shall have our own modest celebration of it here, and think of you and yours on that holy night. Should the day ever come when we can be of service to you, or to your great cause, beyond being faithful to the Stone, then so shall we be.

'Meanwhile, on those days when the weather is clear, and we can see Duncton Wood, we shall be pleased to think that the Stone Mole was born so near to us, and to know that he found his love across our heaths, and in our little tunnels.

'Mistle brings light to an indulgent old mole's heart, but I know she is too good a mole to mind me saying that Sleekit here is the mole *this* mole will not forget – for her wit, her wisdom and her youthful looks!'

Tubney beamed and Sleekit smiled with pleasure at this graceful compliment. The others laughed and Mayweed leered around at all of them.

Then with touching and with tears they left, taking the northern route along the riverbank, among the shrubs and grass and to the sound of a solitary wood pigeon among the trees, and the muffled sobs of Crocus from down below.

When they had gone the Bablock moles, disconsolate, went their separate ways, and Tubney went down to comfort his beloved. It took some time, but at last her tears were gone.

Then Tubney re-emerged and looked about the place. Up, down, along, behind. He went to his favourite spot on the riverbank, the very place where Mayweed had first discovered him. He snouted a little at the ground, smoothing the place, setting it back to rights, and then he slowly stanced down. He eased his snout along his comfortable paws, sniffed the winter air, and began to watch the Thames flow by. Bit by slow bit his body relaxed, and slowly, as if after a dull day a setting sun was showing itself once more, a smile spread across his face.

He whispered a name, and the dark gentle water of the river spoke it back again.

'Bablock Hythe,' it said.

How dark the journey of Mayweed and the others to Rollright seemed. Under the rising heights of Duncton Wood, over the dangerous cross-over at Swinford, then on through interminable heathy fields towards the north.

Mayweed took them to the very spot where, so long before, he and Tryfan had led the Duncton moles under the river with such disastrous results. They stared back over the river, and thought of the friends they had in the rising wood they could see so near but whose trees seemed dark and impenetrable; then Beechen said a blessing in memory of the moles who were no more, and a prayer for those even now in Duncton Wood.

For a long time Mayweed stared across the river with Sleekit at his flank. His snout was low, and he seemed not to want to leave.

'It looks so murky by this light,' whispered Mistle.

'That's the Marsh End you can see from here,' replied Beechen. 'I lived there for a long time with Tryfan. Are you sure you still want to live in Duncton?' Mistle had told him about the fancy she had when she had first seen it from the hill above Bablock.

'It's the only place,' whispered Mistle, 'but I couldn't be there without you.'

'I'll always be with you,' said Beechen strangely, and his paw touched hers. But she felt his fear.

'And I with you, *always*,' she said.

536

In front of them Mayweed stirred and looked about himself as Sleekit reached out and touched him.

'Humbleness is unhappy,' he said, 'because he does not like to be so near Tryfan and unable to go to him. A long time ago Mayweed promised himself he would always be near Tryfan when he was needed.'

'But it was he who wanted you to guide Beechen out, and you have done. After Rollright, my dear, you must return to him.'

'And you, my lovely love?' said Mayweed, full of foreboding. Beechen had warned them they would part. Sleekit only sighed.

'Mayweed looks at the trees of Marsh End across the marsh, and he thinks they look beleaguered and upset, waiting. If Mayweed could swim this great river he would go now to Tryfan's flank. Mayweed may be humble, but he thinks that Tryfan will need him soon.'

'My love. . . .'

But Mayweed was not to be comforted or consoled, by Sleekit or any other mole there, and he led them on silently, his normal good cheer not returning until they were far from the place and the mole he had grown to love.

They journeyed on, and each day that passed seemed a lifetime shed since their stay at Bablock. Roaring owl threatened them, a dog and the twofoot it pulled chased after them, heron flapped and shadowed the December sky.

Yet on they went, Mayweed leading, Buckram taking up the rear. Few moles but grikes in those derelict parts, little to do but have faith they could reach Rollright by Longest Night. They were glad when the ground began to rise again, and took them off the clay vales of the Thames and back on to more sandy soils once more.

The days were shorter still, Longest Night was almost on them, they travelled close, as if all the better to keep out the cold.

One day, two days more and Mayweed took them quickly on until, on the morning of Longest Night sensing at last that Rollright was near, Mayweed grew suddenly cheerful once again.

'Tum-to, tum, tum, te-dum,' he sang tunelessly as they went along.

'My love, it's very annoying for some, your singing,' Sleekit said.

'But I'm excited. It is Longest Night and we're here in time. Stones are near, we're getting there, and that means that though Mayweed has shed an acorn cup full of tears at losing his new-found friend Tubney, he is already thinking positively about the pleasure to come of meeting once again his long-lost friend, not so hapless Holm. Grubbiness himself! Yes, yes, yes!' Then he raised his voice and called out across the heath ahead, 'Holm, be happy! Holm, be prepared to speak! Humble me is coming back. Humble me is almost here! Yes!'

The ground rose ahead, they climbed to its summit, and there, across a shallow vale the ground rose more. Dark and stolid the place, and Mayweed said, 'Sirs and Madams, beloveds one and all, see there our destination. Rollright! Danger calls, friends beckon, what will be, will be.'

With that, and no more said at all, Mayweed led them over the heath towards the system made famous by the Rollright Stones with no sign yet of guardmole grike, or mole at all.

They approached the first entrance they saw with extreme caution –Mayweed going ahead with Buckram lest there was guardmole trouble. But there was none, none at all. Nor did they find a guardmole at the second entrance they came to, or the third. Then when they entered the tunnels, they were silent but for the echoes of their own paws.

Mayweed's brow furrowed and his pace quickened.

'Sirs, Madams, Mayweed likes it not. No guardmoles, nomole at all, nothing. His snout quivers with apprehension. He stops, he turns and he asks Beechen and Mistle to do as he will ask them.'

He turned and faced them, and they saw how deep the concern he felt was.

'But maybe there aren't any guardmoles on this side of the system,' said Mistle. 'Especially on Longest Night.'

'Maybe, Madam, maybe. Buckram, you stay here with your charges, my love and I will go on and find out what we can. Hide here, do not move, one or other of us shall come back for you.'

Mayweed and Sleekit went carefully on, but only after they got nearer to the heart of the system, by which time they would normally long since have been challenged, did they hear mole.

Then . . . laughing mole, oh most jovial mole!

'Follower!' whispered Mayweed peering round.

He and Sleekit came out of the shadows and found a group of five moles having a good time.

'Greetings, brother!' cried out one. 'Hello, sister. Have a worm!'

'Where is everymole?' asked Sleekit.

'At the Stones, of course. Readying themselves for Longest Night.'

'Salivating stranger,' said Mayweed, 'forgive my dimness, but where are the guardmoles? Where the eldrene? Where . . . ?'

'Oh, *them*! Gone, most of them. They left a token force at the Stones, but they're just joining in the fun. The eldrene and the others all left *days* ago. It's liberty for all. Eat a worm and have fun!'

'Where have they gone?' said Sleekit urgently.

The followers looked at them as if they were indeed dim.

'The bloody fools have gone to Duncton Wood,' said one of them. 'The lot of them, grikes, sideem, Master-elect and some of our moles as servers. We warned them of the disease they'd get but the silly bastards went all the same. So for the first time in a long, long time Rollright moles can enjoy the Stones and have a revel and a feast for Longest Night!'

'A revel,' repeated Sleekit faintly. 'A *revel*?'

But Mayweed said nothing, but only stared dumb-struck. A revel was one thing, but Longest Night was a holy night and the revels came after the reverence, not before. And grikes and sideem and the Master-elect gone to Duncton?

'Mayweed is unhappy,' said Mayweed.

'Come, my dear, this bodes ill. We must fetch the others and decide what to do.'

'Yes, yes, yes, yes, because no, no, no, no, no, Mayweed is *not* happy.'

Chapter Twenty-Five

By the time Mayweed got back to Beechen and the others, dusk was beginning to fall on Longest Night. The wind hissed on the high grass hills around Rollright, and the moon showed low on the horizon beyond thin trees.

The moment Beechen heard from Mayweed that a large and powerful body of grikes had gone through Rollright and on towards Duncton Wood, a striking change came over him.

'You say the Master-elect was among them?'

'*They* said, agitated Beechen, they did,' said Mayweed.

Beechen suddenly shed that youthfulness and lightness Mistle had brought out in him, and seemed to take on once more the burdens of leadership and spiritual resolve. He moved apart from them, and looked somehow bigger, and strangely menacing.

When Mistle tried to speak to him he seemed not to hear. Instead he ignored them and snouted slowly all about as if in search of something. He seemed angry and tense, and as they watched him, they saw he grew distressed as well. Mistle went to him.

'Mayweed, guide me,' he whispered. 'Mistle . . . and you, Sleekit . . . and Buckram. Guide me.'

They all went to him, and to their alarm he broke down and wept, though why he would not say. But as they sought to comfort him he finally whispered, 'Father, guide us, for we are so few, and the light we bear so weak against the darkness that shall fall this night. Stone, help me, for you have made me but mole and I am weak.'

Then he reached out a paw to Mayweed, and snouting south said, 'Which of the Seven Systems lies there?'

'Duncton,' replied Mayweed, 'and Uffington far beyond. And Avebury to the south-west.' For a long time

Beechen stared that way. 'And there?' he asked, turning north-westward.

'Caer Caradoc and Siabod, where the holy Stones of Tryfan rise.'

'Yes, oh yes,' he said. Then the Stone Mole slowly turned to the north.

'And there, Mayweed?'

'Why, bold Beechen, strange Stone Mole, not one of the Ancient Seven lies in that direction.'

'What is there?' whispered Beechen.

'Beechenhill, Stone Mole, proud Beechenhill is there.'

'Beechenhill,' whispered Beechen, and it seemed to be spoken like stars across the sky. But then, 'How dark the northward way seems, how dark,' he said.

He turned back to face the direction in which he had started, towards Duncton Wood, and Mayweed said, 'Stone Mole, if the grikes, and the Master-elect Lucerne, and even the eldrene have gone to Duncton Wood then . . . then what shall we do? I must go there myself, for they shall be defenceless and Tryfan will need me. But you. . . .'

'Did Bablock and its moles teach you nothing, Mayweed?' Beechen said fiercely. 'Tonight is Longest Night, the most holy of nights. You shall not leave us tonight but go as we all must to the Rollright Stones and pray for Silence. It is what all moles should do tonight. Only that, for it is enough.'

He stared the Duncton way some more and then, seeming to gain his strength said, 'Mistle, Sleekit, Buckram, come now. Mayweed, guide us to the Rollright Stones for we are needed there. Come now.'

The trek was a rough one because Mayweed chose to go by the surface and the last stage was upslope. But if they had wished to prepare themselves reverently for the rituals to come, they could not. Long before they reached the Stones they came upon followers indulging in wild revels and ribaldry, laughing and singing, and playing jokes.

'Greeting, mateys!' one shouted to them, though Beechen tried to go on by, serious and forbidding.

'Oh! Sorry I spoke! Some moles . . .' The mole called out again, but he fell silent when Buckram loomed out of the shadows and glowered at him.

More moles were making merry at the Whispering Stoats, that sombre group of three stones that lean into each other a little to the south of the Rollright Stones themselves. Laughter, innuendo, males and females chasing each around, and even, so it seemed, a guardmole giving up trying to control the rabble of moles and joining in their lewd celebration.

'Look at them lot! Dear, oh dear! Hey, give us a smile then!'

The moles paused and stared as Beechen and the others went by, their quiet order in contrast to all the moles about.

'The Stones are not far ahead,' said Mayweed, 'let me just . . .' He went to a group of revellers and asked, 'Have you seen Holm or Lorren?'

'Up by the Stones I should think, doing his nut,' was the immediate reply. 'He was down here just now trying to lay down the law, the little runt, and we told him to piss off. Which he did! Ha, ha, ha. . . .'

The mole turned away from him, others stared, laughter broke out again, and Mayweed and the others moved unhappily on.

The noise up at the Stones themselves was so great that they heard it from a long way off, and when they reached them they saw a pandemonium of milling moles. Some played games even among the Stones themselves, some sang songs, the odd fight or two had broken out, and some even sought to mate in public.

Appalled, Mayweed stopped at the edge of the circle and simply stared in horror and disgust. In Rollright it seemed the holiest of nights had become the unholiest of feasts.

So busy were the moles enjoying themselves, along with at least three guardmoles they could see, that nomole saw the group in the shadows just outside the circle. None saw

Beechen staring blankly, nor Mistle shocked. None saw Buckram, all protective behind Beechen and muttering fiercely to himself.

There *is* a place for revelry on that special night which marks the seasons' greatest change when darkness gives way once more to light. But first let moles be reverent, let them give thanks for what they have had, let them turn to the Stone and be silent for a time. Only then let them make their way graciously with the rest of their community and enjoy what grateful revels they may make.

But not *this*, not the blasphemy the Stone Mole saw at Rollright. Never that again.

'Look!' said Sleekit quietly to Mayweed, pointing through the noisy throng, 'Oh look, my dear.' But she could not bear to look more and turned to Mistle and Beechen for comfort.

Yet Mayweed looked, and saw, and knew what he must do.

For there in the midst of that assembly of so-called followers of the Stone, stanced by the greatest Stone of that great circle, was a grubby mole. Small he was, his fur dusty, his talons dirty. He was staring up at the Stone and trying, despite all that went on about him, to say a prayer. Which was hard, for he seemed unable to say anything. Anything at all. And mute tears were on his face, and he was unable to find the words of prayer, and at last he lowered his snout as if he dared not look at the Stone any more.

While at his flank, vainly trying to console him, was a female, grubby too, and though small herself she was bigger than her mate. Her paws were on him as if vainly trying to protect him from the noise all about them, and she was turning this way and that, shouting at the moles to be still and be quiet.

''Tis Holm,' said Mayweed blankly. ''Tis Lorren at his side.'

Then telling the others to stay where they were, Mayweed moved into the circle and among the moles, and slowly, resolutely, began to cross towards where his old friends stanced.

Quite when Lorren first saw him would be hard to say, but suddenly her hopeless shouting stopped and she stared across the circle and was still. There was surprise on her face, and then hope, and then, as Mayweed got nearer, incredulous relief.

She turned to Holm, whispered something to him, and he too turned to look.

At first he seemed perplexed, but then his eyes filled with joy, and as swiftly as they did, his face fell with grief and shame and, like a mole gone mad, he shook his head as if to say, 'Not, not now, this is not how I would meet *you* again.' But Holm was never one for words, and so he shook his head, and cried.

As Mayweed went near enough to greet them both, Holm made such a helpless gesture of despair that Sleekit gasped and gulped for the pity of it.

Mayweed reached out to them both, talked with them, and then as the revels went on unabated around them, slowly turned towards where Beechen stanced, still unseen.

Mayweed whispered more, and then a look of disbelief came over Holm's face, and he reached to hold Lorren close, and his look turned to wonder. For out of the shadows, slowly, mightily, as if one of the Stones themselves was on the move, Beechen came.

There was no gentleness on his face, no kindliness.

Nor did he look at anymole in judgement, but rather in a terrible despair at the great Stone before which Holm and Lorren had been so pathetically stanced.

His eyes seemed to catch the shining lights of stars and moon, his fur to glow with a fearsome light, his talons to shine. Buckram, Mistle and Sleekit came behind him, and as he advanced a hush began to fall. Moles fell back from him, moles who had not seen him and still sang or argued or made a noise were shushed by those who had. Moles crept about to see him better, moles stared at him in awe.

545

Then as he came closer to Holm and Lorren a light seemed to cast itself across their faces, and then up on to the great Stone.

One of the guardmoles began to remonstrate, joking and wondering what was going on, but a mole who moments before had been laughing and shouting turned on him and he fell silent.

'There is no shame in joy,' said Beechen, 'unless it be the false joy of those that hide a frightened heart, or mask a fear of their own emptiness. Therefore if you be unafraid, and if your life be full, dance, sing, and I shall join you now.'

He looked about him, first at one mole and then another. He reached out his paws, and smiled. But his smile was bleak. Nomole danced, nomole sang.

'This is moledom's holiest night,' said Beechen, so softly that it was no louder than a breeze across the face of a wind-smoothed Stone. 'It is the night we of the Stone give thanks for what we have, the night we pray for those who need the Stone's help in the dark winter years ahead, and a night to be reverent of ourselves.'

The moles were utterly still, and one who could not quite see or understand what was going on, muttered, 'Who is he? What's he saying?'

Then Beechen said, 'Your brothers and your sisters in Duncton Wood are enshadowed by the Word tonight. Across all moledom darkness has fallen, yet here in Rollright I hear but one prayer spoken tonight.'

Beechen rested a great paw on Holm's shoulder.

'But how can moles pray for others who are not still themselves? This mole is praying that the Stone forgives him for he feels he has failed it. He has not failed it, for the Stone hears well a prayer from a mole whose voice is weak, whose voice is drowned by a thousand who dance and sing when they should pray. Yes, the Stone hears his prayer well.'

'Who is he?' muttered a mole again.

'What's he on about?' said another.

'I am what you shall make me,' cried out Beechen suddenly. 'I am the Stone Mole come amongst you. Your weakness is my burden, your faithlessness is as talons on me, the shadows you cast are as black to me as the shadow of the Word. Is it then for you I have come?'

A terrible silence had come to the Rollright Stones, and it seemed to have spread to the Whispering Stoats nearby, for the sounds of revelling had ceased there as well and the hurried pattering of pawsteps told that moles were coming to see what was going on.

'It is well that you are quiet. For tonight, the holiest of nights, I shall speak the prayers and rituals of our faith as they have been taught us from Balagan's time. The liturgy was taught me by Tryfan of Duncton, and they were taught him by his parents, and by Boswell of Uffington who is my father. We shall start our vigil now, and cast out from ourselves the noise that is within us, and discover once more the reverence that should be in a mole before the Stone.

'If there be any here who would not pray with me then let them go in peace.'

There was silence until a mole, an older female, pointed a talon at one of the guardmoles and cried in a strange, half-hysterical voice, 'What about him then? *He's* not one of us, he's of the Word, *he* is.'

Others began to shout the same thing, pointing towards the other two guardmoles there, who began suddenly to look very afraid. The follower's cries grew louder and full of hatred, and some of the stronger ones crowded forward to try to strike the guardmoles, and others jeered.

'Strike them and you strike me,' cried out Beechen. 'Strike me and you strike the Stone.'

He pointed a talon at the great Stone whose light seemed so strong about them.

Then more gently, his voice calming them, he said, 'The mole that strikes the Stone is like a hunted vole and much afraid.' As he said that he quietly moved over to the guardmoles and said, 'Would you pray with us?'

One of the guardmoles nodded his head, too afraid it seemed to speak.

'And you, mole, would you pray with us? And you?'

The other guardmoles nodded.

Then Beechen smiled, and to one of those who had been loudest in their shouts said softly, 'And you?'

And then, softer still, 'And you?'

In the peace of the night the anger was gone. Then Beechen said, 'Know that all of us are one in our intent before the Stone, which is to share our sorrow and our joy, to release our fears and find our strengths. Before the Stone it matters not whatmole you are, but only that you truthfully seek to open up your heart. And in *that* silent place what word is there for "Word"? What word for "Stone"? No words at all but only the wordless cry of blind pups caught up in all the confusing fears and wonders of the life they have begun.

'Therefore as you would help a pup to grow, help each other now and know that as you help each other you shall help yourself; and as you love each other you shall love yourself, which is the Stone's great joy. As a parent would see its pups grow whole, so would the Stone see you grow whole. As a parent flinches and feels the hurt of its pups, so does the Stone feel your hurts and, all the more, your hurting of each other.

'Now, let us begin to rejoice at last, for tonight is most holy. . . .'

So began Beechen's teaching and rituals before the Rollright Stones, and the moles who heard him knew him to be the Stone Mole come among them, and were glad.

Already for days before Longest Night, Skint and Smithills had warned Tryfan that the long-feared move of the grikes into Duncton Wood was imminent.

The few watchers Skint still had available were old now, and nearly all the few who had been active in the summer years had died in the cold of late November. Nevertheless, thin on the ground though the watchers were, they had succeeded in confirming a strengthening of the patrols at the cross-under as December began.

Sometimes now the guardmoles dared come inside the system, and the watchers would peer out at them and wonder at how young the guardmoles seemed, how strong, how formidable a force to keep such old moles confined.

But the guardmoles had not only become more inquisitive and courageous about entering the system, but more aggressive as well. Where once they mocked and chased the old moles in the wood, now they hurt them if they could, as they had hurt Sorrel. In December a 'hurting' led to another death, and Tryfan advised that the watching activity cease.

Yet the guardmole training of Skint and Smithills was too ingrained to let them do nothing at all. A system needs watchers, as a mole needs eyes, they said. But unwilling to embroil other moles with watching they moved their quarters down to the Pasture slopes, and took it in turn to watch the cross-under with only Marram occasionally keeping them company.

Skint said little these days, Smithills was getting slow, but watching was one thing they could do – though what they would do if they saw something threatening neither knew any more.

In truth both hoped, Skint especially, that before their days were done they might one day see the impossible, and a party of grikes come through the cross-under and up the slope to say that the struggle was over now, nomole had won, none lost, the Word was, and the Stone was, be at peace now!

It was old moles' dreams, no different in quality than the longings they often shared for Grassington, and the River Wharfe, where once they had been pups, and the Word and the Stone were all the same, which meant nothing at all. They had been happy then.

But the truth was very different than the dream, and they knew it. The grikes were massing, the patrols were getting tougher in the way they looked each day. Great trouble was apaw.

Yet concerned though they were for the system, Skint and Smithills were strangely untroubled for themselves by the growing threat. They had begun to tire and to leave fear behind them, and now it was more the anticipation they disliked, rather than any violence yet to come.

Indeed, one said to the other more than once, 'Well, old friend, if they come I'll go down fighting. Let's take some of the bastards with us!'

To which the other replied, 'My feelings too, but don't let Tryfan hear you say that!'

But in any case, their warnings of the grike threat did not disturb the growing calm that spread throughout Duncton in the wake of Beechen's departure. Moles talked to moles, worship at the Stone increased, and comfort was given as best it could be to those who were taken by the November cold. A community, Tryfan had told them, cares for its dying as much as for its living.

There was good spirit in the system, and some said that no sight expressed it better than the way grumbling Dodder, a diehard mole of the Word, followed Madder and Flint up to the Stone from time to time, and crouched outside the clearing, watching his friends say their prayers. Afterwards, very slowly, helping each other along, they would pick their way back down through the wood to the Eastside, and resume their noisy but amicable enmity once more.

Tryfan never went back to the Marsh End after his declaration of the Rule, but stayed close by Feverfew in the southern burrows where they had reared Beechen.

How quiet the system was, how old the moles who were left, and how many counted the days to Longest Night, saying with a touching optimism that if only the Stone would spare them until then, they might see the winter through and struggle into spring. But age had caught them up, the young mole who was their triumph and their glory had safely gone, and their wrinkled, weakening eyes could only peer up at the December skies and wonder where he was, and how he was, and pray that the Stone would give him strength.

December seemed so slow, and Longest Night a lifetime away. Some, indeed, fell then, surprise on their faces. Borage died, quite suddenly, and Heather, so gaunt now, cradled and spoke to him to the end, seeming to think he was the pup she never had.

Teasel weakened, and Feverfew hurried to her. Yet the loving old female pulled round, saying *she'd* see Longest Night in if it was the last thing she did.

Rain, mist, cold, clear days, and trees leafless: the very wood itself seemed to have grown old.

In the second third of December, with Longest Night near at last and after Skint had come his frail way up from the south-eastern slopes to warn him that the grikes were massing even more and seemed poised for something, Tryfan went to the Stone once more and kept a vigil there.

Others who came heard him say that should moles of the Word come to Duncton, they must be treated with every courtesy, 'even unto death'. So he said, and those who were not nearly senile themselves said that finally age had caught up with him. Yet none dared say so to his ravaged face, nor look in his poor eyes and say what they really felt. Even now, he carried himself with authority, and though his head shook, and sometimes Feverfew had to reach out a paw to stop his paws from their involuntary trembling, there was greatness in his gait. And in his presence a mole felt he or she might do great things.

When the day of Longest Night finally dawned not a mole woke in Duncton who was not glad to be alive. Such a day, grey though it looked, was one to cherish, knowing that its night was holiest of all, and a mole might give thanks for the past and what was to come, and that he could say a prayer at all.

One by one, those still left from the now distant-seeming day when they had said farewell to Beechen, helping each other as they had done then, old, lame, blind, weak, they made their way up to the Stone.

Most were followers of the Stone, but even those few like Dodder who were not came too. A very few might still be called 'young' – though 'not old' might have been the best description – Hay for one, and Feverfew was younger than some, Bailey younger than any, and these moles helped where they could. Until by dusk-fall all but Skint and Smithills were gathered at the clearing, and hushed, and glad to be together.

'My friends Skint and Smithills will soon be here,' said Tryfan simply, 'Marram and Bailey have gone to find them and when they come we shall begin. But until then, let us be quiet unto ourselves, let us give thanks for the good things our lives have brought us.'

Then did the moles of Duncton begin their humble and quavering prayers.

Time and again since she had arrived at Duncton's cross-under, with but a few days to go before Longest Night, the eldrene Wort, accompanied by her personal henchmoles, had gone up a little way on to the south-eastern slopes and stared up at the mysterious wood that rose beyond the Pastures.

She had looked at it often enough from Cumnor, but from this side, it looked more formidable and its slopes awkward. No wonder Henbane's guardmoles had had trouble taking it in Wrekin's day.

But she did not worry now about what outcast moles were there – she knew. Her guardmoles had taken one of the Duncton moles prisoner and before they killed him had got information enough to tell them that there was going to be precious little opposition from the moles in the system, since they were now few in number, and most old.

Even so, she would have preferred to invade the system before Longest Night, just to ensure there would be no trouble and nothing untoward happened when the Master-elect Lucerne came for the great ritual ordination, which was designed as a desecration of the Stone and about which all followers would soon know.

But Lucerne had made his wishes absolutely clear, which were that the system was not to be entered properly until he came. But perhaps, Wort smiled to herself, that was as well. What she and her guardmoles had discovered from the tortured mole was that a mole called Tryfan was still alive within it, the very same who had once been to Whern. What joy Wort felt to hear that news; how much more would be her Master's joy.

What was more, the Duncton mole had told them that Longest Night was one night when all the moles, even the lame and sick, would be conveniently gathered in one place all at once.

How elegant the justice of the Word! For Tryfan was Lucerne's father, and the Master-elect would be well pleased. Almost as good was this: a mole Feverfew was said to be the mother of Beechen the Stone Mole. Well, well, well. This was evidence to Wort that Beechen was no more than an ordinary mole, however inspired he seemed. All this talk of eastern stars followers made!

Had she permitted herself the vanity of thinking it, she might have reflected on how wise Lucerne had been to elevate her as he had. First among equals she had quickly made herself with Drule and Slighe, of *that* there was no doubt, and powerful though they were and remained in their respective ways, it was the eldrene Wort who put the fire of zeal into their unholy trinity.

The three of them had come ahead of the Master-elect after waiting impatiently for him at Rollright for several days. Days, however, which Wort had put to good use by reviewing Rollright and finding its eldrene and guardmoles gravely lacking in Word zeal. Indeed in her view the system was more lax than the reporting trinity had made it out to be, but Slighe had prevailed on her to moderate her views that a snouting of the eldrene and senior guardmoles there might do everymole a service. This was not what the Master-elect *wished*.

'Humph!' said Wort. 'Does not their evil sicken you?' She asked the question with such fierceness that to say 'No' was almost to suggest support for the Stone. Slighe said nothing.

Drule outwardly agreed with Slighe about not killing moles, but he privily suggested that an accident or two to the right senior guardmoles, which is to say a crippling and a disappearance of the most lax and most disliked, might achieve as much as a public snouting. Wort accepted this most sensible compromise, and it was done, and proved its worth, for the rest asked no questions and looked to their devotions more assiduously.

Lucerne had come, visited the Stones with interest, found them miserable things and declared magnanimously that all the guardmoles bar a very few could come to Duncton for his ordination. Wort privately disapproved. 'They have not earned the right!' she said, adding, 'But the Word speaks better through the Master-elect than any of us and we do not always understand it.'

But in truth, Lucerne had arrived in Rollright with only twenty key sideem and the Twelve Keepers for the ordination, and was thinking that more moles should witness his elevation. It was a matter of the glorification of the Word. But then, others would be coming from Buckland and other southern systems, for messengers had gone ahead to summon them.

Now, two days before Longest Night, the area around the cross-under was beginning to get congested with moles, and for this reason if no other Wort would have liked to direct moles into Duncton Wood, but she abided by the Master's edict.

The last day had gone slowly, then the dawn of Longest Night came and the advance guard arrived soon after from Rollright, with the Master-elect on the way.

It was a dramatic and historic moment, and the eldrene Wort found herself in the unexpected position of organising many moles. Her own Cumnor moles had been summoned, and their discipline, humourlessness, and austerity set a tone to the growing gathering. Moles were quiet, voices low and a sense of coming holiness and worship was all about. While over it all loomed the unknown heights of Duncton Wood, and the knowledge that moles would die tonight, and the Word make judgement of the Stone by desecrating one of its most holy places.

Lucerne came at midday, accompanied by his entourage of Keepers. Few of the guardmoles had ever seen such a thing and a dark, expectant hush settled in the tunnels about the cross-under. Keepers prayed, sideem chanted, and Terce was everywhere, cold as ice.

The eldrene Wort knew her place, and how to keep it, and only when she was summoned did she go to Terce, and brief him of what she had found out.

'You think Tryfan is here?'

'I know he is here,' she said, explaining what they had learnt from the tortured mole.

'And Beechen, the Stone Mole?'

'Unlikely. He left the system in September as we know, but our informant told us that there was no intention that he should come back. We also think Feverfew, the Stone Mole's mother, is still in the system – unless she be dead she cannot have got out.'

'Beechen got out!' said Terce acidly.

'That was before my own moles had taken control of the cross-under, Twelfth Keeper.'

'It is well. You have done *very* well, eldrene Wort.'

'I serve only the Word and the Word's will, and through it the Master-elect and his agents,' said Wort archly.

'I know it, eldrene Wort, I know it well.'

The day was cold, grey and still, but when afternoon came the sky began to clear and the wind to freshen from the north.

Terce disappeared, Lucerne and Mallice were not to be seen, guardmoles on duty shivered and looked at each other and dared speak no word at all. The Word hushed them, the Word awed them, the Word would show its strength tonight.

Gradually, dusk came, colour left the vegetation and the ground, above the place they waited the roaring owls became more plentiful, and as their sound increased and their gazes became brighter the sky darkened.

Short, sharp commands brought more guardmoles into positions preparatory to entering the Duncton system, and Clowder, who had taken overall command, stanced at a point where he could oversee them all.

With nothing left to do now the eldrene Wort stanced to one side of the cross-under, the better to see the advance begin. She peered through to the darkening slopes beyond and her talons fretted. She saw Drule was nearby, and Clowder further off, but Slighe was in attendance on the Master-elect and unseen.

'Holy Word, my mother and my father, bring peace to thy servant Lucerne, and to all thy servants here; teach us to be humble before thee, teach us all things we need to know to prosecute your glorious way; holy Word, my mother and my father . . .' So Wort whispered her prayers.

'He's coming!' one guardmole warned the first troop of guardmoles who were going to enter the system. Paws shifted, snouts straightened, eyes alerted.

Wort watched. The movements of the guardmoles, the ritual to come, the glory of the night, was not in her control and she need not fret: she could enjoy all that was so soon to come. She had done her part, and now the entry of the moles of the Word into the system would begin, and lead to its culmination in the first southern ordination of a Master of the Word. She shed tears of gratitude to be where she was at such a moment as this.

'Holy Word, my mother and my father . . .' she said softly, as the order was given for the first troop to advance. 'Holy Word, now let glory be, and on the pitiful Stone command that thy final darkness fall. . . .'

The dusk all gone, nothing more to do, Smithills was already on his way upslope from the cross-under when Skint's worst watching nightmare came true.

556

He could not believe his old eyes, and simply stared as first one, then two, then *three* lines of guardmole columns emerged out of the cross-under and began to trek up the slopes below, one to his left, one to his far right, and the biggest up the central slope straight towards the High Wood.

Nomole knew better than he, not even Smithills, the import of what he saw. So great were their numbers and so resolute their purpose, that for a few moments he could only stare aghast.

'Smithills!' he turned and urgently called, not caring that he was heard. That mattered not, for he knew there was nothing anymole in Duncton, even if their years were halved and their number quadrupled, could do against such a force. On and on they came, and still they came.

'Smithills!' he called out again, moving as quickly upslope as his old paws would allow after his friend.

But Smithills was well ahead and seemed not to hear, for Skint had told him not to wait, saying he wanted to be alone for a moment or two and would then come on up after him. Smithills knew that tonight was the last time Skint would ever watch for even if they saw anything, where were the messengers, where the back-up watchers, where the moles that could stance and fight? All gone, all old, all long since dead. Then, '*Smithills!*'

Smithills, almost up to the wood's edge by then, heard the call and turned, surprised and then alarmed. He could just see his friend in the murk below moving fast across the slope, as if he was cutting a mole off.

'*Smithills!*' came the urgent shout once more.

Smithills turned back at once downslope, moving as quickly as he could, which was not fast, for his great limbs were half lame now. Why, what a couple of failing watchers they made! Well, they weren't so old they couldn't head off a couple of guardmoles gallivanting about on Longest Night.

It was only as he approached Skint, that he began to realise that what his friend had seen was more than a couple of guardmoles. Skint was stanced low at the edge of a flatter part of the slope, looking down at something Smithills could not yet see.

'Look!' said Skint as the bigger mole arrived.

Then Smithills saw where he pointed far below, and he gasped. The area around the cross-under was black with moles, and they came up in three formations, the main one steadily towards where they themselves were stanced, the others rising faster still in the distance on either side.

'But 'tis Longest Night!' said Smithills. ''Tis bloody Longest Night. They should be. . . .'

'Go quickly up to the clearing, warn Tryfan, *order* him to hide our moles in the Ancient System.'

'Aye, and what'll you do, mole? Pass the evening with them?'

Skint turned to him, his eyes fierce. 'Do it, Smithills, and that's an order.'

Smithills looked back downslope at where the grikes advanced inexorably up the slope, then back at Skint, and he turned and was gone up into the darkness as fast as he could.

Skint watched him go and then, satisfied, calmly assessed the slopes all about. He knew the ground well, and had already placed himself at a patch of ground where a natural buttress gave him an advantage on those coming from below.

He moved from one side of the patch to the other and calmly waited, one mole against the many.

The moles below him came slowly but steadily, well trained in climbing such slopes, knowing that the best way to leave a mole ready for fighting when he got to the top was to go steady. The formations to Skint's far right and left were already higher up the slope than he was because the slope there was a little less steep and he had the sense of being surrounded by an army of grikes. Smithills would have to be quick to reach the clearing in time.

Skint had never felt calmer in his life. He waited until the leaders of the middle formation were near enough that

558

they could hear him – so near he could hear the grunting of their breath – and he called out, 'Halt!'

He knew they could not see his numbers yet, and would have to stop and assess. It was a bluff that would last but moments and already others were spreading out from the middle formation, and gaining ground on either side of him.

'Halt!' he cried again.

But they said nothing, dark moles advancing, and he guessed they must know his numbers were nearly nothing.

He heard an order from below.

'You two, round him off. Do not kill him yet.'

Do not kill him yet. . . .

Anger overwhelmed him for a brief moment, and then his training and his inclination settled him. All thought of Tryfan's order not to fight left him. He was the mole he had been years before, decades before, the mole that had left Grassington in the name of the Word, his strength and intelligence ready to do what it was commanded. He had been trained to fight.

Do not kill him yet.

'I'll take as many of you buggers as I can,' he said quietly to himself.

The moles below had stopped, but near enough that he could see the shine of night sky in their talons, and the flash of their teeth. Stealthily, their colleagues came up the slopes on either side.

'There's just one of them, Sir!' he heard a mole hiss.

'You four, take him from either side!'

Skint readied his paws on the ground, settled his snout, and waited to see from which side they came first. He did not mind dying now, but he wished . . .

He turned sharply as a shadow loomed behind him and even as he saw who it was Smithills' much loved voice said, 'You're a silly bugger, Skint, always have been and always will be. Did you think I could leave you to face them alone?'

'The others . . .' began Skint.

'No good going on above, even if I'd wanted to. There're outrunners in the wood ahead of me and they'd have cut me off long before the clearing. No, my place is here with you, old friend. I'll take the right flank, and you the left.'

'Another's joined the first one, Sir!' they heard a grike call out.

'Stop buggering about,' an impatient command came back. 'Deal with them.'

The grikes advanced on them slowly and confidently, for they saw two old moles, their fur grizzled and patchy, their paws withered.

'Come on, you two, we'll not hurt you.'

'Come off it, mate,' said Smithills, 'we've heard it all before.'

'Kill them if there's any delay,' a senior guardmole barked out from below. 'We must keep on moving.'

'Try it,' muttered Smithills.

Four moles converged on Skint and Smithills simultaneously, two on either side, and all four were unready for what they met.

With a roar Smithills struck the first one down and, using a technique he knew so well, pushed him mightily back into the next advancing mole who, off guard and off balance, made himself vulnerable.

'Bastard,' cried out Smithills, and plunged his talons straight into the mole's belly.

The mole screamed and rolled downslope even as Skint dealt the first who came to him a talon straight in the snout, and throated the second with his paw.

Then as more came at them, back to back they fought, the whole advance slowing before them as moles, uncertain of what was happening, paused, turned and shouted.

All that Skint and Smithills knew then was the rush of moles upon them, the grunt of killing breath, the raised talons, as each protected the other and they both fought stolidly on, using the ground, surprise, anger and the confusion of numbers about them to their advantage.

Each felt the support of the other's back and haunches, each knew the other was still fighting, and then each felt the first flow of blood across his flank, not knowing if it was himself or his friend that bled.

On they fought, and roared, thrusting out at the enemy with guardmoles falling where they were hit. On and on they struggled until each felt the other weaken, felt the tiredness coming, felt the inexorable approach of his own death by the pause and judder of the other's haunch.

'Skint, you're an old fool!' gasped Smithills as he raised his talons one last time.

'Smithills, words have always failed me where you're concerned!' rasped Skint. But it was the last thing he said, and Smithills heard his friend grunt in sudden pain, and turning from his adversary with no more thought for himself tried vainly to protect poor Skint from further blows.

On Smithills broad back mortal blows fell, on and on, until he weakened and red darkness came, and he knew no more.

'Bastards!' said a grike, wounded and bloody from the fight, as he stared among the bodies at the two moles who had fought to their very last breath.

Another guardmole came up and looked at them.

'They were brave bastards,' said the mole Romney.

The second guardmole looked at them and said, 'They were our own kind that we killed.'

'And if you'd been first on to them they'd have had you 'cos they knew a thing or two about fighting.'

'Stop dawdling there! On, on, on!' a commander shouted and the two turned from that spot on the south-eastern Pastures, re-formed, and moved on remorselessly upslope to enter the southern edge of the High Wood.

While below on the slopes bodies lay still and were lost in the gloom, and far beyond them from south to north, from north to south, roaring owls went by endlessly, their gazes cold, their calls an unceasing roar.

For the briefest of moments Tryfan and the others thought it was Skint and Smithills coming through the wood, but the sounds increased beyond what their two friends would make, and moles came from all about, spread wide around the clearing, too wide to flee if any of them had thought of doing so.

But they did not. Instead they stanced closer to each other and Tryfan turned his snout up to the Stone and cried out, 'Stone, we of Duncton are old and weak and uncertain of ourselves, guide us now. Help us do thy will with all our strength.'

He had no sooner said this than three stolid males came into the clearing and looked about. Then two more on the other side, and then four more. Shouts echoed through the wood, orders to go this way or that and the sense of being possessed, and being impotent.

The Duncton moles, many afraid, some angry and some confused, seemed overwhelmed by the suddenness of the grikes' coming and instinctively clustered closer around Tryfan and Feverfew at the Stone. Perhaps if the grikes had attacked them physically they might have fought, but the grikes did not.

They mustered about the clearing, young and strong and intimidating in their stares and silence, and the only contact they made with anymole was with Teasel on the edge of the clearing who seemed confused by all the moles and had stayed where she was. Not unkindly, it seemed, a senior guardmole helped her join the others and said, 'That's right, my love, you stay there. Now, you lot, if you behave yourselves nomole's going to get hurt.'

'Some chance!' muttered Madder.

'Who said that?'

The voice came out of the murk beyond the clearing, thick and menacing.

The Duncton moles were silent, none saying who it had been.

562

'What do you want with us?' called out Hay, struggling to break through the moles to the front.

'Be still, mole,' said Tryfan, putting a restraining paw on him. 'Be still.'

In the space of moments the clearing seemed full of guardmoles, several of whom stationed themselves around the beleaguered Duncton moles, and there was no doubt at all that resistance of any kind was useless.

'Is that the lot?' a voice called. 'Well?'

'None about the place, nor did we see any flee. Could be some in the tunnels, but it seems unlikely. It *is* Longest Night.'

'None on the far Pastures either, Sir.'

'Right. The Keepers will be here soon, so let's sort these moles out. We know which one we want.'

The voices seemed disembodied, coming sharply from one side of the clearing to the other, as yet more moles crashed unseen about the wood and the guardmoles organised themselves.

'Found Tryfan yet?'

'Just about to, Sir.'

The voice came from a group in the gloom behind the Stone.

'Don't identify yourself, Tryfan!' whispered Hay urgently. 'If you don't we'll not say.'

'He's right,' responded Dodder.

'Speak only the truth, do not fight, love them. This is our only way,' said Tryfan. Feverfew came close to him, her paws about him.

'Well, mole, found him?'

The voice was nearer, and deeper, and full of authority.

'No, Clowder Sir, not yet. He'll be among that lot by the Stone . . . Drule's about to sort them out.'

'Is he now?' said Clowder.

These disembodied voices from out of the gloom had been menacing enough, but nothing could have prepared them for the sight of the mole Drule who now emerged into the far side of the clearing, the light of the risen moon and stars on him. He was huge and stared about in a fat, grotesque and disinterested way, before stancing down confidently opposite the Duncton moles. He looked up at the Stone, sucked his teeth, spat, and said, 'Which one of you is Tryfan?'

His pig eyes stared at them. His gross size, his stubby talons, his moist snub snout, everything about him was unpleasant, and cruel. It was clear that he was not going to waste any time, for after only the briefest of pauses while he waited for an answer he pointed a talon at the nearest female, who was Teasel, since she had been the last to be taken to the group.

'Bring her here.'

As two hefty guardmoles moved in on her there was a movement among the Duncton moles led by Hay to protect her, but six more guardmoles came on aggressively to stop any possibility of effective resistance.

'Well, which one's Tryfan?' he asked Teasel.

She stared at him blankly.

'My name's Teasel,' she said, 'and I do not know why you're here. This is Longest Night.'

Drule nodded to the two guardmoles who brought Teasel within reach of him. He stretched out a great fat taloned paw and grabbed her by the throat and pulled her bodily to him.

The action was so fast and violent that the watching group gasped and stared dumbstruck.

Then he held Teasel out from his side and slowly raised her up, his talons tightening about her throat and her cries muffled and choking. Her old paws struggled pathetically at the air and her mouth opened in pain.

'She's not Tryfan,' said Drule looking away from her and back at the defenceless moles huddled by the Stone, 'so which one is?'

The group parted and Tryfan came out from among them.

'Leave her be,' he said. '*I* am Tryfan of Duncton.'

564

Slowly, too slowly it seemed, Drule lowered Teasel to the ground. His grip did not slacken.

'Keep him by the Stone,' he ordered. 'Group the others behind me and take no nonsense from any that resist.'

He let go of Teasel and she fell sideways on to the ground, her mouth open to the soil, her left paw trying pathetically to reach up to her throat. The atmosphere was heavy with fear.

'Let me go to her,' said Feverfew, trying to struggle past a guardmole.

'Hold her,' said Drule. 'Now separate them off. . . .'

Despite Tryfan's earlier request, there was some attempt at resistance, led now by Hay and Madder, and there were shouts and struggles as none of them wanted to leave Tryfan, least of all Feverfew.

'Myn luve, myn luve. . . .'

In the brief and hopeless fray, Hay was taloned unconscious, Madder was viciously mauled, and Feverfew was dragged bodily away, her paws literally pulled out of Tryfan's as she was taken to the others, and he was surrounded by guardmoles and forced to stance still by the Stone.

Herded at the far end of the clearing in the shadows away from the Stone, some of the old moles wept, but most slumped and stared, and a few tended to those who had been hurt. Then two moles came and dragged the half-conscious form of Teasel back to where the others were.

'She's dying!' cried out one of the moles. 'You've killed her.'

Drule smirked and picked his teeth while outside the clearing Clowder gave quiet orders. 'Aye, stay there . . . the Master-elect will come this way . . . no, the Keepers first . . . oh, aye, they've got the mole Tryfan by the Stone.'

For his part the old scribemole stanced still in the Stone's shadow, unheeding now of the commotions around him, dignified, gentle.

565

He looked at Drule and asked, 'Why do you hurt us and ours?'

There was no answer that Drule could make, but nor did he try to or care. He turned to one of his minions, out of sight beyond the clearing, and said, 'Tell the Twelfth Keeper we have the mole Tryfan here.'

''Tis done, Sir.'

The sense that Tryfan and the others already had – that the events that were overtaking them were quite beyond their control – was now increased by the sound of a deep and guttural chanting that began to come out of the High Wood about them.

Nomole can adequately describe that sound nor the growing horror they felt as it began to be accompanied by the tramp-tramp of paws through the undergrowth, getting ever nearer.

Then suddenly two columns of moles, chanting their processional more loudly, came out into the clearing and began to circle the edge of it, one column on either side. The impact on the Duncton moles was all the worse because they had no idea what they were seeing, or that these moles were sideem and senior guardmoles come to welcome the Master-elect to his place of ordination.

For Tryfan and the others the sounds were so alien to anything they had ever heard, so in opposition to the grace and Silence of the Stone, so freakish among the wintry trees of the High Wood, that the feathers of a raven might have turned red in the sky and its flight left a trail of blood among the clouds and it would have seemed less strange, less ominous.

Deep the chant, incomprehensible the words, as over it a guardmole commanded, 'Be still for the Keepers there, stop shifting about.' At this moment the eldrene Wort slipped into the clearing, and took a stance adjacent to the place the moles of the Word were using as an entrance.

'What's happening?' one of the Duncton moles began.

There was a tussle, a sickening thump, a moan, and he was silenced by a guardmole. The rest were mute.

The chant deepened and quickened and into the clearing came the Keepers who, but for Mallice and Clowder, were old and slow, and moved unrhythmically, their very discordance evidence of their seniority and importance. Some looked about, some kept their snouts to the ground, Mallice, eyes alight, gazed up at the Stone and then, whispering to Clowder, pointed at Tryfan.

The Keepers were disposed by Slighe near where Drule had been watching over the proceedings, and he retreated to the side, and near the Stone. Now, except for Tryfan, who remained captive by the Stone, the Duncton moles were barely visible at the back.

As suddenly as it had started the chanting stopped, and a dreadful, awesome silence fell. The summary assault on anymole that spoke seemed to have quietened the Duncton moles, though sometimes one of the confused ones spoke loudly or cried out, and one mole was softly sobbing.

'Shut the bitch up,' hissed a guardmole.

'It's all right,' whispered one of the females, herself half crying, 'she'll not make another sound.'

'She won't if she does!' growled a guardmole.

Two figures moved in the gloom beyond the clearing in the direction from which the sideem and Keepers had come. But for Tryfan, all the moles looked that way, the Duncton moles too, for as well as fear there was a terrible fascination about the scene. Only Tryfan did not look, but stared at the ground before him, though his posture did not speak of defeat or subjection but, rather, of deep sadness.

Then from out of the gloom came Terce, and just behind him, looking at his most powerful and healthy, came Lucerne, his head up, his eye first on the Stone, than on Tryfan beneath it.

'Is that the mole Tryfan?' asked Terce of Wort who was just nearby.

'It is, Twelfth Keeper. Tryfan of Duncton.'

Lucerne came forward and whispered to Terce who, moving to one side, came forward with him. Any fears the Twelfth Keeper had that the Stone might dominate the moles of the Word in general were proved false. It was the tension between Tryfan and Lucerne which dominated, each facing the other, the younger mole staring at the older arrogantly, the older still and looking at the ground.

'So,' said Lucerne, 'you are Tryfan.'

Slowly Tryfan looked up and stared back. By the pale light that shone down, the scars on his face and about his eyes were impenetrable shadows. Certainly he was sad, but it was hard to judge if he was angry as well.

'This is a holy night,' said Tryfan, 'and we are worshipping. Join us.'

A faint smile came to Lucerne's face.

'Do you know whatmole I am?' he asked. 'Look at me, Tryfan of Duncton.'

'I know whatmole you must be,' said Tryfan.

'Then look proud when you look at me!' said Lucerne. Did some hint of recognition come to Tryfan's face then? Some mixture of alarm, of hope, of surprise, of horror? Whatever he felt he did not betray it, but said icily, 'I have many failings, mole, but pride in you is not likely to be one of them.'

There was a brief laugh from Hay among the Duncton moles followed by a thump as he was hit, and from Wort there was a sharp intake of breath expressing horror that the Master-elect had been insulted.

'Release the moles of this system, celebrate Longest Night with us though you be of a different faith, be not afraid of us,' said Tryfan.

'I am thy son, Tryfan. I am Lucerne of Whern; I am thy Master-elect come to be ordained. Welcome me in the spirit in which I come.'

The guardmoles maintained their solid silence, Mallice stared with unadulterated glee, Wort half closed her eyes and prayed and only the Duncton moles moved and expressed anything – and it was surprise, confusion, disbelief.

'His son? Master-elect? Lucerne?'

'We welcome all moles, Lucerne, whatever moles they are, whatever their faith,' said Tryfan. 'We welcome them in the spirit of the Stone.'

A mole watching that scene then would have seen Lucerne stiffen a little before this reply, and two others shift their gaze from Tryfan to Lucerne: Mallice and Terce. They saw anger in Lucerne, and knew it came not from what Tryfan said, but what in Lucerne's eyes he had not done: he did not respond in any way to Lucerne's declaration that he was his son. It might have been anymole who had come, anymole Tryfan was welcoming.

'Renounce thy Stone,' said Lucerne, his voice suddenly harsh. Never had three words spoken in that hallowed place seemed more threatening or more bleak; but never did a reply sound more final.

'I cannot.'

Son to father, father to son; Word to Stone, Stone to Word.

'I shall make thee, mole.'

'Lucerne, you cannot,' replied Tryfan, speaking for the first and only time in a voice that sounded like a father to a son, but it was a voice of weary warning, not of love.

Lucerne tried one last time.

'This holy night, here, now, might be your proudest moment, Tryfan of Duncton. Your son shall be ordained the Master of the Word. In the name of the Word I abjure you to renounce thy Stone that we may rejoice together.'

'Moule, Tryfan moule shal nat renege upon owre Stane,' said Feverfew from behind, her voice warm and maternal, as if she spoke to a youngster. 'He cannat renege upon himself. The Stane ys and namoule may gainsay ytt.'

'She speaks true,' said Tryfan, slowly turning from Lucerne to face the Stone. It was a gesture of such final dismissal that some say the two guardmoles at his side were later executed for allowing this insult to the Master-elect to take place. But from that moment on the fate of Tryfan, and perhaps the other moles as well, was sealed.

If Tryfan had intended to speak out a prayer to the Stone he was prevented from doing so, for he was dragged, at Drule's quick command, to one side, and, shrugging, Lucerne turned to Terce and nodded, and without more ado, or chance of change, the ordination of Lucerne of Whern, Master of the Word, glorious in his faith, learned of the Twelve Cleaves, began.

Terce, Twelfth Keeper and most senior, spoke the first words, saying, 'A Master is called by the Word to work with his fellow Keepers and with the anointed sideem as servant among the moles to whom he has been sent. It is a holy office and he is successor to great Scirpus, receiver of the Cleave. Hear now. . . .'

What the disbelieving followers heard was a recitation by the Twelve Keepers of what being Master meant, as expounded in the scrivenings of past Masters since the first beginnings of that malevolent office. So long did this go on that they might have been forgiven for thinking that they had no role in the rites they were witnessing.

But then the infamous litany and suffrages of that rite began, when each Keeper in turn cried out to the Word to spare the Master from a succession of sins he might commit. . . .

'From all evil and mischief; from sin; from the crafts and assaults of the Stone; from thy wrath . . . *Spare us, good Word, and accept this the Master's anointing!*'

From the first of these pleas in the litany the waiting followers knew what their terrible role was to be. For as it was uttered Hay was dragged, struggling and angry, from the Duncton group and held helplessly against the Stone as Drule came out and stanced hugely over him.

Then Terce asked him, 'Do you, mole of the Stone, accept the Word's rule and this thy Master?'

'I do not!' cried out Hay, eyes blazing.

Terce turned to Tryfan and said, 'Thou hast the power to save the life of this sinning mole: renounce in his name.'

570

'Do not do so,' said brave Hay as Drule readied his talons for a crushing strike.

'I cannot speak for anymole but myself,' said Tryfan.

There was no second chance. Terce nodded grimly to Drule and then was the Word's way known, then was the power of its way seen. Back went the talons of dread Drule, and with a sudden intake of breath his talons thrust down: foul the crushing life-taking noise as he thrust hard into the snout and face of Hay.

But worse came then and evil was seen before the Stone.

'Holy Word, my mother and my father . . .' As the eldrene Wort whispered her obscene litanies a Keeper came forward, thrust his own talons into the still-living head of Hay and, taking his blood, anointed Lucerne across the brow.

'By this blood of Atonement thy sins shall flee, by this first sacrifice the Word shall be satisfied in thee as Master.'

No sooner was this rite complete than another Keeper came forward, another suffrage spoken, and another victim dragged forward to the Stone.

'From all blindness of mind; from pride and hypocrisy; from envy, hatred and malice; from desire of the flesh, and thy wrath . . . *Spare us, good Word!*'

So harmless Thrift, who had once stanced at this spot and saved Tryfan's life, died. Then another Keeper, another demand for renunication of the Stone, another refusal, another death. . . .

From lustful thought, from wrong fornication, from deceit, from plague of mind and spirit, from thy wrath . . . *Spare us, good Word!*'

Teasel, already half dead, had her head crushed by Drule against the Stone. Another Keeper, another victim. . . .

Even the most steadfast mole who heard of that grim time finds that a pall of horror numbs his mind, and he sees the events that now followed with disbelief. Why did not Tryfan speak? Why did not a mole like Hay fight more? Why do such things happen at all?

571

A mole may be unable to answer such questions, but he cannot turn his back on them. If he is to reach the Silence that the Stone brings he must know that such obstructions to his getting there as evil, or wickedness, or greed, or the desire for power such as Lucerne had, cannot be bypassed. No route exists to Silence, nor tunnel be delved, that does not pass through the shadow of suffering, the mists of moles' selfish ambition, and the bleak dark of evil.

Tryfan, who had seen and felt so much, now saw and felt much more than anymole should bear.

For constantly, in the hours that followed in the ritual ordination of Lucerne, he was asked, 'Renounce the Stone, Tryfan, and these moles need not be sacrificed. The Word shall take your renunciation in place of the sacred anointing by their blood, the Word shall be merciful. Renounce.'

On and on they were brought to the base of the great Stone. While between each murder – or sacrifice as the Word liturgists would have us call it – Terce and other of the Keepers proceeded with the arcane and filthy rite of blood anointment which Lucerne chose, and all about, obscene in its growing rhythm, like the mating of two mutant grikes, the sideem on each side of the Master-elect, chanted their blood-lustful chant.

Madder, most pitifully calling out for his friend to forgive him, as if, after so long, Dodder had anything to forgive.

Then Dodder quickly followed.

'Do you . . . ?'

'He is not of the Stone,' growled Tryfan.

'He is lax to be with thee,' hissed the eldrene Wort, the only words she said.

'I do not renounce, and nor must Tryfan for me,' said Dodder with dignity.

A nod and Drule killed him, and his warm blood was touched (this time) to Lucerne's mouth and his sickening whispered prayers underlay the chant.

Flint. Crying. How great the Stone seemed over him, how shining now its face. Flint died.

Feverfew, and whispers.

'This is the mother of the Stone Mole, Master-elect.'

'Does she renounce?' Lucerne's voice was indifferent to Feverfew and what she was, but driving on towards the climax of the ordination.

The very trees seemed stricken then, the crescent moon to bow its head, the wind to haunt among the roots, and flee.

For the first time Tryfan broke down, his head bowed low, and began to speak to save her life. But Feverfew, unafraid, her eyes filled with love as she looked at him, said, 'Myn luve, do nat doe so. Wat wee yaf hadde, ytt was ynough, ytt yss far more yan thidde trublit moule Lucerne canne ever hav.'

Terce nodded, Drule thrust, and the very Stone seemed to shudder in the night as Feverfew slumped and died at the very place where she had given birth to the Stone Mole.

So the last anointing was performed and all was still, all chanting done for now.

Then Terce, who had begun the rite, now brought it to its conclusion with the concluding liturgy.

'Receive the Spirit of the Word here now, Lucerne of Whern, as I Twelfth Keeper place my paw upon thy head in token of the faith that all moles of the Word have in thee. Remember that thou strengthen the weak and faltering spirit which is in us by thy supremacy as exemplar of the power, wrath and purpose of the Word. Teach, exhort, and impose upon us the Word's holy will by whatever means you choose and we shall be obedient to thy will. Minister discipline, show no mercy to the lax and to the wicked, or to the Word's enemies. Lead us and we shall follow thee whom now at last, for the first time and forever, we call Master. Master Lucerne, Master of the Word!'

'Master Lucerne! Master!' The sideem joyously cried

out his name, and the moles milled forward, reaching out to touch him. The guardmoles smiled, the Keepers nodded and looked pleased, and all talked and revelled, and were glad for the Master before the Stone.

But Tryfan, still close-guarded, could only stare blankly at the broken bodies of his friends, blankly at the blood-anointed thing that was his son, and blankly at the Stone. And weep for Feverfew.

The moon turned in the sky, Longest Night was long in its Word revelries by the Stone, until at last, in groups, the guardmoles and the sideem and the Keepers left to go back down through the night to the cross-under, leaving only three moles by the Stone: the new Master, the creature Drule, his talons red with gore, and fated Tryfan.

Lucerne came close to Tryfan, for the old mole seemed half dead.

'Father, I ask you one last time, renounce the Stone.' He whispered the words, and there was a pleading in them that only Drule would have been allowed to hear.

Tryfan shook his head, his eyes low.

'Look at me, mole. I am thy Master now. Thy Stone is dead. Look at me.'

Slowly Tryfan looked at him.

'I . . . I . . .' Then he struggled in Drule's great paws to look at the Stone and cried out in anguish, 'Forgive me, Stone, I cannot love him. He is of me, but love him I cannot. Take the sight of him from out of my eyes, for the burden is too great. Let me die.'

Lucerne stared at him, puzzlement giving way to an anger and hatred all the more horrible for being so controlled.

'The Stone shall answer your prayer, mole, in the form of Drule it shall do it. But not of death. There is no need for that. But thy Master whom you cannot bear to see, you shall not see again. Drule, blind him, just as my grandfather Rune should have done long ago.'

Then Lucerne turned from his father, turned from the

Stone, turned from the clearing of Duncton Wood and, as Drule's talons lunged down one last time, the Master left the place of his ordination behind. Then Drule pulled back from where Tryfan lay, his face all blood, looked up at the Stone with a sneer, stared at the blood and bodies that lay about its base, spat on them dismissively, and followed his Master out of Duncton Wood.

Cold, cold that Longest Night. The sky, the stars, the moon uncomforting. How slowly the darkness waned away to dawn. When it did, and light crept to Duncton's Stone again, the bodies there were all turned white, white with frost.

While before them on the ground lay Tryfan, his breath light steam before him. His face was encrusted with blood, and his back fur thick with rime, his breathing slow.

Dawn light touched the Stone above, but where Tryfan lay was a darkness blacker than the night.

PART IV

Beechenhill

Chapter Twenty-Six

Yet though the tide of the Word was running strong with the new crusade, and had spread across moledom once more and threatened to engulf the Stone for ever more, one place succeeded in rising above it that notorious Longest Night. There the Stone shone bright and its followers found growing hope and faith in themselves. That place was Caer Caradoc.

Already by the morning that followed Longest Night Word messengers were hastening from Ginnell's emplacements on the Marches, and the news they carried would not well please the new Master when it reached him.

To make sure he got it, some went to Cannock, others by the south-western route to Buckland, but the message was the same: 'Master, Caer Caradoc is taken, grant me permission to re-take it with all the freedom for severity and punishment at our command.'

Meanwhile, Ginnell was fretting and furious, unable to take his eyes for very long from the prospect that dominated his north-western view: the arduous incline of Caer Caradoc.

'Now, now we should attack,' he muttered angrily to himself. '*Now!*'

Yet he dared not, for his orders expressly forbade him making any assault at all along the Marches, for fear that it would be premature and might lead to a uniting of the Welsh followers and an action that would take matters out of control and divert attention from Lucerne's main aim, which was not war but utter subjugation, death of the very spirit of the Stone.

In this Ginnell shared the frustration of all commanders in the field, who see battles and wars lost because they cannot act when they know they must.

'Sir, we must attack, we *must!*' said Haulke, one of his youngest commanders, and the best. 'Each hour that passes means days, months and many more lives lost later.'

'I cannot allow you to do it, Haulke, right though you may be. The Master is Master of the Word, to disobey his orders is a blasphemy for which we would all be culpable.'

'But he's only Master-*elect*, surely.'

'He *was* Master-elect until last night, but then he was ordained. I warned you what I would have to do, Haulke. He is the Word's representative on earth, and I know what his orders are, or were when I saw him and Clowder in Cannock.'

'If he was here. . . .'

'He is not, Haulke. When I was in Cannock he made as clear as anymole could what his strategy was: *no* attacks. A single strike would be made for now, a mortal blow upon the Stone. The killing phase of the crusade comes later.'

Haulke stared disbelieving at the harsh profile of Caer Caradoc and said, 'The Master is a bloody fool.'

'Haulke, if you were not my best commander I would have you dismissed for that. But as it is . . .' Ginnell turned his battle-wearied gaze towards the object of their argument, 'I agree that *not* taking it is a folly beyond my wish to start imagining. But as for bloody fools, I shall pretend I did not hear what you said.'

'Pretend what you damn well like, Ginnell *Sir*, but this failure will result in more dead to capture a position we could have taken without a struggle two days ago, and might have taken last night if those guardmoles had done what I damn well said.'

Haulke stormed off and stopped some way downslope, stared once more and then roared, 'Shit! I'm looking at the biggest disaster in all the campaigns of the Word. If the Master . . .' But guardmoles were listening, and Haulke thought better of saying in public what he had already said in private to Ginnell.

Which was just as well, for had he done so, Ginnell would have had to have him killed.

Their argument had started over what had seemed a trivial thing, though one whose origins they could not have known.

At the conclave called by Alder in Siabod in the autumn years it had been decided that while Alder attempted to reoccupy the lower slopes of Siabod, Troedfach of Tyn-y-Bedw would travel east and occupy deserted Caer Caradoc, more as a matter of caution and pride than anything else.

So it had been, and the moles of the Marches had left Siabod cheerily, with great Alder saying that when he had succeeded in dealing with the 'little matter of the grikes in lower Siabod' he would leave that system in the paws of young Gowre, and travel on to Caer Caradoc himself for old time's sake – he felt he had started his Welsh campaign at Caer Caradoc and had a fancy to see the place again; and anyway, it was best to leave a mole like Gowre to do what he must alone, once he had been put in charge of Siabod itself.

Troedfach and Gareg of Merthyr, the best of the younger leaders, had travelled east together with Caradoc in their company, and by the time they neared the Marches once more Gareg had persuaded Troedfach to let him and a few moles take Caer Caradoc.

'You can assess its defences and later we'll privily send moles up there and occupy it properly,' said Troedfach. 'No need to draw attention to ourselves or Ginnell will be up there in no time and our task will be hard. He's no fool, that one: I know, I've been fighting him for years.'

So it might have worked out, but for the accident, unknown to the Welsh followers, of Ginnell's absence in Cannock at that time. For Haulke had been left in charge and, as ambitious young commanders often are, he was critical of the command above him.

There had long been a tradition that neither side

occupied Caer Caradoc. Because the Stones there were unattractive to more traditional moles of the Word, and because the Welsh moles of the Marches did not have the local molepower to garrison it, neither side had bothered with the place.

But staring up at it and in sole command, with that acquisitive abandon younger moles without responsibilities and a knowledge of the broader issues so often enjoy, Haulke decided that the traditional view was wrong.

He had therefore chosen an idle moment in early November to lead a few guardmoles up to Caer Caradoc and, finding not a solitary mole in sight, had there deployed them for a time. He called it 'campaign practice' and replaced the first patrol with another, knowing well that when Ginnell returned he could call his moles down once more and matters could go back to normal. On the other paw, he might just persuade Ginnell that he was right, and the occupation could remain in place. The more he thought about it and got to know the site, the more certain he became of Caer Caradoc's importance.

Naturally, having no reason to think that Caer Caradoc was other than unoccupied, as it always had been, Gareg began to ascend its western slopes, guided by Caradoc himself, thinking of the climb merely as an opportunity to see an Ancient System that was unlikely –whatever old Caradoc might think – to be colonised again. They took four moles with them and proceeded slowly, for Caer Caradoc is rough and steep and not a place moles go up fast.

It was Caradoc, who knew and loved the place so well, who first sensed that something was not right. Initially he simply scented uneasily ahead, thinking not of mole but predator and scanned the skies, for kestrel hover there and raven have been known to stoop on moles. Then he slowed, narrowed his eyes and looked all about.

'Something wrong?' said Gareg, signalling to his well-trained moles to keep an especially low snout.

'No, no,' said Caradoc, 'I'm just getting tired, see? 'Tis old fears of mine surfacing. There's surely nomole here.'

But Gareg, cautious, experienced and respectful of hunches, called a halt and snouted at the rising slope above.

'Tell me the way the ground lies on the top,' he said.

''Tis more flat than sloping, though if there's high ground it's to the north where the Stones rise. The way we're climbing will take us to the centre of the place.'

'Any cover there?'

'Not much, just grass.'

Gareg snouted about again.

'So any moles on top would see and hear us?'

'See – yes, but hear, that all depends. The wind can deafen a mole up there. As pups we used to make sure we were downwind on Caradoc, and not a mole can hear you come.'

'If there were mole up there, *occupying* moles, where would they be?'

'But. . . .'

'Just supposing, Caradoc. Just supposing.'

'The Stones are near the high north end but the old system lies south of the Stones. There's some shelter there they'd use.'

'And routes?'

'Central, like the one we're using, and southern, but not to the north. Too steep, too dangerous. But why. . . ?'

'Because I am a cautious mole who has never yet been defeated by the grikes. One thing I know is this: if we have thought of occupying this place all of a sudden, then somemole of the Word has done the same. If you sense danger ahead then I shall proceed with care until I know we're safe. Anyway, I like this kind of ground and the grikes generally don't. Eh, lads?'

His guardmoles, all of whom had travelled from Merthyr in the south with him, nodded grimly. They were small, dark moles, and between themselves spoke their own soft-accented dialect.

'We'll contour round and take the north slope up, at its *steepest* point,' he said finally. 'The wind will carry sound away from the top, and scenting will be in our favour.'

'Gareg . . .' began Caradoc uneasily.

'Do you want Caer Caradoc for the Stone one day?'

'It is already of the Stone, mole,' said Caradoc.

'Aye, like that Avebury, like Duncton Wood. They were too. No, mole, I know ground like this. But if it's heights you're afraid of, stay by me and you'll be safe enough.'

They proceeded exactly as Gareg had suggested, though it took them much longer than they had expected. Only when they reached the very top of the north end, climbing between great buttresses of rock, did they stop. There they were so sheltered that the wind was all gone, but Caradoc had warned them what to expect. Suddenly, in a matter of a few paces, they rose out of the wind-shadow into the wind itself and it seemed set on blowing them off their paws, roaring in their ears and parting their fur.

To talk they had to shout, and Gareg did not want that so they proceeded in single file and in hunched silence until they reached the most northerly of the Stones and, breathless, eased thankfully into its shelter.

It was immediately plain that Gareg's caution had been wise, for mole paw-prints old and new covered the muddy ground about the Stone. Gareg's moles knew their job well and quickly deployed themselves to right and left while Gareg himself crept carefully around the Stone, with Caradoc just behind him.

There, not far downslope of them, stanced two grikes, eating and having one of those fierce and cheerful arguments males who know each other well sometimes enjoy; while yet further off, one on either side of a narrow strip of land at that end of Caer Caradoc, watched two more. The wind blew from the south and so sound and scent favoured the followers and unless they were unlucky there was no likelihood the grikes would see them.

One of Gareg's moles crept down to him.

'We can take them any time we like. From this upslope position and against the wind they'll not know we're on them until they feel our talons plunge, and then it'll be too late.'

Gareg nodded, and agreed it was tempting. Very. He looked about him for the first time, relaxed, and said, 'This is a place and a half – why all moledom lies at our paws!' It was true enough, for the country spread out east and west and north of them, while to the south Caer Caradoc itself ran, its great Stones and rock outcrops giving way to the shallow slopes of grassy, heather-bound fell which much of it comprises.

'Shall we take them, Sir?'

Some inner instinct cautioned Gareg against it. If they took the grikes now then others would quickly be on to them and then it would depend on who had the biggest force. . . .

Even as he pondered it there occurred one of those shifts of circumstance that force moles to act so quickly that only through experience, nerve, and a sound grasp of tactics can they hope to gain advantage from it.

They heard a good-natured roar from one of the eating moles below them, their argument suddenly erupted into a mock fight, one buffeted the other and chased him straight upslope towards where Gareg and the others stanced in hiding.

Some strategists who have analysed the long and tragic campaigns between moles of the Word and Stone go so far as to say that the decision Gareg of Merthyr was forced to make in the few moments he then had was more critical than any other single decision a commander ever made. In that moment he showed the command and decisiveness that was later to be so much needed by the forces of the Stone.

Most moles would have said there were but two choices: to wait their moment and emerge fighting, or to turn and flee, hoping surprise and superior speed would take them safely out of harm's way downslope.

But there was a third option, and it depended on Gareg's extraordinary analysis of the implications of either course of action, and his appreciation, as he stanced there, of the strategic potential and its importance for morale that Caer Caradoc had for the moles of the Stone. If Caer Caradoc was to be taken, it was best done in the way and at a time that suited moles of the Stone, not hastily in a skirmish, which if they won it – and Gareg had no doubt they could – would force the grikes to reoccupy from their strong base, while moles of the Stone would have to defend a position they were not yet ready to. Better to bide their time and choose their moment well. Yet if they were seen – whether fighting or fleeing – the grikes would know they had an interest in the place, and either take it back in force, or occupy it and make it impregnable.

These were the thoughts the young mole had and with no more time at paw he gave the riskiest command a mole could at such a juncture.

'Freeze!' he cried. '*Freeze!*'

His own moles were obedient to his word. Caradoc, not being a fighting mole, was inclined to protest but as the two great guardmoles all unawares rushed nearer he saw the sense in Gareg's order. The slightest movement would be seen.

Up came the guardmoles, turned, joked, played, so close that the breathless moles of the Stone could smell their sweat, then closer still. Why, one seemed to pause and look straight at Caradoc but he stanced as still as ice and the mole saw him not. Were they made invisible as some have said? Perhaps. Gareg never thought so, but only said that if there was ever a time he believed the Stone loved him *personally*, it was then.

Tiring of their play the grikes turned and went back downslope, and as soon as they were out of the line of Gareg's and the other moles' vision he ordered the retreat, and not until they were far down the steep northern slope did they dare breathe again.

By then poor Caradoc's ragged fur was wet with sweat

and strain, and he was shaking his head and saying, 'I never thought that *not* fighting would be more of a strain than fighting, but so it seems to be.'

This secret retreat had been the preface to what must have been one of the most clandestine occupations of an important site in all mole history. For the moment Troedfach heard Gareg's report he too saw the implications and approved what Gareg had done.

'Aye, we must make them think we have no interest in the place and then build up our forces until we have the strength to take it quickly and hold it so strongly that the grikes will not risk taking it back.'

'Longest Night,' said Caradoc without hesitation. 'That'll be the time they'll least expect us to occupy it. Plenty of time for us to build up our forces until then.'

'Aye and meanwhile we recce the place and establish the best way of taking it over,' said Gareg. Troedfach nodded and growled, 'You make me feel old, Gareg. When I was your age I would have stayed where I was and fought it out, but now it's all feints and shadows and calculation. I wish I were younger than I am. How differently I'd do things!

'But be patient with me over this for it will take until Longest Night at least to get all the moles we'll need from other parts. We do not want to weaken ourselves just north and south of here.'

Troedfach's watchers reported every grike movement from that day on, and naturally could not understand the inexplicable withdrawal of moles from its heights soon after the first incident. They were not privy to the fact that Ginnell was back from Cannock, and Haulke had felt it prudent to withdraw his patrols.

Meanwhile, well hidden and without even the moles themselves knowing the reason, forces were brought in from Troedfach's system to the south, and Gaelri's to the north. The decision was made to persuade Alder to delay the occupation of the lower Siabod slopes lest that action encourage more activity and movement along the western front and delay the arrival of Troedfach's reinforcements. But even without that precaution Ginnell still put pressure on along the line, and slowed Troedfach's movement of moles up so that even the day before Longest Night moles were still not assembled in numbers, or quite near enough, to complete the rapid assault Gareg proposed.

'Well, we'll hurry them, mole,' promised Troedfach, 'for I agree that it would be a good time to reoccupy Caer Caradoc in the name of the Stone. Should have done it moleyears ago.'

But that same day, all unknown to Gareg, Haulke at last prevailed on Ginnell to let him occupy Caer Caradoc. His own spies had seen the moles of the Stone showing an interest in the place and he used the dubious argument that if the deed was done before Longest Night and the Master's ordination – in short, while Lucerne was still 'merely' Master-elect – it could not be said to be breaking the Word's law. Then, too, there was a certain satisfaction in taking an Ancient System of the Stone at Longest Night, even if it was a disregarded one.

'Should have done it years ago!' said Ginnell, in unknowing echo of his great adversary. 'But you've got only until the moon begins to wane on Longest Night, for that's when Lucerne's to be ordained. After that, if you've not occupied the place you'll retreat. Understand?'

'Yes *Sir*!' Haulke had cried out.

But what instincts drive fighting moles to know where to be, and when? How was it that a day before Longest Night Gareg was moved to take an especially strong patrol up the northern incline to the very top? Was it 'just to have a final look' as he said? On such hunches the outcome of fighting moles' lives depend.

Why, too, that same day, did Haulke suddenly get concerned about what seemed a simple unopposed occupation, and decide to bring forward by half a day his massive occupation of the top, approaching from the south-eastern side? Nomole can say, but so it was.

And so it was, too, that at dusk of the last night before

588

Longest Night there took place the first of what moles have come to call the Battles of the Caradoc Stones.

Gareg ascended to the Stones shortly before the light began to fade, and decided to do the one thing he himself had not done ever since he first mooted the best way to take Caer Caradoc, and crossed past the Stone to look at the flat, exposed slopes of the central part of the place.

Then, just as chance had so nearly permitted the grikes to know he was there, so now chance beckoned him and brought him to the very edge of Caer Caradoc's south-eastern edge as Haulke's force of many moles confidently ascended towards the very top.

The plan that had so long been in the making now seemed on the very brink of foundering even before the occupation of the moles of the Stone had began. So many assembling, so many almost ready, but most too far off to deploy with speed.

Gareg watched the moles below approaching and assessed the position rapidly. His own force of eight moles looked pitifully small against the many coming up towards him, and yet . . . and yet his had the advantage of height, surprise and, surely, purpose. Perhaps if Longest Night had not been almost on them Gareg would have retreated, but he looked balefully around, saw the Stones and Caer Caradoc which courageous Caradoc had so long argued for, and summoned his moles to him.

'We are eight and they are many, many more. You all know me well, and know that I am not a mole to hesitate.' They nodded, and one or two who had not already peered down at the advancing moles went and did so and came back looking dour. Then he continued: 'Yet here and now I do not know what to do. To retreat is the sensible thing, and we shall be safe, but we shall never reoccupy Caer Cardoc. If we stance firm and fight all we can hope for is to hold them off until Troedfach can be informed and gets moles up here, but even then I doubt if we're enough to hold these moles off for long. If

589

they get over the steep edge here then I fear our chances of survival are low.

'I shall not issue an order but ask you to agree to this: if all of us say we stance, then all shall do so. But if only one of you declines, all of us will leave, and that one who decides against shall not be harshly judged, but respected for courage to retreat and we shall follow. So, all or none of us. Which is it to be?'

There was no sound then but that of wind in heather, and among the distant Stones.

Gareg looked at each mole one by one. He knew them all, and well: five were of Merthyr, and close to him, the other three were Troedfach's and strong moles. Only one of them was younger than Gareg.

Some nodded their agreement immediately, others more slowly, and the last, the wise fighter Brecon, went and looked again and came back and said, 'If we stance here and do it we'll be bloody fools and chances are we'll die. But if we live then it's heroes that we'll be, and after so many grubby years scurrying about being a hero will suit me well. As for retreating, if we do it we'll never know what might have been and I'd not like that. Aye, I'm for it. Eight of us can kill four times as many grikes.'

'Seven of us,' said Gareg, 'for I'm ordering one of you down to warn Troedfach. You, mole, you'll go.' He pointed to the youngest and waved away his protest. 'Go on, mole, you're the fastest of us, and we'll promise not to finish them all off before you get back.'

Then quickly, with dusk falling, those brave seven were deployed by Gareg in such positions that each supported the other well, and had room to move back and forth along the top so that the grikes coming up would find it hard to tell how many were there.

They gave no warning of their defence but, knowing that surprise would demoralise the grikes, killed the first guardmole as he unsuspectingly came over the ridge's top, and then the next and then a third.

Those were the easiest deaths. For the grikes retreated,

reformed, and began to mount a determined assault on what they naturally assumed was a heavy force of followers. But Gareg had chosen his ground well, and there was something about the looming Stones as night fell that worried the grikes and slowed them down.

On and on into the night went the fight, bloody, violent, a struggle to the death. Only when three of Gareg's moles had died did the first grike succeed in coming over the edge. Even then, most cleverly, using every hollow and shelter they could find, Gareg's moles, all wounded, all tired, succeeded in confusing the grikes and making them think there were many more defending than there were.

Only as dawn light came did the stark truth become plain to the astonished grikes – their adversaries numbered only four, and all were wounded, all retreating up the rising ground north towards the Stones.

If Haulke had brought up all his moles at first there would have been no contest. If his moles had not been fooled into thinking that the position was held by many more moles than it was, then he might have pushed much harder much sooner. If Troedfach could have been reached sooner than he was. . . .

So many ifs.

But by dawn the battle was all but lost, and Haulke, seeing now how few were against his moles, himself advanced to the very front and shouted out his terms. He was, like Ginnell, a mole who respected other fighters.

'Surrender now and you'll get away alive but if you don't. . . .'

'Aye, and if we don't?' cried out Gareg, emerging from behind the greatest of the Stones and staring down at where so many moles were ranged against him, their bodies cut, their looks murderous, their numbers too great to resist for more than seconds now.

For a long moment Haulke looked at the mole who had resisted his might for so long.

'. . . And if you don't, and try to retreat down the northern slope, we'll have you all dead.'

No good crying 'freeze' now! Yet to his enemies it seemed that Gareg was about to give an order, for he half turned and spoke to one of the three who still stanced with him.

'Well?' roared Haulke.

'We are protected by the Stones!' cried Gareg.

'Protected by shit!' shouted Haulke. 'Take them!'

Gareg came forward and with an ancient shout seemed to call a Welsh curse of the Stone upon the grikes. As Haulke and his moles hunched forward to climb up the slope and take Gareg and the others, there occurred that which even the moles of the Word never forgot.

For out of the dark dawn sky behind Gareg loomed a great mole, and at his flanks others, and then all about the Stones, and they came past Gareg, and the great mole took command by giving the oldest command of them all.

'Charge!' thundered Troedfach. 'And kill!'

Aye, up the night-dark slopes they had come guided by Caradoc to the very point where Troedfach had rightly guessed they must retreat. And out of the dawn they charged.

Yet Haulke, a great commander in the making too, did not panic. He and his moles retreated quickly, back and back again to the edge where they had first encountered Gareg, even to those positions that Gareg had until then used so effectively.

'We've until the moon's wane!' cried Haulke, and so the bigger, even bloodier battle began. Through the day it went, the followers outnumbered yet fighting with the Stones behind them, and mightily. On and on, using those few reinforcements they had at the best moments, retreating deliberately to counterattack again, on and on that day.

Until dusk came once more, and Caer Caradoc was littered with dead, and the followers were in retreat again. Yet on they fought, into Longest Night as the moon rose and each felt that even to raise a paw to strike again was beyond his strength, yet raise his talons he did.

592

Disarray, mayhem, brutal fighting. The moon rose over it, on and on until at last it seemed that even Troedfach's intervention had not been enough and the battle was swinging back Haulke's way once again.

But, as it seemed to the followers, a miracle happened.

'Retreat! Retreat!'

'The buggers are retreating!' cried Gareg in astonishment.

'Ginnell says retreat!' and with that strange cry, Haulke and all his moles were gone and in Caer Caradoc the Word lost the night.

Troedfach did not hesitate one second. He entrenched his exhausted moles quickly, he sent messengers down and ordered a further advance up into Caer Caradoc the moment reinforcements arrived which, before dawn, they began to do.

Dawn came, the dead lay untouched, the wounded moaned their agonies untended. Entrench! Position! Deploy!

'Get our moles up here. Fast!'

Haulke's spies saw them do it. Haulke's spies said they could see that Troedfach's position was still insecure.

'Sir, we can still take Caer Caradoc, but we must move now, *now*.'

It was then that Ginnell had finally forbidden it, and yielded up Caer Caradoc to a force which at that time he might have destroyed, but soon, if it was increased and well deployed, a grike force five times as strong would find difficult to displace.

'But Sir . . .!' cried Haulke, coming back and trying one last time.

'No!' said Ginnell, 'it is too late.'

And by the end of the first day after Longest Night it was.

Thus did the first Battle of the Caradoc Stones come to an end, and a stirring tale it is, often told by moles of the Stone to keep their beleaguered spirits up. For what a contrast it is to the tragedy that befell the moles of Tryfan in Duncton that same night. Yet, when all is said, a mole must think and ask: whatmole did right? Tryfan, who did not raise a single talon to defend himself, or encourage others to do so? Or Gareg and Troedfach? Which of them was closer to the Stone? Which most in the spirit of the Stone Mole's teaching?

What might a mole lose if he kills others to save himself? What does a mole gain if he saves his enemy yet lets himself and his own be killed? Which is the way to Silence?

These questions old Caradoc asked himself as he wandered among the bodies strewn across the ground he loved.

'Not like this,' he whispered and wept. 'Not like this, Stone. Bring peace to this place and send thy Stone Mole that I may know thy peace will stay. Grant it to an old mole who has faith in thee, Stone.'

The wind took his words, and blew them about the Stones, and then out across moledom's darkened land.

Chapter Twenty-Seven

The Word may have prevailed in Duncton Wood on Longest Night, but it had not won the hearts of all the guardmoles who witnessed the deaths by the Stone, and by their presence were a part of them.

One guardmole, Romney of Keynes, the same who had witnessed the brave struggle Skint and Smithills had put up against such overwhelming odds and had muttered their rough epitaph, 'You brave bastards', had been more appalled than awed by the bloody rite of ordination.

Not that Romney was a weak mole, or one who until that night had ever faltered in the Word. But it happened that one of the moles he saw killed that night was one he knew and had special reason to be grateful to – Dodder. So he had tossed and turned all night in deep distress by the cross-under, quite unable to join in the celebrations that accompanied the new Master's triumphant exit from Duncton Wood.

For Romney had served with Dodder in days gone by and knew the old rascal well, knew him to be true to the Word and true to everymole under his command. More than that, Dodder had once saved Romney's life. So, seeing that old mole appear suddenly among the other moles put a face and personality to moles which until then he, like most others there, saw as mere fodder for the Word and for a rite.

Romney knew Dodder did not deserve such a death, and guessed that if such a mole as him stanced unflinchingly by the others then they did not deserve it either. Nor was Romney the only one who felt that way, for he heard others mutter their doubts, and had not moles like Drule and the eldrene Wort been about they might have muttered more.

595

But of them all, Romney was the only one so upset that the following morning he took advantage of the confusion and euphoria that followed the ordination, and wandered off to be by himself.

It is at such moments that a doubting mole gets confirmation of the truth that the Stone, silent though it usually is, is about us all the time, and sees what we do, and directs us to its way. When a mole prays 'Guide me! Help me!', the Stone, almost always, brings him help through another mole as much in need of help as he. Romney did not pray to the Stone for he was of the Word. But yet he gave out a heartfelt prayer for help to whatever power might help him, and a curse of anger against the Word that had just wreaked vengeance on a harmless mole he had once loved. Unable to get the sight of Dodder's final moment of defiance and of Drule's talons out of his mind Romney wandered bleakly about not knowing what to do with himself.

Of the moles from Rollright who had travelled with the mass of the sideem to serve their needs of food and tunnelling, there was one we know: Rampion, Holm's daughter, and one who had been witness to the touching of the Stone across the seven Ancient Systems that day in June with her father at the Rollright Stones.

Her father and she had made their escape from the guardmoles that distant day and, the system being lax and the summer languid, had succeeded in the course of time in returning to their different tunnels and resuming their life once more, sharing the common hope that one day the Stone Mole would come and the Word be put into retreat at last.

The experience in June had strengthened her and increased her faith, and, despairing of the Rollright followers who compromised themselves for favours from the eldrene and a comfortable life, she felt isolated in her faith. She served the guardmoles, she abased herself, she watched, and most of all she waited: for one day the Stone

596

Mole would come, he really would, and moles must be ready then, and strong, and knowledgeable.

So in her own way, with but her father Holm believing in what she did, she debased herself and curried favour with the guardmoles, and knew her time would come.

But the way it came took her by surprise. For when the eldrene Wort came to Rollright Rampion briefly saw her, and had that same shocked sense of recognition that Mistle had had in Hen Wood.

But Wort travelled on, Lucerne and his entourage came and Rollright bulged with guardmoles and sideem. It was a simple thing for trusted Rampion to have herself chosen as one of those to travel on to Duncton Wood to serve.

But such moles as she, though they knew the ordination was to take place, were not allowed near the cross-under itself. Nor were they told what had really been involved in the rite of ordination. But when dawn broke and they heard what some of the guardmoles were saying, they knew something bloody and evil had been apaw at the ritual. There was a look of violence in the eyes of the guardmoles, a wildness, and Rampion who had never been to Duncton Wood, nor knew much –though her father had come from there – beyond that it was outcast, feared something dire had happened.

She was curious and worried, and in half a mind to try to find a way past the sideem and the guards into the system itself. It was in the course of this abortive search for a route into Duncton that she saw the guardmole Romney, and sensed immediately that far from challenging her he was upset and needed help.

She knew enough to know that such moles talk.

'Mole, you are troubled. Was it . . . ?'

It needed no more than that. Romney saw a female, a server from Rollright, he saw her sympathetic stance, and he began to talk. And talk. The world grew still about her as she heard, for the implications of what she heard were plain enough. These same moles who had, it seemed, massacred Duncton moles by the Stone on Longest Night, would very soon return to Rollright. There, she surmised, they might easily massacre a second time. She must escape and return at once to Rollright.

She stared at the troubled guardmole, she saw his loss of faith, and the Stone guided her.

'What are you going to do, mole?'

'I don't know . . . I shouldn't have spoken. I cannot ever forget. I should not have spoken. If you. . . .'

'Mole,' said Rampion, and though her voice was gentle her spirit was firm, her purpose resolute, and she sensed that the Stone was giving her a task, 'I have no reason to speak of what you have told me, indeed I have a special reason *not* to. Well then, mole, let *me* tell *you* something that I should not: I am of the Stone.'

Romney looked surprised at such a confession, as well he might, for at the least it would normally mean an Atonement, at the worst it could mean death.

'Aye, it is so,' continued Rampion. 'Now listen. I am leaving here. I am going back to Rollright and I am going to warn the followers there that what this Drule and others did here in the name of the Word may soon be done in Rollright.'

'It was a rite,' said Romney defensively. 'They won't do it again so soon.'

Rampion laughed cynically.

'I am going anyway.'

'What do you want of me? To let you go without restraint? Of course I shall. . . .'

'No, I want you to come and bear witness for me. You saw what happened with your own eyes, I did not. They're a weak lot in Rollright and though my father would believe me most would not – or if they did they would not act on it. Therefore mole, if you would serve the memory of the mole Dodder you saw killed, come with me! But now, for we must travel fast so that we are there before anymole from here.'

At such a moment the direction of a mole's life may change for ever.

'Come with me, mole!' urged Rampion again, 'and you may once more find the peace that you have lost.'

'I . . . I shall!' said Romney with sudden resolution, and within the hour they had set off for Rollright.

Nor was Lucerne idle. For one thing he did not much like the cross under as a place for moledom's business. He had lost all interest in Duncton Wood and nor did he like the clay vales he had had to cross on his way there, or the sense that roaring owls were all about the south, day and night.

His original intention, which was to press on to Buckland, now seemed much less appealing than before and yet he knew he needed a strong presence there. Matters could perhaps be left in Clowder's capable paws – a suggestion already made by Terce, who had warned that Clowder was under-used and could provide the strong, military-minded mole needed to impose the kind of rule the south had not had since Henbane's departure from it.

Wyre, it seemed, had been a disappointment, and the more relaxed policy against the Stone that Henbane had introduced through him was failing.

'No, Terce, I like it not, not at all. If I turn north again now I may not come this way again. I know so many of these systems from the scrivenings that I would like to see them with my own eyes. Mallice has a mind to see Uffington.'

'It may be wise, if unpalatable. The south does not suit me well either, but if Clowder is to be left in charge we should take a few weeks to see what it is he will be administering.'

'In any case this is the Stone Mole's heartland and the eldrene Wort's view is that he is most likely to be hiding hereabouts. It would be amusing to make his acquaintance.'

'It would,' agreed Terce.

The whereabouts of the Stone Mole was taxing Terce considerably, and thus far Wort had not tracked him down, though in fairness the ordination had diverted her

as it had everymole else. Yet Wort was confident, and had
done the right things. They had been here but a few days
but already trusted henchmoles of hers had gone out in all
directions to ensure his whereabouts might be found.

There had been no sighting of him in her absence and
she regretted now her decision to order the Cumnor moles
to lie low. A mistake, she now agreed, but then she could
not have predicted the success the Word would honour
her with. But one thing she had succeeded in doing was to
persuade Lucerne that she would be better operating by
herself and without Drule and Slighe. The Master surely
had better things for them to do?

The Master had. He missed Slighe's efficiency, and
Drule's usefulness, for there were all sorts of services that
that mole could perform.

'Well, eldrene Wort, we have considered your request
and grant it willingly and with amusement. It seems that
Slighe here and my friend Drule are quite exhausted by
your sincerity and zeal. Your task does, I agree, need the
flexibility that one mole can have working for herself. But
do not take any major decision about this Stone Mole
without my permission, and know that at all times you
shall have my ear.'

'My Master, I am most grateful and praise the Word for
giving us a Master *so* able to decide *so* fast.'

This business done, Lucerne gave himself only one day
to decide which way to go, and finally the south-west
seemed best, but only as far as Buckland. Mallice would
have to forgo Uffington. They would travel fast, and when
they got there he and Clowder could review the plans for
the next strike against followers. But Terce had been right
– Clowder needed a task, and the south was more than
enough. With him down here, Ginnell in the west, and
himself back at Cannock, moledom would be primed for a
final assault or crusade upon the followers which would
make this brief business in Duncton seem like nothing.

Before he left, Lucerne briefed the sideem who had
travelled with him and told them what the Word would

600

expect them to say about Duncton: how the Stone was outfaced and bloodied by the Word.

'Did we not come in good faith, could we not have ended the outcasting of Duncton and brought it back into the community of moledom?' Lucerne declaimed to the willing sideem. 'The moles' pride, the moles' failure to Atone and renunciate, killed the system. Let it be known wherever you go.'

These lies sown, Lucerne left for Buckland, while other sideem and guardmoles travelled back towards the midlands once more, to return to their systems and prepare for the final assault on the Stone.

But Wort stayed where she was, free now to act entirely on her own authority without the wimpish Slighe and doltish Drule to concern herself about. She would visit Fyfield and the area about it, but be ready to set off once again the moment one of her henchmoles sent news of which way the Stone Mole had gone. She felt well pleased . . . and yet, so guilty to feel well pleased and in need of the special chastisement her henchmoles gave her.

'Holy Word, my mother and my father, punish me for the pride I feel, drive the wickedness of vanity from my heart . . .' And her henchmole serviced her with his talons, that the pain might be penance for the sin of conceit she knew she sometimes felt. And as she suffered the penitential talons of her henchmole she sighed and gasped with pain, and thought of the Master of the Word, Lucerne, and imagined the beauty of him in her mind.

It was not until the evening after Longest Night that Beechen was able to escape the attentions and demands of the moles into whose presence he had come with such extraordinary effect.

Not all the Rollright moles were glad to see him, for he had spoilt their revelry; nor did all believe that he was the Stone Mole, or any other special mole come to that.

But there were enough there, including those three guardmoles whose lives he might well have saved, who felt that in his words, and presence, something that had been missing from their lives had at last been found.

Many of these found it hard, impossible indeed, to take themselves from him, and simply hung about and stared as if to leave him was to desert themselves. Others sought his help for problems of healing and comforting, and everymole that came to him he talked with, and many he touched, turning none away.

So many indeed that Sleekit and Mistle, seeing he had grown tired, tried in the course of the mid-morning after Longest Night to get him to rest, and Holm offered to lead him to a burrow where he might find privacy.

But no, he could not leave moles who still needed him, and continued to talk gently with some, and pray with others, and even to debate issues of the Stone with a few.

He declined to speak of Duncton Wood, or of the danger of grikes, or whether it was safe for him to stay in Rollright for very long, though Mayweed and Buckram, concerned as one was for Duncton and the other for Beechen himself, tried hard to make him. But Buckram was discovering what Mayweed already knew, that when Beechen was ministering to moles he seemed to disregard all else and especially his own needs. When moles that cared for him tried to make him talk of these things it was as if he did not hear what was said to him.

'Yes, yes, Buckram,' he would say absently, 'but I must just talk to this mole here and I must do it now. Now is the time, Buckram, not later . . . now.'

Only in the afternoon, when the crush had eased and moles who still sought his counsel began themselves to say, 'Stone Mole, you are tired, what I wished to ask can wait' . . . Only then did he agree to rest.

It was to Holm and Lorren's lowly burrow, downslope and muddy, that he went and there settled down and ate. Even then Buckram found it impossible to make him address the matter of his safety until he had spoken at length with Holm and Lorren, and enjoyed listening to

Mayweed and Holm together, a one-sided conversation if ever there was one.

'Mute mole,' said Mayweed to his old and dear friend, 'you have been missed.'

Holm stared with wide eyes at Mayweed and said nothing.

'*Much* missed, slovenly Sir. As humbleness was saying to messy Madam here, "There's only one Holm in all of moledom," and me myself would have liked to see more of him these years past.'

Holm opened his mouth to speak, thought about things a bit, and then closed it again.

'Mayweed surmises that Holm is pondering an utterance. He hopes it will be made, for Beechen the Stone Mole would like to hear your voice. And Mistle here, Beechen's much-beloved; and Sleekit, too. We wait, we pause, we scarcely dare to breathe. Be eloquent, dusty mole, speak out!'

Holm stared at them all, eyes even wider, and then at Lorren, and blinked. Lorren shook her head, seeming to understand what it was he wanted to say but not wanting him to.

Then Holm looked desperately about, from floor to ceiling, from mole to mole, from light to shade, and then, as if grabbing it quick and placing it down in front as if it might otherwise throttle him, he spoke a word; a name.

'Bailey!' he said.

Then, that being greeted by blank silence, and seeming to gain his courage, he spoke four more words by way of explanation: 'Lorren needs to know.'

'I miss him,' said Lorren. 'And Starling too.'

For once Mayweed was stuck for words. Only days before he would have smiled and declared in a great many words how well Bailey was when he last saw him, one of the youngest moles in Duncton Wood. But now . . . but now? Sleekit, understanding Lorren's need better, took over.

'Bailey's your brother, isn't he?'

603

Lorren nodded bleakly.

'My dear, how long is it since you've seen him?'

Lorren stared at Sleekit but if she knew she could not speak, but only stare at them both.

Lorren looked at Holm, and then at them all and then at Holm again. She lowered her snout and Holm shifted about uncomfortably and together they gave the impression of moles who, had they been alone, would have comforted each other but that they could not do in front of others.

Suddenly Mayweed struck the side of his head with a thump and, rolling over on his side, kicked his legs about.

'Humbleness is abject. The idiot is a fool. The fool is dim as a dead lobworm. A lobworm is better than Mayweed! Madam, strike Mayweed. Go on, hit him.'

Mayweed leapt up again, dashed over to Lorren, and thrust his flank towards her, declaring, 'Mayweed is an insensitive mole, heartless mole, amnesiac mole. Let him suffer! He had forgotten that the likeable Lorren has had no news of the once-youthful Bailey since before he was a youth.

'Madam, your long-lost Bailey misses you. Notice humbleness uses the present tense and not the gloomy past participle "missed", which would indicate that Bailey is deceased, inanimate, inert or, to use another word, dead. No, no, no. To continue. . . . Bailey misses Starling. Mayweed knows it. How? Because humbleness thinks. Bailey has never once mentioned you or your sister to him, Mayweed, not once. Which must mean he *more* than misses you. Bailey knows his moles. When you were separated something in himself was lost and will not be found again until the day you see him once again.' Mayweed stopped talking and allowed Lorren to speak at last.

'I miss him,' Lorren said, 'very much. When he was young I was horrible to him, but I loved him and I just wish I had told him once, just once, that I loved him, before he, before we, *before* . . .' She paused, and stared, and her eyes brimmed with tears for the unrequited memory of the brother she thought she had lost in a flood.

There was nothing anymole could say and so nomole tried. But then Lorren added, 'It's different with Starling. I survived the flood with her and when we parted we both knew it would probably be forever and ever.' The others smiled, for even now, so many years later when she was a mature if not quite aging mole, when she spoke of her siblings a sibling look came to Lorren's face – protective and guilty where Bailey was concerned, and like a younger sister when she spoke Starling's name.

Sleekit, who knew much of the truth of Bailey's long subjugation by Henbane in Whern, noted with approval that Mayweed had not gone into that, but created an image of Bailey in Lorren's mind which though not quite untruthful yet left something positive and good.

Perhaps Beechen sensed this too for he said, 'Bailey was always my friend when I was young. I think he would have liked to have pups of his own but he never had the opportunity, for the females in Duncton were old and sterile. Even now, perhaps it is not too late. . . .'

Then, at last, Beechen told them what he thought they must do in the light of the grike descent on to Duncton.

'Wherever my next ministry takes me from here I shall not rest until I know what has happened in Duncton. Hopefully the grikes who came simply passed it by but we all know that Tryfan has long believed that trouble might come, and that his urging for me to leave was partly due to those fears.

'But I cannot continue my task until I know the truth, though in my heart I do not feel the Stone wishes me to return to Duncton yet.'

He looked sadly at Mistle, whom they all knew had set her heart on going to Duncton Wood, and they reached out and touched each other and waited for him to say more.

'I am much afraid,' he said quietly. 'Afraid for the moles in Duncton whom I love and who made my life; afraid for you; and afraid for myself. When we were on the surface at the edge of Rollright last night and Mayweed told me what had happened here, I snouted in a circle all about moledom and felt, as I have before, that my way lies northwards, towards where Tryfan once went, and my father Boswell as well.

'Mayweed and Sleekit know that I have believed for some time that the Stone shall part them, though I think it will only do so knowing that what they have discovered in each other means that, in truth, they can never be apart. But that is their own business and I shall not speak of it more.

'But Mayweed's task lies with Tryfan now and whatever anymole might say I know that to Tryfan he will go. Sleekit has been with me throughout my ministry in the vale, she has wisdoms that I have not and a different kind of faith, and followers, especially female ones, often go to her in preference to myself. More than that, she was witness to my puphood and witness to Duncton's quiet discovery of itself with Tryfan, and she has much to give to other moles of love, of faith, and of the community that is Tryfan's greatest teaching, and which we must all strive to live and teach. If I go north I shall need her at my flank, though I hardly dare ask it.'

Sleekit looked deeply at Mayweed, and it was clear that they had talked and resolved these eventualities. She went to Beechen and held him close as a mother might her son, and said, 'My dear, you shall not have to ask. My way will be with you and what the Stone makes for my future and for my beloved Mayweed we shall accept and trust, though parting will be hard.'

Then Beechen turned to Mistle, looked into her eyes and said, 'The Stone knows the love I have for you, and I have grown in the love you give to me. These friends have witnessed it. I never want to part from you but if the Stone should ask it of us I pray that we shall have the strength to keep each other ever in our hearts as we are now, alone and with our friends. May the Stone help us to act true in the difficult days ahead.'

It was a strangely affecting moment, for though Beechen had not said they must part, or why they might have to, yet there was the sense that there was little time left for them, and as a great tree must bend and accommodate the winds of change if it is to survive, so their love might soon be tested by the storm of darkness by which moledom was already beset.

At that tender moment, the most stolid of them all seemed to be Buckram, who was stanced firmly behind Beechen, his great flanks and paws like walls and buttresses of strength to protect them all.

'I'm not much of one for speaking,' he said, 'unless it be to order moles about, in which I was well trained. But right now what I want are the words for a prayer, and I wish somemole here would tell me what they should be.'

'Say what's in your heart, Buckram. It's all the Stone ever wants to hear,' said Beechen. 'Say a prayer for all of us.'

'Well,' began Buckram in his rough way, 'it won't be much and I'll keep it short: Stone, moledom seems a dark and dangerous place to my friends and me and we're not sure what to do. We don't none of us want to part but we may have to if we are to serve you best. Help us find our best way towards your Silence; help us believe we can find that way; Stone, you help us now.'

When he had finished they all nodded and Buckram, a little embarrassed, added, 'Well, that's what I want to say to the Stone and I'm glad I have. But I'll tell you one thing: since I met the Stone Mole I've been parted from him twice. First when he left me to recover myself at Sandford, and the second when we got to Bablock. Now, you can talk till worms fly, but I'll not be parted from him for a third time, so whatever happens, whatever mole goes where, Buckram here goes with *him*!'

Something about the way that Buckram prayed and spoke changed their mood and raised their spirits, and Beechen said, 'There's seven of us here all unsure of ourselves, and all with good reason to know about

607

Duncton. I think we should set off towards it very soon, taking the quickest way, and see what we can find out.'

'Straight into trouble?' said Buckram dubiously. 'Believe me, once the grikes have rumbled that the Stone Mole's about – and they must have started to at Cumnor – then they'll be on the lookout for him, *especially* near Duncton.'

'True, true, worthy Buckram, but Mayweed's observation is that moles looking for others look everywhere but in front of their snouts. They won't be expecting us to come the obvious way, and as we shall expect them we shall see them first. Elegant that! When do we all start? Now?'

It was as well that Mayweed's argument prevailed, for if they had set off on a more circuitous route, then two days later, when they were approaching Chadlington, they might easily have missed two moles travelling fast towards them: Rampion and Romney.

But there they were and there they met, and there the terrible news of Duncton's Longest Night was shared between moles who had no wish to impart such tidings and moles who had no wish to hear them.

First Rampion described the scenes outside the cross-under before Longest Night, and the scurrying and hurried preparations that were made to ready the guardmoles for their mass entry into Duncton Wood. Though brief, her account left no doubt in the minds of those who heard it that hours before the invasion itself all there had guessed that the guardmoles' intentions were murderous.

'If I could have found a way into Duncton Wood to warn the moles I would have taken it, but all of us servers were watched, and I did not get very near the cross-under itself. The only other way was over the great embankment of the roaring owl way and they guarded even that. The eldrene Wort who had gone ahead from Rollright was in charge of the organisation and she made sure that moles stayed where they were meant to. Everything seemed so *dark*, and I feared something terrible was going to happen, and it did.'

Then Romney took up the tale, speaking quietly and somewhat shakily, because even after three days the memory was still as vivid as if it was happening as he told it and he could guess how much what he was saying must mean to his listeners.

Almost at once, as he described the unexpected opposition by two old moles on the south-east slopes, Mayweed, Beechen and Sleekit guessed with mounting grief the names of the moles he was describing, and the full horror of what he had been part of came to them.

'You say one was small and spare, one large and scalpskinned and dark-furred?'

'Yes, they fought together and I've never known moles, young or old, fight as those two did.'

'And they . . . ?'

'Yes,' said Romney, 'yes. They both died.'

There was silence until Sleekit whispered their names: 'Skint and Smithills, that's who they were. It *must* have been them.' Then she said, looking strongly at Romney, 'You know they were once both moles of the Word, guardmoles like yourself. They stanced their ground as moles who believed that others could live as they wished, provided they hurt no other mole.'

'Well they died fighting for their freedom, and no death could have been braver than theirs.'

Beechen said gruffly, 'What then, mole? What happened next?'

Romney told them, trying his best to make something coherent of the confused succession of horrific events of that night. His account was sombre enough until he got to Dodder and then, hardy and experienced guardmole though he was, he broke down, mixing his description of Dodder's defiant end with that of his memory of the mole who had trained him when young.

After that all of them wept, and all sought to comfort the

three Duncton moles when it was realised from Romney's description that the last mole to die was Beechen's mother Feverfew. All the other moles in the wood as well, it seemed, must have been killed, but for Tryfan himself, whose stolid defiance throughout and unwillingness until Feverfew was threatened with death to renounce the Stone was like no trial of mole any of them had ever heard.

'He was left alive to suffer,' said Sleekit. 'Oh, poor Tryfan, he will be so lost.'

Mayweed wept, terrible inconsolable tears intermingled with mutterings and self-accusations that he should never have left, or should have gone back sooner.

'You would be dead yourself if you had,' said Romney quietly. 'I tell you, not a mole but Tryfan survived. I have done many things in the name of the Word in my time, many with my own talons, but nothing matches the wrong I feel I did that night when I did nothing but watch. I cannot put it from my mind.'

Nor could the others, all of whom but Buckram and Mistle had lost moles they knew and loved.

'There is one more thing,' said Romney, who wanted to tell them all he knew, however hard it might be, 'but it is not something I could bring myself to tell Rampion these past days nor something I witnessed myself. I heard the senior guardmole Drule, who was the last mole with him at the Stone, say that Tryfan was . . . blinded. It was their final act, and he was left there to fend for himself.'

'Blinded,' whispered Mayweed. 'Tryfan! Sleekit, I must go to him *now*. Sleekit, my dear. . . .'

Tears, anger, grief, confusion, all and more were with them then.

'But *why*?' whispered Lorren, for whom the great tragedy in what she had heard was the loss for the second time of all hope of ever seeing her brother Bailey again, 'why does the Stone allow such things. Where was the Stone's power when it was most needed?'

The question hung in the air about them, a voicing of what most of them felt, and somehow then it was to

Beechen that they all turned, who had lost a mother and all the moles of his life, and more than likely Tryfan as well, for how could he have survived alone and so dreadfully wounded?

Beechen was stanced in their midst, his snout low, his eyes half closed, and he said as if speaking to himself, 'The Stone's power comes from ourselves alone, and from our past and our present. It was moles that failed in those hours on Longest Night by the Duncton Stone, not the Stone itself. Until moles understand that, they shall not be true moles, but dependents on a Stone that can never satisfy their needs and cravings. I tell you, this failure is *all* moles'. There shall soon come a day when moles know this and they shall see that what *is* is what they are. Then will moledom tremble between final darkness and the discovery of the way to light and Silence. That day is near to us, and we who live now must prepare for it.'

Hearing him a mole might have thought he was angry, but he spoke rather with a kind of savage disappointment, and there was apprehension in his voice, and despair.

Then Romney spoke, saying, 'I'll tell you one more thing then, Beechen of Duncton, before you decide what you must do. The rumour among the guardmoles is that the eldrene Wort of Fyfield has been given the task of rooting you out and delivering you to the judgement of the Word. Her reputation is fierce. Therefore one thing is certain: every pawstep you take towards Duncton is a pawstep nearer to this Wort, and, whatever your task may be, if you are taken by her it will not be well served.

'More than that, the gossip is that Tryfan betrayed his friends and that's why he was allowed to live; and no doubt they'll say the Stone Mole is a coward for escaping Duncton at such a time as this.'

'Yes, I had thought *that* might be,' said Beechen wearily. 'I am beginning to understand the mind of grikes. So now does our trial and despair truly begin, for now we must part. Now we must put much behind us and turn to the tasks the Stone is giving us.' They nodded, grateful in

611

a grim way that one among them was taking charge at such a time.

'I shall take my ministry northwards as I thought I must. I have teachings to make, and word of the Stone to impart before moles such as this Wort catch up with me. Sleekit, you have said you shall come with me.

'Buckram, you too shall come with us, to help protect us along the way, not with your talons, though if they frighten away our enemies that will be no bad thing, but with the growing strength of your spirit.

'You, Mayweed, must surely go to Duncton, for if Tryfan has survived, and he has survived much before this, then nomole in moledom can serve him better than you can. You, Mistle . . . you must go with him, for your task lies in Duncton and not yet with me. Our day shall come. Romney, I charge you to go with her, and as you regret the passive part you played on Longest Night, the Stone shall know those active things you do to help Mistle in the great task she shall find awaits her in Duncton Wood.

'As for you, Holm and Lorren, you must decide, for I would not part you. Perhaps 'tis best now if you returned with us towards Rollright where we can leave you to continue the Stone's work there.'

'I wanted to go to Duncton to find Bailey, but he is taken from me!' wept Lorren. 'And now, now I shall lose my Holm. Tell them what you must do, my dear! Tell them!'

Holm stared miserably about him, then at Lorren, then at Beechen. Eventually he turned to his friend and said desperately, 'Mayweed, tell me!'

'Tell you what, unhappy Holm?'

'What to do.'

Mayweed looked from Holm to Lorren and back again, he leered, he shook his head, he scratched himself.

'Grubbiness,' said Mayweed at last, 'me Mayweed always thought next to him you were the best route-finder he ever found, and in wet and muddy places perhaps even better. You are better than Beechen here, Mayweed knows that, and it's saying a lot. Yes, yes, yes. Now, humbleness knows that though the Stone Mole, Buckram and his beloved Sleekit make a splendid trio, they are lacking a route-finder to help them along. Holm must draw his own conclusion and decide. Whatever he decides Mayweed loves him.'

Holm looked this way and that in continuing desperation, and then opened and shut his mouth several times before saying what he wanted to.

'Holm will route-find for the Stone Mole. And.'

'And what, arrested Sir?' said Mayweed.

'And come home again.'

Then he rushed up to Lorren, touched her in a quick, jerky, yet most tender way and made what for him was a long speech. 'Holm will come back to you because he loves you very much. Rampion, stay by your mother!' Then all three hugged each other close, and grubby Holm was lost in the loving paws and heartfelt tears of the two females he most loved, as if they were saying goodbye there and then.

'Come,' said Beechen to them all, 'we must part. Lorren and Rampion, we shall see you safely back to Rollright and then go on.'

Then the others said their distraught farewells, Mayweed and Sleekit first, and then Buckram to Mayweed and Mistle whom he had grown to love.

For a time Beechen and Mistle remained alone, the two sorry groups ready to leave on either side of them.

'Mistle, you are my life,' he said.

'And you mine, my love.'

'The Stone shall guide you to your task in Duncton Wood. Make a community once more. Lead it. Teach it. Be its mother and its father and trust the Stone.'

'Will you come home to me?' said Mistle with terrible despair.

Beechen looked at her for a long time, and then held her close. He moved back from her and gazed into her eyes.

'One day I shall come back to you, but. . . .'

'But what, my dearest love?'

A look of loss and trouble was in his eyes.

'I don't know. I fear what I feel I must say. I shall come back to you and yet you may not know me, or want to know me then.'

Mistle smiled tenderly, and said, 'My love, I shall know you always, love you always, and wait for you until the Stone sends you back to me safeguarded.'

'The Stone is with us both,' replied Beechen. 'Yet I feel that I have been searching for you from the beginning of time and that our parting now, when we have barely found each other, is a final test for us, and for moledom too. I do not understand quite what it is the Stone shall ask of us but one day perhaps we shall be free to love each other as we were meant to do.'

Mistle reached out her paws to him and held his face and whispered, 'I shall know you always and none other but you.'

Then with one final embrace they turned from each other, and joined their separate groups.

Then Beechen cried out, 'Stone, help us all fulfil our tasks, and go like warrior moles towards the future that lies before us now!'

Then one group turned for the north and darkness, and the other turned south to seek once more the light of Duncton Wood, and not a single mole among them paused or turned, or looked back to the life they left behind.

Chapter Twenty-Eight

There is no doubt, none at all, that without Mayweed to lead them, Mistle and Romney would not have reached Duncton Wood alive.

Grikes seemed everywhere along the route they took, and the first they came across – but a few hours after they left the others at Chadlington – were four thickset guardmoles hurrying rapidly along, and clearly under orders not to dally in their northward journey.

Mayweed heard them before he saw them and, always ready for such problems, made sure they were well hidden in the scrubby ground they were then crossing, and the guardmoles went on their way none the wiser.

'I hope the grikes won't catch the others up,' whispered Mistle doubtfully.

'Humbleness trained Holm himself,' said Mayweed. 'They will be more than all right!'

It was typical late December weather, wet, gloomy and cold, and as they neared Duncton at last their route took them alongside the roaring owl way under which they would finally have to pass if they were to get into Duncton Wood.

They had already passed under it after leaving Rollright, but there the cross-under is almost underground and rises further off from the way itself. This was the first time Mistle had been so close to so large a roaring owl way and, with the embankment rising on their right, the sound of the roaring owls heavy and sending a rain of dirty spray out over the steep slope above as their gazes rushed by, she was awestruck, and stopped more than once to look.

'Dangerous it is, Madam, never go up there unaccompanied. Moles die on roaring owl ways.'

'Do they talk? Like moles?' asked Mistle.

'They roar,' said Mayweed, wanting to get on, 'like owls.'

'And their gazes, what do they look at?'

'The way ahead, humbleness should think, but sometimes when they cross the countryside in the distance on smaller ways they gaze all around.'

'Do you think they think, like moles?'

'Persistent Madam, Mayweed doesn't know. He avoids them like the plague but if he must use a roaring owl way route he looks down at the way, and breathes out of the corner of his mouth away from them, to minimise the fumes. He hopes they think, but if they do they never seem to change their minds, which negates their thinking, doesn't it? No good thinking if change does not result.'

But the approach of more grike guardmoles ahead of them ended the conversation abruptly and Mayweed once more led Mistle calmly into hiding and the grikes went unknowingly past.

'Madam Mistle and Romney Sir, follow closely now because we're near to the cross-under. Rather a dirty route I fear, through a pipe, but it takes us to where we can observe what moles are about without being seen.'

They followed him silently, and for Romney, who was the biggest of them, it was a tight squeeze, and he could see nothing much ahead but Mistle's tail and an occasional flash of light at the pipe's end far ahead.

When they reached the end Mayweed watched and waited for a long time before he would get out. But when he did he leapt nimbly down, snouted about, went straight into the centre of the cross-under and said in a voice that echoed off its concrete walls, 'Astonishing, incredible, amazing, I never thought I'd live to see the day!'

They followed after him and saw that the cross-under and beyond into Duncton Wood were quite unguarded with not a mole in sight.

'Remember, Madam, if we're stopped we're Romney's prisoners and we're to act dumb and pretend to be followers and if there's *real* trouble run in opposite directions and hope for the best.'

But no moles appeared as they hurried through the wet and echoing cross-under. Everywhere had a derelict air and looked forlorn. The sound of the roaring owls was muffled and apart from the drip-drip of water from the way above on to the concrete floor of the cross-under, the only sounds were the ugly caws of distant rooks high on the slopes above.

Despite Mayweed's natural desire to get up through the High Wood and to the Stone as quickly as possible, Mistle could not help stopping and staring upslope in awe at the system she had only seen from a distance with Beechen.

They were nearing the top when Mayweed called out from above in a distressed voice, 'Mistle Madam, please, please come.'

She went quickly up to him and saw that he was looking ahead up the slopes to just below the edge of the wood itself. The rooks they had heard were pecking there, and then rising a little into the air, stooping at each other and then dropping in an untidy way to the ground again and stalking about. Four of them. It was all too plain that they were feeding off carrion, and that the carrion was the dead bodies of moles that lay scattered about a little promontory or knoll that jutted out of the slope.

'That's the place the two moles I mentioned made such a fight of it,' said Romney grimly. He and Mayweed eyed the feeding rooks uneasily, but Mistle, well-used to surface travel, went boldly ahead, saying, 'They'll fly off if we make ourselves obvious enough. Come on, Mayweed.'

'Oh Madam, Mayweed knows that,' muttered Mayweed. 'He was not born yesterday. It's what the rooks are feeding on that distresses him.'

'Come on,' said Romney with surprising gentleness, 'let's get it over with.'

They followed quickly after Mistle and reached her flank as the rooks, irritated and made noisy at their approach, rose and hovered low, their white bills dangerous, before suddenly angling into the light breeze and disappearing up into the trees beyond.

They found themselves surrounded by a scene of stark devastation, the bodies of moles scattered all about, and some of them dismembered by the rooks.

'Stone, may they be at peace and brought to your Silence safeguarded,' whispered Mistle, a look of pity on her face. She put a paw out to stop Romney from going to Mayweed, who had gone ahead among the bodies and was searching for his friends.

'Let him be,' she said. 'It's best he's alone at such a moment. He'll call us when he wants us.'

Rarely had Mistle seen so touching and pathetic a sight as the thin and ragged form of Mayweed wandering disconsolately among the bodies of fallen moles, reluctantly looking at each one to see if it was Skint or Smithills.

'I wish Sleekit was here,' said Mistle, 'it's her he needs.'

'He's quite a mole is Mayweed.'

'He's a great mole,' said Mistle passionately, 'and if you knew what he'd done in his life, and the moles he's helped. . . .'

'Yes, I'm sure,' said Romney placatingly, looking unhappily over the bleak scene.

They saw Mayweed stop on the furthest point of the promontory where several bodies lay, they saw him peer down and then pull away the large body of a young-looking mole. Then he stared down at two bodies that lay so close they seemed to be touching each other, and they heard him sob, and stance still a long time, staring.

Then he looked round and Romney said, 'Go to him, mole, you'll know best what to say.'

She went, and as she reached him Mayweed gestured at the two moles she knew must be Skint and Smithills. Both had suffered terrible talon wounds to face and flanks.

'That's good-natured Smithills,' said Mayweed, pointing to the larger of the two, 'and that's Skint who found me in a seal-up in the Buckland Slopeside. They were never apart those two, and even now. . . .'

Mistle gazed down at them, and guessed that they must have fought for each other back to back to the very last.

But there was something more than that. After they had been overwhelmed and the grikes had moved on, Smithills must still have tried to protect his old friend before he died because his broad back showed signs of having taken many talonings.

'They came from Grassington,' said Mayweed, 'and knew each other as pups. They were my friends.'

Mayweed wept some more and Mistle stayed comfortingly close to him, as she imagined Sleekit would have done. She stared at the dead moles, and wondered how it was that two such old moles as these had found the strength and courage to have battled so hard as they had done.

Mayweed sighed and said, 'Mistle Madam, there'll be other sad sights today, but I feel I've wept my tears now and am ready to move on.'

They looked on up the slope and saw that already the rooks were circling out of the leafless trees and coming down their way again.

'Come on, Madam, and you, rough Romney, this mole Mayweed is ready now to go on up into the High Wood and leave the rooks to do their work here.'

The rooks flapped and snapped above them in the sky as they moved on with heavy hearts towards the trees of the High Wood.

How sombre the wood seemed to Mistle as Mayweed led them through it, not at all as she had imagined it when Violet had first spoken to her of Duncton. The towering grey-green trunks of the beech trees utterly dwarfed them, and the smooth rustling floor of fallen beech leaves, which seemed half golden even in that dull winter light, stretched endlessly in all directions about them. The only relief was the occasional raft of dog's mercury stalks, and a sporadic holly bush which had rooted in the deep leaf litter.

'Wondering moles, the Ancient System lies beneath us

and is not a place to venture down without extreme care, so don't. The Stone rises straight ahead on the west side of the wood.'

'Aye, I remember the direction well enough,' said Romney, 'but the wood itself looks a lot grander in the daylight.'

Mistle said nothing, for she was full of apprehension as well as having a curious and contradictory sense of excitement now she was among the trees. It was what they would find that concerned her, not the wood itself which, despite its size and the way it made a mole feel small, gave her a sense of belonging quite unlike anywhere she had been on her long journey here.

'I was meant to come here,' she kept saying to herself, 'and I was meant to come without Beechen at first so that I can get to know it in my own way. He said he'd come back, and I know he will, and I know that if I'm true to the Stone then this system will look after me.'

The trees ahead thinned, they clambered over the surface roots of another beech tree, the ground dropped away slightly, and there, before them through the trees, they saw the great Stone of Duncton, its colour greener and more brown than the beech trees, but its surface having the same strange shining quality they held.

Remembering Mayweed's reluctance to go first on to the Pasture slopes, Romney went to the front saying, 'I'll take the lead, for it'll not be a pleasant sight about the Stone.'

On they went, past the last tree before the clearing and then out through the undergrowth before the Stone itself. Mayweed kept his snout low, and Mistle could hardly bear to look.

But when they did so it was somehow not so bad as it had seemed on the slopes. There were bodies there, and owls and rooks had been, but somehow the trees surrounding them, and the Stone especially, put them into a different proportion. The clearing was peaceful, nature would take its course and the bodies would be gone.

'Madam and Sir, if Tryfan has survived then where is he?' said Mayweed. 'For he is not here.'

Mistle stared up at the Stone whose face seemed to catch light in strange and subtle ways, even on a dull day like this. Romney shifted about uncomfortably.

Mayweed snouted about a bit, stanced with his head on one side, ran hither and thither and finally came back, stopped, turned, and stared north out of the clearing.

'Please to follow me,' he said, 'and quietly.'

As dusk fell on Longest Night and the grikes came, Bailey had not been in the Stone clearing, but hurrying over the surface of the Ancient System in the company of Marram.

He should have been at the Stone but he had grown bored and, seeing Marram setting off to tell Skint and Smithills that everymole was waiting for them, had gone along to keep him company.

Neither had suspected anything was wrong until they reached the edge of the High Wood and heard shouts and commands coming from the slopes below. Bailey had peered out from the cover of the wood with Marram and been faced by the most terrifying sight coming up out of the gloom below that he had ever seen.

Dozens and dozens of grike guardmoles came inexorably up towards them. Even as they saw them they heard grikes crashing into the wood on either side of them and knew it was too late to even attempt to get down and reach Skint and Smithills, assuming they were still there.

'We must go and warn the others,' said Marram, turning and starting back the way they had come.

But it was too late, the moles on either flank had heard them and even as they rushed back towards the Stone clearing the grikes turned to cut them off, hissing commands to each other. Bailey felt he was about to die.

'Hide there!' commanded Marram, 'There! Now! And don't move whatever happens, *whatever happens*.' Then, shocked and in a daze, Bailey scurried into the shelter of some roots and dog's mercury. Even as Marram turned from him and had moved no more than a few paces away, he was confronted by grikes coming from all directions.

Bailey heard a strong confident voice say, 'Here's the one we heard.'

'What's your name, Stone-lover?' said another.

'Marram, I. . . .'

Then there was a sickening thump, a weak diminishing cry, a grunt, and then the grikes rushed on as more came up behind them and Bailey's world seemed to turn mad around him.

He began to shiver and shake, and as moles went here and there and all about, he covered his head with his paws and kept them there for what seemed an interminable time.

Then as things fell silent and the last of the grikes seemed to have run past, Bailey heard a rasping voice he did not at first recognise.

'Bailey!' it called, and it might have been death itself speaking his name.

He dared to peer out of his hiding place and saw poor Marram stretched out and dying.

'Bailey,' rasped Marram, 'hide. Go down into the Ancient System. Hide. One must survive: you. Hide.'

'But Marram, b–b–but. . . .'

'Bailey . . .' It was the last word Marram said, for he coughed and died even as Bailey reached out to him.

Nothing can describe the talon-crumbling, mind-numbing, heart-stopping panic that Bailey then felt. Not a thought did he have for Tryfan and the other moles in the clearing nor, as he turned and rushed blindly from Marram, for anymole else but himself. He ran about, stumbled over roots, crashed into fallen branches and then, when he heard a grike call out, 'Whatmole's that?' he tried to scrabble at the leaf litter and chalky soil beneath him and make good his escape.

'Hey! You!'

He gave up trying to delve and dashed off, first here and then there until he tried to delve once more, desperate to escape from the death that seemed about to descend on him.

Once more the ground was too hard. He heard moles coming for him and he ran blindly on again until he scented the ground below was more moist, and he delved down and succeeded in tunnelling out of sight. His breath came out in grunts of fear despite all attempts to silence it, his mouth was full of soil and he pushed wildly on. Then he stopped, listened, realised nomole was following, pushed a paw forward and found himself tumbling headlong into a pitch-black tunnel.

'Where's the bugger gone?'

He heard death's hard voice on the surface above, soil and litter dropped down into the black space around him, sweat poured down his face, and then the voices were gone.

He stayed quite still until the cold began to get at him and, feeling his way along in the blackest tunnels he had ever known, he began to explore. Had he not been to the Ancient System before, which he had as a pup in Henbane's day, and more recently when Mayweed had shown him where his father Spindle had hidden his own and Tryfan's texts, he might have felt more nervous, for the windsound is most attenuated and strange, and that night seemed full of rushing above, and ominous cries and screams.

At first he did not know where he was or where he could go, but after a long and increasingly miserable wandering he came to a tunnel he knew, lit by moonlight. He decided to go to the secret place Mayweed had shown him and somehow he got himself to it: a burrow hidden among the roots of a beech tree, itself empty but leading most cleverly by way of a tilted flint through a concealed entrance to a safe burrow for texts.

There he stanced down and stayed still, listening, very afraid, unable to move more. Finally he dozed off, only to wake when new sounds came: moles laughing and joking, their voices guttural. He knew them to be grikes.

He realised that they were leaving, but he did not dare move. Fear of them had been replaced by fear of what they had left behind. It was not until two long, wretched days had passed that thirst and hunger finally drove him out of the chalky burrow and from among the bark texts where he had felt safest, and up on to the surface. He crept about, gulped down some water he found in the interstices of a tree root, and grubbed timidly about for some food, starting at every slightest sound.

The wood was silent, the trees still, the place felt dead. Eventually, not knowing what else to do, he went timidly to the Stone, and what he found there was unspeakably worse than anything he could have imagined. It seemed that everymole he had ever loved was lying there, cold, stiff, frosted over, taloned and crushed to death before the Stone.

He stared numbly about him, at the wide empty clearing, at the bodies, at the Stone, and at the bodies again. Feverfew, Madder, Teasel all crumpled . . . they were all there, all dead.

'Bailey. . . ?'

For a moment his heart seemed to stop and he half screamed in fear.

'Bailey. . . .'

The voice was familiar and yet unlike anything he had heard before, coming from a place Bailey had no wish to go.

'Bailey,' it said. And if Bailey could have died himself he would have done so then, so fearful was he of turning and peering into the shadows from which that voice came. But then he heard the slow drag of steps behind him in the gloom and terror made him turn and stare in horror at the bloody apparition that came.

Tryfan, blinded. His face and what had been his eyes all open and raw, his face fur no better than gore, his paws bespattered with his own blood.

'Is it Bailey?'

'Yes,' whispered Bailey. 'What have they done to you? What have they done to Duncton?'

'I knew you were safe, Bailey. I knew you were hiding. Where did you go?'

How could he speak so calmly? Bailey answered him, not knowing where to look. Blankly he told him about Marram, and about how he had hidden in the Ancient System.

Only after that did Bailey come to himself sufficiently to ask of Tryfan himself, and what had happened.

'I am in pain, though not as much as it was. The cold has helped me, Bailey. I have found food, for my snout is unharmed, but I could not find water. Take me somewhere I can drink. You must guide me. . . .'

Slowly, pathetically, still barely aware of what was happening, Bailey led Tryfan along to where he himself had found water and helped the old mole drink.

'Now keep me warm, Bailey, for I must sleep, and then I shall need your help. Do not be afraid, mole.'

'I feel ashamed,' said Bailey suddenly.

'No, mole, there is no time for that now. The Stone has protected you as, in its own terrible way, it protected me. We still have our tasks.'

'But you can't do anything,' said Bailey bitterly.

'There is one thing I can do, and I shall need your help to do it, but I must sleep first . . . Now keep me warm. . . .'

Bailey did his best for the mole who had given so much of his life to so many, and for the next few hours he felt each painful breath, each suffering shudder as if it were his own.

Once during that first night, Bailey found himself crying for Tryfan and the old mole stirred and woke and said, 'Bailey, do not cry for me. I can bear this pain and darkness. I bore it before when Rune's sideem hurt me in Whern; oh yes, I can bear it . . . weep not for me.'

Dawn came and Tryfan stirred and said, 'Now find me food and lead me to the place to drink again.' When Bailey had done that, Tryfan said, 'Now listen, mole, and do as I say. You have seen the texts hidden in the Ancient System and on what they are scribed. Go now to the Eastside and find me some bark of silver birch. Do it now. I shall not move, but wait for you impatiently. Go now. . . .'

Bailey went, and got the bark, and came back and found Tryfan stanced where he had been before.

'Now, mole, guide my paw to the bark and keep it still for I must scribe one last time. Why, I thought the Rule I made was the final thing but it cannot be! One day moles shall live in this place again, one day a community will be here. They must know what happened, and be warned of what can be. They must know that not one single mole who lived here renounced the Stone. Not one! Scribing of it is what your father Spindle would have done. Then help me, as he would, and if my talons slur off the folio, buffet me and keep me to my task.'

Then, despite everything, Tryfan found the strength to scribe a final text, so that future moles might know of the events that had led up to that Longest Night, and on the night itself. In all of scribemole history, perhaps, no text is more moving or more fearful for the mole who snouts it than that one, scribed, it seems, from the heart of a dying mole. Rough, hard to make sense of in places, torn, scribed out of pain by a mole who believed in the future.

With passion and anger was it scribed, and yet, strange as it has seemed to some, it never once scribes badly of the Word or even of the grike guardmoles. Rather it talks of a mole called Lucerne, and one named Drule, and how they lost their way, led others astray, and why that might have been.

It tells of moles who would not renounce the Stone even in the face of death, and names them all, one by one, and describes each affectionately, their good parts and their bad. It finally commends the mole Bailey, who helped the scribemole make his final testament, and asks for the prayers of those who follow. It counsels moles to reflect that even when all seems lost to mole, all hopeless, the Stone may yet bring comfort and encouragement to moles with faith; and as Bailey had come out of the darkness to help him, so others struck down may hope that they are not abandoned.

For two days Tryfan made a scribing which got progressively more slow, and Bailey knew him to be a dying mole, for towards the end he could barely move his paw and Bailey had to hold his talons as he scribed.

'. . . And you shall not be abandoned, for the Stone is with you and at your flank, and attends you. Wait and you shall hear its Silence. This was scribed by Tryfan of Duncton, ordained by Boswell in Uffington.' So ends the final testament of Tryfan.

When it was done, Tryfan said, 'Now, mole, I have completed it and it is well. Take it to that hiding place you know, and then return to me, for I have one last request to ask of you. Hurry, mole, for the darkness comes on my mind and I begin to be afraid. Hurry now.'

Then poor Bailey took the text and hurried into the tunnels of the Ancient System and back to the hidden place where his father and Mayweed had long since made their secret library. There he carefully put the text, and sealed the place up once more to make it hard to find.

When he reached Tryfan again he found him only half conscious and muttering, and afraid of some imagining that had come to him. Indeed, when Bailey reached him and touched him poor Tryfan started as if Bailey was his enemy and began to defend himself, thrusting out this way and that.

'It's only me, Tryfan. It's Bailey.'

'Bailey?' said Tryfan with relief. 'I thought, I thought. . . .'

'It's *me*,' said Bailey. 'I won't hurt you.'

Tryfan gripped his paw and said, 'Bailey, mole, take me down to Barrow Vale, take me there.'

'It's a long way, Tryfan, and you're weak.'

'Take me . . . please.'

The painful, slow journey took a night and half a day, but at last they reached Barrow Vale.

'I'll wait on the surface, not below.'

627

'Wait for what?' whispered Bailey.

For the first time since he had found him, Bailey saw Tryfan smile. Then he looked conspiratorial.

'For a mole who's coming to me,' he said softly. 'He always said he would come when I needed him. He will come now.'

'Whatmole, Tryfan?' asked Bailey, looking about the deserted place and knowing in his heart that nomole could come now.

'A mole who is much loved and most loving. He will know that Tryfan needs him.' Then Tryfan shook and shivered and out of his lost eyes there came what might once have been tears, but now it seemed all blood.

Bailey thought to ask Tryfan some questions, to take his mind off his thoughts and fears.

'Tryfan, tell me about my father.'

'Of all moles I have ever known, I loved Spindle most of all. He was a mole I met at Uffington and. . . .'

There on the surface in Barrow Vale, Tryfan began to talk about his life, with Bailey staying close to him as he slowly began to sink towards a place of darkness of which he was afraid. Sometimes he seemed to feel he had slipped into it, and all sorts of images of horror and fearful things came to him, and he fretted, and shook, and tried to fight Bailey away. But Bailey stayed close, and talked to him, and sometimes Tryfan would emerge once more into a safer world where the darkness did not close him in.

Sometimes, too, he would say, 'Is he here yet? Is he come? I need him now, Bailey, I need him at my flank to guide me on. Is he come?'

But Bailey could only hold frightened Tryfan close and do his best to comfort him, and whisper his hope that soon that mole would come . . . soon.

So a long night passed, and then a day, and then another night, a night when owls stooped close, yet still Tryfan would not go underground. The best Bailey could do was cover him with leaf litter to keep him warm, and hope the owls, who scented blood, would not dare come too close to a living mole.

Yet sometimes Bailey had to leave him while he fetched food, and poor Tryfan cried feebly out and seemed to think that he had been utterly deserted. Then when Bailey came back Tryfan would say, 'Is it you come at last, mole? I have needed you!' And when Bailey said, 'It's Bailey,' he knew he was not the mole Tryfan meant.

So Tryfan clung on to life, but full of fears and doubts, and the belief that he was lost and in a place of darkness, shaking and crying out and even then, feeble as he had become, stancing vainly up to Bailey.

'Help him, Stone,' prayed Bailey. 'Take his suffering from him, bring him safely to thy Silence. Help him now. . . .'

Then in the afternoon of the second day in Barrow Vale, Bailey, only half awake, heard moles coming. Down through the wood from the Stone, more than one mole, but Bailey was almost too tired to care. He felt they must be grikes but he was not afraid now, and if a hundred guardmoles had appeared at the edge of Barrow Vale, he would have stanced in front of Tryfan and defended him to the last.

Indeed, he stanced forward towards the coming moles and, though never a fighting mole, cried out, 'Halt! Come no further or I shall . . . I shall attack!'

It was a brave effort, but words are one thing and deeds another, and poor Bailey knew the moment the great guardmole came into view that he had no chance.

'We're hurting nomole!' he said, still trying to sound as bold as he could, and keeping himself between Tryfan and the mole. Then another appeared, a female, and stared at him. Then, finally, Mayweed appeared and Bailey's mouth fell open in astonishment and relief.

'Mayweed,' he said. 'Oh Mayweed!' and gesturing to Tryfan with his left paw as he held him with his right, he cried.

Romney and Mistle crouched down some way off and Mayweed went forward quietly to where Tryfan lay near Bailey.

'Bailey, mole,' said Mayweed gently, 'I shall look after him now. Go to my friends and rest. I shall guide him now.'

Even as Mayweed spoke Tryfan stirred and snouted weakly up and reached out a rough old paw and felt Mayweed's face and flanks. The wood was quiet about them as Bailey crept away and stanced with Romney and Mistle.

'Mayweed, I told him you'd come,' said Tryfan.

'Torn and wounded Tryfan, Mayweed is here now and here he'll stay.'

'I'm in darkness, Mayweed, and cold and much afraid.'

'Much-loved mole, keep your paw on my flank and listen to my voice, and you'll not get lost.' Mayweed did as Bailey had done and surrounded him with leaf litter to keep him warm. He looked at his torn eyes and shook his head.

Tryfan was quiet for a long time until he said suddenly, 'You've been gone so long.' His voice was calmer than it had been, and he sounded more secure.

'Humbleness has been rushing about doing things, but didn't want to be gone so long.'

'Beechen. . . .'

'He has gone north to preach of the Stone.'

'They came and hurt so many moles.'

'Mayweed knows.'

'Even Feverfew, Mayweed, even her. But not one of them renounced the Stone, not a single one. Bailey's safe, but Marram died and Skint I don't know. . . .'

'Died fighting, he did, with you-know-who defending his rear.'

'Told him not to fight. Skint never listened. Loved Skint. Smithills too . . . all of them died. Not you, Mayweed. You know how to survive. I've missed Spindle these hours past.'

'Great mole, myself I know that, humbleness knows lots of things.'

There was another long silence, and Tryfan's breathing grew heavier and more laboured. But then he spoke again.

'What do you know, Mayweed, eh? Tell an old mole what you know.'

'Humble Mayweed knows a thing or three. Knows Tryfan loved and was loved more than most; he knows he loved moles others did not love, like Henbane, like himself. Mayweed knows lots and lots and lots. . . .'

'Mole, don't leave me,' whispered Tryfan, now frantic again and afraid of something that wasn't there. 'Wanted to be here in Barrow Vale when I left. Nomole now, Mayweed, nomole to carry on. What's to become of Duncton Wood, who's to show them the way to go?' Tryfan began to cry, terrible weak sobs.

For a moment Mayweed was at a loss, but then he turned to Mistle and signalled her over.

'Terrific Tryfan, I've got a mole with me, one you'd like to know, a female. . . .'

'No,' whispered Tryfan, though whether he was denying something he feared, or saying that he did not want to meet another mole was hard to say.

Mayweed brought Mistle closer and, raising Tryfan's frail paw to her face, got him to touch her. Slowly, fumblingly, Tryfan felt Mistle's face, and then her flanks.

'Who is she, Mayweed?'

'She's Beechen's love.'

'Ohhh. . . .'

No words can describe the sound of pleasure that Tryfan gave when he heard this, and he said, 'Come here, mole, let me touch you again.'

He caressed her face with touching tenderness and said, 'Tell me your name.'

'I'm Mistle of Avebury.'

'And you're Beechen's love?'

'Yes. He wanted me to come to Duncton Wood because –

because he thought . . . he said my task was here until he comes back.'

'He said your task was here?'

'Yes,' said Mistle.

'Hear that, Mayweed? Beechen's sent a mole to carry on until he comes back. He *will*, my dear, when his task is done, but you know that.'

Mistle nodded, unable to speak.

'It's a good system, Mistle, but it's seen hard times. One day it will be found again.'

'I know,' whispered Mistle, 'and Beechen will be here when it is.'

'And you, Mistle?'

'I'll wait for him always.'

'Is she beautiful, Mayweed?'

'Inquisitorial Sir, she's a marvel of mind and body. Beechen is a lucky mole.'

'I think he is.'

Tryfan grew tired then and began to sleep once more, and Mistle crept quietly back to the others. Then Tryfan awoke, much troubled, and spoke in a jumbled way of Stillstones and Seven Barrows.

'You must go there, Mayweed,' he said.

'It's a long way for a humble old mole like Mayweed. Why, it's beyond Uffington itself.'

'I went,' said Tryfan, 'and you must. *She's* been, I could tell. You'll find everything there just as Spindle and me left it. The Stillstones are all there waiting to be found. Their time's coming soon . . . Seven Stillstones, Seven Books made . . . soon now. Beechen's Mistle here, you there. Yes. It's all coming right now, Mayweed, it's coming right and Duncton's trial is nearly over. The Stone guides us well. . . .'

He slept some more and dusk came, bringing with it a cold breeze that whispered through the wood and among the branches above.

With a sudden start Tryfan awoke again and seemed much afraid.

'I'm here, Tryfan.'

'It's dark and dangerous, it's always been so dark and it never stops, not ever. . . .'

'Listen to my voice, good Tryfan, great mole, listen. . . .'

'Where are you? Guide me, guide me.'

'I'm close, I'm just ahead. Follow me, Tryfan, you're nearly there where the darkness ends, follow me. . . .'

Tryfan gripped Mayweed's paw and seemed to stare up at the sky, and then around, fear on his wounded face and his breathing growing faster.

'The way is so hard but Boswell made me go on it. He did, he did, and I was not worthy. I'm so frightened. How did you learn the way, Mayweed?'

'Great Tryfan, I learned the way from you. You've just forgotten it for a moment, that's all. Now, Mayweed is here, just here, and the darkness is nearly ended, so follow him a little more. You are so much loved, Tryfan, by so many moles.'

Darkness was coming to the wood, and the two moles huddled together right in the centre of Barrow Vale.

'Stone, help him,' prayed Mayweed for his friend, 'embrace him with thy Silence.'

'Why, Mayweed, that's what Boswell prayed when he ordained me scribemole so long ago.' There was a pause and the listening moles were astonished to hear Tryfan chuckle softly and then say, 'Mayweed, you're a *clever* mole. Humbleness my paw! I knew you'd guide me at the end . . .' His voice sounded young again, and firm, and snouting forward a little he added, 'Do you know, I think we're almost there . . . yes, it's just ahead now, isn't it?'

These were the last words that Tryfan of Duncton, son of Bracken and Rebecca, last scribemole ordained in Uffington ever spoke aloud. His friend and guide, the great route-finder Mayweed, held him close as he neared his end, and whispered, 'Terrific Tryfan, you can find your way there now without me. You can, you know the way.' Then, with a contented sigh, Tryfan stirred one last time and breathed his last.

Yet Mayweed held him for some time more until, at last, he was ready gently to lay the scribemole's head on the leafy floor of Barrow Vale and very slowly, very quietly, went to where the others stanced.

Where Tryfan lay they saw a slow light come in the dark, not powerful like the sun, or shining like the moon, but gentle, soft, and quiet. A great light that came over Tryfan in the heart of Barrow Vale, and gathered him into its Silence.

During the days that followed they were all subdued. Mayweed seemed suddenly to have grown old and grey, as if the death of Tryfan had robbed him of anything to live for.

Bailey was disconsolate with grief and shame, for he felt he had been a coward and had no right to live. Romney, too, was low, seeming to think that the emptiness of the wood and the lack of mole life there was his own fault. The sound of feeding rook and calling owl seemed to fill the wood.

The grey, cold weather continued into January until one morning they woke to find the lightest powdering of snow on the surface of the wood between the trees. The sun broke through and suddenly the wood looked beautiful once more. Rooks flapped and were gone; the owls fell silent once again.

That morning Mistle went to the Stone and, with the sun on her flanks, stanced before it to pray in silence for a long time, her snout low. When she had finished she looked up and her eyes were bright, clear and purposeful.

She went and found the other moles: Bailey stanced by a tree doing nothing, Romney fretting at a worm half-heartedly, Mayweed asleep.

'I want to talk to you,' she said to the first two, and then prodded Mayweed awake. 'And you as well, Mayweed.'

Reluctantly, and looking truculent, they gathered round her.

'Somemole here's got to say it, so I shall. Duncton isn't a system for gloomy moles. Gloomy moles don't look right here. Now I am not and have never been a gloomy mole. One day my Beechen is going to come back, and when he does I want him to come to a system *sparkling* with life. So, what are each of you going to do towards that?'

She looked at each of them in turn.

Bailey shrugged and said he didn't know.

Romney said he'd do anything to make amends, even if it included trying to be more positive, but that wasn't easy in the circumstances.

Mayweed said, 'Magnificent Mistle, you are a felicitous fillip to this mole, who is not by nature gloomy either. No, no, no. He has a thought and will utter it. What did Tryfan mention before he died? Well?'

'He mentioned Seven Barrows,' said Mistle, 'and he was right to say I have been there. The Stone must have told him that. He said you should go there.'

'Got it in one, Madam Mistle. "Go there, young mole!" he more or less said. Well, Mayweed may be old but he's not one to vegetate and would prefer to die while he's route-finding rather than stancing still. So . . . Seven Barrows and Stillstones seems a good way for Mayweed to go in search of death! Humbleness has therefore decided to be off. Oh yes, and he's taking Bailey with him.'

'But. . . .'

'But, but, but, but, but,' said Mayweed. 'Me, Mayweed, really doesn't want to know. Trouble with you, Bailey, is you have never got over losing Lorren and Starling all at one go. Very careless that. Still, Lorren's alive and well as I told you, and Starling could be too. Come with me, see the world and come back when you've got yourself sorted out. You'll be no good here and that's a fact, a very gloomy fact, eh, Mistle?'

He grinned and she laughed. The sun shone in the wood about them.

'And Romney?' said Mistle wryly. 'Since you've got it

all worked out, Mayweed, you better tell us what your plans for him are.'

Mayweed leered.

'Best way of ridding yourself of guilt is to work so hard you don't think about it. Work him, Mistle, work him hard! Plenty to do, and one day moles will come back to this place that's been a home to me and find it just right. *I* won't come back, but others will.'

'But. . . .'

'Bothered Bailey, don't bother. I've heard it all before. If you say "but" once more we'll leave *immediately*. Be warned!'

'When will you go?' said Mistle.

'Before I think about it twice.'

'I *have* been to Seven Barrows,' said Mistle. 'It was magical.'

'Amazing Mistle, if I was younger I could love you, but as I'm not I'll merely say they didn't make moles then like they do now. Except, of course, for Sleekit who is one in a million.' He smiled that happiest of smiles, which is that of a mole who has known true love and has no need to speak of it.

'But,' said Bailey.

'Ah! The third "but". The moment has come. Goodbye, Madam, goodbye, Sir, I don't want to leave you but I think Bailey ought to go. A long journey suits him. Last time he lost weight. This time he'll find himself. Farewell one and all!'

'Er, goodbye, Romney. And you, Mistle,' said Bailey.

Mistle gave them both a warm hug and started to go a little way with them.

'No, Madam, no, Sir, do not accompany us! Mayweed hates goodbyes and a route-finder likes to leave others standing exactly where they are. It gives him a sense of identity. Ha, ha, ha. Perturbed Bailey, get your snout straight and your paws set, Mayweed's going to make a mole of you at last!'

With that they set off across the wood, and were gone into the morning sun.

'Just like that!' exclaimed Romney, wondering. 'You moles of the Stone are like nothing I've ever known.'

Mistle was smiling after Mayweed and Bailey, with tears in her eyes.

'So what do we do now?' said Romney looking around and feeling a little daunted.

'Why Romney, we work, that's what we do! To make Duncton live again, to make Beechen know that the Stone is loved and cherished in the system in which he was born.'

'But if . . .' began Romney, sounding one last doubt.

'But he will, he will come back,' said Mistle fiercely. 'He told me that he would, and so he will.' And that was an end of that.

Then she put her paw to Romney's, and said warmly, 'Come, let us explore the system to which the Stone has sent us. Let us see the place that is our home.'

The winter sun was all about them, and the leafless trees of Duncton shone bright; and if the breeze made any sound at all, it was like whispered welcomes among the trees and tunnels from old moles of faith and courage, filled with joy to see their young back home at last.

Chapter Twenty-Nine

It is many moles' hope to see snow on Longest Night, and as systems of the Stone go, Beechenhill, being northerly, was normally luckier than most. But that cycle of seasons, though the weather was cold, the snows did not come until the third week of January.

Then, when they came, they were sudden and severe, as easterly winds drifted deep snow across the lower slopes and covered the higher parts with a crust of fluted ice through which the ends of mat grass stuck stiffly.

Treacherous though this surface was, two moles struggled at that time to find a route through the frozen, fractured communal tunnels there to get as near to the Stone as they could. They should not have done so, but Harebell insisted that she wished to go to the Stone, and Wharfe refused to let her go unaccompanied.

The day they chose was clear and bright, and when they finally stanced unsteadily on the exposed and icy surface by the Stone, all their adopted system lay stretched out beneath them, glinting in the south-east where the sun had risen low. All was white, all beautiful. The only sound was the thin whine of wind in the wire fence that lies north of the Beechenhill Stone, the only movement the flick-flack shift of sheep's wool caught on the wire's barbs.

'We must not stay here long, Harebell,' said Wharfe.

'I know. I just want . . . just for Betony.'

'I know you do,' said Wharfe, for ever since Betony had been lost, Harebell had come regularly to the Stone to pray for her, whatever the weather and whatever anymole said.

That day, despite the difficulties of getting there, the system looked purer and more peaceful than they ever remembered, even on the gentlest summer day. White, pure, good.

'When will moledom's darkness and the siege of Beechenhill ever end?' asked Harebell. 'It has been going on so long. I'm so tired of it, Wharfe. But I'm sure the Stone Mole has come and that he'll find Betony for us and she'll be safe.'

Wharfe smiled bleakly but said nothing. He wished he could go out and look for Betony, but he did not know where to begin. While Harebell felt the loss emotionally, he felt somehow responsible, as if he had failed Betony, and more than once before he had wanted to go off in search of her. The winter years were beginning to seem long and slow, and he had never thought a system could change so much, and come to seem so hateful. It was no consolation that Squeezebelly had warned him that it would be so.

'When the worms go deep, and moles follow them and are confined, then trouble starts; always did, always will,' Squeezebelly had told him. '*That's* when a system shows its strengths and weaknesses.'

'Stone,' said Harebell, 'bring our Betony back to us safeguarded and send the Stone Mole to us here in Beechenhill.'

'Yes . . .' muttered Wharfe, too tired and dispirited even to speak a prayer.

Then Harebell turned back the way they had come, and Wharfe followed behind her and they went back down out of the light.

Such a harsh season is a difficult and fractious time in any system, for just when moles want to be out and about and beginning to think about a mate they find themselves confined below ground and inclined to be restive and quarrelsome.

In Beechenhill the situation had been made worse because since November the grikes had successfully caused dissension and disaffection in the system with a policy for which there seemed to be no precedent. On the one paw, they had steadily increased the sense the system had of being besieged by closing more and more of the routeways out, especially to the west, which had always been the best source of news. On the other paw, and most dubiously, the unheard-of had occurred – a sideem and some guardmoles from Ashbourne had made friendly contact with some watchers before Longest Night and claimed that they were interested in an exchange of views on matters of faith.

Even more surprising was the fact that the Ashbourne sideem, Merrick, sent a messenger to inform Squeezebelly that he was willing to have the discussions in Beechenhill or in his own system, whichever they preferred.

The moles of the Word could not have found a more effective way of dividing the system, for while moles like Squeezebelly and Wharfe believed it was merely a way to spy on them, many others, including Squeezebelly's son Bramble, and the now well respected Mallerstang mole Skelder, argued that they should respond positively.

'You're beginning to see shadows where there are none,' said Bramble, who, since Betony's tragic disappearance had become bitter and estranged from Squeezebelly, and Wharfe and Harebell too, as if he blamed them for the loss of Betony.

'My dear Bramble . . .' began Squeezebelly.

'But I agree with him, Squeezebelly,' interrupted Skelder. 'If we don't even try to talk to them then they can rightly say to anymole in moledom that we're closed to all discussion, and afraid of the Word.'

'What's more if we talk to them there might be a chance of finding out something about Betony, or had you forgotten about her altogether?' said Bramble.

'That's unreasonable, Bramble, and you know it,' said Wharfe.

'No, Wharfe, I think Bramble's got a point,' said Squeezebelly, a master of compromise and diplomacy, who had put up with worse things from Bramble and some other of the younger generation of moles than their present anger and dismissiveness. He had been through the winter years before.

'I remain very suspicious of their true intentions, but if they really want a "discussion" about our beliefs and theirs (the Stone help us all!) then perhaps they can demonstrate their new spirit of cooperation and tell us what happened to Betony . . . It's the not knowing I cannot bear.' Squeezebelly sighed and shook his head sadly.

He had aged since Betony had disappeared, and his face had lost its normal good cheer and humour. He felt he had lost not only a daughter but, indirectly, a son as well, and he was aware that matters were not helped by the now obvious fact that of all the new generation of moles Wharfe not Bramble was the most able successor to his role as first among equals in the Beechenhill hierarchy.

But they had all been much affected, though in different ways. While Wharfe remained passionate with anger about Betony's loss, Harebell, partly because of her close friendship with the Mallerstang female Quince, had had more recourse to the Stone.

On the very rare occasions that news came to Beechenhill through itinerant moles who had made a successful entry into the system, she now always asked of matters of the Stone, and whether any news had yet been heard of the coming of the Stone Mole.

Just as she clung on to the belief that Betony was still alive, so too she had faith even now that the Stone Mole would come. Indeed, she often asked Squeezebelly if she might not attempt to escape the system by the well-concealed escape routes through the limestone tunnels that lay to the north, but he said no, arguing that it was bad enough losing Betony, but if *she*, daughter of Henbane and therefore sister of Lucerne, were ever discovered or caught, her life would no longer be worth living. Of that Squeezebelly had no doubt, for he knew the ways of the Word and its moles. For that reason, too, he could guess all too well what, if Betony was still alive, she might be suffering, and wondered if it might be best if she were not alive. . . .

Squeezebelly knew, too, that Bramble's present discontent, exacerbated by being winter-bound in the system, arose as well from the fact that he had vied with Wharfe for Quince's affections, and as everymole knew he would, he had lost.

Not that Quince was giving much away – after all it was not even near springtime yet – but the time she and Wharfe spent together, and the impressive pair they made, left little doubt what the outcome would be.

Bramble's chances were not improved either by the fact that Quince, like Wharfe, was dubious of the sideem Merrick's intentions with their proposed religious discussion, saying that it was not the nature of the Stone to be evangelical. Moles must learn from each other by example, not the spoken word – words, she argued, were only a means by which moles got themselves into a *position* for doing things. Bramble was a talker. She, like Wharfe, preferred to be a doer.

Squeezebelly was too wise and experienced a mole to involve himself directly in such matters, but he did what he could to keep Bramble and Wharfe apart, and sent them, as he did other moles, out into the wintry system to help repair tunnels against the ice and snow, and to delve them deeper where need be. Physical activity, he knew, was good for moles. Meanwhile he used the excuse of Betony, and his suspicions that the sideem of Ashbourne must know where she was, to keep the discussions at bay.

Only at the end of January, after repeated denials by the sideem of Ashbourne that he knew anything of the female in question, Squeezebelly finally yielded and agreed that discussions could take place – in tunnels at the edge of the system where nothing about it would be given away.

The discussions were as innocuous as Squeezebelly expected, but he attended them with some interest if only to meet the sideem Merrick directly, for until then their contact had been through intermediaries. Merrick was harmless looking enough, and might have been mistaken for diffident but for the firmness and clarity of his

642

arguments when he was pressured by the Beechenhill moles. Squeezebelly observed with fascinated distaste the way in which this clever sideem's apparent reasonableness seemed to impress moles like Bramble and Skelder. Nothing that was said changed his mind that the Word was merely a heartless system of oppression which made moles ruled by it miserable.

Then, after several fruitless days, the discussions were suddenly terminated by the sideem Merrick for the unconvincing reason that the Beechenhill moles were 'not cooperating'. This, it seemed, referred not to the discussions but because the moles of the Word felt insulted not to be let further into the system. Rarely had Squeezebelly's leadership and command been so sorely tested, for Bramble and Skelder argued he was being unreasonable, but he succeeded in asserting his wishes, sensing that the slow attrition of the Word might one day be too much for Beechenhill moles if too many of them were like Bramble. He hated to think such a thing of his own son, but thank the Stone for Wharfe!

In fact he was too canny a mole to believe the reason given for terminating the discussions, and observed to Wharfe and some other moles, 'Something has happened outside which they are not telling us about. Did you notice that there were fewer of their moles there today, and only very senior and dependable ones?'

'Aye, and hardly any of them spoke at all in contrast to previous days, leaving it all to the sideem.'

'Something has happened which they do not want us to know about, something important, and we must find out what it is.'

'You know, I'm willing to try to get out,' began Wharfe.

'And me,' said several voices.

Squeezebelly allowed himself to smile.

'I know perfectly well that you're all very willing to leave the system to go and find out what you can . . . and I also know that the grikes will be waiting for you. Even so, I must say that if the weather was not so severe I would let

643

one or two of you go but you know as well as I do, better in fact for I don't venture out much these days, that the chances of them getting you in these conditions are too high to be worth the risk.'

Some of the less experienced moles there muttered that they did not agree, but others, including Wharfe, knew that what Squeezebelly said was true. In warmer weather the surface provided good safe cover, but when the ground was frozen then a mole driven to the surface was dangerously exposed, and could not rely on snow for cover. Drifts were safe enough, though they disoriented a mole, but clear frozen ground was treacherous. As for the normal routes – grike guardmoles watched over them day and night. The watchers confirmed that.

Indeed, within hours of the curiously sudden cessation of the discussions, Beechenhill watchers reported that guardmole patrols had been doubled, and even obscurer routes to north and west were over-watched at their far ends where a mole must exit.

It was most frustrating and strange.

'There must be some way of getting out!' said Harebell.

'There is,' said her brother drolly: 'Go to Ashbourne, and you'll get out right into the paws of the guardmoles and that will be that.'

'It might be the quickest way of finding out where Betony is,' said Harebell with that mock light-heartedness with which she tried to hide the agony she felt.

'When the spring comes, Harebell, and the ground's thawed, I'm afraid that my patience is finally going to snap and I'll leave the system and find out about Betony once and for all.'

It was plain that if he ever did so, Harebell was not going to try to stop him and she said, 'At least we know that the mole who took her was called Mallice – it's not a name a mole forgets and I'm sure the sideem *does* know who Mallice is. She *must* be senior.'

But at such a time, and in such conditions, what could moles do but talk, and hope, and plot their dreams of love, or change, or journeying? But it was small consolation that in such conditions it was unlikely that the grikes would mount an attack.

Older moles than Harebell and Wharfe let the days drift by and stayed quiet and by themselves, and tried not to think too much. Hoping was a young mole's game. Best to take things slow, best not to think much at all. Beechenhill had survived well enough for a very long time and as long as Squeezebelly was alive all would be well, so why waste energy getting agitated?

Then, quite suddenly and unexpectedly, one mid-February night, when the wind battered at the ice-bound entrances, and moles sought out the warmest part of their burrows, a brave mole appeared in the system as if by magic, having come to one of the north-east approaches in the night, and the news he brought changed all their lives. And Squeezebelly discovered that he had been right, and what it was the Ashbourne sideem hoped he and other Beechenhill moles might never hear.

The mole was no more than a cycle old, strong and tough, and tired and breathless though he was, worn and bleeding though his paws, he would not rest or answer any questions until he was taken to great Squeezebelly himself.

News of his arrival got about, and Wharfe and Harebell, Skelder and Bramble and many others hurried to Beechenhill's communal chamber to hear him speak.

The mole bore himself with strength and purpose, and yet to his eyes there was wildness, and to his speech great passion.

'Mole, I am told you will not even speak your name,' said Squeezebelly, 'and yet you inspired enough trust in our watchers and those you've met to get this far. So tell us your name, and your purpose, and then have rest and sleep before you speak more.'

'Well!' declared the mole, nearly in tears. 'I never thought I'd be in your presence, Squeezebelly. You and the moles you lead are respected far and wide beyond Beechenhill. We who are followers of the Stone in other systems know you as a great light for our faith and . . .' Then he stopped and looked suddenly distressed. 'But no other moles have reached you? You have not been told?'

'You have a chamber of moles hanging on your every word. If you don't want rest and food, tell us your name and tell us why you've come.'

'My name is Harrow, son of Winster, snouted eldrene of Ashbourne.'

A hush fell across the chamber, for most of them knew of Winster's death, and that she had been a brave and privy friend of Squeezebelly and Beechenhill, and of the Stone; she had lived a dangerous double life of faith for many years. Her death, and those of moles close to her, had been the beginning of the closing of the outside world to Beechenhill.

'My mother had suspected that when Lucerne of Whern took over as Master-elect in June, her days at Ashbourne might be numbered.'

Squeezebelly nodded and said, 'Aye, Harrow, I heard as much from moles she sent.'

'Well, fearing that, and knowing how much I was of the Stone, she sent me to Tissington, a safer system than Ashbourne, though it too has since had its troubles with grikes. But she felt it was far enough off not to be affected if she was suspected at last, and punished.

'She did not tell me all the routes into Beechenhill – I think you are too careful for that – but she spoke of some of them, and other moles helped me as well. In this weather, if a mole can stand it and risk attack from rooks and owls, guardmoles do not watch the surface too well. The only hurt I had was to my paws when I slipped down icy slopes. But this is of no consequence.' He spoke well and clearly, and without false modesty.

'I asked if others had come because several of us have tried, and two have been lost, caught, I fear by the grikes. Outside we know you are beleaguered, and my mother

Winster was always aware of it, and charged me to do all I could to keep you informed when matters of importance arose. Well, something has arisen, something you must know.'

He looked around at the assembled moles, and if there had been a hush before, there was dead silence now.

Then Harrow said, 'Moles of Beechenhill, a glorious time may soon be on us. We have news all followers wish to hear. The Stone Mole, for whom we have waited for so long, is come at last to moledom. He is alive, he is among us, his day has come.'

Before Harrow could say more he was interrupted by shouts of incredulity and exclamations of joy.

'What is more, this is more than just a rumour or wishful thinking by followers. We heard it through the grikes in Ashbourne, for though my mother died and others too, yet some followers remain there secretly and pass much on to those of us in Tissington who still struggle for the Stone.'

'But where and whatmole is he?' asked Harebell, her eyes gleaming, for in the Stone Mole's coming she felt much would be resolved.

'His name is Beechen, and he was of Duncton born.'

'But we heard Duncton was outcast,' said Squeezebelly doubtfully, 'and that the grikes had put their own diseased and miscreant there.'

'Well, so it was, but the Stone's ways are wonderful and mysterious. The mole Beechen was born there. He is not in that system now, but coming north, and the grikes are much perturbed by it. They say he is not the Stone Mole but an imposter, a Stone-fool with madness in his head. Some among the followers say the same, but the stories that we've heard tell of healings and miracles he has made. Everymole is confused by it all, not knowing what to believe.

'What *is* certain is that the sideem of Ashbourne is much worried that if you Beechenhill moles hear of it you will rise up and go forth to meet the Stone Mole. They have recently strengthened their complement of guardmoles at Ashbourne and I think secretly they hope you will make a break out their way, for they would be on their own ground. I have come to warn you of that, and that their numbers are great now and you would certainly be crushed.

'Nevertheless, if this mole is the Stone Mole as many of us believe, then this may be the hour for us followers to prepare ourselves to fight. . . .'

'Harrow! Our system is not, and has never been, aggressive,' said Squeezebelly immediately, 'and it is because of that we have survived so long, even through this long time of the Word. One day it will end, but it shall not be ended by fighting, for that is not our way.'

He spoke sternly, and a mole might have thought that none there would have dared contradict him. But there was an immediate rumble of discontent, and Bramble dared give voice to it, saying, 'There comes a time when a mole may have to fight for what he believes, and when it comes I hope that moles here will not be cowards!'

'Aye!' said many others.

They'll do so over my dead body,' said Squeezebelly angrily, his normal calm leaving him for a moment. 'But we shall not argue at a moment like this, but hear more of this mole Beechen, and ask Harrow what else he knows. And of other news, too.'

Then to change the subject, and to divert the gathering's attention from the question of whether to fight or not, Wharfe quietly asked if Harrow had heard anything of Betony, explaining who she was and how she had been lost.

Harrow shook his head, but when Harebell said the mole who had taken her was thought to have been called Mallice, he said sharply, 'When was this?'

When they said it had been in October he said cautiously that there had been a mole called Mallice in Ashbourne at that time.

'Do you know who she is?' asked Squeezebelly.

'Oh yes, everymole who has had to do with the sideem knows who *she* is. Mallice is consort to Lucerne of Whern; she is not a mole moles love. I have heard that moles she takes end up in Cannock, Lucerne's new system to the south-west.'

Squeezebelly had no wish to extend what might now become a painful conversation in public, nor to risk resurrecting the calls for fighting which the Stone Mole rumour had provoked. So using his desire to ask further but private questions about Mallice and Betony as his excuse, he took Harrow to his own chamber, not even allowing Wharfe, Harebell or other senior moles there for a time.

'Get Harrow some food,' he said. 'Let him have a little conversation with me and then, once he has rested, I'm sure he'll be willing to answer more questions.'

But the moment Squeezebelly had Harrow alone, he said, 'Well, mole, and why have you really come?'

Harrow looked surprised and impressed.

'My mother said you're not a mole easy to fool, and she was right.'

'Well, this business of the Stone Mole is still a rumour when all's said and done, and you might have guessed that we knew grike numbers have been increased, so it didn't strike me as a reason why a mole might risk his life getting here. Nor would the news you have of Mallice been that important, even if you had known we needed to hear it.'

'Well, as for Mallice, nomole will get near her unless they wish an audience with the Master of the Word himself. Not something to be recommended, I would think.'

'So why did you come?' said Squeezebelly.

'Because something has occurred which I do not know what to do about. Something I dare tell nomole, whether of Word or Stone, unless I can trust him. Before she died my mother said that you are a mole to trust.'

'If 'tis a matter of the Stone, or a matter on which lives of moles depend, then you can trust me. I shall do nothing, nor allow those I command, to do anything against the Stone or its code. What knowledge do you wish to entrust me with which is so dangerous that so few moles must know it?'

' 'Tis knowledge that you will scarcely believe. I did not myself at first. But now I am convinced it's true, more so by far than I am about the Stone Mole, and in the struggle with the Word which I think is coming – whether or not we fight with talons, and I can see you're against that, Squeezebelly! – it is knowledge that may prove valuable for the side that possesses it. Have you ever been to Tissington?'

'In my younger days, yes. My father sent me out on such escapades, saying it was good for my education. Forgive me, but it seemed a nondescript sort of place.'

'Exactly. Not a place moles much remember, not having the advantages of site and location which systems like your own and Ashbourne have. But that very anonymity makes Tissington a good place to hide, which is why my mother sent me there.'

'A good place to hide?' said Squeezebelly sharply.

'Yes,' said Harrow, 'to hide. Sometime before Longest Night a follower came to me with a story so incredible that at first I dismissed it. Very fortunately he was not only persistent but intelligent, and had told no other mole. He told me because he knew I was strongly of the Stone. He said that he had found a mole nearly dead of hunger and exhaustion, and as strange a mole as ever he had seen.'

'What was the mole's name?'

For a long time Harrow said nothing but simply stared at Squeezebelly. Then he looked behind at the burrow entrance, and came close and spoke low.

'The mole is Henbane. Henbane of Whern.'

'Henbane?' whispered Squeezebelly aghast. '*Henbane*?' Then he shook his head dismissively. 'But she's dead, mole. Surely Lucerne would not have taken over Whern unless she was. The Master of the Word is not going to tolerate a former Mistress wandering around moledom. No, it cannot be.'

'My reaction exactly,' said Harrow. 'Nevertheless it seemed sensible to see her because if the grikes got to hear of it they'd have come crawling all over Tissington. I therefore talked to her myself, and more than once. She is . . . remarkable.'

'A remarkable liar I should think.'

'I think not,' said Harrow, 'and I risked my life coming here *because* I think not.'

'In what way is she remarkable?'

'In many ways, but most of all because although she had been ill and malnourished when I first met her she radiated the kind of spirit that defies death.'

'She must have a reason for living, then, whoever she is. It's what I've got. Mine's a desire to see the Word leave Beechenhill alone. What's hers?'

Squeezebelly spoke lightly. It was plain he still scarcely believed what he was hearing.

'Her reason is because she desires to see two pups taken from her at birth. I came here because I believe they may have been reared in Beechenhill.'

Harrow had fixed an unwavering stare on Squeezebelly whose face, for once, betrayed more than he wished it to.

'I see I am right, or if not right I am near the truth.'

'Something about you, Harrow, restores my faith in moles, moledom, and the new generation. You *are* right, and if this mole is Henbane then you have already met her young who are now rather older than yourself. Both were at the gathering you spoke to. But first you had better tell me the whole story, and before that you had better eat. . . .'

At that moment Harebell appeared with some food.

'Well timed, my dear.' She seemed to want to stay, indeed she seemed *more* than interested in talking with Harrow, but Squeezebelly firmly cut that short, saying they still had things to discuss.

When she had left Harrow said, '*That* mole! Who was her mother, Squeezebelly?'

Squeezebelly shrugged noncommittally.

'There's a mole I know, in Tissington, very old, clinging on to life, who has an aged version of *that* mole's fur and eyes,' said Harrow. 'Remarkable, isn't it?'

Squeezebelly grinned, a lot nearer to being convinced.

'It certainly seems so. Eat your food and tell me the story of the mole who says she's Henbane.'

Squeezebelly heard how Henbane – for soon he did not doubt that it was her – had come to leave Whern, and travelled south in long and fruitless search of her young. She had kept to high and desolate places and avoided mole. Bit by bit she had come southward until, in the place Tissington moles appropriately call Hunger Hill, she had fallen ill and weak, and barely survived.

It was there the follower had found her, and to him she had told something of her tale one night. The follower, understanding something of the significance of what she had told him, went to find Harrow in Tissington, and Harrow had succeeded in gaining the trust of Henbane, and offered her his help.

She had given much evidence of her identity, and revealed much of Whern, and of other things that only a most powerful mole could know. But when she had said that the purpose of her journey was the seemingly hopeless task of finding her lost pups, Harrow remembered rumours he had been told by his mother of the identity of two moles in Beechenhill – rumours first told by watchers tortured by the grikes.

Harrow realised that if they were true and this mole was Henbane, and what she had told him of her rejection of the Word was true as well, then her importance to moles of the Stone might be very great. He did not need to say much about Squeezebelly to Henbane, for she knew of him already through her sideem and she was prepared to trust him. . . .

'In fact, she's prepared to trust anymole if it means she gets a sight of the two pups she lost at birth,' said Harrow.

Squeezebelly heard all this with a growing realisation of

its implications. At the simplest level they would be profound for Harebell and Wharfe; at the level of his system he might have further problems with those keen to set off and fight the grikes in the name of the Stone Mole. But there was also the risk that the knowledge that Henbane was involved in any way with Beechenhill would surely precipitate a full-scale invasion by the grikes. It was becoming increasingly plain to Squeezebelly that this was not something they could easily combat.

'I shall sleep on this, Harrow, and so shall you,' he said eventually. 'Meanwhile, say nothing to anymole, least of all Harebell. It is not my nature to hide things from others in the system, but nor is it wise to reveal everything until they have been thought about. Timing is what running a system's all about. But Henbane, Mistress of the Word! Remarkable indeed! Quite remarkable.'

It took no more than a few hours for Squeezebelly to decide that Henbane ought to be brought to Beechenhill. But he felt he owed his first loyalty to Harebell and Wharfe and they must be asked their opinion.

'You shall tell them yourself, Harrow, just as you told me. Let me summon them. . . .'

When he came back, and while waiting for Wharfe and Harebell to come, he said, 'The Stone speaks to us in this, but I know not how. These are strange times, times for moles to watch to their beliefs and stay by them, time to trust the Stone. But this Stone Mole rumour . . . is it really true, do you think?'

'I'm not sure. I like no rumour that comes first from grikes. As you say, these are times when a mole must be cautious, but there's something about it that rings true.'

Harebell appeared and she did not look as happy to see Harrow now as she had before; she looked as if she had been awake all night.

'My dear, this mole has been telling me of something which you should be the first to know. But it affects Wharfe as well.'

'Wharfe is not here.'

'Well, he can't be far.'

Harebell looked alarmed and distressed and said, 'I'm sorry, Squeezebelly, but he's left Beechenhill. He's gone to try to find Betony . . . It was last night after Harrow spoke to us. I tried to stop him, but he's been half mad since she disappeared and when this mole . . .' She turned to Harrow and said, 'I wish you hadn't told us about Mallice as you did.'

'You should have told me,' Squeezebelly said.

'I told him to think about it first. It's not like him to go rushing off. I mean he's always been the most sensible one of us, hasn't he? Anyway he said he would think about it but then he talked to Bramble who said he shouldn't go until he knew more, but if he talked to you he thought you'd stop him.'

'Of course I'd stop him!' roared Squeezebelly. 'Just how does he imagine he's going to find Betony?'

'I've no idea,' flared Harebell, 'and it's all your fault, Harrow, for telling us of Mallice. Anyway, despite everything Bramble isn't completely useless and he's gone with some others to try and stop him, though whether he'll succeed I rather doubt. You know how fast Wharfe can move, and even if Bramble catches him he'll not persuade him to come back.'

'Well, the cold might help, and the ice, and common sense. As you say he's never done anything like this before.'

Squeezebelly glowered while Harrow, caught in the middle, remained diplomatically silent. It was Harebell, trying to calm things down, who broke the silence: 'Well, here I am whatever the circumstances. What did you want me for?'

Squeezebelly, feeling suddenly that things were out of his control, sighed and said, 'This mole did not merely come to tell us of a Stone Mole rumour, or to unwittingly cause Wharfe to risk his life, but also to tell us something which you should know, Harebell. I shall say no more. But, please, please, my dear, will you first agree to stance quietly where you are now and *discuss* what he says like the sensible mole you are before you go rushing off like your brother?'

'I'll try,' said Harebell.

'You do that, try really hard,' said Squeezebelly heavily. He turned to Harrow, 'Now, tell her what you told me.'

Harrow repeated to Harebell what he had already told Squeezebelly, telling the tale slowly and in detail. Apart from a sharp intake of breath, and a stancing down into utter concentration, Harebell betrayed no emotion during Harrow's account, or later when he dealt with the many questions she asked about Henbane's health, condition and state of mind. Even when all was done she did not move, but continued to stare at Harrow as if still taking in what he had said.

'Well then,' said Squeezebelly, 'what are we to do?'

'I shall go to her,' said Harebell simply, 'and Squeezebelly, you shall try to dissuade me but I'm afraid you will not succeed. I shall go to her because she is my mother and she may need me. She must feel very much alone. Harrow here will guide me to her, and we shall bring her back together by another route, one of the more northerly ones. That way fewer moles will know she's come. They should not know who she is. I do not like a lie, but they should not.'

Squeezebelly sighed.

'You will not go to her,' he said.

'I shall.'

'I cannot let you, my dear. First Betony, next Wharfe, now you. I'm sorry, my dear. No.'

'Will you forcibly stop me? Is *this* how a mole of the Stone treats another?' She stared at him and then added, 'Squeezebelly, I *must* go, and you know why.' She smiled and went close to him. 'I *must*,' she said again. 'Do you want to think about it?'

Great Squeezebelly shook his head and blinked back tears.

'No, my dear, no I won't think about it because it's you who must decide. I just cannot bear to think of losing you. . . .'

Harrow quietly left the burrow, and never knew quite what was said. It was plain that these two loved each other dearly, and that Squeezebelly would take Harebell's departure at such a risky time very hard. But eventually he was called back in to them and he saw that she was indeed to go.

'Are you willing?' she asked Harrow. Harrow nodded.

'And is Henbane capable of the journey back here if she wants to come?'

Harrow said he thought she probably was.

'Perhaps some others could go with you.'

'That would be unwise,' said Harebell cryptically, but in the kind of voice Squeezebelly knew better than to argue with, 'and anyway, the fewer moles the better.'

'I don't like it, any of it, one bit,' said Squeezebelly finally.

'You always said that when things began to happen they would do so all at once. Well, now they have.'

'But I don't *like* it. The system needs to be united at a time like this, but it is not. The Stone Mole, Henbane, Wharfe disappeared, now you . . . I am concerned.'

But there was no answer to that and Harebell stared at Harrow, and Harrow back at Harebell, and seeing them both, staring like that and not missing a thing, Squeezebelly shook his head again and decided he must be old.

'But not so old,' he muttered when they had gone to Stone knows where, for Stone knows how long, 'that this old mole can't keep Beechenhill in order a little while longer yet.'

Chapter Thirty

Within a few days of Longest Night the eldrene Wort had gained an accurate and disturbing insight into the true danger the Stone Mole presented to the Word.

She had delayed her journey north for the vain, though understandable, pleasure of briefly revisiting Fyfield to glory in the regaining of her position as eldrene. But the moment had been soured by the discovery of just how profound an effect the Stone Mole had had in the brief time he had made the journey through the northern part of the Vale of Uffington that ended at Cumnor.

When she had returned she discovered that the vale was seething with stories of the Stone Mole, and with incipient rebellion. Eldrenes and sideem reported that the disaffection had spread even into systems which, to all intents and purposes, had seemed utterly converted to the Word. It was plain to the eldrene Wort that the Stone Mole had had a far greater impact than she could have imagined possible, or any other mole yet knew. She had found, in fact, her very worst fears confirmed.

But if the Stone's evil did not thereby seem bad enough, it was made worse by the complacent way (as it seemed to Wort) that the sideem and eldrene regarded it.

'Kill a few of the buggers at the right time and in the right way and they'll stay as pathetic as they always have been,' said one senior guardmole with a sneer. A typical response.

Another was more subtle.

'It's about power and what moles hold it,' he told her. 'I have seen no evidence that these moles have any power at all, and if they gained it they would soon lose it because they have not the organisation to sustain it.'

Wort did not agree, but could not get others to see it her way.

Nothing had alarmed her more than the resolute blind faith of followers she and her henchmoles tortured and killed privily. Indeed it was a matter of fascination to her that a mole could suffer so much for something as patently wrong as the Stone, and this proved the alluring nature of its evil.

'So *deep* does its evil eat into a mole's heart,' she whispered.

Some of the Fyfield guardmoles even doubted her sanity as she repeated the actions for which Wyre had originally demoted her by taking followers to the Fyfield Stone and, with her henchmoles, killing them even as she touched the Stone, as if to test its power against her.

In these semi-secret killings – it is hard in any system to keep such things *secret*, but easy to enforce a rule of not acknowledging them – she was said to repeat that anointing in blood that the Master had delighted in by the Duncton Stone.

At such times, so the whispers went, she repeated his name again and again in a continuous scream of penitential and self-inflicted taloning: 'Masterlucernemasterlucerne-masterlucerne.'

Meanwhile she, like the others, had assumed the Stone Mole had gone south, and so was appalled when one of the henchmoles she had sent out to discover where the Stone Mole was came back in the middle of January and, the winter mud still wet on his paws, told her the dire news that the Stone Mole had fooled them all by celebrating Longest Night at Rollright, and had now gone north and was already well clear of any immediate pursuit.

What concerned her immediately was that the Master Lucerne was in the south when the Stone Mole was moving north with a free paw to foment all kinds of evil and temptation for moles of the Word. She had no doubt that she and her henchmoles could catch up with Beechen, and take him. But if she did, what then? She would need authority to act on her own account on the day she caught the Stone Mole.

She saw immediately that the widespread vengeance planned by the Master against followers must be brought forward, and capable of execution before the Stone Mole himself was punished, so that any revolt was killed before it began.

For these reasons, and some might say an unhealthy desire to be near the Master she now worshipped, Wort fought every instinct she had to follow after the Stone Mole and instead travelled swiftly to Buckland to seek to persuade the Master to go north.

It was a brave decision, but when it came to pursuit of the Stone and its followers, Wort cared nothing for herself and if achieving her end meant annoying the Master she would risk it, just as she had before.

This time, at least, she had no difficulty gaining an audience with him, which was the more gratifying because she knew that Clowder and Mallice, as well as Drule, thought her fear of the Stone Mole overdone. But Terce took her seriously and this was, perhaps, the clue to why the Master was prepared to listen to her again.

'Greetings, eldrene Wort. Have you the Stone Mole for me yet?'

'My Master, holy teacher, the Word tries us sorely: the Stone Mole is escaped. Fled north while our eyes were fixed on thy glorious anointing and ordination in Duncton Wood. Many days have we lost, many to regain.'

'But my dear Wort, our guardmoles will catch him,' said Mallice. 'He cannot flee for ever.'

'Mistress Mallice, forgive me for I am but a humble eldrene, but you talk untrue. Every day our guardmoles fail to catch him – and I blame myself for thinking he would come south and have suffered chastisement of the talons for it – is another day this Beechen is free to ensnare the hearts of moles with the temptations and evils of the Stone.'

'Well . . .' began Mallice dubiously.

'It is not well, it is ill. Our task of suppression becomes harder each time the Stone Mole speaks of the Stone and makes converts. These days past I have been able to assess the impact he made in the brief time he was in the vale. Moles are hungry for the false teachings that he brings, and, hearing him, moles will die for him. Before he went north he even led moles in worship of the Stone at Rollright on Longest Night.'

'What would you have the Master do?' asked Terce.

'Wherefore is the Master in the south if the infection is travelling the north? He should go north!'

She turned and faced Lucerne and said loudly, 'Direct the suppression sooner than you planned. Prepare moles with vengeance now for the capturing and punishment of the Stone Mole which I shall soon achieve. And command me, Master. If I take him before that is done, what shall I do with him? If I keep him he shall be a tempter. If I kill him he shall be a martyr.'

'Then, eldrene Wort, you must yourself find just and fitting punishment for him,' said Lucerne, his voice as smooth and sharp as broken flint.

A light of pleasure came to Wort's eyes.

'So shall I, Master! So shall I. But be warned by me. Go north. . . .'

'And you, Wort, go too far.' He softened his voice and he said, 'The spring solstice, eldrene, is a good time.'

'For what, Master?' she asked, puzzled.

'For taking Stone Moles and doing what you must to them. Enough, Wort. Go and chase the Stone Mole, take him, the Word will guide you what to do with him.'

'Master, bless me, for I am weak. Lay thy touch upon my head . . .' And as Lucerne did so, his body scent was like nectar to her snout, his presence overwhelming in its effect upon her, and she sighed and cried out, 'Holy word, creator of my body, mother of my mind, father of my talons, let the memory of my Master's touch never leave, let it burn within me like a mighty procreating fire, oh let it stay and flourish within me!'

Lucerne smiled. Terce stared. And when she had gone,

Clowder spat. As for Mallice, she mimicked her voice saying, 'My Master, my beloved, how she lusts for you.'

Lucerne's expression was grave as he said, 'Yet she shall find the Stone Mole, and she shall know better than anymole how to do what must be done.'

'I would kill him and have done,' said Clowder.

'You have your strengths, Clowder, she has hers. I have every confidence she shall find him and kill him.'

Terce nodded and agreed that it was so and then said, 'What do you think of her desire for you to go north?'

'I think, Twelfth Keeper, that she is right. Very right. Clowder, you shall command here from now on and we shall leave you.'

'You did not tell her that you agreed with her when she was here,' Mallice said.

'She is already quite smug and self-righteous enough, my dear.'

'When shall we leave, Master mine?' asked Mallice, coming close.

'Tomorrow.'

'And the suppression?'

'This mole Wort offends my dignity. She makes it seem she persuades me, but as Clowder knows we have already planned the suppression for the springtime solstice. We shall have time to inform the sideem in the midlands and the west, and to do what we can for the difficult east.'

Clowder nodded grimly. The systems over which he now had control would not be found wanting. By the end of March very few followers would be left alive.

'It is better then than later in April when they start having young. We shall not fail.'

The eldrene Wort's busy journey to Buckland had, therefore, been all but pre-empted by Lucerne's decisions, but even if she had known that she would have been well satisfied. He had given her freedom to take the Stone Mole by the spring equinox, and when she had taken him to do what she would with him. She could ask for no more.

But in terms of time lost the journey was more costly than she thought, for a day after she left Buckland blizzards drove across the south-east and slowed her down, and it was not until the end of January that she was back in Rollright and able to consult with her henchmoles and decide at last on the strategy that would lead her to the Stone Mole.

Beechen's now legendary journey north, which had begun with the tragic news of the killings before the Duncton Stone on Longest Night of so many loved moles, was almost brought to a premature halt near Rollright as he, Buckram, Sleekit and Holm said their farewells to Lorren and Rampion. They were nearly discovered by guard-moles and only by the skills learnt from her father was Rampion able to lead her mother safely back into Rollright and obscurity.

Holm, too, showed his mettle then, leading Beechen and the others swiftly away by the moist routes he preferred.

He was a mole born in the Marshes beyond the Marsh End of Duncton Wood, and always one for mud, water and dampness. Dykes, streams, pools, lakes, mud flats, drains, conduits and culverts were all bliss to Holm, and he was drawn to them like a bee to pollen. He stopped at running rivers for he had once as a pup, in a moment of curiosity, attempted the feat of crossing the Thames, and been swept away so far that it had taken him three days to get back to his starting point.

But anything less than a river was a routeway to him, and he used such routes with a nearly infallible sense of when he must (often reluctantly) ascend above the waterline once more before the stream, culvert or dyke veered them off in the wrong direction.

There were several problems with Holm's approach. One was that it made moles muddy, very, and his companions had to get used to that. Another was that it was not a way to meet other moles since most were sensible enough to site their systems clear of too much water and the risk of floods. A third was that some creatures moles did not like, most notably water rats and herons, inhabited these wet places and were inclined to attack.

Holm, despite his habit of staring wide-eyed and in complete silence and therefore looking terrified, was, as Beechen, Sleekit and Buckram soon discovered, almost fearless.

The only concession he made to fear was the occasional utterance like, 'Rat, scarper!' and, curiously, 'Bleak!' When he cried this his voice rose a little and it was a sound of extreme danger and alarm that might have been created specially by him from the words 'Bleat' and 'Squeak' with the added bonus that when he spoke it their prospects did indeed usually seem bleak.

But like Mayweed, Holm had the true route-finder's constant awareness of alternative routes, and the ability to utilise them under pressure. When he did use roaring owl ways it was the culverts at their bases that he preferred rather than the often quicker but more exposed parts where the roaring owls themselves ran.

However he did it, they felt safe in his company, and though his watery ways kept them from followers, they also, especially in the early days of their escape from the Rollright region, kept them from guardmoles.

There is no doubt that the whole nature of Beechen's extraordinary and fateful northern journey was influenced by the twin shocks of Duncton's destruction and the nearly fatal clash with guardmoles at Rollright.

Until then, partly because of the sealed-off nature of his life in Duncton Wood, and the skilful way Mayweed had led him out of the system and into the vale, Beechen had seen little direct evidence of the grikes' ways, and therefore had no personal experience of their destructiveness. Even the experience in Hen Wood had seemed charmed, its potential impact lessened by his subsequent and all-important liaison with Mistle of Avebury.

But now he was going on that same journey Tryfan had

long before undertaken, and one which the great scribe-mole had often described to Beechen in stories and teachings, and which he characterised as a journey to the heart of darkness.

The sense that he was now making such a journey himself, combined with the deep and natural fear he had always felt that his destiny would place upon his shoulders a burden he would not have the strength to bear, coloured so terribly by the unknown but well-imagined horrors left behind in Duncton, put into Beechen a purposeful sense that much would depend upon this journey.

But more than that, he believed he would not return from it – for he said as much to Sleekit and Buckram more than once, asking their forgiveness for so confiding his fears and self-doubts, and trusting them not to speak of it to other moles.

In essence, the journey that he now made, for which his entire life and loves had been a preparation, was a paradigm for the journey he felt all moles must strive to make throughout their lives if they were to find their fulfilment through the Stone.

We have Sleekit's account of this, the Second Ministry of Beechen, scribed with Beechen's blessing, and at first it tells of a succession of quiet and often very small meetings, sometimes with but a solitary mole or a pair, often in communities much beset by the Word.

While he had been in the vale with Sleekit and Mayweed, Beechen's teachings were varied and particular to the moles he met, and much concerned with faith and purpose. But during his Second Ministry, whether because of changes wrought in him by his all too brief contact with Mistle, or because he had a growing sense that the journey he was taking was in some sense towards a final if so far mysterious goal, the teachings he gave seemed more linked together. We have not yet found all of the accounts Sleekit made, for much of it was scribed as they travelled and secreted along the way for future generations to find when times were more peaceful and the Stone was strong again.

But what we have shows how deeply Beechen had absorbed the teaching given him by Tryfan in the Marsh End, enhanced as it had been by the texts scribed and collected there by Tryfan and Spindle, and by the wisdoms Beechen had learned well from the moles outcast into Duncton Wood. It seemed to Sleekit that in that limited time he felt was left to him the Stone Mole wished to take his thoughts and meditative practices to the very edge of the Silence which is their final goal.

He travelled with us as if on a journey to what Tryfan had taught him to call the eastern sun, the light of truth and purpose bright in his eyes, his openness to other moles, his *love* for them, ever more apparent, and seeming to fail only briefly when, for short periods, he would turn from them and seek solitude, and meditate.

At such times, those of us travelling with him each had a part to play, and he would choose to be with each of us, often in silence, as if from us he could gain something we ourselves did not quite know how to give.

When he was with Buckram, it was renewed strength he found, and that great and devoted mole understood well that he had to be near Beechen in quiet and silence. Great Buckram would most touchingly bring him food, and make sure he was not disturbed.

With Holm he seemed to touch something different, that curious and questing restlessness which is a pup's, and which Holm, like his mentor Mayweed, possessed in abundance. Together they would peer here and there, and to Buckram's alarm and discomfort would wander out of range, Beechen as happy as Holm to get muddy and dusty. But unlike that route-finding mole, Beechen was very particular about cleaning his fur and washing his paws and talons when his explorations were done.

As for myself, I think he valued much that I had

known his father Boswell in Whern, and had witnessed his puphood, as if in some way I was a continuity from his beginning. He often asked me of Wharfe and Harebell, yet when I spoke of Beechenhill as a system he was always subdued, for I think Tryfan had impressed on him that of all systems in moledom, Beechenhill was the most purely magical. But more than once he asked me, 'Shall I be ready for that place, Sleekit? Shall I be prepared?' I knew not what it was he feared and sought to reassure him.

Yet driven though he was by these needs of solitude and individual companionship, yet he found the strength to see so many, and again and again moles said they felt great calm in his presence, and the sense that they had discovered a home they barely knew they had been seeking all their lives.

Sleekit also says this about him then:

There was no doubt that he was what old Teasel of Duncton often described as a 'goodly' mole, by which she meant physically pleasing — graceful, strong, straight of snout, purposeful without seeking to dominate or be aggressive. But when I heard others describing him the common things they spoke of were the quality of light about his fur, as if whatever light there was in a burrow was most concentrated on him, and the awesome power of his gaze which seemed to anymole that faced him not that he looked at the mole but into his very heart, and they knew for a moment the light and Silence of the Stone.

This was especially true at those moments when he healed moles with a touch, or a word, and sometimes as it seemed just a look. Many came to him with ailments and complaints of body and mind, and he ministered to them, and cured them.

Holm's route at first took them off the heaths beyond

Rollright to the lower moister vales to the east of the roaring owl way, down which Tryfan and Spindle had travelled when they escaped from Whern.

It was here, at Grafham Water, that Sleekit's account suggests that Beechen first began to expound his teachings of the great journey all moles seek, whether they know it or not, towards Silence in terms of warriorship.

Drawing on those myths he had been taught as a pup by Feverfew, and those more arcane teachings Tryfan later instructed him in when he learnt scribing, Beechen now began to speak to those who came to listen to him of the great mythical warrior moles of the past, said to be the sons of Balagan, first White Mole. Sleekit recorded Beechen's teaching thus:

These warrior moles did not live in moledom as we know it, but in that place of light that lies on the far side of the Stone, a place we physical moles cannot quite see, nor quite touch however much we circle a Stone and strain to reach it.

It is a place moles long to be, for it is the place from which they once came and where they do not strive and struggle for what finally they do not need.

That world of the great warriors seems so near, indeed it *is* so near. It is but a moment away. But when they are young, moles think that the way to that place is round the Stone and so they spend moleyears, whole lives, seeking ever more complex ways to get there. But that is not the warrior's way. The warrior mole knows that the only route is through the Stone, which is through Silence. That is called the sacred path of the warrior. It is a path we all must strive to take.

The wise scribemoles of the past, in the days when such myths were real and substantial in the hearts of moles, said that to be a warrior, and to set himself upon the sacred path, a mole must turn his snout towards the rising eastern sun and feel its light upon his face. That light and the warmth it brings is ever a reminder to a mole of what was true from the first moment of his birth – that he is good, essentially good. His goodness is like a warm light within him ever ready to shine out.

As the eastern sun reminds a mole of what he has, so a warrior set upon the path with truth and humility will be an eastern sun to other moles who have need of him, though he himself may never know it. Goodness brings out the good in others, and brings back a warmth and light to moles that has always been theirs.

Therefore, a warrior mole is of good cheer, others feel better for knowing him, life blossoms about him, and the shadows fade. His heart has awakened to the goodness of the life of which he is a part, his life is inextricably bound to all others' lives; he does not exclude others, he is not enclosed. This is the stance of the eastern sun, this the happy, ever-awakening, good reality of the warrior.

When Beechen first gave this teaching a mole called Mallet who lived at Grafham heard it. He was a mole who lived by himself on rising ground amidst low and often flooded meadows.

'Stone Mole,' asked Mallet, 'how shall I take my first step once I have adopted the stance of a warrior?'

Beechen replied, 'With a gentleness of which you do not think, and a harmony of which you are not aware, towards a place that has no name. And with certainty!

'Doubt is not in that first step, nor fear, nor any restraint but that imposed by love for yourself and other moles.

'A warrior does not run, lest he knocks down those who cannot move; he does not turn, lest others have less sight than he; he does not falter, lest others lose their faith. A warrior's first step is most hard!

'But with cheer in his heart, and love and faith, he shall make it true, and find the next step follows on, and the next, and the next after that until he looks behind and sees with surprise how far he has come, and that he goes alone.

668

Then does he see that where he thought he did not run, he ran too fast; and where he thought he did not turn, he knocked many down; and where he was certain he never faltered, he shook and shivered like a pup lost in a blizzard wind. But being a mole of cheer the warrior shall laugh, and that laugh will be joy and reassurance to others that hear it and, knowing that, he shall feel a little less alone.

'But I tell you this: each step a warrior takes is like his first and he must strive to be at once aware and unaware of it, which is most difficult.'

Then Mallet asked this question: 'Stone Mole, how does a mole learn to be a better warrior?'

'By listening,' replied Beechen. 'First, to all that is good in himself, and true, so that he knows himself true. Next, to those other warriors about him from whom he can learn, always remembering that since moments, hours, days and years cannot be replaced he had best be intelligent in his choice of company. Finally, he listens to the world of which he is an essential part so that he learns to be more of it, and less of himself. A mole who rushes cannot listen to the world, another mole, or himself. A mole who does not tell the truth deafens himself to what is good. A mole who self-deceives cannot listen to anything at all, nor be heard by anymole – such a mole is truly miserable. A mole who talks too much does not listen, and yet one who makes a study of humility and silence often does not hear.

'Listening moles are alive, responsive, enjoying, giving, always curious, always learning, exploring the world with their whole beings. Such moles train themselves even as they travel along the sacred path of warriorship.'

'But Stone Mole,' asked Mallet, 'how does such a warrior know when what he hears, he hears true?'

'The Stone has blessed all moles to be a part of life, and to make life, and through this may he set himself upon the sacred path. As a mother who has never had a pup before quickly learns to listen to her young, understanding the troubled bleat and the content mew and responding to it, so can all moles learn to listen out for themselves.'

So did Beechen speak to Mallet of Grafham Water, and after that many came to hear his teachings, and some began to follow him as he travelled northward into the driving snows of winter.

But more than that, news that the Stone Mole was coming travelled ahead of him as well, and now, as he and the growing number with him journeyed on, they found ever larger groups of followers waiting for them. As his meetings grew bigger, and the numbers needing his personal counselling and healing increased, his progress began to slow.

'Stone Mole,' warned Buckram, 'if this continues any moles pursuing us will find us, and if you let these moles travel with you how can we be secret from the grikes?'

'We cannot, Buckram.'

'But we must, Stone Mole, for the grikes. . . .'

'The grikes shall find us soon enough.'

'I cannot protect you by myself, and you will not let me muster others to fight, so how shall you be safe?'

'I have never been safe, Buckram, and nor have any of us, whether follower or grike. The pursuit of safety is the quickest way I know to death.'

'But are you not afraid?'

'Each day now new followers come to me, each day I feel their love; and each day you, Buckram, and others here come closer to me, and I feel less fear. Now I am afraid only that the work I must do shall be incomplete. For this alone have I travelled in these more obscure parts, and so far we have been favoured. But you are right to think that something will happen: it will and soon.'

'What then, Stone Mole?'

'Then we shall be that much nearer to the end of our journey.'

But guardmole grikes had already been appearing at some of the meetings they held in the better known systems: they were at Oundle on the Nene, for example, and again at Stamford some days later. As at Cumnor, they came in packs of three or four, to observe darkly and intimidate.

It seemed that so far they had been prevented from interfering physically with the followers or Beechen by the policy the grikes had adopted of 'listening', but Buckram had little doubt that this could not last long, and some moleweeks later, in mid-February, he was proved right.

Holm had turned their route, with some reluctance, from the flatter and wetter east, to the north-west across the clay vales and limestone rises that stretch south to north in those parts. It was country much more occupied by grikes, and to all but Beechen it seemed all the worse because it took them from obscurity to exposure.

Strangely, just as earlier news of their coming had travelled ahead among the followers, now it went with the grikes, who came more frequently and in greater numbers to stare, mock and jeer at the preaching 'Stone Mole'.

Across the rising vales they went, on into grike country. Again and again Beechen spoke out against meeting violence with violence in defence of himself, themselves or anymole, and warning them that it was not his way to strike another mole, *whatever* he might do to him. This appeal seemed only to increase the numbers coming to his flank, as if they felt that such a gesture was an act of faith and discipline.

Buckram was recognised as the mole responsible for Beechen's safety, and since his size and grave bearing commanded great respect, so did his words which, daily, warned all moles to honour the Stone Mole's wishes and, however much they might be provoked, not to respond in kind.

There was – and is – no doubt that this policy, though it now came under severe strain as the grike intimidation increased, for a time aborted the attempts by the grikes to cause a fight. Yet ironically the very non-violence of the followers inflamed the grikes to shout and threaten even more.

'Stone Mole,' said Buckram, 'I cannot prevent what I

know must inevitably happen if you continue on this route. You have done enough. None shall blame you or call you coward if you turn back or take a safer way. I have been told that tomorrow we shall pass near Oadby, which is a grike garrison and known for its violence. I fear what might happen there.'

Even Sleekit advised Beechen to retreat, but he refused, saying, 'It is the right of mole to go what way he will, with his snout straight and proud and his heart open. That is the way of the warrior. To turn back is to yield up our heart and joy to the agents of darkness and be diminished by them. Now at the moment of hesitation is the time to show our courage and our faith by exposing all our heart. To retreat is the greatest gift a mole can give his enemy.'

The only exception that Beechen made was for the few younger moles and their parents who were travelling with him now to go back, and some infirm moles as well, though most of these insisted on continuing. Beechen asked Buckram to travel with these weaker ones rather than himself, since his presence might help protect them.

'Stone Mole,' said Buckram, who rarely argued with Beechen, 'I would prefer to be with you and see that you are safe.'

'Do you think your talons are mightier than the Stone's peacefulness, Buckram? Do you think the Stone Mole would have protection which much weaker moles than he will not have?'

Buckram shook his head miserably and Beechen's look and voice softened as, smiling, he said, 'The Stone shall protect us, good mole, and thee as well. Warriors do not travel the sacred path without collecting wounds. And tomorrow, remember that though they may not know it the grikes are warriors too, upon the same path, and they may suffer wounds of a different kind: those that do not heal so fast.'

Buckram's fears were more than justified. As the followers came towards Oadby, with Beechen in the front line and

females and youngsters on either flank, grikes asse[m]
on either side of the way in large and ugly numbers.

At first they simply shouted and shook their talons
then, as the followers refused to respond but simply k[e]
their eyes ahead and their snouts straight, singing songs [of]
the Stone, some of the grikes began to buffet the olde[r]
ones in front.

But buffets turned to strikes, and strikes to talon
thrusts, and talon thrusts to hurts. It was a scene of very
slowly mounting violence which took place at that point
north-west of Oadby where the way passes rising ground
on either side. Enclosed, with nowhere to go but backwards or forwards, with grikes striking out as they went by
and some of the bigger, bullying ones running along
beside them and shouting, there was little the followers
could do but suffer the blows and continue.

Beechen was the target of special attention, first himself –
and soon his face was cut and red with blood – but then
those with him. The grikes would strike them and cry out
mockingly, 'Neither your Stone nor the one you call Stone
Mole protects you! Are they impotent or cowards?'

Sleekit was a little way behind Beechen and her flanks
were badly taloned and hurt, but most pathetic, and most
courageous of all, was Holm, a mole who had never struck
another in his life. Strangely, for one whose tendency was
to look terrified all the time, that day his eyes and his gait
did not waver, until he was bodily dragged from the group
and several grikes threatened him.

Buckram had prepared well for precisely this kind of
assault and he and several larger moles, all former fighters
before they turned their snouts properly to the Stone,
quickly interposed themselves between the grikes and
Holm, not striking back themselves but taking blows that
might have seriously maimed the little mole before they
hustled him back to the relative safety of the group.

This sudden show of calm control seemed to cool the
aggression of the grikes who retreated on either side of the

...ursue them once they were clear of
...ering laughter and threats.

...nature of Beechen's journey north,
...went with him on it. Some fell away
...g or unable to take such threats again, but
...not always the strongest —seemed to grow in
...purpose as if the demonstration of hatred by
...s towards Beechen had stripped away all that was
...r vague in these followers' faith to reveal an inner
...e of warrior strength.

Holm had already proved himself, but after Oadby gained an almost legendary respect among the followers, many of whom came specially to see him, though such honour did not change him one bit. He was as grubby and modest as ever. Sleekit, on the other paw, gained the gaunt and courageous look of an older female with great purpose and no fear, while Buckram, always strong, seemed to grow in stature every day and move with something of that strength which moles like Marram and Alder had. Moles who had been trained in fighting and discipline and have found their true way at last.

But if Oadby made those close to Beechen understand the violent nature of the threat that he was now trekking towards, it was what happened a few days later that showed a truer, darker face and made Sleekit, for one, realise all too clearly that this was indeed a journey into darkness.

Some miles west of Oadby the ground rises and hardens towards the bitter granite heaths of Charnwood Forest. This dread and eerie place is no friend of moles, whose eyes might well dart about them to the slopes above which seem to overhang and reveal with each corner turned, each new place gained, a looming black-rock edge, or clump of dying oak trees, their branches a contorted silhouette against the sky beyond.

At Charnwood the winds are fractious and snow seems dirtier and ice sharper: the kind of place where winter lingers on long after it has fled the rest of moledom.

As they rose up into this grim place, their numbers fewer than for weeks past, the followers gathered nearer Beechen as they went and he cheered them with his accounts of the giant moles that myth and legend said once lived among the jagged rocks.

Holm, so far from water, did not like the place, and hurried on ahead of them, pausing only to snout and scent the air, and frown, and then turn round to beckon them to hurry after him.

The highest part of the way took them among some dingy shattered rocks among which stunted hawthorn and gorse sought to find a place to thrust down their roots. Here a mole might stray from the path and not be found before the corvids that lurked about, or the foxes that crept, or the stoats that screamed at night took him.

Here are no good memories for mole.

Here they were benighted and spent shivering, dark hours.

Here, suddenly, as they set off once more, grikes rose up around them like filthy water rising out of bad ground to swamp a mole. One moment nothing but rocks, the next every rock seemed to spawn ten grikes, and every grike to show ten sharp talons.

While there before them all on a flat rock overlooking their way a female stanced, eyes narrow, eyes dark, unwavering.

'Greetings, mole,' said Beechen boldly, and in the old way said, 'Whatmole art thou and whither art thou bound?'

The female laughed, a tuneless sterile laugh which was chillingly echoed by chuckles and guffaws from the grikes who now came menacingly close, though no follower was touched. But evil was as palpable in the air as the stench of a dead sheep that drifted to them from among the rocks.

The mole's laugh died back to a sneer, and then to pity of an arrogant kind, and she said, 'Use not your vile tricks of charm on me, tempter, insulter of the Word. I am the eldrene Wort and I am bound to the place that shall be thy journey's end. Will you pray with me?'

'To what end, mole?' said Beechen, his voice powerful.

'For thy redemption from the evil of the Stone.'

'There is no evil, Wort. Not even in the darkest heart, not even in the vilest act, there is no evil that cannot be turned to the good that is in us all. Let us pray in celebration of that good!'

'Hear him, guardmoles of the Word! Hear his denial of his evil and pitiable plea for good. Lax good. Good indulgence. Good weakness . . .' Then she hunched forward towards Beechen and said this rapid prayer: 'Holy Word, you who are my portion and my sup, you who are my delight, you who make my body glad, help this mole renounce the Stone, help his followers turn from their twisted way, help their eyes see the glory that is only yours. Holy Word, mother and father of us all, chastise this mole that he may see thy truth, chide this mole that he may be sickened by what he is, admonish him that he may sing thy name and know the proper way.'

Wort's voice cried out these last words as if she were desperate and suffering, an impression increased by the way her eyes fixed on some distant point beyond all the moles. Now she half turned back and looked straight at Beechen once again.

'You have nothing to fear if you renounce the Stone, for the Word shall be merciful. I plead with thee to do it now.'

Beechen reached forward slowly and, even as guard-moles to right and left of Wort came towards him, he placed his paw on her head and she did not resist.

'Mole, be not afraid of me,' he said.

Wort closed her eyes and she whispered with terrible intensity, 'Holy Word, I feel thy power flow into me, I feel thy power destroy the temptations of the Stone, I feel thy power great within me. *Un-paw me, mole, un-paw me!*' She screamed the command at him and then her eyes snapped open and a look of disgust and hatred was on her face.

'Renounce, mole, before thy journey ends or you shall be damned by the great Word, and lost.'

'Wort, whatmole art thou, and whither art thou bound?'

This time Beechen spoke with a terrible sadness, and turning to the others signalled them to move on.

Which they did as the eldrene Wort continued her impassioned whisperings and warnings in the Charnwood heights, not hindering them more.

Of this strange incident Beechen did not directly speak straight afterwards. But some days later, at Swadlincote, one of the followers asked him again about it. Was he not afraid, she asked, of the threats the grike moles made, particularly the eldrene Wort?

'A warrior is wise to judge nomole,' he said. Then pointing at a place they had just passed where a tiny snowdrop grew from the dark, wet protection of a root – a flower none had even noticed until then – he said, 'You see what may come out of the darkest shadow? Remember this before you judge another mole.' But of Wort he said no more.

And yet in the moleweeks that followed this confrontation with Wort, Beechen seemed to accept that the eldrene had a part to play in his destiny which was beyond his power or desire to influence. Downcast and silent he became, trekking more slowly, talking to none, looking to Buckram and Sleekit to protect him now from other moles. Dreadful days of worsening winter weather, as driving rain turned to sleet and snow harsh at their faces.

On, on he wished to go, Holm never failing him, more silent even than he was. Until at last, one afternoon, Holm stanced up and scented against the wind.

'Holm knows what's there! Been told! Sleekit knows too.'

'I've never been by this route,' said Sleekit.

Holm turned forward once again with a startled look on his face and dashed forward as if just round the next corner was whatever it was he scented. In fact it was an hour's more travel and they came down upon it over a rise. Deep, dark, sinewy, flowing from the west, flowing to the east.

'See the River Trent!' said Holm. 'North's beyond it, south's this side.'

'Lead us down to it, Holm, and we shall rest.'

So, wearily, unharried for now by grikes, they came to the River Trent.

Even there, in the depth of winter weather, moles found them and Beechen, despite the darkness that had beset him, counselled and ministered to them through the long and desolate days.

Grikes, some of whom had been with Wort at Charnwood, came and stared. Came and grinned.

Beechen ignored them, turning towards the dark river which all knew he must soon cross.

'Father,' he whispered in one communal prayer he made then, 'give us strength for the final days to come. Let the Stone be ever before us, let its light shine upon our way, give me the companionship and love of my friends to the very last, grant me the strength to go on alone, however much I fear. Guide me.'

The others were afraid when they heard him speak prayers like this, and some of the followers complained and said, 'Is this a warrior's prayer? Is this not a prayer of fear and doubt? Where is the Stone in this? Why does he speak of his father and not of the Stone? Why do we feel doubt in his presence? Why does he not lead us differently than this?'

'Father,' whispered Beechen, 'help them in their hour of distress!'

How deep and black was the flow of the Trent, how fearful the prospect on its other side, how restless Beechen's sleep. Close came Buckram to him, comforting were the words Sleekit whispered, loving was Holm's way.

It was one bitter day then, when they lay by the Trent waiting for the weather to improve, that Sleekit found

Holm stanced miserably by the river, staring across to the other side. He had been gone some days by himself.

'What is it?' she asked. 'Couldn't you find a place to cross the river?'

'Ha!' said Holm. 'Easy that! But I'm sad and sorry.'

He turned to look at her, his eyes brimming with tears, his fur spiky with mud.

'Sorry I am,' said Holm.

'For what?' said Sleekit gently.

'Because . . . because I'm not Mayweed. Because he knows what to say and do. Stone Mole needs *him* now.'

'No, my dear, he needs you. You are worthy. Mayweed would be most proud of you. Mayweed loves you.'

Holm stared at her but found no more words that night.

So it was they helped each other; in such ways is community made.

Perhaps Sleekit told Beechen of what Holm had said, but more likely he sensed himself Holm's misplaced anguish. For when the day came that the weather cleared and Beechen was ready to go on he said to Holm, 'Take us now over into the north and keep your eyes open for where the Stone stands proud.'

'My eyes are not dusty like my fur!' said Holm.

'Do you know where to go?'

'Yes,' said Holm. With that he led them off and said no more.

Chapter Thirty-One

Southern moledom put Lucerne, Terce and Mallice into an ill humour. There was something insubordinate about its moles, its vale-ridden landscape, and even the mucky dullness of its winter weather that offended northern moles.

Then too there was the matter of the irritating change that was overcoming Mallice as the breeding season approached. She had been eager for young in the autumn and they had not come. Now spring was stirring beneath the frozen winter soil and there was an urgency for pups about her that Lucerne did not like.

Mating pleasurably is one thing, mating for the desperate purpose of wanting and needing young is quite another.

Now when Mallice purred, 'Master mine . . .' her eyes seemed suddenly aged to him, and her body lost its appeal.

'Not now, Mallice, the Twelfth Keeper and I. . . .'

'Sweet Lucerne. . . .'

'No!'

His voice, when thus harsh, was mirrored by his eyes, all glittering and black without love at all. His turning away from her at such moments was final.

But then, sometimes, as they had journeyed back from Buckland, across the hateful Vale of Uffington with memories of the heights and beauties of Whern a deep longing in them all, he would come to her and she had to suffer him taking her roughly, without words at all. What once she had loved in him, now she began to hate. It was pups she yearned for now, not him.

'But did you not want me, mole?' he would say when he had done.

'Yes, yes, yes,' she said, but still no pups quickened inside her.

Subtly does the seed of dissension and sexual distress germinate and grow, mean and bitter the silent secret fruits it bears, and all the worse for being unspoken and barely seen.

'Master mine . . . ?'

'Yes, Mallice, my love . . . ?'

The weary reply to the eager request.

'Nothing now. No, nothing.'

'Then why disturb us, Mallice?'

Mallice turns, Mallice leaves, Mallice finds others to vent her unscreamed screams upon.

Terce observes the Master's narrowed eyes and hears his acid tongue.

'Henbane, Master . . .' he whispers evilly. It is the true art of the Twelfth Keeper of the Word to know when and how to resurrect such things.

'What of Henbane?' barks Lucerne.

Terce smiles and shrugs.

'She was never found.'

'She is dead.'

'Yes, Master.'

'Mention her not again, Twelfth Keeper.'

Terce smiles again, thinking that one day, when his glorious work is done, Lucerne too will be better dead for then might the greatness of his, Terce's, name be scrivened truly, and that of Rune as well. As age crept upon Terce now, so did the lusts of vanity and recognition. He did not want to die unknown. The completion of his task must now be nigh.

'Yes . . .' hisses Terce to himself. 'But there will be need of succession. Pups.' A mole, hearing that cold creature say the word, would pity any pup that came within a talon reach of Terce. Especially those of his kin.

But we cannot escape. Terce is there, plotting, in tedious tunnels in unnamed systems of the south. A powerful mole acting for himself and the dead Rune.

'Slighe?'

'Twelfth Keeper?'

'Send the sideem Mallice to me here.'

Look how coldly she comes alone.

'Tutor-Keeper?'

'Pups, Mallice: you shall need to make some come the spring.'

'He does not wish to make them. Times will get better. The south oppresses him.'

'Times will not get better. Get with pup, my dear, it shall be the Word's will.'

'But Tutor-Keeper. . . .'

'It matters not how it is done. Get with pup, sideem Mallice. One of them shall make thee matriarch.'

Mallice smiled.

'And that same pup shall link thee in blood with Rune. Is that thy lust?'

'Tunnels have ears, Mallice.'

'Not the dullard southern tunnels, nor memories either but my solitary sighs.'

'Get with pup.'

'Yes, Tutor-Keeper, I shall,' said Mallice coyly. 'I shall give him until Cannock, and then if he fails another shall succeed.'

With such irritations as Mallice's needs and the continuing discovery of evidence of secret Stone worship throughout the south upon his mind, the Master of the Word was in an evil humour by the time he and his entourage arrived at Rollright at the beginning of February. Only to discover, as he immediately did from the guardmoles who had moved in and taken command of the system, the full extent of the worship of the Stone on Longest Night by moles in Rollright, led by Beechen of Duncton himself. It seemed the culmination of many aggravations.

He listened in glowering silence to the account a stuttering guardmole gave of the blasphemous revelries before Beechen's coming, Beechen's subduing of the place, and the subsequent counselling and healing of moles before the Stones.

'Keep this mole under guard, Drule,' he said, turning immediately to Terce. 'And you, Twelfth Keeper, what think you?'

'Because it is known that it happened, and widely known, it is a challenge to thy authority, Master. Severity is in my mind.'

'Absolute severity,' agreed Lucerne. 'Slighe, find out how many moles live in Rollright – of the Word and of the Stone.'

'I know it already, Master,' said Slighe efficiently, quickly telling Lucerne the number.

Lucerne fell into thought. Not a mole moved. There was silence of a mortal kind. Eventually he said quietly, 'Terce, we must act now. We know that the eldrene Wort expects to take the Stone Mole soon. We know where enough of the followers are in most of the systems to deal with them conclusively. The sideem are very ready to act. Then let us act, now.'

Terce stared at his Master uneasily.

'Master, we must not be premature.'

'And nor must we be too late. The Word is insulted by what happened in Rollright. The Word is insulted every day, every hour, that these followers pay their blasphemous homage to the Stone. Well, they shall know vengeance now. Let us heed the warning it took a brave eldrene to give us. Let us act on it . . . Assemble the moles of this system in the circle of Stones tomorrow,' he ordered Slighe. 'There will be a conclave of moles of the Word and Stone, an exchange.'

'Master, I shall,' said Slighe, asking no questions, keeping his thoughts to himself.

'And Slighe . . . on your way out ask Drule to attend me,' he said and then told Terce and Mallice that he wished to be alone with Drule.

Drule came and stanced before him.

'There will be a conclave of moles in the Stone circle tomorrow.'

'Slighe thought fit to mention it, Master. *All* the moles of Rollright.'

'Yes. The Word is displeased with everymole of them. Kill them, Drule. *All* of them.'

For once Drule looked surprised.

'*All*, Master?'

Lucerne nodded coldly.

'Master, it will be our pleasure. We have ensured already that the moles of this squalid place are watched. Now, none shall live.'

Lucerne smiled bleakly.

'For myself, I shall leave at dawn before your pleasant conclave. Terce as well. But there should be one sideem here to witness it.'

'The sideem Mallice, Master?'

'Yes, why not? And do not dally long when it is done. Give her your protection and bring her on along the way. Now leave me, for we have much to do and orders to send.'

'Yes, Master,' said Drule softly, his eyes alight.

The infamous Bloody Conclave of the Rollright Stones needs no further mention here. Word of it is enough to chill most good moles' hearts, details of it would be gratuitous. The Duncton massacre had been but the preface to the succession of bloody pogroms of followers that started now at Rollright, and spread forth across moledom from that time on, a tidal wave of calculated violence against which its innocent victims had little defence. On the crest of this vile wave Lucerne journeyed back to Cannock where he received an unctuous welcome some moleweeks later, in the manner tyrants like: effusive, smiling and most eager to see the Master pleased.

But lest the violence against the followers seems absolute, know that always at such times a few escape to tell the tale. All across moledom, nameless even now, there were followers who were not quite caught by the tightening squeeze of the Word's vengeance. Some by luck, some because they were overlooked, some by foresight and cunning, some by courage. One day, perhaps, their tales will be told.

Of Rollright know only this: that before Lucerne had

even come, sturdy and faithful Rampion, wise already to the ways of the grikes, knowing what had happened at Duncton Wood, rallied a few followers and, with Lorren at her flank, got them out to safety before Drule's killings by the Stones.

As for the east, and north-east, Lucerne decreed that they would be spared for now. Let the rest be killed and the guardmoles gathered, for, as Lucerne himself said in his homecoming speech at Cannock, 'if Duncton was the preface then shall Beechenhill be the epilogue! We know the Word's intentions for that place. To there shall we go last, but most mightily!'

A mole can therefore imagine, that that was not a good time for a follower to be wandering the heaths of Cannock Chase.

A disastrous time, in fact, to be poking his snout about those entrances on Cannock's eastern side that lead down into the doleful depths of the Sumps.

But it was just then, and to there, that Wharfe had come in his desperate search to find Betony, and there he was taken by guardmoles. Though not without difficulty, for it took five to restrain him fully, not counting the two he killed and three he concussed before he was subdued.

'Name?' said a senior guardmole when he was finally taken into the Upper Sumps.

'Brook,' lied Wharfe, looking around at the dark damp place into which he had been brought and where he had good reason now to think that Betony would be.

'Brook,' said the guardmole indifferently, scrivening the name in his clumsy way and nodding to his subordinate to take the mole away.

'Usual, Sir?'

Oh yes, a mole who had killed two, one of them the guardmole's friend, would have the usual all right, and plenty of it.

'In here,' said one of the four guardmoles who carried him bodily along and cast him into a scalable cell in the

Middle Sumps. Once there, as usual, they taloned him; then, as usual, they let him starve a while; then, as usual, they took him to the noisome burrows at the north end of the Sumps and half drowned him for three days. Then. . . .

'That Brook? Surviving?'

'Tough he was, broke yesterday. Weeping, abject, usual things. . . .'

'Clean him up a bit, just enough. The sideem Slighe is coming down today.'

'We've a couple of youngsters for him.'

'Only males will do.'

'Aye, both male. He'll like 'em.'

'Good.'

Slighe came and looked in on Wharfe.

'Name?'

'Brook. It wasn't my fault. . . .'

Slighe looked at the mole coldly. Large, strong once, but weak now it seemed. A pity he had killed guardmoles or else he could have been used.

'It never is "my fault",' said Slighe. 'Where from?'

'Youlgreave,' lied Wharfe.

'What were you doing here?'

'Looking for worms.'

'You're lying,' said Slighe, and turned and left.

'Five days more here,' Slighe told the senior guardmole, 'and then put him down. He's lying, that one, and no fool. He's not hurt as badly as he seems, so hurt him more. Then Middle Sump him and put a peeper on to him. Now, what else have you for me?'

'Two, Sir, waiting for you now.'

'Parents?' said Slighe, his voice a little higher, his eyes shining, his small mouth moist.

'Were followers, Sir.'

'Good,' squeaked Slighe.

Slowly, with a filthy thrill of anticipation, Slighe went back down the tunnel . . . and that same day Wharfe heard worse sufferings than any he yet had. He had to listen as, in a burrow not far off, two young things pleaded, first for their lives, and finally to be allowed to die untouched any more. . . .

Much later Wharfe heard them die, and cursed the Stone for not helping them. And then cursed Slighe and swore to see him dead.

Five days later, Wharfe, his body weak but his spirit as resolute as it had always been, was taken to the Middle Sumps and found bedlam in the murk. Communal cells, murderous, maddened moles, wickedness incarnate, and all the sound and filth of moles reduced to beasts.

From the first moment Wharfe was shoved into that place he guessed what he must do and did not hesitate. He stanced up to his first attacker, buffeted his second to the ground, and picked out the third and nearly throttled him.

'Leave me alone or you shall die,' he said loudly, rounding on them all.

'Bastard!' said one, retreating.

'Don't hurt me,' whined the second, coming near.

The third stared, scratched at his sores and laughed like the mad mole he had become.

Wharfe soon discovered that his was not the only way to survive. Some weaker moles formed gangs, some used their infectious sores as threats, some chose to huddle in such filth that nomole went near them, and some, like him, were too strong (so far) for others to come near.

In truth, it was the guardmoles who were the greatest danger to life and limb, coming when they felt like it and dealing out their blows. Or throwing in the suppurating worms which they called food, and watching as the prisoners did battle for them.

The Middle Sumps consists of a series of interconnected tunnels in sandstone which, since they are lit only by fissures at their higher end, slope down into near darkness. To this bottom and most fetid end, where water oozes and a stream of mud and filth flows slowly in the dark, the weaker moles were driven. The stream flows into

687

a heaving pool, often more mud than water, which sucks and slurps away into some grim depth, and once a mole is lost in that he or she is lost for good.

The poor wretched moles who eke out their lives there do not attack each other, or anymole else, but live in a shivering, wretched darkness, cold, hungry, grateful for the scraps that come their way, hopeless. Some even, it seems, lived on the bodies of others.

It was not until his third day down there that Wharfe finally went searching among these ragged things called moles to find his Betony. For hours that became days he reached out a paw to moles who shrank away from him, or he stanced to watch some muttering form that might once have been a mole, hoping that among them he might find the poor mole he sought.

'Betony?' he would say, but they only shied away.

'Betony?' and they stared.

'Betony?' Silence.

Until at last:

'Betony?'

'Wharfe?'

Where did that voice come from? From his declining mind?

'Wharfe?' Why would the tormented voice not leave his head?

'Wharfe?'

What was this broken, scarred and noxious creature that came out of the cloven rock, where the chamber was its lowest, and stared at him?

'Betony?' he barely dared to say again, for it could not be her. Not this thing with but one talon left on one paw and three on the other, whose back paws dragged upon the rock.

'Betony?' he whispered once again, too frightened of what he had found after so long a search to go forward towards her.

'Bet . . .?'

'Yes,' she said, and in her eyes, which was the only part

of her he recognised, he saw the one thing he would not have thought to see: remorse.

'Forgive me,' she said, 'their tortures were too great.'

Why, she must think . . . she must fear . . . she must believe that he was there because of what she had said.

'Oh Wharfe,' she cried, as he took her broken body in his paws and whispered, 'Yes, Betony, it's Wharfe. I shall take you from here and back to Beechenhill, back where you belong . . .' And whispering on, not letting go of her, letting her weep her dry croaking tears, he did not see the peeper peep, and turn, and go, and whisper to the guardmoles for the favour of a sodden worm:

'His name is Wharfe, not Brook.'

'His name is Wharfe, Sir. The one sent down three days ago.'

Slighe stared.

'*Wharfe?*'

'Seems so, Sir.'

'Bring him up here again, and summon guardmole Drule.'

'He's busy, Sir, if you know what I mean.'

Slighe's face hardened.

'Get him,' he said brutally.

Harebell had borne the trek from Beechenhill to Tissington with Harrow through snow and ice, without a thought, and crept past grikes on the alert without a qualm, but only when she began to climb the final slope towards her mother's hideaway did she begin to feel real doubt.

She was glad Harrow was with her and he seemed to understand her feelings, for he said nothing as she stared up the slope ahead to the rough nondescript and hidden place where her mother was.

'I feel quite scared,' she said.

'I've told you already, Harebell,' Harrow said with a reassuring smile, 'she's just an old mole. Well. . . .'

'Yes! Well!' said Harebell ruefully.

They spoke easily to each other, and their looks were direct and frank. Each had learned to trust and respect the other on their long trek, and more than that, each had begun to want the other. It was the time for young, and they were free and adrift in a world of danger, and excitement too. Harebell did not underestimate the danger of their enterprise, but the further she had got from Beechenhill, especially when they crossed the River Dove on to new ground, the freer she had felt, and a little wild too.

In truth, they had taken a slow way, under the guise of it being more safe. But the company of each other was sufficient reward for what hardships they faced, and when it was time to sleep, then for safety's sake they had slept in the same burrow, getting closer every time, revelling in the privacy they had and the freedom that two moles, young and attractive and unwatched by other moles, can feel when darkness comes and they are sleeping close. Then, rather more . . .

But in truth, neither could quite believe their luck. To Harebell, Harrow was surely the most – well – *male* mole she had ever had the pleasure to be near, and he scented good, very good. The first male indeed that she had ever met whom she felt might stance well alongside Wharfe. How she longed for the two to meet.

While Harrow, who had felt lonely in dull Tissington, had never for a moment dreamed as he set off for Beechenhill that his strange journey would bring him into the presence at one and the same time of the famous Squeezebelly, and a mole he could not keep his eyes off called Harebell.

'Harebell,' he had whispered stupidly to himself, 'now that's a lovely name.'

They slowed as they climbed the final slope towards Henbane's tunnels.

'Did you tell her why you went off to Beechenhill?' whispered Harebell.

690

'More or less, though it was only a hunch.'

They went on a few more steps before Harebell stopped again.

'I'm *terrified*,' she said. 'I've never got used to the idea that Henbane was my mother. Was! *Is*, Harrow, *is*! Oh! You'd better stay here and just let me go on. . . .'

Then Harebell went on until the slope eased off and she saw an entrance ahead.

Assuming Henbane was there, she guessed she must have heard them approach, and probably their voices too.

'Hello!' she called out, feeling foolish. Is that what a mole says to the mother she has never seen? Is that what a mole says to she who was once the most powerful mole in moledom?

'Hello,' said a voice.

Even as she heard Henbane's voice, even then, Harebell knew it would be all right. Something was good about it, something of the Stone was there with them.

She turned a little and saw Henbane stanced on the surface a little to the left of the tunnel entrance among some fallen gorse. A place, she supposed, from which she might have made an escape if it had been necessary.

'Hello!' said Harebell again, too nervous to smile, and feeling too emotional to speak. Harrow had said she was an old mole, but that was because he was male and had not noticed something more important. She was . . . a most elegant mole. She was nearly beautiful.

'Oh!' said Harebell, surprise in her voice, 'I didn't know what to expect.'

Then a soft smile came to Henbane's face, and Harebell saw that her mother *was* beautiful. And more than that there was something about the way she stanced, and the presence that she had, that she recognised from the way Wharfe was. It was authority.

'I heard you come with Harrow,' said Henbane. 'Whatmole are you?'

'My name is Harebell,' said Harebell. 'I am. . . .'

'I think I know whatmole you are,' said Henbane, a slight quaver to her voice.

Which one said 'daughter' neither after remembered, but one of them did and both stared, struck dumb, and still, and much moved.

'I . . .' began Henbane.

'Harrow came to Beechenhill and brought me back here.'

'And your name is Harebell?' said Henbane.

Harebell nodded and still neither mole moved, but each continued to stare at the other as tears came to her eyes.

It was Henbane who looked away, and Henbane who first wept aloud. It was Harebell who moved, and Harebell who came forward and reached out to touch her mother for the first time.

She put a tentative paw to Henbane's face and gently touched the tears there and said, 'The one thing I didn't expect was that you'd be beautiful.'

Henbane, her face lined, her fur flecked white now, but her gloss still good, looked up with that cracked and vulnerable smile a mole has on her face when she weeps and yet feels safe and released by tears, and said, 'My dear, what I have missed in you. How *much* I've missed.'

They looked at each other in silence again until, suddenly, Harebell said, 'Sleekit brought us up. And Mayweed.'

'Sleekit?' whispered Henbane smiling. 'It was the best – the only good – decision of my life to ask her to take you. And she found the courage for it. Is she at Beechenhill then?'

Harebell shook her head.

'No, she went south with Mayweed.'

'There's so much to ask . . . so much! The other. . . .'

'Wharfe.'

'He was male?'

'You didn't know?'

'There was no time, you see . . . Oh, there's so much to talk of.'

692

Harrow came up the slope saying, 'Well! There probably is but can't you do it down in the warmth, and get some food at the same time?'

Henbane laughed. A strange, comfortable, familial laugh, and one she had never laughed before.

She turned to lead them down into the tunnel and Harebell whispered fiercely and excitedly to Harrow, 'You didn't tell me she was beautiful!'

'You're beautiful, too,' he said irrelevantly, but he was glad he did, very glad, as she turned, laughing, and they followed Henbane down into the warmth below.

For some days none of them was inclined to want to start the trek to Beechenhill. For one thing Harrow was tired, having done the journeys there and back in quick succession. Then, too, the weather remained difficult, the cold staying on, and the slopes icy.

But most of all, having found each other as they had, Harebell and Henbane had no desire to move, but wished to stay where they were and to talk and share the time they had, telling each other of the things in their lives that mattered. But of the Word they did not speak, nor of the Stone.

On good days the two females would stretch their paws over the fell behind Henbane's tunnel, and Harrow would leave them to it and travel the little distance down to the mole who had first told him of Henbane's coming and who remained the only one to know that Henbane, and now Harebell, were there. The Stone had chosen well, for he was a trusty mole and one who knew all the news and gossip, Harrow was certain that he would tell nomole of the moles hidden up on Hunger Hill.

As followers they had much to talk about, for in those days the news in Tissington was all of the Stone Mole, and the chances of him being taken by the grikes in Ashbourne.

'No doubt of it, Harrow. If he goes on the way he is their patience will wear thin and he'll be taken. Dammit, he's said to be coming nearer this way every day, and our sources tell us there's a lot of very senior, and very nasty-looking, sideem and guardmoles about in Ashbourne now.'

'Where do you think the Stone Mole's headed for?'

'The whisper is Beechenhill. But that's obvious, isn't it? It's got a Stone and the place has stood out against the Word all these years. But no way is he going to get into Beechenhill without being attacked or taken.'

'Well, they've not taken him yet. Maybe their talk of listening and reconciliation is sincere.'

'Oh yes, Harrow, sure,' said his friend heavily.

A few days later Harrow saw the mole coming quickly up the slope with news.

'The Stone Mole,' he gasped, 'he's going to be in Kniveton tomorrow and a lot of us are travelling overnight to support him. You've got to come, Harrow, you've *got* to. A mole's come up from the south who has heard him before. He says the only reason the grikes have not taken him is that so many followers travel with him that they dare not. You must come, it's not a difficult journey.'

'But I want to stay with Harebell and Henbane. We were thinking of taking advantage of this milder weather and making our way to Beechenhill.'

'Bring them!' said the mole recklessly. 'I'm setting off shortly. The more the merrier.'

When Henbane heard what the fuss was about she said, 'You must go and hear this mole, my dear, the more so because Harrow has been told he is of Duncton Wood. Your father comes from there and spoke so lovingly of it. Perhaps if you could talk to this Stone Mole he would tell you.'

'I don't want to leave you,' said Harebell reluctantly, for truly she would have liked to hear the Stone Mole preach.

Henbane smiled.

'Oh! I'll come too! I got this far. A little further won't hurt me and it's not a great distance. I would like to hear what such a mole has to say, about the Word as well as the

Stone. As for my safety, well . . . if there are many followers about then there'll be safety in numbers. Provided I remain anonymous to them and any guardmole who might be near.'

'You'll be safe enough, Henbane,' said Harrow, always a positive mole. 'And I'll be there at one flank, Harebell at the other. But if we're going, we'll need to go soon. . . .'

They journeyed through the night and met up with many other Tissington followers as they went so that, as dawn broke and they climbed up through Kniveton Wood, the slopes were alive with moles. Progress was slow, not because the slopes were steep but because old moles like Henbane had come, aided by family and friends, and moles weak from illness and even a few who were early with pup. Everymole helped the other, and as the sun rose over distant Madge Hill there was the sense of promise and companionship, and abiding faith.

The Stone Mole had come to moledom, and this great day he was coming here to Kniveton Edge, to speak to them and tell them of the Stone.

Yet there was tension, too, for Harrow's friend was not the only one who had prophesied that soon the Stone Mole would be taken. There was a sense of foreboding in the air, of preordination, a sense almost of helplessness.

As they passed beyond Kniveton Wood they came to a valley that sloped gently eastward and was caught by the sun. This, they were told, was Kniveton Edge. It was pasture ground, and the grass was green and moist, and there was the first distant scent of spring in the air. Moles were already assembling and Harrow found a place for them –though higher up than Harebell wished to go. But Harrow was cautious, and thought that if they needed to hurry away and make themselves scarce then the higher up they were the better.

They had not been stanced down long before they saw a group of moles, perhaps ten in all, coming up the little valley towards them. The sun was in the sky behind them lighting their way ahead, and its brightness made it hard at first to make the moles out.

But on they came, slowly, and a hush fell over the assembled moles, their chattering stopped and they watched in growing anticipation as the group got nearer and the individual moles among them could be made out.

It was quite clear which was the Stone Mole for whatever he did, whether it was to turn to speak to a mole on one side or the other, or come forward or slow down, he always seemed to be at the very centre of the group.

He was in any case a pleasing mole to look on – well made, graceful, and with the kind of fur over which the light played well. If that were not enough to pick him out, a small mole went in front, as odd and grubby a looking mole as Harebell had ever seen; while behind the Stone Mole was a large scarred mole, his paws huge and his manner protective: Holm and Buckram.

As they neared the assembled moles, several of those with them, some of whom Harrow knew to be Kniveton followers, separated and quietly joined the others, and a fourth mole in the Stone Mole's group, an elderly female, became more visible.

'But surely, Harebell, that mole . . .' said Henbane in astonishment.

'The female?'

'Do you know her?' whispered Harrow.

'It's Sleekit,' said Henbane. 'Sleekit!'

There had been doubt in Harebell's face until Henbane said the name, but the moment she heard it she knew it must be the mole who had reared herself and Wharfe so long ago and finally left Beechenhill to travel south with Mayweed.

'We must let her know we're here,' said Harebell eagerly, but Harrow put a restraining paw on hers.

'No need to draw attention to yourself, or to Henbane, and anyway it looks as if the Stone Mole's going to speak. I'll go down and bring Sleekit here when he's finished.'

It was therefore in a state of surprise and delight that

both Henbane and Harebell, their eyes at first more on Sleekit, heard the Stone Mole's first words.

But if, to start with, this prevented them from attending to what he said, it was not long before his calm assured voice, his radiant manner and the words he spoke began to make them forget Sleekit for a time. Steadily they were drawn, as all the moles assembled there were drawn, into the address that Beechen of Duncton then made.

He spoke first very personally of his own life: of Duncton Wood, of the moles there who had raised him, the moles that he loved, of many things close to his heart. Of Mayweed, of Skint, of Smithills, and many more. Then he spoke of Feverfew, and how it had been that she had met the White Mole Boswell in the light of Comfrey's Stone.

How magical it seemed to those moles of the southern Peak, this land to the south where great Stones rose, where the Ancient Systems lay, and where the scribemoles in times past had come from. How mysterious.

'I am the son of Boswell, and the son of Feverfew, and through me soon will those who follow the Stone in humility and truth know a new light. Your ancestors called me Stone Mole, and this I am; and they said I would be a saviour, and come among you by the light of an eastern star.'

'You have!' cried out a follower.

'Yes, I have come among you, but not as a saviour who uses talons, or who can save what talons save – which is physical life. I have not come for a fight of the flesh and fur. Like me, those I love who travel with me, who are most close to me – 'And here he turned to Buckram, and touched him with a smile – 'have renounced that way.

'That mole is stronger by far, and closer to the Stone's Silence, who, though he has the strength of ten moles, bows down his snout before a pup and hurts no life. That mole is more a saviour who, rather than raise a talon in anger or in fear, lets his own life be taken all for love of the Stone. Yes, such moles shall be much favoured.

'Strong moles, loud moles, dangerous moles with bigger talons than they have hearts, strong of body but not of spirit, are shadows in the Stone's light. A gentle mole of the Word is closer to me than such a mole of the Stone.

'I have spoken of Duncton, the place that gave me life, and whose moles taught me how to love. But I have not told what has happened to Duncton, and of that I must now speak. . . .'

Then Beechen told of how the Duncton moles had been killed by moles of the Word, and described what he knew from all Rampion and Romney had told him.

Yet throughout it all he spoke with sadness about the grikes, not accusation.

'Their deed was our deed, the blood on their talons is blood on our own . . . for we have all been weak and frail of spirit, and into the void of our indulgence and spiritlessness darkness has flowed as a flood over a wormful valley.

'We are that flood, moles of the Word are our victims. Aye . . .' And here he had to raise his voice and quell mutterings of dissent . . . 'Aye, each time you are weak of the Stone, each time you put yourself before your kin, your neighbour, and especially your faith, you become the enemy, you become the talon that draws the blood of innocents.

'The Duncton moles were innocent. I knew them, they made me what I am: this was the task ordained them by my father Boswell. Their community made me.

'But one mole I have not named, one mole who has passed this way, one mole whose name many of you know: Tryfan of Duncton, scribemole, as close to me as my mother Feverfew.'

At the mention of her father's name, Harebell reached out a paw to hold Henbane's, and another to Harrow. All three moles listened now in terrible silence as Beechen described something of Tryfan's sufferings as he had heard of them, and of his teachings.

Then he said quietly, 'I am told that Tryfan of Duncton

was blinded by order of the Master of the Word, Lucerne of Whern.'

A gasp went out among the moles, and it was as well that it did for Henbane half screamed, and Harebell was sobbing, yet nomole noticed them, so great was the horrified commotion at what Beechen said.

'Now as you would love Tryfan hear me, and hear me with all the love you have. Listen, listen with all the heart you possess. And learn, learn with all the power you command.

'Tryfan was a great mole, a mole whom those of you who have heard me speak before know I would call a true warrior. A mole whose life was spent listening with a fierce love to what others said, and listening with his heart to others' hearts, and learning, always learning. This was a warrior mole, in the tradition of Balagan, and this mole I knew, and others here knew.

'Yet whatmole blinded Tryfan? I tell you that though Lucerne ordered it he was not to blame, nor that sorry mole called Drule who did the deed. Not them. Who blinded Tryfan?

'Moles, anymole who has ever turned his back upon the Stone had a talon in that blinding; anymole who does what he knows is wrong because he is too lazy to do what he knows is right, his talon was in that blow; anymole who points a talon at others long before he points it at himself – aye, his talon was there on Longest Night in Duncton Wood.'

Silence had fallen, and nomole spoke. Harebell's grip was tight on the paws of Henbane and Harrow. Henbane was as still as rock. Harrow barely dared to breath.

Then, like sun breaking out across a sullen moor, Beechen smiled.

'I believe that Tryfan forgave those moles who blinded him. I believe that whatever anger and rage and loneliness he felt in his time of pain, he remembered the refusals of moles he loved to renounce the Stone and save their lives and from that gained the strength to forgive. In that dark and tragic moment beside the Duncton Stone, Tryfan had his final test. I tell you he knew that not to forgive, not to *love* in that moment, would have been as great a recanting as speaking his renunciation out aloud. Greater, for forgiveness is private and unseen.

'As Tryfan forgave, so soon must you. I shall be taken and in that taking you shall be tested. I shall be hurt, and in that hurting you shall be tried. I may be lost to you, and in that losing is your greatest temptation. Then must you all be true warriors. Your anger you shall meet with patience. Your grief you shall meet with faith. Your hatred you shall meet with love. Put your light to the darkness you find: that is the difficult way warriors must go if they are to find the Silence.

'I was born but mole, as you were, and as a mole I shall face whatever the darkness will soon bring. Fear I shall have, pray for me. Anger I shall have, pray for me. Hatred I shall have, oh pray for me. . . .'

As he spoke some of the moles about him were openly crying for the fate he seemed to presage. Then silence fell, for a ripple of apprehension went among them and then murmurs of concern as they saw coming inexorably across the fell, and over the rise behind, and up from the valley below: grikes.

Slow, steady, determined and relentless, the guardmole grikes appeared and came towards them.

Buckram was the first to move.

'Stone Mole, you must flee!'

Beechen said, 'Where does a mole flee to be from his own dark self? These moles are *us*.'

'Then, Stone Mole, you must let us fight them!'

Beechen said, 'And make my words dry grass to break in the first harsh wind?'

'Stone Mole. . . .'

'Buckram, as I love you, stance by me in peace, and be an example to all the moles who watch and listen here this day.'

So it was that nomole moved but all simply watched as

the grike guardmoles came, with a female at their head whom Beechen already knew – the eldrene Wort.

She stopped just far enough from him that when she addressed him most of them could hear her voice clearly.

'You have blasphemed against the Word one time too many, Beechen of Duncton. You shall come with us and it is best none try to protect you.'

'We welcome you in peace,' said Beechen, his gaze upon her. 'Take only me.'

'We shall,' said Wort.

'And me!' roared Buckram.

'And me! And me!' cried many more.

The guardmoles were astonished at the followers, that they did not fight but all offered themselves to be taken into custody, and were obedient to the Stone Mole's desire for peace.

'One of your own choosing can go with you,' said Wort, anxious to get Beechen and her guard away from there and not argue more.

'Stone Mole. . . .'

'Yes. You, Buckram,' said Beechen with a calm smile.

Then he turned and began to embrace Sleekit and Holm and others there and say farewell, but this was soon cut short by one of the eldrene's powerful henchmoles.

'Come on, get on with it.'

But when he laid a paw on Beechen to push him along the way Beechen turned towards him and gazed on him and the henchmole retreated, not daring to touch him more.

'Come on then, we don't want no trouble.'

'You're the only trouble,' cried out a follower, and several shouted out their agreement and began to move forward aggressively. Then Beechen turned to them and said, 'As you love the Stone, love me and abide by my wish for peace.'

Then they stopped, and that was all the resistance anymole made as the guardmoles jostled around Beechen and great Buckram and herded them off, and away into the Word's custody.

Strange the behaviour of the followers then. Some stared, some turned and ran, some wept. Harrow told Henbane and Harebell to stay where they were and went quickly down the slope and spoke to Sleekit and Holm. They turned and looked and came up the slope, Sleekit staring in disbelief at what she saw, Holm seeming simply bemused.

But it was not a time for happy greeting, nor even to give each other the comfort truly needed as the slow realisation came on them that the Stone Mole and Buckram had been taken from them and might never return. He had warned of it, and now it had happened, they felt numb. All they could do now was to leave Kniveton Edge as soon as possible, and find consolation and hope in each other's company later. Only in the days ahead, when the shock of the Stone Mole's arrest had been absorbed did Sleekit begin to find joy in her reunion with Henbane, and her rediscovery of Harebell – so grown now, so beautiful.

The first night Henbane was tired and they slept near by. A strange, comfortless night of tears that the Stone Mole seemed lost beyond recall. Harebell needed comforting, and Harrow felt distress, and those two moles came closer, and closer still, for the stars were in the night sky and a sense of fate hung in the air, and wildness too. A night when moles needed to be close, a night to fear, a night after which moles could never turn back. For some, for Harebell and Harrow, a night of clinging love in which ecstasy seemed stolen from the stars, and was but cold comfort against what the future seemed to hold.

They had intended to return to Hunger Hill, but when they got to its lower slopes something about the place was wrong and they suspected grikes were there, waiting for their return.

'We must go to Beechenhill,' whispered Harebell, 'for Squeezebelly shall need us now. Harrow, lead us away from here and back to the place where we might be safe.'

Long was the way he took, and most circuitous, for the River Dove was in spate from thawing on the fells to the

702

north and crossing it was dangerous. On they went, Holm helping much to scent out dangers, and spending the nights on guard. Nights that Harebell and Harrow spent close and sighed, because time and circumstance seemed to be stealing back from them the love they had just found; and Beechenhill, though near, seemed hard to reach.

'Master, we wish to speak to you,' said Slighe.

'Both you and Drule?' smiled Lucerne, darting a glance at Terce.

'It must be a matter arising from the Sumps since that's all you two have in common,' said Terce, who knew much, and deduced more.

Slighe could barely conceal his excitement.

'It is a small matter,' he said a little pompously, 'called Wharfe.'

'*Wharfe?*' said the Master silkily.

Slighe nodded and Drule beamed.

'Where?' said Terce.

'Here, Master. Yes, Master. Here,' said Slighe.

'Are you sure?'

'Oh quite certain, Sir,' said Drule. 'The mole told us so himself.'

'If this is true, Terce, the Word is pleased with us. If not, then, Slighe and Drule, you may regret this day.'

But Drule only grinned, and Slighe looked smug.

'Take me to him. And find Mallice. This will please her.'

'So,' said Lucerne softly, gazing down from an observation gallery in the Sumps an hour later, '*that* is my brother Wharfe.'

'It is indubitable, Master.'

'He *looks* like you, my sweet,' said Mallice.

'Well!' said Lucerne, staring.

'Will you not talk with him, Master?'

'*I* would,' said Mallice, 'out of curiosity.'

'I know you would, Mallice. I know you well.'

'Yes, Master mine,' she said, coming close.

'He might tell you more than he told me,' said Slighe.

A look of anger came to Lucerne's face.

'In my own time I shall talk with him. In my own time. Now come, my dear, I wish to be alone with you.'

So Lucerne turned and went, leaving Terce to ponder something strange: for the first time since he had known Lucerne, from the moment he had seen him as a pup at Henbane's teat, Lucerne looked . . . scared. Aye, that was the word for it. Scared. And well he might. Wharfe looked a formidable mole.

'Drule,' said Terce before he followed Lucerne out, 'weaken Wharfe some more.'

'Yes, Sir!' said Drule.

Three days later. . . .

'Master, will you not speak with him?'

'Not yet.'

Six days later. . . .

'Master . . . ?'

'No,' snapped Lucerne.

Ten days later. . . .

'Your brother. . . .'

'Twelfth Keeper, do not mention him again. The best place for him is where he is. Let him and that Betony rot for ever but not be allowed to die. Before he does that I shall wish him to know but two things: that Beechenhill is waste, and Harebell dead.'

'Yes, Master.'

Nor did Lucerne change his mind, or have time to. The following day a messenger came from Ashbourne, urgently and with priority.

'It is a henchmole from the eldrene Wort.'

How Lucerne smiled.

'Show the *hench*mole in,' he said. 'I like everything Wort does, Terce. A henchmole – how very quaint! Well?' he said as the mole entered.

'The eldrene Wort sends the greetings of the Word,

Master, and to say that Beechen of Duncton, the one called Stone Mole, is taken in Ashbourne and that she awaits your pleasure.'

'There, Terce, how the Word does smile on us! The crusade nearly done, this Stone Mole captured, and Beechenhill ripe to take as a female in March.' He turned to the messenger. 'We are well pleased with you, henchmole of the eldrene Wort.'

'Thank you, Master.'

Three days later, guardmoles were mustered and more sent to the east and north. The Master had ordered that the final strikes must now begin. Soon they would depart, leaving Cannock with a garrison under the joint command of Drule and Slighe.

'Master mine, once we leave I do not want to come back to this dull place. It can become ruinous for all I care. Whern is our home and I miss it.'

'Mistress Mallice, get me a pup and Whern shall be yours again.'

'Master love, you know how.'

Lucerne laughed.

'Have I neglected you?' he said, his paws firm on her haunches as he quickly mounted her. His teeth were at her back.

'Yes,' she sighed, 'you have.'

'I want you with pup,' he cried, coming close into her then.

'Oh, oh, oh, I may be soon,' she whispered, 'I may be, my dear.'

From now, *how* she got them was of no consequence. So she let him make his sterile love to her and knew he might soon be pleased.

Chapter Thirty-Two

Mistle set to her great task of preparing Duncton Wood for the life that she passionately believed would one day return to it with a will and many a way. And if, so far, she had but one mole living with her in the wood, well, that would change and meanwhile she must make the most of him!

Romney – a mole hesitates to say 'Poor Romney' of such a strong mole as he – had already had enough shocks in a short time for most moles. Before Longest Night he had been an ordinary guardmole going about an ordinary life, but everything had changed from the moment he saw Dodder killed.

He had been stricken by what he had witnessed, and Rampion had taken him over and dragged him north towards Rollright. Then at Chadlington he had been hijacked yet again, this time by Mayweed, the maddest mole he had ever met, and Mistle, a fervent, passionate, unstoppable younger version of Rampion, and hauled back to Duncton again. There he had witnessed the suffering and death of Tryfan, who in the brief time he saw him alive Romney felt was a great mole in every sense.

Then, before his bemused gaze, the mad Mayweed and insecure Bailey had one moment been doing not a lot and the next, and without (it seemed) any thought at all, they had set off on a journey from which Mayweed did not expect to return.

'If this is how moles of the Stone live,' he grumbled, as he found himself dragged off yet again, this time by Mistle around an empty and derelict system, 'then I think I prefer the more orderly ways of the Word.'

'Fine! Leave now, mole! We don't want half-hearted moles in *this* system, thank you very much!' declared Mistle turning on him.

'"We" as you put it, are *us*, which is you and me,' protested Romney, who guessed that unless he stanced up to her now he would be lost and subjugated forever. 'There are no others. *I*, Romney, formerly a guardmole, am half of *us*, and don't you forget it!'

But Mistle was having none of it.

'Unless we work together for the same purpose then *we* and Duncton Wood will get nowhere. I realise it's all a bit much for you and that you hardly know me, but then I hardly know you. Now, I'm a positive mole and there's lots to do, and even more I want to do, but I don't want to do it grumpily, miserably, or in the company of unwilling moles.'

'But . . .' began Romney.

'No "buts" about it, as Mayweed would say, none at all! I saw "but" scribed over the face of every single guardmole I ever knew in Avebury. It's "buts" that killed the moles by the Stone. "But" is an attitude of mind we of the Stone do not enjoy. Look around you, Romney! Breathe the good air! See the trees! Scent the worms!'

'The air's cold, the trees are leafless, the worms are deep!' As Romney said this, he tried his best to keep a straight face but, faced by Mistle and her excitement with life, and with a wood which the more he looked at it the more beautiful it seemed, he could not help himself, and began to smile.

Which was as well, for Mistle seemed about to burst with frustration at his 'half-heartedness', but now she saw he could laugh at himself she too began to smile, and then she laughed.

'The air *is* a bit cold, but it won't be cold for ever,' she said. 'And the trees will bud soon enough. And. . . .'

'I know, Mistle, the worms will come nearer the surface when everything warms up. Yes, I can see it now, it's all going to be *wonderful* – as you moles of the Stone would put it.'

'Yes, I think it is,' said Mistle seriously. 'But much more than that. You see, Romney, I come from a system that has been oppressed by the Word for so long that its spirit was almost all gone. One day I'll tell you about my grandmother Violet, but for now I'll only say that she taught me all she knew about life, and living, and the Stone, and with her help I was able to leave Avebury. She told me to come to this system because to her, being raised with the old stories of the seven Systems, it was always the greatest system of moledom: with an awesome Stone, with a tradition of great and spiritual moles of whom Tryfan was one, but not I hope the last, and with a site and position that gives it that sense that other systems often lack – harmony and rightness.

'Now by circumstances strange and mysterious which I don't pretend to understand, you and I, a mole of the Stone and a mole of the Word, find ourselves alone here, and it's not even a system either of us was raised in.

'But I feel as if we have been given a great heritage that we must cherish until times change and others can come back and make their lives here once again. In fact I think we are very lucky, and that's why I feel sad and distressed when you start moaning, because Duncton's worth more than that. In fact, anywhere is worth more than that, but especially Duncton!'

As Romney listened to Mistle he had the growing feeling that he was in the presence of a mole who could persuade another mole to do anything. But it was more than her words – there was something grand and alluring about the way she stanced beneath the beech trees, her paws well set on the ground, her fur glossy and her looks magnificent and yet seeming vulnerable. To turn from her, to leave the wood, to have nothing more to do with such driven moles as these had been in his mind.

But now, hearing her, seeing her, he knew he could not leave. But *he* had always been the one to get others to do things for him, and other moles did not trek right over him, and . . . he grinned.

'We'd best get to know the system first,' he said, 'and if

708

ever I'm in doubt about what I'm doing here, just remind me of what you said today.'

She rushed to him and touched him affectionately, her face as excited as a young pup's.

'For a moment I thought you'd leave.'

'I'm sure you'd have stayed on without me.'

'One's alone, two's a community, and three or more. . . .'

'A nightmare!' laughed Romney.

'Leave them to me,' said Mistle.

'Don't worry, that's *exactly* what I intend to do. I'm a well-trained guardmole who knows all about delegation.'

'"Delegation",' she said slowly, enjoying the word. 'That sounds something worth learning about. Will you teach me?'

'Humph!' said Romney, starting off downslope to explore the system.

'Romney,' she called after him, 'do you think Beechen will come back one day?'

He stopped and turned.

'For you, mole? Yes, I do. A mole would travel a lifetime to come back to a mole like you.' He spoke with absolute sincerity.

'Romney,' she said quietly, 'will you always tell me that, whatever may happen in the future and if I begin to doubt it? *Always?* You see, I don't think I'm going to have the strength to do all the things I know we're going to have to do in Duncton unless I believe that Beechen will come back to me. Is that silly?'

'No, mole, it isn't silly,' said Romney. 'I saw Beechen, and anymole could see he loved you. It was scrivened all over his face. But more than that, he is like nomole I've ever seen. There's something certain about him. Why even Tryfan did not have the same certainty Beechen had. If that mole said he'll come back then he will, and I'll tell you that until the day I die because I believe it. Now, let's go, because if we talk anymore like this you'll have me in tears, and until I came to this place tears was *not* my way.'

'Thank you,' said Mistle, with a smile and touch that would win the heart of anymole.

'You can lead the way since you seem to be in charge round here,' he said.

Then, by now won over and thoroughly persuaded that Duncton was the place to be, and the first of many moles whose lives Mistle's charisma and persuasiveness would win to the cause of Duncton Wood and a community of moles such as Tryfan had begun, he followed her down-slope to discover whether or not this was indeed likely ever to be moledom's greatest system.

Mistle knew more than she realised about Duncton and the places in it, from all that Beechen, Mayweed and Sleekit had told her in their time together in Bablock Hythe.

Barrow Vale and the Stone clearing were obvious enough, though she and Romney avoided the Stone clearing in the early days, trusting that the owls and rooks would do their work, and the grim evidence of the killings in Duncton be gone. There is no dishonour or distress in a dead mole being owl fodder for it is the natural order of things, and many mole has decided when he was near his time to take himself off to somewhere open knowing that death would be followed by the stoop of claw and the flap of wing.

But for a time they preferred to go to other places, and, accordingly, Mistle was able to show Romney the Marsh End, and the Eastside, and tell him their names, and show him how it was that the Westside, being wormful, trad-itionally attracted the strongest moles.

When they first arrived in Duncton there had been a succession of frosts before Longest Night which had driven the worms down, and from the way the deeper levels had been cleared to ease the taking of these worms, they were able to tell which tunnels and burrows had been recently occupied.

But these were relatively few and generally the system

was in a bad state of repair and showed evidence of having been long under-used, especially in the Marsh End where tunnels were frequently collapsed and a sense of order nearly gone. Elsewhere, though, the soil being drier, the communal tunnels at least were surprisingly well maintained, and retained that special quality of clear yet vibrant sound which the older systems, whose tunnels have evolved over many generations, often have.

For Mistle, used as she was to the newer tunnels of Avebury where the grikes had moved the moles from their original system, the tunnel sounds of Duncton were a revelation and a delight. Romney, on the other paw, had lived in several other well-established systems, including Fyfield for a time, and was more familiar with how good quality tunnels should be.

'But even so these are something else again, Mistle. Their lines are so pleasing to the eye, and look at the way they used buried flints to aid sound travelling! We can't delve tunnels like them these days.'

'But we can try, Romney, we can try!'

The first winter snows were light falls across the Pastures beyond the Westside in mid-January, and the trees prevented these from settling in the wood. Then the air got steadily colder, and a north-eastern wind drove snow hard into the wood, and formed drifts against the tree trunks so that if they looked one way through the wood it seemed all light, and another it seemed dark.

They had spent a long time debating where to make their burrows, Romney arguing that the sensible place was somewhere anonymous on the slopes below the Ancient System, off the obvious surface routes but near a communal tunnel with good sound properties so they could hear the approach of other moles, and be able to make their escape if danger threatened.

So convincing was he that they even found a suitable place and prepared some tunnels and burrows there. But then, just when Romney, pleased with his set of tunnels and looking forward to his first sleep there, was settling down as darkness fell Mistle came in without a by your leave or thank you.

'We can neither of us stay here, like furtive moles in our own system! We must begin as we mean to go on, and live where it can be seen we are here, and proud to call ourselves Duncton moles.'

'Like where?' said Romney heavily.

'I don't know yet, but nearer the Stone. I'll find the right place soon enough.'

'Well, when you have will you let me know, mole? Meanwhile if you don't mind. . . .'

'Oh we're going to look now, we're not putting it off.'

'But. . . .'

'*But?*'

Romney sighed, and grinned ruefully.

'Where do we begin?'

'Let's start on the slopes between Barrow Vale and the Stone and work from there. The right place will emerge in time. It's a matter of patience.'

'*Tonight?*'

Mistle hesitated.

'Tomorrow then,' she said, conceding for once. 'I suppose we have hardly stopped for a moment since we came here, have we?'

'No, we haven't.'

'Violet used to say a mole should know when to stop and stance still. I'm sorry, Romney. Do I work you too hard? It's only that I want things to be right.'

'Yes, you do work me too hard. I can take it, but one day other moles may come who can't, so you remember that. Now you stance here, mole, I'll get some food and we'll just talk for a change. You can tell me about this Violet you keep mentioning and about the Stone, too, because you forget I'm of the Word. There's things I'd like to know.'

That night, for the first time, the two moles talked, the snowy wood falling into darkness above them, and only the rustle of falling twig and the quick call of tawny owl to break the silence. Mistle told Romney all about her

712

puphood in Avebury, and something of her escape from it, and how she had joined forces with the mole Cuddesdon.

'You know I've hardly thought about him at all since we were separated in Hen Wood. I just feel he's safe and that one day we'll meet again.'

'All these males you're going to meet again.!'

'Only two so far,' she said. 'But I think the Stone meant Cuddesdon and I to part when we did, and for me to find Beechen. I'm sure Cuddesdon got to Cuddesdon Hill and is discovering what it is the Stone wants him to do there.'

'You believe the Stone guides everything, don't you?'

'I think it helps us along, and not always in directions we expect or think are right for us. Beechen told me that Tryfan believed that moles behave most intelligently when they don't think about it too much. The Stone reminds them, sometimes forcibly, what's good for them.

'The nice thing about Cuddesdon and I is that from the day we first met we decided to trust each other. That's why I've not thought about him much since Hen Wood. I trust him to have done the right thing, and I know he'll trust me to do the same. He knew I was going to make my way here one way or the other, and here I am! He'll find me in time. It's how moles should be, Romney.'

'It's how we were as pups with our mother,' said Romney, who had explained that he had been raised in a Midlands system and then put into service of the Word as a guardmole and had travelled ever since. 'But with the Word everymole is judged all the time and I wouldn't say "trust" is commonplace. Senior moles are watching out to see if their subordinates have done wrong. And if they have, naturally they punish them.

'Now, this mole Cuddesdon, what was he going to do exactly when he got to wherever he was going?'

Mistle shrugged and, laughing affectionately, said, 'That was always a joke between us since he didn't know himself. We agreed that the Stone would guide him. But not mate, I think. He decided he wasn't the mating kind.'

'And you?' said Romney softly.

She shook her head and looked away and fell silent, thinking.

'Ever since I met Beechen I know I've wanted young almost more than anything. That, and Duncton Wood! Well, I'll just have to wait until he comes back.'

There was a moment or two of tension in the air and then Romney relaxed and smiled.

'Well! I don't think I'm going to get very far with you!'

'Romney! You and me?' She seemed genuinely amused, and Romney looked a little rueful.

'It would be natural . . . wouldn't it? I mean there's nomole else.'

But Mistle only laughed more.

'It's not that I don't like you, but, well, I've found my mole. And anyway. . . .'

'Anyway what?'

'Nothing.'

'I'm not having "nothing" from a mole who always speaks the truth a little too directly on every other subject.'

'It's obvious, isn't it?'

'What's obvious?' said Romney.

'It was obvious to me, anyway.'

'*What* was obvious?'

'Rampion! She likes you!'

'*Rampion?*'

Mistle nodded, feeling pleasantly sleepy.

'But she's gone back to Rollright.'

'Don't worry, she'll come here. You're too good a mole for her not to. Anyway, Duncton needs your pups.'

'Mistle, you're impossible!'

There was friendly silence for a time until eventually Romney said again, 'Do you really think so? I mean about Rampion?'

'Yes,' murmured Mistle.

'She's quite a nice mole.'

'Very nice,' repeated Mistle, almost asleep.

'I never thought of *that*,' said Romney to a sleeping burrow. 'Rampion?'

Snow fell yet again that night, but evidently deep in the hearts of moles, deep in the soil and deep among the roots of trees, spring was beginning to stir.

'She's quite a good looking mole, in fact,' said Romney to himself sometime in the night, feeling Mistle's friendly flank next to his, and glad to be alive.

An ominous calm settled over Caer Caradoc in the weeks after the victory over the moles of the Word, but hostilities all along the western front soon increased as Ginnell responded to his defeat by putting pressure on those points where he felt the Welsh followers were weakest.

The greatest pressure was felt north of Caer Caradoc in that area controlled by Gaelri, the second of the Pentre siblings, and more than once he had to ask Troedfach to send moles up from Caradoc.

Neither side seemed quite to have the numbers it needed to risk continuing an attack too long if the opposition proved at all effective. Nevertheless, despite reinforcements, Gaelri's defences nearly failed towards the end of January and was only saved by a timely deterioration in the weather which forced the attacking and more exposed moles of the Word to retreat.

Caer Caradoc itself was not attacked again, and after the vulnerable period after Longest Night, when Troedfach hurried to get moles in place up there, it was secure though by no means impregnable, for its top is extended and would need far more moles than Troedfach could afford from the main front to make it truly safe.

'They'll come again when spring starts and the weather turns mild,' said Gareg one day as he stanced with Troedfach high on the top.

'I do not understand why he fell back on Longest Night,' growled the old campaigner suspiciously. 'A few more hours and he'd have had us. He's not a mole who likes that kind of defeat and if I was him I'd be planning even now how to take it back. He's no fool and he knows that we've to hold the place, which keeps moles caught here getting cold and dispirited. Have you thought what he might do?'

Gareg screwed his eyes against the bitter wind and looked out east over Word-dominated moledom.

'Often,' he said tersely. Troedfach nodded, pleased. Gareg was proving his promise as a commander and strategist – a mole who did his best to think as his enemy might.

'Ginnell will begin a heavy and sustained attack against Caradoc at the same time as mounting another some way from here, attacks which will leave us guessing which the main one is. If we increase our strength on Caradoc we weaken ourselves elsewhere, and he'll go hard for us there. If we do the opposite he'll take Caradoc – or try to.'

'I agree, I'm sure that's what he'll do. But what should our response be?'

'What we've always tried to do: what the grikes least expect, but this time in a different way. If he is attacking us in two places then one thing is sure – he'll be weak elsewhere and we can break him there. Perhaps it would not matter if we lost Caradoc again, or another place as well, if we were able to advance rapidly through his line. Supposing then all our force was to attack half of his before he could regroup? Why, we would have a greater victory than we have ever had.'

'Gareg, you young moles have spirit! I hope I live to see the day of such a victory, and look into the eyes of Ginnell whom I have fought so long.'

'And what would you say to him, Troedfach?'

'Say? No, mole, we'd discuss and find out where we went right and wrong. I have no quarrel with Ginnell as a mole, only with the Word he represents.'

'On the other paw . . .' said Gareg, staring eastward as far as he could see.

'Yes, mole?'

'Nothing, Troedfach. A young mole's ideas, that's all! Another time if you've the patience for it.'

'Your day will come, Gareg, I know it will. When it does, mole, remember that it is for the Stone we have fought all these long years, not for ourselves.'

'I'll not forget.'

One result of this conversation was that Gareg was deputed to organise swifter messenger moles along the line, so that Troedfach received news of attacks more quickly than he had before. It was a good exercise for February, a period when little normally happened in those parts, the winter having set in and moles finding surface travel difficult. A good time for tactical attack and harassment, but nothing more.

Yet in a small way the new messenger system soon proved its worth, for news came in from Gaelri's way that Ginnell had sent moles along the line and up towards Siabod, whose long valley was the only real break in the line. Troedfach sent some more moles that way, to help reduce the movement of the grike guardmoles.

The reason for this movement was soon apparent when, to Troedfach's surprise and pleasure, no less a mole than Alder appeared at his emplacement west of Caer Caradoc one day accompanied by a few hardy Siabod moles, all old friends.

'We expected to see you months ago, see?' said Troedfach.

'We had trouble on Siabod's lower slopes, for it was not as easy to clear of grikes as we expected and I doubt that even now we have done so. Ginnell knows his stuff and sent moles in to reinforce the place.'

'We knew of it, and tried to slow them down.'

'Enough came to make our task impossible. But Siabod's in no danger and I've left the place in Gowre's paws. He's glad to be left alone to do it, and he'll not let us down. I wanted to see the view from Caer Caradoc again.'

Alder had been kept well informed about Caer Caradoc. Now Troedfach pointed a rough paw at the great hill.

'There you are, mole. Do you want to stroll up it before or after you've groomed and eaten?'

Alder's wise gaze travelled slowly up the steep slope to the outcrops at the top.

'After, I think,' he said and laughed.

But the weather worsened and he was content to stay with Troedfach and talk of old times, and watched with approval as his old friend delegated the complex day by day business of organising the line to Gareg.

'You've a good one there, Troedfach.'

'He is. He'll help lead us to victory one day, and he'll do it well.'

'I wish I could see that day. I wish. . . .'

He fell silent, his old head lined and grey.

Troedfach said slowly, 'What is it, Alder? Why did you really come?'

'I'm tired, Troedfach, too tired now. All these long years in Siabod, so many memories. I had hoped to leave before Longest Night but that was not to be for Gowre was not ready to take over. But now, I've handed Siabod back to a Siabod mole, and one of Glyder's kin.'

'Did Glyder . . . ?'

Alder nodded.

'Aye, he did. Gowre got him back to Ogwen and stayed with him to the end, which was not long coming. He was not alone when he died. But that's a reason I've come here . . . I wanted to tell Caradoc of it personally. Those two had something in common, something nomole else but me knows about. Where is the old rascal?'

Troedfach grinned.

'About. He's not changed, but wanders here and there telling younger moles about the Stone and the traditions of the Marches. He was much upset by the way Caer Caradoc was taken, not liking to see bodies up there among the Stones. He's not a fighting mole, see?'

'Not fighting with talons, no, but of the spirit he's one of the greatest fighters I know.'

'He lives for the day when Caradoc is free for anymole to

718

wander. If he had his way moles would live up there again, or hereabout and trek up there to worship at the Stones.'

'Does he still believe . . . ?'

'The Stone Mole? Aye, he claims he's coming here. Up that slope you've been avoiding climbing, that's where the Stone Mole will go.'

'I hope for his sake he's younger than me!' said Alder, smiling.

Caradoc came back from a journey south some days later, having trekked through snow and ice and into the teeth of a gale or two to get there, though how he guessed Alder had come he did not say. Many moles believed that the Stone told Caradoc things.

'Bless me, it's Alder himself back here again!' he declared, embracing his friend. 'You're looking older.'

'I am old,' said Alder. 'I've retired. Siabod is in the capable paws of Gowre who, no doubt, has taken to it well. I think he was pleased to see me go. I've been asking Troedfach to find me a task here but he's no use for me either.'

'The Stone shall find a use for one who has served it better than any in all Wales these many years,' said Caradoc passionately. 'You stay here, Alder. This is the place to be now. Caer Caradoc will be clear of fighting one day soon and we'll live to see my dreams come true.'

'They will, Caradoc, I believe they will.'

Troedfach grinned and stanced up to make a diplomatic exit so the two old friends could talk privately, saying, 'Aye and I hope they do, Caradoc, but I'll leave you two together.'

When he had gone Alder came closer to Caradoc and said quietly, 'Mole, there's another reason I've come here to see you. Glyder is dead. He died before Longest Night up in Ogwen, and young Gowre was with him.'

Caradoc nodded sadly.

'I know it, Alder, I felt it *here*,' he said, thumping his breast. 'Here, see? He was the first to die of those of us who touched the Stones in June and helped the Stone Mole. Don't ask me how I know, but I do. One by one the seven Ancient Systems shall be free again, one by one. And each in their different ways shall be won back for open worship in the Stone.

'It grieved me to see my Caer Caradoc won with blood, but the Stone must mean something by it. New times are coming, Alder, and we've helped them along, and that's an honour. But I want to live to see it, see? I want to be up there by the Stones and know it's true. I'd like to hear the sound of pups playing in the wind where I once played. And I want moles like Troedfach and Gareg and yourself, fighters all, to go back to your systems when you've done here, and make peace there among your communities with the same skills you've shown making war.'

'I know it, Caradoc,' said Alder, 'and you're right. I was saying to Troedfach that I'm tired and so I am. I feel I've never had a home.'

'But Siabod, that's been your home.'

Alder shook his head.

'Glyder's home. Gowre's home. Not mine. I've been its guardian and protector, but a home is where your body and your spirit feel at peace.'

'Dreams, Alder, and for a mole like you! You *are* getting old, mole, and your brain's beginning to rot. You've told me yourself all the places you've been in your life – Siabod, Duncton, Buckland . . . Stone knows what before that.'

'I should have given this up long ago and gone back east as Marram did. He was right, you know: there comes a time when the fighting must stop and a mole must reach out to his enemy in peace and say, "No more, we are friends now".'

Caradoc saw how distressed Alder really was and let him talk on a little more before saying, 'Tomorrow it's a climb for you up Caer Caradoc. I'll lead you on ways which will avoid the ice and you can see the finest view and breathe the clearest air in all moledom. Why mole, we'll find ourselves a couple of mates, tell moles of Stone and Word to clear off, and make as fine a home as any you'll find elsewhere. We're not so old we can't make pups!'

'You've never had pups so far as I know, Caradoc.'

Caradoc grinned, a little shyly.

'Never met the right mole. And never the time.'

'Well, if you wait for the Stone Mole to come it might never happen,' said Alder.

They laughed and talked some more, enjoying the evening slowly, as good friends do, their laughter and argument a cheering thing for moles like Gareg and Troedfach to hear, and their conversation inspiring to those moles who, when night came, had the sense to gather round and listen to what Alder and Caradoc had to say.

Next day Caradoc was as good as his word and, refusing the offers Gareg and Troedfach made to accompany them, he led Alder up the slower but easier western flanks of Caer Caradoc to explore its highest parts, and to stare over towards the east.

The garrison was glad to see Alder, and its young commanders showed him how they had placed their limited number of moles. They were astonished at how quickly he understood the strengths and weaknesses of their deployment and predicted where future likely attacks might come from.

'Aye, Sir, we have the occasional skirmish. The grikes like to keep us occupied and guessing.'

'It's a hard position for them to take right enough, but you're vulnerable to a concentrated night attack.'

Caradoc listened with a grin on his face. He was amused to see how quickly Alder had reverted to the campaigning mole he truly was and knew that, though he claimed otherwise, Alder missed commanding Siabod but was too good a leader to cling on to a command that needed a younger mole.

Alder came over to Caradoc and asked, 'Did you really live up here when you were young or was it lower down where it looks more wormful?'

'Lower down,' said Caradoc, taking him to the north-east side and pointing out pastures bounded by a river. 'Down there, see, which is occupied now by grikes. It's wormful and was lived in until the plagues came. In the old days it was the younger moles' task, led by an elder, to come up here for a while and learn things about the Stone. The top will support a few moles well enough, and it does a mole good to live for a time above the world. Makes him get things in proportion.'

Alder looked about a little more, at the Stones and then across the sloping top.

'When Marram and I came you kept us so busy meeting other moles that I don't remember looking about like this. It's a fine place.'

'It's the finest! I tell you, mole, stop here awhile.'

'I'll do that with pleasure until the winter clears. But then . . . perhaps I'll always be a traveller. Perhaps I'll drift back to Siabod. Perhaps I'll go down to Tyn-y-Bedw, where Troedfach comes from, and have a rest. *He* says *that's* the finest place.'

'Stop still, mole, and you'll be content.'

'You're a one to talk, Caradoc. You've wandered the Marches all your life. Despite your fine talk you're no more likely to settle down now than I am!'

The two moles continued to argue and talk until, the day drawing in, they began their descent to Troedfach's emplacement once more, to get back aburrow, and watch the winter through.

So Alder came to Caer Caradoc, to share the military life with moles he loved and felt most comfortable with. On clearer days he wandered off with Caradoc, but when the weather was bad he stayed underground, and many a mole was sent by Troedfach to talk with him, and to learn the many things that his conversation and experience told them. None more than Gareg when he had time, who respected a mole like Alder and enjoyed his company.

The Marches, like the rest of moledom, were gripped

by winter, until at last the rough tunnels of Troedfach's position began to drip with thawing snow and ice. A busy time then, an exciting time, a time to go out on the surface with energy once more and enjoy the approach of spring.

'And a dangerous time,' warned Troedfach, and moles like Alder and Gareg knew what he meant. A time for the resumption of fighting once more.

'But a time of promise,' said Caradoc to himself, adding a prayer to the Stone: 'Make it the time when promises come true, the fighting begins to end and Caer Caradoc can become my home once more.'

Even February's cold and cruel progression through Duncton Wood – when starving foxes falter in the night and are found frozen at the wood's edge when morning comes, and ragged birds peck at the barren soil – did nothing to dispel the excitement and purpose from Mistle's determined heart.

She and faithful Romney got to know their system well, and though they heeded Mayweed's advice and avoided the Ancient System, they got the measure of everywhere else, and Mistle made her plans for the system's reoccupation.

'What reoccupation? By what moles?' demanded Romney – not in doubt, for he had given up doubting Mistle, but in curiosity.

'*Duncton* moles, of course! And if you ask me what moles they may be I'll tell you now! Moles of good heart, moles of good faith, moles of good humour, and moles with paws and spirits willing to work and make this place alive once more.

'I don't know where they'll come from or who they'll be, but come they will and they'll be made welcome by you and I and by these tunnels in which for now we wander all alone.

'Barrow Vale, where Tryfan died, shall be the centre of the community once more, and the Stone shall be loved and often visited. At first I shall not allow moles to settle just anywhere and that's why we've had to get to know how the tunnels run, so I know where moles must go.'

Romney laughed.

'You mean you'll organise everymole here?'

Mistle grinned.

'Only at first, just to get them started. Somemole's got to do it and ensure we don't have those arguments and divisions which Beechen said he had been told by Tryfan were common here before the plagues. In those days the Westsiders didn't talk to the Eastsiders, the Marshenders were regarded as scum, and hardly anymole bothered with the Stone at all.

'There was a system of elders, but it became dominated by a mole called Mandrake, and then Rune who later became Master of the Word.'

'Rune was *here*?'

'It seems so. Henbane was, too, for a time. And most recently Lucerne, of course . . . There's something about Duncton that attracts moles, Romney. Even moles like them.'

She might have added, too, that there was something about Duncton Wood that changed moles as well.

But if Romney had not changed by then, he certainly did when March came, and the snow began to thaw, the wood's great trees dripped and ran wet, and its floor began to rustle and bustle and seem to shine and glimmer with the new-found life brought out by the warmer winds and brighter light.

Then, one day. . . .

'Mistle! Mistle!'

Romney ran upslope through the wood from Barrow Vale, a different mole than when he had first come. His fur was rougher now yet glossier, his eyes brighter, his movements easier and more confident.

'Mistle!'

Mistle too had changed, and the fairer weather suited her. She came out to greet him and he stopped before her, breathing heavily and half laughing.

'What is it?' she said, laughing too, for his humour was infectious.

'Come with me! What I want to show you isn't far,' he said, and turning, he led her back the way he had come.

She hurried after him, and the light of the sun was caught in the budding trees above them, and shone in the new bursts of leaves that were breaking out along bramble stems which, when they had first come, had all lain moribund but whose last dead leaves had now fallen away.

Past these he went, turning across towards the Eastside among a shooting bed of pert dog's mercury, the shining green of their leaves bright across their path, and then great rafts of new shoots of bluebells down the gentle slopes below them. While between them the leaves of wood anemone were showing, dark, more delicate, their flowers still hidden too.

'Come on, Mistle!' he called behind him, and in the joy and pleasure of his shout she lost the sense of flagging she had had and bounded on, the sweet-scented humus beneath her paws seeming the gentlest surface she had ever run across.

All about the wood seedlings were suddenly bursting up, as shiny as the dog's mercury, frail-seeming and yet pushing litter out of their way to reach the light above.

'What do you want to show me, Romney?' she called out.

He paused just before breaking through the wood's edge onto the eastern Pastures.

'Look!' he whispered, creeping forward like a pup who has found a new exciting thing. He parted the brambles in front of them and beckoned her to his flank.

Here the March sun came unimpeded down and she saw among the grass at the wood's edge the first peeping yellow flowers of celandine. Just two plants of them were out, but others were there, their flowers nearly ripe, their dark green veiny leaves abundant. The stems of the plants already out rose up with the pale yellow petals of the flower spread out like the rays of the sun. Above them, echoing

725

the flowers' colour, the catkins of a hazel hung, trembling in the light breeze off the slopes.

Romney looked at her, his eyes moist.

'I came this way and saw them and it seemed to me suddenly that winter was over and I saw the real promise of the spring and Duncton Wood. These are just the beginning, aren't they, Mistle?'

She nodded, unable to speak, joyful for his joy.

'So much that's good is going to happen here,' she said. '*So* much.' She gulped the fresh air in as if overwhelmed by the excitement of it all and said, 'Oh Romney, I can hardly breathe!'

In the days that followed, spring continued to spread its delightful, sudden, sporadic way across the wood, not yet in its full glory, but stirring and rich, and the two moles had much to discover in the magic world that was theirs.

One day then, with March well under way, Mistle said she was willing now to go to the Stone again, for if they were going to perform the rites and say the prayers that Violet had taught her they must begin to become acquainted with their Stone.

'You don't have to join in, Romney. Just listen and take your time.'

So they went, and on the way Mistle told him of the four great turnings of the seasons, which start with Longest Night and occur again in March and June and September.

'Violet taught me the prayers to say, and I'm going to begin when the March equinox comes. But we'll start now just by getting to know the Stone, and telling it that we're *here*, and we have faith in it and in ourselves. The Stone likes to know that *we* know, because it gets tired of just supporting moles who only turn to it when times are hard.'

They reached the clearing and ventured into it a little diffidently, lest there was still evidence of the massacre, but there was not. The winter snows and winds had turned and cleaned the leaves, and owl and rook had done their work.

At the Stone's base, where so many had died, no trace of mole remained.

'Beechen was born here,' she said, reaching out to touch the Stone. Romney hung back, somewhat intimidated by the Stone's rising mass and the many dire associations the eldrenes of his youth had inculcated in him regarding it.

'There's no need to be afraid of it, Romney,' she said, realising his concern.

'You would be if you had been told since a pup that the Stone's the most evil thing in moledom.'

She was about to reply when, to their mutual alarm and astonishment, three moles suddenly emerged from the undergrowth. They were thickset and fit, two males and a female.

'Stone followers!' said one of the males shortly.

'Don't just stance there!' snapped the female. 'Tell them to scarper.'

'Well, I mean. . . .'

'Oh fine and splendid!' said the female, who had a preening pouty way about her. 'If you're too cowardly then *he* will, won't he?' She smiled coquettishly at the second male.

'He will!' declared the second male in a voice and with a look that suggested that, though dim, he had a nasty streak in him. Indeed, he came past the female and appeared to prepare himself to attack Romney and Mistle.

The most alarming thing about it all was that the three moles spoke as if neither Romney nor Mistle were there, as if being 'followers' had rendered them anonymous annoyances that should be got rid of.

All this took but seconds and Romney, not a slow mole nor a coward, was in the act of putting himself between the grikes and Mistle and assessing his best chances of warding them off and getting away to safety when, to his astonishment and concern, and even more to the alarm of the three aggressors, Mistle reared up in a violent rage, rushed forward, thrust her snout within a hairsbreadth of the preening female's, and screamed, 'How *dare* you?'

The two males backed off immediately and the female looked utterly stunned.

'Have you any idea where you are?' shouted Mistle, bringing her right paw forward and prodding the female in the shoulder. The female opened her mouth to reply but was no match for Mistle in voice or ferocity.

'You're in Duncton Wood, and you're before its Stone, *and* you're forcing me to disturb the peace.'

By now the first of the two males had recovered himself. He pushed a paw between the two females and seemed about to buffet Mistle away. Once more Romney came forward to intervene but Mistle was proving quite capable of looking after herself and, turning to the male, she brought her paw hard across his snout.

'Don't you dare get fresh with me before the Stone, or anywhere else for that matter. Go on, get out! We don't want moles like you here. Go on, *out!*'

To Romney's amazement the three moles, at first thrown in to disarray, then looking uncertainly at one another, finally retreated before Mistle's anger. But even then she did not let them merely slink away, but followed them through the wood among the beech trees, harrying them, stopping them answering her back, prodding them unpleasantly.

'It's not that we don't want moles here,' she cried out as they hurried from her blows and invective, 'but we'll not put up with *your* kind of insensitive asinine aggression. Go on, hurry up, I haven't got all day, and I'm not stopping until I see your rears scarpering, as you put it, downslope towards the cross-under. Yes, and *especially* yours, playing your games with these two males and don't think I don't know what you're about! If they've got any sense they'll tell you to get lost! Go on . . . !'

She finally stopped harassing them halfway down the south-eastern slopes and the only comment any of them made as they escaped was from the first male, who looked dolefully past Mistle at Romney and said, 'Better you than me, mate! You wouldn't catch me setting up burrow with her.'

'No you would not!' said Mistle. 'Out!'

She turned back upslope, still angry and raging it seemed, and it was not until they had reached the wood again that Romney caught her up and she turned to him, half laughing and half crying, and then shaking as he held her, and said, 'Oh Romney, they really went! They really did!'

'Whatmole wouldn't, Mistle?'

'I don't know what came over me. But the moment I saw them it was as if I knew what I must do. But I'm not *like* that.'

'Remember, no "buts",' said Romney. 'And I think we've just seen you *are* like that. Like a mother protecting its pups you are in this system!'

'We've got to start as we mean to go on. Moles must know where they stance.'

'Next time you might get ten grikes, not just three.'

'The Stone will protect us . . .' Her voice faded, her eyes grew alarmed, she seemed to cock her head on one side as if listening, though he could hear nothing, and she whispered, 'Romney!'

Her face became full of fear. Romney sometimes felt he could not keep up with her.

'What is it now?'

'I don't know,' she said quietly. 'I don't know. Lead me back to the Stone now, *please*. Please, Romney!'

How different the quality of the wood seemed to Romney as he led Mistle urgently through the wood and she at his flank, almost leaning on him, gasping and distressed.

How much more awesome the Stone seemed to him now, yet how much closer to it he came. Something in her earlier defence of their wood, something in her need now, made the clearing a comforting place, a haven and a base, an end and a beginning.

'Stone,' Mistle said, staring up at its face but not touching it, 'protect now those who need thee. Give them courage. Give them strength. Help them. Guide them.

729

Let them feel thy love, and the love of those who love them. Stone, I feel thee close to me. Let those who need help feel thee close as well. Give them the strength you give me, remind them of thy love. Stone, hear my prayer.'

She bowed her snout before the Stone, she trembled, she sighed in despair, she was silent and her paw reached out for Romney's.

'What is it, Mistle?' he said. 'What's wrong?'

'It's Beechen,' she said, 'he needs us again like he did once before. He *needs* us. . . .'

Romney took her in his strong paws, and held her as she shook and wept and prayed.

'Needs who?' he asked, not understanding. But she made no reply.

Finally he looked up at the Stone and whispered, 'Mistle, he will come back.' As she stilled against him, reassured, her body weak from the strange day, he looked higher at the Stone, and spoke to himself his first prayer as a follower.

'May it be so, Stone, that Beechen returns one day.'

And he knew then that he would stay in Duncton, that Mistle needed him and he would stay until Beechen came home again.

Chapter Thirty-Three

There was an unpleasant look of self-righteous pride on the face of the eldrene Wort as she finally led the captured Stone Mole, close-guarded by her henchmoles, into Ashbourne.

No matter that thin snow sleeted down; no matter that the only audience was a desultory few of the grike guardmoles who, under the command of the sideem Merrick, had taken over the running of the place after the snouting of the eldrene Winster; no matter that Wort was still uncertain what she was going to do with her prisoner.

She was triumphant. She had done the will of the Word, and the Word would guide her towards what was right. For had not the Word already showed its trust in her, weak though she was, and guided her well until now?

'He has abused my holy name for far too long' (it had seemed to say to her) 'and you, eldrene Wort of Fyfield, mole whom I supremely trust for this great task, must take him, humble him, and do with him as I shall command!'

No doubt of it! She had prayed, she had suffered her body to be chastised, and out of her suffering the Word in its endless mercy had directed her; and she had obeyed.

But, oh, how much mightier was the Word than mere mole could understand, how much *cleverer*. One thing only she regretted now: that in her molish failure to have faith in the Word's might she had felt it necessary to take such a strong force of henchmoles to the Kniveton meeting, thinking there would be resistance. Thinking, indeed, that if there was she would not hesitate to personally attack the mole Beechen and ensure that he did not escape, whatever the cost to herself and her henchmoles might be.

Sheer fantasy and vanity! The Word had put fear and

731

respect into the hearts of the followers, and they had not dared in the face of its might to raise a single talon towards a mole of the Word. Not one!

'Holy Word, forgive me for not putting enough trust in you. Let these blows and talons on my body' – she was muttering this abject prayer as she suffered her habitual chastisement at the paws of one of her young henchmoles – 'remind me of my sin and failure. You have entrusted me with the great task and temptation of bringing the Stone Mole Beechen of Duncton before your eternal judgement. Word, who loves me, I beg that I may fulfil this task unto its very end.'

For all her prayers and trust that the Word would see things right, the eldrene Wort had a practical streak and so, feeling certain that the Master would be pleased with what she had done, she had, within minutes of securing Beechen at Kniveton, sent a messenger off to bear the good news to the Master at Cannock.

She had prayed for guidance about what to do next very frequently on the way back to Ashbourne, and had had the henchmoles take Beechen and the former guardmole Buckram, whom she had once punished at Fyfield and wished now she had snouted, away from her, for she felt weak and tempted towards pity and love in their presence.

So now here she was, Wort, mere eldrene of Fyfield, empowered by the Master himself to have sole decision upon the moles Beechen and Buckram. The question was what was she going to do with the Stone Mole until such time as the Master got her message and came to Ashbourne? If indeed he was coming.

Despite her posturings of modesty, it was a blow to her vanity that the only mole at Ashbourne who showed the slightest interest in her arrival with the Stone Mole was the resident sideem in the place, Merrick of Hawe, one of the new sideem, and the kind of mole Wort did not like: cold, close and – worst – dubious of her authority.

But Merrick had already been insulted by the way eldrene Wort had ensconced an unpleasant group of

732

taciturn henchmoles in Ashbourne before she had set off to Kniveton, and so on her return with Beechen he was waiting to assert his authority.

The encounter was unpleasant and extended since neither mole was willing to yield to the other. At issue was which of them was to have control over the Stone Mole within Ashbourne. Merrick quickly discovered what many others had since Wort had begun her resolute progress north in pursuit of Beechen: that a mole with the purpose of the Word in her heart, and sincerity, however misplaced, in her eyes, and an overriding belief that what she was doing was more important than anything else in moledom, is not easily thwarted.

But Merrick was not just another senior guardmole or eldrene, nor even 'just another' sideem. He had after all – though Wort had no reason to know it – been the first to survive at the Midsummer rite when Lucerne himself was anointed, and this had required a rather special desire to survive.

Unfortunately, since then he had been confined to more northerly systems and at the time Wort met him in Ashbourne he was feeling undervalued and rejected. In this meeting, therefore, between Wort and Merrick, the driving zeal of an eldrene met the thwarted ambition of a sideem, and initially the eldrene seemed to win.

But Merrick had been trained by the First Keeper of the Word very well, and knew that persistence would eventually find its reward. Though he thought Wort overzealous to a fault, and found the overt – almost physical – passion with which she had espoused the Word distasteful, yet he saw he might make it her weakness even as it appeared to be her strength. He had been dismayed by the eldrene's patent disregard of his authority, thinking at first that it was an expression of her desire for power. But the more he studied the eldrene the more it seemed, incredible though it was, that her sole concern was to maintain her possession of this irritating mole, Beechen of Duncton.

Naturally sideem Merrick had heard of the Stone Mole

and his reputation, but he dismissed it as an inevitable outcome of faulty oppression that such moles thrived in the backwaters and grubby places of moledom where followers eked out their lives.

His view was that the sooner such apostles and Stone-fools were disposed of the better, in spite of the Master's orders. He had himself been instrumental in having several such moles quietly killed. The fact that this insolent eldrene had not harmed the Stone-fool suggested to him two possibilities: first that she was afraid to because the Master had instructed her not to; or second, and more sinister, she was herself infected by a desire for the Stone, and could not bring herself to kill the mole. Both were, of course, good reasons to encourage the eldrene to do so. . . .

Even as Merrick weighed up these devious thoughts an idea, yet half conscious and half formed, came to him and he found himself saying, 'Eldrene Wort, I am sure you are aware that one of the difficulties we have in administering Ashbourne and providing extra quarters is that the Master is planning strikes against followers. They have already started in the south, and guardmoles and others are coming north to be ready for the assault on evil Beechenhill.'

As Wort's eyes lighted up at his use of the phrase 'strikes against followers' and then positively glowed at the mention of 'evil' Beechenhill, he quickly added, 'You probably know that it has been one of my long-standing ambitions to be the mole that is responsible for the final annihilation of that wretched system.'

He turned to the two senior guardmoles who had come to give him support in this curious confrontation, and nodded at them in such a way that they echoed his sentiments about Beechenhill with frowns and a general eagerness to rid moledom of the pestilence of the Stone.

Wort, who now looked as if tasty morsels of worms had been placed before her after a long fast, said, 'The holy Word must indeed long for the destruction of Beechenhill,

734

whose notoriety is known to us in the south and is something, I am forced to say, we do not understand. You cannot have will enough for this task! But sideem Merrick . . .' Merrick smiled and came closer, all friendliness now, all willingness to help.

'Eldrene?'

'These strikes you mention against followers. I had understood, indeed it is no disloyalty or betrayal to say I understood from the Master himself, that they would not be started quite yet. . . .'

'No, no, eldrene Wort, they began in February, earlier than originally intended, and I understand they have been going on at an ever increasing pace.'

'Successfully?'

'Very. But naturally it is most frustrating that we here in Ashbourne have not been told positively that we can attack Beechenhill.'

This was a little misleading. Ashbourne had been told not to mount an attack until given the word, and it was reasonable to assume that this was because the Master wanted to oversee it himself.

'Of course, the Master will be well pleased when it is done,' he added, turning the talon in the wound of Wort's over-weening ambition towards the Word.

Wort could not resist saying confidentially, 'Sideem Merrick, I have good reason to think that the Master may soon be with us. He had a particular interest in the capture of the Stone Mole and instructed me to let him know when it had been effected, which I have done.'

'How glad he will be to know of it. And how I envy you that honour, Wort, indeed I do! If he is coming here – and clearly you have his ear in a way I could not hope to have – what pleasure it would be for him to arrive and find Beechenhill taken.'

'Taken and laid waste by the order and vengeance of the Word!'

'The Word triumphant at the Beechenhill Stone!'

'Oh yes,' said Wort, filled with sudden passion, 'the

blood of followers desecrating the Stone's face, the blood of followers red upon the talon of the Word. . . .'

'This Stone Mole. . . .'

'Stone Mole?' said Wort immediately, and Merrick thought he had lost her again for her eyes narrowed as if she sensed a threat to her jurisdiction.

Merrick kept smiling and said, 'Beechenhill would be a fitting place for the Word to end the life of such a mole. If he is the *Stone* Mole, what more fitting judgement than to desecrate the Stone with his life? If he is not, but merely a vile and evil imposter, then no punishment is too great for him, and the sooner the better.'

'Holy Word, our mother and our father,' cried out Wort suddenly, 'guide us here in this hour of need and doubt, to find the way thou desirest us to go that we may go that way in thy name and no other.'

Merrick nodded in an agreeable kind of way at the end of this impassioned prayer and said, 'But, eldrene Wort, such a course is not open to us, is it? No, no, tempting though it would be I cannot let my guardmoles loose on Beechenhill.'

'The Word shall guide you, sideem Merrick!' declared Wort with conviction. 'You shall do what you must do and be guided by the Word.'

'Would that I had your confidence, Wort. Would that I always knew my way forward with the Word. Sometimes we are faced with problems that seem beyond the possibility of mole to resolve . . . but no matter. I shall not burden a mole who has barely ended such a long quest as you have. Another time.'

'We are put into moledom to help one another,' said Wort, warming to her new-found role of spiritual counsellor, especially to a sideem, 'and if there is anything. . . .'

'Yes, there *seems* to be a problem. Is it anything or is it merely a figment, like a nightmare that seems real at the time but afterwards is not, though the taste of horror remains?'

'Nightmare? Is it a matter of the Stone? My dear sideem Merrick, if it is advice you want. . . .'

Merrick signalled to the two guardmoles to leave.

'No, no, Wort . . . you must forgive me if I seem awkward. There has been something much on my mind for these two days past. But. . . .'

Wort stayed silent, Merrick affected to decide suddenly to tell what he had hoped to tell all along. He opened his mouth, he glanced over his shoulder, and he said, 'I should not.'

'Sideem Merrick, is it a blasphemy you know of?'

'Worse.'

'*Worse* than a blasphemy?'

'Supposing, eldrene Wort, just supposing I told you I knew where another lived, what would you say?'

'I would say, "Does it matter?" And if it did I would ask the name of this other.'

'To the Master it matters.'

The Master! A new way to serve him! The eldrene's mouth moistened at the prospect of a satiation of her spiritual greed.

'Then I must ask, sideem Merrick, the name of this mole that matters to him.'

'The Mistress Henbane,' said Merrick quietly.

'Where?' said Wort with undisguised greed.

'Beechenhill.'

Wort greeted this with a kind of fomenting silence, her face twitching, her eyes hungry for more knowledge, her stance almost lusty with the pleasure of what she heard.

'Are you sure?'

'A mole I trust saw her fleeing into Beechenhill several days ago. He is sure it was her.'

'Henbane,' whispered Wort, her eyes narrowing and staring at a distant place where the name of the eldrene Wort of Fyfield seemed to be scrivened gloriously in stars across the night sky.

'She may escape. She may die. Nomole more accurst. Nomole more fitting for punishment,' said Merrick.

'But the Master, his mother. She cannot. Once he put out an order that she be taken. Now . . . The Master would rejoice to know she's dead, the Master could not kill her if she is alive. Others . . .' Wort was almost incoherent in her musings on Henbane and what it might mean.

Then she said, as if in grip of herself once more, 'Aye, others of confidence must do that deed. Sideem, I hear the holy Word, I hear it cry damnation on that apostate Mistress of the Word, I hear it cry vengeance on Beechenhill, I hear it cry death to the Stone Mole. These cries I hear as one, as one I hear them brutally assail me, demanding that I hear.'

'But I cannot help thee, Wort,' said Merrick, craftily. 'I am restrained by my promise to the Master's order. But thou with thy authority have been entrusted to act as you see fit. Pray this night for guidance, Wort, as I shall. Pray for us all! Pray for those brave moles of the Word whose lives are lost each day that the former Mistress lives and Beechenhill survives. Yield not to that temptation which the Stone Mole offers thee, to let him live. Be resolute, eldrene, for all of us, and pray for us and for thyself. Seek guidance this night!

'As sideem of this place I give thee full authority to use those tunnels that thou wilt, and demand that thou art resolute in the commands for action thou may in future give to thy worthy henchmoles. Though I cannot myself command my own guardmoles to follow thee I tell thee this: if they were to decide to follow a certain devout eldrene that I know, and her henchmoles, on a mission for the Word – as observers perhaps, as support, as moral sustenance – this sideem would not, could not, stop them! And if their destination was Beechenhill, why this sideem would rejoice. But it is for the Word to guide thee in such matters, not a mere mole like me.'

With that Merrick turned with a flourish and was gone, to leave Wort to face the most sleepless night of prayer and chastisement she had ever had.

Harebell's return to Beechenhill with Henbane and the others had nearly turned into disaster on the very threshold of the system, a disaster only averted in a way that left the grike guardmoles who almost trapped them in no doubt that it was Henbane they had seen.

They had finally found a safe crossing over the River Dove, which was in spate due to thawing on the northern moors, and they were ambushed by a grike patrol on the other side. No doubt the grikes had guessed that moles might be forced to use that route and had simply lain in wait, though they could not have imagined that it was the former Mistress of the Word they were about to confront.

But there they were, four large guardmoles against two tired males, Harrow and Holm, and three females, two of them elderly: it was no contest, or should not have been.

'Well, well,' said the commander of the grikes with a cheerful smile, 'patience is rewarded with a little group of faithful followers. Greetings . . . and *don't* move.'

But Henbane did move, in an extraordinary display of authority which made all of them, none more than Harebell, understand how it could have been that this mole was once Mistress of the Word and ruler of all moledom.

'Mole,' she said, coming forward with dignity and complete confidence, 'I like not your tone, your manner or your intent. Nor shall the Word. And by the Word you and your colleagues shall be accursed if you do not Atone for your insolence against my person and that of my companions.'

It was unfortunate that one of the grikes had seen her before, for there was no question that they would have retreated, so formidable was her manner and the threat she made.

As it was, one of them said, 'By the Wor . . . it is the Mistress Henbane herself.'

'It is, mole, and you are fortunate you stopped yourself

swearing by the Word. As thy Mistress I command thee all to stance back and let us pass.'

'But . . .' began the grike.

'Ssh!' one of those with him said in awe.

Quick-thinking Harebell said, 'They should be made to Atone now!' and with that, and her snout in the air, passed on, leading her mother with her.

Harrow had to prod poor Holm in the rump to get him moving again, so terrified was he, but Sleekit, a formidable mole in her own right and well able to think calmly in such moments, made a fitting rearguard to the group, and even gave the patrol a withering stare as she passed. Each of them proceeded slowly up the slope, expecting the patrol to come chasing after them, but it did not and they reached the shelter of the tunnels above without further trouble. Once there Harebell was able to lose any pursuers in the complex limestone tunnels and they were soon picked up by an astonished and delighted watcher and taken on into the main system.

Squeezebelly's excitement at Harebell's homecoming was soon overshadowed by the news they brought of the Stone Mole's capture, and the fact that an attack on Beechenhill seemed certain now that sideem Merrick must know, through the guardmoles who had stopped them, that Henbane was in the system.

Henbane, on the other paw, was more concerned about what her reception might be once moles knew who she was, but Squeezebelly reassured her that she would meet with no hostility if she came in peace, though it might be best if she kept a low snout.

'Surely you can trust Beechenhill moles, Squeezebelly,' said Harebell.

But he shook his head sadly, and said he was not sure that he could any more. The pressures of the winter years, the failure of Wharfe to return and the sense of the omnipresence of the grikes had created divisions in the system which even the combination of Harebell's safe return, Squeezebelly's good sense and the thawing of the snows and return of milder weather could not cure.

'To make it worse,' Squeezebelly said, 'something has happened which I knew was a possibility in such circumstances. Indeed, I'm surprised it has not happened before. Very few of the females have got with pup, very few.'

'The same thing happened in Ashbourne when the grikes first came, according to my mother,' said Harrow.

Squeezebelly nodded. 'Yes, that's right. I heard that too. It's hard for a female to get with pup if she's worried, and downright impossible if she's afraid for her life. But that's how we all are now, so it's not surprising that females aren't fertile.'

'Well, Squeezebelly . . .' began Harebell, unable to contain her own news longer, though she had intended to. 'There's another who is. *I'm* with pup!'

It was true enough, but as is the way of such things, Henbane was the only one to know and Harrow, though he might have guessed, was the one to look surprised. Holm stanced up, looked about in the usual way he did before speaking, seemed about to explode, and said, 'Good luck. You'll need it!' and shut up again. They were the first words he had spoken in nearly three days.

Harebell giggled and there were a few moments of lightness and cheer among the otherwise beset group.

'Well, if I had any doubts before, I have none now,' declared Squeezebelly, 'we're going to have to evacuate some of us from Beechenhill, certainly younger moles, the few females in pup, and older moles of both sexes. It's the only way for us to survive as a community without fighting.'

'Where will we go?' asked Harebell.

'The Castern Chambers,' said Squeezebelly, quickly explaining about them to the non-Beechenhill moles there. 'There'll be a communal meeting about it, there'll be a lot of complaints, Bramble will sound off again as he has for molemonths past, but believe me it will have to be done.'

'And what of Beechen? What can we do for him?'

Sleekit asked the question, but in their hearts all there knew there were no easy answers, and that Squeezebelly was unlikely to allow heroics.

'If the Stone Mole had been taken forcibly,' said Harebell, 'it would be different. And he expressly asked that we do not take any violent action.'

'Something might be possible with surprise and a good disciplined assault,' said Henbane, who in her day had been, alongside Wrekin, a great leader in campaigns.

But Sleekit shook her head.

'I have travelled with him ever since he first left Duncton Wood and again and again he has begged his followers not to resort to violence. I have known him almost from the moment of his birth and never seen him strike another mole. He would not want moles hurt on his behalf. It is against all his teachings. The only good thing is that he has Buckram with him, and he's a mole of resource. He might find a way to get him free. But Beechen wants no violence.'

Holm nodded his head vigorously, and then shook it.

'Yes, no violence,' he said.

'We have followers among the grikes guardmoles in Ashbourne,' Harrow said. 'If, as I think, that's where they've been taken, they might get help, or perhaps moles will try to get a message to us. They're likely to know where we are now that Henbane has been seen coming into this system.'

But it was small comfort to Sleekit and the others, who could still barely comprehend that Beechen had been taken from them.

The meeting that Squeezebelly called was rowdy and unpleasant and it was as well that Squeezebelly decided that Henbane should not be there, for even in her absence it was plain that he had underestimated the hostility felt against her. Truly, the pressures were showing and Beechenhill was not what it once had been.

742

Bramble was the main cause of trouble, first attacking the whole notion of Henbane being allowed in the system at all, and then going on to suggest that she could be exchanged for the Stone Mole.

When Squeezebelly stopped this suggestion short, even though several other moles seemed to agree with it, Bramble went on to argue that if they were going to evacuate they should do so immediately and then the males could return and fight it out.

'Fighting is not to be our way. It is only by not fighting that we have survived, as you know well, Bramble.'

'There's others here who agree with me,' said Bramble, indicating Skelder and Ghyll, who had changed their tune considerably since they came as refugees from Mallerstang. Their peaceable philosophy had gone, and they were all for using their fighting skills now to attack the murdering grikes.

But Quince bravely spoke up against them, and others too, and it was plain that by a small majority the Beechenhill moles believed they should leave the system, at least for long enough for the few females who were with pup to have them somewhere safe. They all knew about the Castern Chambers and they would be safe there for a time.

As for Henbane, it was clear, too, that had she not been the much-liked Harebell's mother, and had Squeezebelly been a weaker leader than he was, she might not have survived long in Beechenhill.

Squeezebelly had been especially glad to have the support of Quince, for she had been subdued and upset since Wharfe's departure on what would surely be a vain search for Betony, and he had feared she would go the bitter way Bramble had. But she was tougher than Squeezebelly's son, and bore Wharfe's loss well. She was a mole who seemed to flourish in adversity. He prayed that one day Wharfe would come back to her, for she was the kind of mole of which the future must be made.

'We shall begin the evacuation over the next few days,'

said Squeezebelly finally, 'and Quince shall oversee the care of the females who are to pup. We should aim to be clear of the system by the March equinox, and until then our watchers shall be doubled and warned to be especially vigilant and all moles should keep in close touch. If we need to go quickly we want no stragglers.'

'We should leave sooner than that!' said Bramble.

'We must ensure that the Castern Chambers are secure, and though I have no doubt that all the lower valley routes are watched by grikes, at least there are hidden higher exits which will give us respite from being underground. Believe me, Bramble, and you others who are for leaving now, once you get to Castern you will not want to stay confined in the chambers there for longer than we need.'

'And if Castern is not secure, do we drop this cowardly inclination not to fight?' asked Bramble.

'We shall decide that when it happens, and be guided by the Stone,' said Squeezebelly strongly, looking around the gathering for support that the discussion was now closed.

But though he did not betray his unease, yet he felt it. Was a mole really to do as his conscience and the Stone Mole himself suggested, and do nothing in the face of violence? He hoped that if and when the time came he would have the courage of his peaceful convictions, and the qualities that would be needed to lead these moles in such a crisis.

'She is with pup, Terce, the sideem Mallice is with pup!'

For once Lucerne seemed as young as his years, young and delighted, and Terce, too, was able to be pleased. At last his daughter had got herself with pup and he felt the thrill of knowing that his plans for moledom and for the Mastership were going right.

'*Everything* is beginning to go right, Lucerne,' he said.

Lucerne nodded his agreement, for it was true enough. In the last few days confirmations had come in with growing frequency from the trinities that the murderous strikes against the followers had been almost entirely successful; quietly, efficiently, and in a sufficiently co-ordinated way that the followers had not had time to group and fight back.

The strikes had begun ruthlessly in the south-east in February with a campaign led from Buckland by Clowder which had then spread to the west and into the Midlands just as he and Lucerne had planned. Before long the strikes had gained a momentum of their own, and as the grikes acquired taste for them they were spreading northwards. The Word was supreme.

So much so that Lucerne decided shortly before his departure for Ashbourne and Beechenhill to send word to Ginnell to begin the final rout of the Welsh Marches, strengthened as he would be by the guardmoles in the Midlands and south-west.

'Yes, Terce, all is coming right,' smiled Lucerne, 'and today we shall leave for Beechenhill.'

'Whatmole shall you leave in charge?'

'Drule and Slighe can manage it between them, I think. Now, I shall go and prepare my beloved for her departure. I would have preferred her to have the pups in Whern but that is hardly possible. But Beechenhill is within a safe range for a journey, and for the future Master to be born there would be a fitting desecration of the place.'

Lucerne smiled again and left. Terce watched him go, but his pleasure in the sharing of the news that meant much to both of them slid into concern and unease. He frowned, his sleek face lined and old, his eyes wrinkled and cold, his fur thin. Austerity had made the bones of his body prominent and they formed gaunt shadows at his shoulders and rear.

Why uneasy? He did not know. Something about the reports of the strikes. Something wrong.

Too easy. No opposition from the followers at all? Was the Stone, their enemy of centuries, so weak? Terce could not believe it. The original counts of followers might have been wrong, or more had emerged since and remained undetected. No, no, something was wrong. Perhaps the followers had been better at dissembling than the sideem gave them credit for, and there were more than anymole had thought living isolated and quiet and waiting. Waiting for what? The Stone Mole was what they were always meant to say when asked that question. But what could a solitary mole do – especially one now in the safe paws of Wort?

Terce had not risen to his position of power as Twelfth Keeper by asking such questions merely rhetorically. He trusted himself that when he felt uneasy there was reason for it, and if a question asked itself in his mind it might have another answer than the obvious one.

So . . . what could a solitary mole do against the might of the Word? Nothing much, surely. Not even if he was martyred, and Wort would not be so stupid as to kill him before the Master got to Ashbourne. Would she? She might, yes, she might. Martyrdom then . . . well, there had been martyrs on both sides over the centuries. Yet Terce, who knew his history as a Keeper must, knew of nomole through the centuries who had achieved power through death. Martyrdom was a temporary thing, soon forgotten in the living affairs of moles. And yet . . . he was uneasy.

Did not his own task on Rune's behalf depend on having Rune's memory elevated to something higher than a mere history of his life? Aye, through the death of his grandson Lucerne – a death that would be his, Terce's, greatest achievement on behalf of Rune – their dynasty would become divine; would become in moles' minds the once-living incarnation of the Word, living on through memory, worship, and liturgy. Divine Rune! Divine Lucerne! And then the emergence, once moles had forgotten the truth, of divine Henbane. And after that, one of the pups Mallice would bear, pups of which he, Terce, would be grandfather . . . and thus he would be part of that divinity.

What was the matter? The western front, always a running sore. Siabod never truly taken. The followers not quite as destroyed as sideem and the Master might think. And always the memory of Wort's warnings that the Stone Mole had a quality about him that might destroy the Word. What quality could that be? One mole . . . *divinity*. Terce did not move as he thought, and now was very still indeed. Barely breathing.

Rune had always known that there were risks in his great strategy towards the elevation of his kin to holiness, and Terce had long since guessed that when the day came for Lucerne to be killed, in pursuance of the Word's need, there would be risks, and tensions, and doubt. All that he felt now.

The Stone Mole, born in Duncton Wood, the one place where none could have expected it. Duncton, Tryfan's system. Duncton, where Rune had found moles for the first and only time who thwarted him. But how sweet the Word's revenge to ordain that a son of Tryfan should be Master of the Word! Terce smiled and for once felt excited.

Yes, yes, oh yes . . . it was, as Lucerne had said, coming right, but for an objective only he, Terce, could know. Obviously the Stone Mole's death must be at one with Lucerne's fate and thereby the opposition to the Word of which Duncton was the symbol would be finally crushed, and then . . . divinity. Terce liked it.

But I like not Wort having the Stone Mole in her power, he thought. She has fulfilled her task, and now she must be relieved of anything more. He was glad Lucerne had decided to leave today. Three days, a little less time perhaps, and they could have their paws on the Stone Mole, and all would be safe, and well.

So . . . Mallice was with pup! Good. Wasn't it? More doubts now in Terce's endlessly seething mind. He had noticed something *unenthusiastic* beneath Lucerne's enthusiasm.

Perhaps Mallice had not been as clever as she should have been. Whether the pups would be Lucerne's Terce had no idea – he had planted an idea in Mallice's head, but

747

it was one she had not discussed or even acknowledged since, nor one he ever wished to know more about. If she had pups and they were Lucerne's he would be satisfied. If they were not, why, they were still pups of his own blood and might be deemed to be of Rune's and that was sufficient satisfaction of Rune's great scheme.

What would Lucerne do if he thought they were not his? Kill them, no doubt. It had been what Rune himself had intended to do with Henbane's pups, and what, in truth, he, Terce, loyal only to Rune himself, intended to do to Lucerne.

To seem to father a future Master and to die gloriously and so create the hallowed dynasty was all Lucerne needed to achieve. Yes, yes, it would be well enough. Terce frowned in the dark, his eyes narrowing as he thought.

Then Terce smiled.

'I could never have been Master,' he whispered to himself. 'I would have worried too much. I am content that a mole of my blood will succeed Lucerne soon. Content with that, and thankful to the Word and glorious Rune for making it so, for it shall be.'

Terce was right to worry so far as Mallice was concerned. For just prior to his meeting with Terce – the one where he had seemed *too* pleased – Lucerne had seen Drule privily, very especially privily so that Mallice could not overhear. Out on the surface above the Sumps, in fact.

'There'd better be a reason for this, Drule.'

The big mole looked warily back and forth and said, 'Master, there is a reason.'

'Why, Drule, I have never seen you look afraid before. Discomfited, yes – as when I sent you off to Duncton with the overzealous eldrene Wort; but not afraid.'

'I am afraid, Master.'

'Of what?'

'Of nothing but yourself. But yet I must speak out.'

'Then speak,' said Lucerne sharply. He liked this not. He liked this not one bit.

'Master, my loyalty is to thee alone, thee even before the Word.'

'I know it, Drule, I trust you absolutely.'

The mole managed a brief smile of satisfaction at this, but it did not last long.

'Master,' he continued hesitantly, 'it is the sideem Mallice. Of her I must speak to you.'

'Something you know?'

Drule nodded, but his eyes dared not meet Lucerne's.

'Well?'

'She is with pup.'

'I know it. Well?'

'They are not yours, Master.'

Perhaps only Lucerne could have kept his gaze steady and betrayed not one single tremor of surprise, anger or doubt. Only his voice revealed how shocked he was: it was a trace more quiet than it might have been.

'Tell me, Drule, what it is you know,' he said evenly.

'The father, Master, is the guardmole Weld.'

'I know him not.'

'He is one of those whose task is within the Sumps.'

'Tell me more.'

Drule's mouth curled.

'He brags, Master. Brags of having her.'

'You have no doubt?'

'None, Master.'

'Bring him to me now, here, quick.' Lucerne's voice betrayed more of what he felt now. Its tone was one of controlled violence.

'Drule, tell him not why, nor whatmole he is coming to see. Do it now.'

The cold March wind drove over the heather above the Sumps and among the sandstone rocks which outcrop there. Lucerne waited, eyes half closed, heart steady, heart cold.

He had suspected it. Something about the way she had been. Too eager, yet enjoying it less than she had before. A

749

disconcerting combination. Too, too eager, her sighs not fooling him. Oh yes, he had suspected it.

Lucerne hid in shadow until the mole was almost up to him. Drule was very close behind. The mole Weld would not escape.

'What's the secrecy abo. . . ?'

Lucerne appeared.

'I am told you brag of having sideem Mallice.'

'I . . . did not!' said the mole.

'Ask him, Drule, do it quick.'

Drule's massive paws went round the mole's neck, but only to get a hold. That done he took the talons of his left paw and began to insert them into the now whimpering mole's snout. Then he slowly turned them. Done too fast a mole can die of pain that way; too slow and a mole goes mad; done right a mole confesses all.

Drule did it right. Before blood came the mole was beginning to confess and the astonishing words he screamed were these: 'I was not the only one!'

'Shall I kill him, Master?'

Lucerne shook his head and stared at the pathetic mole. It was jealousy he felt, and rage at being taken for a fool. It turned him icy calm, and Drule, who knew him well, saw that Weld would die.

'Tell me everything, Weld, and you might live.'

He told the tawdry tale of how Mallice had two others, and had them killed – by him. Then she had him and he, not quite such a fool it seemed, got clear before she could have him put down. Then nothing, but news that she and the Master were leaving to go north, and he had hinted that he knew something about Mallice others didn't. A hint, a laugh, a jest is all it needs to make a brag, and brags get passed on to Drule.

Drule told Lucerne and here they were.

Lucerne smiled and said, 'Weld, I am grateful to you, more than you know.'

Weld stared hopefully.

Drule said again, 'Shall I kill him now, Master?'

'Always too fast, Drule, too eager. No, put him in the Lower Sumps, and leave him there to die.'

A look of horror came over Weld's face, for he had put moles in that place himself. But Lucerne saw not his face, for he turned away and left Drule to do his task.

He must see Terce and play his part. But first he went to Mallice.

'Master mine, so soon?'

'Now,' he said coldly, and he took her violently.

Her screaming done she took to sighing over him. But when he wanted her again she said, 'No, no, my love, you are too eager. Think of the pups: you would not want to hurt them.'

Lucerne contrived to look contrite.

'Well then, I shall go and tell Terce the news.'

'I told him myself, but he would like to hear it from you.'

So, affecting joy and happiness, Lucerne had told Terce with convincing enthusiasm and, that done, he had gone back to Mallice.

'We leave soon for Beechenhill. I wish to take the journey slowly, so that our pups are unhurt.'

'You think of me at such a time!' said Mallice.

'And the pups as well, my dear,' he said. The odour of evil hung about them both.

Lucerne saw Drule one last time before he left, and Slighe as well.

'Together shall you administer Cannock well. Is all as it should be, Drule, with the guardmoles? Am I leaving enough behind?'

'Yes, Master. Each and every one is exactly where you would wish him to be.' He beamed at his uncharacteristic subtlety. The bastard Weld was already sealed in a darkness from which he would never escape, and whimpering too for the talons Drule had ripped out of him. Drule knew how to pain a mole. Weld was already wishing he was dead.

'Master Lucerne, it shall be a pleasure to keep Cannock

running smooth in your absence,' said Slighe. 'But are you sure. . . ?'

'Yes, Slighe, you are to stay here. I need one mole at least to keep my friend Drule in check.'

They laughed, moles three, easy with each other.

'Good luck, Master,' said Slighe.

Lucerne smiled and was gone. They would leave within the hour.

But at first he did not hurry the journey to Beechenhill, for he wanted to think.

Did Terce know of Mallice's infidelity? He could not tell, but time would reveal the truth of that. Probably he did, for Terce was not Twelfth Keeper for nothing. Almost certainly he did. In which case . . . it needed thought. His punishment of Mallice would be to kill her pups in front of her once born. But Terce . . . what punishment for him?

They travelled on. They rested. Night came. Dawn broke. Terce appeared.

'Master, we are travelling slow and I cannot but think that we should travel more swiftly.'

'Why so?'

'Because now she has got the Stone Mole I do not trust the eldrene Wort.'

'Tell me why?'

'Because she is obsessive. And obsessive moles are inclined to think they are right and everymole else is wrong. We do not mind her killing the Stone Mole, I suppose, but we do not want him martyred.'

'How many days to Beechenhill now?'

'Two or just over perhaps – if we do not dawdle.'

Lucerne sighed.

'The Master is not Master of his destiny, it seems.'

'True of us all,' said Terce. 'Shall we go faster?'

'We shall. I wish to meet this Stone Mole before he dies, and martyrs can be tiresome things, no doubt.'

'And dangerous, too,' said Terce.

It was at the coming of that same dawn that Wort knew the Word had spoken to her.

'Summon Merrick,' she told a henchmole.

When he came he saw that her eyes were glittery bright and she was trying to contain her restlessness and seem calm.

'Sideem,' she began, 'I am glad you have come quickly for I have something of importance to say. This night past I had a vision of the Word and it commanded me what we must do, with vigour and without fear. The Word is with us.

'It said, "Wort, eldrene of Fyfield, thou art commanded to strike hard into Beechenhill and purge us of the former Mistress Henbane. Thou art commanded to take with thee the curst mole Beechen, called Stone Mole, and there before the Stone to make him Atone for his insults against the Word. Do it in my name." I saw great lights, and great darkness, and my body felt as if it was tossed on a wild river of great waves which were the tears of the Word for the sadness it feels that such moles live in moledom. Sideem Merrick, blessed are we to be appointed agents of the Word and resolute must we be!'

Merrick, who had half expected some madness of this kind, had rehearsed in his mind what his response might be, and he now said, 'We are honoured, eldrene Wort, to have you in this system. I doubted you when you first came, but now I see the Word is truly with you, and shines from you like a light to us all. But I am afraid to act against the Master's wishes. Should we not wait until he comes?'

'There is a time, Merrick, as one day you too will know, when a mole must abide by the Word's wishes, knowing that when it speaks directly it says only what the Master would were he here. Yes, great is the honour but great the responsibility. I understand your fear, but you must be true only to the Word's will. Each day, each hour, each minute that Henbane and the Stone Mole live unatoned before the Word is an insult, danger and temptation to us all. Now, are thy moles willing to be led to Beechenhill?'

'They would follow a mole with the power of the Word in her talons.'

'Then I and my henchmoles shall lead them.'

'But have you no fear of the Beechenhill moles?'

'The Word shall protect me as it protected our force against the might of the followers when we arrested the Stone Mole. They shall not dare fight us, though our numbers may be smaller.'

'When shall you act on the Word's commandment?'

'This day, this hour, now! Henchmole, bring the Stone Mole and the mole Buckram here, and double the guard on them and command them to keep their snouts low lest others look in their eyes and are tempted.'

'Surely, eldrene, they are but moles. . . .'

'Be warned, sideem Merrick, be warned. The Word has made its commandment to me of all moles for the good reason that it knows I have the strength to resist the enticements of this mole. Pay heed, for he is dangerous.'

'I shall stay and see him, eldrene Wort.'

'You must ready your own moles.'

'They shall be ready. Muster yours and your prisoners over at the North End of Ashbourne and ours will follow after your lead.'

'Then make haste to do it, for the Word's judgement shall not tarry. If you would see the Stone Mole, see him even as we leave to take him to his Atonement before the Stone.'

Which, with some curiosity, and the satisfaction of knowing that the jumped-up arrogant Wort was doing precisely what he wanted, was what Merrick did.

There had been no difficulty in getting his guardmoles ready, none at all. For some weeks they had been hearing reports of others having the pleasure of striking against followers, and now they had the opportunity – under the guise, as he would need later to claim, of watching over mad Wort's henchmoles – to strike against the most notorious system in all moledom. Oh yes, they were ready right enough, and willing, and very able.

So Merrick came with his orderly troops of moles to the North End and there saw Wort's admittedly impressive henchmoles – an unsavoury, taciturn and mean-looking bunch – gathered round the two prisoners.

One was the large mole known as Buckram, scarred from disease and now evidently lacerated with wounds and blows from the rough treatment Merrick assumed he had been getting at the paws of Wort's moles.

The other was harder to see, for he was close-guarded by the henchmoles.

'Be not tempted by his guise,' Wort whispered hoarsely at his flank, 'for his innocence hides duplicity, and his seeming gentleness masks vileness.'

She passed him by and went on to the front of her moles and cried out, 'The holy Word is with us this day and we shall be its talons and its teeth, its power and its purpose, and we shall wreak vengeance upon dread Beechenhill!'

There was a great cheer at this, mixed with laughter and the unpleasant sound of moles grunting their aggression.

'Holy Word guide us! Give us thy courage! Give us thy truth on this a mission for thy holy cause!'

The moles began to thrust at each other in their eagerness to leave and with more cheers and ugly roars they started to move, and the sideem Merrick looked curiously towards the prisoners.

He saw Buckram pushed and shoved and jeered at, and saw that great mole shrug off the blows with unexpected dignity and without retaliating. Then he saw him turn and try to reach back to the second mole, the one they called the Stone Mole.

Merrick pressed closer, and tried to see over or between the guards surrounding him.

'Come on! Move!' he heard a guard cry.

He saw a taloned paw thrust cruelly down, the group around the prisoner swayed, and then it moved. In that moment the guards separated and all too briefly Merrick saw the Stone Mole for the first time.

It was a moment that seemed to last forever, for he found that the mole's eyes were fixed on him. He saw blood on the mole's face, and wounds in his shoulders; he saw that movement caused him pain.

But it was the eyes that transfixed him, for though they showed suffering yet they shone like nothing the sideem Merrick had ever known or seen before; they shone with a love that seemed for him alone. They *were* love.

Quite involuntarily he reached forward saying, 'But this mole . . .' But he knew not what he tried to say.

Then the moment was lost, the column moved on, and the prisoners were gone on the long march upslope towards Beechenhill.

'Come on, Sir!' one of his own moles shouted, easing him along. 'Our moles are moving off!'

The sideem Merrick stared uncomprehendingly, for in his eyes he seemed still to see that gaze, and knew, knew terribly, that what they did was wrong, and worse than wrong.

'We must not . . .' he whispered.

'Too late now, Sir!' said the senior guardmole. 'Look!'

On and on the guardmoles went past him, a column of darkness spewing out of Ashbourne to Beechenhill.

Merrick sighed, and followed on as well.

No. Nomole is true master of his destiny.

Chapter Thirty-Four

It was as first light began on the cold day of the March equinox that the three watchers deputed by Squeezebelly to the Ilam end of Beechenhill, the most likely route for an invasion from Ashbourne, saw Wort's henchmoles approaching through the grey shadows beneath Bunster Hill.

They knew exactly what to do. As one headed west to warn the watchers on the slopes overlooking Ilam itself and another went to make contact with watchers in the lower Dove Valley, the third calmly sent the waiting messengers to alert Squeezebelly.

Then he watched as morning light came, and he was able to confirm the scale of the attack, and be certain that this was not a mere skirmish or minor assault, but the massive invasion they had all expected for so long.

Squeezebelly had had time since the return of Harebell and Harrow to get the arguments out of the way, and whatever lingering doubts there had been about evacuation were dispelled when one of the followers in Ashbourne had been able to get through the lines and brought news of the appalling atrocities that had been committed against followers across moledom in the name of the Word at the order of Lucerne.

There seemed little doubt that the grikes would try to commit such a massacre in Beechenhill, which put even more pressure on those moles – still the majority – who followed Squeezebelly's lead in wanting to commit no violence.

But their informant had said one thing which, ironically, had made Squeezebelly think that there might after all have been another way. He had overheard the sideem Merrick and others talking, and discovered that the strikes had been made only after the same 'friendly discussions' that he had agreed to so reluctantly in Beechenhill. From these the sideem in the different systems had gained sufficient knowledge of the followers' numbers and locations to enable the strikes to be mounted very accurately, and by surprise.

'So there has been no organised resistance by followers at all?'

'None, so far as I've heard. The grikes were simply killing groups and communities of moles who were not expecting to be attacked and had no time to organise themselves.'

'A mole might wonder how the followers would have fared if they had been organised and led, as the grikes were,' mused Squeezebelly, who, though philosophically a believer in non-violence, was by temperament stubborn and disinclined to go down without a fight.

'They would have fared better,' agreed the follower, 'but be in no doubt about the numbers massing in Ashbourne now. They are surely too great for your community here to resist for long.'

'I am in no doubt that we must leave,' Squeezebelly sadly told the last meeting of their community, 'yet what might followers have done if they had been organised and held on to a resolution of purpose rooted in faith! But one thing at least we may feel cheered by: there is no report of the Siabod moles failing, and perhaps there will always be a stronghold of followers there and in the famous Welsh Marches.'

It was a thought, an overly optimistic thought perhaps, that he repeated again that March day when the message had come through from the Ilam end of the beginning of the invasion and the last main group of moles in Beechenhill made their pre-arranged mustering at the Stone.

They looked back downslope towards Ilam and saw where the force of the grikes were coming.

'If they could be once turned,' said Squeezebelly, 'and

moles stanced up against them, what strength would they have to resist? Moles brought up on fear, and an ethos that conquers fear with might, do not always know what to do when their defences are broken.' Squeezebelly shook his head and sighed.

Then he said, 'We are too isolated to resist them, too separate from our brothers and sisters in other systems, as we long have been. Perhaps we should have tried to join forces with others but . . . that would have been hard to control and would have ended with a meeting of talons with talons and it is not my way nor, more important, the Stone's. Nor, I may add, from what Sleekit has told us, and she should know, is it the Stone Mole's. The view that Tryfan expressed here so many years ago, that the *only* way is non-violence, remains the only way.'

'And how it will ever return our system to us, let alone save our lives in the weeks and months ahead, I don't know!' said Bramble.

'The Stone shall show us,' said Squeezebelly. 'And though the Stone Mole be taken I am not yet so downhearted that I do not believe he will find a way for followers to carry the Stone's faith forward once more. Let us be glad that our waiting is over and the critical time come. Let us be alert, and positive, and faithful to the Stone. Let us listen with all our hearts in the days and nights ahead. The Stone Mole has come, and now must his hour be.'

Squeezebelly had agreed that a few moles would stay secreted in the system as watchers, willing to risk their lives to see what happened when the grikes came, and filter back their information to the Eastern Chambers as and when they could.

For these moles Squeezebelly said a blessing by the Stone, and a final prayer for the Stone Mole. Then they turned north-west underground to make their way to their hiding place.

Yet despite the ominous circumstances there was a sense of guarded excitement among the moles that Squeezebelly led out of Beechenhill. Most moles knew the

Castern Chambers by name, but very few had ever been there, for their precise location and the route into them had been a well kept secret for generations.

These tall limestone caverns, formed over the millennia by the drip and run of water dissolving the limestone, are not directly accessible from the surface that lies above them. The routes to them are all underground, and so full of changing twists and sudden turns, not to mention tunnels that split continuously, that a mole is easily lost among them.

Nor do they at first look promising, for so deep and sterile are they that there seems no promise of food or life ahead. Whatever mole first found and explored them must have been an optimist indeed! Yet they repay the journey and the risks, for once past the mazy entrance tunnels, the darkness and the confusing echoes, and through the fords and subterranean streams, a mole comes to the great chambers themselves, and finds them open to the sky through fissures above which, on the surface, the limestone outcrops.

Through these fissures light streams down to the chamber floors so far below, and where there is light there is life: bats above and, among other things, cockroaches feeding on their dung below. Hundreds of thousands of them.

There too is water, dripping and flowing underground, and strange white-green etiolated plants, among which white creatures crawl. Here, if driven to it – and the Beechenhill moles had been – moles could find food of a kind and hide for days and months, their lair unknown to moles above; and easily defended against moles able to find them underground.

This was Squeezebelly's secret retreat, and it was to here that he now brought the last group of moles to join those already there. He did not expect to find them full of cheer, and they were not. Yet this pale subterranean place, with cockroaches for worms, and frail plants instead of grass, was better than a cruel death at the talons of grikes.

That at least was the theory, but Squeezebelly knew well that the practice might be different. Having got his reluctant community that far, the problem would be to keep them from getting too fractious and unhappy there.

In truth, even as he arrived he himself felt depressed, as if coming here was slinking away from the responsibilities above. Yet he could think of no other way to see that his moles survived, unless it be through violent and hopeless resistance. And yet . . . was not that better than this? He smiled and made his greetings as cheerfully as he could, but in his heart was dismay as he looked about the high enclosing walls, and at the distant fissures to the sky above.

There was a general air of dejection, and almost immediately moles began to say that they hoped there might be news from the watchers soon.

'Soon enough,' said Squeezebelly noncommittally. He could see that moles like Bramble and Skelder, who had been vocal in their reluctance to come, were already priming themselves to complain. Well, he would deal with that.

He went the rounds of the moles, most of whom had explored the interconnected chambers already and, as moles will, found a space they liked to settle in. Sentries and patrols were long since deployed at the different entrances and all there seemed to do was wait.

He spoke to them as a whole – or rather in each main chambered grouping they had made – and was careful to lower their expectations, and tell them that it might be a day or more before they had any news of what the grikes had done in empty Beechenhill.

'Swear, I should think!' said one senior mole.

'Bugger off, I hope,' said another, ' 'cos then we can all go back tomorrow and forget this place.'

'Hear, hear!' cried several with feeling. Well, thought Squeezebelly, for now they're manageable.

The older moles and females with pup, including Harebell, were in a higher, drier chamber a little way beyond the main ones, through one of the innumerable tunnels in the place. It was warmer, and lighter, and seemed safe enough. Henbane was there and Quince was in charge. The only surface exit, as complex as the rest, was guarded by two moles and so narrow that they thought it would be impossible for grikes to come in that way.

So now the deed was done, the evacuation complete and there they were, subdued, waiting for nomole knew what, and with Squeezebelly, who had worked so hard to get them there, beginning to think that this, surely, was not where they should be at all. . . .

'Stone Mole . . . Beechen!'

'No talking! Any more trouble and it'll be your snout next time.'

Tears welled up in brave Buckram's eyes as he sought so vainly to give comfort to Beechen behind him as slowly, painfully, they climbed the final slopes to the Stone of Beechenhill.

'Buckram,' whispered Beechen, 'Buc . . .' trying to reassure his friend ahead. But another talon came down upon his flank, already red raw from the talonings he had had and he was thrust forward again.

'Go on, you bastard, nearly there now before your precious Stone,' a guardmole snarled at Beechen.

Another heavy talon drove into him, pushing him forward up the slope and he grunted with the pain of it. He stared at the grass, new green mingling with old brown, and another blow came into him and a wave of pain exploded in his back and his limbs and stumbled his weakening body on.

Until they had got to Ashbourne the henchmoles had not touched them, though they had given them too little food, and not let them drink. It seemed they knew about such things, and how to make a mole suffer without taloning him too much.

But then, in Ashbourne, the mood of their captors had turned ugly and wild, and the eldrene Wort had come and spoken to them, words of the Word, words of threat, and Beechen had tried to touch her, for she was a mole who needed that almost more than anymole he had ever known.

She had shied away and cursed him, and told the henchmoles to 'subdue' him and they had asked if that meant the other bastard too and she said yes.

So then the talonings had started, not heavy but persistent, drawing blood and weakening them by the hurt and continual pain.

The eldrene Wort had come to them in the night and asked Beechen one last time to renounce, but he would not, and nor would Buckram. Then she had gone and they had been kept awake by more talonings, and the first direct threats that they would soon die. Then the first mention of Beechenhill.

'Stone Mole . . .' Buckram had whispered.

'Shut up, you,' said the henchmole, and a pawful of talons went into Buckram's face and for the first and only time he had risen up with his full strength and thrown three of them off.

Beechen had had to watch as they beat him for such insolence. Prayers did not take the pain away.

Then they had been dragged from the place they had been kept in and brought to the surface close-guarded by so many moles they could barely see each other. They had set off north from Ashbourne, and as they went moles had come to stare.

Some said, 'What moles are they?'

When the henchmoles said, 'Moles of the Stone being taken to suffer the vengeance of the Word,' those watching laughed and said, 'Kill them well!'

Their progress had been slower than the henchmoles wanted, and so they had begun to buffet and talon them to hurry them up.

At Broadlow, Buckram was unable to go on for a time, and they let him stance still there, and gave them something to drink and eat at last.

'Let him eat my food, let him drink my drink,' Beechen said to one of the henchmoles.

'I cannot,' said the henchmole, frowning and unhappy.

'What is thy name?'

'Mole, I cannot,' said the henchmole thickly, turning from them and letting others guard them for a time.

The next part of the journey, to the slopes by Thorpe Cloud where moles can cross the River Dove, was yet slower, and Wort ordered that the talonings cease.

'We shall cross here and rest until nightfall. I would have us reach Beechenhill at dawn, and the Ashbourne moles say that from here the journey is not so far.'

She did not talk to Beechen or Buckram, or look at them, nor say her prayers to the Word. She was like a driven mole, her eyes only on the journey ahead and the coming day. This time Beechen and Buckram were allowed to rest near each other, but not to talk. When they laid their bodies down they slept the restless sleep of the tired suffering.

Deep in the night Beechen was woken by a henchmole.

'Eat,' he said.

Beechen looked at him and saw it was that same henchmole who he had sensed had wanted to help them before.

'Give it to my friend.'

'He has already said the same, mole,' whispered the henchmole with a half smile.

Beechen took the food and ate it and felt better for it.

'Whatmole are you?' he asked.

'I know not any more,' faltered the henchmole. And he wept.

Beechen reached a hurt paw to him.

'Then you too have begun your journey, mole,' he said gently.

'You will die tomorrow,' said the henchmole.

'He will not die,' rasped Buckram. 'He shall never die.'

Another henchmole stirred at the sound of Buckram's

voice and a third came in and that was all that was said by the Stone Mole that night.

Before dawn came they left the Dove behind them and began the long climb into Beechenhill, following routes which their Ashbourne guides seemed to know. They saw little and remembered nothing but the endless painful struggle up the slopes. Except one thing: in the dark the henchmole who had spoken to them was able sometimes, under the guise of buffeting him, to help Beechen along.

First light, dragging, bloody steps; dawn, talon thrusts and pain; morning, and now this final climb, so slow, and the Stone rising ahead beyond the henchmoles' swaying bodies, the sky cloudy and sheep's wool fretting on the barbs of the wire that stretched across the field beyond the Stone.

'Stop!'

They stopped, and were turned, and through their pain, nausea and fatigue, saw the eldrene Wort stanced proudly by the Stone, staring at them.

Her eyes were blank, her mouth was whispering prayers to the Word, one paw was raised in a parodic benediction over them, as if she were the Master himself; as if she were the incarnation of the Word.

Beechen tried to speak, to tell her not to be afraid, for it was plain to him that she was afraid of much, but even if words had come she wished not to hear them, or anything else he might say.

She nodded her head and a henchmole hit Beechen again, so that he slumped and slewed to one side, while to his right Buckram was hit as well, and fell likewise.

In that moment, as Buckram fell, Beechen knew fear. He saw the Stone and the spirit of the evil Word in the form of the mole who stanced before it. He heard the distant chuckle and rumble of angry henchmoles. He heard the rattle of Buckram's breathing. All of this and a spiralling darkness in the morning clouds, and he knew fear.

Slowly, desperately, he tried to turn his head to see

Buckram, but the grass, the hard earth, the whole of moledom perhaps, seemed against it. He felt a crushing blow to his left paw which made him roll and crush it more and he found himself staring into Buckram's eyes.

'Stone Mole,' whispered Buckram, his mouth twisted and bloodied, his teeth broken now, 'forgive me, I cannot stay with thee.'

A henchmole loomed over Buckram, and to Beechen, watching sideways on from where he lay helpless on the ground, it seemed the henchmole was part of the mounting dark cloud above, as if it had come down to wreak vengeance on stricken Buckram here before Beechenhill's Stone.

'You should not have spoken,' said the angry cloud that was a mole.

Beechen saw the great taloned paw raised and saw the mole look towards the eldrene Wort, wait, nod his understanding of her command, and then bring down his paws one after another in two great thrusts into Buckram's back, and then he moved and dealt a third blow, this time to Buckram's neck.

For a moment Buckram's mouth stretched wide in pain and he grunted deep and gutturally. The rear of his body seemed to twist and turn and then go limp and as blood poured down his side he strived to reach a paw to Beechen, and he said, 'Forgive me. Be not afraid.'

And there, before Beechen's gaze, in the shadow of the Stone, great Buckram died.

Then Beechen turned and tried terribly to stance up and all there heard him cry out to the Stone: 'We are but mole and much afraid!' He faltered, and fell sideways, and cried out again towards the Stone saying, 'Father, you have made me but mole!'

Then the henchmole who had killed Buckram came and stanced over Beechen and raised his bloody, taloned paw and turned once more to Wort.

Wort stared, and, most terribly, she smiled.

'Not yet,' she said, 'the holy Word would not have him die so easily.'

'Shall we snout him then?'

It might have been any of them that gathered there who asked it. It might have been all of moledom that spoke it, so loud did it seem across Beechenhill.

Shall we snout him?

'*Now?*'

'No,' murmured Wort, 'not yet.'

Then she stanced up, and came forward, and peered down into his eyes and reached out a paw as if to touch him, but she would not, or dared not.

'I do not hate you or anymole, Wort,' said Beechen feebly.

Then, for the first and only time, the eldrene Wort struck him, her paw and talons across his wounded face.

As his head fell back further on the grass she stared at her paw and saw his blood on it and a look of disgust and horror came to her face.

'Now, eldrene?' grinned the henchmole.

She seemed to want to say, 'Yes', but then she whispered, 'It is temptation to want him dead, the temptation of pity to put him from his misery. Yet cruelty too, for he might yet redeem himself before the Word. So . . . kill him not yet. The Word will have its vengeance of him and choose its own time.'

Then, she wiped her paw hard and harder on her flank as she sought to clean it of the Stone Mole's blood. But she seemed to fail in that and turned off downslope to where other moles were coming, led by sideem Merrick. And Merrick looked uneasy.

And well he might.

He saw the eldrene Wort coming towards him spattered in blood. He saw that behind her by the Stone the big mole Buckram now lay dead. He saw a cluster of blood-lusty henchmoles gathered about that other mole, the mole with eyes that were like talons of light into a mole's heart. He saw that that mole was beginning to die.

And beyond it all were stretching barbed wires of a

fence, black against the strangely mounting sky, taut in the heavy tense air. Merrick felt oppressed.

'And where are the Beechenhill moles, sideem?' said Wort. Her eyes were wild and her mouth a little open with her quick, sighing breathing, almost as if she had just been pleasured by a male. Merrick felt afraid of her, and of all of *this*.

'We think they have hidden underground just to the north-west.'

'All of them?'

He nodded abstractedly. 'Yes, yes, all of them.'

'Then it is your duty to the Word to flush them out.'

He laughed, a little out of control. Some grass by the Stone was touched by a freshening wind and suddenly moved. His head felt pressured and strange.

'They might be got out, eldrene Wort, if we knew exactly where they were, had a moleyear to do it and could find a way of attacking them in a probably inaccessible place. But they cannot escape, of that we are sure. They are probably in the Castern Chambers, of which we know a little from information extracted over the moleyears from watchers we have captured. It won't help us get at them, but at least the lower exit routes are covered, and I presume they cannot hide forever.'

Wort looked disgruntled for a moment, but then her face cleared.

'The Word shall find a way of bringing them to us. The Word is all-powerful and will not be frustrated for long. Perhaps they will guess that we are avenging the Word through the Stone Mole, whom they value so highly, and will vainly seek to save him from his salvation in the talons of the Word.'

Merrick looked at the mole who lay injured and suffering before the Stone, and at his dead companion nearby.

'He looks no danger to anymole,' he said. 'But if he is, then he should be killed forthwith.'

The truth was that Merrick felt pity for the mole, and

did not want his death drawn out. A quick death would mean he could forget this troublesome mole, and more easily blame Wort for this invasion of an empty system. The more the affair dragged on the more he was concerned that the Master, presumptuously summoned by Wort in Ashbourne, might end up here in Beechenhill, and then Word knows what punishments might be meted out. Yet having come, he would make the best of what had happened, and perhaps in the end the retreat of the Beechenhill moles played into his paws. Of course, if they could get their paws on Henbane, the Master would forgive their transgressions in coming here in the first place; he would forgive them everything.

Yet as Merrick weighed up these possibilities his eyes drifted involuntarily once more, as did his mind, towards the mole who lay beside his dead companion staring at the Stone. Indeed, Merrick found he could not keep his eyes *off* the mole, for there was something about him that seemed to make everything there, even Wort herself, seem secondary to his presence. Not just visibly but mentally too. Merrick had the uncomfortable feeling that his convoluted thoughts, his sideem thoughts, were, in this mole's presence, utterly inconsequential.

'Temptation,' said Wort, her eyes sharp upon him. 'You are suffering the first temptation that the Stone Mole's cunning creates in moles' hearts. I see it in your eyes, sideem Merrick, you are thinking nothing else matters, that only this mole matters. I too was so tempted, but conquered it with the Word's help.'

Conquered it! thought Merrick with an inward laugh. Mole, you are obsessed by Beechen of Duncton Wood!

Wort said, 'Now pray with me, mole, and help save yourself: holy Word, I feel the temptation of the Stone thrusting its talons in my heart, I feel the caressing of the Stone upon my flanks, I feel a false ecstasy that makes me forget thy glory and power and my loyalty to thee. Help me, Word, help me!'

Merrick found himself mouthing this prayer, but even

then thinking of the Stone Mole, and finding his eyes drawn to him even more.

'I do not understand,' he whispered.

Which is the beginning of all understanding.

The hours were dragging slowly in the Castern Chambers and were not helped by the growing sense, gained from a darkening of what sky they could see and a heaviness in the air, that outside and above a storm was coming.

An air of dejection had come over the moles. They lay still and so far as any of them talked it was to wonder if, and when, one of the watchers might get through with news of what was happening in Beechenhill.

But one mole was not still, but stanced up and staring all about, twitching with nerves: grubby Holm.

He had been nervous from the first moment they had entered the limestone tunnels, and grown more so as they had gone deeper in. He had tried at one point to turn back but Sleekit had stopped him, and now she crouched near him talking to him softly, trying to get him to tell her what was wrong.

He was stanced nearly upright, snout whiffling and sniffling at the damp air, and looking extremely unhappy as he had done from the first.

'You can tell me, Holm, and I won't tell anymole else unless you want me to. What's wrong?'

He turned his head sharply towards her, opened his mouth to speak, frowned, narrowed his eyes, widened them, breathed in and out several times, and just when she thought he was once again going to say nothing, said, 'Wrong? Everything's wrong. We can't stay here. Can't. Mustn't. Won't.'

'Why not?' she said, hoping that he might be soothed by talking.

He would not say immediately, but stanced tensely and getting tenser until he spoke again.

'Explore, Sleekit, you and me,' he said.

So they did, Holm leading her here and there through

the chambers, pushing his snout up even the smallest and dampest clefts in the limestone, going everywhere.

'No. No, no, no,' was all he said.

They went eventually to the higher chamber where Harebell and the others were and this he did not like either, having to paddle through the water of an underground stream to get there.

'No, no, no,' he muttered urgently to himself.

'No what, Holm?' said Harebell, smiling. Being with pup had made her calm, and the pups were clearly showing. She was stanced close by Henbane, and not so far above, but out of reach, a fissure opened to the sky. They could see the day was darker than it had been.

'Holm doesn't like the Castern Chambers,' said Sleekit.

'Why not? Is it the cockroaches?' asked Harebell.

Holm shook his head.

'Do *you*?' he said unexpectedly, darting a look at Henbane.

'No,' said Henbane quietly, 'I don't.'

'She's from Whern. Mayweed told me about Whern. Water's the worry here, not the food.'

'Water?' said Harebell, puzzled.

'I think by water Holm means floods,' said Henbane.

'Oh!' said Sleekit looking around. 'Oh dear.'

Holm had been with Tryfan and Mayweed when the tunnel had collapsed and so many moles were drowned.

'*Is* it flooding you fear?' said Sleekit.

Holm stared at her, nodded his head, and his wide eyes filled with tears.

'Once is enough,' he said.

'I doubt if they'd flood here,' said Henbane. Then she lowered her voice and said, 'I did think about it when we came but really the risk is small, less than facing the guardmoles on the surface. But I did not mention it because moles panic so easily.'

'Floods,' said Holm.

'Holm, if I tell Squeezebelly, would that satisfy you?'

771

'Getting out would satisfy me,' said Holm, 'but telling's a start.'

On their return Squeezebelly listened to what they had to say, but said talking about it would hurt morale, and that he had been down here when it was wet above and the water levels did not rise.

'Depends, that does, doesn't it?' said Holm. 'Holm knows his water. Let's leave now.'

Squeezebelly smiled and shook his head.

'No, no, but we'll keep a weather eye open, Holm. In fact, would you do that for us?'

Holm nodded, pleased to be asked, and left them.

'He's not usually wrong about such things,' said Sleekit.

'If we have to go up on the surface we shall all die,' said Squeezebelly wearily. 'It's as simple as that. Now, let's see how we can pass the rest of this first day and the coming night. . . If there's any sign of a real storm we'll get moles to the higher places, Sleekit.'

The 'sign' was coming.

At the Stone the wind, which had grown persistent by midday, died off again in the afternoon, and the previously noticeable heaviness to the air came back threefold.

Merrick had gone off to lead the searches for the hidden Beechenhill moles and left the eldrene Wort in possession of the Stone. She had been still and praying for an hour or more, and Beechen half conscious and limp, when she suddenly stared up abstractedly at the Stone, then at the Stone Mole, and then back to the Stone again. Then she turned and looked behind him to the wire fence.

'Henchmole,' she said softly.

'Eldrene?'

'Barb him on the wire.'

'Eldrene?'

'The Word has spoken to me at last. Barb him.'

'To die?'

'To die slow.'

'He is weak.'

'It shall be fitting that he lasts a full night and at least until this time tomorrow.'

'He may not.'

'The Word shall decide.'

One of the other henchmoles came forward and whispered to their leader who listened, nodded, and turned back to Wort.

'Eldrene, we . . . we have not eaten since dawn.'

'Nor have I,' said Wort sharply and frowning. 'Barb him now, and leave two watching him. The rest may eat.' She glanced down at Beechen, and then immediately looked back at the henchmoles.

'Do it *now*,' she said, turning quickly away towards the Stone and beginning to mutter her prayers again.

It was a scene to which the others there seemed indifferent, but then such moments of punishment and torture upon followers had been repeated too many times in the moleyears past to attract much interest. A snouting was always worth watching, of course, but a barbing. . . The only interest was predicting when the mole would die. The weakest-looking often lasted the longest.

Two of the henchmoles grabbed Beechen under the paws and dragged his limp body towards the taut wire. They stared up at the barbs appraisingly and chose one which was angled upwards. Some of the barbs were corroded and there was the smell of sheep's urine about, and a piece of fleece fretted nearby on the wire.

The two dragging Beechen looked towards the leader for directions.

'Which paw?' said one. Back paws killed quicker, front paws made it more difficult to get the victim on.

'Front paw left. She wants him living for a time and facing this way. High up. We don't want it ripping through like with that Rollright mole we did.'

'Yes, Sir.'

They pulled him to a position directly under the fence and looked up again at the barbs above. Beechen was conscious now, but he seemed not to understand what was happening to him.

'Nearer the post where the wire's higher,' they were commanded. 'When he's up we want his back paws clear of the ground and giving him no support.'

It was not as easy as a snouting, and Beechen was heavier than they expected, and so only at the third attempt and with a heave and shove and a helping paw from their leader did they get him in the right position. Now Beechen seemed to understand what they were doing and he was looking about as if for help.

He did not struggle, but as they pushed him up in the air and got his paw where they wanted it he gazed at the Stone and began to pray.

Then with one reaching up to hold his left paw in place, the other two girdled the lower half of his body with their paws and pulled him suddenly and violently down so that the barb caught his flesh and then drove sickeningly among the strong sinews and bones of his paw.

He let out a terrible cry at this, and again when they cruelly let him go and his body swung briefly back and forth and up and down with the rebounding of the wire, until it was still. He groaned, the immediate pain over, and his body hung angled and strange. Only the longer talons of his right back paw touched the ground. His upper right paw seemed to strive to reach over and try to gain a purchase on the wire to lift himself off it, but the effort was futile and the henchmoles evidently knew it, for they had already turned away.

'You two stay here, we'll relieve you when we've had food,' said the leader.

Looking irritable and disgruntled the two henchmoles stanced down. Neither of them looked at Beechen, not even when after a short time he began to groan with pain, his mouth half open, his eyes staring terribly at the Stone.

Nor did Wort look back at him. But as his groans came

774

to her she began to speak her muttered prayers more loudly, as if to drown out the sounds he made.

And so, in the midst of an almost indifferent world, with the muttering of the alien prayers of Wort his only litany, with nomole of his own to watch over him, with no light of sun nor light of hope to shine upon him, Beechen's suffering on the barb before the Stone of Beechenhill began.

'Stone,' he whispered, 'take Buckram to thy Silence, and be my companion now.'

Then from over the fells beyond the fence, flying obliquely to the Stone and some way from it, a pair of mallard flew, birds far out of their territory and habitat. Like dark forms they rushed out of the northern sky and the henchmoles watched them as they went by, not far above the fence, and then southward into the better light. For a moment the head and neck of the drake glossed green, all bright and beautiful, and then they were lost over the fields below and among distant trees.

'Watch it, mate!' whispered one of the henchmoles. 'The eldrene's coming to.'

Slowly Wort turned to face them as they stanced up to seem more on duty, and slower still her eyes lifted up to stare at the Stone Mole. Then with the Stone behind her, and the glorious bright sky in the distance beyond she approached him where he hung.

'Holy Word,' she whispered, 'mother and father of us all, bring thy understanding to him, bring him the words of renunciation of the Stone, bring him the wounding vengeance of the Word's talons, that he feels the evil drained from him as his blood drains from these wounds he has. Thrust thy avenging judgement into him as the barb is thrust now into his flesh and bones, let him feel his pain as the searing of thy great might. Holy Word, our mother and our father, be mother and father to this evil mole that is humbled before you now; holy Word. . . .'

Beechen's eyes, filled though they were with his

growing pain and despair, looked down on her, and then at the Stone.

'Forgive her, Stone, for she is full of fear. Help her, Stone, to see thy light through me. Guide her, Stone, towards thy Silence, which she longs to. . . .'

But Beechen's prayer ended in a terrible cry, for the henchmole, to silence him, mounted up and struck the wire on which he hung, and his body swung and his own weight pulled against his paw and racked the sinews and muscles of his shoulder.

'No!' said Wort fiercely, her mouth curling and trembling with anger, her eyes wide in what some might indeed have called fear. 'Let the Word be his judge and tormentor now.'

She stared at Beechen, hatred in her eyes, and, never taking them from his face, she whispered, 'Holy Word, now is the hour of my trial, now is my greatest temptation, give me strength before the evil urge to pity that mounts up about this mole, give me words to fight him, give me power to meet his word.'

Beechen stared at her, and his eyes softened.

'See the light that rises in the sky behind you, mole. It is the coming light of the Stone you fear to love.'

The henchmoles looked at each other and backed away as if they felt they were caught between two moles that fought and either of which might kill them in the war.

'Word, great Word, maker of us all, bring down thy soaring darkness upon him soon, bring down thy fierceness, that we may know thy power.'

Then suddenly Beechen cried out so violently that the wire stirred, and even as he spoke his pain added force to what he said so that it seemed to come from the great and ugly clouds behind.

'It is thine own darkness you see, mole!'

As he spoke the words 'thine own darkness' the sky behind him broke open from its highest point down to the distant ground itself in a great and jagged line of lightning that lit the faces of Wort and the henchmoles and seemed to reach a sense of their growing fear into the very air where they were.

Again he cried 'Thine own darkness!' and the words seemed to gather about the eldrene Wort and become the cracking burst of thunder that crashed down upon them, as the roof of a great chamber of rock might fall upon a group of moles.

As it died away the maddened eldrene Wort shouted, 'Temptation of the Word! I shall not suffer these vile effusions to corrupt my heart.' Then screaming out her words, her mouth distorted and her breath sharp and painful between each word, 'I have faced thee all my life, all the filth and infection that thou art, and the Word strengthens me against. . . .'

'Love her, Stone,' the Stone Mole whispered quietly, 'and be my companion now.'

The sky darkened above them, the air was heavy at their ears and eyes and mouths, the henchmoles retreated still more as their companions emerged from the ground to stare aghast as Wort retreated too, to stance between the Stone and the barbed mole, from where she screamed her curses on him.

The sky to the south grew brighter than before, but about them now a strange, leaden light seemed carried on a driven breeze, now warm, now cold, and the leading henchmole whispered urgent instructions.

'Get others here, summon guardmoles, I like this not. We shall take this mole. . . .'

Even as he spoke, the sky above the Stone Mole, dark a moment before, seemed to open up as clouds parted and great light shone beyond, and the light on the ground seemed more lurid still.

'. . . down. We shall take the bugger off the barb and kill him now. I like this not.'

'You shall not!' commanded the eldrene Wort, turning from her stance and rushing over to him to thrust her snout within inches of his own, her eyes red and fierce. 'Now, mole, is the temptation, now is our test. See this mole, see the darkening sky, see the corrupting Stone that helps him not!'

'I see *trouble*,' said the henchmole. 'Let's end it now.'

'I am empowered by the Master himself, and if you touch this mole you shall be blaspheming in that act. *This* is the temptation, *this* the corruption. In him does the Word do battle with the Stone, in him shall we find proof of the Word's might.'

'We'll get others here,' said the henchmole, 'let us at least do that.'

'Aye! Get others here! Get everymole here that you can. Let them witness this mole's suffering and death, let them see what the Word shall show them!'

She turned from him as the sky above darkened again, and whirled and turned about them.

'Here now, in vile Beechenhill, last bastion, here shall the Stone finally be broken and scattered, and we moles of the Word are privileged to witness it. Watch, listen, see that I am right!'

There was something so powerful in the way she spoke, so fierce and passionate in the stances she made, that nomole there could have gainsaid her.

The most the henchmoles could do was to whisper again that others should be brought here, as if whatever was taking place should be guarded rather than witnessed. Among all the henchmoles there had come a palpable sense of foreboding, and they looked at one another fearfully as the dark wind whipped at the thistles and grass around them; and they looked up at the Stone and the hanging mole opposite it with undisguised apprehension. The sense of unease they gave off was increased by the fact that they were normally strong moles, fierce moles, not prone to fears and doubts. To such moles as these, fear itself is frightening and often masked by anger, and anger overtook them now. They went up to where Beechen hung and began to shout and jeer at him while Wort, who had returned to her stance between the Stone and Beechen, encouraged them.

778

'Cry out your hatred of him, expel it from yourselves upon him, disgorge the temptation he creates inside you back upon him, let your hatred be your strength, my moles. *Hate* him and purge yourselves of evil.'

As she spoke the moles gathered about her, and like a pack of creatures from the darkness of past times they bayed and roared at Beechen, and willed the Word to take him, and the northern darkness that mounted once more behind him to engulf him in its mighty paws.

And Beechen *was* engulfed, lost in the sterile darkness that they were, lost in their cries of hate, alone and lost; lost in the sense of his own fear.

'Oh Stone,' he cried, 'bring comfort to me now, let me know that thy light shall be seen and my life not lost in vain.'

The henchmoles thought it was of physical pain he spoke, not understanding that Beechen's agony was of the spirit and the mind.

'Comfort he wants, is it?' said one.

'Relief from his suffering? He can have that!' said another.

Then, laughing, they turned to the corpse of Buckram and several of them dragged it towards the spot above which Beechen hung.

One put his shoulder under Beechen's rear and eased him up a little as the others laid the broken, bloodied body of Buckram beneath him. They let him go so that he gave the appearance of half standing on his friend's broken back.

'There's comfort!' they shouted.

'There's relief!' they jeered.

'Dear me!' mocked one. 'Haven't you got the strength to raise yourself from off the barb? Stone not being friendly to you today?' It was true enough that had he had the strength Beechen might have raised himself and freed his paw.

There was more laughter among the henchmoles, and vile Wort whispered and prayed and said her incantations to the Word, the very mouth of evil.

Then tiring of the sight of him half propped on Buckram's body two of them ran forward and with a sudden shove pushed Buckram from under him. The effect of this on Beechen was very cruel, for his body and the wire listed over for a moment and then, as all support was taken from him, his full weight was borne by his paw once more.

There was a crack and tear, then Beechen screamed and his left back paw began to shake and his mouth opened into a cry of pain so terrible that it seemed to sear the dark sky.

His suffering was so plain that even that rabble was struck into silence as they stared at him, a kind of fascinated morbid awe in their eyes and about their mouths.

Out of that silence, the first agony of the new pain receding, Beechen whispered, 'Stone, comfort me, and show me a sign of thy love that I may have strength to forgive them.'

Even as he spoke one of the henchmoles, the one who had given him food in the night on the journey there, detached himself slowly from the group and went forward towards the Stone Mole. Thinking that he had found a new torment for their victim the others watched him with amusement, but instead, when he reached the hanging body of Beechen, he turned to them and said quietly, 'Finish it now. He's suffered enough. Finish it.' And so it might have been, for several others there seemed suddenly to feel the same.

But detecting the twin dangers of pity and weakness in the hearts of her henchmoles, the eldrene Wort screamed, 'See the face of temptation! See the corrupted mole! See the new enemy!'

'He's suffered enough,' said the henchmole again, his voice beginning to break with emotion.

The eldrene's words were enough to put fear into the hearts of those who might have agreed with him and he found pitiless eyes staring at him.

'Don't be a fool, mole,' said the leader among them, seeing a new danger now.

But the mole turned suddenly from them and whispered, 'Forgive them, mole, for they are weak and know you not.'

'Mole!' warned the leader once again.

One of the others laughed and with a jeer said, 'Forgive us! Why not lift the bastard off the barb if you like him so much? The Stone will help you and the Word might just forgive you.'

Once more the mole spoke, saying, 'Forgive me.' He gently put his paws about Beechen and tried to raise him up. But he had not the strength and his struggles only caused Beechen more pain.

'Forgive me, forgive me,' whispered the henchmole as Beechen's blood coursed down his body and fell upon the mole's paws.

'Thou art forgiven,' said Beechen, 'the light of the Stone shall be thine. Look, mole!'

And the mole turned from his vain labour and looked with wonder in his eyes beyond the jeering henchmoles, beyond the Stone, and saw the clouds all filled with a light so bright that it was across his face, and upon the Stone Mole where he hung.

'Snout this mole!' cried Wort. 'He has blasphemed, he has the blood of a blasphemer's forgiveness upon him! Snout him!'

Then there was madness, and the rise of paws and talons, and a forgiven mole was raised up towards the northern sky and then that mole's snout was brought down hard upon the barb.

Even as this happened Beechen said, 'Stone, let thy light and peace be with him. . . .' Then Beechen cried out the terrible bubbling scream as of a snouted mole and received to his own body the pain of the henchmole who died at the moment he was snouted, and hung at Beechen's side.

It was a moment that struck terror into those executing

the snouting, who jumped back from the dead mole as if they themselves had been hurt, and seemed almost to cower from the scream of pain that came from the Stone Mole.

Though it was still afternoon, such was the ghastly shifting light about the environs of the Stone that it might have been any time, spring or autumn, summer or winter, when the sky and earth appears out of order with itself and clouds and wind and light seem fraught and confused.

Out of this unnatural gloom, henchmoles and groups of Merrick's guardmoles returned empty pawed, drifting from across the fields, frustrated of their prey, disgruntled at the lack of mole to hurt, their expectations of violence utterly thwarted by the disappearance of the Beechenhill moles.

It was known that Squeezebelly and the rest were not far to the north-west, but were safely sequestered in tunnels and chambers which, those who had tried to go there confirmed, nomole could safely attack.

But by now the rumour had gone about that perhaps the guardmoles should not be there at all, that they were on a mission which was not approved or ordained by the Master. And worse: the Master himself was coming, if not to Beechenhill then to Ashbourne. Now was added to this news of the strange and ominous happenings associated with the barbing of the Stone Mole, and the sense that if they were to be anywhere here it was not near the Stone.

Perhaps fortunately, Merrick had established a firm discipline in Ashbourne and the large gathering of moles about the place now was under the eyes of forceful and respected guardmoles, themselves as aware as any of the risk to themselves should the Master appear.

For the most part, therefore, the guardmoles settled down some way from the Stone, and left the tormenting of the mole on the wire to the henchmoles. If there was any sport to be had at all it was to watch and hear the violent ramblings of the eldrene Wort by the Stone, who seemed to be trying to invoke the wrath of the Word upon the barbed mole, though why it was hard to see since the mole seemed all but dead.

This sullen, dreary scene was made the stranger by the looming of heavy air as the afternoon wore on, accompanied by the fearsome sight of the clouds above them swirling and turning violently above a land from which all wind had fled.

A few moles sought comfort in the tunnels below, but there the air was heavier still and such worms as they found were limp and sweating, and made a mole ill to look at. It was a day to endure, an afternoon in which a mole dozed in fits and starts and nightmares, and shuddered awake again.

Chapter Thirty-Five

Yet even in a place of such spiritual dereliction as Beechenhill had become that afternoon, courage and hope may still be found.

Among the brooding guardmoles there came privily, by routes surreptitious, yet still exposed should a grike have looked the wrong way, one of those brave watchers Squeezebelly had left secreted within the system.

The watcher had learnt a little of what had been going on, and guessed that a mole was being tormented near the Stone, but more he knew not. Yet something in the heavy atmosphere, and something about the sense of waiting in the system, gave him courage to venture forth, and the Stone guided his paws and took him by degrees to that part of the system beyond the wire fence where few grikes had gone.

How near to the Stone Mole he went we cannot tell, but near enough it seems to sense that the barbed mole was more than mole.

He stared aghast, uncertain what he saw, or what moles hung there, knowing only that one was alive, and about him there was strange light. He watched, which was his task, and listened, and sensing deep suffering, he prayed.

The hanging mole, the one alive, stirred in the morbid light, and half turned the watcher's way, and the watcher saw a staring eye, and the eye looked gently and was full of care. The watcher knew he looked upon a holy mole.

'Pray not for the Stone Mole but for these lost moles who torment themselves through him,' he heard Beechen say, and knew it was the Stone Mole he saw hanging there. Then the Stone Mole turned back again and cried out as best he could, 'Stone, what more can I do here? What more?'

'Renounce the Stone,' the watcher heard a female whisper, 'and yield thyself to the peace and discipline of the Word and we shall let thee live.'

The Stone Mole was silent a long time, and then he stirred and said in a rasping voice filled with pain, 'Grant that my thirst is satisfied, grant it to me, father.'

The watcher heard the female reply, 'Aye, mole, thy thirst shall be satisfied but only by the Word . . .' Her voice faded as the air was suddenly heavier still and then with a cracking roar the skies opened up with a thundering downpour of rain.

In the first moments of its beginning the watcher turned back underground knowing he must go to the Castern Chambers and tell Squeezebelly what he had seen. The deluge was so great that when he reached the tunnels he was deafened by the rain above, and as he ran on he saw that in places the walls were darkening with wet and great drips were coming down. On he went, and quicker, as Squeezebelly had trained him to, for hanging there by the Stone his system loved was the Stone Mole, and he needed aid.

On and on he went, the sound of his racing paws matching the drumming of the deluge coming from above.

But even as the watcher ran frantically on, the image of the hanging Stone Mole before him all the time, the rain brought havoc into the Castern Chambers, and the worst fears of Holm came true.

Holm had felt the air grow heavier as the afternoon wore on, and again and again had urged Squeezebelly to get them out. The great mole had resisted that, but agreed to evacuate his moles from the deep moister chambers, though that meant they had become short of space and even more irritable, whilst separating them still further from the elderly moles and pregnant females who stayed on in the small and most distant chamber because it was the driest of them all.

'No, no, no!' Holm said again and again. 'Out, out, out!'

Yet when the rain first began there had been no change at all in the water in the chambers – the streams flowed the same, the lakes' levels were unaltered, and all that got wet were the white-green plants underneath the roof fissures, where water fell from outside.

This seemed to prove Squeezebelly's point, and the moles stayed where they were, though because of Holm's insistence none yet returned to the deeper and more comfortable chambers, except for one who volunteered to go down through the tunnels and ensure that the elderly moles and pregnant females were dry and safe.

They were, and the little stream that separated them off was quite unaffected by the rain outside. But then a new noise came, and the chambers were filled with a frightening roaring and raging of approaching sound.

'Sir! Out! All of us!' shouted Holm, and his conviction communicated itself to the others.

'Out, out!' they cried and but for Squeezebelly's mighty shout and command to keep calm they might have panicked and rushed for the exits. This was not like Beechenhill moles at all, but there was something in the oppressive air, something unsettling and violent, and even Sleekit, as calm and disciplined a mole as could be found, felt it now.

But one thing the roaring did was to make Squeezebelly determined to get Harebell and the others back through to them now, and accordingly he deputed two trusted moles to go down to fetch them, along with Sleekit and Harrow, who wanted to be with Harebell, and Holm as well, since he would stay calmer if he did something.

The distance was not far, but it was downslope and each step they took the roaring seemed to grow louder, and the air, previously quite still, was rushing and almost gale force against them at some tunnel turns.

When they came to the greatest of the chambers, the one at the far side of which, through a short tunnel, the others were hiding, they heard and then saw a new flow of water. It was a rushing, threshing fall into the lake from a

786

fault that had been dry before, and it was plain that the lake was rising and inexorably spreading out and flooding the chamber.

At first they tried to skirt it but this took too long and so they splashed their way across what had formerly been a dry floor. The silently moving water's edge was a mass of fleeing cockroaches, each scrabbling over others in their efforts to escape, and many already engulfed by water and swimming; and some drowning.

Up the short tunnel they went, the roaring ever louder and the sense of imminent flooding greater still, and up into the chamber where Harebell and the others were hiding. There a scene of horror met their eyes.

The stream they had formerly been able to ford so easily was now a torrent rushing by and threatening soon to overflow the eroded channel in which it ran. Beyond, though now unreachable, the chamber was dry enough but where seven or eight moles had been there were now twenty. Grike guardmoles had fought their way in and attacked the Beechenhill moles. Squeezebelly's plans had gone more than awry: they had failed.

Such future as Beechenhill had was taken now, and with it Harebell, whom they could see rounded up against a wall with others there, including Quince.

Harrow stanced by the torrent of water and cried out his rage and loss as he watched Harebell being pushed from the chamber and out of sight. The helplessness of the watching moles was made worse by the fact that the guardmoles did not hear them against the noise, and worse still as they were forced to stand by as the grikes rounded on the elderly males who had been separated off from the females and now horribly taloned them down towards the rushing, sucking water of the swollen stream. They shouted, they cried out, and then, more terribly still, the seeming loss of Harebell, followed by this cold murder of moles, became too much for Harrow.

As Holm, who knew water better than anymole, cried 'No!' and tried to stop him, a madness of anger or loss gripped Harrow and, heaving little Holm off, he dived into the water in a wild, hopeless bid to reach the other side and . . . and what? What could he have done? This was but the first of the madness seen in the hours just begun.

Harrow's front paws made only one stroke and then half a second before his body was grabbed and turned in the water, and half sucked down, and then rushed along hard into a rock. They saw him struggle for a moment, they saw his snout gasp up and a paw reach feebly out, and then he was gone from them forever into the dark, sucking place into which the torrent flowed.

Grikes on the far side saw them, and gesticulated and jeered, as Holm and Sleekit and the other two were forced to watch those old Beechenhill moles taloned into the stream that had just taken Harrow.

Numbed now with shock, Sleekit took command of the abortive expedition and, turning them round, ordered them all back the way they had come. Back they went into the great chamber, and found its floor was all wet now and the air was thick with cockroaches seeking to escape the water yet unable to fly far. Through it all the moles half splashed and half swam until they reached the far side, where they paused and looked back and saw water gushing out of the tunnel from which they had just escaped. On, on through a nightmare of flooding, Holm leading now, and Sleekit behind, the place littered, crawling, slimy with dying and drowned creatures which the flood had driven from their subterranean lairs.

They arrived back at the high chambers to find that Squeezebelly and the others had all but given up hope that they were alive. Already half the moles had been got out to the tunnels nearer the surface, and Squeezebelly was overseeing the evacuation of the rest.

His joy at their return was immediately destroyed by the desperate news they brought: Harrow lost, moles murdered, Harebell, Quince and the others, including Henbane, taken. . . .

788

While their own relief to have reached Squeezebelly again was overtaken by the news a watcher had brought of the barbing by the Stone of a mole who might be, who surely was, from all that the watcher said, the Stone Mole himself.

There was wildness now in Squeezebelly's eye, the same Sleekit and Holm had seen already so fatally overtake Harrow. At his flank Bramble and Skelder and other such moles were angry and working towards a fight, and it was plain that if Squeezebelly did not lead them out against the grikes they would take themselves there anyway.

But he was not reluctant now, nor doubtful, but rather looked as if the care of years had gone from him and he was ready to do what he must have wished to do long before.

He got the moles together in a chamber along the way, with every tunnel off it packed with his system's moles. Though there was no rain for now on the surface, here below the tunnels were wet and dripping.

'Harebell and the other females with pup have been taken,' Squeezebelly shouted, 'and no doubt if we go in search of them up Castern way we shall be ambushed and taken or killed ourselves.

'Our better chance is to attack the grikes in the very centre of Beechenhill: at the Stone. We know they are there because we have news of a desecration before our Stone, news that suggests that the Stone Mole himself is being barbed there even now.' The moles were hushed at this, and angry too.

'For long I have resisted the temptation to fight the grikes, for reasons you well know. Others here have argued in favour of war and today I put my support behind them. I cannot any more resist their call to fight and if I must go by myself I shall. I pray that one day a mole shall come to this place who knows better than I the non-violent way. But I do not, and that way has nearly led to the loss of us all, for surely we would have died here in the Castern Chambers but for the warnings by Holm.

'I do not believe we can win this day. I do not think that

789

if we give ourselves up we shall be allowed to survive. We can only hope that under cover of this ominous weather, and knowing the ground as we do, we can deal the grikes a blow on behalf of all moledom that they shall not forget.'

There was a great and terrible cheer at this.

'Yet one thing I shall ask of you!'

'Ask it, Squeezebelly!' several shouted.

'Then it is this. If the Stone decrees that most of us must fall before the talons of the Word it shall, surely, let some survive. Let such moles, whoever they are, be not ashamed to flee from Beechenhill as opportunities come. They shall have the task of going out to other systems and telling such followers as they can find what they have seen happen here in Beechenhill.

'I believe that one day the Stone will live again across moledom, and if we in this great system can pass on to others news of all that happened here – of our doubts, of our retreat to Castern, of how the Stone seemed to call us out again, of whatever aid we may bring to the Stone Mole – then other followers in other systems shall gain courage from it; and wisdom too. For surely violence is not the way and there shall be a day when a better way is found!

'Now, up and out we shall go, keeping together, having courage to bring our help to bear upon the barbed mole before our Stone. May we be given all the strength the Stone can give, and if we do wrong, may each of us be forgiven!'

With that, and a mighty shout, Squeezebelly led his moles out of that chamber, and up onto the surface to make their final return to Beechenhill from the northern side.

So hard had the downpour been at first that the surface of the Stone seemed surrounded by an aura of mist where the rain bounced off; so hard that the body of the henchmole hanging next to Beechen twisted and turned under its force, and his fur turned gleaming black.

Yet barely a guardmole moved, for the rain initially

seemed good, seemed cool and cleansing, and its coming marked a sudden easing of the pressure in the air. They saw Wort stance up in the rain as if trying to combat its might against her body, and they saw her shouting against it, but heard her not for the rain was so loud and violent on the ground.

They saw the Stone Mole pull his head back and open his parched mouth as rain darkened his body and cleansed it, and then shone on him, and reflected the violent light in the sky above.

Down, down it came, in ever more powerful tranches until soon in places across the grass small rivulets began to flow, while lower down the slopes water began to gush out of tunnel entrances and moles and other creatures were forced to come running, blinking and closing their eyes against the violent fall, their paws and fur filthy with yellow mud.

The tunnels underground being flooded, there was no shelter from the rain there and the moles had to stay where they were, and if they moved at all it was to cluster together more and to stare at the Stone Mole, who seemed to command the very rain itself.

Heavier, and yet heavier it came, seeking to bow a mole's snout down, thundering in his ears, stinging his body, squelching between his talons, splashing up violently into his face.

Yet there was an urge, an addictive urge, for everymole to keep his snout up and stare at the Stone Mole to whom the rain seemed to have brought a strange and awesome kind of life.

His head had arched further back, his mouth was open as if to quench his mortal thirst, and his free paw reached and turned and went up as if in benediction upon the eldrene Wort who stanced beneath, or upon the Stone, or perhaps upon them all.

Then with a sudden rush of wind and lightning in the sky the rain stopped, leaving everything and everymole chilled and dripping. Yet still barely a single mole moved.

They stared instead at something on the northern horizon, far, far beyond the Stone Mole, barely thicker at first than a stretch of taut barbed wire.

Yet it seemed to grow towards them, though how slow or fast none could quite tell.

'Look!'

One mole shouted it, but all saw, all were amazed.

For running, gathering towards them, seemingly carried by the driving wind and cloud itself a force of moles came, a great and commanding mole at their head.

''Tis the moles of Beechenhill!' cried out Merrick then in surprise. ''Tis Squeezebelly himself that leads them!'

As he said these words, the first winds of the new storm hit them. The eldrene Wort reared up again as if against the very storm itself and as the new and heavier rain began to fall into their eyes and faces, and the first shouts of the Beechenhill moles were heard, she cried out, 'Tear down the Stone Mole. Kill him! Talon him! Make him die! Now does the Word put us to its greatest test! Tear him down and talon him!'

Her screamed words seemed to release an instinctive fear among the henchmoles, so they felt that if they did not do as she said they would all be lost.

But as they lunged forward to do Wort's will, the great wave of Beechenhill moles also rushed forward with Squeezebelly's roaring command in their ears: 'Save him! In the Stone's name, save the Stone Mole!'

The darkness of the heart of the storm came then, and rain turned the ground to mud beneath the frantic paws of moles of Word and Stone as they joined in a killing battle for possession of the Stone Mole.

While he, dying now, hung still and silent above them all, and the rain that was upon him washed his tears and blood into the soil of Beechenhill below. And darkness began to come.

In Duncton Wood, as night fell at the Stone, the madness that had seemed to be with Mistle for several days past began at last to reach a climax of violence and distress. She screamed and cried as if trying to reach out to something she could not touch and Romney, though tired with watching over her for so long, only stopped her from dashing herself against the Stone by exerting all his strength. Instead, she began to sob, 'No, no, no, no,' into that dreadful night.

Minutes or hours later, he did not know which, she went quiet, her eyes open as she watched through the long night, her body trembling, and her pain terrible to see.

'Yes,' she whispered, utterly beyond comforting, 'yes, my dear, I am with you before the Stone, I am here.'

When Romney tried to speak to her she only stirred and turned, as a mole stirs when another seeks to wake it from deep sleep, its brow puckering, its paws feebly seeking to push the disturbance away.

'He will come back,' said Romney through his tears.

'Yes, my love, I am here,' she whispered.

'He will come back, Mistle.'

'No, I shall not go. No, no. . .' she whimpered then, 'my love is dying.'

'Your love lives still, the mole you love will come back home to you one day,' Romney whispered again and again; when she said 'No', he whispered it more, on and on, his faith confronting her despair.

'Stone, help me help her,' he said. 'Mistle, he will come back to you.'

Above them in the still clear night the first new beech buds trembled, while below the flowers reached up towards the sky, and had there been light a mole might have seen that the promise of spring was already bright across the wood. But there was none, all was dark, the promise was not seen.

'My love. . . .'

'He will come back,' said faithful, loving Romney. 'One day he will, one day. . . .'

On through the night he whispered it, and whatever other comforts he could find as well, holding poor Mistle close, and watching and hoping that when dawn came it would bring respite.

Sometime in that long night of violence across Beechenhill the Stone Mole cried out, 'Father, let them know thy Silence now! Father, let them be still at last!'

But they were not still. Madness had gripped them all, a madness that drove them on through rain and storm, through pain and fear, thrusting their talons at anymole that moved, a madness of slaughter in the driven dark in which mole of the Stone and mole of the Word could not tell each other apart, and yet killed on. It was a night of screams lost in the wind, a night when taloned paws grasped the heads of fatigued moles and thrust them at the wire's barbs; a night of utter shame.

Nomole knows what dread deeds were done in the name of Word and Stone, nor truly why it was that such a bloody mayhem as that was fought around the body of a near-dead mole. Yet so it was, and so history must record it.

And dawn revealed the dead.

Squeezebelly, slumped still near the Stone, with the blood of many a mole of the Word upon his paws. His son Bramble dead nearby. No sign of Skelder though, lost perhaps among that throng of fighting moles who seemed to roll downslope from the Stone and lay there now, all dead, just spread about like leaves in a wet autumn. He might be there.

And yet . . . look close beneath the Stone. Wort lives, bloodied yet not badly wounded, staring where the Stone Mole still hangs, motionless but alive. Look closer yet: her eyes are full of tears and though she whispers still, her prayers of obsession and hate are all quite spent; her tears are tears of compassion, her words are words of pity.

Sleekit lives, but only because grubby Holm, grubbier than ever, had the sense to stay close by her, and when she fell and would have been killed, slumped on top of her and stayed there shivering. They live.

But then a pile of dead. A mass of dead. A field of

muddied, bloody dead; and along the wire, contorted silhouettes against the coming dawn, moles hang; of Stone, of Word, whatmole knows?

Most are dead, yet some are alive, some groan. Beneath them Merrick lies staring at where the Stone Mole hangs, still unwon by either side. Merrick stares, but his eyes are sightless now.

So he does not see the Stone Mole stir, nor hear his rattling agony, or see where his left paw has pulled still further out, and bone and sinew have ripped apart. One touch of wind, one turn of his body, and he'll be off that barb.

Tears are dried now on his worn, hurt face and, as Merrick stares but does not see, Wort stirs, stances up and comes to where the Stone Mole hangs.

She reaches up, but by herself she cannot lift the Stone Mole off. She looks up and sees Holm there.

Holm looks at her, and knows her, and is not afraid.

'Help me,' she says, and he comes.

He strives to girdle the Stone Mole's lower half with his paws, and she reaches up and does the same, and then with a heave they lift him sideways off the hook and gently set him down.

The scene is desolate and slow. The moles are moles of moledom now, nomole knows the Stone, none the Word. Moles groan and stir all across Beechenhill. Sleekit stirs, stares, sees, and stances up. She is the third to reach the Stone Mole, the first to stretch out a paw and touch his face. His eyes are open from their pain and look on she who was there almost from his birth. His eyes smile on her and are sad.

'Turn me towards the Stone,' he says.

They help him face that way and he says, 'Go to the Stone and touch it, and pray that what I pray the Stone may grant.'

'Beechen. . . .'

'Do it, Sleekit.' She goes.

'Stone Mole. . . .'

'Do it now for me, good Holm.' And he goes.

'Mole. . . .'

'Eldrene Wort, I love thee, open up thy heart now to the Stone for all the darkness of the Word is almost gone from thee.'

'I would have it all gone,' she whispers.

'Then you must find the courage to face your darkness to its end and see my light beyond it.'

He reaches a paw to hers, and she looks into his eyes and sees the love that waits there for her.

'Go now with the others to the Stone, and fear much to look back. But if you do, be not afraid to bear witness for the Stone of what you see.'

Wort is the last of three to turn towards the Stone.

Together they hear his voice whisper this last prayer: 'Stone, my father, the burden was too great for me. You made me but mole, and I alone cannot turn the world nor touch all moles at once, even with thy love. Thy Silence waits for them to discover for themselves. Show them the way to it.'

The Stone is silent, the three moles touching it are still, the Stone Mole stirs one last time and says, 'The way to Silence for allmole shall be through one, through she who loved me and thee, most of all. Father, I am but mole. The task is too great for me. Wilt thou not lead them there?'

Silence was at the Stone as Sleekit, Wort and Holm humbly prayed, each with a paw upon the Stone. Such gentle silence, and gentle light, as the dawn sun began to rise on Beechenhill.

Then trembling and much afraid, the eldrene Wort dared turn and look at where the Stone Mole lay, and to what she saw she whispered out this prayer: 'Stone, my mother and my father, forgive me for all that I have done.' Then a light was on her face, great and good, and it shone within her eyes as she saw what mole it was she had persecuted so long, and watched him rise again, and go.

Then she turned back to the Stone and to her right side Holm reached and touched her, and to her left Sleekit reached out a paw as well, and the eldrene Wort was alone no more.

Survivors stir across the slopes of Beechenhill; moles call one to another, moles of the Word help moles of the Stone because, for now, fear has gone from out of their hearts, and so the violence has fled their minds.

The three moles turn from the Stone and see that where the Stone Mole lay, before the sun came up, moles are quietly gathering. His body is not there, yet light and peace are there, and to it the moles have come.

The moles on Beechenhill look about, puzzled, wondering, hurrying here and there, afeared. Some even venture into the sodden tunnels to search, but nomole is hidden there, nomole nor corpse.

The mole they fought for, none has won. The mole they killed is gone.

Then a whisper begins and then a shout, 'Ask the eldrene Wort, she will know. She is closest to the Word. She was his persecutor. Ask *her*.' The shouts are ugly, mocking, and similar in tone to some of the jeering at the Stone Mole as he hung dying.

'Aye, where is he gone, this Stone Mole?' asks one of the henchmoles aggressively.

Can fear return so soon? It can.

The eldrene Wort stances still by the Stone, her fur bedraggled, and by the new light of morning she looks much aged. Yet on her face is a look none who knows her has seen before. It is soft, it has suffered, and now it grieves. Yet beyond that, it is at peace.

First she turns to Holm and Sleekit: 'Go from here,' she says, 'bear witness of these hours. Go now, for you should not be taken.'

'But you . . .' says Sleekit.

'He looked on me with love, and took my fear from out of my heart. Go now while it is still safe and these moles are subdued . . . Lead her, mole.'

So it was that Holm began to lead Sleekit out of Beechenhill towards the final tasks they both must find.

Once more a henchmole cried out to Wort, and as Holm and Sleekit left her they heard her reply, 'He has gone from here, I saw him go and the Word did not beset him, for he is stronger than the Word. I saw him go among you. I saw him . . . there!' She pointed to a place just beyond the Stone.

'Why, mole,' she said to one of her henchmoles, 'he stopped by thee . . . and you, mole, you there, you stanced aside to let him pass.'

The moles looked at each other in puzzlement as one turned to another and said, 'What did you see?'

'I saw no Stone Mole here. Just an old mole among the crowd, one of the followers I thought.'

Then a Beechenhill follower said, 'I saw him, too. He touched my paw but I thought him one of you.'

The puzzlement was replaced by slow wonder, for the more they spoke among themselves the more clear it was that a mole had been there.

One asked, 'What did he look like, this mole you saw?' Some said he was young and strong, others that he was old and weak; some were sure that 'he' had been female, some claimed he was barely more than a pup.

The arguing mounted up amongst them until one turned to Wort and said, 'You started this, you finish it. What did this mole look like?'

Wort said softly and with a gentle smile, 'Old, so old, his fur more white than grey, and as he went he had a limp where we had hurt him long, long ago and hurt him now. And his eyes were like two suns. . . .'

Some laughed at her, some whispered she was mad.

'And where's he gone, this white old limping mole?' mocked one.

'To find a mole who shall know him true,' she said. 'For we failed him, didn't we? All of us failed him. But the Stone Mole said it would need only one to see him as he is and that way the rest of us must go to find the Silence.'

That was the last Holm and Sleekit heard of what the eldrene Wort said of what she saw. The sun had risen, its light red upon the Stone, and they saw coming up the southern slopes some moles.

Moles of the Word. Assured moles, well-guarded.

'What moles?' whispered Holm, eyes wide.

Sleekit looked.

Terce she knew.

Other sideem there she knew.

The dark female who was with pup she knew not, and she liked not.

The leader of them all, beautiful to see, fur elegant, she had seen once before. Tiny, wet and slippery with the blood and muck of birth he had been then. Yes, yes, she knew him. Like mother, like son.

'That is Lucerne, Master of the Word.'

Holm stared.

'Lorren. Not believe a word of it,' he said.

Sleekit smiled.

'You'll see more yet, good Holm,' she said. 'Come, lead me from here.'

'Where to?'

'Harebell,' said Sleekit. 'We must try to find her.'

'Harebell!' said Holm, protesting.

'You're a mole who likes watery ways,' said Sleekit. 'There's plenty of those north-west of here around a place called Castern! It was on the far side of there that she was taken, wasn't it? Use the cover of the flooded tunnels to find her. Nomole could do it better than you.'

Holm stared at her, opened his mouth to speak, shook his head, looked exasperated, and then turned to the north-west.

Chapter Thirty-Six

Terce liked it not; Mallice liked it not; the sideem and the guardmoles of Lucerne's entourage liked it not.

But the Master of the Word revelled in it. There was something *right* to him about the devastation they discovered at Beechenhill. Visually he thought it was . . . magnificent. And if that is the way a mole chooses to see a scene of death and dying about the Stone of a system which had resisted the power of the Word for so long then so it must be.

A scene lit that day by a red rising sun, an effect that began to fade as the morning wore on and the Master inspected the place. But the image lingered on, and seemed even to redden his eyes as he gazed about, content to see that, though his orders had not been obeyed, yet Beechenhill seemed to have been destroyed.

What was more, and what became plain as he and Terce listened to the guardmoles' reports, the eldrene Wort had had a paw in it. She had manipulated the whole thing. She had achieved it.

A pity, really, she was mad, but so she seemed to be for the Stone Mole was all she talked about. If Drule was here there would have been ways. . . .

'Take her to Ashbourne and let us hope her ravings of the Stone Mole stop,' said Lucerne. 'Have her close-guarded, and honour her. She may be unorthodox, but she got results. Even so, I think her time is done.'

Lucerne smiled round at Terce, but Terce looked bleak. He liked it not, Lucerne knew that. Well, let them hear the reports through first and then they could discuss the implications of it all. Meanwhile he decided that they should inspect the dead more thoroughly.

'Master mine, I would prefer not.'

'Mallice, you will come.'

His voice was sharp and thin with her, and he had deputed two trusted guardmoles to be at her flanks all the time. For her safety, he said.

'I wish not to see corpses, Lucerne. I am with pup.'

'Bring her,' he said savagely. Even before they saw anything the sick sweet smell of death made her retch and she protested yet again: 'I am near my time and this. . . .'

'This will hurry it along, my dear,' he said.

'This is Squeezebelly, Master.'

Lucerne turned from Mallice and looked down curiously at the slumped corpse. Death is a tedious thing.

'Master, this is Merrick of Hawe, sideem of Ashbourne.'

Lucerne stared. Mallice retched and was sick.

'And these?' said Lucerne, pointing at the corpses on the wires.

'Moles of the Word and of the Stone. The fighting was at night. Some did not see the wire they ran into, others used their greater strength to force weaker ones on to it.'

'So moles of the Stone *snouted* our guardmoles?'

'It seems so, Master.'

'For a peace-loving system this was strange behaviour, was it not?' said Lucerne cheerfully. 'Let it be known what Beechenhill moles did. Eh, Mallice, eh?' He grinned unpleasantly at her.

'Master mine . . .' she said weakly.

'The sideem Mallice is ill, take her from here. Let me know when her time comes.' His voice was chill – and full of mock concern.

'You are cruel,' hissed Mallice at him.

'And you and yours,' he said with menace.

For the first time Mallice showed him the fear that he had been building in her all along their journey from Cannock.

He smiled, charm itself.

'Go slowly now,' he said more gently. 'Before, you always liked me to be harsh.'

He watched her go, and Terce watched him watch her go and saw the contempt he felt.

He knows, thought Terce. And Terce's eyes went round the slopes of Beechenhill and he scented the odorous air with distaste. No, no, no, no, he liked it not at all. Something was wrong, very wrong indeed. Something incomplete.

'Master, forgive me, but I too feel a little faint. May I leave thee and go among those moles further down the slopes?'

'Do it, Twelfth Keeper, and when you have talked to them, you come back and tell me what it is that troubles you.'

They smiled coldly at each other, and each was thinking that the other's time of usefulness was done. Beechenhill was taken, the Word triumphant, and now. . . .

The Master must die, thought Terce.

Terce must be made eliminate, thought Lucerne. Drule, I would have had thee with me now; leaving you behind was a mistake.

'Have Wort sent to me before she goes to Ashbourne,' Terce told a guardmole a little later on.

He managed a smile when she came, and stanced her down.

'You have done well,' he said.

'The Stone has done it all,' Wort said immediately.

'Ah, yes. And the Stone Mole?'

'Lucerne won't find his holy body,' said Wort matter-of-factly.

'Why don't you tell me what really happened here?' said Terce. 'From the beginning, and taking your time.'

So Wort did, right from the beginning, the strangest, maddest tale that Terce ever heard, except for one thing. All the evidence supported the truth of it. Moles called in for corroboration after Wort had been taken away described it just the same. And all spoke in awe of the Stone Mole, describing his suffering as if it had been their own. And the strangeness of his parting, or disappearance, or whatever that was. . . ! No corpse, no sudden recovery. Nothing, but images out of the confusion of fighting and a tired dawn of a young mole, an old mole, a White Mole.

No, Terce liked it even less. It stank of martyrdom and mystery. It stenched of just the kind of nonsense that whatever followers were left could rally round. It was rank with danger to the Word.

Yet here and soon, in this confusion, in this possible disaster, the Word would guide him. Terce trusted that. Always, always, it had been a risk, but somewhere here in all of it was a way of ending Lucerne's mortal life and beginning the immortalisation of Rune's dynasty.

That would be. For now, his concern was Mallice and her coming pups, of whom he would glory to be grandfather. His task might have been harder if Drule had been here, but he was not. The guardmoles who close-guarded her were moles he knew; they owed him favours. Let her have the pups here, and soon. She would be safe.

Meanwhile he must listen and learn, and the Word would, as the eldrene Wort might once have said, show him the way.

The Word did, and very soon.

'The Master asks for your presence with him,' a messenger said. 'He is up near the Stone.'

He went and found Lucerne looking smug, and a tired and travelled guardmole stanced nearby.

'Ah, Terce, the day's good news is not over yet, for there is more. Harebell, sister of Wharfe, sister of another mole you know, is caught. More than caught indeed; she is with pup.'

'It is the season for pups,' said Terce easily.

'And mothers too.'

'Mothers, Master?'

'Old mothers. Mothers with dry teats. Mothers do grow old, Terce, very. Or had you forgotten?'

803

Terce was silent, thinking, frowning. Then he let out a little sigh of disbelief.

'The Mistress Henbane, Master?'

'This mole's commander has her *with* Harebell. And others, too, of rather less interest to the Word.'

'Then we must see them!' said Terce, almost jubilant. Henbane! The Word had spoken.

'It is a little way, I fear, for they are half a day from here. They were found hiding and caught napping, literally it seems. And just as well by his account or floods would have drowned them dead, and thus denied us the pleasures yet to come. Think of it, Terce: united once more with Henbane on the very day of our greatest triumph.'

'There are matters we must. . . .'

'They can wait,' said Lucerne sharply.

He turned to the guardmole and dismissed him with more smiles and compliments, but the moment he had gone the smiles faded.

'I know you, Terce. These matters . . . they will be to do with something that troubles you, and no doubt you are right to raise them and I am derelict to avoid them. Well, Terce, I like not my mother; I like not the idea of my sister, though her pups may be a very different thing. Yes, they may well be. These are matters I wish to attend to. What is yours that it is more important?'

'The Stone Mole, Master. The Stone Mole is dead, long live the Stone Mole. I tell, you Master, the Word is in danger now.'

Then he told Lucerne his fears, powerfully and convincingly, and sought to persuade him to have Henbane brought here.

'Harebell is too far gone with pup, according to that guardmole. She is imminent and my dear mother naturally wishes to stay with my dear sister, and since for now I wish nothing more than to see them, why, the Master will be the one to move.'

'As you will, Master.'

804

'Yes, as I will.'

Terce was expressionless and, despite all he said, inwardly pleased. The Word had sent Henbane as guidance to Terce. She was the way. The one mole in moledom who might yet conquer Lucerne.

'Is she well?' asked Terce. 'The Mistress Henbane, I mean.'

'Elderly and fit, just as you always said Rune used to be. Just as one day I shall be.'

'I hope so, Master, though I shall not live to see it.'

'No, you won't,' said Lucerne, and laughed. Somewhere here in Beechenhill, somehow for reasons neither fully understood, the relationship of the Twelfth Keeper and the Master of the Word had turned a corner into hatred.

'Oh, and Terce,' said the Master, so gently. 'Summon Mallice. She shall come with us.'

'But Master, she is near. . . .'

'Near her time? Ah, yes. But then she always wanted to meet Henbane, and – who knows? – my mother may not live too long.'

'Yes, Master,' hissed Terce.

'We shall simply have to wait,' said Sleekit firmly, frowning.

Holm frowned back, jerked his head about a bit, looked around the running muddy tunnel they were in and sighed.

'Wait,' he echoed faintly.

'Yes, wait. I thought you liked this kind of place. You *like* being grubby.'

'With Lorren, not you. You're Sleekit, not my mate. Not nice with you. Nice with her.' Holm was indeed grubby, the grit and wet sand on the walls and floor of the limestone tunnel he had finally brought them up was thick in his fur and between his talons.

Sleekit, on the other paw, contrived to look surprisingly clean, but then at the first opportunity she was inclined to wash herself in any running water she could find, and if that was not available then drips of water were nearly as good. And failing even that, then if there was a current of air she would dry herself and shake her fur clean.

'Gets dirty again,' Holm would say.

'Lorren would love you more if you were clean,' Sleekit would respond.

But it was only friendly banter between two moles who were now living on the very edge of disaster, and needed all the lightness they could find.

Holm had led them on a fur-raising journey back through the Castern Chambers, which had involved wading, swimming, and diving through sumps and emerging in lightless pockets of air, until, miraculously as it had seemed to Sleekit, he had got them to the torrent beyond which Harebell and the others had been captured.

The water level was much lower than when they were last there, though dangerous still, and Holm had explained and then demonstrated how Sleekit must swim across, and somehow they had made it.

After that it had been a relatively simple matter of following clues and probabilities until they had found a place along the Manifold Valley where a small grike garrison was stationed. They had lain in wait and watched, and Sleekit had recognised two guardmoles she had seen during the flood in Castern.

'I hope they will not recognise me,' said Sleekit.

After that Holm had lain low, while Sleekit used her former sideem ways and risked direct contact with the grikes, claiming she was journeying northwards on the Master's business. She felt safe enough, for the spot was isolated and unlikely to have another sideem there who might have identified her as false.

She was with them a few hours, and the fact that she was female and the grikes all male was helpful, for they soon revealed they had taken five female prisoners from the rabble who had escaped from Beechenhill and they were not certain what to do with them.

'Pupping, aren't they?'

'All of them?' asked Sleekit.

'All but one.'

They said this oddly and she soon found out why. They knew, and this explained their caution and their doubt, that the odd one out was Henbane, former Mistress of the Word. Or that was who she said she was.

'The sideem would not by any chance know what Mistress Henbane looks like?'

'I saw her once,' said Sleekit, realising that this was at least a way to contact the captive moles. She prayed they would not reveal that they recognised her.

'What will you do with this mole if she is the Mistress?' asked 'sideem' Sleekit as they went into the tunnels to see the prisoners.

'Keep her and tell sideem Merrick double quick. The others are a useful source of pups and could be used for breeding. Not many fertile females about these days . . .' The grikes grinned and laughed and nudged each other at the prospect. But they went serious again: sideem never laughed at such things.

Sleekit was taken to the captive moles and was able to establish where they were hidden so that Holm might find a route through limestone tunnels to it. A slim chance, but just possible.

She was careful to talk loudly just before she reached them, making clear by what she said that she was here as a sideem and, therefore, not to be recognised. She found them all being kept together in a cramped burrow, and well guarded too. Along with Harebell and Henbane was Quince and two pregnant females she did not know.

At the sight of Sleekit, Henbane, more used to hiding her feelings, stayed expressionless and, as best they could, the others took their cue from that. But even so it was all Harebell could do not to express her joy at seeing Sleekit so unexpectedly.

'Well, sideem,' said the senior guardmole, 'you tell me which you think is Mistress Henbane, if, that is, any of them is.' It was a tense moment, for whatever she said would sentence Henbane to punishment and death.

Sleekit thought quickly and decided what to do. She lowered her snout towards Henbane, and said, 'Mistress, I am grieved to see thee thus.'

'So she is who she says she is?'

'She is.'

'Yet you greet her deferentially.'

'A long word for a guardmole,' said Sleekit haughtily. 'I hope you know its meaning, and remember that Mistress Henbane did much for moledom before her apostasy, so treat her well.'

This was the best Sleekit could do for Henbane. As she looked at them she guessed that the moles had realised when they were caught that the grikes were only keeping those who were with pup alive and Henbane had decided to give her real name rather than be drowned with the others in the stream.

Quince stared at her and Sleekit realised that she must have claimed she was with pup to survive as well. . . .

'These others, sideem, I don't suppose you know their names!'

It was said more as a joke than anything for before she had even framed a reply the grike guardmole said. 'Don't worry. That's Harebell there, and that's Quince, and . . .' And he gave all their names correctly and with an unpleasant proprietorial leer, as if the pups they carried were his own.

'They seem near their time.'

A look of minor alarm came over the grike's face.

'Well, I've already sent a couple of moles down to Ashbourne – one via the valley, one over the hill by way of Beechenhill – to tell them who we've caught. They should be pleased. But we don't want pups *here*. It's a garrison, not a bloody birth burrow.'

'You'd better find them more suitable quarters then, hadn't you?' said Sleekit, seeing an opportunity for getting them out of here to somewhere from where it might be easier to help them escape.

'Well . . . maybe,' said the grike.

'Do you know what happened to the Beechenhill moles?' said Sleekit, trying to mask any hint she may have given that she had the captives' interest in mind.

'Drowned, we thought. Drowned in Castern.'

Sleekit shook her head, and though she hated to give her friends information in such a way she felt it was for the best.

'No, killed. I heard they escaped from the chambers and most died by guardmole talons down by the Beechenhill Stone. I doubt if any got away at all.'

'Blest be the Word!' said the grike.

'Aye, blessed be the Word!' agreed Sleekit.

Sleekit emerged from the garrison and went on her way northward, being very cautious about deviating back lest the grikes were watching. It was therefore some time before she found Holm again, and they were able to seek out an alternative way into the garrison tunnels. Though they were not able to get to the chamber where Harebell, Henbane and the others were being kept they did at least succeed in reaching a point where, with a squeeze and a slide, they could see down into the main tunnel into the garrison, and overhear some of what the grikes' guard-moles said when they were at rest.

'We must wait patiently, and an opportunity for doing something will come along,' said Sleekit. 'The Master Lucerne will send moles here to get Henbane and the others, or perhaps even come himself for Henbane must matter to him. And if he realises who Harebell really is she will matter too and, I fear, need all the help we can give if she is to be saved. But at least Henbane and Harebell now know that I am here nearby and that may give them courage to try to escape.'

Holm sighed again.

'I like route-finding, not waiting,' he said. 'Waiting *drags*.'

'Then use the time to clean yourself, but do it quietly. And while you're doing it consider ways of getting moles out of here under pressure, for we may need to.'

Holm sighed some more, dejectedly looked at his fur, and wondered where to start.

Lucerne, Terce, a few guardmoles and a very pregnant Mallice reached the garrison as dusk fell, and while Mallice was close-guarded in a quite separate tunnel and burrows – against her will but 'for her own protection' – Lucerne and Terce went immediately to see Henbane and Harebell.

'See' was the word, for just as he had with Wharfe, Lucerne preferred to spy on them from a distance first and then retreat, delaying direct contact until it best suited him. He stared at them unseen for an hour or more before he left.

'I shall speak with them later,' he said, and Terce saw that he looked excited and cruelly pleased, 'but now I will visit Mallice.'

'Master, I should like to come too,' said Terce carefully. So far he had made no comment about Lucerne's rough treatment of Mallice, feeling, perhaps rightly, that his loyalty was being tested.

'No, but be ready this night.'

Lucerne found Mallice out of sorts, irritable, and tired. She was in a high, rough, damp chamber, and it was cold. What little nesting material there was was mouldy and lank.

'Master mine,' she whispered, 'send Terce to me, I am near my time. I cannot have my pups in here. Send him to help me.'

'He is engaged,' lied Lucerne, 'and I have need of thee alone.'

'But I am near my time, my dear.'

'I said I have need of thee, and I will have thee.' His eyes were full of hate.

'But . . . no!'

810

'I have seen my mother and my sister this night.'

'And, my love?' said Mallice, hoping for a diversion.

'I hated to see them close. I hated to see them talk. I hated all of it, Mallice, and now . . . I have need of thee.'

His voice had become thin and strange, almost pleading. She knew him well. Seeing Henbane had not agreed with him. Seeing Henbane with Harebell had agreed with him even less.

'Gently then, my dear,' she said, and near her time and heavy though she was, she proffered herself to him.

Then that perverse mole took her one last time, and for a moment forgot his mother, and for a moment more forgot his sister, and for a brief moment forgot even himself.

'Master mine,' she tried to sigh as if she had enjoyed herself.

'Now have your pups,' he said, 'have them well.'

'I shall, my dear, I shall, but send Terce to me.'

'He does not want to come. He says you disgust him now.' Lucerne laughed, a laugh to put fear into another's heart. 'Your fat body disgusts him. And it disgusts me too.'

'My . . . dear . . . please send him.'

'It's company you want, is it, mole? I'll send you moles to keep you company, oh yes I shall!' He laughed again. 'When your pupping starts I want to know so tell the guardmole.'

'Am I captive then, my love?'

'Are not thy pups captive of thy body? Not for long perhaps, but certainly they are victims.'

'Of what?' she said sharply.

'Of thine infidelity.' His eyes narrowed as hers widened.

'Infidelity to thee?' whispered Mallice.

Lucerne only laughed and left with no word more, while she, uncertain, shrank back with a paw to her flank and wondered how long she could delay before she must say that her pupping was begun.

Lucerne instructed the guardmoles, who were moles of Terce's choice, to admit nomole to those tunnels, *nomole*, on pain of death and then went and summoned the senior guardmole of the garrison, who was plainly a mole of purpose and ambition. Yet he wished once more he had Drule here. He was the mole for *this*.

'Master?'

'Senior guardmole . . . I need two moles obedient to the Word and to their Master.'

'We all are here.'

'Obedient and unquestioning.'

'What must they do, Master?'

'Obey me only.'

'I am one, and I can find another. Tell me what we must do.'

'If I asked you to kill your own mother would you do it?'

'If the Master asked it, yes I would.'

'And pups?'

'My own. . . ?' The grike faltered at this.

'Not thine. A follower's brood, and bastards.'

'I would, and another here would too.'

'Be ready for a summons from me this night. Speak to nomole of this, for it is business of the Word. Do it well and the Word shall be pleased.'

'Yes, Master,' said the grike guardmole, eyes purposeful.

Such opportunity for advancement might come but once in a lifetime and he intended to take it with all paws.

Darkness falls in the deep, incised valley of the Manifold like a close and clinging dankness that catches at a mole's throat. Things move muffled, the hazed moon moves slow, stars seem too far away, the night crawls; screams are barely heard.

Terce did not sleep, but lay angry and thinking. The Master had ordered him not to see Mallice and then said,

'Be ready this night!' But for what he did not know, and so he did not sleep. Something with Mallice?

What was plain to Terce was that from the time the Master had spied on Henbane and his sister Harebell he was cold with sibling envy. And Mallice was in danger, that was plain as well.

How hard the Word tested him! How small the difference between triumph and disaster yet might be. But how sweet and divine the triumph when it came. So Terce was restless, waiting, expecting his summons.

A scream, barely heard in the distance, sometime in the night. Mallice's? Perhaps. Terce had never felt so ready for new life as he did now. 'I shall be the grandfather of the new Master of the Word, and his name shall be divine. I shall . . .' Terce waited, ready for it all.

Henbane was awake, listening to Harebell and knowing her time was very near. Her movements were heavy now, her breathing shallow and a little desperate.

'I am afraid,' whispered Harebell in the dark. 'What will they do to my pups?'

'I was afraid, my dear, when it was my time, yet here you are. I shall see that they will live. I am here.'

'I am glad you are. . . .'

In the cloying darkness Henbane heard her daughter, and shed tears for her. She knew her fear.

'Help us,' she prayed to that great unknown to which she gave no name, neither Word nor Stone, 'help us all. I shall be their grandmother, show me what best to do.'

'Mother,' whispered Harebell again, 'I think my pupping will soon start.'

'I am here, my love, I am close.'

In the distance, down the tunnels, muffled, they heard a scream.

'Holm!'

Holm stanced up in the dark.

'The scream is from where that Mallice went. She's pupping. Something will happen now. Be ready.'

Holm's eyes were wide open, and they stared unblinking at a murky tunnel wall.

'Very ready,' he said.

Yes, the screams were Mallice's and hearing them the guardmole came.

'Have you begun?' he said. 'The Master. . . .'

'I have, mole,' she sighed between the pains, 'tell him.'

Running paws in the dark, another scream. 'Oh yes,' whispered Lucerne, Master of the Word, all to himself. 'Mallice has begun and soon they shall all be punished of the Word, and all Atone. Eldrene Wort, you would be proud of me!' He was laughing aloud when the guardmole came.

'Master. . . .'

'I heard. Summon the senior guardmole. He will be ready. And Terce as well. Get him.'

Quickly the guardmole came with a companion and they waited hushed and silent.

Then Terce arrived, a little slower, a good deal older. They heard Mallice scream again.

'Mallice has begun,' said Lucerne calmly, moving not at all.

Terce was watchful, and silent.

'What would you say, Twelfth Keeper, if I told you that the pups she is about to pup were bastards all? Eh? What would you have me do?' Lucerne's voice was cold, his eyes black, his fur glossy with night.

Terce said nothing.

'Well, Twelfth Keeper, father of this bitch, you shall hear what I shall do and we will know your loyalty then.'

'My loyalty is to the Master and the Word,' said Terce.

Lucerne laughed at this and, turning to the guardmoles, said, 'Go to your prisoners. Take the moles Henbane and Harebell to the entrance of the tunnels where the sideem

814

Mallice is held. Brook no argument with them, use force if need be. Do it now.'

Lucerne turned to Terce and loomed over him in a posture that was almost bullying, and certainly insolent.

'Come with me,' he said. It was an order, not a request.

'Yes, Master,' said Terce softly, and they went. But the eyes of Terce were not those of an abject mole, but of one who awaited his time.

The surface was chill and damp, the clouds above were lit up with the equinoctial moon, off below them down the slopes the Manifold, still full with the rain of the day before, flowed and roared in the gloom.

Shapes came out of the dark, two great guardmoles each guiding a female. The first to come was breathing heavily, and in some pain.

'Hello, Harebell,' said the stranger in the dark, his voice mock warm and therefore cruel.

The second guardmole brought the Mistress Henbane.

'Hello, mother,' said Lucerne. 'I have found a challenge for thee greater than any you have faced before. You will not like it, but I shall – very much – and so shall the Word.' This was Lucerne's greeting to his mother after so long: cold, cynical, matter-of-fact.

Henbane's eyes widened fractionally, and though when Harebell turned and looked at her in alarm she nodded a sign to keep calm, she herself felt shock. He was here sooner than she could have expected; and vile Terce as well.

With that instinct she herself had bred into him, and which Terce had trained and refined still more, she knew why he had come: he was here for the kill.

'Now follow me, all of you,' he said, and she knew their true ordeal was beginning. To Harebell he spoke no more.

While in the shadows near that place Holm stared at Sleekit, and Sleekit stared at the tunnel entrance, empty now of moles. She turned to Holm and said quietly,

'Listen now, my dear, and listen well. You are a route-finder; you never were and I think the Stone never desired you to be, a fighter. I do not know what is going to happen tonight, but I think there will be much violence. It is plain that Harebell is near her time, and already Mallice has begun. Lucerne means no good in bringing them together here.

'Yesterday, when Squeezebelly spoke to us, he asked that survivors should seek to escape while they still could. I trust that some did so. *We* got away, this far at least, and I think that others might have done. For myself . . . when I said goodbye to Mayweed at Chadlington I knew that I was beginning a task from which I might not come back. My beloved Mayweed knew it too. We have had our time, and he is always with me, as I am with him.

'But you and Lorren, your time must not be yet. So promise me, Holm, that you will escape from here and not try to fight. Promise me, my dear.'

Holm looked at her in the dark, his eyes wider than ever, and he said, 'Sleekit, I don't want to travel alone. I don't want to leave you.'

'Promise it, my dear. I need to know to have the strength for what I think that I must do. Henbane needed me once before like this, she needs me now. I owe it . . . I owe it to myself, and to the memory of Tryfan, who knew her truer than anymole, and loved her as I do. But this is not your fight and not your task.'

'Could help though,' said Holm miserably.

Sleekit smiled.

'Yes, you could! The others will not be so well guarded this terrible night. There might be a chance for them. Soon you can leave me, go back to the tunnel into the garrison and wait your chance, for a mole there might need guidance.'

Holm perked up.

'But first,' she whispered, 'guide me into the tunnel the Master has taken Henbane down. We need a route by which we can escape. Will you do that?'

Holm nodded.

'Stay here, don't move, I'll come back,' he said. And soon he was, grubbier than ever.

'Found one.'

Then, secret as water in the night, he led her upslope above the tunnels and then through faults and solution crevices in the limestone and so into the tunnels below.

Mallice was near pupping when Lucerne and the others reached her, and the guardmole there was much concerned.

'Dismissed,' said Lucerne quickly. He wanted moles loyal to him alone here now.

'Yes, *Sir*!' said the guardmole, and scrabbled to get away.

Lucerne turned to Mallice and said pitilessly, 'You needed company, my dear, and now you have it. This is the Mistress Henbane, and this her daughter, my sister, Harebell. Near pupping too, it seems! Well, well, and what shall we all do? I'll tell you what you'll do, and I'll tell you once only. But first I'll tell you why.

'Sweet Mallice here, whose very life I once saved – remember, mother? I'm sure you do – Mallice carries bastards in her womb and now they struggle to get out.'

He held up a paw to stop Mallice's whimpering her feeble protest as she screamed out a contraction again.

'Harebell too will soon start pupping and I intend to leave. She, like me, is too young to remember it, but mother does. We were made separate at birth, and I was reared and groomed in Whern for the Mastership. She I know not as a sister, but as a rival she . . . exists. That will not do.

'But now I need an heir. I thought Mallice would provide and so she might, if the Word allows it. The pups she carries might well be mine. Who knows? She does not, nor I. Nor the mole Weld who is at this moment cast down into the Lower Sumps of Cannock.'

He turned to Harebell as Mallice screamed again.

'Where, you may like to know, certain other moles are kept. Poor Betony for one, mindless now. Wharfe, for another, our dear brother. Yes, yes, he is there, forgotten, dying slow.

'Now you, Harebell. . . .'

Harebell gasped with coming pain, and turned to Henbane in horror at what she heard, and at the coldness she saw. Henbane stared out rejection and contempt at her son. Harebell gasped again.

'Males are not wanted here, Terce, so we shall go, but for safety's sake these guardmoles can remain. Know only this. I want to see none of you alive again, not one. But your pups, well, that's a different thing. One will do. Yes, one. Guardmoles, bring the last surviving pup to me. He, or she, shall be the one. The Word shall judge which one is best. If Mallice's, why, then the Word surely intends me to know that the pups she carries were mine after all. If Harebell's, then at least they are my kin. One will do. As for you, my mother dear, you have been dead to me for many moleyears past, and you are dead still.

'Terce? No comment? We'll leave it to the Word and a mother's love to decide. One only of you all shall survive, and that a pup. Sort it out between yourselves. Now we shall go, and you guardmoles shall kill anymole that tries to escape. And when the pupping is done let these females decide among themselves which is to survive.

'Questions?'

The guardmoles frowned and shook their heads. Talking was not necessary.

'Come Terce, let us leave the future to forces greater than ourselves.'

With one last look at Mallice, who was now in a corner of the unpleasant chamber and breathing fast and ever faster, Terce turned and left. Lucerne smiled, the madness of evil on his face, and followed.

The guardmoles raised their talons, and forced Henbane and the weeping Harebell fully into the chamber.

'Get on with it, you bitches,' the senior guardmole growled.

Some of this – enough – Sleekit and Holm had heard in the shadows of the tunnel Holm had found. They had frozen where they stanced when the dismissed guardmole had gone by, and then again when Terce and Lucerne left.

'You will wait here until I come back, and guide anymole with me out of this place. Then you must go as you promised,' breathed Sleekit.

Holm stared at her.

'When I go home, and if I see Mayweed, what shall I say to him from you?' he whispered.

She smiled, tears in her eyes.

'My dear, I think I know where my Mayweed will be and that I shall see him there before you do. But if you find him before me, you shall know what to say on my behalf! Now, I must go, and when your chance comes, as it will, take it knowing the Stone is with you. And then get yourself back to Lorren as quickly as you can!'

'Bitches!' muttered the guardmole again, and Sleekit prepared herself for the bloody hours soon to come.

There are times when anymole, even a Chronicler devoted to the truth, hesitates to scribe, still less to speak. He turns from the evidence in grim despair, tears in his eyes; he turns back to it and tries again but cannot; he ventures to the surface and seeks comfort in the trees and in the skies, but sees them not, for the shameful images of what he knows fills his mind and sickens his heart.

Nor is there consolation in knowing that even worse horrors than what happened at Lucerne's command in Mallice's birth burrow that night have happened elsewhere, and are recorded. No doubt they have. But what he knows is here and now, and that is quite enough.

Of what happened that night this Chronicler has scribed, and then been forced to scratch his talons across it all. Horror happened there. Pups were pupped to die.

Mothers defended their own to the very death. Darkness was red with blood. Mewings started and then died. Seven pups born and Henbane and Harebell forced to defend half of them. Half? Three and a half is half of seven, and this much we can say: if it had come to ripping into two the one who survived the others then had they had the chance Mallice and Harebell would have done it. Aye, mole, it would have come to that and was beginning to when the guardmoles intervened. Their task was to see that one pup alone survived and nomole else. They turned on Harebell and then on Mallice, both already weak from pupping and from wounds the other had inflicted. It was in that moment of murder Henbane took up the one surviving pup.

Whose was that pup?

Perhaps one day your Chronicler will know.

'The bitches have decided, give it to us,' they said to Henbane, reluctant to go for her lest the pup was hurt.

'*No!*'

It was then, with Henbane's terrible cry, that Sleekit came out of the dark behind the grikes.

The only one there who had never had young, fighting as if all the world were her own pups.

'*No!*' she cried as well.

Fighting with all the life she had.

Fighting for the life of the pup she saw was left and Henbane held.

The scene she saw she had lived and heard a thousand times in the minutes that preceded it. Mallice dead; Harebell dead. Pups all . . . but of that we cannot bring ourselves to speak.

Henbane, potent, dangerous, stancing with the solitary pup that was left and shouting that great '*No!*' at those males who loomed angrily over her, demanding the pup of her before they killed her.

'*No! It is not thine to take from me. It is my kin and it shall live!*'

That was the scene that Sleekit routed.

And then those guardmoles found they faced not two females in disarray but two as one, defending a solitary pup. They might as well have faced an army as face that!

No training could have prepared a mole for the force that Sleekit was. No courage could have bettered the courage that Henbane had.

So Sleekit came and violently taloned one guardmole to one side, and then she and Henbane taloned at the other.

'Take it, Henbane, take it now and run!'

So Sleekit cried and so Henbane did, taking the pup up by the neck and running from that burrow of blood; and Sleekit followed her. Their advantage was not much, but it was enough to give Sleekit hope that Henbane and the pup might be got away.

'Run, Henbane! *Run!* When you see Holm, follow him and look not back. Oh run. . . .'

Desperate, panting, the grikes now close behind and angrier than storms, Sleekit ran and urged Henbane on. Ahead, a shadow. The shadow moved, had eyes, saw, and heard. Holm was ready there.

'Go, Holm, lead her, take her to safety now. *Go!*'

Then Holm turned and Henbane followed, but then turned briefly back as if hesitating at the final moment of escape.

'You gave me your pups once and gave me life,' gasped Sleekit, 'now take this for yourself, Henbane, and give back to it what you once lost! Oh, run!'

Then Sleekit turned and as the two great guardmoles bore down upon her, she gathered all her strength and, raising her talons, launched back at them as she had done before, striking, and striking more, taloning, her strength, her speed, her instinct quite beyond their ken.

'*No!*' she cried, and even as they struck mortally, she had the sense and strength to retreat into that tunnel, to block it, to hold them off still more.

'*No!*' she cried again more quietly now.

Yet the last words that she spoke were not 'No!' or 'Run!' but gentle, and to a mole she had once known, and knew that when the Stone willed it, she would know again. 'Mayweed . . .' was the last she spoke.

But Henbane had never felt so alive as she did then. She ran out into the night where Holm had led her and quickly laid the pup down and stared at him.

'What did Sleekit say to thee?'

'She said I must not fight.' Holm stared at Henbane who looked wild and dangerous and loomed over the pup as if she felt the whole of moledom endangered it, even him.

'Leave me now, Holm. Make your own way from here, for what I must do I had better do alone. I thank you, Holm, and one day this pup I bear shall be told your name and he shall honour it. Now go, and look not afraid for you are as brave as anymole I ever knew.'

'Not Tryfan,' said Holm.

Henbane almost smiled.

'Not *him*, perhaps!' said Holm, looking at the pup that lay between her paws.

'Him. . . ?' she said staring at the pup. Her voice was a mother's voice, gentle and concerned.

Holm saw her take the pup from off the ground, saw it dangle in the night, saw her look to right and left.

'Up's best,' he said, 'then east.'

He watched her off to safety in the dark, and then turned and stared downslope and sighed, indeed he almost bleated with distress. He shook his head. He stared some more. He opened his mouth and closed it. He listened, and he swallowed, and he blinked in the dark.

Downslope below him at the tunnel entrance to where Mallice had been captive he could hear angry guardmole shouts. In the ground beneath his paws he could feel the vibration of moles in tunnels, big moles.

He slipped downslope in the dark as the most senior of the guardmoles emerged where Henbane and he had come.

'Here!' Holm dared to cry . . . And drawing the guardmoles away from where Henbane had gone, he darted among the shadows of rocks and scrub until, familiar with the ground, he left the guardmoles utterly confused, and made his way back into the grubby tunnel that led down to the garrison.

There, breathing heavily, he stopped and watched and before long his patience was rewarded.

'Quick, out you lot!' a guardmole shouted down the gloomy main tunnel.

'But Sir, there's nomole else on guard.'

Running paws, a hurried conference beneath where Holm watched down.

'There's trouble where they kept that Mallice bitch. The Master's *mad*. He wants us out and searching for the Mistress Henbane who's escaped.'

'*She* won't get far. But what about the ones in here? There's nomole to cover for me.'

'Threaten them. Tell them that if one so much as moves they'll all be killed. We'll not be long. Get on with it!'

He did, and Holm heard him snarl a warning to the captives there and then come on out again, and set off for the hunt.

Holm waited until he had gone, scrambled down with some difficulty from the narrow ledge where his fissured tunnel came, and hurried quickly to where the captives must be.

He found them cowering in a corner of their chamber, and felt scared himself just seeing them.

'Come!' he said. 'Quick, quick!'

Two of the three shook their heads.

'Please!' he begged. 'It's safe for now.'

'He's Holm, the mole who came with Harebell,' said Quince. 'He's all right.'

Holm stared and they stared, looking petrified.

'They'll kill us if we move,' said one.

'Come *on!*' pleaded Holm. Then turning to Quince he said, 'Make them, Miss!'

But she could not, and they would not and uselessly stared and trembled, and kept their snouts all low.

'You come then,' said Holm firmly to Quince.

Then he turned and ran and Quince, with a final look of despair at the trembling females, followed him.

As they went they heard the pawsteps of a mole coming towards them and Holm ran faster, gasping with fear as he hurried to get back to his point of entry into the tunnel. Quince, who was bigger than him, ran at his flank.

'Here!' said Holm triumphantly pointing up at the ledge he had scrambled down from. But his triumph faded, for try as he might he could not quite reach up to it, and the limestone walls which had been easy enough to scramble down were too slippery and awkward to climb up again.

In any case, it was too late, for round the corner came a guardmole.

'What the. . . ?' he shouted angrily when he saw them.

Holm gulped.

'Luck's run *very* out,' he said.

'Stay where you are and don't move,' said Quince of Mallerstang, an adept of an ancient martial art, very quietly. She went a pace forward and, as it seemed to Holm, leapt upward, turned slowly in the air and merely touched the guardmole on the flank with her paw. The guardmole fell back as if a hillside had hit him.

'What's. . . ?' he began.

Quince struck him but once more and Holm could see the surprise in his eyes as he turned, fell back, smashed against the opposite side of the tunnel and slumped, unconscious for all Holm knew, upon the ground.

'Oh dear,' said Holm. More pawsteps were coming down the tunnel.

'Is that the way you came in?' said Quince, pointing a talon at the fissure out of Holm's reach.

Holm nodded bleakly, and was still nodding as he felt a paw thrust under his rear and he was lifted bodily up and found himself scrabbling into the tunnel.

'Pull me up,' ordered Quince from below.

Holm turned round, peered down, and saw a paw reaching up to him.

'Quick,' said Quince.

The pawsteps were getting nearer, and across the tunnel the guardmole was beginning to stir and mutter darkly to himself.

Holm grabbed the paw and tried to pull Quince up.

'You're big, I'm small,' he said hopelessly.

'Imagine I'm something you want,' said Quince.

Holm grabbed her paw tighter, closed his eyes, and with a mighty shout of, 'Lorren!' heaved Quince up and with a scraping of her back paws and another heave from Holm she was into the tunnel as well and they were gone.

Lucerne liked it not, not at all. He liked it so little that by dawn, and once he had got what information he could from the two senior guardmoles to whom he had entrusted the culling of the pups, he had them both snouted on the spot for failing him.

Then, when it was discovered that the mole Quince had escaped as well as Henbane and the pup, he had two more of the garrison guardmoles killed. So mad with anger was he that had he had the means he might have had everymole in the place killed there and then.

How much *Terce* liked it not was hard to say since when he was taken by Lucerne to see Mallice dead, and Harebell, and their pups all mingled, he said nothing, but stared and blinked. His daughter dead and a father blinks! For such is the training of a Twelfth Keeper!

'Well?' hissed Lucerne. 'Henbane gone and with the one surviving pup. The Word speaks strange in this.'

'Yes, Master,' said Terce cautiously.

'To find her myself . . . or to send others out for her. Which? There is much to do just now in moledom, much to consolidate. I have not time to find her, Terce. You warned that the Stone Mole might become a martyr, and so he might. We must stop that soon.'

But Terce was thinking, and nor was he so sure.

825

'The pup that survived, Master, it might be thine,' he said slowly. 'If it is the mole Harebell's, then it is still thy kin and a potential threat to us. All the more so in the apostate paws of Henbane.'

Terce watched the seed he planted take root and as he did so he mused upon the supreme power of the Word. With what elegance it was using Henbane to lead Lucerne towards the darkness of divinity! He, Terce, was but the guide along the way.

'She will not kill the pup, Terce,' said Lucerne. 'She shall fawn and fondle it, as once she fondled me. She must be found and then the pup will be mine to train.'

'I agree, and it must not be long, Master, before we take her lest she trains the pup to become your enemy. She is a Mistress of such arts. No, I should have pressed you harder to find Henbane when she first fled Whern. Nomole in moledom has greater powers than she, nomole but yourself. Worse by far is the undermining of your authority by the fact of Henbane's existence, not forgetting that of the pup's. This will be known, for rumours spread upon the wind of discontent, and discontent there always is where power is fragmented. Master, you must seek Henbane out, you and only you must kill her.'

The rooted seed thrived in the fomenting soil of Lucerne's jealousy.

'I saw her smile on the mole Harebell,' he said, 'and that troubles me. For that alone I will kill her.'

'Master, you must do it.'

'And who shall bear witness of it in moledom? How shall the memory of her be corrupted and its effect neutralised?'

'I shall be with you. I, Terce, thy tutor and Twelfth Keeper shall bear witness for thee to the Keepers and sideem. By powers great shall you kill her, powers . . . divine.'

'Divine,' whispered Lucerne, eyes narrowed with bitter ambition. 'I shall suck her power to me as once I sucked her milk.'

'It is thy right,' said Terce. 'Her death shall be a fitting seal upon thy ascendancy to divine power.'

Lucerne's eyes glittered.

'It might be so,' he conceded, and the rooted seed now began to flourish well. 'I must find her, Terce. I *must* find her.'

'Master, you must, and since the Word guides you, you shall. Nothing is more important to you now.'

'And you, Terce? And Mallice? Can you forgive me that?'

'She betrayed us, Master, and the Word. She is nothing to me.'

'But her pup, if so the one Henbane took proves to be, what then?'

Terce permitted himself a smile.

'Then I shall be . . . pleased, Master.'

'And I, Twelfth Keeper, pleased for us both. It shall bind us again, and take this chill between us quite away. I like that not.'

'Nor I, Master.'

'Come, let us use our powers to find the former Mistress Henbane.'

He turned away, not seeing that behind him Terce's eyes were black barbs of hate.

Chapter Thirty-Seven

If a mole would know why it is that beauty and comeliness can sometimes fade so fast in moles as the years go by, let them seek the answer in the opposite: why is it that some moles start life plain, and end it beautiful?

The answer is that true beauty is but slowly made, and rarely quickly born. While in the corrupted mole beauty is soon lost.

Through the many molemonths of early summer that followed the Stone Mole's barbing at Beechenhill, and Henbane's escape with an unnamed pup from a burrow of death in the Manifold Valley, Lucerne of Whern lost those looks that once made moles call *him* beautiful.

Perhaps they were lost in that single bloody night when, on his sole orders, Mallice and Harebell were slain. But more likely, the canker of the Word had long been eating at the inner spirit he might have had, and finally erupted into his eyes and the set of his mouth in those strange obsessional weeks and months when he set off in search of Henbane.

No, he was not beautiful, nor even comely now. Handsome perhaps, powerful certainly, but where once moles warmed to him, and were charmed by the smile he gave, now they were afraid. Small wrinkles of age were on his face, and lines of loneliness, and the acid etchings of a cold, cruel heart whose only love is self. His fur still had its gloss, his talons their shine, his eyes their glitter, but all this dark light was confined now to a body in which something had begun to die.

This was the mole who roamed the valleys and moors around Beechenhill in an endless search for Henbane, knowing that every day that passed was another day lost when that growing stolen pup might have been reared unto his own will.

'I must find them, Terce, I must!' was nearly all he said.

While moledom and the Word's hegemony, and the many matters that the sideem were demanding must be resolved, were left undone, half done or, even worse, when he gave them time, badly done.

Clowder could get no sense from anymole and began to go his own way unrestrained.

Ginnell gave up trying to get sense from Cannock, and began a venture in the southern Marches.

Cannock, under Slighe, became slow and over-cautious, and sideem who came there waited for weeks and months on end for answers that never came.

Not that the Word did not seem ascendant. Had not the strikes on the followers succeeded? Were not systems like Beechenhill and Rollright now laid waste of followers, and able to be garrisoned by a mere pawful of guardmoles? They were.

Yet whispers were abroad, whispers heard by guard-moles as well as the seeming few followers who survived. Whispers that the Stone Mole had died, yet now lived again.

Aye, the Word made impotent.

'Master, I beg you to hear these reports,' one brave sideem said, who had risked his snout by venturing north to the obscure place where the Master was lurking believing that the Mistress Henbane was nearby.

'I have heard more reports than you have eaten worms,' was the Master's sane reply. Except his look was not sane, the look that peered and darted here and there, and made him say, 'And did you see an old female and a pup, or youngster now, on your way to me?'

'No, Master, I did not, but these rumours of the Stone Mole are getting dangerous now, and. . . .'

'*Now get out!*' the Master cried in rage. '*Get out!* And you as well, Terce, if you cannot help me here!'

In such a situation the Twelfth Keeper was a marvel, considering his age; so tolerant of the Master, so skilled at knowing what to do, so essential now. By creating such impressions Terce now enhanced his reputation, and undermined Lucerne's, and so moved towards the completion of the scheme whose purpose, though not its detail, Rune had long since devised.

Yet where was Henbane? The search, Terce knew, might yet go on too long.

'Master, we can deal with these trifling reports which the sideem bring even as we draw near to the end of our search,' said Terce.

This phrase 'near to the end of our search' was one much used to and by Lucerne in those long molemonths. It seemed to give him encouragement.

'Yes, yes,' said Lucerne absently, 'see to it, Terce. Do what is best. Now . . . any news today?'

'None yet, Master, but more moles are due back soon.'

The system that Lucerne had obsessionally devised to uncover Henbane and the pup was this: a team of guardmoles, organised by Lucerne personally, were searching every valley in all directions from where Henbane had escaped and interrogating anymole they came across for information that might lead to the discovery of the fugitives.

These contacts produced many blanks, the discovery of a number of *other* fugitives (duly punished) and a large number of false leads which were the result, in Terce's view, of moles trying to get the interrogators off their backs.

For a time the upper Manifold had looked most promising; then the pursuit switched across the fells to Tissington where, it was discovered (and correctly too), that Henbane had lived secretly for a time, and, claimed a mole, had been seen there a few days after 'Beechenhill', as moles now called that grim incident.

This took the best part of April. In May, a positive sighting came from the Dark Peak. No doubt of it: Henbane had been seen up wormless Grindsbrook Clough below Kinder Scout. To there, with some reluctance, they had gone, and when they reached it a mole with a pup was there all right, except she was not Henbane, and the mole the local guardmole had been keeping such a careful eye on proved to be a vagrant with a lost pup she had found nearby.

Terce might almost have felt pity for Lucerne, for he seemed broken by the disappointment – a response made more extreme by the relative proximity of Whern, and all it represented to the Master of the Word.

'Whern is where we would have gone, Twelfth Keeper, where Mallice and I would be now, if . . .' He stared bleakly across the Dark Peak and said no more.

But then the urge to find Henbane returned, and the hope that she was north of Kinder Scout – a hope, because it would have taken Lucerne nearer to Whern – was dashed by a report that she had been seen down near Beechenhill again, so back they went.

May brought a pleasant summer, but Lucerne enjoyed little of it. While Terce, beginning now to think they would not find their quarry Lucerne's way, tried something else.

One day in June, one of the guardmoles routinely brought a follower in and Terce thought to ask him this: 'As a fugitive with young, where would you hide?'

The follower, intimidated and scared, and hoping for his freedom back, saw no harm in answering.

'I'd seek the protection of a Stone, especially if I had young I wanted to teach matters of the Stone to. That's what I'd do, Sir.'

'Then, mole, in exchange for your freedom from our custody I want you to tell me the names of all the places where Stones are in the area around Beechenhill for a distance of . . .' And Terce named a distance beyond which it seemed unlikely Henbane could have gone with a young pup.

'Don't know them all, but I know some at least.'

Terce scrivened down the names, and added others as more followers were interrogated and then, without a word to the Master, he devised a scheme by which guardmoles set off to report on each of the Stone sites on the list.

It soon became plain that until then the guardmoles had been avoiding such sites. 'Hadn't thought of them,' they claimed. Afraid of them, Terce thought. The venture soon threw up a disturbing fact: followers were thicker on the ground where the grikes looked least for them. There was hope yet of finding Henbane.

The names meant little to Terce, but one by one the reports came back. No sign of Henbane or her pup.

No sign.

Forgive me, Twelfth Keeper, but no sign again.

Until Terce began finally to despair.

Until a day in mid-June when a guardmole arrived.

'Guardmole?'

'Twelfth Keeper, I have news.'

'Henbane?'

'It is certain.'

'And her pup?'

'Him too.'

'You know he is a male?'

'I saw him myself.'

'Is she guarded?'

The guardmole shook his head.

'Not in this place, Twelfth Keeper. I felt it best to go by myself. Thought that if I was her I'd find a place and lie low. I think that's what she's done, and been there all this time. She did not see me at all. But at night, when she came out, I saw her well enough.'

'And?'

'She is old, Twelfth Keeper. Old and slow. She'll be no trouble.'

'The pup?'

'The youngster, now! He's well enough. Stays close by her, closer than a shadow. Not dangerous.'

'Is this place far?'

'Not far.'

'Have you told any other mole?'

'None, Twelfth Keeper.'

'It is well. Tell me the place. Whisper it. In my old age I grow suspicious.'

The guardmole whispered.

'You are sure?' said Terce.

'Certain.'

'I sometimes think that if there was another false report the Master would go mad.'

'I have heard . . .' The guardmole stopped himself.

'Rumours? Speak freely, I shall not harm you.'

'That the Master is . . . unwell. Without him in command we are adrift, Twelfth Keeper.'

'Well, mole, this news may change all that. I shall inform him, and we shall leave as soon as he is ready.'

Terce found Lucerne, who was on the surface and staring.

'Have you news, Terce? I need news.'

'Master. . . .'

'You have! I see it in your eye. You have!'

'Master, I think there is a chance.'

'Where is the bitch?'

'She is at a place called Arbor Low.'

Henbane's flight to the fell above the Manifold might have been encumbered by the mouthful of pup she was carrying but, rather, it was driven by it, as if this limp frail life gave sustenance to her.

Certainly it gave her purpose, just as Lucerne's birth so many years before had. But that was dark purpose, this was light. This was a last opportunity to give life back something good and sweet, to save life, to make it right. This pup she carried might be the very making and resurrection of her flawed life.

She had run as Holm directed her up the slope and across the rising fells to the east. Her mind was only on escape and survival, and so she did not think yet of the horrors she had seen, though perhaps unconscious thoughts of them drove her on as well to escape the place she saw her lovely daughter, and those pups, crushed and killed.

Grike guardmoles followed her, closer than she ever knew, and forced her sometimes to stop and hide in shadow, stancing over the pup. To keep it warm for one thing. And to be ready to fight with all the strength she had, to the death if need be, to protect it.

Through the night she travelled until, growing tired and fearful for the pup's safety – for the air was cold, the pup too limp for comfort – she sought safe shelter. She knew it must be somewhere secure and quiet, for the pup would not survive such travel for too long. She must feed it, warm it.

But that first night she found nowhere, and was forced to delve a temporary burrow and use heather for nesting material and dig out a worm or two. These she ate into a pulp, and mushed with spit, and fed as best she could into the pup's mouth. It seemed that it swallowed nothing, but only mewed and grew weak.

Yet in the morning there he was, curled in the circle of her warmth, pink-grey, his eyes closed, his tiny bones and sinews visible through his nearly transparent skin; suddenly beautiful to her. Her own to nurture the very best she could.

Her spit, with a touch of worm, was still all she had to give, and this she did, judging it best to lie still and keep him warm. Only once she left him, and that briefly to gather worms for them both. She bit their heads to keep the worms from straying far.

Grikes came near, the pup mewed when he should not have done. She huddled in the burrow, and nomole heard them.

But the place was not ideal, and the soil was wet. Not a place to bring up young! She knew she must soon move on. The pup was living at least, though pathetic in his desire for milk and questing at her empty teats.

'I can't suckle you, my dear. I am too old,' she said. Then more spit and worm she gave, and it had to do.

Four days she was there and then when a warm day came she journeyed on, praying to that greater thing, which she refused to call either Word or Stone, that she would be guided well.

Going east, as Holm had said, had served her well at first but now proved slow and arduous with pup in mouth, and so when she came upon a rough stony way – for roaring owl, perhaps, for it had the distant smell of them – she turned north upon it. At its edge the worms were good, and that night, mercifully warm, she slept among the grass, and the way the pup nestled up to her almost made her weep he was so beautiful.

Despite the dangers all about, and what seemed the impossibility of the pup surviving, Henbane felt happy that night: the happiness moles feel when they have good purpose, and their bodies and their minds are stretched and tried and proving strong. The pup was alive, they were warm, the sky was good across the fell.

'You shall live, my dear, and find a happiness I shall never see or know you had. You shall live!'

The way she had found was straight and went on northward. She followed it the next day and it took her to a derelict twofoot place high on the fell where metal rusted and rattled in the wind, and great tunnels were delved into the slopes. The twofoots seemed all gone.

She looked about, she pondered, she found worms aplenty, and water, and no moles at all.

'This might do,' she said, speaking to the pup who lay flat upon the ground, his paws spread out and struggling to make sense of themselves and the body to which they were attached, his mouth mewing and questing once again.

She picked him up and took him into the echoing tunnels there, huge places, tall and regularly arched, all made by twofoots. They were larger than most of the tunnels of Whern, and seemed to lead a long way into the hillside.

But Henbane did not explore that far, for the air was

cold inside and dank, and the ground wet and filled with puddles. There were several of these tunnels and she chose to stay near the one whose entrance faced south and would catch the sun.

Here, in contrast to the fells over which they had come, the ground had been openly delved long since, and a rich variety of plants had come. The rough ground before it was already covered in creeping stonecrop, and where brambles ran there were violets and some primrose. On the sunny banks were all manner of things – tormentil, sweet woodruff and lower down the spread leaves of herb robert whose flowers had not yet come.

It was a gentle spot, a safe spot, and there was evidence of only vole to disturb them. Before them, in an area long since churned flat by roaring owls, the ground was waterlogged and not a place a mole would happily cross. While behind them the banks of the place rose steep and they could not be easily attacked.

'Besieged, perhaps, my dear, but not attacked. There's the tunnel to escape into, and places in there to hide I'm sure, and plenty of worms hereabout. A good enough place for us.'

She made tunnels into the bank, using some old vole ways and even, in one place, a broken rabbit burrow. It was rough but obscure and good, and to find it a mole would have to have come a long way looking.

'It feels safe here,' she told him, speaking to him as if he understood. It was here, a few days after they arrived, that his eyes opened and it seemed to her they were the most beautiful she had ever seen.

'You *are* beautiful,' she whispered to him, 'the most beautiful mole that ever was!' He supped her spit and worm, and soon after his eyes opened he began to crunch in a feeble way at the parts of unchewed worm she gave him.

'You will survive, my dear, you will, and so I must find a name for you.'

For days she pondered it, speaking out all the names she

knew, and some she made up, and wondering if they suited him. Tryfan, she tried, of course. And Bracken, too. Even Mayweed of whom Sleekit had spoken, and Wharfe, and *all* the names she knew.

Then one day, the pup well fed and wandering gently here and there and then running back to her, she lay in the sudden warm sun that comes sometimes in May and marks the first of many summer days. Her snout was along her paws, her eyes were closed, the pup was busy, and her snout twitched and scented the small pleasurable scents of spring.

The very pleasant scents; the *sweet* scents.

She opened her eyes, peered to her side and saw that the woodruff was out, its petals white and fragrant, and beneath it the pup snouted up as well, as if he too scented it.

'Sweet woodruff,' she sighed, remembering a time when she was young and her mother Charlock had left her alone and she too had scented at such flowers and her mother had not known their name. It was one of the few happy memories she had.

'Sweet woodruff,' she said once more, and then, looking at the pup, she knew his name at last: 'Woodruff, that's what it must be.' She watched him with great pleasure, and when he came near she encircled him in her paws and whispered again and again, 'Woodruff,' until his darkening cheeks wrinkled, his growing paws scrabbled and he struggled free and went to the puddle's edge and surveyed it as if it was a mighty lake.

That place was where Woodruff's puphood passed, and where he first spoke words, and learnt that tunnels have echoes, and rain hurts when it falls hard, and live beetles are near impossible to catch, and adults are warm things to run to when things hurt.

That place, it might be said, was where Henbane grew young again, as she tried to give Woodruff a puphood and security she never had herself.

In that place they saw the weather warm, and the puddle that had been Woodruff's lake, in which he learnt to play, turn dry. There they saw the brambles flower, there Woodruff watched his first bumble bee; and there, one never-forgotten evening, they watched a fox pass through.

Grikes came twice, and once quite close, but so careful had Henbane been about not leaving signs, so marginal did the little place they lived seem, that they were not found. The first time was when Woodruff was too young to care, but the second was more fraught. . . .

'There's two moles here,' was the simple and chilling way he announced their arrival. He had been playing out in the open when suddenly he had seen them and dashed back to her.

She had grabbed him and pressed him in among the grass and stared around and saw them over by one of the twofoot tunnel entrances. They were great dark guard-moles with thick talons and heavy snouts who snuffled and peered about the place, and then moved nearer where they lay.

Henbane and Woodruff watched them, absolutely still, the youngster's eyes wide with fear. The guardmoles laughed deeply and tussled with one another and their strength was obvious and unlike anything he had ever seen before.

Then they turned and came straight towards them, and Woodruff felt Henbane tensing ready to fight and she whispered, 'If they come you must run, run anywhere.'

For the first time he had realised it was possible that one day he might lose her, and he was still as death.

But the guardmoles stopped, were distracted by rock and water sounds down in the nearer twofoot tunnel, and after an interminable wait in which they shuffled and peered here and there, they turned and left.

There was nothing Henbane could do to stop the nightmares that came after that but be there and offer comfort. The image of the grikes stayed with the young mole, and he lost a little confidence and stayed close to her for days. Woodruff had discovered fear, and it did not easily leave him.

It was some time then, in the molemonths of early May, in an effort to combat this first and seemingly disastrous sight of other moles, that Henbane decided to tell him stories of the real moles and moledom that she had known.

'Other moles have siblings, and neighbours, fathers and all sorts of moles,' she said 'and there are. . . .'

'And big moles,' he said.

'Yes, there are some of those. . . .'

'Who are not nice. . . .'

'Some of them aren't, but most of them are, my dear. Your grandfather Tryfan, for example, was a big mole, much bigger than the ones who came here, and he was not one to hurt others at all even though he could have done if he wanted.'

'What did he look like? What did he do?'

Woodruff saw Henbane's eyes soften, he heard her voice go gentle, he felt her paw reach out to him, and he was lost in the tale she told and began to learn about moles other than grikes.

In this way, as the summer days passed by, Henbane discovered in herself stories that she barely knew she knew, and gave them willingly to Woodruff, as if to make up for the family and life his puphood and youth did not have.

At first these tales were light and simple things, but gradually, as the moleweeks and months went by and Woodruff grew a little older, her tales became more fulsome, richer, and told of the light and dark that had been Henbane's life.

In the telling of them her old passion returned, she seemed to live the characters she portrayed for him and in but a few words could turn the twofoot tunnel that loomed nearby into the darkest parts of Whern; and transform the pretty bank in which they lived into the warmest, quietest glade in Duncton Wood.

It was perhaps inevitable that in this world she made for Woodruff, Whern should be the dark place and Duncton the place of light. Inevitable that names like Scirpus and Rune, Weed and Charlock should be names he was made to doubt and fear, while others, like Tryfan and Spindle and a few of the Duncton moles she remembered Tryfan telling her about – Comfrey was one, old Maundy another –became in the world she made for him moles to whom in imagination he ran and found love and safety.

A few there were who were not so dark or light as these – moles like Wrekin, her commander in the south, and others that she knew.

But there was one whose role in the stories that she told evolved and changed as those precious, loving, mole-months went by, and that was Boswell, whom she had known in Whern, and observed.

'Is Boswell in this one?' the youngster would ask eagerly as she began a new tale, for he always liked a tale that ended (if it had not begun) with some account of the old White Mole who limped and had gentle eyes, and who, though often impatient, was always there and would always be.

'Yes, my love, I think somehow he'll be in this one today. . . ' she would say. Or, sometimes, just to be mischievous, 'I don't think he is, but you never know with Boswell, do you?'

'No!' Woodruff would say excitedly. Adding a little later, as the tale drew ominously near its close *without* Boswell having made an appearance, 'He will be there, won't he? At the end?'

How Henbane loved her Woodruff then, and how impossible for her imagination to deny him the appearance of that strange White Mole of whom her own memory was so strong.

Had she not herself taken him into custody at Uffington? Had she not, through him, begun to discover that slow and painful yet infinitely rich other way of being which her rearing in the Word so long denied her: the way

840

of truth? Had not knowledge of him at Providence Fall in Whern, where her father kept him, made her heart open to the love that Tryfan finally brought?

How then could she deny Woodruff the gift that Boswell gave her? Boswell was part of her history, part of what she was.

In this way, and barely knowing what she did, Henbane gave to Woodruff the father that life itself had denied him, and as time went by she found that in the games that Woodruff played with the characters she described, Boswell was the arbiter and final recourse when all seemed confused, all lost; all still to be found. Boswell was the strength and safety in his world.

As Woodruff had begun to mature, he would come and ask Henbane to tell him a story she had told before and as it unfolded once again would ask for details she had not previously given.

How high were the highest tunnels of Whern? Is a White Mole's fur really white? What were the names of Bracken's siblings? (She remembered Tryfan naming only one of them.) How far is Uffington from Duncton Wood? What sound does a mole make when he dies?

Darkness came to the questions, and sometimes prurience, and sometimes mere morbid curiosity. But most of all there was what Henbane came to see as a kind of determination for detail, for fact, for knowing that one thing which nomole can ever know – *all* that had happened.

Of the Word and the Stone Henbane naturally had to talk, but feeling absolute trust in neither, she did not make him believe in one against the other. The tales she told, the facts she gave, surely revealed as much to him of the Word and of scrivening as they did of the Stone and scribing.

Yet it was of scrivening that one day she began to teach him, since that was her better art; and of the rituals and rites of the Word in Whern he inevitably knew more than of the Stone, since she knew more of them herself.

Yet again and again she would say, 'I cannot tell you all I

would like since I do not know it, and you must do as other moles do and seek out the answers for yourself. You must do it in what I heard the Stone Mole describe as a warrior-like way, but if you ask me what that is I can only tell you to remember all I have told you of Tryfan, for he was surely a warrior among moles.'

When June came and after much persuasion on his part (and despite her fears), she agreed to take him out from the place they had hidden in for so long and on to the fells. For him that climb up through heather and grass towards the sky was the beginning of an exploration of moledom that could never stop; for her it was the discovery that she had aged, and was slow, and her balance was not what it had been.

It was he who turned them back, he who slowed for her, he who helped her down the final slopes. She knew then that her days with him were numbered now, and that one last thing she might do was take him on his first real journey into moledom.

By now his fur was thickening fast, and his body was sturdy. He was not as large as Tryfan had been but strong enough, with well-made paws. His eyes were good, yet cautious too, as if he knew there were dangers in the world; his look was a little earnest.

'Where shall we go?' he asked with all the eagerness and innocence of youth when she told him what she had decided.

'Somewhere not *too* far to be daunting, but not so near that we will not have adventures on the way,' she said. 'You'll learn much and we may meet other moles.'

'But *where?*'

She pondered it for several days before she decided.

'Did I ever tell you about my journey south from Whern?'

'The first or second time?' he asked. 'When you were leading the moles of the Word south, or when you were fleeing from Lucerne?'

'It was both times, really. Wrekin showed me a place

that first time which was a haven to me on the second, much as this place has been. I think I would like to go there now. I wonder why I have never mentioned it to you.'

He looked at her and settled down for what sounded like the beginning of a tale, but she shook her head and said, 'Woodruff, I think our time for tales is over now. We must go from here and you must begin learning about moledom as it really is. This journey shall be the start of that.'

His brow furrowed.

'It's because you felt old when we went on the fell, isn't it?'

She nodded and sighed.

'I shall have to let you go one day, my love. Before I do I want to share a journey with you so that you remember me in a different way than . . . this!' She waved a paw around at the place that had been their only home and suddenly it seemed small and inconsequential to her. It was certainly time to go.

'What's the name of the place we're going to?' he asked.

'It's a place called Arbor Low. It's a circle of white and fallen Stones. It's . . . a very ancient place, a good place for a mole to journey to. We'll set off early tomorrow.'

'Arbor Low,' he repeated, 'Arbor Low.'

That night he came to her and looked at her in a way she knew followed much thought and usually preceded a question he found difficult to ask,

'How did my mother die?'

He stared at her, resolute, and in one so young there was something so touching about his purposefulness that she almost wanted to weep.

She stared back at him, and she saw the blood and terror of Harebell's awful death. Her body tensed again, she saw pup after pup die, those of Mallice and those of Harebell, and she heard the screams and her eyes were fixed on one pup, instinctively cowering, the one she had protected, the mole that stanced before her now.

Henbane stared at memory and wept, and Woodruff stared at Henbane, still resolute.

'Why did she die?' he whispered.

Then Henbane knew what to say.

'My dear, when you have made the journey we will make, and seen at least a little of moledom, if you ask me that question again I shall answer it as truthfully as I can.'

'All right,' he said. And that, for now, was that.

Arbor Low lies north of Beechenhill and Tissington, on the way towards the Dark Peak. Some say that the north starts here, for after it the ground begins to rise, and worms grow scarce.

Many a legend attaches to the pale Stones of Arbor Low, which lie in a circle in pleasant rolling ground some way to the west of the deep valley of the Higher Dove. They are limestone, and all but one Stone on the western side of the circle lie flat and white, half buried in the pasture there.

Here, the scribemoles used to say, the powers of the scribemoles ended; and the influence, if not always the full power, of the Word began. To Henbane, whose heritage was of the Word, but whose heart had been stolen by the spirit if not the ritual of the Stone, it was a natural place to come.

The ground undulates hereabout, but round the fallen Stones themselves there is a bank of earth, quite steep in parts but flat and broken in the north, with a narrower, less distinct entrance to the south.

It was to here that Henbane brought Woodruff in early June, as evening fell and the flat sides of the fallen Stones caught the light of the sky and seemed like a circle of lights in the dusk across the ground. These were the first Stones the youngster had seen, and he was as excited as a mole could be to see and touch such Stones at last, after hearing so many descriptions and tales about them from Henbane.

Naturally it was the solitary one that was still upright in

the west that awed him most, and to a mole who had never seen a Stone before it was awesome indeed.

'Why are they all fallen but this one?' he asked.

'My mother Charlock told me that here a great scribe-mole of the past was defeated by one of the early Masters and the Stones lay flat. But this last one stayed upright against the day when the Stone prevails here once more and the Word begins to die.'

With such tales as these in his mind, Woodruff helped Henbane make a tunnel and burrows in Arbor Low, and though he was not yet as skilled as her, what he lacked in experience he made up for in enthusiasm. There were worms enough, and a few troublesome rooks that flew over from their roosts in the great stands of trees that rose on adjacent hills, the highest of which, Gib Hill, was across a shallow valley to the south-west.

There was no question but that Woodruff had matured on the journey they had made, and that Henbane had aged more. But of that journey they had much to share and talk about – the meeting with moles at Alstonefield, the attack of the tawny owl at Steep Low when Woodruff had raised his talons against another living creature for the first time, and found they worked! There had been the failure to cross the Dove at Wolfscotedale and the trek to the north to find a better crossing point. Much else besides, but grimmest of all the roaring owls at Parsley Hay that had nearly crushed them both before, finally, they came within sight of Gib Hill and Henbane knew they were nearly there.

They settled in quickly. The days were warm and slow and suited their mood of talking and quiet. Henbane needed help with finding worms now, and even climbing up the bank about the Stones was hard, and she did it only twice. She felt as if the last of her strength had gone on the journey to get there and she had no more, yet she was not sad or low. Each day it seemed to her that Woodruff grew more and she was glad, wishing each morning that came, 'One more day, give me one more day,' and when the sun set, she did not fail to thank whatever it was that held their destiny for the day just past.

The Stones were peaceful and Woodruff asked much about them, and what they meant. Nothing disturbed them except that one day Woodruff thought he saw a mole off down the western slopes. Dark and big, like those guardmoles he had seen when young.

'Which way was he going?' asked Henbane, worried.

'Away from here,' he said.

She frowned and said it was probably just a vagrant and there was nothing to worry about. But then, after all, what could they do? The hiding time was over, the living time begun and they must take their chances.

'Keep an eye out, my dear, that's all. Caution hurts nomole.'

It was now, as well, that he asked again about his mother's death and she told him all she remembered: with quiet passion and outrage, and often with tears on her face. A mole must know the truth, and as best she could she told Woodruff of it. Lucerne she talked about more than before, and Sleekit too, describing how her old friend and aide had defended her and gave them the chance to escape.

It was then, too, that Henbane first told Woodruff about Mayweed, for though she had never met him herself Sleekit had told her much in the short time they were together after they met again at Kniveton when the Stone Mole had spoken.

But it was Lucerne who seemed to shadow her thoughts, for he was kin of Woodruff, and of him the mole's questions were inexhaustible.

'So he had my mother killed?' said Woodruff at last.

'He wanted power over you – or whichever pup survived.'

'Are you sure I was Harebell's pup and not one of Mallice's?' he asked.

'I am sure,' she said.

'But it must have been so . . . terrible.'

She looked away. Distress at the memory? Or doubt? He dared not ask her more.

As for Henbane, she preferred to talk of something more positive. He was nearly mature, and Midsummer was near.

'When it comes, my love, I am going to ask for something that will be hard for both of us. I am going to ask you to leave.'

He said nothing. She had spoken of it before but he knew he could not leave. His world was her. Apart from her, there were only the names of those moles she had told him her tales of. Apart from her, there seemed nothing real at all.

'I would prefer to see you go as I see you now – young, strong, purposeful, excited.'

'Well I won't,' he said. 'How could you live alone?'

She smiled weakly. She could not live alone, yet she felt he was more than she deserved.

'And anyway, where would I go to? You're my home.'

'You'll have to go one day, my dear,' she said, 'and Midsummer is the traditional time. I wish I knew the words that Tryfan said the moles of Duncton Wood used at such a time.'

'Special words?'

'Ritual words, I think. Well, you'll find them out one day.'

'I'll find out lots of things,' he said. 'I'll go. . . .'

'Where will you go?'

'To the places you mentioned.'

'Some of them may be dangerous with grikes, and if moles ever know who you are your life will not be easy. Tell nomole who or what you are, Woodruff. Just say you came from Arbor Low.'

He looked at her, and saw her frailty, and was frightened of the future that seemed suddenly so near.

'Well, now, you tell me a story for a change,' she said.

He laughed, pleased, and just as he had learnt from her

847

he thought for a moment and lured her into a world of make-believe.

'Did I ever tell you about two brave moles who tried to cross the River Dove and failed? Now *that's* a story you should know about!'

She shook her head and whispered that he had not told her that tale, but she would be grateful if he would and did he mind if she closed her eyes so that she could imagine it all the better?

The seasons of moles' lives turn, young mature, parents age, and the old begin to slow and live on through the young. This is the passage that Midsummer sees through, this the passage into the years of summertime. For some moles the passage is peaceful, for others the Stone demands a different way.

Out of the talons of a bloody death Henbane had taken Woodruff and saved him, and now the Stone had one last task for her.

'Soon,' she was inclined to say in those days of June. 'Soon will be Midsummer, and then, my dear, I think I can say I've done enough!'

Soon . . . but not quite soon enough.

It was an afternoon a day or two before Midsummer when three moles crept among the shadowy ways a mole can find if he looks hard enough on the slopes below the west side of Arbor Low.

We know these moles. We have been expecting them. Perhaps, indeed, the Stones have been expecting them as well. Perhaps, in truth, Henbane too had expected them and known no other way to prepare Woodruff for their coming than to rear him as she had, and to bring him here and trust that in some way the Stones would, finally, protect him well. Perhaps.

It was Lucerne who came that day, wild now and strange; and Terce, aged too like Henbane; and the guardmole who had first discovered Henbane here sometime in the days past and whom, too briefly, Woodruff had caught a glimpse of.

Now they crept, unseen this time, up towards Arbor Low on a summer's day when skylarks sang above and insects scurried among the fresh grass.

'Master, the top of that bank ahead looks down upon the Stones and that's where I saw them,' said the guardmole quietly.

'Good,' said Lucerne, eyes staring, eyes hungry, mouth open, breath quick. 'You stay here.'

'Master, the pup's no pup now but a sturdy youngster. Shall I come with you?'

Lucerne glared coldly at him.

'I said stay here. This is a private matter.'

'Yes, Master,' said the guardmole, and as they turned from him and crossed the field to the bank and climbed up it he shrugged and muttered, 'Yes Master, please Master, and bugger *you*, Terce.'

Travelling here with them he had come to the conclusion that Terce was as vile a mole as ever he had met, and the Master was mad. He muttered for his mother in his sleep. Gazed at his paws for hours on end. Couldn't settle in a burrow until things were arranged just so – which could take him hours to achieve. Barmy. Daft. Dulally. *Mad*. The guardmole stanced irritably. Since Beechenhill something had changed in him and he was tired of fighting, tired of guarding moles like . . . *these*. Bugger the lot of them!

The guardmole stretched out his snout along his paws, felt the summer sun begin to warm his fur, and thought of the home system which he had left so long before.

Henbane saw them first, a sudden blackness breaking the line of the bank behind the only standing Stone. Then another. Both staring.

If luck can ever be said to have been in Henbane's life it was there then: that Woodruff was close by. He might have been caught by them on the slopes; he might have been below ground. But he was there and when he heard her sudden sharp call he sensed its urgency and came to her immediately. He saw where she looked and looked there too and saw two moles beginning to descend the bank towards them.

His instinct was to go forward and protect her but already she had put a restraining paw on his, calm and still. She was not Henbane, former Mistress of the Word, for nothing.

'Listen, my dearest,' she said softly, not taking her eyes from where the other moles came. 'I want you to do exactly, *exactly* what I say, whatever it may be. Will you do that for me?'

He nodded.

'Come close,' she whispered, 'yes, just so. And if they speak to you say nothing. Your life may depend on it.'

He was a little in front of her, with her right paw on his neck. She lay on her side, her belly exposed.

'Who are they?' he said as they came past the Stone and stopped.

They were two males, both frightening in a way far worse than the two guardmoles he had once seen. Both still, and both with eyes that stared. About them, it seemed to Woodruff, the summer air was cold.

'Who are we?' smiled the younger of the two. 'This is Terce, Twelfth Keeper. And I am Lucerne, Master of the Word.'

They came a fraction closer and Woodruff felt Henbane's talons tighten on his shoulder, and her body stiffen. The sunlight was across their faces and Woodruff could see every line, every piece of fur, every wrinkle. Their eyes were black and dead, not like Henbane's at all. There was . . . nothing in them but dislike, and in Lucerne's pure hatred. Woodruff felt as if his breathing had stopped, as his heart thumped in his chest and trickles of sweat were on his neck and flanks.

'Well, mother, and so we tracked you down,' Lucerne said. 'And this is the pup?'

'He is,' said Henbane.

'Now tell me,' said Lucerne, 'whose pup is he? The sideem Mallice's or my sister Harebell's?' Woodruff saw the Master's talons fretting at the ground. He seemed poised to leap forward. He was not large so much as powerful of presence, almost overwhelming. There was something *suffocating* about him.

For a moment Henbane's talons stayed tight on him and then to his astonishment he felt them begin to relax. Something . . . she was going to do something. The world seemed very still to him.

Henbane said, 'He is the pup of Mallice. He is thy pup, Lucerne.'

Woodruff saw the Master's talons still. He saw him lightly smile. Yet as he saw it her words seemed to repeat themselves within him: 'He is thy pup, he is thy pup.' It was not what she had ever said before. More words thundered in his head. 'He is thy father, the Master is thy father.'

Lucerne turned his head and looked at him.

'He is thine own, Lucerne, but I have trained him to hate thee and you will never win his heart.'

It seemed to Woodruff that her voice was strange, lulling, unlike the way he had ever heard her speak. Her body was relaxing at his flank. Her haggard belly breathed slowly in and out. Her black teats were empty things that showed. The grass. . . .

'Yet I shall have him now. Mother, make it easy for us all. Give him to me.'

The place they were in seemed to move slow, the air was chill and cold and still. At Lucerne's flank and just a little further back, Terce stared. Behind him was the solitary upright Stone. Woodruff glanced again at Lucerne and saw he was watching Henbane's every move and that surely there was nothing anymole could do against such a mole. They were looking at the poised talons of death.

Suddenly Henbane laughed, a strange young laugh, the laugh of a passionate mole, the laugh of one who is used to having her way. Not the laugh of one afraid at all.

'No,' she said, shaking her head a little. Then she turned her gaze from Lucerne to Woodruff, eased herself back so that her belly showed more and her ancient teats were proud, and said in a gentle voice as her paw pulled him down towards her, 'Come, suckle me, Woodruff, and be my love.'

The words were smooth, incestuous, mocking, but most of all, the words were exclusive to him. Not for Lucerne, nor any other mole. He was the one she suckled, he was her love.

He stared down at her teats and disgust came into him, but her talons tightened again and he seemed to hear her voice, 'Do exactly, *exactly*, what I say!'

Woodruff had time to see the look of jealous outrage suffuse Lucerne's face before he bent down towards her. As the nearest teat came close and his mouth opened towards it he heard Lucerne's roaring cry of '*No!*' and all suddenly was wild and terrible.

He heard Lucerne move wildly forward and felt the powerful grasp of desperate talons at his flanks.

Even as Woodruff sought to do the unthinkable and take Henbane's teat within his mouth he felt her thrust him violently aside and he saw the mistress of the killing art begin to kill Lucerne.

For in that moment of enraged jealousy that Henbane had provoked in him, when he had rushed forward and sought to oust Woodruff, Lucerne exposed the upper half of his body to her.

What she had made she could take back again. With a sudden shocking cry she thrust her talons up into Lucerne's snout and throat, and then, more terribly still, she pulled out the talons in his throat, raised them, and stabbed them down into his eyes and kept them there.

Blood was everywhere, and more than blood. From Lucerne's mouth came an unforgettable bubbling scream, and up in the air went his paws as Henbane clung on and tightened her terrible hold.

'Run now, run now!' she cried out to Woodruff.

He saw Lucerne's talons thunder down into Henbane's belly. A gasp, a second fading blow and Woodruff had time to see Henbane's talons thrusting even tighter in. Lucerne's snout burst, his whole body seemed to scream and his left paw taloned its dying thrust into Henbane's throat. Mother to son, mole to mole, they were caught in a tearing, bloody embrace of death.

Then Woodruff turned, and saw Terce triumphant straight ahead —triumphant! Worse, he looked smug. In that moment Woodruff looked upon the face of evil and, though he did not know it then, he saw a mole who believed he had achieved his end: Lucerne and Henbane passing beyond life towards a divine history he would fabricate. Terce fixed exultant eyes on Woodruff, but the last thing Woodruff saw in them was surprise at what he himself did next. Without thought of what might happen, he pushed hard at Terce so that he fell against the Stone behind.

Then he was trying to get past him as angry Terce shouted, 'No! You! Come with me! I can make thee immortal.' And he felt an old mole's talons grasping thin and tight at his right paw. He heaved and pulled and floundered past, and up the bank and over, Terce just behind.

Woodruff, hampered by Terce's grasp, tumbling and turning down, fell into the dry ditch below the bank. He looked up, saw that enraged austere face falling towards him and, turning to one side, thrust up his talons into its cold eyes. He felt a shuddering pain up his paw and shoulder, and down his back. A terrible pain from the power of his blow. Terce slumped beside him and blood dripped upon the ground.

Woodruff stared down at his talons and found them impaled in Terce's face. He pulled them out with a terrible cry of horror at what he had done, then turned round to run, and there, over him, more powerful than him by far, a great guardmole stanced.

The guardmole looked at him, and then at the dead

853

Terce. Woodruff was quite still but his breath rasped in and out as if he had climbed a mountain for his life and there, on its summit when all his strength was gone, he had found death waiting. The guardmole looked down again.

'Shit,' he said.

The guardmole grabbed his paw, pulled him almost off the ground, and in a few mighty steps was up and over the bank and back to where Henbane and Lucerne lay. Lucerne was dead, Henbane nearly so.

They gazed down at her, their shadows across her head. Her eyes were still half open.

'Live for me, my dear,' she said, and slowly her eyes closed, and slowly, slowly she breathed her last.

The guardmole's grasp was tight, and he stared down at the Master Lucerne and the former Mistress Henbane in a state of shock. He stared about the Stones of Arbor Low, which lay peaceful and white in the sun.

Then back at the two bodies before him.

'Shit!' he said again.

Slowly his tight grasp of Woodruff's paw slackened, and then it let go altogether.

Woodruff was too shocked to move. He gazed at Henbane and then up at the great guardmole.

The guardmole looked wearily at him.

'Scarper,' he said.

But still Woodruff could not move, but gazed on at where Henbane, all his world till now, lay dead.

The guardmole bent down towards him and roared, 'Go on, get out of here.'

'But . . .' began Woodruff, not understanding, 'I've nowhere to go.'

The guardmole sighed and put a rough paw on Woodruff's flank, steered him back up the bank and down the other side past Terce, and out on to the grass beyond.

'Well, mole,' said the guardmole, 'I'm going to report this but, for myself, I've had enough and as soon as I can I'm going home where I belong, and a lot of other guardmoles will do the same. As for you, go and do what she said, and live. *I'll* not say I saw you. Go on!'

Then, not knowing where he went, Woodruff set out alone from Arbor Low.

PART V

Duncton Found

Chapter Thirty-Eight

Now, moles, *now* is the time to heed the Stone Mole's words. Now when we have lost friends we loved – good Squeezebelly, bold Harrow, loving Harebell, caring Sleekit – and when moledom seems bleak indeed, *now* is the time to point our snouts forward as warriors and trust in him.

He taught us that the warriors' way is not to *not* despair, but to see moledom for what it is and ourselves for what we are and, being strong and having faith, to dry our tears, to put our best paw forward, to seek beyond the darkness that besets us and our friends.

Therefore, though we have come by different routes, let us journey on as friends together, flank to flank, along the way this last part of our Chronicle describes. Together then, let us turn to moles we know have shown the strength we need: Caradoc, for one – no more faithful mole than he! – Mistle for another – few more faithful moles than she! Are they not much beset as well? They are, and yet they still press on!

Let us hurry to their flanks, and see what new hopes, and new courage, we may discover there. . . .

Since moles of the Stone under the leadership of Troedfach and Gareg secured Caer Caradoc on Longest Night, the Marches had entered a seemingly endless phase of attack and counter-attack between Word and Stone as each sought to out-think and out-manoeuvre the other.

'They're not sure what to do!' became Troedfach's refrain, and Gareg, and old Alder too, were inclined to agree.

A period of uncertainty seemed to have settled on the front. There had been a brief and exciting time in the winter when a captured mole of the Word had revealed in passing that a mole called the Stone Mole had been heard of to the east, but he knew nothing more than rumours and despite all their best efforts to find hard news nothing had come through.

Yet one thing the news of the Stone Mole, vague though it was, achieved was to make them realise how truly cut off they were from moledom. There had always been moles willing to cross the front – as Gowre of Siabod had done successfully before the Siabod conclave the previous September – but it was Troedfach's view that it was not worth the risk. Such expeditions lost moles, and rarely brought back information which was actionable. Better in his view to interrogate captive moles of the Word – that got results.

Sometimes Gareg, under pressure from younger moles who wanted to do something more adventurous than defend a front, argued that sending a few patrols across the line would not hurt too much, and might get new and more useful information.

But Troedfach was concerned with other things. It had been his view that the longer the stasis went on the better the prospects might be for the Welsh moles, for as the winter had passed by and spring had come he had sensed a weakening on Ginnell's part – a weakening which had started, he saw later, with that surprising retreat on Caer Caradoc on Longest Night.

It would have been nice to attribute this to the supposed Stone Mole – which Caradoc had tried to do – but the more realistic Troedfach put it down to a harsh winter and poor leadership.

Yet every time they themselves tried to break the line, whether to north or south, Ginnell or Haulke, his number two, seemed to have read their minds well.

'Maybe they're saying, "They're not sure what to do" as well,' said Caradoc ironically, for as spring and then summer came he grew increasingly impatient with the fighting. He wanted to be up on his beloved hill and among his Stones without the impediment of patrols and garrisons. He wanted the war finished.

'You're probably right, Caradoc,' said Alder, 'but it's one thing for defenders to be reactive and another for the aggressor. No, I'm sure Troedfach is right and they're uncertain. Leadership from the top, that's what's wrong. If Wrekin and Henbane were still in charge then I doubt we'd be stancing here today, but then I doubt if Gowre would be stancing pretty in Siabod. We may count ourselves lucky that Wrekin was old by the time he got to the western front, and tired. Ginnell does not have Wrekin's brilliance.'

'If you're right and they're uncertain of themselves,' Gareg said, 'then we should take the initiative and attack boldly.'

Troedfach thought for a while. 'Gareg is right,' he said. 'As Midsummer approaches there'll be more moles about, and some going spare, and it's a good time to build up our strength still more. But let's do rather more than that. Let's have faith that my hunch is right and the Word's leadership is faltering . . . Let's send a call out across all of Wales and ask for volunteers to come. Let every system, however small, send us some moles. They won't be fighting all along the front for years to come, but they could be part of one mighty surge forward across the line in an attempt to break the deadlock. Gareg, you've talked of this before, and Alder too. Let us bring all our strength to bear in one place at one time!'

Troedfach was rarely so passionate as this and the others caught his enthusiasm. He turned to Alder and Caradoc and said, 'And you two could be of special use! Aye, the retired commander and the pacifist. Caradoc, if you're with us, and I know you are, you'll help us now. Alder's only old when he's stancing still.

'Therefore, Caradoc, take him off into the Marches and start getting some of the younger moles in the mood for fighting. The way to change things now is for us to come on strong, very strong. To be bold we need moles. Get them for us and we'll show them what to do.'

'Well, you know I'm not one for fighting, but I suppose if there's a possibility of ending this once and for all it's worth a try. But use the moles we send well, and make your campaign short.'

'We'll use them very well,' said Gareg. 'But it'll make sense to keep them behind our lines here so that neither the moles of the Word nor even our own moles get wind of them.' He held up his paw as they expressed surprise and went on, 'That'll be best, believe me. After all, a lot of our best information comes through moles we capture and you can be sure that if moles of ours are taken then Ginnell's lot would find out we're massing moles and where they are and he'll wonder what we're planning. No, we'll do it secretly, and we'll train them well too. There's some advantages in using moles who've not been fighting on the line before. Easier to train!'

The others nodded their agreement and then Troedfach said, 'If we get good moles, and we do our job, then I'll tell you this: things are changing, our chance will come, and I wouldn't be surprised if the moles you send will be back in their home systems by next Longest Night with brave tales to tell, and ready to breed pups when next spring comes around.'

'You speak well, mole, and convincingly,' said Caradoc. 'But I hope it'll all be done *before* next Longest Night because I'm too old to wait much longer, and Alder here's on his last paws! But just one thing: I'll be telling them it's the Stone they're fighting for, and for peace, not for power or glory or revenge. If that's their way there'll be no peace. Don't forget it, Troedfach, nor you, Gareg. If the Stone is with us, and our strategy works, there'll come a time to turn back and leave well alone, and if the Stone Mole was here that's what he'd say.'

'I'll not forget it,' said Troedfach.

'Nor I,' said Gareg, but the light of war was in his

younger eyes, and the cruel glint that the hope of victory brings.

Caradoc and Alder were as good as their word, and through May and June moles came drifting in. Many had never fought before, some did not even speak mole, and a few were too old or too young to fight.

But there they were, full of the spirit and purpose that Alder, whose name all knew, and Caradoc, whose passionate belief all respected, had put into them. They settled willingly down to wait in those secret places which Gareg arranged behind the lines near Caer Caradoc.

'What's good about these moles,' said Troedfach one day to Gareg, after the two had been reviewing some more recruits, 'is that they've come believing that they're going to be part of a great push forward, and not feeling that this is the last stand.'

'That'll be important when the time comes,' said Gareg, 'for we'll be leading them eastward, into flat unfamiliar vales, among moles they'll hardly understand and they'll need to believe in themselves and the Stone. They must be disciplined as well, though, and ready to follow orders, and have the ability to act fast.'

'You've time yet to instil that into them,' said Troedfach. 'But one thing's certain: come Midsummer, when the grikes have seen their pups to maturity, they'll be pushing forward once again as well. That's when the trouble will start and our chance come, and it'll be sudden and unexpected.'

'And we'll be ready!' said Gareg.

So summer came with the moles of the Marches building their strength, and by Midsummer they were ready. But for quite what they did not know.

As the moles at Caer Caradoc prepare to make war against the Word, and Caradoc struggles to help them find a way towards a non-violent peace, Mistle in Duncton Wood has a struggle of a different kind – to find the way beyond the sense of loss she feels.

For already, long before news of the barbing of Beechen at Beechenhill, Mistle had seemed to know that something final had happened that would change all their lives.

In the wake of those terrible nights by the Stone during the March equinox when she had suffered so much, she had stayed subdued and wan. The promising spring had turned into a delightful summer about them, but she had seemed to see it not.

So it was that Romney was forced to take charge of things for a time. The projects of cleaning and renovation she had so cheerfully started he busily continued, trusting that the summer sun, and the new spirit in the air that he began to feel just then, would bring a change in her.

Yet nothing seemed to, not even the best of news. In April the first new moles had come up the slopes, the female pregnant, looking for a place to make a home and scarcely believing it when Romney told them that this deserted, beautiful, shimmering place, was *the* Duncton Wood.

'Where are you from?' asked Romney.

'He's asked where we're from!' said the mole to his quiet mate. 'That's a laugh! We're from all over, aren't we love? Eked out a living where we could, kept our snouts clear of grikes, and when you appeared we thought our number was finally up. Didn't we, my duck? Yes, Sir!'

'What are your names?' asked Romney.

'Whortle and Wren,' the mole replied.

'Whortle and Wren!' repeated Romney with pleasure. It seemed to him as good a pair of names as there could be for the first breeding pair back in Duncton Wood for a very long time. 'Welcome to you both! I'm Romney.'

'You look like a guardmole to me,' said Whortle frankly.

'I was once,' replied Romney.

'Yes, well, there's a few of *them* about. Doesn't have quite the allure it once did, does it? Well, I'll be direct: if there's no disease here we'd like to stay. Been wandering about from portal to post and Wren's tired of it.'

'I said you're welcome, and that means welcome to stay.'

'What's the way it works here then, mate? Is there an elder or eldrene or what? 'Course Duncton used to be of the Stone but then . . . we'll go with whatever's going so to speak. We're followers of a kind but that's more for her than me.'

'There's only Mistle of Avebury and myself here so far. And the Stone, of course. Duncton's going to be what we make it.'

At the mention of the Stone, Wren's eyes had lightened a little, and she spoke for the first time.

'You mean there's no rules? Nothing we've got to do?' Romney laughed.

'Mistle's the one to answer that, but she's not well at the moment.'

'Oh dear,' said Wren, with quite genuine concern. 'With pup, is she?'

'No, no. She's missing a mole just now . . . but she'd probably say that provided you tell the truth, respect other moles, give help when it's needed, and do your bit looking after the communal tunnels and the meeting places, then that's all the rules we need. Something like that anyway.'

'Er, yes,' said Whortle.

' "Er, yes," my paw!' said Wren. 'We should help others and look after the communal tunnels, but let's start with the truth. Like where we really came from, for example.'

'Must we?'

'Begin as you mean to go on, that's what I say,' said Wren.

'Buckland,' muttered Whortle reluctantly. 'We deserted. Bloody awful place, Buckland, so we upped and left when Clowder began his strike. We were lucky to get away.'

'Strike?' Romney said. 'What's that? We're rather cut off here, you see.'

'Against followers. You mean you don't know? Well . . .' Then for the first time Romney heard about the strikes that Lucerne had ordered. Presumably the massacre at Longest Night had been the strike here. Oh yes, then he knew about strikes!

'Thing was though that the grikes thought they knew who the followers were but a lot of them kept quiet, ourselves included.

'And others, seeing what was going on, lost faith in the Word –especially in some of the systems like Fyfield and Cumnor where guardmoles betrayed each other to settle old scores. Happened in Buckland too. Aye, Clowder bit off more than he could chew and now there's confusion all about and moles are looking after their own interest first.'

Whortle went on: 'All we want is a place to call our own where we can settle down. If that includes cleaning a few tunnels then it's not asking much, is it? Whortle's your mole, and if he's not then Wren here will make him be! Being with pup, she's not her usual self. You should see her afterwards!'

'I hope I will and that you decide to stay,' said Romney with a smile, but his mind was on what Whortle had said. Moledom was in change. Mistle, these moles, he himself, and Duncton Wood were all part of it. He did not like to hear of the strikes against followers, yet he felt cheered by the sense of change; and there was a refreshing directness about these two.

'Look,' he said, 'up there is the High Wood. On the far side of it is the Stone, where likely you'll find myself or Mistle. But if you go up that way you'll come to the Eastside and it's reasonably wormful. You go and sort yourselves out a place and in a day or two we'll talk again. When are the pups due?'

'Three days, maybe four,' said Wren, looking pleased to be asked. 'We started a bit late.'

'Your first?'

'Mine too,' said Whortle as she nodded.

'I'll get Mistle to come over and say hello soon, then.'

'That's the Eastside, you said?' repeated Whortle, looking up the slope.

'That's what he said,' said Wren. 'Now say "thank you". This isn't Buckland, you know. Moles treat each other with respect here.'

'Er, thank you,' said Whortle.

Romney waved and left them to it.

'Moles treat each other with respect here,' she had said. Why, if he could scriven or scribe he'd put that right across the south-east slopes for everymole who ever came here to learn!

Mistle did not show much interest, although Romney supposed that the pair's arrival was good news to her, and nor did she say much when Romney reported a few days later that three pups had been born. But his good cheer remained: another pair came later in April with their young, followers who had escaped the purge at Cumnor, and then in May three solitary moles appeared as well and took up burrows on the Eastside.

Mistle kept to herself and matched the quiet and hidden mood of the system in a way that Romney, who went about and tried to be of cheer and seemed the only one who knew them all, felt he did not quite manage. They often asked after Mistle, especially Wren, who was a direct and kindly mole.

By the end of May the pups had become youngsters and one day when Mistle was out with Romney she met them for the first time. She seemed glad, and smiled at them, and they were shy and silent and in awe of her; but even the adults, Romney noticed, were in awe of her.

'You're the Mistle who lives by the Stone,' said Wren.

'My name is Mistle, yes, and I am a follower of the Stone.'

'Well, there's a question I'd like to ask.'

Mistle looked at her and waited.

'It's about Midsummer. I mean, are we celebrating it or what?'

'Why, yes,' said Mistle, surprised. 'Of course we are.'

'You'll be preparing the youngsters then?'

'Preparing them?' said Mistle.

'It's what my parents had others do with us, you see, and I've been worried sick that my youngsters wouldn't be prepared. Wasn't much, I suppose, but things should be done right.'

'What did they do?'

'Told us stories about the Stone and things,' said Wren.

'I'll willingly do that,' said Mistle. 'Mole . . . Wren, I'm sorry I. . . .'

'You've been ill, haven't you? We know 'cos Romney told us. It's all right, there's time yet to get acquainted, isn't there?'

As the youngsters played about them Mistle said, 'Where are you from?'

'Buckland, but my parents came from Charney, which was a system of the Stone.'

'Did they raise you to the Stone?'

Wren shook her head.

'Not what you'd call "raised". They . . . here you, come here and stop hitting him; he's a rascal, that one . . . couldn't do much in Buckland. Just the Midsummer stories because they said that was what they remembered being done to them, but anything more. . . .'

'Was lost?' said Mistle.

'Yes, it was all lost. Never met another mole but Whortle from Charney in my life.' She smiled a little bleakly. 'You couldn't call Buckland a home.'

'This is your home now,' said Mistle.

Wren nodded, unable to speak. She looked at her youngsters playing with the leaves, and she stared about.

'We can't believe our luck, can me and Whortle. A great wood like this, and we've got it almost to ourselves. Done nothing to deserve it, have we?'

'That's what I think too,' said Mistle. 'Others will come

one day and we'll have a chance to make Duncton like a system ought to be. But that won't be easy, Wren, and it'll need all of us working together.'

'You can count on us,' said Wren, gathering her brood together. 'Whortle really likes the place, and you should hear him tell this lot off when they get the communal tunnels dirty. I never thought I'd live to see the day! So you'll prepare them then?'

Mistle looked down at the three youngsters and reached a paw to each in turn and smiled. They looked shyly back, one turned and thrust its face into its mother's flank, not one said a word.

'I'll come down and find you again before Midsummer,' said Mistle.

It was, thought Romney, a beginning and he had seen with his own eyes how a community heals its own. Yet as Mistle had implied, nothing is won easily, and that he soon discovered too.

In June, just before Mistle was going off to the Eastside to see Wren's youngsters, one of the single moles who had come to the wood in May, came to Romney to report that she had seen some grikes peering up the slopes from the cross-under. He ran swiftly to tell Mistle.

'If they mean no harm they are welcome,' said Mistle calmly, and asked Romney to go and meet them. As he went he remembered wryly the first time grikes had come and how Mistle had dealt with them. Now it was him she sent. She was not the mole she had been then and he wished he knew how to bring her out of the lonely place in which she had lost herself.

The grikes, three in all, were not unfriendly, indeed they seemed a little intimidated by Romney's bold and unexpected appearance at the wood's edge as they came up the slopes. But then Romney was skilled in such things, and knew that sometimes a bold appearance at the right time is enough to keep trouble at bay.

'This is Duncton, isn't it, chum?'

Romney nodded.

'Just wondering where the Stone was. Just curious, that's all, and as we were passing by. . . .'

'It's not far,' said Romney. 'I could show you.'

'Many living here?' one asked as they went.

'A few,' said Romney cautiously. 'Where are you off to?'

'Buckland. Replacements. Shouldn't be here really.'

They were not talkative, and indeed the deeper among the beech trees they went the more nervous and uncomfortable they became.

'You sure this is the way?' said one.

'It isn't an ambush if that's what you mean. Duncton isn't that kind of place.'

'Bit of a spooky kind of place, isn't it? How far's this Stone now?'

'Not far.'

Nor was it. When they got there they went to the Stone but seemed hardly to want to stay, peering hurriedly up at the Stone, and around the clearing.

It was at this moment that Mistle appeared.

'Welcome,' she said.

'Yes, well, thank you,' said one of the moles. They looked almost guilty.

'Is this what you wanted to see?' asked Romney. 'Just this?'

'This is where that mole Beechen came from, isn't it? The one they called Stone Mole?'

'Yes,' said Romney quietly. He dared not look at Mistle. 'Why?'

'Just curious, after all the stories about Beechenhill. As we were passing we thought we'd have a look.'

'What stories?' said Mistle. Her face was expressionless.

The grikes looked increasingly uncomfortable.

'Well, when he was barbed and that, and he made the weather change and brought moles out of the ground where he hung; and how after the barbing the Stone sent

870

the Master mad. A mole dreads to think what's happened since. We just wanted to see Duncton for ourselves.'

Mistle seemed to sway where she stanced and then smiled briefly and said, 'Tell my friend what you know. Tell him.'

Then she was silent, and the grikes did not know what to say, and she said to one of them with a shaky laugh, 'You're stancing just where the Stone Mole was born.'

'Oh!' said the mole, moving back sharply. 'Well, there's a thing!' They all stared stupidly at the spot near the Stone, and Mistle turned and left.

'She's a funny one. Say the wrong thing, did we, chum?'

Romney shook his head and decided to explain nothing but to get them to talk instead.

'Nothing much to add. Thought everymole knew about Beechenhill,' one of them said. 'Since then the Master's been wandering all over the place and nomole knows where to look for him next. They say he's mad and Clowder will be Master now, but he's gone off up to the Marches to deal with some trouble there. We got orders from Slighe in Cannock to go to Buckland but by the time we get there they'll be changed again! In some systems it's been murderous but we're just looking for a cushy task. Keep your snout low at a time like this, eh? But you look as if you know the score, mate!'

They turned from the Stone and wandered slowly back across the High Wood, and told Romney a little more about Beechenhill, basing their account on what a friend had been told by another mole who had seen it with his own eyes.

'The Stone Mole was killed, was he? You merely said "barbed" before.'

' "Barbed" or "killed" – same thing in the end. He didn't get down off the wire and dance, no. You can take it he was killed, though they never found his body. Funny, that. Then the Master went spare, chasing after his mother Henbane. Shouldn't of never left Whern, not the Master's *job* to go round the place. That's for the likes of Clowder.'

'Are followers still being killed?'

'Died down, that has. Weren't many left. Mind you, they seem to come out of thin air, do followers. Like all the followers in Duncton was meant to have been killed but here you are. It proves my point: killing will never get rid of followers, even if you wanted to, which I don't!'

They did not speak aggressively at all, and Romney saw that things had changed more deeply than moles knew.

They reached the cross-under and looked upslope towards the wood.

'Nice place you got here,' one of them said.

'Come again,' said Romney.

'You're on there, mate. In my old age I'll come and put my paws up here.'

'You do that,' said Romney.

But that news of Beechen . . . Romney hurried back quickly to Mistle and found her in the High Wood, stanced still and quiet.

'He will come back, won't he Romney?' she said immediately she saw him.

Never had he found it so hard to say what he said, for everything about Mistle, and about the community they hoped to build, had to be based on truth. The Stone Mole had been barbed: how *could* he come back? Yet he had promised her. . . .

'Yes,' he said, 'he'll come back.'

She came to him, leaned against him, and said, 'Thank you, Romney.' And then, a little later, 'He will, you know. He will.'

Despite himself, despite everything, sometimes when he went about the wood he almost could believe it.

She was gone from her normal haunts for days after that and he wondered if she would remember to go down to see Wren's youngsters, and decided she would not.

I'll go myself, he thought, though what I'll say I just don't know. A mole of the Word preparing moles for the Stone's Midsummer! What a place Duncton is becoming!

872

Yet when he got to where he knew Wren and Whortle lived, they were all gone. And so were the others, all of them. He waited a night, snouted towards the Marsh End, and then on a hunch went west to Barrow Vale, and even before he reached it he knew his hunch was good.

For there in the centre of Barrow Vale was Wren and her family, and the other youngsters too, all gathered around Mistle who had them silent and rapt in some story she told.

'Ssh!' said a youngster as he approached. 'Ssh, ssh!'

So he settled down as Mistle finished her tale.

'She taught us a rhyme, and told us about a mole called Balagan,' said one of the younger ones from the late litter.

'And about Tryfan, who used to live here long ago,' said one of the older ones.

'And about Midsummer!'

'And what did the mole who lives by the Stone tell you about Midsummer?' asked Romney, as one of the smaller ones settled comfortably against his great paw.

'She told us that her grandmother Violet said that if you close your eyes and say a prayer for somemole else you'll get a good surprise.'

Romney laughed.

'Are you going to?'

'Of course we are.'

He glanced at Mistle, and though she looked tired still, yet something in her was coming free again.

'It'll be a good Midsummer, Mistle, won't it?' he said.

'I think so,' she said.

Midsummer came, and perhaps the youngsters did close their eyes and make a prayer for another mole; for certainly a surprise came a few days later.

Whortle brought it to Mistle, the youngsters and Romney when they were working to clear part of the communal way that ran from Barrow Vale up to the Stone.

'There's a strange mole asking for you, Mistle, up in the High Wood. I said if I saw you I'd tell you.'

The youngsters looked up, excited. A new mole to meet!

'Did he tell you his name?' For the briefest of moments Romney thought of Beechen, and he looked over to Mistle. He saw that she seemed resigned now to the fact that he was not coming back, even if she would never say so.

'He said he was called Cuddesdon,' said Whortle.

'Oh!' said Mistle, her paw going to her mouth in delighted surprise. 'Romney! It's Cuddesdon!' And then. . . .

'Mistle's crying!' said one of the youngsters.

'No, she's laughing,' said another.

'Let's go and meet him then!' said the third.

Then up through the wood they went, almost all the new inhabitants of Duncton Wood, the youngsters running ahead, Mistle explaining to Wren who Cuddesdon was, Romney chatting to Whortle. Upslope they came, through the trees to the clearing, and then all together bursting out towards the Stone where a mole, an odd mole, a friendly mole, a quickly grinning mole, was stanced.

'Welcome!' said one of the youngsters. 'You know what you are, don't you?'

'A surprise I should think,' said Cuddesdon.

'Not half,' the youngster replied.

'Mistle's crying again,' said his sibling.

'Moles do, and so will I shortly,' said Cuddesdon, who with the youngsters milling all around embraced Mistle and was quickly introduced to the others.

'This is the mole who I travelled with nearly from Avebury itself, and we haven't seen each other for a long time. He's called Cuddesdon because that's where his family originally came from, and he was going back there.'

'Sounds like a good tale!' said one of the youngsters.

'A rattling good tale,' said Whortle.

What was it then about them all at the clearing? About the

light upon them, and the Stone, and the sounds of the wood all around? What rediscovery did Mistle make in the time between the telling of her first stories to the youngsters in Barrow Vale, and Cuddesdon's coming?

She looked at the adults, and at the youngsters playing, and there came back to her at last that same excitement and purpose Romney had seen when they had first come, and which he had missed so much.

'Duncton's beginning again,' Mistle suddenly said. 'It's here and now where we are. Can't you feel it?'

The same old impatience was there, too, the impatience that had once scolded Romney, and the confidence that had sent the first grikes running. The belief that life was there to live, not there to die. Romney saw that Mistle had come out of darkness into light again and he knew that she was stronger for it. He knew that she was the mole that Duncton would need if . . . if what? If Duncton was to be the place to which the Stone Mole would want to come back, that's what!

'Well, can't you?' Mistle almost shouted. 'Can't you feel it?'

'Yes!' said Romney with a laugh.

'Certainly!' said Cuddesdon.

'Yes, Ma'am!' said Whortle, grinning. 'This is the place to be all right, isn't it, Wren?'

Wren wasn't listening, but was stanced enjoying the company of her youngsters by the Stone, and they did not look so young any more.

'Did you find Cuddesdon Hill?' asked Mistle.

'I found the place but not the spirit I was looking for. I don't think I was ready for that task so I thought I'd come and find you.'

'How did you know she'd be here?' asked Romney.

'Mistle? She was *always* coming here from the first moment that I met her. Weren't you, Mistle?'

Cuddesdon nudged her in a friendly way, and Romney warmed to see her close to another mole like that.

She looked around at the rising beeches, she listened to

the sounds of the wood, she scented the summer air. She touched a paw to Cuddesdon and then one to Romney.

'Yes, yes, I was always coming here,' she said. 'This is the place where moles will always find themselves.'

Chapter Thirty-Nine

It was in July that suddenly and quite unexpectedly the breakthrough at Caer Caradoc came. Just when Troedfach and Gareg were beginning to have difficulty keeping the morale of their secret army of moles up, one of the small volunteer patrols that had crossed the line came back in June with real news for a change, and not just rumour. Sensational news that would change everything for them all the moment it was heard.

Better still, they brought with them a mole who knew the news was true, or most of it at least. He had been there.

The leader of the patrol, his eyes alight with excitement, told Gareg, 'Sir, you're going to want everymole in the Marches to hear this mole's story. It's not all good, and it's not all bad, but it makes a mole's talons itch for action!'

A meeting with Troedfach, Caradoc and Alder was quickly arranged, and then all the senior commanders nearby, and many others were hastily summoned, and the mole came to speak to them: a mole we know. . . .

'Ghyll's the name, and I am of Mallerstang in the north,' he said clearly, eyeing the moles carefully. 'I don't know much about you here except that you're of the Stone, and the war you've waged has gone on for many a year.'

'That's true, at any rate!' said Troedfach with a smile. 'A whole lifetime in some cases.'

Ghyll nodded and said quietly, 'Where does a mole begin? From what the patrol that picked me up tell me, you've been cut off from what's happening in moledom and not much has filtered through.'

'Not much,' said Gareg. 'That's why we sent out patrols.'

'You don't even know about the Stone Mole then?'

They shook their heads, and went very quiet indeed.

'Well,' said Ghyll, 'I'd better begin with him because I've a feeling he's where it all begins, and where it all may end.'

'And did he come then, the Stone Mole?' said Caradoc.

There wasn't a mole there but Ghyll who did not understand how important Caradoc's question was to him.

Ghyll looked at him in that clear, direct way the Mallerstang moles had, and he seemed to sense something of Caradoc's faith and trust.

'Greetings, mole,' he said, lowering his snout respectfully.

'My name's Caradoc of Caer Caradoc,' said Caradoc formally, pleased to be well greeted, 'and I've waited all my life for the news you bring this day.'

'And I!' said Alder.

'Aye, and all of us here!' said Troedfach.

Ghyll was moved by their faith and eagerness and he said, 'Then moles of the Marches, I'll tell you this: your wait has not been in vain. I have seen the Stone Mole with my own eyes.'

There was a clamour of questions, and Ghyll raised his paw and the hubbub slowly quietened. But most remarkably it was not the moles' eagerness to know that truly quietened them, but something about the way Ghyll stanced, and the look of faith in his eye. A hush fell.

'The Stone Mole is dead,' said Ghyll. 'I saw him barbed by the moles of the Word with my own eyes. But the Stone Mole lives, and shall live in everymole's heart.'

'Tell us your tale, mole,' said Caradoc in a compelling voice, 'and tell us it slow. From its beginning to its ending as you would tell it to youngsters on a Midsummer night, for are we not pups who must learn the Stone Mole's ways? We must know of his coming, and of his ministry among us, and of his end.'

'Then know that the Stone Mole, as moles call him, was born of a mole called Feverfew in Duncton Wood,'

878

responded Ghyll, 'and his name was Beechen, and if he died – aye, I said *if* he died – then it was at Beechenhill. But first. . . .'

So it was that the moles of the Marches first learnt of the Stone Mole, and of Beechenhill, and of those teachings that Ghyll had heard Harebell and Sleekit talk about when they returned to Beechenhill.

Quietly he spoke, and with reverence, telling what he knew for fact, what was hearsay and what was his surmise. Through the evening he spoke, and halfway into the night, and he ended by telling them of that terrible night of death and the barbing by the Stone of Beechenhill.

'Before then I was one of those who had come to believe that fighting was the way – and I a mole, as I've explained, who had come from a system where non-violence was the code. But years of pressure from the grikes at Beechenhill changed that, and I'm not proud of it.

'Nor was Squeezebelly, I'm sure, as he led the charge on the grikes at the Beechenhill Stone. But is a mole to stance idly by while his own kin and ones he loves are killed? You answer me that, for I never have!

'Yet I know this too: I've seen an extreme of violence that I never want to see again. As I crossed moledom from the north-east where Beechenhill lies, counting myself lucky I had escaped and fulfilling Squeezebelly's hope that those who did would spread word of what they saw, I have felt the violence that still waits to erupt across moledom. There's anger, there's vengeance and there's confusion. Perhaps violence must have its place.

'But if *you* must fight, and I think you will, then moles of the Welsh Marches I beg you to do it swiftly, and to stop it soon. And when you stop it, stop it for good.'

'Aye,' cried out Caradoc, 'that's how a mole should speak!'

And later, when Caradoc got Troedfach and Alder alone, he said, 'Let me take Ghyll of Mallerstang to talk to the moles who wait so impatiently behind the lines. He'll instil respect for the Stone Mole's way in them.'

'I had thought of it and so had Gareg,' said Troedfach. 'But you, Caradoc, what of you and the news he brought?'

'What of me?' said Caradoc sharply.

'He said the Stone Mole was barbed to death,' said Alder. 'And you've always said. . . .'

Caradoc stared up at Caer Caradoc.

'He'll come,' he said fiercely, 'and I'll be there to greet him when he does. He'll come, see?'

It was but a few days after this that the grikes began the assaults along the line that Gareg had so long ago predicted they would do, and the new war they had prepared for finally began.

The period and its events is rich in varied and often conflicting sources, but the two main accounts that cover what historians now regard as the final part of this long period of conflict* agree on the basic facts.

The first major assault on the Marches came in the south and was led by Clowder – though at the time that was not known by the Welsh moles. He had privily concluded a secret agreement with Ginnell and had left Buckland and the south-east in the paws of a group of eldrenes and travelled westward with a heavy guardmole force.

A few days later a second attack, and one cleverly arranged to seem heavy and likely to be sustained, began on Caer Caradoc, no doubt to turn moles away from positions further north on that old line across the Marches in Gaelri's territory which led towards Siabod itself, where the biggest attack of all was to be mounted.

Clearly the grikes hoped, with good reason, that the Welsh moles, never well co-ordinated before, would split up their effort by reacting to each threat as it came, all the less effectively because of the need to protect their hard-won Caer Caradoc.

Troedfach and Gareg had been so long prepared for this

*See Gareg's *Strategy and Attack* and his more philosophical *On Ending Wars*; and, of course, Haulke's *Memoirs of the Western Front*.

renewed war that when it came they were calm and efficient, and at first did nothing but put up the normal resistance and slow the attacks down. The swift messenger systems Gareg had established brought news fast, but it was not until some eight days after Clowder's first attack, and when the moles of Merthyr in the south were beginning to weaken, that Troedfach made his move.

The mood at Troedfach's headquarters was serious, and moles like Caradoc and Alder found that suddenly there were a lot of new faces around, young moles trained by Gareg whose task was to co-ordinate what was to be one of the biggest and most astonishing campaigns in moledom's history. Troedfach had talked of Wrekin's 'brilliance' but he might well have talked of his own – or at least of his and Gareg's together. It was the perfect partnership of the old campaigning mole of experience with a younger more imaginative commander.

But significantly, it was to Caradoc that Troedfach first revealed his plans, feeling that the mole who had sustained them all for so long should be the first to know what they were going to try to achieve.

'Caradoc, stance down here and listen. You want this new phase of the war to end quickly and finally and I think that I know how it will. But it wouldn't be right if I didn't tell you what we plan to do. . . .'

'Does Alder know?'

'Aye, he's given his advice.'

'You military moles are thick as thieves.'

Troedfach smiled.

'Now listen, mole. You know that Cacr Caradoc is under attack from the east and we're defending it? Well, tonight we're going to start weakening up there – not much, but enough to call the grikes' bluff and make them commit more moles to the hill from their headquarters thinking they'll win an easy prize.

'Well, they will, for in three nights' time, when we've "retreated" even more, we're going to clear out altogether and give them the prize. Aye! And as we do we shall attack their headquarters in force and take it.

'That will only be the beginning. Today orders have already gone out for all the moles along the Marches south of here to retreat in such a way as to encourage the attacking moles there to go after them, and extend their lines. They will be hurrying into the paws of half of Wales, paws very eager to say a brusque hello. These moles will stay along the Marches to make sure that the grikes do not occupy the void we've left behind, and to keep those on Caer Caradoc busy. We don't want any minor raids disturbing things.

'Meanwhile our moles here, or rather on the far side of Caer Caradoc as they then will be, will turn north up towards Gaelri's patch, where I believe we will find Ginnell or Haulke or both. Gaelri's moles will move to counterattack from the west as we come from the direction Ginnell will least expect – the east. That will be the critical part and on the speed with which we can achieve success much else will depend.'

'And afterwards?' asked Caradoc, a little dazed, for the prospect of *giving* Caer Caradoc to the grikes did not seem a cheerful one.

'Why, mole, the grikes on Caer Caradoc will be urgently recalled, probably by Ginnell to the north, though possibly they'll go south to the aid of those moles there, and you'll have your system back again with not a military mole in sight. More seriously, Caradoc, we will have to decide later if we continue the attack on the grikes beyond the line, perhaps even heading an attack on the Master himself. We shall see. That's the theory anyway, but I believe it is going to work.'

'What of Siabod, which is where this war began?'

''Tis secure under Gowre who has had reinforcements and knows what to expect – nothing! We shall see. We have assumed that Ginnell will not get through to Siabod. It's on our front that the war will be won or lost, not in Siabod.'

Caradoc fixed Troedfach with a gaze.

'Remember 'tis for the Stone you fight: if you and Gareg never forget that, your moles will not either.'

'I know it, Caradoc,' said Troedfach, 'and I believe it.'

'Then may the Stone be with thee, Troedfach of Tyn-y-Bedw, and may the moles of the Marches and all of Wales remember your name with gratitude as the mole who brought them peace.'

'As for you, Caradoc,' rejoined Troedfach, 'you are advised to retreat from here for a time. It's possible that this area will be attacked from Caer Caradoc.'

'I'll not move from sight of Caer Caradoc.'

'No, mole, I didn't really think you would.'

'Is Alder going with you?'

'No, he's staying as your bodyguard, old mole.'

'Humph!' said Caradoc.

Of the extraordinary campaign that now ensued moles have been told enough in the past, and the outline is well known. In only two days Troedfach's large and well disciplined force had taken the grikes' headquarters south-east of Caer Caradoc and cut off the force that had been lured on to the hill.

Several grike senior commanders were taken, including Haulke himself. It was then that Troedfach learnt that the mole Clowder was in charge of the southern campaign of the grikes, and that his force represented a considerable addition to what the grikes already had deployed along the front.

But though tempted to send more of his own moles south he kept to his plan and moved immediately north with Gareg for the assault on, as he had correctly thought, the force led by Ginnell. These were the critical hours, when Welsh moles in the south retreated before a larger force than they had expected, and the outcome in the north was unknown.

But at the bloody battle that was waged in the north for four days over difficult waterlogged ground at

Cefn-Mawr, the main northern force of the grikes was all but wiped out. Less by skill, perhaps, than by the sheer number of moles that had been so brilliantly mustered, and by their ferocity. Nor did Troedfach hesitate to order that all grikes caught be killed and his action there, though often criticised, effectively destroyed the grike strength along the northern Marches.

While in the west, the Siabod moles under Gowre, seeing the grikes forces retreating east to support the failing forces of Ginnell, went in pursuit, and at Corwen caught up with most of them. The Corwen massacre – or plain 'Corwen' as moles of those parts know it – was a vile and dishonourable act against a retreating force, though Gowre himself did not order it, and was what Caradoc had warned so often against.

The struggles to the south were more drawn out but effectively ended when Clowder himself retreated as news of the Master's disappearance and rumours of his death reached him. He hurried north, and began his infamous attempt to win the Mastership, which reached its notorious climax at Whern the following December.

These general facts are well known, and the victory of the moles of the Welsh Marches is usually taken to have been when, one late August day, the grikes now besieged on Caer Caradoc did not retreat, but yielded to two old, brave moles of the Stone: Alder and Caradoc.

Overtures had been made, the grikes had refused to surrender, so Alder and Caradoc decided to try to stop more bloodshed on their own initiative. Up they slowly went, knowing that the chance was high they would be killed.

Perhaps lesser moles might have been, but those two had strength in their grizzled paws and wise eyes, and peacefulness, and the grikes recognised them for what they were.

'Not one of you shall be harmed, I pledge that upon the Stone itself,' said Caradoc. 'You'll be prisoners for a time, until our campaign is over, and I've a grim feeling you'll be safer as prisoners than roaming the countryside. After that you can go home.'

'Yonder's my home,' growled a grike, pointing south-east to the slopes below the hill. 'I may be of grike stock but my father was stationed here before me and I was born of a local mole. Where shall my home be now, eh, mole?'

Then, in a memorable gesture, Caradoc said, 'Mole we may not be kin by blood but by birthplace we are, for the place you point to is as near to where we stance now as my own birthplace is.'

Then he put a paw to that grike's shoulder, and pointed out the slopes to the north-east where he had been born.

'What's your name, mole?'

'Clee,' said the grike.

'When peace comes, Clee, and it will come, you climb this hill again and I'll give a welcome your good sense and faith in our justice this day deserves.'

'That's well said for a mole of the Stone,' said Clee. 'What's *your* name, mole?'

'Caradoc of Caer Caradoc,' said the old mole proudly.

'Then by the Word, Caradoc, I'm not ashamed to yield to you. But if the day comes when I climb this hill again I'll expect you to yield to me for a day, just for old time's sake, mole to mole!' Clee laughed, a great, rough grike laugh, and Caradoc looked at Alder, and Alder at Caradoc, and they laughed as well.

'It shall be so, Clee.'

But it was at Cefn-Mawr in the north Marches, when the Welsh moles discovered their true strength, that the war and its direction really changed. Not for the first time in moledom's sometimes bloody history, a force of moles, well-led locally, won a battle and then a local war, and suddenly all looked different.

What had seemed established and permanent forever was suddenly seen as vulnerable, its weaknesses exposed. For from the few captives taken at Cefn-Mawr, Trocdfach and Gareg discovered that the Master Lucerne was in all probability dead, Clowder's force was stuck in the obscure south Marches, and contained, and no other coherent force ruled moles but a bunch of sideem and eldrene, each with their own patch to scheme over.

But more than that, within days of the Cefn-Mawr victory, moles began appearing at the Welsh moles' quarters. Followers and well-wishers, of course, but moles of the Word as well, who said that for too long they had suffered the rules and restrictions of the Word and were changing their faith. . . .

The Word and its weakness was indeed exposed. But Troedfach was not impressed: all that Alder had told him over the years suggested that the moles of the Stone had been equally fickle and weak when Henbane had come down from the north against them. Perhaps the Stone Mole *was* needed to give moles the strength they lacked in themselves.

Nevertheless, if the Word's power had still been at Whern Troedfach would not have thought to advance much more. But when he learned it was at Cannock, which was not too far off at all. . . ! If his forces were able to take that as well then the Word would be well broken. It seemed, too, that on the way, there were systems that needed to be liberated of the Word. . . .

In this way, what had begun as a campaign now became a crusade that in its early enthusiastic weeks was only just controlled by Gareg and Troedfach, but controlled it was. Gradually, methodically, they journeyed east and south, splitting first into two groups and then into four, and meeting little or no opposition at all except in some of the bigger systems and that desultory.

What surprised Troedfach was the ready disloyalty of the moles of the Word to the Word itself. It was as if the rumours of Lucerne's death, and the failure of Whern to provide a successor who could bring the moles of the Word together had caused faith in the faith itself to die.

'We have the Stone, Gareg, and that is always there. But the Word seems to need a Master or a Mistress to give it strength, and failing that it looks an empty thing. Remember the Word started with Scirpus, a *mole*, not with the Stone.

'We shall continue to advance on Cannock, and perhaps we'll find tougher opposition there, but after that our real task will be to turn our moles back. Victory is a heady thing, and freedom to kill across these vales may become more alluring than the rough Welsh hills.'

'Aye,' said Gareg grimly. 'I've had to discipline some of my own moles harshly to stop them running wild. Caradoc was right to warn us as he did.'

Yet there was something more abroad than mere failure of the Word, something that a military mole like Troedfach was not able easily to understand, for he had never lived under the thrall of the Word, nor seen the corrupting years of eldrene rule; nor known the snouting of his kin and the stealing of his pups.

Such things make moles harbour hate, and though they may live for years without their masters knowing what they feel, the hatred thrives with each fresh injustice. Take away restraint and the evil pus of that hatred spews out and vile killing starts.

This was the force that now threatened to unleash itself where the Welsh moles went; this the dark side of the smiles of the moles who suddenly emerged into the daylight of freedom once more. And, some might say, this was the beginning of the new Word. Aye, revenge is often how it starts; freedom spawns its own failure.

This danger was very real, but thus far Troedfach's restraint, and Gareg's good example, hindered it.

A sense of these truths must have begun to come to Troedfach before the battle at Cannock, for sensing that his moles were fast becoming marauders, he re-formed the groups of four from two, with himself and Gareg in supreme command. More than that, he personally spoke to all the commanders under him, and had Gareg do the same, and told them that if Cannock was a victory then it would be the final one. After that the fighting must end, and moles of these parts must find their own way. Whatever happened now, the Welsh moles had proved that they could defend their own, and it would be many a moleyear before any force ever tried to attack Wales and Siabod again. This restraint marks Troedfach out for greatness, and did much to set the tone for moles of the Stone for a time.

Yet Troedfach could still be ruthless if he felt it justified, and in Cannock, most infamously perhaps, his moles were violent for a final time. To that place all the sideem and Keepers who could get there had fled, and so too had many of the guardmoles from the systems in the Midlands, which explains why so many had fallen so fast.

Troedfach had learned that Drule and Slighe had been deputed by Lucerne to be in charge of Cannock before his ill-fated journey to Beechenhill. These two, at least, he no doubt hoped to take, though he would not have had the respect for them he had for Ginnell and Haulke, who both survived the war.

We may imagine the miserable inability of Drule to deal with the military crisis that faced him after Lucerne and Terce had vanished and when the Welsh moles appeared, and all without Clowder nearby to help. We can guess the difficulties Slighe faced as the structure of reports and counter-checks that Lucerne had made ground to a total halt.

Under those two Cannock ceased to work. Yet there, panicking, arguing, even murdering perhaps, the sideem and the guardmoles rushed; and there they had to wait their fate as, inexorably, the Welsh moles approached nearer to them and, to make matters worst, Gareg took a force of moles round to the eastern side of Cannock and prevented a retreat.

Then, just as at a single blow Troedfach had stopped the fighting on the Marches by ruthless killing, so in Cannock he desired to destroy the hierarchy of the Word. Nomole knows how many died, or what moles they were, but after Cannock if a Keeper lived he did not speak his rank; and if a sideem lived he lied to survive. In Cannock, as in Cefn-Mawr, few prisoners were taken.

In Cannock the grikes' power died. In Cannock the Word died. In Cannock Whern itself lost its hold on moles' hearts and minds.

And Drule? And Slighe?

Oh, *them*?

We know their fate.

It seems that when the last killing in Cannock was done, and the Welsh moles were finishing clearing out the system and picking off the last moles hiding there, they heard a cry, a subterranean cry.

Then from out of a deep and fetid tunnel, like a creature from a lost vile world, a mole staggered up bringing with him one other mole, a female, who looked all but dead.

Those who first discovered them were aghast at what they saw, but the more living of the two, the male, seemed to roar at them and threaten them in a voice that was no more than a rasping croak, and with a body that was nearly broken. His face and flanks were hollowed out with hunger, his paws and body had wounds that had congealed and yet been torn again as if he had been in a fight for days.

His companion, if that's what a mole could call so ghastly, broken a thing as she seemed then, lay motionless, her eyes swollen and closed, her body nothing more than ragged fur half hanging off her bones.

The Welsh moles recoiled from them in horror, and uncertain what to do summoned senior commanders to the place. But though these tried to approach they were threatened more, and the male cried out at them, such sounds as he made at first making no sense at all.

It was not until Troedfach himself came to the mole that any sense was made of what he said. All that was plain was that anymole who touched the weak mole he had carried out would have to kill him first. Yet when they retreated he still whispered on.

'I think he wants to know what moles we are,' said one of the Welsh moles.

'We're from Caer Caradoc, we're. . . .'

'We're of the Stone,' said Troedfach, suddenly understanding. 'We're of the Stone.'

The mole stanced down and turned to his companion, and seemed to whisper to her, to comfort her.

'Bring them food,' said Troedfach softly, 'bring them good worms. This mole is not threatening us. He is defending himself, and his companion too, and I think he has had to do so for a very long time.'

The worms were brought and Troedfach told all the others there to leave. He placed a worm before the mole, who stared at it in disbelief and suddenly grabbed it, guarded it, and with one paw poised to defend it, to the very death it seemed, he chewed some of the worm and then fed it slowly to the female.

Troedfach guessed that the scene he saw was one that had been enacted many times before, and that somewhere below them where the mole had been was a place nomole should ever have to go. He put more worms before the mole and watched as he fed the female again and then, finally, took food for himself. His stance, though still feeble, grew stronger.

'Mole, I am Troedfach of Tyn-y-Bedw, commander of the Welsh Marches. I am of the Stone. Cannock is no longer of the Word. Cannock is free and you are free as well. You shall not be harmed more. What is your name?'

The mole did not reply, but turned instead to his companion, and Troedfach heard him whisper again and again, 'Betony, did you hear that? Did you hear? He's of the Stone. We're safe now, we're safe. Betony, we're all right now. . . .'

'Mole, what is your name?' asked Troedfach.

The mole looked at him with strong, proud eyes and said, 'I am Wharfe of Beechenhill and I too am of the Stone.'

'What is this place from which you come?'

'The Sumps,' said Wharfe.

'Are there others like you in the tunnels below?'

'Only a few are left, but we must try to get them out.'

He tried to stance up as if to lead Troedfach towards the tunnel but he was too weak and fell back again.

'I'll send moles in.'

'Tell them to beware of mud, and if they find moles to say they are of the Stone or otherwise they may be killed. The others must be dead by now.'

'What others?'

'Grikes who fled down there, but we killed them in the end. As for Drule and Slighe, they were still alive when I last saw them. I doubt that they survived.'

As moles went down Wharfe told how Drule and Slighe and a few other grikes had come down into the Sumps, though Wharfe did not realise then it was to hide from the Welsh moles.

Their coming was preceded by weeks in which the moles in the Sumps had been abandoned, and amid scenes of utter horror most had slowly died. But Wharfe had fought and killed for worms the grikes brought down, and these he fed to Betony and himself and they had managed to survive. They stayed clear of the anarchy that began when the Welsh moles approached Cannock and some of the guardmoles, and Drule and Slighe as well, fled down to the Sumps in the hope they would be thought prisoners and set free.

'What happened to them?' asked Troedfach. 'Were they killed?'

Wharfe shook his head.

'They put them in the Lower Sumps,' he said matter-of-factly, but as he named that place Betony recoiled and shivered and it was a long time before Wharfe could settle her again.

The patrol Troedfach had sent to the Sumps returned, bringing out nine moles alive, each but the ghastly shadow of a mole, each driven to the edge of sanity by what they had experienced.

As for Drule and Slighe, the patrol found them alive all right, but there was nothing they could do but watch them go to a ghastly death. It was the senior member of the patrol who described their end.

'We were taken down to the Lower Sumps by one of the survivors and he showed us a slimy, muddy pit and said that weeks past, when it rained heavily, the ways down into there had crumbled and fallen in. Off it was a tunnel, a black tunnel with no light which we were told led on to the many damp burrows and cells where prisoners were sometimes confined.

'The pit was full of seeping mud that was slowly rising up towards the tunnel entrance, and into this mud Drule and Slighe had been thrown along with several of the grikes. These had all fought for their lives, trying to use each other to climb up out of the pit. When we arrived only Drule and Slighe still lived, the latter huddled in the tunnel entrance where he had retreated, while huge Drule, having killed all others there, was trying to find a way out of the rising mud.

'There was no helping him, for a mole could not reach that far down. What was worse was that their struggles had churned the mud and made it worse and as we watched, slowly, very slowly, it surged and turned revealing bodies in its sticky depths among which Drule floundered and cried out in fear. More and more we saw him driven back towards the tunnel out of which Slighe now attempted to come as he realised that if he stayed there and the mud rose higher he would be sealed into that fetid roaring darkness. But Drule would not let him out. He crashed his talons on him and pushed him screaming back inside.

'We watched helplessly as Drule was driven back to the tunnel as the mud rose. We saw him push Slighe into the darkness as he himself sought the hopeless refuge the tunnel gave.

'Nomole can describe the horror we felt as he desperately tried to push the mud's sticky, suffocating mass back from the tunnel entrance. The last we saw was a paw pushing helplessly at the mud before he retreated into darkness forever, the mud very slowly but relentlessly pursuing him and Slighe into those dreadful depths.'

Such is all we know of the end of Drule and Slighe. Of their final end, in claustrophobic darkness, pursued by suffocating mud, nomole will ever know, nor be able to guess how many days it was they survived down there. There was dripping water enough perhaps for drinking, but we can contemplate only with horror what the last survivor among them, Drule probably, was forced to use as food. . . .

The Welsh moles stayed on in Cannock for some time more and in that time the moles from the Sumps were able to recover. Some might never fully have done so, but Wharfe and Betony had better luck than most, or greater faith perhaps.

Then some days after the fights were all over two moles came to Cannock, saying that they had heard there were survivors from the Sumps and asking if certain friends of theirs might be among them. There were many such in those days, many moles coming and going and few noticed those two as they were led through the Cannock tunnels to see the survivors.

One was but a small and modest mole, and grubby too, the other a quiet female. . . .

'Holm,' said Quince, 'do you really think that Wharfe. . . ?'

He could not know. After all the struggles they had had since their escape from the Manifold Valley, and a long period of waiting near dangerous Cannock in the hope of better times coming in the wake of the Stone Mole's passing, it seemed unlikely that Wharfe had survived – if he had ever got here, for even that they did not know.

'The survivors?' said one of the Welsh moles kindly. 'Aye, there are a few living in warm burrows up this way . . . you go on and see if the moles you want are there.' He pointed to a pleasant but small tunnel. Not many survivors there!

'Is that all the moles who lived?'

'Aye, that's all, Miss.'

Quince stared at the clean tunnel, and scented its good air. At one or two of the entrances she could see a paw or a flank moving.

'Holm, I dare not go, I daren't. Will you?'

'I don't know what Wharfe looks like.'

Quince smiled.

'You knew Tryfan, didn't you?'

Holm nodded.

'When Squeezebelly told me the truth of Wharfe and Harebell's parentage, he said that Wharfe looked much like Tryfan.'

'I'll look,' said Holm.

She watched him go down the tunnel, peering into each burrow in turn. Her heart beat hard and she barely seemed to breathe as one by one he turned back to her and shook his head.

One by one Holm went, and saw moles thin and gaunt. Some whispered to themselves, some stared, some lay fast asleep.

But then he came to one burrow where two moles were. He saw the female first for she was facing towards the burrow entrance. She smiled at him.

Then the male slowly turned to face him. He was gaunt as well, but his body was big, his shoulders broad and his paws and talons were large. He had the bearing of one who had suffered and survived and still retained the good spirit that he had always had; and as his gaze fell on him, Holm saw his eyes were like Tryfan's.

Holm stared, stanced up as he usually did at such moments which were always so difficult for him, looked round the burrow for inspiration and said, 'Quince has come.'

Quince saw Holm pause at another burrow, almost the last

indeed, she saw him stare, she saw him stance up and look desperate and she saw him speak.

Then a mole came out of the burrow, and he turned towards her, and she knew him not from his thin flanks, or his scarred shoulders, but from his gait and his gaze. Her Wharfe was still alive.

'Wharfe!' she said as he came to her. And his great paws were on her shoulders, and for a time they spoke no words.

'Betony?' she said at last.

'She's here.'

'Harebell?' he asked, but even as she shook her head he seemed to know the answer.

'Bramble?' he asked.

'No, my dear, we understand that few in Beechenhill survived.'

They held each other in silence some time more before he said, 'Come and meet Betony now, but be warned she has suffered much and is very frail.'

'Then Beechenhill will help her recover, for soon we must go home.'

Then with cries of pleasure, and tears as well, those moles came together once again and what had been their little group was, as moledom itself was, not the same as it was before, yet not altogether lost.

It was Gareg who suggested what they might do.

'Troedfach has asked me to take some moles from Cannock and travel north as far as Whern, just to be sure that there are no moles of the Word still wishing to impose themselves on moles who do not want them. They can believe what they like provided they don't try to bend others to their will. Anyway, that's for me to worry about, but these are troubled times and you might like our protection for the journey back to Beechenhill if you're willing to go back now after what has happened.'

They nodded their agreement.

'Also,' continued Gareg, 'you can tell me a lot about

moledom that I don't know. We're cut off in Wales, see, and when I go home I'd like to know more than I did.'

'Like what, mole?' said Wharfe cautiously.

'Places; moles; incidents. I've heard so much about moles like Lucerne and Henbane, Tryfan and Beechen of Duncton and as you come from Beechenhill you must know something about all that. It seems to have been a kind of centre for the Stone.'

'But hasn't he told you whatmole he is?' said Quince surprised.

Wharfe put a restraining paw on hers and smiled.

'Who is he?' said Gareg.

'I'll tell you about that on the way to Beechenhill,' said Wharfe. 'Not afterwards, mind, because we're going to have our work cut out and you. . . .'

'Me?'

'Well, mole, you'll not be coming back from Whern. Didn't you know? Giants live up there!'

Gareg laughed.

'Aye, like giants named Troedfach come out of Wales!'

It was soon after this that Troedfach, leaving only a small garrison at Cannock, said farewell to Gareg for a time and turned his great and disciplined force back towards its homeland. Then Gareg was set to leave.

Many farewells were made then, and many tears were shed. The whole of moledom seemed to be on the move, but Holm was not a mole to enjoy saying goodbyes and, knowing that, Quince held him close for a time and would not let him go.

She told him how much he meant to her, and how much he had achieved, and that he had fulfilled every task the Stone had set him.

'What will you do now, Holm?' she asked as she said the last goodbye.

He stanced up, he stared, then he waved in a southerly direction and grinned happily and said, 'I'm going home!'

Chapter Forty

The victory of the Welsh moles over the forces of the Word at Cannock, bloody and terrible though it was, brought to an end the hegemony of the Word over moledom as a whole. To be sure, the struggles of moles for the Mastership, principally that between Clowder and the sinister Thripp of Blagrove Slide, would occupy the northern parts for many a moleyear yet, but the Word of Rune and Henbane in her prime, the true Scirpuscan Word, the Word of darkness and dismay, was no more.

Where did it die? At Beechenhill, when Beechen was barbed? At Caradoc, when Troedfach first led the Welsh moles out? Or at Whern itself, when Henbane first knew doubt?

Would that it were so, or that we truly knew what the Word was. For after Troedfach had retreated with his forces the violence that his moles had contained broke out as all the hatred of moles of the Stone against the Word burst forth. Now the revenge for those sideem strikes was taken. Now moledom saw begin a wave of retaliation that would spread like fire across a wood, and burn fierce indeed before it died. Whole systems of the Word were slain, even the moles who professed to a belief in the Stone, youngsters, old moles, females. Everymole killed.

The scenes we witnessed at Beechenhill, aye and even the cruelty we saw in a burrow on the Manifold were repeated again and again now, and shaming it is for us, for they were done in the name of the Stone.

Aye, this was so, moles; this was so. Forget it not.

Yet knowing it we may more easily understand the despair the Stone Mole expressed upon the barb, for the scene of violence he saw acted out across Beechenhill as he hung dying seemed to show that violence must ever be met with violence.

What then did he do? Two moles, Holm and Wort, two of those who had helped him touch the Stone that distant June in Duncton when his commitment to moledom truly began, helped him from the barb and laid him down.

He took the form then in which he had been before, a White Mole's form, and he left that violence far behind thinking perhaps that if he could find but one mole of true peace, one mole who could touch Silence in this life, then through that mole others might know there is a way which ordinary moles can take.

Therefore we should turn our backs on the violence that now erupted across moledom and seek rather to know the way the White Mole might have gone to find that one mole.

But we may guess where it was he went.

In moles' hearts he searched, in ordinary moles' hearts. Some by virtue of the Stone Mole's example, some for the natural love of others that they had; some because the Word's baleful sound was no more, and they could hear Silence and see the Stone's light once more.

The full Chronicle of that recovery would be the story of moles beyond counting. Yet one thing is sure. As the moleyears began to unfold after Troedfach's victory, and his historic decision to turn back to his own homeland, it is to Duncton Wood that the story returns, where the Stone Mole's heart had been, and where the hope and purpose he had when he was alive might now be found.

Four moles, close related, will tell the story of many more. In their lives, certainly, much of the Stone Mole's purpose and teaching is bound. To one of them indeed, good Bailey, a great task will soon be entrusted. While for the others of this quartet tasks have been well done and new ones may yet wait. Starling, Lorren, Holm, these are the moles we think of most when we speak good Bailey's name, and their stories now will surely lead us along the

White Mole's way to waiting Duncton Wood. It is with Bailey we begin.

Mayweed and Bailey first learned of the death of Lucerne a few days after they reached Seven Barrows in late July.

Theirs had been a long and meandering journey of which, as all moles know, Bailey was in time to scribe his own account in which he incorporated many things that Mayweed told him of the history of those times.

As was Mayweed's way, they had gone where his snout took him and spent so much time with many a mole, chatting and laughing and making friends, that Bailey had finally urged Mayweed to straighten up his snout a bit and make more directly for Seven Barrows.

'Bothered Bailey, you lead us there then!' said Mayweed, and Bailey, very bothered indeed to be leading such a route-finder, did manage to get as far as Uffington, though not without running into all kinds of danger from grike guardmoles and informers.

'Just my luck!' grumbled Bailey, after a particularly gruesome chase near Wantage when they were both nearly caught.

'Exactly, self-destructing Sir, exactly. "Just your luck." You're kind, Bailey Sir, you're well meaning, but you're still sorry for yourself even after all these years. You attract disaster.'

'Wasn't me who drowned half Duncton under the Thames.'

'Cruel, cutting and unfair, Bailey, and all you'll do is come cringing and creeping to this humble mole and apologise.'

'Well I am sorry, I mean I didn't. . . .'

'Enough, half-hearted Sir. If you're going to be nasty, be nasty; if you're going to lead, lead. Don't dither because dithering ends up as disaster.'

After that Bailey was more forceful in his leading, and even had the sense when they reached Uffington Hill, and spent the days of Midsummer there exploring the desolate tunnels, to ask Mayweed to take over again. Peering southward towards Seven Barrows, where the light was hazy and odd, he could see he would be out of his depth.

'Bailey, I love you, you have a charm especially your own, like buttercups,' said Mayweed amiably.

From this historic site they eventually turned to head southward only in late July to that different and most mysterious place where the Stones of Seven Barrows rise. This – or rather the tunnels of the forgotten system nearby – is where Spindle, Bailey's father, was born, and from here he was sent by his mother to serve his time as a cleric in doomed Uffington.

'Much improved Bailey,' declared Mayweed as they ascended the slopes towards Seven Barrows, 'humble old me feels good to be here, feels right. You should too: a mole who travels to where his kin were born travels closer to his heart.

'Scholarly Spindle would have been proud to see you here, and I am pleased, in fact I'm even moved, to be here on his behalf and say what a father should say to you.'

'Which is what?' said Bailey, himself well past middle age.

'Bailey, be bold at last, discover a task by which all moles shall remember you, make your mark, enjoy! Loss has lingered about your loins too long! Ha! Good that! Humbleness does not lose his touch with words, even at his end.'

Bailey's brow furrowed.

'Your end?' he said.

'This humble mole's journey's end.'

Mayweed looked around at where the stonefields spread, and to the rising Stones among them. They seemed indistinct, all shimmery in the summer sun. Flying insects buzzed and lazed amongst the taller grasses, and over the small stones an occasional ant ran busily.

'*You're* fitter than *I* am,' said Bailey, for though the journey had slimmed him down yet thin Mayweed always went faster than him, and much more restlessly.

'Never been fitter in my mind, Bailey mole, never! But in my body, well! Enough said! Anyway, I have to go somewhere you can't follow. I don't think you'll want to try somehow. Humbleness has a snout for such things, a thin and raddled snout it's true, but a snout all the same for . . . such things.'

'What things?' said Bailey, very concerned now.

'There's a mole I love. . . .'

'Sleekit?'

'That's her name, acute Sir. Sleekit.' He fell silent and peered towards the Stones across the fields. Bailey noticed that his head shook a little now, and sometimes when he blinked one of his eyes was slower to open than the other. Age had caught Mayweed up on their journey here, and now it had overtaken him.

Once, a few weeks past, Bailey had noticed that Mayweed's old sores had begun to open again.

'Yes, yes, yes,' Mayweed had said, 'you are right. Tryfan closed them up with healing love, and later Sleekit kept them closed with her own special love. Without those moles this pathetic and much hurt body that is mine would long since have died. But, well, the Stone was kind to me and put loving moles my way.'

'It wasn't the Stone, it was you yourself!' Bailey had burst out. 'Nomole is more loved than you, Mayweed, and you know it. You have been . . . you've been like a . . . like a . . . I don't know what you've been like!'

'Blubbering Bailey,' Mayweed had said, his own voice close to tears, 'if I've been like anything to anymole, I've been like a humbleness and, you know, all moles need one of those. But now . . . my sores have opened because I'm old and because the mole I love is far from me and I fear – I know, Sir, I know – I shall not see her again. I miss her, Bailey, I miss her enough to die.'

That's what Mayweed had said on the journey there, and now Bailey saw him staring out towards the Stones. His sores were worse than they had been then, and hurt him (though he would never complain of it), and Bailey knew it was of Sleekit that he was thinking.

'Yes, Bailey mole, I have to go somewhere now.'

'Where?' said Bailey.

'Innumerate mole, how many Stones do you see across those sunny fields?'

Bailey looked and counted, not once but twice.

'Six,' he said.

'There's seven, Bailey sir. Seven, seven, seven.'

'I can only see six,' said Bailey firmly. 'I *can* count.'

Mayweed grinned and said quietly, 'Ah, but can you see? It seems not. And that's why you can't follow me there. Later perhaps, when you're old and thin and scabby like me, but not yet. Anyway you've got better things to do, haven't you?'

'Like what, Mayweed?'

'Learning to be truly bold. Sometimes, Bailey, humbleness thinks you're dim, but he imagines that it's an impression you give because you had a deprived puphood. Not as deprived as mine, but we mustn't boast. Ha! Mayweed jokes! Ha, ha, ha! Well, before I go, I think I can find time to point you in the direction of the task I think will suit you. Anyway I'm curious myself, always was. Curiosity will kill me. That's a joke as well, though it's true enough.'

Bailey's eyes drifted off across the fields again, but hard as he tried he could not see where he looked, nor see more than six risen Stones.

'She is there, you know, and she and I will watch others come and stay until the seventh comes,' whispered Mayweed. 'Humbleness won't be humble then, nor anything else; but just himself with those he has loved so much . . . He drifts in thought, he doesn't want to leave you but he thinks he ought to go . . . He's said that before! Humbleness must be very near his end if he's repeating himself! Quick, quick, quick. . . .'

Mayweed, leering, grabbed Bailey's paw and hurried

him from the stonefields and began snouting about the Seven Barrows themselves.

'Nearly bold Bailey, stay there! Mayweed, that's me, has to remember what Spindle told him once, corroborated by great Tryfan . . . yes! No! Tum-te-tum-te-tum . . .' He wandered off and Bailey stanced down patiently, looking about and trying to imagine his father Spindle as a young mole here. Did he run up and down the barrow slopes? Did he venture out into the stonefields? Did he ever think that life would take him so far from where he was born?

His reverie was interrupted not by Mayweed but by the arrival of a worried-looking mole with unkempt fur who wandered up short-sightedly and stopped suddenly.

'Mole?' he said.

'Yes, Bailey's the name.'

'That's a relief. You looked like a vole from a distance. There's another one about, I can hear him.'

'That's Mayweed.'

'Humph! What are you doing here?'

'I'm not sure really. I've sort of come along with Mayweed.'

' "Sort of come along". What's that mean?'

Mayweed joined them suddenly, saying, 'It means, untidiness, that our friend Bailey here is a sloppy mole when it come to speech. Mayweed's the name, being humble is the game. Whatmole are you?'

'Furze. Live south of here. Came because I wanted to.'

'To what?'

'Celebrate. But didn't think I'd meet another mole, let alone two.'

'Share, share, share, exasperating Furze.'

'Lucerne's dead. Henbane's dead. Heard it yesterday.'

After a very long pause Mayweed said, 'That's it, is it, investigative Furze?'

'Yes,' said Furze. 'It's enough. It's more than enough I should have thought.'

'How did the deceased die, a mole might wond'

Whatmole did the deed? And where? These are questions that spring to mind.'

'Well they don't spring to mine, Humble. What springs to my mind is good riddance.'

'Ha! He calls me Humble and he thinks "good riddance" – learn from him, Bailey. Learn. Furze, share a worm with us!'

And so he did, all evening and all night, and they chatted of much and especially living alone, and they discovered that Furze had seen Mistle and a mole call Cuddesdon pass by moleyears before.

That night Mayweed spoke of what he knew of Seven Barrows, and told Bailey and Furze the story of the Stillstones, and how Tryfan and Spindle had come to this very place, and with great difficulty, hurled the seven Stillstones out across the stonefields, where they lay, even now, waiting to be found by moles who would be part of moledom's discovery of Silence.

Bailey was spellbound, but Furze said, 'Humph! Moles of the Stone are a superstitious lot.'

'Moledom needs more moles like you, unfuddled Furze,' said Mayweed, 'but not too many. Mayweed asks if you have a task?'

'Minding my own business mainly,' said Furze.

'Want a better one?' said Mayweed with a friendly grin.

'Wouldn't mind,' admitted Furze.

'Bailey will find you one before he leaves,' said Mayweed.

'But. . . !'

'Oops! The first "but" in months, Bailey.'

'Sorry.'

'Ask him when I've gone,' said Mayweed.

'Ridiculous,' said Furze, but Bailey noticed he looked pleased. Moles like to have a task, that he knew. What then was his now? Mayweed began to talk some more. . . .

Furze left the following morning and promised to return

the next day. Late nights did not suit him. But they seemed to suit Mayweed, for the moment Furze was gone he leapt up and hurried to show Bailey what he had found just before Furze had arrived.

Without a word he led Bailey in among some thick tufts of grass and thence down past a half buried piece of flint and into an old tunnel. The soil was dry and smelt clean, and the windsounds were deep.

Down, down they went, this way and that, until, deeper still, they made their way into a great chamber.

'Be proud, Bailey,' said Mayweed, pointing to the end of the chamber. 'Scholars of the future will revere your father's name and say this was his greatest work! Behold, look, see, and believe: this is what remains of the great library of Uffington.'

There, stacked carefully, were rows and rows of texts, and fragments of texts, all covered with bark lest dust or grit fall from the chamber's high roof above.

They went up to them, and at first barely dared to touch them. Yet they did so eventually, looking through them with increasing interest, snouting them, feeling them.

'Great Tryfan told me that your father carried each one of these from the ruins of Uffington and that it took him all the moleyears from November to March. A labour of love and courage it certainly was. He also told me that among them. . . .'

But he paused and watched Bailey with a gleam in his eye, for the younger mole had gone on looking among the texts and had come upon a separate row of them, six in number.

They looked of different ages, and the oldest was old indeed. This one Bailey gingerly took up, and touched a paw to its scribed title.

'It says "Boc aef Erthe",' he said.

Mayweed said, 'Bold Bailey, you touch my heart. For a moment you looked just like your father. That book you hold, what do you think it is? "Boc aef Erthe" you say. Why, surprised Sir, those six are six of the Seven Books of

905

Mole and Mayweed imagines that this one you hold as if it's going to bite you may be translated as ' "The Book of Earth".'

'We can't just leave them here.'

Mayweed laughed wildly and clutched his stomach.

'Can't very well move them, can you, Bailey Sir? No, no, no. They're doing very nicely here, harming nomole. Moles can come here in due time and study them. That'll keep them occupied! Ha! But no, no, no, your task isn't here I shouldn't think. Live the book, Sir, live the book!'

But Bailey had wandered on and was looking at another text.

'Strange,' he whispered. He ran his talons over its folios, beetling his brow and scratching his head.

'Puzzlements? Perplexities? Ponderments?' said Mayweed. Bailey passed the text to him, and Mayweed touched it in his turn. Then he crouched over it, and turned its folios and became more and more intent on it.

'Live the book, Mayweed! Live the book!' Bailey said, smiling.

'Bailey is droll,' muttered Mayweed to himself. Then he cried out suddenly. 'Ha! I have it! It is an astonishment! It is an utter amazement. A scribemole of the past has done what I imagined could only be done in the future.' He crouched over the strange book some more.

'Not very well, mind you, not brilliantly, as Mayweed might. But not bad at all, no, not bad at all.'

'What is is?' asked Bailey, much intrigued.

'Maps,' said moledom's greatest route-finder with a sigh. 'Maps. My idea snitched from me by a dead mole at the end of my long life.' He leered.

'What's a map?'

'It's a two-dimensional representation of a three-dimensional space showing where places are relative to each other, bookish Bailey.'

'I don't understand.'

'Well, imagine that this mark here' – he made a mark on

906

the floor – 'is Duncton Wood, and this is Whern. Now, where's Siabod?'

Bailey frowned, and looked very puzzled.

'North, east, south or west, dim mole?'

'North-west of Duncton Wood and south-west of Whern, sort of,' said Bailey.

'Brill, brill, brill,' said Mayweed. 'We have a genius among us. Mark it on the map.'

Bailey tried to do so.

'Yes, if you want to send all of moledom into the Wen "here" will do very nicely, thank you.'

'Here then?'

'Near enough,' said Mayweed. 'Now . . .' And Mayweed became utterly absorbed, his paw moving here and there, scratching out and scratching in, scribing and de-scribing, and, as it seemed to Bailey, going around the floor in circles.

'There!' he said proudly when he had finished.

'What is it?'

'Mayweed's Map of Moledom,' said Mayweed.

Bailey studied it.

'Do you remember us leaving Whern?' he said, peering at Mayweed's representation of that place.

'You were tubby in those days, and unhappy, but Boswell sorted you out.'

'Yes, he did,' said Bailey. 'I miss him sometimes.'

'We all miss him, good Bailey. All of moledom has missed him for a very long time. Mind you, it never occurs to moledom that *he* might not only miss us but *need* us. Cryptic that! Most deep! Now, let's go up to the surface and talk about old times.'

When they got there they found a whole day had passed and that Mayweed felt tired.

'Bailey mole, sleep near me tonight,' he said, and with that he curled up in the puplike way he usually did and went to sleep. And soon Bailey followed suit.

When he awoke again, it was deep night, and Mayweed

was still asleep, his breathing heavy and irregular, his body twitching. Bailey stanced up and decided to watch over the old mole for a time.

He felt at ease with himself, glad to have had the chance to travel with Mayweed, pleased to see the texts his father saved. He stared up at the stars, and thought of the places he had been, and imagined where they might be on Mayweed's map.

For now . . . he looked at the silhouettes of the barrows against the starry sky and decided to go and look at the stonefields beyond. Just for a moment, just to see if he could see the Stones at night – all six of them!

As he moved to go Mayweed stirred, and woke.

'Insomniac Sir, I'll come with you.'

'I didn't mean to wake you.'

'It wasn't you who woke me,' said Mayweed.

Together they went over the grass, among the barrows and round the last one. The stonefields stretched before them, misty, strange, and Bailey shivered.

Mayweed looked round at Bailey and said, 'Bailey mole, this mole Mayweed, this humbleness, is going to say something he's not often said. Ahead, over there, across the fields and in the night, rising with light that's clear enough to him, is the seventh Stone, and Mayweed sees it. But what he says is, he doesn't think that there's a route to it he can find. He wonders what Bailey says to that?'

Bailey stared at him, and felt Mayweed's strange fear and awe and knew that somewhere here tonight Mayweed would leave him. For Mayweed to ask another mole the way could only mean he was afraid. But to ask him! Bailey!

'If I could show you the way I would, Mayweed,' he said, 'but if it helps I'll get you started by leading you a little way. I'll do my best anyway.'

Mayweed stared into the night and said, 'Good Bailey mole, what you've just said is the most loving thing you could say, and Mayweed is touched. Me, or Humble as Furze called me, would like it if you led me a little way because I've been leading moles all my life and now I'm feeling tired. So I say to you again what I've said before: be bold, Bailey. Be bold, and lead the way!'

So then Bailey set off across the stonefield, quite slowly because Mayweed seemed unable to move as fast as he usually did, and bit by bit they put the Seven Barrows behind them and came to the first of the Stones.

'It's hard,' whispered Bailey, 'but I think I can go a little way more . . .' And so he led old Mayweed on, turning to him sometimes to make sure he was at his flank.

On and on they seemed to go, to the second Stone and then the third, turning this way and that, finding their way among the stonefields whose little stones glinted and glistened like stars at their paws. Sometimes Bailey's paws stumbled, and his eyes seemed unsure of what Stone he saw ahead, and yet he managed to lead Mayweed on.

'It's getting harder,' said Bailey, faltering at last, 'and I'm not sure I can go much further now, because. . . .'

'Be bold,' whispered Mayweed at his side, 'and you'll be all right. Get me to the sixth Stone. Go on, just a bit more.'

Then Bailey told himself to be as bold as he could, and not afraid, and he put his snout forward, peered ahead so his eyes were not distracted by anything on either side, and pushed on; but the stony ground, the misty air, the very stars seemed set against him now, as if they all wanted to push him back.

'I can't, I can't . . .' he said, and yet he saw the sixth Stone there and by putting one paw in front of the other, one at a time, he just managed to get Mayweed to it.

Ahead – too far ahead for him, he knew – he saw, or thought he saw, another Stone rising in the dark.

'I can't lead you further, Mayweed. I'm sorry, I just can't.'

'Bailey,' said a voice he knew and had not heard for a very long time, a voice he loved and missed, 'I can lead Mayweed on from here. You've done well, very well, so now let me lead him on. . . .'

Bailey saw a mole stancing just ahead. He was old, his fur was grey in the night, his eyes gentle.

'You've been a long time getting here, Mayweed,' he said.

'Humbleness was scared,' said Mayweed, 'and humbleness still is.'

'Mayweed,' whispered Bailey, 'Boswell will help you on now.'

The light of Silence touched them both as Boswell came near. He touched Bailey briefly and with warmth and then took Mayweed's paw in his own.

'There's a mole waiting for you, Mayweed, and I must take you to her where you'll never be apart again. Your task here is done now.'

A look of joy came over Mayweed's face and yet even then he thought of the younger mole who had accompanied him so far.

'Bailey mole,' said Mayweed, turning to him, 'I must leave you. You know what you've got to do, so do it; and you know how to do it, don't you?'

'Boldly,' said Bailey.

'Ha!' said Mayweed, 'with persistence and this humble mole's guidance, he learnt in the end!'

'You be bold too, Mayweed.'

'Ha, ha, ha!' laughed Mayweed, and with that he straightened his snout and peered ahead. 'Is it far?' he asked. 'Not far,' said Boswell going forward. Then with a last look round at a moledom to which he had given so much, and which he wanted so little to leave, Mayweed set off, flank to flank with Boswell, towards the seventh Stone.

It was only a loud shout and the bright morning sun that woke Bailey.

'Sir! Bailey Sir! There you are! I was worried about you!'

Bailey opened his eyes and saw Furze peering at him.

Bailey wriggled one front paw and then the other.

'I couldn't see you, Sir!' said Furze.

Bailey wriggled his back paws, extended his talons and

snuffled his snout. He was himself but did not feel like 'Bailey'. He smiled happily as Furze said, 'Funny place to sleep. Are you all right?'

Bailey nodded and knew who he felt like: *bold* Bailey, that's who he was.

'I'm very well indeed!' were Bailey's first words as his new self.

Something glistened on the ground a little to one side of him and he knew what it was before he even looked full on it.

'What's that?' said Furze, as Bailey picked it up.

'It's a special stone,' he said. 'A very special stone.'

He stanced up, looked all about and Furze said, 'Where's Mayweed?'

'He hasn't gone very far, but he won't be coming back,' said Bailey, grinning suddenly. He had spoken just as Mayweed might! Other moles are catching!

He tucked the first Stillstone under his paw and turned and headed back towards the barrows. His paws felt light, the air smelt good, the sun was clear, and moledom was all before him.

'Sir, Sir,' said Furze, who seemed to be having trouble keeping up with him, 'where are you going?'

'Where am I going, Furze? To Duncton Wood, of course. Where else would a mole go who is going anywhere?'

'But what about me? I mean it was good talking to you and Mayweed for a whole evening. I was thinking we could do it again.'

Bailey stopped.

'I think there'll be other moles coming,' said Bailey. 'Quite a few. One for every Stone you see rising here. They'll be glad to be welcomed here by you, just as we were. You could make welcoming them your task.'

'Welcoming isn't much of a task, is it?'

'It's a very important task, as a matter of fact,' said Bailey, who felt that everything he did, everything he said, was clearer than it ever had been before.

'Well, I'll miss you, and I'll look forward to some other moles coming.'

'Good!'

'But I don't know what I'll do until then.'

'Be like me, Furze.'

'Like you?' said Furze peering at him.

'Be bold!'

'I always said,' said Starling, 'that if and when this happened I would leave the Wen and go back to Duncton Wood.'

'And will you?' asked Heath lazily, basking in the September sun despite the noise all about.

'*We* will!'

'I wish you were joking, Starling, but sadly I know you're not. When you decide to do something, that is usually that.'

'Just look!' she shouted, pointing a talon across the broken ruins of where an hour before Dunbar's ancient tunnels lay. 'The place will never be the same again and I'm very cross about it.'

Age must be infectious, for both seemed old and a little grey.

Heath looked in a bored way at the great ditch that the yellow roaring owl had been threatening to delve for days, and which was now there before their eyes. Further downslope, the roaring owl was resting noisily, and fuming all about. Twofoots had been about the place for weeks before. Now Dunbar's tunnels, whose strange, mysterious sound Heath had tentatively explored and left well alone ever since; but which Starling had come to love, were all quite gone. And with them an irreplaceable part of moledom's lost heritage.

'There's still the old library,' he said. 'They've never come near that.'

'Humph!' said Starling.

'And our place is safe enough, and I like it. I don't want to leave. I'm old. Look at me!'

'You don't look old at all.' Then she smiled briefly and added, 'You weren't old in the autumn when I got with pup again.'

'You didn't this spring past, thank the Stone. That's age.'

'No, Heath, it's being sensible. Well, maybe we *are* older than we were, but not too old to leave.'

The roaring owl stopped roaring, and peace returned.

Below them, spreading far and wide, lay the Wen, blue, hazy and beautiful in the sunshine.

She stanced down companionably by him and said, 'I shall miss it all. I've got used to it.'

'I shall miss *you* when you leave,' grumbled Heath. 'But you've been saying you'd go back to Duncton for years and you never have, and I don't believe you will. What's special about this time except that a few old tunnels and burrows have been destroyed? There's still plenty of room, and anyway we could always follow the youngsters up to the Heath and find a spot there.'

'Too many dogs,' said Starling with distaste. 'What's special this time? I don't know. Something.'

She looked up at the bright sky and said more softly, 'Something *is* special now. I sometimes feel we've just been watching over this old place, and guarding what little there is left.'

'Well, the texts are safe enough – Spindle and Mayweed saw to that. I wonder . . .' He stopped himself from wondering. Heath preferred reveries in the present, not reveries in the past. But Mayweed . . . he often thought of him.

'Why, what is it, Heath?' said Starling gently, seeing the tears suddenly in his eyes.

He shook his head and pretended to push her comforting paw away. 'It's nothing,' he said. 'It's just me getting old and remembering moles I liked.'

But that night, when Heath was dozing in their burrow, Starling slipped out and climbed up to that spot of ground that lies above Dunbar's old library in the Wen where moles who wanted to be closer to the Stone went, and none normally disturbed them.

She had first started going there with Feverfew after Tryfan, Spindle, and Mayweed had left, and here they had talked and shared their dreams and hopes.

Not that Starling was much of a dreamer, nor much of one to think of the Stone, though she lived by it as well as anymole, and had brought up her many pups to speak its prayers and rituals, and celebrate its seasons.

But more than that . . . why, that had been more Feverfew's thing. She had been the one with dreams. She had been the one who followed the call of the eastern star.

'Not me,' sniffed Starling, discovering she was fighting back some unaccustomed tears.

But something had changed and she did not know what it was. Not having pups this spring past, perhaps, which meant that despite all her protests to Heath and his worry about age, she too was getting old.

'Has this been my life?' she whispered to herself, staring across the Wen, all lit up with lights and to her even more beautiful than in the daytime, with its familiar night-time roar and orange glow on the clouds above.

She had become the acknowledged elder of the place, and it had been her young that had ventured off to Hampstead Heath and come back and brought others with them, so that now there were new moles in both places, and each system survived.

'That was my work and Heath's,' she said.

High above the stars were bright, the air gentle on her snout, and she sniffed again and did not mind the tears that came.

'In autumn Duncton must be so beautiful, and if we left now . . .' She could just remember the great trees with the light all shimmery, and Lorren and Bailey to keep charge of and Bailey saying, 'Look! Look!' He had always looked at so much and she had envied him the things he seemed to see.

914

Some of her male pups had reminded her of him, with their wide eyes and eagerness, and trust. Their heart-stopping trust.

Up the slope and out of the darkness Heath came.

'I was worried about you,' he said.

She heard his voice, she saw his warm, familiar shape, but only when his paw reached out to her did her snout go low, and her tears freely come, and she whispered, 'I failed him, I wasn't there when he needed me, I failed him, Heath.'

Heath was silent for a time, and let her weep. It wasn't a thing she often did.

'A mole never forgets some moles he's known. With me it's my sister Haize, lost in the Wen, and that madcap Mayweed. I'd do anything to see them again. With you it's Bailey and Lorren, isn't it? You know why you never went back? Guilt. Fear as well, probably, but guilt mainly. Well, the way Mayweed told it there was nothing you could have done, nor any other mole.'

'But he trusted me, Heath. Reason does not restore broken trust, only love does. I failed him.'

'And all those pups you've loved and raised? And me? And all of us here in the Wen, and those up on the Heath? There's none would call *you* a failing, mole! But as for Bailey, I can't help you there. And anyway, I suppose I feel I failed Haize. But then, being a very much older mole than you, I've got used to it.'

She smiled, and felt loved, and brushed a paw where her tears had been. But then. . . .

'Heath?'

'Starling?'

'Thank you! But would you mind if I ask you to leave me now? I suddenly want to be alone. Please don't mind.'

Heath grinned in the dark.

'Feel like that myself often enough! But if you do decide to leave I'll be coming with you. You'd never make it through the Wen alone, and anyway, I'd like to see Duncton Wood.'

Then with a squeeze of her paw he was gone.

She felt sudden excitement and gazed up at the stars all bright above her. She *was* loved, and she had done right by all her pups, and it was wrong what the yellow roaring owl had done . . . and, and, and.

And suddenly she knew the time was right to leave. There was more for her out beyond the Wen – if she could get there – than there was here. She had been the one to stay, first when Tryfan left and then when Feverfew had gone. Now others could stay because it was *her* time to leave.

She ran down the slope, not old at all, and into where Heath was trying to sleep, and she prodded him to wakefulness.

'We're leaving, you and I. We've been here too long.'

'Have we?' said Heath.

They lay in silence together, Heath dozing, but Starling's mind was racing.

'We'll take some of the texts in the library with us, the ones Spindle said were old.'

'They're all old.'

'Well, the old, old ones then. And. . . .'

In the darkness Heath smiled.

'And how will we find our way out of the Wen?' he asked.

'The same way Feverfew did, because I'm sure she did. The Stone will guide us, won't it?'

'It's what I was hoping!' said Heath.

Chapter Forty-One

All summer long there was a steady arrival of moles in Duncton Wood so that by October it was beginning to have the feel of a system once more.

Many were younger moles born locally, who had left their home burrows earlier in the summer and were looking for a good place to be, and learning that Duncton Wood was accessible again thought they would try it out.

A few of the arrivals, who came from the pastures beyond the cross-under and south of it, preferred to take up residence on the pastures below the wood, drifting to the better ground that lies west of the High Wood where the soil is more wormful. But most followed Whortle and Wren to the Eastside and settled into long-discarded burrows there.

In fact these two moles, and their offspring, Dewberry, Rush, and the studious Kale, proved solid and dependable additions to the system from the start, for Wren's sense of determined responsibility was balanced by Whortle's kindness and sense of fun, and if he could be stubborn and go off in a huff by himself once in a while, well, a system wasn't worth the name if it couldn't cope with that. And anyway, at such times, which usually arose when Wren was ordering Whortle about too much, he ended up passing the time of day with Romney or any other male he could find, and helping them out in some way.

As for working the communal tunnels, what had begun as a joke with Wren had become his special concern by the time the autumn came. 'Going a Whortle' was the expression moles began to use of the task of renovating yet another stretch of communal tunnel that moles found abandoned from the long years of neglect the system had suffered.

Wren's youngsters had all found places of their own by late summer and after trying various combinations of tunnels and burrows were all well ensconced in time for the autumn, and the places they chose reflected their different characters.

Rush, a male, was the strongest of the three and, like his father, quick-witted and generally light-hearted – a happy combination – and he established his place up the slopes at the junction of the High Wood and the Eastside, where the soil is drier and chalky and not easy for worms. But he liked the clean line of tunnels there and enjoyed wandering onto the pastures. He was often the one to greet a newly arrived mole, and he knew how to make them feel welcome without being too overbearing about it.

Kale, even as a pup, decided that he wanted to live near Barrow Vale, and was one of the first to go down that way.

Dewberry, the female, seemed, to all appearances, rather dull. She stayed in tunnels near Wren, and there was rarely a day when she did not seek out her mother's company and the two could be found stanced down together busying themselves – Wren always the more restless, her daughter always the more serene.

Mistle had stayed in tunnels near the Stone, and Romney on the slopes some way below her. They worked well together and when most moles first met them they assumed they were a pair; but it was not so, which was a mystery in the wood since they looked so well together.

Mind you, as Whortle would observe when he was having a rest and an idle chat, she was clever with the males, was Mistle. Take that Cuddesdon for example, now what was a mole to make of him?

Quite a lot, in fact. With his gawky paws and quick, direct manner, Cuddesdon was not a mole others could ignore, and like Mistle herself he was unselfconscious in his belief in the Stone; he liked to say grace before eating, and tried to spend time every day in contemplation by himself.

Sometimes Mistle would join him and, as time went on,

others would do so too, particularly Dewberry, who liked to be silent in company near the Stone.

In this way Cuddesdon began, by force of his own example, to establish a pattern of worship in Duncton Wood, but one to which no other moles were forced in any way to subscribe: some did, many didn't, and of those that did there might be long periods when they did not. But without Cuddesdon building the pattern in the first place, moles with less purpose and will than his own in such matters would never have thought much about the Stone at all.

He lived rather roughly, and wherever he took a fancy to, but there he was, rain or shine, soon after dawn each morning when the wood was waking, to whisper a morning prayer in the Stone clearing, such as one he first learned from Mistle:

> *'This dawn*
> *Let us honour you.*
>
> *Stone, you have raised us freely from the black*
> *And from the darkness of last night*
> *To the kindly light of this new day.*
>
> *Let your light lighten our heart,*
> *Let your light lighten our desires,*
> *Let your light lighten our actions,*
> *Let your light lighten our faith.*
>
> *Stone, you have brought us freely to your light*
> *To travel with us through the day*
> *In heart, desire, action, faith, this new day.*
>
> *Let us honour you*
> *This dawn.'*

Yet despite the fact that it was Cuddesdon who was the outward face of the quiet worship of the Stone in the newly established system, it was Mistle who remained its inner heart. All moles sensed her faith, and from the tales she told and prayers she often made, the description of her as 'the mole who lives by the Stone' was a potent and true description of not just where but how she lived.

Slowly but surely she was becoming the mother and father of the new system, and was the mole about whom so much so subtly and quietly seemed to revolve.

But if those who grew to know her realised that neither Romney nor Cuddesdon was likely to be her mate, they naturally wondered who might be, not quite believing the rumour that it was, in some strange way, the return of the Stone Mole she was waiting for.

By the autumn all had heard of the Stone Mole's barbing, and knew he must be dead. Could Mistle then be waiting for *him*? Surely not! She was too attractive and sensible to wait on a dream! No, the truth really was – so moles said – that there was a mole who had been out in the wars of moledom and would one day return, a mole of faith who had gone fighting for the Stone.

Gradually then, as young pups like Dewberry and Rush grew to adulthood, this notion of Mistle waiting for a mole to come back took a hold on the system's collective imagination and the truth of Beechen and Mistle, so far as it had ever been known (and Romney was never one to talk about it), receded and the Stone Mole was no longer directly associated with Mistle. *Her* mole was much more real than that. Indeed, Wren and Dewberry enjoyed themselves describing him, and supposed him to be large and strong and purposeful, brave and good, and yet he had about him (they said) that touch of ruthless dedication which had taken him so far and so long from a mole as beautiful as Mistle!

'He'll come back one day,' Wren would say, 'and that'll put Romney's snout out of joint.'

But moles, inclined as they are to get hold of the wrong end of the worm in their haste to make deductions about other moles, were wrong about Romney. It was he who found a mate, not Mistle.

In mid-October, when the winds were beginning to blow lustily and the beech leaves to fly in droves through the wood and deliver a sharp shock to a mole's snout, there was a sudden influx of more moles. Unlike the ones who had come through the summer, these were older moles and travellers, who often came from afar, having obeyed the instinct that overtook many in moledom after the defeat of the moles of the Word by the Welsh moles.

Like Holm, like Starling, like Bailey indeed, they too had felt an urge to find somewhere that, after so many moleyears of displacement and disarray, might be a home for them. Some of those who now came to Duncton Wood, like Mallet of Grafham, came because they had heard Beechen preach on his way to Beechenhill, and having been much affected by his teachings and being appalled by his barbing, set off for Duncton Wood to dedicate their lives to his precepts.

Others who had met Beechen, like Poplar of Dry Sandford where the great Buckram had been healed, now made their way with their families to Duncton because they began to hear good reports of it, and felt that to find a home in the system in which the Stone Mole had been born would make sense.

A few were descendants of the survivors of the ill-fated evacuation from Duncton led by Tryfan, who had heard tales of Old Duncton, and wished now to see where their forbears came from.

These new moles found the system already established but brought with them experience, their own histories, and a willingness to occupy other parts of the system than the Eastside. Now it was that the wormful Westside began to attract moles, and the slopes between Barrow Vale and the High Wood where Kale, Wren's son, was already established, and he became an advisor and help on tunnels and territory to many a new mole.

But the Marsh End remained unoccupied, for few moles saw its attractions and many were positively frightened of it, as if, each system needing its darker place, this northern part of the wood fulfilled that need.

Mistle, who knew that in the old days the Marsh End was a community rich in lore and its own rituals, would have liked to encourage more of the newcomers down there, but though a few tried it none yet stayed.

'They will in time,' she said, 'for the Stone likes to see a system well occupied. But we have still got far to go before we're ready.'

'Ready for what, Mistle?' Romney asked.

Mistle smiled, and Romney guessed: ready for *him* when he came back. But of that, by then, they did not speak, for whatmole but Cuddeson perhaps would understand?

It was at the end of October that Romney's life changed, and moles like Wren came in for a surprise, for that was when Lorren, formerly of Rollright, came to Duncton Wood and with her, her daughter Rampion. We who have journeyed through the Chronicles already know their tale and unlike the new inhabitants of Duncton will not be surprised that the first thing Lorren did when she was through the cross-under and up the slopes was to say, 'Rampion, take me north! I'm not going to talk to a single solitary mole until I have snuffled my snout in the moist Marsh End soil, and scented its once familiar air!'

So down there they went, with Rush for company since he had come to greet them and liked their down-to-earth manner.

When they reached the Marsh End Lorren sniffed and said, 'What memories it all brings back! We should have come here years ago, Rampion. I think I'm going to cry.'

'So you lived here before?' said Rush.

'Born and raised here I was, in the days of Tryfan and Comfrey, and would have been back sooner if travelling had been safer around Rollright. Now let's go and look at the Marsh itself. . . .'

They wandered on, and Lorren had to be supported when they got to the northern edge of the wood and looked

922

at where Holm had been born and raised.

'I'm sorry,' said Rush, 'but I think a lot of your generation lost mates.'

' "A lot of our generation lost mates"? Humph!' said Lorren, looking up at Rush with indignation. 'Holm was never lost in his life. As for "our generation", young mole, we're doing very nicely and we don't need moles of your generation, or even Rampion's here, to suggest anything otherwise, thank you very much.'

Rampion and Rush exchanged a grin.

'As for Holm,' said Lorren more quietly, 'he'll be coming back now the troubles are easing. He said he would and he will, and since we've moved from Rollright and wandered about a bit avoiding guardmoles and saving ourselves he'll not find us where he left us. Now I know my Holm and he knows me, and where he'll come when he finds I'm not in Rollright is where he thinks I think he'll come! Which is here, to this Marsh where he was born and which he loved and where Mayweed first found him. And here in the Marsh End, within sight of it, is where I'm going to stay until he does, and a lot longer after that!

'However, Rush, before I talk about myself, Rampion and I want to know everything you can tell us about the moles in Duncton Wood, don't we, Rampion? Starting, because Rampion won't ask and she's itching to know, with the important question of whether or not a mole called Romney is still here.'

'He is,' said Rush, 'and very much so, and if it's half helpful, he doesn't have a mate.'

'That's a relief,' said Lorren, 'isn't it, dear?'

Rampion smiled with the loving but weary look of a mole whose mother cannot help but tell all and sundry about their family's affairs.

Nevertheless Lorren's instincts were right because the romance of Romney and Rampion was the talk of the autumn, and they all watched as Mistle 'lost' Romney to an older mole (and was left all alone), and then agreed that as Romney had been a guardmole and Rampion was definitely of the Stone there would be problems . . . But even before all the ins and outs had been fully discussed, possibility became reality and the two moles took tunnels together on the slopes. 'As far from that Lorren as she could be!' every mole pointed out and said that Lorren would be lonely.

But Lorren was not having any of that sort of nonsense. The friendship she soon developed with Wren, and the willingness with which she talked to younger moles like Kale about the old days, soon diverted them to other topics of the moment.

But in truth the gossip and back-biting that many systems develop was not prevalent at Duncton Wood, and there was a good reason for it: if there was one thing Mistle did not and would not do it was to gossip about others behind their backs. Moles tried it once with her, and got a very sharp reply. From the first Mistle set the example that the system came to live by.

Aye, Mistle could be sharp if she needed to be and nomole was going to get her to do something she didn't want to do. *She* could be relied on to stance up to a mole even when others didn't, or couldn't.

Like the time in early December when two pairs of Cumnor moles who thought they were the bee's knees came up the slopes and, without a good morning or a please and thank you, made their way straight across the wood – and 'right across Romney and Rampion's patch without even a greeting' – to the wormful Westside, and proceeded to occupy some tunnels.

A noisy, mucky, bullying lot they were, but moles must live and let live, and that's what the new moles of Duncton did. But then there was a bit of an argy-bargy when Poplar was going a Whortle near their tunnels and it might have been worse if Poplar hadn't quietly stanced his ground and stayed passive. A lot worse! Nor was that the first time. But the next time . . . Mistle herself went down all alone.

There was neither sight nor sound of her for three days

during which, it seems, she decided to go and live with them. 'Hello!' says she, 'I thought I'd join the fun!'

Dirty, wasn't she? Noisy, wasn't she? Intrusive, certainly! They didn't seem to have the nerve to throw her out and it was not long before they got the message loud and clear: think of others or you'll find others don't think of you, like me.

There she stayed and wouldn't give in though they threatened, shouted and pleaded with her to leave *their* burrow. On the evening of the third day some of her friends, including Whortle and Wren, turned up and had a bit of a singsong which went on, and on. And on.

That was the end of three of those four Cumnor moles, because they upped and left saying that Duncton moles were an unfriendly lot, but the fourth, crafty Cheatle, said, 'It looks like you're having a better time here than we've been having. I'm staying.' And he did, right there where he was, and he even had the nerve to ask Mistle to join him, seeing as he was alone now and so was she as far as he could tell, and maybe they could get it together for the winter months?

'No thank you,' said Mistle-who-lived-by-the-Stone, 'but you're welcome to stay. I like a mole who changes his mind for the community's sake.'

'Community be buggered,' said Cheatle. 'It's you I want, Mistle my mole!' But he didn't get her then, and didn't get her later, and nomole at all did either. But that was Mistle, wasn't it? Knew what to do at the right time to make moles delve for the sake of all.

In December, too, the saga of Lorren (who by then was well established in the Marsh End with a few others of her generation, all of whom she had got on the watch out for Holm's return, which she said was bound to be any day now) took a new turn.

Wren it was who first heard the news, and Wren it was who hurried down to the Marsh End to break it to Lorren, who emerged from her burrow as dusty and grubby as ever

925

she had been when she heard Wren's hurried pawsteps.

'There's a mole here!' gasped Wren, barely able to catch her breath.

'A mole?' said Lorren. 'Here?'

'Asking for you up on the slopes.'

'It's him, he's home!' says Lorren, running round in circles and trying to tidy up herself and her tunnels both at once and making them all the worse.

'Holm's back!' goes the cry through the Marsh End as all Lorren's friends run about and look at each other in astonishment, and pretty themselves up a bit because they imagine from all Lorren has said that Holm is a large, handsome mole like none have ever seen before.

'He's really back, is he? Well I never! Where is he?'

'No, no, no,' says Wren. 'I've been trying to say it's not Holm, it's. . . .'

'Starling?' says Lorren in astonishment, looking at a mole who's come with Wren. This wrinkled mole, fur thinner, paws and talons worn, is she really Starling?

Oh yes, she is . . .

'Starling!' Large as life, the same eyes, her fur clean, neat and tidy like it always has been.

Then. . . .

'Lorren?' This nearly old mole, this little grey mole, this dusty mole, is she Lorren?

'Oh Lorren!' Plumper now, happier, untidy still, looking like a stranger.

But whatmole cares what who looked like? Not them! They weren't any younger, but they were alive, and suddenly the years rolled back and all that talking they had missed, all that chat and sharing and the things an older sister talks to a young sister about, all of it was coming out, and paws were touching faces, and questions were tumbling into answers, and a celebration started that seemed to go on for days.

Then Heath appeared with Rampion, and *they* had soon got to know each other, and there was Romney grinning to be part of a family that had suddenly grown, and all of them went off to meet Mistle who lived by the Stone and whom Starling would find a most interesting mole! And Cuddesdon, must just mention him, there's so much to tell . . . and how Lorren told it, and how Starling was glad to listen, for her own long journey through the Wen, how Heath and she helped each other along, could wait until another day, for they were here now and that was past.

Then when they met Mistle, and all said a prayer of gratitude, there were more tears for Starling, because she discovered at last that Bailey *did* survive the flooding under the river, and survived the grike invasion, and survived much else.

So where was he?

Then Mistle had to tell Starling what little she knew of Bailey, namely that he had gone off with Mayweed to Seven Barrows, which is a holy place, and she thought it was for his own good.

'One day he might come back, like Holm will,' said Lorren.

'One day Bailey *must* come back,' said Starling, and it was more an order or directive than a hope, the kind that older sisters often make. . . .

So Duncton Wood became an exciting living place as December passed and Longest Night loomed once more. The community of moles delved itself in against the coming winter months, and the upper slopes were busy with moles for days before Longest Night itself, all come to hear what Mistle and Cuddesdon and Mallet of Grafham had to say about the meaning of that time of renewal for all moles of the Stone.

Mistle set the tone for those few days of preparation as somewhat sombre days, for she did not forget, nor did Romney, that here in Duncton Wood, a cycle of seasons before, the Master Lucerne had come with the grikes, and where the beech leaves now blew in the wet winter winds in the clearing before the Stone, many moles had died in the name of the Stone.

'None renounced the Stone, not one,' said Romney, who was witness to the truth of the terrible tale he told. 'Yet in their courage that night moledom surely saw the true beginning of moral resistance to the Word, and now here we are, free of its talons; free to worship and rejoice.'

They were serious days and yet, intermingled with them, was that growing cheer and excitement all moles feel come on them at that time, knowing that Longest Night will give way to longer days once more and the season's turn.

It is traditionally a time when moles come home, but if all the moles who lived in a system once have died, what moles are there to come back? Not many, it seemed, to Duncton Wood, whose slopes were empty of returning mole in those last days before Longest Night. All gone, all dispersed, so many dead: the hope, surely, lay in the new ones here, and the spring to come, when more pups would be born and the tunnels sound once more with new life.

Yet why, the day before Longest Night, did moles drift, by themselves, over to the edge of the High Wood, and stare for a time down the slopes towards the deserted cross-under and sadly shake their heads and go away again? What loved ones did they remember and dream might come up the pasture slopes whole, alive, and make a mole feel he could reach back and touch his past again? Many then, many.

Starling quietly went, and Heath knew it, for he waited for her in the wood, and let her stare out over the slopes and think of the brother she had lost when young, and who in a way she had lost again, for he had come back to Duncton Wood before she had, and gone off once more far away.

Lorren, too, had her quiet, sad time, for secretly she had hoped that as well as Bailey Holm might have been to Rollright by now, and had the sense to travel on to Duncton Wood where he *must know* she must be. Unless . . . but no, Lorren refused to think the unthinkable. She was like Mistle as far as that was concerned. Their moles would one day come back to them, they would!

Yet by the time dusk was coming on Longest Night itself, and moles were mustering through the wood and coming up the slopes among the darkening trees towards the Stone, these cares were gone again. Moles were excited and content, and could laugh and chatter of the good things they had, and of all their hopes, and look forward to the night of celebration soon to come.

Yet before we set our flanks to theirs and join them by the Stone, let us pause and think of other moles in other systems on that Night of nights, for surely there are many whom we love and who must celebrate alone. Moles who could do with company and companionship.

We cannot know them all, but there is one especially we can turn our snouts towards and trust that the Stone will find its way of bringing him its light.

A wintry place it is, with blustery winds and sleety rain, and up there the Stones seem to shine wet and cold: Caer Caradoc. Yet its Stones are not deserted, nor will they be when the darkness replaces the present grey dusk and the holiest night begins.

Here, all day, old Caradoc has been, but here even he, a mole of such great faith, has felt wan and low, and wondered how a mole holds on to hope when hope never seems to be fulfilled.

Not that he had need to be alone. Gowre of Siabod had long since asked him to spend Longest Night there; and Troedfach, too, at Tyn-y-Bedw, while Gareg had almost ordered Caradoc to journey down the Marches to the south.

But no, he chose to stay alone where he was born, and make the trek upslope to spend the day in contemplation of the long dark years just past. Bitter they had been, and more violent in aftermath than he had wished, and then the long distress of Alder, who had ailed in November and asked that he might be helped to the Stones of Caer Caradoc to stare across to the east to which he never did return.

'I never had a home to call my own, old friend,' he said to Caradoc towards the end. 'Never a place where Alder was at peace.'

Then Caradoc had gone close to him and said, 'Look about you, mole, see the place I love. This shall be your home, here where on a clear day you can see Siabod which you saved, and to the east the homeland that you left. This shall be your home for ever more, here in the very shadows of the Stones whose faith you taught us to defend, and when the Stone Mole comes I shall speak your name to him.'

Alder smiled and said. 'He will come, mole, for you he'll climb this great old hill and be a light among the Stones. He will. . . .'

There it was that Alder died, and there among the rocks at dusk he may sometimes still be seen, snout straight, paws strong, a mole of strength and courage. Some moles who go that way say they find him in the west, looking Siabod's way, others fancy they see him to the east, his snout towards the places which he loved, but which he never did call home.

So there until the dusk Caradoc had wandered, and thought of old times and friends, and hopes he'd had. Then as the rain had eased, and it grew cold and gradually dark, he had settled by the Stones and felt suddenly so tired. He hadn't minded all the rain, thinking it cleansed Caer Caradoc of the blood spilled there and prepared it for the spring years.

'You'll come,' he whispered fiercely to himself and to the Stone, 'you'll come! And moles shall know it yet and say old Caradoc was right! "The Stone Mole came!" they will say. "Have faith like Caradoc and live the way you should! The Stone Mole hears all your words."'

But when he was silent and staring at the empty shadows, he wished he could have seen young moles on his hill just once more, and seen them listen as he had done to old moles telling their passionate tales of the Welsh

Marches, and crying out their passionate prayers. And he wished. . . .

But then sounds came. Scrabblings. Whisperings. Slidings and slippings and heavings. The sound of moles climbing a steep hill in the dusk and not sure where they are. The sound of *excited* moles coming up into the mysterious unknown.

From east they came, from west. From south across the top and even – even from behind his stance – some hardy moles up the steep north face.

'Phew! That was a climb!' said one out of the gloom.

'What do we do now?'

'Look, there's the old Stones, over there.'

'They're . . . big. Let's go together.'

Caradoc could scarcely believe his eyes, but there they were, moles of all sorts and ages, all come up here, all here now, all coming where *he* was.

'There's the old mole here.'

'There's lot's of moles here!'

'No, him . . . but he's not the one. He said. . . .'

'Stop!' cried Caradoc, as moles seemed to gather all about, chattering, laughing, excited and then, bit by bit, falling silent about him.

'Happy Longest Night!' called out one.

'But what moles are you?' cried Caradoc.

That was a mistake, for what conflicting answers they started to give as all wanted to tell how it was.

But then one came forward and said powerfully, 'Greetings, Caradoc of Caer Caradoc. Remember me?'

Caradoc peered at him and shook his head.

'Clee is my name and I am the mole who yielded to you for the Word on Caer Caradoc last summer. I was free by autumn and made my home nearby.'

He embraced Caradoc warmly, as moles of those parts do, and at his flanks Caradoc saw a female and some youngsters from an autumn litter. They and all the others there looked at him as if they expected something from him.

'I'm glad you've come,' said Caradoc, 'all of you, but I did not expect to see moles up here this rough evening.'

'But it's Longest Night,' said Clee, 'and though I can't speak for the others here since I don't know them, for ourselves we were wondering how to celebrate. Then an old mole came and told us to join him on top of Caer Caradoc. I said. "That's a bit of a climb for anymole, let alone our youngsters," and he said, "Not if they're going to remember it all their lives, and anyway, if I can make it surely they can!" And then he limped away.'

'An old mole?' said Caradoc. 'Limping up the hill?'

'Aye!' cried others. 'That was the one we saw. Said to come up on Longest Night.'

'I thought you were him,' said one of Clee's youngsters, staring at Caradoc and putting out a soft paw to touch his grizzled fur.

'Me?' said Caradoc responding to their cheer. 'No, I'm just a dreamer who lived here once . . . but if it's a prayer you want. . . .'

'It is!'

'. . . and a song in a cracked old voice. . . .'

'That's it!'

'. . . and a tale that'll have your fur rising and your talons tingling, and bring a tear to your eye and warmth to your heart at the end. . . .'

'All of that, Caradoc!'

'. . . then I could try to be your mole, as the dusk fades and Longest Night begins.'

So Caradoc began to show them how, when he was young, and before even that, old moles showed younger moles how Longest Night was done, and faith in the Stone was ritually renewed once more in the hearts of moles who lived about Caer Caradoc.

And as he did, and the night came slow across the high place he loved, and the moles' eyes were all on him, he saw come among them and share the night with them, an old mole with a paw that had been hurt once by a barb. He saw his gaze, and the way he put his spirit among those moles, and then old Caradoc knew the Stone Mole had come to him at last.

As the night drew on, and their celebration grew loud and joyful and full of love and faith, that old mole called to Caradoc, like wind among the Stones, 'I have need of thee, good Caradoc, I'm glad you put your faith in me. But not yet, not quite yet, for these moles must remember you. We'll tarry with them for a while. . . .'

Then Caradoc told great tales of the past, as old moles will, and towards the end, when moles were tired yet did not want to sleep, one youngster said, 'Who was the greatest mole you ever knew?'

And Caradoc replied, 'Well now, there's a thing to ask a mole of the wild Welsh Marches, where so many great moles have lived. But if it's not the Stone Mole you mean. . . .'

'A *real* mole!' said the youngster, making Caradoc laugh, for what could be more real than the Stone Mole, who was there limping among them now and they too busy to see him?

'If it's a real mole you want, then Alder's the mole I'll name.'

'Where was his home?'

'Look around you, mole, look among the Stones. This is that great mole's last home.'

Then he told them the tale of how, in this very spot, Alder first came with a mole called Marram, and of how he inspired the moles of the Welsh Marches to struggle against the Word, and how it ended, and come to think of it was ended here and now this very night all over again as moles of all sorts made their prayers, and sang their songs, and told their tales.

Late, late in the night, when all the moles turned to sleep, to Caradoc the old mole came again. 'You can come with me now, good Caradoc. Your task is completed here.' And Caradoc went, but where he had been in the place he most loved he left a community behind.

*

Yet that same night, even though the hour was late and the celebrations over, a sense of community had not quite come about Duncton's Stone.

Prayers had been said, songs sung, tales told, but that special quality that great Longest Nights can sometimes have had not come. Moles might say and were saying that they had had a good time and had plenty to look forward to in the cycle of seasons ahead, but excitement was not entirely with them, and now tiredness was overtaking them.

Mistle had done the best she could, and no mole would say she could have done more, but perhaps what they knew had happened at the Stone the previous Longest Night was too harsh and dark a thing to easily forget. Or perhaps it needed something more than simple celebration to bring in the wonder of the night, and a true sense of its holiness which lingered still outside the clearing of the Stone, but had not brought its light within it.

For most of the evening they had been gathered in the old chamber a little way from the Stone, where traditionally Longest Nights had been celebrated. In the past, though they did not know it, the chamber had been crammed to overflowing, and festivities continued in the tunnels, and even on the surface. But the system was not yet so occupied that that was so, and there was space for all.

Yet some sense that something might happen yet, and the conviction that thus far Longest Night would not leave a memory to conjure up in the moleyears of hard work that Mistle knew lay ahead, persuaded her to suggest that even at that hour they all go out to the surface again, and gather by the Stone to pray as one.

There were moans and groans at this, but Cuddesdon said it seemed a good idea, and Romney too, and then when Lorren declared that she thought it as good an idea as any, and some fresh air would do nomole any harm, off they went cheerfully enough.

Round the Stone they gathered once more, and together

934

whispered a prayer for themselves, and the health of their community. Above the stars shone rather dim for there was cloud about, and the beech trees swayed a little in the cold wind.

Before them the Stone rose up darkly, massive and still. Heath and Starling were close to one another, Lorren nearby too, and Wren and Whortle, and Rampion and Romney, and all the moles who had come to put their future in that place.

'Mistle mole,' said Starling, 'say a prayer for all of us.'

Then Mistle lowered her snout, and all fell silent about her as she spoke this prayer:

'O Stone, who brought us from the darkness of the years
Unto the joyous turning of this Night,
Bring us safely now towards a new dawning,
Be our guiding light into the Silence yet to come.

O Stone, from the darkness of the years
Bring us to the Silence yet to come.'

Then as they stopped their praying and the group began to break up and drift off into the night, Romney cried out suddenly, 'Look! Look!'

He pointed to a spot before the Stone where, when moles crowded round and looked more closely, they saw what seemed a stone upon the ground that glistened, or glowed perhaps, or perhaps simply shimmered.

There was no doubt that it was there, for when Whortle bent down to look closer its glimmering glow lit up his face brighter than the stone itself.

More than that, there was about it a strange stillness and allure that hushed a mole and made him shiver a little with some thrilling fear – not for himself but for moledom as a whole. Yet soon, here, where that stone was, was peace, and from here nomole wanted now to go.

'What is it?' asked a mole quietly.

Another said, 'Where's Mistle? She's the one who'll know.'

Mistle came and stared down at it, and her face too was lit.

She looked from it to the Stone, and then at all of them in turn and asked, 'Whatmole among us placed it here?'

But nomole answered.

Then again she asked, 'Whatmole placed it here?'

But nomole came forward.

'What is it, Mistle?' asked Wren.

'It is a Stillstone,' said Mistle, and there were gasps about her, for all had heard the Stillstone tales and knew what a Stillstone was.

'I ask again,' she said. 'Whatmole placed it here?'

This time, though nomole spoke, there came an answer of sorts, or a hint of whatmole had placed it there at least. For on the slopes below them, from the direction of Barrow Vale, they heard the sounds of moles coming. It must be said that they were noisy moles, cheerful moles, moles who could not quite speak clear but did their best. And the nearer they got the more it seemed that these were moles who had imbibed rather too much of the juices of the aspen tree, and the dubious drink of winter-decayed foxglove root. Aye, the nearer these over-cheerful moles approached the more certain it seemed from their jolly shouts and suppressed mirth, that they were more merry than was good for them.

And yet the light of the Stillstone still glowed, glowed stronger perhaps, and the hush was still there, but now filled with the cheer, the rather good cheer, of the moles, who were almost there. . . .

Earlier that evening, after all the moles had given up any hope that some last journeyer would reach the cross-under and had gone off to start their Longest Night, a mole had come that way. Cheerful he was until the moment he set paw to the southern slopes, when, not unaccountably at all, he started feeling weary and depressed.

Bold Bailey had come home at last, after his moleyears of travel and self-discovery when he had left Seven Barrows, but now something about the chilly cross-under took his boldness right out of him. He knew what it was, and had been fearing it for days. It was guilt, which was especially affecting to him since that Night of nights when, a cycle before, he, Bailey, had fled and hid when the grikes came and massacred Feverfew and the others, and blinded Tryfan. He alone survived unscathed and now, as he began to climb up towards the place to which in all of moledom he most wanted to go that night, he felt gloom, depression and anxiety come upon him, and what had been Bold Bailey become Poor Bailey once again.

Yet he struggled on, hoping perhaps that if there were a few moles about, especially Mistle of Avebury whom he had liked, they might cheer him up. Yes! That was it! They might . . . and so Bailey had gone on.

When he reached the High Wood he had heard the moles about the Stone and crept guiltily towards them, hardly daring to show his snout because he felt so bad about himself.

He reached so near that he could almost touch a mole as he parted some twigs, peered out, and found he was staring straight at the face of Lorren. Lorren! Gulp! And next to her – the shock and surprise even greater – Starling. Oh no, Starling! Gulp again!

But . . . but! How ashamed of him they would be, for surely they must know he had run away in the moment of Duncton's crisis. And then . . . and then, what about the dreadful things he had done in the past? They were sure to have heard of them. He had been Henbane's pet for many years; he had renounced the Stone to save his life and taken to the Word; he had lived in Whern and, for a time at least, *enjoyed* it.

Now here they were, his adoptive sisters Starling and Lorren, looking older it was true but no less sisterly than they always had.

No way! thought Bailey to himself. I can't! I am so ashamed!

So there he hid as the night darkened and the little community of Duncton Wood celebrated Longest Night so cheerily (as it seemed to him). But he could only hide, and watch, and dab and sniff at his tears. It got worse as it went on, for the more he stared out at Starling the more she began to look like she had when they were young, and there was nomole in the whole of moledom whose embrace he wanted more. Yet in the circumstances she was the very last mole he could run to. Then there was Lorren, and she looked even grubbier than she had done when they were young and yet she was just the same. No, happier! *Plumper* – that was it. 'Oh Lorren,' he whispered achingly as he stared at her, 'I wish I didn't feel ashamed. Starling, I wish I knew *now* how to be bold. But I don't because I'm not bold, and I'm no good to anymole at all.'

Then he had taken out that little stone he had carried all the way from Seven Barrows over so many moleyears and miles, so proudly at the time, so sure that this would be a worthy thing to bring back to Duncton Wood, and placed it on the ground in front of him because he felt he no longer deserved to carry it.

Then he lowered his snout and wept all unseen and uncomforted into the leaf litter, and listened to the celebration in which he so much wanted to join. Sometimes he heard Starling laugh, sometimes Lorren spoke, and once they sang, and once, most dreadfully, they said a prayer for absent friends and kin, and he was sure he heard Starling say 'brothers too'. His tears were all the worse that he could not let them hear, and so, silently, snout so very low, he sobbed that celebration away.

But when much later on they all went off, laughing and joking, to the communal chamber underground he raised his snout and thought, I could just go to the Stone and say a prayer for *them*. Which is what he did, and how heartfelt it was. Then, thinking how far he had carried it, he ˹rried back into the wood where he had been, took up

938

the little stone and brought it back and placed it before the
Stone.

'Stone,' he said humbly, 'I carried it all the way for you
from Seven Barrows. Well, it's not much, and I'm not
much of a mole after all, but there's something of me in it,
and so I'll leave it here. Maybe if Starling and Lorren come
out again tonight they'll stance down near it and you'll tell
them I was here. I wish I'd led a better life. I wish I'd had
more courage like other moles. I wish, I wish. . . .'

But he could not say more, but turned from the Stone
and ran from the clearing, downslope on and on, past so
many familiar places in the dark where he would have
liked to stop. On he ran to Barrow Vale, where, years
before, his father Spindle had taken him. He did not stop
but, weeping still, and feeling that his life must be over
now, and that he was nothing and worthless and *poor*
Bailey indeed, he ran into the Marsh End and on towards
the dangerous Marsh beyond.

Once out of the wood he stopped and wept some more,
because at that very spot he had emerged, muddied right
through and only just alive, after he had nearly drowned
when the tunnel collapsed as Duncton was evacuated.

'I wish I'd died then!' he sobbed, weeping wildly,
bumping his head on the ground in absolute misery.

He heard a coot's call, he heard the mallard fly unseen in
the night. Ahead of him in the dark he felt the surge of the
dark Thames there, and to it, wildly, across the soft
ground he ran, determined now to end it all and do at least
something thoroughly and well.

He reached the river edge, peered out into the darkness,
contemplated the flowing water, and was just wondering
what part it would be best to throw himself into when he
heard the one thing that could have brought him to his
senses.

'Help!' cried a bleaty voice. 'Help, Help!'

There was a floundering in the water not far off, a rustle
and bustle of sedge and mud, and a gulping and a spitting
and general splattering.

939

'Help!' it said.

Bailey's good nature got the better of his gloom and, casting his misery aside, he shouted, 'Over here! Come here! The shore's here!'

That seemed to help, and after more shouts and directional calls from Bailey, out of the dark waters floundered a mole.

'Here, take my paw,' said Bailey.

'Where?'

Bailey reached down from his precarious pawhold on the shore and got his talons to the mole who floated and spluttered there, and pulled him out.

He was muddy. He was grubby. He was slimy. He was Holm.

No, so far Holm's Longest Night had not been of the best. He had always intended to join Lorren at Longest Night and had duly reached their burrow in Rollright some days before, feeling pleased with himself. On the long, dangerous journey from the north he had often rehearsed what he would say at the moment of return and decided that 'I'm back!' would do well. But it was all wasted. She was not there, and the few moles he found were only able to tell him that there had been a massacre by the grikes and most Rollright followers had been killed. But Holm's worry and distress lasted only moments. Lorren and Rampion killed? Impossible. Not them! Rampion would have got her mother to safety and when she could she would . . . she would. . . .

Holm had a long think.

'What would Lorren think I'd do?' he rightly asked himself. Go to the Marsh End, that was it! But time was short, impossibly short, and the only way to reach it by Longest Night was to do something nomole had ever done before. Now *that* was a thing Holm had often wanted to do. And what had nomole done before? Why swim across the Thames, of course!

Do that, and he'd make it by Longest Night. But go the

long, safe boring way by the cross-under to the south and he'd be too late. To see Lorren's face as he arrived home on Longest Night was almost worth drowning for!

All he knew about the venture was what he had learned when he had tried it when he was young: the river flows fast and it was best to go a very long way upstream and hope for the best.

Which is what Holm did, and having done so, he wished himself luck, dived in and set off. The end of the journey we know, the middle he preferred to forget. Being afloat in darkness, not being able to see, feeling the numbing cold, wondering about pikes at his paws which the legends said had teeth as big as foxes . . . it was all too horrible, and there was nothing heroic about it at all.

Yet on he struggled, on he was swirled, on he swam until, very tired, he found himself caught up in rushes, his limbs numb with cold, and he knew he was about to drown.

'Help!' he had cried. 'Help!'

'Over here!' a voice unexpectedly shouted back, and so, floundering and muddy, very, he ended the adventure nomole had had before.

The two moles looked at each other blankly, and all the more blankly because many moleyears had passed since they had last seen each other, and then Bailey had been barely more than a pup. Yet each found something vaguely familiar in the other.

'Hello. I'm Bailey.'

'H . . . H . . . Holm,' said Holm, his teeth chattering with cold.

Holm! Bailey peered closer. Yes, it was possible, it was even likely. This waterlogged and muddy mole certainly looked similar to the mole Bailey remembered. The one who rarely spoke.

'Holm!' he exclaimed. 'It *is* Holm!'

'B . . . Bailey?' said Holm. 'Starling's Bailey? Lorren's Bailey?'

'Yes!' said Bailey masterfully. 'Now come on, you've got to keep moving to keep warm. Let's get you back to the Marsh End.'

The Marsh End! The bliss of those two words to Holm! The tears he shed!

'What's wrong?' Bailey asked.

'H-H-Happy,' Holm said.

'Aspen juice is what you need,' said Bailey when they got to a warm burrow. 'Or foxglove root. Leave it to me.'

The trouble is that both are intoxicants for mole, very. There was no trouble finding them but it was hard to stop imbibing them. And since Holm was cold and *must* for health reasons, Bailey thought he would as well. Just a bit. Just *enough*. Just . . . too much!

'Bailey?' said Holm.

'Holm, my friend?' replied Bailey cheerfully.

'What were you doing waiting for me on the River Thames is what I'd like to know.'

'Holm,' said Bailey, 'you know what I think? I think that's the longest speech you've ever made. Have some more.'

Holm did.

'Well, what were you doing?'

'If I told you you wouldn't believe me,' said Bailey grinning widely, for his mouth seemed beyond his control.

'Bailey, old chum, try me,' said Holm.

'I was about to kill myself.'

For a moment Holm managed to look like his old self. He stanced up, stared, and after several attempts said, aghast, 'You weren't!'

Bailey nodded in a roundabout sort of way.

'Why?'

'Because . . . because . . . well, because. Something about being ashamed of myself.'

Holm half laughed.

Bailey grinned again.

'No!' said Holm falling backwards and wagging his paws with nearly uncontrollable mirth.

'It was when I saw Starling at the Stone earlier this evening,' said Bailey mournfully.

Holm's paroxysms increased.

'Lorren's there too,' said Bailey very sadly.

Holm's paws stretched out in an almost terminal rigor of laughter. His breathing became irregular. His eyes streamed tears. Then for a brief moment he pulled himself together and said, 'You know what? If you'd succeeded I'd have had to break the news of your recent death.'

Bailey clutched his stomach at the thought, his whole body shaking with laughter he could not control as he spluttered, 'Starling would not have been pleased!'

The two moles lay breathless, aching with mirth, until at last, Holm stanced up and said, 'Bailey, you're coming with me. Now! While you've got the courage! You can't avoid your sisters forever! Come on!'

Which Bailey did, letting the little mole lead him back up through the wood which he had been sure he would never see again.

Up and up they went, and it seemed a very long way, and their paws were very tired but there was so much to joke and laugh about. Then at last, shushing each other lest there were moles about, they tottered into the Stone clearing and found themselves in a waiting circle of moles.

Not just that, but a glowing light as well. A beautiful light.

'Whash that?' said Holm.

'Mine,' said Bailey.

What laughter was there then! What community! What love, what pleasure, what great joy as Starling and Lorren greeted their brother once more, and he greeted them most boldly.

Then he moved aside and presented Holm to Lorren and said, 'He's back!' and Lorren said, 'You haven't changed a bit!' and embraced him warmly, mud and riverweed and all.

When they all discovered that in a sort of way Holm and Bailey had each rescued the other from the cold talons of the Thames, somemole shouted, 'That's a tale we want to hear more of, and now!'

'And how you carried the Stillstone here, bold Bailey! That's another tale!'

Ah, the Stillstone. Duncton's community fell silent before it. Awe and a sense of holiness were suddenly with them.

'Tryfan told me once that Boswell found the seventh Stillstone under the Stone itself, through the Chamber of Roots,' said Bailey. 'I think this is the first Stillstone, which is of Earth.'

They all stared at it glowing on the ground.

'What else did Tryfan say, Bailey?' asked Lorren.

'Well, he said that only a special kind of mole could go through the Chamber of Roots for a Stillstone,' said Bailey. 'I think he went once when he was very young, and again to help Boswell.'

'And I think perhaps, Bailey, that since you've brought the Stillstone this far, you could take it down through the Chamber of Roots now, and put it under the Stone for us all,' said Mistle quietly.

'Me?' said Bailey, looking around with some concern. The last mole's eyes he met were those of his sister Starling.

'I think you're the only mole here who can take it there,' she said, and proudly too, not like an older sister at all. 'We'll all wait for you here.'

Then Bailey slowly took up the first Stillstone once more.

'There are others there in Seven Barrows, all waiting for moles to bring them here. Mayweed told me that, and I want to tell you about him and what happened there. And I shall. But first. . . .'

Then he took the Stillstone and went to one of the
trances into the Ancient System and disappeared from

The moles encircled the Stone, and as their flanks and their paws touched and they called on Mistle to say the last prayer of the night, all of them knew that Longest Night had truly come to Duncton Wood again.

The first Stillstone had been brought back by one of their own, and in time, in their lifetimes perhaps, all of the Stillstones would surely be brought here, even the seventh and last, which is the Stillstone of Silence.

'O Stone,' Mistle whispered for them all, 'from the darkness of the years, bring us to the Silence yet to come. . . .'

Chapter Forty-Two

Now began great years of recovery in Duncton Wood, and moledom too. These were the years when the teachings of the Stone Mole, and the gospel of his life, were first scribed by Mallet of Grafham, and told and retold by many a mole. This the time when the Word had truly died and moledom was free again.

In Duncton Wood it was Mistle's time. For as the years went by and the system regained its complement of moles, it was her purpose and example most of all that helped Duncton towards what it gradually became: a place to which moles might freely come, a place where moles could speak their minds and share their passions without fear, a place of scribing and scholarship, a place of devotion to the Stone.

This was the place where there was the growth of the true community that Tryfan dreamed of and for which he had prepared his Rule. An exciting place, a place of change, a place of moles who did not waste their time on feuds and lies and deceit, but lived by truth and openness, and spoke their minds with love, and stanced with humility before the Stone, and before each other.

Most of moledom's great moles of those years passed through Duncton Wood, and brought to it their experience and wisdom. Ghyll of Mallerstang, who brought the good news of the Stone Mole to the Welsh, ended his days in Duncton Wood; Mallet of Grafham, perhaps Beechen's greatest disciple, set off from Duncton Wood at the start of his ministry to bring the Stone Mole's teaching across the south and west. His *Life of the Stone Mole* was his finest achievement.

Gowre of Siabod, he too made his pilgrimage to Duncton Wood, to see where his ancestor Rebecca had lived. Many the exciting tale he told of Glyder, and Alder, and Caradoc, and when he spoke in his deep Welsh voice, the chamber was always hushed.

Quince, mate of Wharfe, Tryfan's son, came to Duncton after Wharfe's death and brought with her the teachings of Mallerstang that they might be forever preserved. And many more. . . .

When such moles came they marvelled at the richness and variety of the thought and faith they found in Duncton's moles. Not always moles others remember now, perhaps, but real moles who lived their lives fully, and kept their faith. Here were moles like Holm and Lorren, who brought the Marsh End to life again; and Bailey, who after his return began his work of recovering moledom's greatest texts, and teaching scribing to moles to whom in decades past it was the greatest mystery.

Through his offspring by Dewberry, who made his last years full of such content, the great tradition of Duncton's learning was revived again, and the tunnels of the Ancient System were worn and polished by the paws and flanks of moles visiting Bailey's library there.

Nor did Duncton's moles stay still. Many travelled forth and took to other Systems that natural sense of faith and trust in the good nature of mole which was such a refreshing discovery to those who came to the system itself. Most famous, perhaps, was Cuddesdon, who set off at last to fulfil his task at Cuddesdon Hill and established there a community of moles dedicated to a life of what he liked to call 'peaceful warriorship'. The number of such Cuddesdon communities across moledom soon began to grow.

Yet how quickly those years passed by! How soon it seemed that moles others had loved so much passed on! How soon others grew and matured and turned memory to history, and pointed history towards legend.

Throughout that time, most wonderfully, the grand tradition of moles seeking to recover the lost Stillstones was revived, for moles knew now of Seven Barrows and the stonefields there. And naturally, what young mole did not dream that he might travel to Uffington as Bailey had done, and thence to Seven Barrows, and be the one to find among those stones a true Stillstone, and bring it back that its light might be seen again.

Many went on such a quest despite Mistle's warning that moles rarely find what they set out to seek. Many did come back with a stone, but few brought back a stone that touched moles' lives as Bailey's stone had done. Their stones were not what they had hoped. Yet, gradually through those years, always unexpectedly, and often quite modestly and without a song and dance, the Stillstones were brought into the system.

Gowre it was who brought the Stillstone of Fighting: and Quince who bore the burden of the Stillstone of Suffering. Great the moles who carried them, stirring and moving are their tales, and touching their reports of how modest Furze stayed on after Bailey's departure and watched over Seven Barrows.

Always it was to the Duncton Stone they came and laid their holy burden down. Mistle it was who welcomed them, for she seemed the very spirit and power of mole in the place, and to her even the greatest moles deferred.

Not that it was always easy for her or the moles she watched over with such strength and love, for a true community does not stance still and often only grows through pain.

The years following the second Longest Night after Bailey's return, when the mole Tor of Tiverton brought the Stillstone of Darkness, seemed so hard to her, so bleak. How much she needed lost Beechen then!

Yet she stayed strong, and soon the Stillstones of Healing and of Light were brought and Duncton's community emerged stronger still, though by those years Mistle was growing old and slowing down.

But with six of the seven in Duncton now, she often recited the text whose words Boswell first brought to light in Uffington:

948

> '*Seven Stillstones, seven Books made*
> *All but one have come to ground.*
> *First the Stone of Earth for living,*
> *Second, Stone for Suffering mole;*
> *Third of Fighting, born of bloodshed,*
> *Fourth of Darkness, born in death;*
> *Fifth for Healing, born through touching,*
> *Sixth of pure Light, born of love.*
> *Now we wait on*
> *For the last Stone.*
> *Without which the circle gapes. . . .*'

Now we wait on . . . Aye, it was after the Stillstone of Light was brought to Duncton's Stone and taken through the Chamber of Roots and laid to rest with only the Stillstone of Silence left to come that the sense of waiting seemed somehow to overcome Mistle again. And since it overcame Mistle, it permeated the system as well. . . .

It was early summer. Mistle had seen four Longest Nights through and was old, and for the first time she gave over some of the preparation of the pups for Midsummer to younger moles and began spending more time alone. That March she had heard that Cuddesdon had gone to the Silence of the Stone during the winter years, and so all the moles of her generation had died, but for Romney, now old too.

What Comfrey and Maundy had once been to Duncton Wood those two now became: valued, loved, held in awe, and their relationship as much in debate at the end of their lives as it had been when they were first in Duncton Wood. But if ever it was true that two moles were 'just good friends' it was true of them, and now as Mistle seemed to age faster, and sometimes to wander and be a little lost, it was to Romney that moles came and asked for help.

'She's out on the slopes again, and staring like she does, and won't answer any question that I ask! You go to her, Sir, for she'll listen to you. The evening's setting in and there's owls about so you go to her quick. Shall I help you there?'

'I'll go,' Romney would reply, adding a little testily that he did not need help quite yet, but when he did he would not be such a fool as not to ask for it.

'Where is she?'

'Where she usually is.'

Romney knew where that was, and what it was she watched for. In truth it had started all those years ago when she had first heard of Beechen's barbing, and he had found her up at the edge of the High Wood staring, as he had thought, at the cross-under, her eyes lost as she whispered that he would be there one day.

He had replied, as she had asked him to, that the Stone Mole would come back and she had said, 'No, no, no,' and then stopped and seemed glad of his comforting.

When Gowre of Siabod came, Mistle had taken to him and enjoyed and been interested in the tales he told; but none more so than that of Glyder, half-brother of Tryfan, and how he had retreated to Ogwen and climbed Tryfan to touch the sacred Siabod Stones at the same time she herself had reached out and touched the Avebury Stone.

But it was the strange and cryptic account of the fallen twofoot in the nameless cwm that Glyder had given at the Conclave of Siabod that seemed to fascinate her. More than once she had Gowre repeat some of what Glyder had said so that she might memorise it. 'But the twofoots . . . it's where the future is, where the Silence will be found. I knew it when that twofoot's gaze dimmed; I knew it on top of Tryfan where the wind was still. I know it now. It's what I've come to tell you. It's why the Stones kept me alive. Listen. There are many paths to Ogwen, all easy to find. But it's taken me all the moleyears since June to find the way out again, and that twofoot never did: so it's got more to learn than we have. Stop the fighting, moles! Tell yourselves and your enemies the Silence will be found where the twofoots are. Aye, where the roaring owls go. Silence there for mole!'

These strange words Mistle remembered and repeated often in later years, and it seemed to Romney that she associated them with the return of Beechen to Duncton Wood. She would go out onto the slope, and the little promontory where years before Skint and Smithills had fought their last and died was where she would stance.

She liked to be there of an evening because then the gazes of the roaring owls began for the night, and she watched as they passed on their endless missions north and south.

There Romney would join her during that last summer, stancing nearby and watching over her, and knowing when to go to her and say softly, 'Come, my dear, I think it's time we went back to the wood. Moles worry about you staying here.'

Mistle would nod, and permit herself to be supported on one side as Romney, himself grown frail, took her back across the High Wood to her tunnels.

It was a time of day younger moles would seek them out, waiting for them in the dusk, and quietly accompanying them for a while in the hope that Mistle might relent for once and tell them a story before she went below.

June passed to July and that exciting time came when the young leave their home burrows, and travellers set off and others arrive came upon the wood. How bustling the tunnels were, how much was discussed and debated there, and how busy Barrow Vale seemed. Yet subtle, rarely spoken, was that sense of waiting that beset Mistle, and which permeated the wood and, in a way, unsettled it. It seemed as if all was hanging fire for something nameless and mysterious that soon might be.

All knew, or thought, that whatever it was it had to do with the return of the seventh and last Stillstone. A few thought it might be more even than that. A quality of tranquillity was sometimes with Mistle now, despite the doubts and fears of age that troubled her. Beyond that was a growing light, a sense of holiness.

The trouble was that 'Stillstones' were forever coming

951

to the wood, brought by hopeful moles whose only claim
to fame was that they had been to Seven Barrows; and
truth to tell, even that was sometimes in dispute. But
moles trusted Mistle, ailing though she was, and knew
that if the last Stillstone came to the wood in her lifetime
she would know it.

It was one warm July evening, then, that a travelling mole
passed through the cross-under and set his paw, with a
curious mixture of curiosity and doubt, upon the south-
eastern slopes.

A mole or two who were there greeted him, but he was
silent, even morose. He was past middle age, and
somewhat lined and grey, his eyes a little watchful, his
brow a little furrowed, and his gait slow and steady, like
that of a mole who has travelled far and conserves what
strength he has lest he finds he must soon travel on.

Up the slopes he went, up to the very promontory upon
which Mistle still sometimes stanced but nomole was there
that day as the woods rose beyond, all full of rustling
leaves and the hollow drifting sounds of wood pigeon.

The mole stopped still and stared for a long time at the
High Wood, and then he turned and looked back down
the slopes, and across the way where the roaring owls were
gazing their first gazes of the dusk.

He took from under his paw a stone and placed it on the
ground. For a long time he stanced there, staring out and
sometimes looking at the stone. Then, with a sigh, he
moved a little from that place and delved. And there he
placed the stone, and covered it again, and stared about
the place some more before setting off up into the High
Wood.

Somewhere there some young moles saw him coming
and, as was the Duncton way, came up to greet him, and
ask where he was from and where he was going. But he
answered them rather brusquely and they, intimidated by
his size and dark presence, retreated and found other
things to do.

Yet he called after them and, striving to put a smile across his face, said, 'The Stone. Where is the Stone?'

'It's that way,' they said, pointing and watching as, with a brief nod of thanks, he turned from them and went his lonely way among the trees.

It was Romney who found him by the Stone, stanced still and staring at it. The mole tried to move away but even in old age Romney was not a mole to be put off, and he had a ready smile which few moles could resist.

'Come far?' he asked, sensing that the mole was not easy of conversation.

'Far enough,' was the dour reply.

'My name is Romney, I. . . '

The mole nodded quickly, and said, 'Romney of Keynes', almost as if it was scribed before him and he was speaking it out.

'There's not many know that!' said Romney in surprise.

'Not many been to Keynes either,' said the mole with the flash of smile. 'Not much there these days.'

'How did you know?' said Romney curiously, but he saw immediately that the mole was not inclined to say. It seemed a lifetime ago that anymole had called him 'Romney of Keynes'.

'Long time ago,' said the mole as if he read his thoughts.

'It is!' said Romney. 'But I can remember it now as if it was yesterday. . . .'

Then he found himself talking to the strange mole and telling him about his puphood, and the terrible circumstances in which he had first come to Duncton Wood.

'Was it here that the massacre took place?'

Romney nodded. Even now it was not something he liked to talk about.

'And where was Tryfan when Drule blinded him?'

'I had left the clearing by then. None of us saw that. It was Lucerne and Drule alone that did it.'

'I never knew that,' said the mole. 'I thought you must all have been here then.'

Romney shook his head.

'And apart from Tryfan only one survived,' he said.

'Aye, that was Bailey,' said the mole, 'and he's one of the moles I was hoping to see.'

'He left us last winter,' Romney said, 'but his sons are alive, and Dewberry, his mate.'

A look of real disappointment and loss came over the mole's face.

'So, I've come too late, then, for Bailey. But I've heard he made a library here.'

'In the Ancient System, and there's moles will show you that. Whatmole are you then, and what's your interest?'

'My name's Woodruff of Arbor Low,' Woodruff said shortly.

It was neither a name nor place Romney knew.

There was an awkward silence, then Romney said,

'You're interested in the past, I take it?'

Woodruff nodded and asked, 'Are there any other moles from Duncton's past here now, or have they all gone?'

'Mistle knew them all, and I myself, but there's not many of the old ones left. You'll find a few down in the Marsh End who knew Holm and Lorren well. The past soon goes, doesn't it?'

'I don't think so,' said Woodruff tersely. 'I think it always lingers on. Would anymole mind if I tarried a little in Duncton Wood and talked to a few moles here and there?'

'No, mole, none will mind. You could try Kale down near Barrow Vale, he's always been interested in the past and was one of the first pups born after Mistle and myself first came.'

'I'd like to meet Mistle as well,' said Woodruff.

'She sees few moles now . . .' Romney began.

'She was mate to Beechen of Duncton.'

'Why mole, few moles know that!'

'My mother heard the Stone Mole preach at Kniveton, and was there when he was taken by eldrene Wort of Fyfield.'

954

Many moles came through the wood who told of how one or other of their parents had heard the Stone Mole preach.

'I would like to meet Mistle,' said the mole again. He was as persistent in his uncomfortable way as Romney was cheerfully in his.

'Well, if she has had a good day and you're near, then perhaps. . . .'

'I'd really like to,' said Woodruff. 'Tell her that I was in Bablock Hythe, and there's moles there who speak her name to this day with pleasure, and that of Beechen too. Will you tell her that from me?'

For the first time Romney found Woodruff gazing straight at him, and he saw his gaze was strong yet troubled, and that he was a mole who had travelled alone too long and never quite found himself.

'I'll tell her that, mole,' said Romney, 'and if she was here she'd want to welcome you and say that Duncton is a place these days where travelling moles may rest their paws, and feel under no pressure to stay or leave.'

'That's well said, Romney,' replied Woodruff with a sudden smile that lit up his creased face, and warmed his eyes. 'And thank you for it.'

From time to time in the weeks ahead Romney heard of the mole Woodruff who was about the wood and asking questions of the past. Moles seemed to notice him, for he had a strange ability, despite his seeming awkwardness, to make moles talk about themselves, and remember things they did not think they knew. Yet he rarely talked himself, or of himself.

The only mole he seemed to strike up a friendship with was Kale, and more than once the two moles travelled about the system and Kale expounded on his favourite topic, which was who had lived where, and when. But for Woodruff of Arbor Low it never seemed enough.

'You must have some idea where Bracken was born!' he

955

would say in exasperation, 'and where Rue's burrows were. She was the mother of Comfrey.'

But Kale shook his head and said, 'It's all too long ago, long before my time. I've never even heard of half the moles whose names you know.'

'Well, I could tell you sometime. . . .'

But with most other moles Woodruff was not so outgoing as with Kale. He was not quite rude when some of the more inquisitive moles of the Eastside tried to get him to tell them more about himself, but his eyes grew cold and his manner distant, and they did not persist.

'He's a funny mole, that one! Gives nothing away at all!'

Yet one evening, in Barrow Vale, when moles were gathered round chatting of times past, Woodruff did give something of himself away. Enough, indeed, to make Romney, who heard it, realise that there was more to Woodruff than there had at first seemed.

It had grown late and the moles, mostly males, some of whom had been north when young, were exchanging tales real or imaginary about the days of the Word's great power in Whern, and all it stood for.

Woodruff was listening with Kale, as he sometimes did, when the subject of Henbane came up.

'She was a right bitch, she was,' said one of them, 'and it's hard to think she was ever in Duncton Wood. But this is where old Bailey, bless him, got caught in her clutches, though it wasn't something he ever talked about. Of course, she got her come-uppance! She was killed by her own son Lucerne, who subsequently died lost and mad in the tunnels of Whern.'

'She caused more trouble to moledom than anymole before or since. She . . .' said another.

'She wasn't all bad,' growled Woodruff suddenly, 'and as for Lucerne, he did not die in Whern. He never even got back there.'

'Oh!' said one of the moles. 'That sounds interesting. Lucerne didn't die in Whern when everything I've ever heard, including from a mole who knew a mole who was there at the time . . .' There was a pause for meaningful and significant looks around to emphasise the strength of his evidence, '. . . suggests that's precisely what happened to Lucerne!'

'Well it wasn't,' muttered Woodruff, obviously regretting he had spoken.

Romney saw all this and was intrigued.

'I must say that there have always been those who said that Henbane had good qualities which belied her bad reputation,' he said, hoping perhaps that this sympathetic remark would persuade Woodruff to say more.

But immediately another mole, who liked such arguments, said, 'Ah, but that was part of her genius for evil, that she made moles think she was better than she was. No, that mole was wickedness incarnate.'

'Yet Tryfan loved her, didn't he?' said Woodruff quietly.

'Humph! Fooled by her more like!' said one of the others dismissively. 'It was only by his force of character and prowess that he got away from her grikes without more injury.'

'I don't think either Tryfan or Henbane ever fooled each other,' rejoined Woodruff. 'And he didn't get away by his "prowess" and nor did Henbane's grikes have anything to do with it. It was Rune's sideem that inflicted injuries on Tryfan, and it was Rune that let him leave alive and Spindle leave unharmed. It was one of many mistakes that Rune made.'

There was silence at this, for it was plain to them all that Woodruff knew more than they did on the subject, even if what he said was not anything like the stories they usually heard.

'You are well informed, Woodruff,' said Romney quietly, 'and we in Duncton like to hear the truth. Would you. . . ?'

'No, I wouldn't!' said Woodruff brusquely. 'I do not wish to speak of those times.'

It was a strange moment, of the kind by which a system

or community is sometimes put to a test without quite realising it. A group of moles debating, a sudden outburst by one of them, and then, too often, a retreat to blandness or unforgiving silence on all sides.

But a true community responds in better ways at moments such as that. Duncton had long since become strong, and sensitive, in its groups as well as its individuals, and many of the moles in that chamber understood immediately that Woodruff's ill temper ran deep to something that mattered much to him. Perhaps they knew that better than he did.

Silence followed his remark. Not an uncomfortable silence but rather a waiting silence, in which a mole can come closer to himself if he is allowed, and can speak his heart without fear of rebuff.

Woodruff had been in the process of stancing up to go, but so quiet was the burrow, and so friendly – so warm – that he stayed himself and settled back and stared at the ground.

Still nomole spoke.

The mole Woodruff had said 'I do not wish to speak of those times', then let the mole Woodruff say what it was he did wish to speak of!

'Henbane loved Tryfan,' he said eventually and very quietly, into the deep and caring silence in the chamber below Barrow Vale. 'To her he was the greatest light in her whole life. I believe that to him she must have been the same, and certainly she believed so – or so I have been told.'

The hasty addition of 'Or so I have been told' achieved the opposite effect than that intended, which was perhaps to distance Woodruff from what he was saying, and make it seem that his information was at second paw. But the trembling passion in his voice and the conviction with which he spoke could not but make a mole think that he had knowledge of Henbane few moles had.

There was a continuing silence, and one it was plain nomole would interrupt.

Woodruff throught some more, hesitated, and then suddenly seeming to decide to talk, said, 'Few moles know the truth of Henbane's puphood and how she was raised by her mother Charlock on Rombald's Moor. If they knew that they would understand how it was that Tryfan's love was such a revelation to her, and, too, what great courage she must have needed to turn her back on the Word and on Whern as she did that grim Midsummer.'

His voice both deepened and softened as he spoke, and Romney, who sensed the importance of the moment, was touched that the mole nearest Woodruff turned to him with a smile and said, 'There's not a mole here, Woodruff of Arbor Low, who would not feel it a privilege if you'd tell us more of what you know of Henbane. It's been a puzzle to me for years that a great mole like Tryfan loved a mole we have been taught to hate. So if you will, tell us what you know, mole.'

Woodruff seemed to find it hard to respond immediately to this, not because he had nothing to say – it was plain he had a great deal – but because the gentle way the mole had spoken, and the atmosphere of care and interest in the chamber was not something he was used to at all. Indeed, he looked round at them for a time, his mouth opening as if he wanted to speak so much, but was not quite able, and tears were in his eyes.

' 'Tis all right, mole,' said Kale, 'you take your time, we can wait.'

'Aye, fetch a worm or two for Woodruff over here!' said another. In this way that awkward moment passed, and it was so plain that the moles were as much concerned for Woodruff as the story he had to tell that nomole could not have felt warmed and cheered by their response. Indeed, he was not the only one with tears in his eyes. Romney had them too. For what he saw before him that night was indeed a community of moles, and one which knew well how to take into its heart a mole who some might have said was not of their number. But there they were and there he was among them, feeling safer, Romney suspected, than he had ever felt in his life. And feeling valued too.

The task that Mistle set herself finds a fruition here tonight, he thought.

Then Woodruff chewed some worm, unashamedly touched a paw to his tears, and said in the old way, 'Of Henbane of Whern, born of Charlock and Rune, former Mistress of the Word, shall I tell as best I can, and from my heart to your heart I shall tell it that you know it to be true.'

So then began the first telling of a tale by Woodruff of Arbor Low in Duncton Wood, and the whisper soon went out that a great tale was being told by a mole who knew what he was telling, and others came quietly to the chamber, and settled down into the silence there, and listened as, once more, Henbane of Whern came alive in Duncton Wood. But now it was through a mole who had loved her and who, it was plain the more he spoke, and the more he told, and despite all appearances to the contrary, loved all moles.

A long tale it was, and the night was late when it was done, and many a mole went up to Woodruff afterwards and said, 'That was an evening I'll never forget, I hope you'll tell us more when you've a mind to.'

'I shall,' said Woodruff, looking surprised and embarrassed by how warm the moles were towards him. 'Yes, I think I shall!'

The following day Romney went to Mistle and said, 'There's a mole came to Duncton Wood some weeks past whom I think you should meet. His name is Woodruff of Arbor Low.'

'Whatmole is he, Romney?' said Mistle.

'Just a mole I'm saying you should see.'

'Why?' She peered at him, half sceptical, half amused. It was not often he told her what to do, and this was the nearest he ever came to it.

'Because,' said Romney with a smile. 'Because you trust me.'

960

'All right, all right, I'll meet your mole, but first tell me what you know of him. . . .'

Woodruff came to see her that same day and stanced down close by her. Like so many before him he was struck by the beauty of her eyes, and the grace she had. But she was old now, older than he expected.

'Why have you come to Duncton Wood, Woodruff of Arbor Low?' she asked. Her gaze was direct and clear.

'I wanted to see the system that most in moledom say is its greatest glory now,' he said.

She gazed on him more and said nothing.

'I wanted to know about the past.'

Still she said nothing.

'I wanted to know about my past,' he said.

She nodded, satisfied, and thought. Then she said, 'And what were you afraid of that it took you so long?'

He stared at her and she at him, and he felt that his heart and mind were plain to her.

'What is it you hope to find here, mole?' she asked.

'I . . . don't know, but I know I have been much afraid of coming.'

'Well, that's plain enough.'

'I was hoping that you might tell me how you began here. . .' he said.

She laughed gently.

'Yes, Romney said you're good at making other moles talk, but I have a feeling that the story of how you began might be more interesting than our recent history,' she said.

He smiled but said nothing.

'Whatmole are you?' she said suddenly, and quite fiercely, her gaze on him all the time.

'I . . . don't think I know,' he replied very quietly. 'I'm not sure. I . . .' His snout lowered.

She reached an old paw to his, and waited until he was ready to look at her again. Her eyes were wise, and he saw there was good light about her, and peace.

'You can tell me,' she said, 'and Romney here.'

Then Woodruff knew he could, and for the first time in his life he began to tell the tale of how he came to be, and all his story after the deaths of Lucerne and Henbane at Arbor Low, and how he had travelled moledom in search of an understanding of his past.

At its end he said, 'When I was young, Henbane often told me that I should go to Duncton Wood. But I was reluctant . . . and yet wherever I went, whatever stories I heard or moles I met, it seemed to me that the story of these times started from here and points back to here.'

'And now you're here?' she said at last, her paw still on his.

'If Harebell was my mother then Tryfan was my grandfather. . . .'

'And Henbane your grandmother. . . .'

'And perhaps here I'll find a sense of peace I've never found elsewhere,' he said.

'Perhaps,' said Mistle thoughtfully. 'Or perhaps you're the mole to find much more.'

'Well, I came here by way of Seven Barrows in the hope that I might find a Stillstone but instead, like others before me, I am sure, came to see that what I had carried for so long was but vanity, and I discarded it before entering the High Wood.' He smiled ruefully.

She was silent for a time, not interested in his stone it seemed, but when Woodruff offered to leave her and let her rest she shook her head.

'No, mole, there's a task I think I have for you. If you'll consider it. Yes, a task. . . .'

Romney smiled. He had heard *those* words before. How many times had wise Mistle said them to moles who until that moment were floundering in life? How many moles had found their life's way directed by Mistle's infallible sense of what their task should be? Romney should know. She had found his task for him.

'Yes?' said Woodruff.

'From what you've said you know as much of the history of recent times as anymole I've ever met. Much more, perhaps. How many moles can say that they were raised by Henbane herself? How many moles saw Lucerne die? How many moles have trekked as you have to Whern, to Caradoc, and to many places in between?

'Not many, Woodruff of Arbor Low. How many have talked with moles, as you have, who heard the Stone Mole speak, and saw him barbed? Not many. How many know so much of the Word and can scriven as you say you can, and yet have faith in the Stone, and can scribe as well? Not many.

'I am old now, and tired, and cannot tell the tales I've told much more. Nor can Romney. But when we hear others tell them, they change them, and put into them stories of their own. I'll be a myth or legend in my own life if that goes on and our history will be lost.'

'You're a legend already, Mistle!' said Woodruff. 'So what would you have me do?'

'You said that all the ways you went, and all the moles you spoke to, seemed finally to point to Duncton Wood. You said that here you believed the Silence might be found. Do you know what that Silence is?'

Woodruff shook his head.

'Have you heard of a mole called Glyder?'

'I have. And I've heard what he said at the Conclave of Siabod.'

Mistle looked surprised, and pleased.

'What did he say?'

'I heard it from Gareg of Merthyr, and it was confirmed by Gowre who was the last mole who saw Glyder alive.'

'You are thorough, mole.'

'It is the only way to be with truth.'

'Aye, it is so. And what was it you heard that Glyder said, that you remember?'

'He saw a twofoot die and it much affected him. He broke out from his retreat solely to tell moles that we should contemplate the twofoot if we would know Silence.'

'Aye mole, so I've heard, so I've heard.'

'But now, what task would you have me do, Mistle?'

'Those that follow us shall need to know what happened here, and the story of our times. Bailey, son of Spindle, made a library here and had begun to collect texts from other places.'

'Aye, there's some I know hidden here and there which I'm sure nomole has seen.'

'Well mole, collecting texts is one thing, scribing them another. I would like to die knowing that a mole I trust shall scribe with truth the history of our times, and of this system here. Will you do that, mole, for me?'

Woodruff was silent and thinking.

'Will you help me, and ask others to help me?' he said at last.

'I will.'

'Will you and others trust me to scribe as I judge best?'

'We shall.'

'Will you tell me all you know of the Stone Mole, for he is at the heart of Duncton's story and I know too little of him. I have heard you never talk of him and yet you loved him as mole, not Stone Mole.'

'You try me hard, Woodruff of Arbor Low, grandson of Tryfan, but I will, I will.'

He smiled.

'And how do you know for sure I am Tryfan's grandson, after all I've told you today?' he said lightly.

'As I remember Tryfan, you have his eyes. And his paws as well perhaps. They are a scribemole's paws,' she said. Then turning to Romney, she said, 'This shall be a great task he does. Help him in whatever way he needs. But for now, leave me, for I am tired.'

All summer and into the autumn Woodruff wandered around and talked to the moles of Duncton Wood. When they knew what his task was and that he had Mistle's blessing, they helped him all they could; and more so that he willingly talked to them of the many things he knew of moledom's history. So it was that slowly he became the

964

mole to whom all moles turned when there was a dispute about the past. His knowledge was so great, his judgement so sound, and the love of mole he felt beneath his sometimes awkward manner was so plain that soon he was as much a part of the system as anymole.

They would welcome him where he went, and tell him of old moles here and there who might know things he would find interesting for the history he was making, and he would seek them out and talk to them for hours, and sometimes days.

Mistle too he spent time with, though with the colder autumn weather she ailed still more, and there were days when she did not speak clear at all.

Yet she seemed to like him and since he was strong, and Romney was ailing too, it was Woodruff's paw she took when she wanted to go across the High Wood onto the slopes to watch the roaring owls.

'The Silence is there, isn't it?' she would say.

'Somewhere it is, but I'm not sure where.'

'Not sure of anything anymore, not even . . .' she would mutter to herself.

'Not even what?' he would say, unable to stop himself asking questions of moles, even old ones whose minds wandered.

'But I am sure! He *is* coming back. You ask . . . you ask. . .' and then she would clutch fearfully at his paw.

'Romney?' he said.

'I forgot his name,' she said in distress. 'I forgot Romney's name.' But then, growing more confused. . . .

'Is Romney coming back?' she might ask with sudden fear. As if. . . .

'You mean Beechen . . . Oh yes, he's coming back,' said Woodruff, 'he'll come back one day.'

'He said he would,' she whispered. 'Oh dear, he said he would.' Then she cried and needed comforting.

As October came again and the beeches began to shed their leaves these wanderings and tears increased and it became harder for her to go to the slopes at dusk and watch the roaring owls. Then, at last, she was confined to her burrow for most of the day, able only, with pain and difficulty, to climb up to the surface and go to the nearby Stone.

Yet sometimes she was coherent, and with Woodruff and Romney at her flank would ask how Woodruff's history of Duncton was coming along, and when it would be scribed.

'It's still the years before you came that I cannot fully rediscover,' he would say, repeating names that were all but lost in the hope that she might know them: 'Mekkins, Hulver, Rue, Rose, Mullion, Cairn. . . .'

But she only shook her head and fretted her talons.

'When I know a little more I'll be ready to make the Chronicles of these woods.'

'Go and watch the roaring owls,' she would say suddenly, 'and he'll be there.'

'He'll come back, my dear,' said gentle Romney.

'Who?' shouted Mistle. 'Eh? Whatmole's ever coming back to me?' And she laughed in a wild old way that tilted now towards bitterness and made them want to weep.

It was plain to the moles of Duncton Wood that Mistle had lived almost past her time, for she was sometimes senile now, and slipped into a strange savagery which was not Mistle at all. Whatmole would have thought it would happen to her? A mole must hope the Stone would take her soon, in her sleep perhaps, for she did not deserve to be what she was becoming. Not that for Mistle, whom they loved.

'He's coming, my dear, I know it's so,' Romney would still say, though she seemed not to know what he meant and if she did, and was her coherent self again, she denied that she knew who he was talking about.

But when she was young, and much in love and had faith in a mole she called Beechen and others called the Stone Mole, a mole with whom she stayed awhile in lovely Bablock Hythe, Romney had promised that to his dying day he'd tell her that her love would come back home to

966

the system she had remade with such love for him, and so he told her still.

There came a dawn in November when the air was cold and clear. The sky was light blue, and the sun began to catch the last of the colours among the trees – a clutch of beech leaves upon a graceful branch, dew on a half-brown bramble leaf, and red berries up on the dry Eastside.

Woodruff was about early, for he had spent the night at Kale's place, talking, as ever he did, about the Chronicles it was his task to scribe. Now, this morning, he was almost ready to start scribing at last, wishing only that he knew, he really knew, just where the task began.

'The beginning's here in the wood, Kale,' he had said, 'waiting to be found. How often I wish the tunnels and trees could talk!'

Kale had agreed, as he always did, about the elusiveness of the past, and how a mole could never quite reach back far enough to know what his true beginnings were.

So, like the good friends they had become, they had talked, and then slept, and Woodruff awoke refreshed, and ready for the day. Ready indeed, to begin. Though where. . . ? Well, the Stone might help!

So he had said farewell to Kale and come out into the wood, just as the sun was rising and giving everything a last autumnal glow. He was going upslope, when, on impulse, he turned back the little way to Barrow Vale, a place to which so much of Duncton's history was tied.

Here Tryfan died, and before that had made his stand against moles who sought to kill him in the time the system was outcast. Here the plagues had hit hard, and once fire had razed the trees nearby.

'But what else?' he muttered to himself. 'What else happened here that I don't know about? If only. . .'

'If only what, mole?' an old mole said to him.

He turned towards the morning sun and saw a mole there he had not seen before and said, 'If only I knew more about the history of the wood.'

'Well, I can tell you one thing about where you're stancing now.'

Woodruff stilled. He liked to hear a titbit or a tale he had not heard before.

'What's that?' he asked.

'It was just there, or very near by, that Mandrake first stanced in Barrow Vale. That was a to-do, that was! He charged in from the pastures killing moles left, right and centre, stanced where you are now and roared a bit, then found an entrance and went down and challenged the whole system at once!'

'They must have been wild days,' said Woodruff.

'Oh, yes, I think they were! You know about his daughter?'

'Rebecca?'

'Yes. She was actually raised in a burrow not far from here.'

'Could you show me?' asked Woodruff.

He did not need to ask, for the old mole was already up and off and Woodruff had to hurry after him.

'There you are, just down there, that's where Rebecca was born. She used to come at dawn to Barrow Vale and dance, which Mandrake did not like. Her mother . . .' Then he talked and talked about the past telling Woodruff things he had so long sought to know, only ending with a sudden: 'But look, come with me, there's somewhere I've not seen for a long time . . . yes, let's go there.'

'Where?' said Woodruff, finding it hard to keep up, hard even to quite see the mole, for the sun was clear and strong and dazzling all over the tree trunks and shining on the ground.

'Mekkins' tunnels in the Marsh End. Now, there was a mole. Which reminds me, did you ever find the Marsh End Defence?'

'The what?' asked Woodruff.

'The Marsh End Defence, delved by Mayweed and Skint, I believe, and lived in for a long time by Tryfan . . . it's on the way, more or less, to Mekkins' place, so let me show you. It's easy enough to find when a mole knows how.'

'Whatmole are you that you know all this?' asked Woodruff, but the mole went ahead of him in the light, and seemed not to hear, and to Woodruff it seemed suddenly best not to ask, but to listen to all the mole told him about Duncton Wood as it had been before the Word came south, before the plagues, just at the time that Bracken was born. . . .

So Woodruff listened and let himself be led through a system that was filled with light that morning by a mole who seemed to know and love all the moles of Duncton Wood, every one.

Through the Marsh End they went, across to the Eastside, and thence to the slopes and into the Ancient System, which did not seem quite the same as the Ancient System he knew. Yet what stories Woodruff heard then and how much began to fall into place as he learnt about Bracken's love for Rebecca, and was shown the places where so much had happened in the past.

But then, gradually, the old mole began to tire and slow, and his memory seemed to slip and his paw to falter.

'There's so much, so much . . .' he said, his voice a little cracked. 'Yes, yes, so much for mole to remember, so easy to forget. Now you help me along here, Woodruff, and I'll see if I can't show you, since we're not far from it here, where Comfrey was born. Not many know that now! Why, I might be the only one, and you now! It was here, and his mother's name was Rue, and she was a love of Bracken's. Yes, that was it.

'You know, I'm getting rather old for this, rather slow, and I've got to go back upslope and that's a long way.'

'There's one other place I'd like you to show me,' said Woodruff, wondering why after so long the sun was still barely risen in the sky.

'What's that?' the old mole said.

'I'd like to know where Bracken was born, because I think a lot began with him.'

969

'Yes, yes it did. But it's right over on the Westside and I don't think. . . .'

'I'll help you there, and help you back. I'd really like to know.'

'Well, come on then.'

So, slowly, helping the mole along, his weight leaning on Woodruff's strong paw, the mole took him to a spot on the Westside.

'There! Delve down there and see what you find.'

So Woodruff did, delving down and down, until he found himself in an old and musty tunnel.

'Yes,' said the mole from the surface, 'that's the place. That's where Bracken was born, and I think you're right: that's where it all began.'

Woodruff bent his head and went along the tunnel and found a family chamber and some burrows off it. So, thought Woodruff, Bracken was born here, and from here he set off when he was older for the Ancient System, and began a quest for Silence that Tryfan had carried on, and then, and then. . . .

He paused suddenly. There was silence. No sound of mole at all.

He turned and hurried out, anxious not to lose touch with the old mole, but when he surfaced he saw that he had already gone off limping through the wood upslope. How old he looked, and how the light seemed to shine in his fur.

'Wait!' Woodruff shouted, running after the mole. 'I said I'd help you back upslope.'

'You did,' said the mole, and let Woodruff support him under his withered paw as they went steadily up towards the south-east with the sun in their eyes. A sun that seemed not to have moved higher in the sky from the moment Woodruff had met the mole.

'You know a lot about Duncton, don't you?' said Woodruff, feeling a sense of awe coming over him, and a knowledge of who this mole was and surprise that the paw he supported was real and that he could feel it on his own.

'I know about it in the old days but these days my

memory goes, and my time here is very nearly done. I. . . .'

'You're Boswell, aren't you?' whispered Woodruff, not daring to look at the mole at his side.

'I've been many moles,' said Boswell. 'Yes, yes, many moles and I can't remember them all. But Boswell? Yes, perhaps I am still him for now.'

They seemed to have gone right through the southern edge of the High Wood and were coming to the pastures where the sun, not filtered by the trees, was brighter still.

'Where are you going now?' asked Woodruff.

Boswell seemed to stumble and falter, and then he stopped and stared downslope across grass whose dew was like a hundred thousand golden stars. Beyond they could see the roaring owl way, and on it a few slow roaring owls, their gazes pale in the sun.

'I promised I'd go back to *them* one day,' said Boswell, 'and I think perhaps they need me more than you moles do now. I think my task with you is done.'

Then he took his paw from Woodruff's and set it down as best he could upon the grass and began, slowly, to move away downslope.

At first Woodruff felt unable to move, but simply stared as if it was right that Boswell must go now. Yet it did not feel right. It did not look right. It was not. . . .

'Boswell!' called Woodruff. 'Boswell!'

Boswell turned back.

How old he looks, thought Woodruff, and how alone. That was what was not right.

'Yes, Woodruff?' Boswell said.

Woodruff opened his mouth but did not know what to say. He wanted to ask . . . he wanted to know. . . .

Boswell began to turn from him once again.

'Boswell?'

'Yes, mole?'

'Are you all right?' Woodruff gently asked. Then he found he could move, and he did move and he went to where old Boswell stanced so shakily.

He reached a paw to Boswell and said, 'You looked a little lost.'

'Did I, mole?'

Downslope behind him, going north and south, Woodruff saw the roaring owls, and they glinted in the sun.

'Not many moles have asked me if I'm all right,' said Boswell. 'Not many at all. Bracken did. And Rebecca. And Tryfan, too. And you, Woodruff, you asked me.'

'Boswell. . . .'

'Yes, mole?' said Boswell softly.

'Would you wait for a little before you go? Would you promise to wait?'

Boswell smiled.

'Why, mole, you can't stop life itself.'

'Just for a little, because there's a mole here in Duncton Wood, who has waited for you for a long, long time and she's not far from here. Would you wait for her?'

'For how long, Woodruff?' Boswell smiled again and looked down at his old paws.

'I'll find a mole who will talk to you while I go and fetch her. Just wait a little, just a little. . . .'

Then Woodruff turned and ran back into the wood. Fast and faster, and the first mole he saw was Romney.

'Romney, there's a mole out on the slopes. Go and stay with him, don't let him go. Go to him, Romney.'

'But. . . .'

'I think he's the mole Mistle's been waiting for. Go to him.'

But he needed to say no more, for Romney turned and, as best he could, ran into the rising sun and towards the slopes. Then as Woodruff ran towards the Stone, he felt himself crying out, as if to rouse the wood, to rouse everymole in it, to tell them that now was the time when they must show their snouts and stance up for Mistle, for now was what she and they had been waiting for.

Like the sounding of the Blowing Stone at Uffington his call was across the wood that morning, and moles hurried from their tunnels and burrows and all seemed to know that it was to the High Wood they must go, and fast! Quick! Hurry now! For the light is all across the wood, and moledom waits, and Mistle, who has given them so much, needed all their strength, and all their love.

So they gather and they hurry upslope through the early morning light, across the dewy leaves, in twos and threes upslope towards the Stone. There they find Woodruff, helping Mistle, who can barely stance at all now and is muttering and wondering and rather afraid. But her paws and flanks only shake, and she stares uncomprehendingly at him.

'He's come back for you, Mistle. He's here, he's waiting for you,' says Woodruff, his strong paws about her as the others gather and turn the way he turns her, which is towards the east, towards the rising sun.

'Come on, Mistle. You need your last strength now, but you and he will help each other on from Duncton Wood, because he needs you too.'

Slowly, bit by bit, tree after tree, Mistle progresses through the wood, Woodruff supporting her, and her snout shakes and her eyes stare, and often her paws stumble. But all the moles are there to lend her their spirit and their strength and urge her on.

'He came back for you, Mistle, because you were the one who had most faith, you were the one who loved him most as mole.'

'He came back?' she whispers, and for the first time she dares let hope be in her eyes.

'It's not far now, not far . . .' And slowly, so slowly, they break out of the wood and into the sunshine beyond.

Romney is out there on the slopes, and with him is an old mole, waiting, his eyes no more certain than Mistle's have been.

Leaving Boswell, Romney comes to her.

'He came back for you as you knew he would, Mistle. Go to him.'

'He's not *Beechen*. He's not young as Beechen was,' she says.

'I think he's many moles, and I think if you can find the strength to go to him, my dear, he will know you again and you'll know him.'

'Then help me, Romney,' whispers Mistle.

Romney smiles but shakes his head.

'I am too old now, my dear, to do more than watch you go, but Woodruff will lead you to the light in which Boswell waits.'

Then Woodruff, grandson of great Tryfan, put his paw to Mistle's and, with all the moles of Duncton Wood urging her on with love and prayers, he helped her make her slow and painful way across the slopes beyond the High Wood to where Boswell stanced waiting for her, near the promontory from which she used to watch the roaring owls.

The light was behind him, and his face was hard to see, but it seemed that as she came nearer to him he started forward towards her a little, as if he almost knew her. She too, with each step she took, seemed to know him more, and where they were a light was too, greater than the sun, for it filled the air about them all, and held the sound of Silence.

'Beechen?' they heard her say.

'Mistle?' he whispered back to her.

'Oh my dear, I've missed you so much. . . .'

Then they touched each other in the light and turned to Woodruff who stanced by them, his snout low.

'Woodruff of Arbor Low,' said Boswell, 'you have fulfilled the great task the Stone ordained that you should perform. Born of violence, raised by Henbane, and traveller in pursuit of truth, you are the mole who brought the seventh Stillstone to Duncton Wood. Delve it up, mole, from whence you buried it.'

Then Woodruff, hardly daring to look at where Boswell and Mistle stanced before him in the light of Silence, delved and found the stone he had buried.

The watching moles gasped as he took it up from the broken soil and its light was upon them all.

'Now mole, what will you do with what you carried for so long and now show us here?'

Woodruff took the Stillstone and touched it first to the withered paw of Boswell, and then to Mistle's beloved face. Its light was great, and whiteness was upon them both, and where they were the moles seemed to see Boswell's paw grow whole, and he and Mistle grow young again, and both to laugh as surely once she and Beechen had laughed. Then they turned, or seemed to in the light, and began to go down towards where the roaring owls went endlessly.

'They are our task now, they are our task . . .' their voices seemed to say. And then, 'Woodruff of Arbor Low, your restless search is over, for here in Duncton Wood you are and always shall be much loved, so much loved.'

Then where they had been only Woodruff stanced, and on his lined and once troubled face was the look of a mole who knows that he is loved most true, and who knows at last from where all Silence comes.

Then he held the Stillstone up that they might see it, and carried it back into the wood, and all of them went with him to the Stone.

They gathered together to give thanksgiving and make celebration as Woodruff of Arbor Low took the Stillstone down through the Chamber of Roots and placed it with the others about the base of the Stone.

When he came among them again it seemed that all celebrations were in one that day, and mole touched mole with love, as the sun rose through the trees and they knew at last their Duncton found.

Epilogue

Woodruff's Duncton Chronicles were finally started on the Longest Night following, as a tale told to a community of impatient moles.

'We're not going to have to wait until you've scribed them all down, are we?' asked one of them.

He shook his head, smiled, crunched a worm and said, 'I'm ready to begin it now if you like.'

'You do that, mole! But wait while we get comfortable.'

So Woodruff did, and started in the traditional way: 'From my heart to your hearts I tell this tale . . .' Then he paused, and smiled again, and began like this: 'Bracken was born on an April night in a warm dark burrow, deep in the historic system of Duncton Wood, six mole years after Rebecca. . . .'

So began Woodruff's first telling of the Chronicles of Duncton Wood which took place over the cold wintry weeks that followed his last Longest Night. When it was done, and old Woodruff had told his tale just as he had scribed it, moles noticed that he was silent, and seemed to have little more to say.

Yet though the scribing of the Chronicles seemed to be his greatest task, yet he left one more gift to moledom.

For aging though he was, he still found strength to direct others to create a great Library at Duncton Wood, wherein all those texts scattered from Uffington and other places during the war of Word on Stone were joined in safety with those left behind by Spindle, Mayweed, great Tryfan, and holiest of all, by Beechen when he was young.

At the end of his life Woodruff would often say that nomole's task is ever complete, and that all he can do is to leave what was left to him ready for those yet to come.

'One day,' he said, 'others not yet born will inherit this great Library we have made. To it they will bring new texts, or old texts that our generation has not yet re-discovered. A few texts,

*and very few perhaps, will be scribed here, using all that we
have left behind and the experience gained after.*

'*Indeed, though the Chronicles are done, one last task seems
to remain if the ministry of Beechen, and the work of Tryfan
and so many others, is to find permanence, and not be lost
through the erosion of time and moles' forgetfulness.*

'*Aye, there shall yet be another mole to come out of obscurity
and show future generations what the Stone Mole's teachings
were. A great mole shall he or she be. More than scribe, more
than a warrior, more than a leader . . . .*'

*Strangely, in his last weeks Woodruff, spent much of his
time in the obscurest part of the Library to which he had
contributed so much. There, amongst that collection of texts
which librarians call Rolls, Rhymes and Tales, Woodruff
found comfort and solace. Those nearest to him spoke out
again the tales he loved, and which for one reason or another he
had not included in his Chronicles.*

'*There's a Book of Tales here,*' *he would murmur dreamily,
'*but another must begin to scribe it. And that mole that shall
teach others of the Stone Mole's work, shall come here one
distant day, and finish it. Now tell me a tale of the moledom
that I love . . . .*'

*These were the last words great Woodruff of Arbor Low
spoke, for during the telling of that last tale, Woodruff heard
the Silence of the Stone, and went into it.*

*Some moles say the tale he was being told was never finished
and awaits completion still. Others believe its end is to be
found in a tale told long after he had gone.*

*For the scribing of the Book of Tales which he thought must
one day begin, and the coming of the great mole who would
complete it, these things came to be as he said they would. Only
in that way was Woodruff's task complete at last, and
Tryfan's too, and Bracken's before him. For the past becomes
the present that we live, and for good or ill, the future lies in the
present we pass on. May our lives make a blessing then on the
lives of the moles that follow us . . . . and may moles find
solace, comfort and inspiration, in the Book of Tales that
Woodruff foresaw would one day come . . . .*

978

PUBLISHER'S NOTE

Since *Duncton Wood* was first published in 1979, William Horwood has received thousands of letters from readers asking about the conception and writing of what has become a fantasy classic. He has been able to provide some answers through correspondence and at a limited number of public talks. However, now that *The Duncton Chronicles* trilogy is published, and a companion volume, *Duncton Tales*, is complete, William Horwood has felt able to record the true and full answers to these questions – and the many more that lie behind the strange, sometimes painful, sometimes inspiring story of *Duncton Wood's* creation.

Molelovers, and anymole else, who would like more details of his work should write to William Horwood at P. O. Box 446, Oxford OX1 2SS

Acknowledgements

My thanks to the Scottish University Press for permission to quote, and translate into mole language, passages from the graces and invocations in Alexander Carmichael's *Carmina Gadelica*.

Readers often ask what the sources of the key spiritual and religious elements are in the *Duncton* books. Although I am no longer a Christian it will be plain that the Gospels are a prime source. Two essentially Buddhist texts have been constant companions in my study and on my travels: Chogyam Trungpa's *Shambhala* (Shambhala Publications, 1985) and Matsuo Basho's *The Narrow Road to the Deep North* (Trans. Nobuyuki Yuasa, Penguin, 1966). I have also found M. Scott Peck's *The Road Less Travelled* (Rider, 1985) and *The Different Drum* (Rider, 1987) very helpful, the latter especially with *Duncton Found*.

A work as long and complex as *Duncton Chronicles* makes exceptional demands on its publisher, and particularly its editors. My own have done far more than readers can ever know, or perhaps care to believe, to correct my many errors at manuscript stage regarding whatmole was with whom, when, where, and why, and other matters editorial. My warm thanks therefore to Peter Lavery, Ann Suster, Victoria Petrie-Hay, and to Pamela Norris, who between them turned *Duncton Found* from an idea into a book with such professionalism and good cheer.

Duncton Quest and *Duncton Found* could not have been written without the love, support and help of my partner Debbie Crawshaw, and nor would the last months of writing *Duncton Found* have been so happy without the presence and pleasures of our newly born son, Joshua.

Bestselling General Fiction

☐ No Enemy But Time	Evelyn Anthony	£2.95
☐ Skydancer	Geoffrey Archer	£3.50
☐ The Sisters	Pat Booth	£3.50
☐ Captives of Time	Malcolm Bosse	£2.99
☐ Saudi	Laurie Devine	£2.95
☐ Duncton Wood	William Horwood	£4.50
☐ Aztec	Gary Jennings	£3.95
☐ A World Apart	Marie Joseph	£3.50
☐ The Ladies of Missalonghi	Colleen McCullough	£2.50
☐ Lily Golightly	Pamela Oldfield	£3.50
☐ Sarum	Edward Rutherfurd	£4.99
☐ Communion	Whitley Strieber	£3.99

Prices and other details are liable to change

ARROW BOOKS, BOOKSERVICE BY POST, PO BOX 29, DOUGLAS, ISLE
OF MAN, BRITISH ISLES

NAME...

ADDRESS ....

....

....

Please enclose a cheque or postal order made out to Arrow Books Ltd. for the amount
due and allow the following for postage and packing.

U.K. CUSTOMERS: Please allow 22p per book to a maximum of £3.00.

B.F.P.O. & EIRE: Please allow 22p per book to a maximum of £3.00.

OVERSEAS CUSTOMERS: Please allow 22p per book.

Whilst every effort is made to keep prices low it is sometimes necessary to increase cover
prices at short notice. Arrow Books reserve the right to show new retail prices on covers
which may differ from those previously advertised in the text or elsewhere.

A Selection of Arrow Books

☐ No Enemy But Time	Evelyn Anthony	£2.95
☐ The Lilac Bus	Maeve Binchy	£2.99
☐ Rates of Exchange	Malcolm Bradbury	£3.50
☐ Prime Time	Joan Collins	£3.50
☐ Rosemary Conley's Complete Hip and Thigh Diet	Rosemary Conley	£2.99
☐ Staying Off the Beaten Track	Elizabeth Gundrey	£6.99
☐ Duncton Wood	William Horwood	£4.50
☐ Duncton Quest	William Horwood	£4.50
☐ A World Apart	Marie Joseph	£3.50
☐ Erin's Child	Sheelagh Kelly	£3.99
☐ Colours Aloft	Alexander Kent	£2.99
☐ Gondar	Nicholas Luard	£4.50
☐ The Ladies of Missalonghi	Colleen McCullough	£2.50
☐ The Veiled One	Ruth Rendell	£3.50
☐ Sarum	Edward Rutherfurd	£4.99
☐ Communion	Whitley Strieber	£3.99

Prices and other details are liable to change

ARROW BOOKS, BOOKSERVICE BY POST, PO BOX 29, DOUGLAS, ISLE OF MAN, BRITISH ISLES

NAME...

ADDRESS...

....

....

Please enclose a cheque or postal order made out to Arrow Books Ltd. for the amount due and allow the following for postage and packing.

U.K. CUSTOMERS: Please allow 22p per book to a maximum of £3.00.

B.F.P.O. & EIRE: Please allow 22p per book to a maximum of £3.00.

OVERSEAS CUSTOMERS: Please allow 22p per book.

Whilst every effort is made to keep prices low it is sometimes necessary to increase cover prices at short notice. Arrow Books reserve the right to show new retail prices on covers which may differ from those previously advertised in the text or elsewhere.

Bestselling Fiction

☐ No Enemy But Time	Evelyn Anthony	£2.95
☐ The Lilac Bus	Maeve Binchy	£2.99
☐ Prime Time	Joan Collins	£3.50
☐ A World Apart	Marie Joseph	£3.50
☐ Erin's Child	Sheelagh Kelly	£3.99
☐ Colours Aloft	Alexander Kent	£2.99
☐ Gondar	Nicholas Luard	£4.50
☐ The Ladies of Missalonghi	Colleen McCullough	£2.50
☐ Lily Golightly	Pamela Oldfield	£3.50
☐ Talking to Strange Men	Ruth Rendell	£2.99
☐ The Veiled One	Ruth Rendell	£3.50
☐ Sarum	Edward Rutherfurd	£4.99
☐ The Heart of the Country	Fay Weldon	£2.50

Prices and other details are liable to change

ARROW BOOKS, BOOKSERVICE BY POST, PO BOX 29, DOUGLAS, ISLE
OF MAN, BRITISH ISLES

NAME...

ADDRESS ....

....

....

Please enclose a cheque or postal order made out to Arrow Books Ltd. for the amount
due and allow the following for postage and packing.

U.K. CUSTOMERS: Please allow 22p per book to a maximum of £3.00.

B.F.P.O. & EIRE: Please allow 22p per book to a maximum of £3.00.

OVERSEAS CUSTOMERS: Please allow 22p per book.

Whilst every effort is made to keep prices low it is sometimes necessary to increase cover
prices at short notice. Arrow Books reserve the right to show new retail prices on covers
which may differ from those previously advertised in the text or elsewhere.